Dexterity watched the princess out of sight, his own grief for the dead princes rewoken.

Poor girl. Such a burden she carries. People watching her wherever she goes. Whispering behind her. Whispering before she arrives. Dissecting her life even as she lives it.

Of course, things would probably turn out all right. More than likely her ailing father would rally. Physicks could do amazing things these days. The king *had* to rally, Ethrea wasn't ready to lose him yet. With the untimely losses of Ranald and Simon there was no prince waiting to take the throne. There was only Princess Rhian. Not yet at her majority and a girl to boot. Ethrea had never been ruled by a woman . . . and there were those who thought it never should.

Prolate Marlan for one. His views on women are stringent, to say the least.

Dread chilled him. Were King Eberg to die without a male heir only misery could follow. Ethrea's past was a tapestry of betrayal and bloodshed, the desperate doings of six duchies wrestling for the right to rule the whole. In the end duchy Fyndle had emerged triumphant, was renamed Kingseat and became the traditional duchy of the king. Peace reigned sublime and for more than three hundred years the cobbled-together̶ ̶ ̶ ̶ ̶ ̶ lesser principalities ha̶

But if Eberg ̶ ̶ ̶ ̶ ̶ ̶ ̶ ̶ ̶ ̶ ̶ ̶ ̶ ̶ here'll be. All the natio̶ ̶ ̶ ̶ ̶ ̶ ̶ ̶ ̶ ̶ ̶ ̶ e will swoop down on u̶

Praise for Kare̶

Books by Karen Miller

Kingmaker, Kingbreaker

The Innocent Mage
The Awakened Mage

The Godspeaker Trilogy

Empress
The Riven Kingdom
Hammer of God

Writing as K. E. Mills

The Accidental Sorcerer
Witches Incorporated
Wizard Squared

THE RIVEN KINGDOM

GODSPEAKER: BOOK TWO

KAREN MILLER

www.orbitbooks.net

New York   London

Copyright © 2007 by Karen Miller
Excerpt from *Hammer of God* copyright © 2008 by Karen Miller
All rights reserved. Except as permitted under the U.S. Copyright Act of 1976, no part of this publication may be reproduced, distributed, or transmitted in any form or by any means, or stored in a data base or retrieval system, without the prior written permission of the publisher.

Map by Mark Timmony

Orbit
Hachette Book Group USA
237 Park Avenue
New York, NY 10017
Visit our Web site at www.orbitbooks.net

Orbit is an imprint of Hachette Book Group USA, Inc. The Orbit name and logo is a trademark of Little, Brown Book Group Ltd.

Printed in the United States of America

Originally published by Voyager, Australia: 2007
First Orbit edition in the USA: September 2008

10 9 8 7 6 5 4 3 2 1

*For Glenda Larke, a great writer
and even greater friend.*

THE RIVEN KINGDOM

PART ONE

CHAPTER ONE

The King of Ethrea was dying.

Rhian sat by her father's bedside, holding his frail hand in hers and breathing lightly. Her world was a glass bubble; if she breathed too deeply it would shatter, and her with it.

This isn't fair, this isn't fair, this isn't fair . . .

Droning in the privy bedchamber corner, the Most Venerable Justin—one of Prolate Marlan's senior clergy, sentenced to praying for her father's soul. His shaved head was bowed over his prayer beads, click-click-clicking through his fingers till she thought she would scream.

I wish you'd get out. I wish you'd go away. We don't want you here. This is our time, we don't have so much that we can share.

She had to bite her lip hard to quell fresh tears. She'd wept so often lately she felt soggy, like moss. And what was the point of weeping anyway? Weeping wouldn't save her father. He was broken, he was slipping away.

I will be an orphan soon.

She'd been half an orphan for ten years now. Without the portraits on the castle walls she might not even remember Queen Ilda's sweet face. A frightening thought, to lose her mother twice. Was she destined to lose her brothers twice as well? Ranald and Simon were dead only two months, she still heard their voices on the edge of sleep. She thought it was likely, and after them her father twice. All these double bereavements. Where was God in this? Was he sleeping? Indifferent?

Mama, the boys, and now dear Papa. I know I'm the youngest, nature's law dictates I'd be the last one left . . . but not this soon! Do you hear me, God? It's too soon!

As though sensing her rebellion, the venerable paused in his bead-clicking and droning. "Highness, the king will likely sleep for hours. Perhaps your time would be better spent in prayer."

She wanted to say, *I think you're praying enough for both of us, Ven'Justin.* But if she said that he'd tell her personal chaplain, Helfred, and Helfred would tell Prolate Marlan, and Marlan would be unamused.

It wasn't wise, to stir Marlan to anger.

So she said, her heart seething, "I do pray, Ven'Justin. Every breath I take is a prayer."

Ven'Justin nodded, not entirely convinced. "Admirable, Highness. But surely the proper place for your prayers is the castle chapel."

He may be a Most Venerable, but still he lacked the authority to command a king's daughter. She looked again at her father's cadaverous face with its jaundiced skin pleated over fleshless bone, so he would not see her anger. Her voice she kept quiet, sweet and unobjectionable. *Be a lady, be a lady, be always a lady.*

"I will go to the chapel by and by. For now, Ven'Justin, even if he is asleep I know His Majesty takes comfort from my presence."

Click-click-click went Ven'Justin's prayer beads. He picked up his droning where he'd left off.

On his mountain of pillows, her father stirred. Beneath his paper-thin eyelids his eyes shifted, restless. The pulse in his throat beat harder. "Ranald," he muttered. "Ranald, my boy . . . I'm coming. I'm coming." His voice, once treacle-dark and smooth as silk, rasped like rusted wire. "Ranald, my good son . . ." His exhaled breath became a groan.

A basin of water and a soft cloth sat near at hand, on the bedside cabinet. Gently, Rhian moistened her father's cheeks and lips. "It's all right, Papa. Don't fret. I'm here. Please try to rest."

"Ranald!" said her father, and opened his eyes. So recently the deepest blue, clear and clean as a summer sky, now they were rheumy, their whites stained yellow with the failing of his liver. For a horrible moment they were clouded, confused. Then he remembered her, and sighed. "Rhian. I thought I heard Ranald."

She dropped the cloth back in the basin and took his hand again. His fingers felt so brittle. Hold him too tightly and he'd break into pieces. "I know, Papa. You were dreaming."

A single tear trailed through his grey stubble. "I never should have let Ranald go voyaging with Simon," he whispered. "I was selfishly indulgent, I cared more for Ranald loving me than I did for what was best, and now they are dead. My heir is dead and so is his brother. I have failed the kingdom."

It was by now a familiar refrain. Rhian kissed his cold hand. "That's nonsense, Papa. Every great man's sons go abroad. Your father didn't forbid you the world, even though you were the heir. You could never have denied *your* sons that adventure. Ranald and Simon had bad luck, that's all. It's not your fault. You aren't to blame."

In the corner, Ven'Justin's beads clicked louder. The Church frowned on superstitious beliefs like *luck*. She spared the man a warning glance. Venerable or not, she wouldn't have him upsetting her father.

"Rhian."

"Yes, Papa?"

His fingers tried to squeeze hers. "My good girl. What will become of you when I'm gone?"

She could answer that, but not in front of Most Venerable Justin. Not in front of anyone who would carry her words straight back to Helfred and Marlan. "Hush, Papa," she said, and smoothed her other hand over his thinning hair. "Don't tire yourself talking."

But he was determined to fret. "I should have seen you betrothed, Rhian. I have failed you as I failed your brothers."

A single name rang like a bell in her heart. *Alasdair.* But there was no point thinking of him. He was returned to duchy Linfoi and his own ailing father . . . and besides, she'd not yet come near to softening the king towards him.

"Papa, Papa, do not excite yourself," she soothed. "You need to rest. God will take care of me." Another glance, over her shoulder. "Isn't that so, Ven'Justin?"

Grudgingly, he nodded. "God takes care of all his children, to the length and breadth of their deserving."

"There," she said. "You see? Ven'Justin agrees." Then added, even as she felt the hot tears rise, "Anyway, you're not going anywhere. Do you hear me, Papa? You're going to get well."

He smiled, a gummy business now, with all his teeth rattled loose in their sockets. "Throughout my life I have not been the most reverent of men. But even I know, Rhian, that God does as God wills. I will leave when I am called and not even you, my bossy minx, can dictate I'll stay."

My bossy minx. It was one of his pet phrases for her. She hadn't heard him use it in the longest time. "Yes, Papa," she said, and again kissed his cold fingers.

Soon after, he drifted back to sleep. Ignoring Most Venerable Justin and his pointed sighs she held her father's fragile hand and, defiant in the face of God's apparent decision, willed him to live, live, *live.*

It was a small room, made smaller still by an overabundance of powdered and perfumed ladies, plump with platefuls of sugared cakes and creamy drinking chocolate served in fine china cups. Rustling in taffeta and satin, swishing in muslin, sighing in silk, they laughed and squealed and squabbled like children over the dolls, toy bears, stuffed piglets and pussy cats, wooden archers, painted marionettes, tin whistles and whatnots the toymaker had brought for their inspection and delight.

Lady Dester, wife to council secretary Lord Dester, poked an impatient, jewel-crusted finger at the tumbled pile of toys in her lap and sighed. "Dear me, Mr Jones, I just don't know. I mean to say, they're all lovely, aren't they? You make it so hard to decide. And goodness gracious, if I don't choose exactly the right one, well, little Astaria is likely to sulk for days, bless her precious heart. My sweeting is so *particular* when it comes to her toys . . ."

Dexterity Jones, Toymaker by Royal Appointment, gritted his teeth behind his smile. What was there to say? Little Astaria would have the head off whatever doll she was given in five minutes flat and then he'd have to fix it so that the joins didn't show, and no matter how hard he tried or how perfect the repair, little Astaria would shriek that it wasn't the *same*, Mama, it *wasn't*, so *there*, she wanted a *new* dolly . . . and Mama would kiss her and coddle her and buy her another dolly . . . and so it would begin again.

An aristocrat-in-training if ever there was one, God bless her and every other spoilt darling in the kingdom . . . for who else kept the roof over the head of a humble toymaker?

Lady Dester sighed, which set her rouged cheeks quivering, and cast a cold grey eye over the fluttering flock of lesser court wives who had gathered with her to purchase toys for their sons and daughters and nieces and nephews and brothers and sisters and flower-children. Plucking a lace-edged kerchief from her considerable cleavage, she flapped it in their direction.

"Marja, oh Marja, dear! Do come and help me decide!"

Keeping his expression as bland as butter, Dexterity watched Lady Braben pinch her lips and roll her eyes, clearly put out, then turn full round and join Lady Dester as bidden. Her husband Lord Braben was a mere pretender to the King's Council, so offending Lady Dester wasn't wise. Lady Braben was many things but feather-headed wasn't one of them. She'd chosen a painted wooden dog and a doll's tea set in three minutes flat.

With one sly, sliding, sideways glance at him she bent solicitously at Lady Dester's side. "Yes, Violetta, dear?"

Violetta dear thrust an armful of dolls, stuffed bears, marionettes and rattles at Lady Braben. "Choose one, Marja, do! Then if Astaria doesn't like it I can say it was your fault and she won't take it out on me."

"I'm honoured," Lady Braben murmured, clutching the toys.

"As you should be," Lady Dester retorted. "Little Astaria is—"

"Good afternoon," a cool, contained voice said from behind them.

Lady Dester squirmed around on her footstool, saw who it was and let out a genteel little shriek. "Your Highness! Goodness, what an honour!" The remaining dolls, stuffed bears, marionettes and rattles in her lap erupted ceilingwards as she surged to her feet.

Still smiling—after a while, one's face set like marzipan—Dexterity launched himself, arms wide, to catch his precious merchandise. One booted toe caught under the edge of a hand-woven Icthian rug and he fell sprawling, clutching at teddy bears, at the feet of the king's only daughter.

She raised an eyebrow. "Really, Mr Jones. Bodily prostration is reserved for greeting His Majesty. A simple 'Good afternoon, Your Highness' would've sufficed."

With a grunt, Dexterity heaved himself to his knees and held out his hand. "Good afternoon, Your Highness," he repeated obediently. "Care for a rattle?"

Princess Rhian smiled, ruefully amused. Then she extended one slim sun-browned hand, grasped rattle and fingers and pulled him smoothly to his feet. "You're a cheeky rogue, Dexterity Jones."

"I know, Highness," he agreed. "I could have sworn that's why you like me."

She glared at him in mock outrage, releasing his hand. "And which misguided fool informed you of that?"

His smile now was genuine. "A royal one, with hair like midnight, eyes like sapphires and a laugh to put the songbirds to shame."

"Then she was a fool indeed to encourage such a flattering knave as you," said the princess, and turned to Lady Dester. "Violetta, you look flustered. Can I be of help?"

Lady Dester blushed and simpered. "Well, goodness, Your Highness, I mean to say, at least, it's just that—"

Dryly, Lady Braben said, "Lady Dester is having some little difficulty choosing a gift for Astaria, Highness."

The princess nodded. "I see. And how does my flower-daughter, Violetta? I confess I've neglected my honorary children these past weeks."

She'd been nursing the king. Dexterity looked up from rearranging his goods so the damaged items were hidden at the back. "I trust His Majesty goes along better, Your Highness?"

The scented chamber fell silent. Smothering the frenetic gaiety the shades of Ranald and Simon, Ethrea's dead princes. Its dead heirs. This young woman's dead brothers. The court and the kingdom were out of formal mourning, determined to thrust aside grief and dismay. Gatherings like this little toy fair pretended nothing was wrong . . . and everyone believed it, at least for a while.

Until some fool of a toymaker spoiled the mood with awkward questions.

Nothing in the princess' polished expression changed, but Dexterity thought he knew her well enough to see behind the royal mask. "He's a little better, Mr Jones," she said, her voice colourless. "Thank you for asking."

Oh dear. So things were very bad, then. Ignoring the court ladies' daggered glances, he said, "If you will forgive me mentioning it, Highness, I have a friend, an excellent physick and a fine woman. It would give me great pleasure to—"

Before he could finish, Lady Dester was on him. "Mr Jones, you forget yourself! Know your place and stay in it, if you please! My husband Lord Dester recommended the physick that labours day and night to ease His Majesty's suffering! If Physick Ardell has not prescribed the cure then you can be sure it is not worth so much as this!" And she dismissed all non-Ardell remedies with a snap of her fingers.

Tight-lipped, Dexterity bowed. "Apologies, madam. I was only intent upon—"

Lady Dester turned her back on him. "Now, Your Highness, as to your most gracious enquiry after *dear* little Astaria, she blossoms more each day. A most beautiful child, if I do say so myself, the very picture of me at that age—"

Dexterity risked a quick exchange of looks with Lady Braben. Her lips twitched, once. An eyelid flickered. Their shared thought was clear on her face: *What a future dear Astaria has before her.*

Lady Dester was oblivious. On and on she prattled, Astaria said this, Astaria did that, and Your Highness wouldn't *credit* what the little poppet had done just this morning . . .

Dexterity, with no choice but to stand alertly by and nod in all the right places, allowed his eyes to rest impertinently on the princess' face. She looked drawn, shadows like twilight beneath her glorious eyes, hollows deeper than beauty below her high cheekbones. Her exquisite blue and gold silk brocade dress sat too loosely round her waist. She stood tall and straight as a young pine, but tension sang in the spaces between her bones and the whisper of a frown lay across her brow.

Oh dear, oh dear. For certain things are very bad.

"—and only last week, Your Highness, if you can believe it, the darling little thing undid the door to the dovecote and let all the birds out!" twittered Lady Dester. "Well, didn't the cottier have a time getting them back in, knowing that the cost of any bird not accounted for would come from his stipend! Oh, how we laughed, little Astaria and I!"

"An amusing trick, dear Violetta," the princess agreed. "And now I think I have an answer to your dilemma. Why don't you give precious little Astaria all the toys? The ones that have yet to be spoken for, I mean."

Lady Dester was taken aback. "*All*, Your Highness?"

"Think how thrilled she'll be, knowing she has the most generous mama in the kingdom," said the princess earnestly. "When she sees these wonderful dolls and toys and discovers every last one is for her, I'm sure you'll see a smile wide enough to swallow the moons."

Dexterity stepped forward. "At a generous discount, Your Ladyship, naturally, to show my gratitude for your bounty."

Lady Dester's eyes narrowed. "How generous?"

He swallowed. "Twenty percent?"

"Thirty."

"Twenty-five?"

Lady Dester opened her mouth to argue, caught the princess' observing eye, and snorted instead. "Very well. Twenty-five. Follit! To me!"

As Lady Dester's page obeyed the summons, Princess Rhian said, "Ladies, it's been a pleasure taking time with you but I'm afraid I must return to the king. Do continue your shopping, and give my fond affection to your families." She accepted their curtsies with a smile, and withdrew.

Dexterity stared after her, frowning, then excused himself to Lady Dester. "A moment, Your Ladyship, there is something I forgot—"

Lady Dester squawked. Feigning deafness, he slipped through the jostle of perfumed women and ducked through the open door into the corridor. "Your Highness!"

The princess, about to turn a corner, hesitated. "Mr Jones? Is something wrong?"

Catching up to her in five swift strides, he sketched a quick bow. "Not with me, Highness. I just wanted to say, well, thank you."

She shrugged. "There was no call for Lady Dester to be so rude. You were only trying to help. God knows His Majesty can use all the help he can get."

He resisted the urge to pat her arm. "I meant what I said, Highness. Ursa is a fine physick, the best I've ever met. I'm sure she could help. She could ease the king's pain at least, I'm certain."

"If you say so, Mr Jones, then I've no doubt it's true. But I'm afraid it's not quite as simple as that."

"Lord Dester," he said, and grimaced. "Of course. I understand."

Her head tilted to one side as she regarded him. "I believe you do," she said at last. "You understand a great deal about court politics, I think, for a simple toymaker."

"A simple toymaker who's trotted in and out of this castle since he was big enough to hold his father's tool bag," he pointed out. "I'd have to be a sight deafer, dumber and more blind than I am not to see the way things work around here, Your Highness."

Her brief smile was sad. "Yes, I expect you would."

She was poised to turn away from him, but he couldn't let it go at that. The poor girl was heartsick and clearly near the end of her endurance. All alone in the world, almost, and sore in need of help.

"Truly, Highness, at least let me speak to Ursa," he said, cajoling. "She has prodigious experience with fevers and fluxes and the like. She could make up a little posset of something then give it to me, and I could—"

"You don't change, do you?" said the princess. "Ever since I can remember you've been fixing the broken things in my life. Do you recall that dappled grey rocking horse I rode to pieces? The one I inherited from Simon, who inherited it from Ranald? Three times you mended it, till we had to concede that the poor old thing had pranced into its last battle." The affectionate amusement died out of her face, leaving it pale and older than its nineteen years. "Do you recall what you told me, a child of seven, as you held me on your lap and let me cry? You said, 'Little princess, don't grieve. The old horse has had a good life, and a long one, and all things in their time must turn to dust.'"

Abruptly the brilliant blue eyes were full of tears, and her lips trembled.

Floating through the nearby open door, a strident, querulous cry. "Mr Jones? Mr Jones! Come back here this instant, Mr Jones!"

The princess took a deep, shuddering breath and dashed her hand across her face. "You're wanted, Mr Jones, and so am I. I'll pass your good thoughts along to the king. He'll be touched to know how his people care." Impulsively, she clasped his wrist. "Thank you, Dexterity. You're a dear, true friend."

And she was gone, long swift strides hampered only slightly by her dress. Dexterity watched her out of sight, his own grief for the dead princes rewoken.

Poor girl. Such a burden she carries. People watching her wherever she goes. Whispering behind her. Whispering before she arrives. Dissecting her life even as she lives it.

Of course, things would probably turn out all right. More than likely the ailing king would rally. Physicks could do amazing things these days. The king *had* to rally, Ethrea wasn't ready to lose him yet. With the untimely losses of Ranald and Simon there was no prince waiting to take the throne. There was only Princess Rhian. Not yet at her majority and a girl to boot. Ethrea had never been ruled by a woman . . . and there were those who thought it never should.

Prolate Marlan for one. His views on women are stringent, to say the least.

Dread chilled him. Were King Eberg to die without a male heir only misery could follow. Ethrea's past was a tapestry of betrayal and bloodshed, the desperate doings of six duchies wrestling for the right to rule the whole. In the end duchy Fyndle had emerged triumphant, was renamed Kingseat and became the traditional duchy of the king. Peace reigned sublime and for more than three hundred years the cobbled-together edges of the five lesser principalities had rubbed along tolerably well.

But if Eberg should die what an unravelling there'll be. All the nations with their interests invested here will swoop down on us like a murder of crows . . .

Dexterity felt his heart thud. If the king recovered he could find himself another wife and sire a son to replace the two who'd died so untimely. Eberg wasn't old, just three years senior to himself. It was barely middle-aged. The king had a *score* of sons left in him, surely. If the worst came to the worst and he died before this hypothetical son turned eighteen, well, there'd be a regency rulership but that could be survived. A king in nappies could be survived. But what kingdom could survive without any king at all?

Stop scaring yourself, Jones. His Majesty will be fine.

Lady Dester appeared in the open doorway. "*Mr Jones!* What are you *doing*? Must I remind you who I *am*?"

"No, Your Ladyship!" said Dexterity. "My sincere apologies. I'm coming right now!" And he fled his dire thoughts as though they pursued him with raised hackles and bared teeth.

While the storm of Lady Dester's displeasure raged about him he nodded and apologised and bowed and packed up her purchases, then the other court ladies' choices. When he'd finished and was blessedly alone, he allowed himself a moment to sit and sigh and heft with pleasure his coin-filled purse.

"Even with that outrageous discount not a bad day's work, my love," he remarked to the air. "I'll stop in to see Javeson on the way home and order the new parlour curtains, shall I? Midnight blue, with perhaps a touch of silver. What do you think, Hettie? Do you think blue would suit best?"

I think we've more to worry about than curtains, Dex.

Dexterity froze. Looked from side to side. Over his shoulder. Behind the couch. Nothing. No-one. The room was empty.

He cleared his throat. Feeling ridiculous, he said, "Ah . . . is anyone there?"

No reply. He sat down again, pulled his kerchief from his pocket and wiped his brow.

"You're overworking, Jones. Time you put your feet up and relaxed with a pint of cold ale."

You can't be drinking ale at a time like this, Dex.

With a strangled shout he leapt to his feet, the kerchief fluttering abandoned to the floor. Beneath his best brown waistcoat and second-best yellow shirt his heart was beating a wild tattoo. It was impossible, but he asked the question anyway.

"Hettie? Hettie? Is that you, Hettie?"

The kingdom's in trouble, Dex, and you have to save it.

"God preserve me!" he muttered, even though he'd stopped believing in God twenty years ago. "I'm going mad!" He scrambled together his trunk and his knapsack, tied his purse to his belt, cast a last horrified look around the empty castle chamber and fled.

Ursa was pruning a boil-free bush when he burst into her physicking workshop. Her narrow face was grave with concentration, her thin fingers sure and steady as she snipped, snipped, snipped at the boil-free's spiky red leaves. Her shoulder-length salt-and-pepper hair was hidden beneath an unflattering old scarf; her short, spare body clothed, inevitably, in a stained baggy smock. Workbenches lined the low-ceilinged room, thicketed ropes of dried and drying herbs dangled from its rafters. Trapped sunshine warmed the air which was redolent of mint and rosemary and sweet julietta.

For once the workshop's rustic welcome failed to soothe him.

"Ursa, I'm sick!" he panted, clutching at the corners of the nearest scarred bench. "Or losing my reason!"

Still snipping, she swept him head to toe with her measured grey gaze. "You look fine to me, Jones."

"No," he insisted. "I'm sick. Quick, you have to do something!"

Sighing, Ursa set down her shears, folded her arms across her flat chest and regarded him in silence for a moment. Then she pulled out a rickety stool and pointed. "Sit."

He sat, carefully, and watched as she rummaged in a handy drawer, withdrew a wooden hammer and laid it on the bench.

"Do you have nausea?" she asked.

He shook his head. "No."

"Dizzy?"

"No."

"Headache?"

"Not really."

"Shooting pains? Pins and needles? Faintness?"

"No, no, and no."

She glared at him. "You'll be more than sick if I find out this is some kind of a joke, Jones. I'm a busy woman, I have no time for jokes."

He clasped his hands between his knees to stop them shaking. "Ursa, trust me. This is no joke, I promise."

Her expression was sour. "It better not be." She crossed to the windowsill, where a neat line of potted plants drank the last of the sinking sun. With an impatient *hmmph* she plucked a leaf from a delicate purple vine, came back to him, spat on it and slapped it on his forehead.

"Do you have to spit?" he complained. "It's disgusting, Ursa."

She looked at him, unimpressed.

"It *is*!"

"Do I tell you how to string puppets, Jones?"

"Yes. All the time."

"And if you paid more attention they'd last twice as long."

With Hettie gone, she was his closest friend. Which wasn't to say she didn't drive him to distraction. "Huh," he muttered, under his breath. "Well, what's happening?"

"Hush up," she said, frowning. "Fevertell takes a minute or two to react."

A minute passed in toe-tapping impatience.

"No fever," she declared, twitched the leaf from his forehead and tossed it in a compost bin. Then she struck him on the knee with the hammer.

"Ow!" he said as his leg kicked out without him asking. "That hurt!" Anxiously, he looked at her. "Was it supposed to?"

"I just hit you with a hammer, Jones, what do you think?"

He swallowed. "I think . . . Ursa, I think I'm losing my wits!"

That made her grin. "If you had any to lose, Jones, I'd be worried for you."

He pounded his fist on his knee. The memory of that loved, longed-for voice in the empty castle room still had the power to raise the hair on his head. "For God's sake, Ursa, this is no laughing matter!"

"And nor is blasphemy, Dexterity Jones. You bite your tongue before God bites it for you!"

Irate, they glared at one another. He was the first to look away. Rubbing wet palms against his best velvet breeches he whispered, "Truly, Ursa, I'm afraid."

Her astringent voice gentled, and so did her face. "Yes, I can see that, Jones. Why? What's happened, my friend, to scuttle you into my workshop like a frightened rabbit?"

CHAPTER TWO

Dexterity opened his mouth to reply, then closed it again. Here, now, brought to the telling, he felt suddenly foolish. What would she think of him, sensible Ursa in her sensible workshop, if he babbled of his dead wife's voice speaking to him in an empty room? No. He was just over-tired . . . and it was spring. A difficult time of year. The ache in his heart, that constant companion, was magnified by memories and regrets.

Ursa was waiting for him to speak, staring with the forthright gaze that turned braver men than him to water. "Dexterity?"

He slid off the stool. "I'm sorry, Ursa. I shouldn't have disturbed you. I—"

"Sit down, Jones!"

He sat again. "Oh dear."

"It'll be more than 'Oh dear' if you don't stop shilly-shallying." She drummed her short, grimy nails on the bench top. "Just tell me what happened. All of it. No prevaricating."

Oh dear, oh dear. He gave her a half-hearted smile. "You'll think I'm a noddycock."

"I've thought that for twenty years, Jones. Spit it out."

"Well . . ." He rubbed his damp palms on his breeches again. "You see, it's like this. I was up at the castle, it's my day for selling to the ladies of the court. I saw the princess, too—" The sharp pity stirred. "I'm worried for Her Highness, she's not looking well. She—"

"Isn't the point of this story, is she?" said Ursa impatiently. "Jones, you are the *most* distractable man!"

No-one scolded like Ursa. He gave her a look. "Yes. Well, after the ladies departed I chatted to Hettie about the new curtains I'm planning for the parlour."

Ursa's fingernails resumed tapping on the bench top. "You're always chatting to Hettie. Do get to the *point.*"

"The point?" he repeated, his voice caught in his throat. "The point, Ursa, is that this time Hettie chatted back."

Being Ursa, she didn't shriek or throw her hands in the air or gasp, even a little. Being Ursa she blinked like a cat stretched out in the sunshine.

"Hmm," she said, after a considering pause. "That's interesting. What did she say?"

What did she say? *The kingdom's in trouble, Dex, and you have to save it.*

He couldn't tell Ursa that. "I—I don't know! I don't remember! It didn't occur to me to write it down, Ursa, please, you have to take this seriously. Hettie *spoke* to me! I *must* have a fever. Or else—or else—" He stared at her in horror. "Perhaps I'm losing my mind!"

She laughed. "That's ridiculous!"

"Easy enough for *you* to say! You're not the one hearing disembodied voices!"

In one of her mercurial mood changes Ursa patted his shoulder, all solicitous sympathy. "Now, now. Just you take a nice deep breath and come down out of the branches, Jones. You're no more losing your mind than I am."

"How can you be sure?"

"Because I'm a physick. It's my job to be sure."

"But—but *Ursa*—"

She rapped her knuckles on the top of his head. "Be quiet. You're going to calm down, Jones, and drink some ginger root tea."

Comforted by her lack of alarm he watched as she set her battered kettle on the hob and poked up the embers with a fire iron. He'd never known anyone so comfortable inside her own skin as Ursa. She moved briskly, with as much concentration and purpose while spooning dried ginger root into the teapot as she showed stitching a wound or splinting a broken bone. Her faded old scarf was fixed in place by the tortoiseshell clasps he'd given her last Kingdom Day. It warmed him to see them.

On the point of boiling, the kettle burped a wisp of steam. Ursa glanced at him, lips still quirked in her mocking smile. "It's been a while since you and I sat down to gossip."

Yes. A while. And not only because he'd been busy working and she regularly disappeared into the countryside hunting for herbs.

It's this time of year. After so long we still find it awkward. Silly, really. We both know there's no blame on either side. She did her best for Hettie and so did I. Some things just aren't meant to be . . .

He shrugged. "Ah, well. The days get away from you, don't they, if you're not careful."

Her mocking smile faded. "Yes," she said softly. "Yes, they certainly do."

The kettle boiled properly. Ursa poured hot water into the teapot and a rich ginger aroma billowed forth.

His stomach growled. "Don't suppose you've any plum duff about, have you?" he asked hopefully. "I rushed off without my breakfast this morning and I'm always too busy to eat when I'm up at the castle."

Ursa gazed heavenwards in silent beseechment. "When are you going to get yourself organised, Jones?" she said, reaching into a cupboard and bringing out a dented cake tin and a knife.

"I am organised! I just overslept. I had this wonderful idea last night for a new marionette, a shepherdess *and* her little flock, and I wanted to get her face started. But when I looked at the clock it was past midnight and I still hadn't packed my goods for today."

Ursa cut two generous slices of moist plum duff and put them on plates pulled down from a shelf. "It's always something with you," she said, handing him one. "You're a dyed-in-the-wool dreamer and no mistake."

Hettie used to say that, too, in the same amused and scolding voice. If she had lived he was sure she and Ursa would have become fast friends.

If she had lived . . .

To distract himself from that melancholy notion he took a big mouthful of plum duff. "Oh, this is wonderful!" he chumbled through Ursa's delectable cooking.

"I know," she said, and poured the tea into two chipped mugs. Looking at him through the rising steam she added, "It's one of Hettie's recipes. She pressed it on me, asked me to make sure I kept on baking plummy duff for you, not long before . . ."

She'd never told him that. He'd eaten her plum duff, oh, too many times to count, and she'd never told him where the recipe came from. *Oh, Hettie. Hettie. I miss you, my darling. I miss you so much.*

Ursa handed him a mug. "Perhaps I shouldn't have mentioned it."

"No, no, of course you should," he said, staring at his tea. "It's quite all right. No need to apologise."

"Hmm." She pulled out another stool and sat. "All right, Jones. About this voice you think was Hettie . . ."

Abruptly, perversely, he didn't want to talk about it. All he wanted to do was sit here eating Hettie's plum duff and drinking ginger root tea, pretending it wasn't nearly the anniversary of his beloved wife's death which was also, cruelly, the anniversary of their wedding.

And Ursa wonders why I've no time for God.

Around his last bite of cake he said, indistinctly, "I really am worried about Rhian, you know."

Ursa's severely disciplined eyebrows rose. For a moment he thought she'd challenge his refusal to answer her question, but she didn't. She just smiled at him and rolled her eyes.

"Rhian, is it? Dear me, how very cosy. And did the princess kiss your cheek on seeing you, Jones, and beg you to advise her about matters of state?"

Warm-faced beneath his unruly beard he washed down the last of his plum duff with a mouthful of tea then longingly eyed the closed cake tin. Seconds would be lovely but he knew better than to ask. Ursa, secure in her lean angularity, had caustic views on overindulgence.

"That's not fair," he said, shifting on his stool so the cake tin wasn't a direct temptation. "I've known the princess since she was a babe-in-arms. Why, I'm more than old enough to be her father! Can I help it if I think of her as Rhian? It's always *Your Highness* to her face, you can be assured."

"I can be assured that if there's trouble abroad you'll be the first in line to buy a ticket."

"I resent that, Ursa!"

She sniffed. "You'd resent the ground for slapping you if you tripped and fell down."

She was treating him like the fractious children who came to her with their cut knees and sore throats and busy beestung fingers. Briefly, he was cross.

"Ursa, I wish you'd take me seriously."

"Says the man hearing voices in an empty room," she murmured.

The kingdom's in trouble, Dex, and you have to save it.

He thrust the echo of Hettie's voice to one side. "This is important, Ursa. Things aren't going well with the king,

I'm certain of it. I think—" He swallowed, his mouth suddenly dry. "I think his health is far worse than we've been led to believe."

Ursa inspected her half-eaten slice of cake. "Really? Going into physicking, are you?"

"No, of course not! But—well—since *you're* a physick I wondered—you know—"

"Jones, I haven't a clue," she said, still eyeing her cake.

He leaned forward, as though her plants might be eavesdropping. "I thought you might've heard something. Something other than the official news from the castle."

"I haven't," said Ursa, after a moment. "But I'm not the physick our loftiest nobles call upon for their hangnails, am I?"

No, she wasn't, more fools them. Ursa had never been fashionable. Her choice of patients was dictated by need, not the size of their purses. Oh, she had her small share of important clients . . . those rare men and women who judged her on results, not the names she could drop at a posh dinner party. But they were few and far between.

"What have you heard of a Physick Ardell?" he said, sitting back. "He's attending the king."

"I know," she said. Typically, she needed no time to rummage through her memory. "Ardell's twelve years younger and eight inches taller than me. Bad teeth—he's far too fond of candied orange. Studied with Physick Runcette in duchy Meercheq. Darling of the nobility despite the fact he's keen on purges, pistillations and leeching."

"But he's a good physick?"

"Why?" asked Ursa, and finally ate more cake. "Is the princess dissatisfied with his services?"

Shadows cast by an uncertain future darkened the

bright, whitewashed workshop. Dexterity sighed. "She didn't say, exactly. But she does look sick with worry, Ursa. I tried to convince her to send for you, but—well, there are complications."

Again, Ursa's quirky smile. "Politely put." She drained her mug in one long swallow and set it on the bench. "And kindly done of you. But even if I did attend His Majesty I doubt there's any more I could do. Ardell's a touch too attached to his own self-importance for my tastes but he's as good a physick as any in Kingseat. In the kingdom, most likely. If the king is gravely ill despite Ardell's best efforts then . . . well, I think it must be hopeless."

"Hopeless?" He felt his mouth go dry again. His heart was pounding. "Do you mean His Majesty's *sure* to die?"

"Nothing's ever sure in physicking, Jones, but I have to say the facts don't bode a good outcome. The pestilence the princes brought home with them from Dev'karesh killed everyone it infected, poor souls. If the princess hadn't been out of the capital when her brothers returned I suspect we'd have long since buried her beside them. I've never said so but to my mind it's a miracle the king's lived this long." Ursa shook her head. "Thank God the outbreak was contained quickly or we'd likely be a kingdom of corpses by now."

That made him stare. "You've been *expecting* this?"

"I'm a physick, Jones. Disease is my livelihood. Of course I've been expecting it."

"You never said a word!"

She shrugged. "To what end? What's done is done. No point stirring people to a panic over what can't be changed or helped."

"Oh dear. And all this time I thought there was *some*

hope." He slapped the bench top. "It's so *unfair*! Rhian's young and beautiful, she should be dancing at balls, breaking hearts, being courted by some young lord, riding her favourite horse through the woods . . . not spending every waking moment cooped up in a sick-room watching her father die!"

No-one should be forced to watch a loved one die. *If only I could help her through this nightmare.* But he couldn't. He was nothing but a toymaker, the plain, unimportant man who'd made her giggle as a child and smile with fond memory now she was grown. He wasn't a great lord with the right to speak to her as an equal and offer his shoulder's strength in this time of woe.

"There's little point fretting yourself about it," said Ursa sharply. "You can't help the princess or the king and that's all there is to it."

Moodily, he rubbed the edge of his thumb over a knot in the bench between them. "I know. It just hurts to see her so . . . wounded."

"You may be as irritating as a shirtful of ants, Jones," she said, softening, "but I can't deny it—you're a good, sweet man."

She didn't often pay him compliments. Any other time he'd tease her for it but his mood was too sombre. "I hate to think what will happen to Rhian if you're right, and the king dies."

"What do you mean?" said Ursa, surprised. "You know what will happen. With no prince to wear Eberg's crown she'll marry a son from one of Ethrea's great Houses. He'll leave his name behind, become a Havrell and take the throne as king. She, as queen consort, will give birth to the Havrell heir."

He tugged his beard. "You make it sound so simple, but I fear it won't be. Rhian's unspoken for. The dukes have sons, and brothers, and nephews. They'll see the king's death as a bright opportunity to further their own fortunes. Who knows what kind of pressures will be placed on the princess to choose *this* man instead of *that* one? And not for *her* benefit or even for the kingdom's, but for the benefit of a virtual stranger." He slapped his knee. "It's a great pity she wasn't matched before the king fell so ill. Now she's got no-one to protect her from the scheming and the politics and the men who see her as nothing more than a pawn to further their own ambitions."

"She has Prolate Marlan," said Ursa. "As the kingdom's leading man of God he'll see she's not importuned or harassed."

Ursa, so acute in all else, had this one blindness. Like every faithful church-goer she set great store by Prolate Marlan. For himself, he wasn't so sure. Ethrea's prolate had always struck him as unctuous and intolerant, an unattractive combination. But it did no good to say that to Ursa.

"I hope so," he said. "Certainly it's his duty to protect her."

Ursa was watching him closely, narrow-eyed and purse-lipped. "You're taking this very *personally,* Jones."

He managed a faint smile. "Call me foolish but she could be my daughter. Hettie and I . . . we dreamed of a daughter." The old, familiar ache caught him. They'd dreamed of many things beneath the willows fringing the duck pond at the end of their lane. He closed his eyes. *Time to face facts.* "I did hear her, you know, Ursa. I just don't know why. I don't know what it means."

Ursa's hand closed over his. "Jones, my dear friend. Hettie is dead. What you heard was wishful thinking."

"No," he said, and looked at her. "It was more than that."

Instead of arguing, Ursa cleared the bench of plates and mugs and stacked them neatly in the sink under the window. Her face, in profile, looked troubled. When she finally turned to him her eyes were the grey of storm clouds.

"You've come to me as your physick and asked for my opinion. Here it is. I don't believe the dead speak to us. Not unless we're a prophet like Rollin, and Jones, you are surely *not* a new Rollin. But I don't think you're sick, either. You've no signs of fever or wilting or addlement. I say you're missing your wife more than usual because it's that time of year again and you should let it rest there."

He wished he could. He wanted to. But . . . "I can't."

"Jones, what did she say to you? At least—what do you *think* she said?"

Braced for scorn he whispered, "She said the kingdom's in trouble and I have to save it."

No scorn. Only pity. He thought that was worse.

"Oh, *Jones.* Do you hear yourself? Does that really sound likely?"

Of course not. It was the most *un*likely thing he'd ever heard. But unlikely or not . . . "I can't help that it sounds ridiculous, Ursa. I want to disbelieve it. But I was there. I heard her. Hettie spoke to me."

Ursa pulled a face. "Then I don't know what to tell you. I'm a physick, not a devout. If it's advice on miracles you're asking for, Jones, put your nose round a church door. It's been long enough."

There was more than a hint of censure in her voice and gaze but he refused to be shamed. The day he buried Hettie was the day he and God fell out and that was that. Ursa knew better than to try and change his mind on that score . . . or should do, after all these years.

Her scolding frown eased and she said more kindly, "There's no mystery here, Jones. The answer's staring you in the face. Next to no sleep last night and no breakfast to set you up for a busy day. That's what's ailing you. A decent meal and a good night's rest is the cure you're after. Go home. Cook yourself a proper dinner and get some shuteye. In the morning you'll laugh and forget all about this."

Something tells me that's easier said than done. He glanced out of the window at the fading sky. "It's not even sunset, Ursa."

"Early to bed and early to rise makes a man healthy, wealthy and unlikely to hear voices coming out of thin air," Ursa prescribed flatly. "You've got my advice, you can take it or leave it. Now stop being such an old hen and leave me to get on with my work."

He pushed himself to his feet. "You're probably right."

"I'm the physick. I'm always right."

Snorting, he kissed her cheek. "Your modesty overwhelms me. Goodbye."

She smiled. "Goodbye. Sleep well."

Outside in the laneway, Otto, his little grey donkey, was lipping at some dusty grass and practising put-upon sighs.

"I did hear her," Dexterity told him, unhitching the reins from a handy tree branch and clambering onto his brightly painted cart. "I'm not frazzled or addled or underslept. I heard Hettie. And I don't understand what it means, Otto."

Otto's ears indicated that he didn't understand it either, nor did he much care and could they just get on home to the stable and dinner, please?

"Go on then," Dexterity said, and rattled the reins. "Shake a leg."

With Otto-like perversity the donkey shook his head instead. Then he leaned into his harness, broke into a grumpy trot and aimed his long ears towards home. There was no time now to see about the parlour curtains. And given the state of the world, perhaps redecorating the cottage should wait.

The sun was just sinking below the horizon as Otto turned in at the cottage gate. By the time Dexterity had unhitched and tended the donkey and stowed his emptied trunk in his workshop, then smothered his day's earnings in the kitchen's flour barrel, lit the lamps, pumped water for his bath, heated it over the flames in the parlour fireplace and filled the tub, stars were pricking the night sky and moths were gathered at his cottage's glowing windows. He tugged the old green curtains across the glass, shutting out the world.

The flickering lamplight warmed his rose-pink parlour walls, sinking the corners and crannies into shadow so the commonplace was made mysterious. Hettie smiled at him from her place on the mantelpiece, pleased by the buttercups he'd vased beside her that morning. The portrait was fading now, with age and the heat from fires in this little home they'd created all those years ago. The picture frame was cracked in the bottom right-hand corner, the paint chipped on the left. He'd dropped it a week ago, while he was dusting. She wouldn't like it much, could she see it; neat as a pin and twice as sharp was his Hettie.

"I'll make you a new frame, my love," he promised as he peeled off his clothes, dropping waistcoat and shirt and breeches and smalls and stockings in a pile by the door. "As soon as I've the time. I'll paint it blue and gold, would you like that?"

Her silent smile lamented his untidiness, but gave no answer.

He dipped his toe in the bath water and sighed. Just right. Hettie would have added lavender oil and rose petals to it and laughed at his complaining. An unscented bath, breathing heat, deep enough for drowning: just what he needed at the end of a trying day. He clambered over the side of the tub and sank inch by inch into the steaming water until his beard touched its surface. Closing his eyes with a groan of pleasure, he surrendered to hard-won luxury.

"Dex? Dexie love, pay attention. This is ever so important."

Heart thudding, he held his breath and cracked one eye open like a man unlatching his door to the tax collector.

"Hettie?"

She was standing before the hearth, not a moment older than the day he'd buried her, with her fair hair curling against her cheeks and her brown eyes warm with love for him. She was wearing her green dress, the one with pink ribbon threaded around the bodice. He'd always loved it on her. The small parlour smelled of lavender and roses.

A sob rose within him and he fumbled out of the bathtub, heedless of dripping water, of naked skin, wanting only to touch her, to hold her, to fold her into his empty arms. But he was too afraid . . .

"Hettie?" he whispered, hardly daring to believe. "Is it really you?"

"Yes, you great daftie, of course it's me," she said, her voice a familiar muddle of affectionate exasperation. Tears sprang to his eyes to hear it. "Now listen, for I've not much time and a deal to tell you. There's terrible trouble coming to Ethrea, Dex. Darkness and despair the likes of which our folk have never known."

"What do you mean?" he demanded. "What kind of trouble? And why are you telling me? There's nothing *I* can do about it. You should be telling His Majesty, or the prolate."

Hettie shook her head. "They wouldn't listen. I can't tell this to a dying king or a prolate arrogant and deaf in his office. You're the one man I can reach, Dexie, and the only man who can reach the princess. This is her fight as well and she'll need a good friend. As for your importance . . . well, you may be a simple toymaker now but in the days to come, my love, you'll be the most important man in the kingdom."

"Me?" he said, incredulous. "I don't think so, Hettie. What I think is that Ursa's plum duff on an empty stomach has given me the collywobbles! I'm *dreaming*. I must be."

Hettie's arms were folded under her plump bosom and her chin was lifted in the way that meant she was serious. "Dexie, it's no dream. You've been chosen to aid Ethrea in its greatest hour of peril, when the future of this land and all its people, great and small, will hang by a thread no stronger than cotton. There's no point fussing about it or saying you won't because you must and that's all there is to it."

"Must?" he echoed. "Don't I get a say in the matter? Who is it tells me I *must*?"

Her eyes were sorrowful, as brimful of sadness as the day she'd kissed his hand and told him she was dying. "God."

He laughed. "Lass, you're addled. I've got no use for God."

"Maybe you have and maybe you haven't," she replied, tart as unripe apples. "But God's got a use for you, Dexterity Jones. Now *listen*. On the morrow, as the sun rises, go down to the harbour. Search out the slave ship with the red dragon figurehead and speak to the sailor with the triple-plaited beard. For a few coins he'll let you on board. There you're to find the man with blue hair and buy him, no matter what he costs."

And that dropped his jaw all over again. "*Buy* him? Hettie, don't be silly. Slavery's for uncivilised foreigners, not us."

"Remember well, my love," she said, and rippled like a reflection on wind-stirred water. "The ship with the red dragon figurehead. The sailor with the triple-plaited beard. The man with the blue hair. His name is Zandakar. You must take care of him till I can come to you again."

She was fading before his eyes, he could see right through her to the fire-danced hearth and the mantelpiece and the cracked picture frame. "No, Hettie, don't go!" he cried. "I don't understand. Why must I buy him? What do I do with him? Is he the cause of our troubles? Hettie, tell me!"

She was smiling, and his heart was breaking. "Don't

be afraid," she said, thinned almost to nothing. "Remember I love you."

"No, Hettie! Don't go! Don't leave me, not again! *Hettie!*" Desperate, he lunged towards her, threw his arms wide to catch her to him . . .

. . . and tripped and found himself half pitched over the side of the bathtub, choking and gasping and coughing in a tidal wave of cooling water that slopped onto the carpet and up into his face. Shaken and shivering he fell back into his bath and covered his eyes, his heart pounding as wild as the harbour waves at storm's height.

Beyond that, the only sound in the room was the tock tick tock of the clock on the mantelpiece.

Minutes passed. After some time he felt able to uncover his eyes. The room was empty. Hettie was gone . . . if she'd even been there at all.

"Hettie?" he whispered to the lamplit room. "Are you there, Hettie?"

The curtains stirred as though tugged by living fingers, and in the air a sweet pungency of roses and lavender.

"Hettie . . ."

He sighed, a deep groaning of air. Mad, he was *mad* to think she'd been here. Red dragon figureheads and sailors with triple-plaited beards and men with blue hair. Whoever heard of a man with blue hair? Or with an outlandish name like *Zandakar*.

Dexterity Jones, chosen by *God*? Chosen by indigestion was more like it. The whole business was impossible. Outrageous. Ridiculous.

"Ridiculous!" he said out loud, daring the shadows to contradict him. "It never happened. It was nothing but a collywobble dream. And I'm not going to pay a dream any mind at all. The only proper place for a man at sunrise is where he should be. In bed. And when the cock crows on the morrow, that's where I'll be. In bed."

Then he sank himself to the bottom of the bathtub, to make his point to whoever might, or might not, be listening.

CHAPTER THREE

R hian . . ."
      Startled awake, Rhian dropped the book she'd been dozing over. "Yes, Papa? What is it? Do you need something?" Taking his hand between her palms she chafed the dry skin and tried not to think of his brittle bones, snapping.

"What time is it, Rhian?"

She glanced at the clock. "Early. Would you like the curtains opened, Papa?"

He nodded, wincing, so she slipped from the chair and drew back the windows' heavy crimson drapes, spilling the sunrise all over herself. The spring light felt clean on her skin, chasing away the shadows of another long, painful bedside vigil.

They were alone. Ven'Justin had mercifully departed at midnight and was yet to return. But return he would, with his droning and his bead-clicking. If she and her father were to talk of things that mattered they must talk now.

Although he was a little restored with sleep, his pinched face told her, unequivocally, she could no longer delay.

If I wait until later I might be too late. God, give me the words. Please give me the strength.

As she slid back into her chair her father said, "I wish you would not coop yourself in here with me."

"What's this?" she said, striving for humour. "Are you saying you're tired of my company, Papa?"

With an effort, he stretched his hand towards her. "Silly girl. You know my meaning well enough."

She had to blink away tears. "There's no place in the world for me save by your side, Papa. I'll be with you until the end."

As he stirred on his pillows she could see the pain in him. It hurt her so cruelly that for a moment she couldn't breathe. He said, "That end is almost upon me, Rhian."

"I know," she whispered, and let the tears fall.

"Rhian," her father said when she had composed herself, "we must speak of what will happen when I die."

I know what will happen, Papa. I'll be alone. "Yes," she said, and sat a little straighter. "I know we can't put it off any longer. I've been thinking on the matter, I—"

"No," said her father. "Where the succession is concerned you will vouchsafe no opinion, Rhian. I speak not as your papa now, but as your king."

Oh, she wasn't going to like this, was she? "Yes, Papa," she said, and folded her hands. The early sunshine no longer warmed her. She felt cold and small and cornered, like some pitiful creature fighting for its life.

"Had God willed it Ranald would have worn the crown after me," said her father, his sunken eyes fixed on midair, on the past. "Or Simon, had he survived that pestilential infection. But my heart's hope was denied me when God took your brothers in their prime." He paused to catch his breath, the air bubbling in his chest. "You are my only daughter, Rhian. You know what you must do, for me and for Ethrea. You must bear a fistful of sons. All that remains to decide is who will take my place on the throne."

And sleep in my bed. Rhian felt the heat of anger flush her head to toe. *He talks as though I'm a prized broodmare, and he the studmaster who must choose the best stallion. But I'm no fecund mare, I'm a royal heir as much as Ranald and Simon. The only royal heir now. Why will no-one recognise that?*

"Papa," she said, schooling her voice to a passionless murmur, "I feel I'm too young to marry."

"Too young?" Her father frowned, displeased. "Your mother, God grant her peace, was two years younger than you the day we wed. *Too young!*" Scorn withered his failing voice. "Such notions arise from an excess of bookishness and a want of attention to the womanly arts."

She sat very still, her heart a drumbeat in her ears. "That doesn't sound like you, Papa. That sounds like the prolate. It's a wonder Marlan can pronounce on such matters, sworn celibate that he is."

"Mind your tongue, Rhian!" her father said, sharp with anger even though he was dying. "Marlan is God's chosen man. Do not take so lightly his office or the God-given wisdom of his preaching."

She rose from her chair and walked back to the window, not daring to show him her face till it was the very image of contrition. He never used to speak like this.

Before the boys died he had scant affection for Marlan and his mean-spirited pronouncements. Nor had he been overpious. But grief and illness had shaken her father to the bone. Cast him adrift on a sea of uncertainty.

If I'm not careful he'll drown me with him.

"Forgive me, Papa," she begged him at last, turning. "It's wrong of me to criticise the prolate."

Her father nodded, weakly. "Excessively wrong."

"But Papa, Marlan is unfair when he accuses me of lacking the womanly arts. Mama took great pains to teach me all she knew of such things, while she could."

Her father's severe expression softened. "So she did, most excellently. No woman born had more gentleness, grace and breeding than your mother."

"And after we lost Mama your own sister, God rest her, taught me everything else I should know."

"Yes. Arabella was a fine woman, too."

"Indeed. And as for excessive bookishness, Papa," Rhian pressed, "upon whose lap did I sit every day in the library, learning my alphabet and then, in time, reading the great histories of Ethrea, the geographies and biologies and religious treatises deemed essential to the education of any royal prince?"

"I know full well I encouraged you to study every book you could lay your hand upon, Rhian, but—"

"Furthermore," she continued, relentless, "who was it presented me with my first foil and taught me to fence like a master? Who gifted me with my first bow and instructed me in the finer points of archery? And who sat me on my first pony and pointed me after hounds?"

Her father's sigh became a rattling cough. "It was me,

it was me, I freely confess it," he said, when he could speak again. "But that has nothing to do with—"

"Papa!" She returned to his bedside. "It has *everything* to do with it. All my life you've treated me as a third son. Never once did you send me away, saying 'This pursuit is unwomanly, you may not take part'. I was Ranald's shadow, Simon's echo. You used to laugh about that! But now you would *chide* me?"

Her father groped for her hand with palsied fingers. "Rhian, my dear daughter. I do not chide you, I only remark that you have often favoured manly activities over and above the matters that should concern a young woman ripe for marriage." Another pause, so he could catch his thin breath. "To be sure I took pride in a fancy riposte or an unbroken string of bull's-eyes, but I hazard a prospective husband might look more favourably upon a fine piece of tapestry or a pleasant tune on the flute."

"Papa," she said, excessively reasonable, "tapestries and flutes are all very well but they have little to do with ruling a kingdom."

He released her hand. In his face, weary understanding and the intent to deny. "Do not be foolish, child."

"Why is it foolish?" she demanded. "I'm of the blood royal, a legitimate daughter of the House of Havrell! You've said it yourself, I'm as thoroughly educated as any prince. Truth be told I'm better educated than Ranald was. He never cared for books and learning. Don't make a face, Papa, you know I'm right! If I were your third son I—"

"But you're not, Rhian," said her father. "And there the matter ends."

"*Why* does it end? Why am I good enough to *breed* a king yet somehow insufficient to rule as one myself?"

He did not reprove her rudeness or demand a more compliant demeanour. He loved her, and was sorry. "Rhian, be sensible. You're barely nineteen, almost a year from your majority."

"If I were a prince I'd have attained it already! That's not fair either, Papa, I—"

"*Fair?*" Her father coughed again, harshly, an ominous wheezing deep in his chest. "You prate to me of *fair*, Rhian?"

She felt her cheeks heat. "Papa—"

"When you say such things I think your fine education was wasted!"

"All I mean," she said, her fingers clenched, "is it's galling to know that Prolate Marlan and the council consider me feeble just because I was born a girl. I'm not feeble, Papa. You *know* that. And they'll know it too, before very long. I'll be twenty in the blink of an eye!"

"Yes," her father agreed. "But Rhian, gaining your majority won't make you a prince. My councillors fear that your feminine characteristics, while admirable in a queen consort, do not lend themselves to the more rigorous demands of ruling a kingdom."

Now she couldn't breathe properly. The air was stifling in her lungs. There were tears in her eyes, she could feel them burning. "And what about you, Papa? Is that what *you* fear?"

He recaptured her hand, his touch colder than ice. "I do not dispute you have much to offer this kingdom, Rhian, and offer it you will." His voice was faint, every shallow breath an effort. "As Ethrea's queen consort, in the bodies of your children and such works of charity and social service as you may choose to perform."

"I see," she said tightly. "So I do get to choose something, do I?"

"Of course!" he said. He sounded wounded. *Wounded*. When she was the one cut to bleeding by his words . . . "Do you take me for a tyrant, Rhian, that I would trammel you about with rules and regulations and give not one whit for your happiness? Is that the kind of father I have been to you?"

With exquisite care she removed her hand from his grasp. "You've been the kind of father who led me to believe that nothing I desired was beyond my reach, that my sex had no bearing upon my value, that whatever I dreamed of I could also achieve if only I applied my heart and mind and will to the task. Are you telling me that was a lie?"

"No," he whispered. "But when I believed it you had two brothers and I had two sons."

As the hot tears overflowed her eyes she said, "So who am I to marry, Papa? Who will be the lucky man?"

Her father averted his gaze. "The council is preparing a list of eligible suitors. When it is completed, you and I will consider their choices."

"But *Papa* . . ." With an effort, she subdued her treacherous temper. "Your councillors aren't impartial. Excepting Marlan, each one answers to a different duke. They'll favour their own lord's son or close relative or someone from a duchy family their duke wishes to court or control. The only way we've maintained Ethrea's unification for so long is by making the business of royal marriage *royal* business, with no outside interference."

"Rhian . . ." Her father sighed. "I am dying, not addled. Of course—"

"Yes, Papa, you're dying!" she interrupted. "And if, God forbid, you're taken from us before the council's list is completed, before I've made my choice with you to endorse it, what then? It's clear your council holds me in utter contempt. They won't listen to my thoughts on this, they'll argue and bully and—"

"They will not," said her father. "Marlan heads the council in my absence, and will continue to head it until a new king is crowned. He will control the dukes' men, never fear."

Control them and me as well, an obedient puppet, if he has his way. I'd rather die. She slid from the chair to her knees and clasped her hands on the counterpane, as though in prayer.

"Please, papa, *listen*. This realm is no more important to you than it is to me. How better can it be served than by your one true heir succeeding you? Our House, our family, was chosen by God to rule Ethrea. How can you break that faith? If the man I marry becomes Ethrea's king our royal bloodline will be broken! More than three hundred years of history thrown away!"

Though his meagre strength had ebbed almost to its lowest tide, her father struggled upright against his pillows. "I break no faith, girl. I throw nothing away. Our bloodline will continue through your children, my grandchildren. And in their children and those children's children. Why isn't that good enough for you? It was good enough to please your mother!"

"My mother's father was not the king! Papa, you say I can't rule in my own right, but *why*? There is no law—"

"Nor is there precedent," said her father. He was sweating, trembling, the palsy in his fingers spreading through his whole body. "Our kingdom's prolate is clear on the matter. There is no authority in law or scripture to sanction the crowning of a queen."

Marlan, again. *He is such a busy man. I must find a way to thank him for his interest in my life.* "Papa—"

"*Enough,* girl. Must I spend my last days in tumult with you?" said her father, tears brimming in his yellowed eyes. "This is not your decision. I am the king. You are my subject. Marriage, Rhian. That is your future. You will marry a fine son of Ethrea and you will have fine sons of your own. When the council is ready it will deliver its list of eligible suitors and together you and I will consider it. Naturally the final choice will be yours, within reason."

Every gasping word he spoke was a dagger point, pricking. "Within reason?"

Drained of colour, her father sagged against his pillows. "Yes. Of course."

She might have laughed, if weeping wasn't so near. "And what of the spurned pretenders to my hand, Papa? Not being of the Keldrave persuasion I have to be satisfied with only one husband. How much trouble can I expect from the eligible men I deem unworthy of a crown?"

Her father nodded. "That is why we must act quickly, to choose the right man and crown him king and you queen consort, before trouble has a chance to stir." He coughed, pressing a kerchief to his bloodless lips. "Before I die," he added, when his breath had returned. "Marlan tells me the list will be ready within two days. But Rhian . . ."

What, there was more bad news? "Tell me, Papa," she said, suddenly exhausted. *I can't be cast any lower than this.*

He was struggling to keep his sunken eyes open. "I know of one name for certain you'll not find on the council's list. Alasdair Linfoi."

"Why don't you like him?" she said, when she could trust her voice. "You've never told me. Ranald was fond of him. Simon, too. You made no objection when he spent time with the boys."

Her father's head shifted, his gaze avoiding her. "Men's friendships are different. And Ranald was to be king, Simon the Duke of Kingseat after him when he took the throne. A king and his dukes cannot be estranged."

He made it sound so—so *practical*. "We all spent time together, Papa," she said, struggling to keep her temper. "Me and the boys and Alasdair. At court."

"And your brothers knew to keep an eye on you," said her father. "And him. They knew how far to let Linfoi run his line."

They'd *discussed* her? *Spied* on her? *What gave them the right?* Sickened, she watched her fingers tighten into fists on the counterpane. "I don't understand. Alasdair's a duke's son, and soon he'll be a duke. Surely—"

"I don't care for his pedigree. And Linfoi's a paltry duchy. It breeds spavined horses and men of slight character. Let Alasdair inherit it, I have no care for that. But I won't have our House allied with his. We can do better."

So unfair! So high-handed! "But *Papa*—"

"Enough!" said her father, almost groaning. "Rhian, enough. Would you crush me with your selfish dissent? Would you poison my last days with fears for your obedience and love for this kingdom?"

Oh. So there are deeper depths into which I can fall.

She pushed herself to her feet and turned her face away to hide her fiery cheeks. "No, Papa. Of course not."

"Then put Alasdair Linfoi from your thoughts, Rhian, and all shall be well," said her father faintly. "I will find you a husband worthy of our name."

Her heart felt like a lump of lead. "Yes, Papa."

"I will," he insisted. "Rhian, look at me."

With infinite reluctance she turned back to the bed. "Papa."

"I know this is difficult," he whispered, with an effort. If she breathed hard on him he'd float away. "Were you some simple village lass you could wed where your fancy led you and frolic from sunup to sun-down with no more thought of politics than a cow gives to astronomy. But you are not a village lass. Your life has ever been circumscribed by matters of state."

If that were true, she'd never noticed. And whose fault was that? *Perhaps I'm not as worldly as I thought.*

"You must rest, Papa. All this talking has tired you out, and Ven'Justin will be here soon to take up his vigil. If you need me, send to the sewing room or the kitchens where I'll be pursuing such tasks as befit a mere woman."

Then she was closing his chamber door behind her, gently, for no-one was permitted to slam the king's door save the king himself . . . and none of the outer chamber attendants, looking at her serene face as she swept past them to the corridor, could have guessed what a stormy passion raged beneath her skin.

These men, these men, these impossible men . . .

"Highness! Princess Rhian! Highness!"

Hearing the cry, Rhian slowed, swearing under her breath. Damnation. *Helfred.* Her entirely unnecessary personal chaplain, yet another debt she owed Prolate Marlan.

In his mind I'm so unimportant I don't even rate a venerable to plague me. But then, Marlan doesn't have a venerable nephew, does he?

"Princess Rhian! Highness! Princess Rhian!"

The querulous, nasal voice could not be ignored. Marlan's nephew would trot in her wake the length and breadth of the castle and all its grounds, bleating like an abandoned lamb until either she heeded him or dropped in her tracks from old age.

She stopped, and turned. "Yes, Chaplain? What is it?" Hopefully he'd take the hint from her tone and scuttle back the way he'd come.

Sublimely oblivious, Helfred hitched his dark blue habit a little higher round his puffy ankles and hurried along the corridor to join her. Such a gormless fellow, looking always as though there should be a drip at the end of his nose. She didn't know exactly how old he was, it wasn't something that came up in spiritual conversations. She guessed he was perhaps ten years older than herself, which would make him a hairsbreadth younger than her dead brother, Ranald. A smidgin older than her other dead brother, Simon. Oh, how she missed them . . . and was angry.

You wretches. If you hadn't insisted on running off adventuring I wouldn't be in this mess now!

"Your Highness," said Helfred as he reached her, touching his thumb to his heart and moist pink lips. "Where are you going?"

She was a full four inches taller than him. At times like this the advantage in height was something of a comfort. "Tell me what business it is of yours and I'll tell you where I'm going," she replied. "Perhaps."

His poached-egg eyes regarded her reproachfully. "Highness, as your spiritual advisor it is my duty to attend you at all times, in case some crisis should arise that requires my intervention."

"So you keep saying," she said, "without any kind of precedent *or* proof, I might add. Very well. What if I told you I'm on my way to the watercloset?"

He blinked, pinking beneath his unhealthy skin. "Are you?"

"As it happens, no. But for the sake of argument let's say that I am. I can't imagine what kind of crisis might arise there that would require your intervention, can you? Unless of course I were to run out of—"

"Highness!" Helfred squawked, blushing like a beacon from his greasy forehead to his pimply neck. "This is hardly a proper topic of conversation!"

"No," she agreed regretfully. "I dare say it's not. Forgive me. I sat up all night with the king. I'm tired and hungry and now that I think of it, I do need to pee."

"Highness!" he called, scurrying to catch up again as she continued toward her privy apartments. "Highness, as I was about to say, given that I have the honour of being your spiritual advisor it is incumbent upon me to remind you that three full days have passed since you knelt with me in chapel and recited the Litany."

She glanced sideways at him, trampling the overwhelming urge to pick up her skirts and run. "Really? As long as that? I swear it seems like only five minutes."

"No, Highness, three days, my sacred oath upon it," said Helfred. "As a good and obedient daughter of the

Church I know you wish to do your duty, and as soon as possible."

Biting back a sailor's oath she'd learned from Ranald, she stopped again and glared at him. "I think you mean, Helfred, that you wish to pick my brains and winnow my heart so you can report my innermost thoughts and feelings to your uncle!"

"*Highness!*" said Helfred, offended, and drew himself up to his full, inconsequential height.

Her temper was like an unbroken horse, fighting at the end of a rope to be free. "Helfred?"

"You are unjust, Princess Rhian," he said, his voice unsteady. "I did not ask to be born the prolate's nephew any more than you asked to be born daughter to a king. These matters are arranged by God, not man. My concerns lie only with you and your soul, and whatever you tell me in confidence I lock in my breast and would not reveal under any circumstance. No, not even were I to be cast into a pit of fire and tortured beyond the endurance of Rollin himself!"

He sounded genuinely hurt. For once she looked at him, really looked, beyond the unattractive surface to the man beneath. The sincerity in his eyes and face seemed real. Conscience pricked her, and she relaxed.

The little worm is right. It's not his fault his mother was Marlan's sister. I suppose, in his own way, he's as trapped as me. Though that doesn't mean I have to like him . . . or trust him.

It did mean, though, she should try to be fair. She sighed, and made an effort to sweeten her voice. "As I can't imagine who would want to torture you for my sake, Helfred, I think you can rest easy on that score." She chewed her lip, then added, "You're right. I was unjust. I know you have my best interests at heart."

Helfred smiled, revealing his small, crooked teeth. "Always, Highness. Please do not berate yourself. The king's illness is a great strain. I think we all feel it, no-one more than you. But in times of trial God's love sustains us. It is wrong of you to turn away from that. Perhaps you don't realise how many in Kingseat look to you as an example of piety and submission to heaven's will. It is your duty to show them how obedience to God strengthens every heart."

Rhian blinked. *I mustn't hit him, I mustn't hit him. Papa would be disappointed if I hit him.* "Yes. Well. That's certainly one way of looking at things, Helfred."

"It is the only way," he said earnestly. "In the love of God even great trials grow smaller. And God surely loves you greatly, Higness, to send so many trials to you in such a short time."

The trouble was, he really believed it. *I could throw rocks at his faith and they'd bounce right off. I wonder where he gets it from . . .* Finger by finger she relaxed her fists. "As you say, Helfred. There have been many trials." *And more to come, with Papa's death imminent, and marriage to an unknown man.*

Helfred looked pleased. "Contemplation in chapel will soothe your spirit, Highness. I know it soothes me when I am troubled."

She really had no hope of avoiding this. "Oh, very well, Helfred. I'll attend you there. You have my word. But first I really do have to pee. And bathe. And eat. And change my dress. I'll need an hour."

This time he didn't react to her lack of maidenly circumspection, only touched his thumb to heart and lips again. "Highness. I shall be waiting for you in God's house."

She watched him retreat, his leather sandals thumping on the corridor carpet, his humble habit swirling around his legs. She had to give him that: even though he was well within his rights to wear silk and slippers like the other chaplains, of his own free will and in the face of his formidable uncle's displeasure he chose the modest attire of an untried novice.

He's gormless and chinless and so often sanctimonious . . . but he's not a bad man. Not bad like his uncle. If I threw rocks at Marlan it's his pride they'd bounce off, not his faith.

She sighed, and put out a hand to the wall. How her head ached. What she wanted more than anything was to fall face-down on her bed and take refuge in sleep. But no. Thanks to Helfred's interference she must kneel for hours in the chapel, begging for help from a God she only half believed in, at best.

You'd go a long way to restoring my piety, God, if you helped me avoid this unwanted marriage. I'm my father's daughter, I know I'd make a good queen of Ethrea. If you did choose my family's House to rule over this kingdom, why turn your face from it now? What have we done to earn your displeasure? What can I do to return us to your favour?

"Go to chapel, Rhian," she sighed aloud, answering herself, and pushed away from the wall. Ah, well. At least it would give her some quiet time to think. And she did need quite desperately to think. To find a way out of her current dilemma or, failing that, some way of reconciling herself to it. "All right. All right. I'm going to chapel."

"Your Highness?" said a startled courtier, in passing. He stopped and bowed. "Was there something you wanted?"

The castle staff had long since been trained to leave her alone unless she addressed them directly. She'd found it tedious beyond bearing to be constantly fawned over just because they met her on the stairs or in a corridor. She knew she was held in awe and reverence, the courtiers and the rest didn't need to prove it every time their paths haphazardly crossed.

With a small effort she found a smile for Laffrie. "No. Nothing. I was . . . thinking aloud. Be about your business, don't let me detain you."

"Your Highness," said Laffrie, with another bow. His eyes were sympathetic. She could feel his concern, like heat from a fire. Even as he withdrew as commanded she could feel his concern. It made things worse, not better. She hated being the object of pity. Yes, her father was dying. Yes, her brothers were dead. It was sad, it was dreadful, life could be so cruel.

But that doesn't make me weak. I'm not weak. I'm not helpless. I'm not a fragile, hothouse flower. I'm a princess of Ethrea, the blood of kings flows through my veins. I don't need men's guidance, as though I were lame or blind or defective in my wits.

And it was past time the council and Marlan and her father recognised that. Unbidden, Alasdair Linfoi's plain, bony face rose before her inner eye.

They say I must marry? Fine. Then I'll marry. But I'll marry a man that suits my purpose, not theirs. A man who pleases me, not them. They're not the ones who'll have to bed him. And if they think they can force me otherwise . . . well, that would be a pity. I'm Eberg's daughter. Let them cross me at their peril.

CHAPTER FOUR

The port of Kingseat never slept.

Even so early in the morning, when sensible people were tidily in their beds or, at the very worst, eating breakfast, heavy wagons drawn by plodding oxen and patient draughthorses stood in line along Harbour Street, waiting to be allowed through the guarded merchant gates to collect the imported goods that had passed inspection by dock and customs officials, or to drop off the goods sold to foreign interests that hadn't come into port by river barge from one of Ethrea's other duchies. Trundling past them, heading away from the harbour, were the wagons already given access to the docks, empty or laden depending on their purposes.

Up and down the long line of waiting wagons stamped food and drink vendors, their trays slung from wide leather straps hooked about their necks. They enjoyed brisk trade, the carters and wagoners readily parting with a few coins to stave off thirst, hunger and boredom. The fresh salt air was ripe with the rich scents of meat and potato and leek pasties, mulled cider, warm milk spiced with nutmeg and hot tea or cold ale for those who didn't feel the nip of an early spring sunrise. Spoiling the sweetness, the ranker stink of horse and ox dung dropped in steaming piles on the cobbled streets. Urchin children with hessian sacks, small spades and nimble fingers darted among the wagons, scooping up the animal shit for later sale to market-gardeners, avid rose-growers and the like in town.

Very little went to waste in this most capital of cities.

Morosely waiting his turn in line, a minnow caught between two whales, Dexterity sat in his little donkey cart and whittled away at the face of his new shepherdess marionette.

He still couldn't quite believe he was here.

I must be mad. One dream brought on by indigestion and I've completely taken leave of my senses.

Beneath his knife and his careful fingers, the face of the shepherdess was revealing itself. She looked like Hettie. He frowned at her.

This is nonsense. I'm a fool.

Lifting the marionette to his lips, he blew, very gently, then sneezed as a wood shaving went up his nose. Woken from his doze, Otto tossed his head. Dexterity snatched at the reins, just in case the donkey judged he'd had enough of hanging about here, thank you, and decided to take them back home. Thwarted, Otto blew disparagingly through his nostrils and went back to sleep. Lucky donkey. Dexterity returned his attention to the puppet he so lovingly carved.

If this is a fool's errand I'll never tell Ursa. She'd laugh me into the middle of next week if I told her I'd come down to the harbour in search of a man with blue hair because Hettie told me to.

He'd woken from restless sleep at the brink of sunrise without the slightest intention of going anywhere near the harbour. No intention of searching for a ship, or a sailor, or a man named Zandakar. *Certainly* with no intention of buying him.

Buying men, like groceries? It's an abominable notion. Bad enough we let the slave ships into our harbour and do business with the nations that truck in slavery. But to become a slave owner myself? Impossible! Not to mention illegal. Hettie, my dear love, what were you thinking?

The wagon in front of him creaked into motion then, and it was time to trundle a few steps closer to the harbour inspection point. Dexterity craned his neck to see round the wagon's bulk. Surely it was nearly their turn by now? Yes. Two more wagons to be assessed, then it was him. He waved away yet another hopeful pie vendor and returned his attention to his wooden shepherdess.

Yet here I am, on Hettie's say-so, waiting to be allowed into the docks. Yes indeed. I'm completely mad.

And entirely incapable of not getting out of bed and coming down to the harbour. Because as he'd lain beneath his blankets in the pre-dawn gloom his squirrelling thoughts had come to one inescapable conclusion: either it wasn't Hettie who'd come to him in the bath last night, in which case all he'd lose was a little time . . .

. . . or it *was* Hettie. In which case there *would* be a slave ship with a red dragon figurehead and a sailor with a triple-plaited beard and a man called Zandakar whose hair was blue.

And if they are there, then it means the other things she said are true too. Ethrea in danger. Princess

Rhian in danger. And my plain life about to become very . . . interesting.

Abruptly and deeply unsettled, he returned the shepherdess and his whittling knife to their leather satchel, woke Otto from his doze and waited impatiently for the line of wagons to move again.

One way or another there's no going on until this is settled.

At last it was his turn to explain his presence to a harbour official. He'd decided he couldn't possibly tell the truth. Who would believe him? Instead he'd concocted a tale about having to meet with a potential supplier of rare woods and fabrics for his toymaking business.

"Ayesuh?" said the harbour official, and spat a stream of baccy juice onto the cobbles. "That'll be seven piggets, then."

"Seven piggets?" said Dexterity, staring. "To drive my donkey and cart along a few piers? *Seven piggets?*" His voice slid up the scale of outrage like a toy trombone.

"Ayesuh," said the official, vastly unmoved. He was a large man, with a straggle of red hair over his battle-scarred scalp and arms strong enough to lift a dozen anchors without trying. "Drive it. Tie it. Occupy space with it and like as not leave donkey droppings for us to clean up after. Seven piggets, Mr Jones. Take it or leave it, makes no difference to me."

Dexterity sighed. Seven piggets. He asked as much for a wooden pony, which often as not took a whole morning's work to put together, and that was before the paint job. But what choice did he have? Trundling about in his waist purse, he produced the coins and dropped them reluctantly into the harbour official's enormous palm.

"Right you are then," said the official, and waved his hand. "Off you go."

"Yes. Thank you," said Dexterity. "Although I wonder if you could help me? I'm looking for a boat with a red dragon figureh—"

"Off you go," said the harbour official, glowering. "You're obstructing a king's man in the execution of his duty."

"My apologies," Dexterity said hastily. "Good morning. Come along, Otto, hup-hup!"

With a distinct lack of enthusiasm Otto hup-hupped his way past the official and a nearby gaggle of wagons and carts, through the noise of brisk merchant enterprise, sailors shouting and singing, dockhands swearing, and the ripe smells of manure and produce and the wafted stink of the fish wharf, some distance away, onto the cobbled harbour apron from which pier after pier protruded like teeth on a comb.

So many sailing vessels from so many nations placidly riding the gentle harbour, tied tight to their moorings like stabled horses. Cogs, smacks, whirlers, fleets, yachts, fourmasters, gigs, deep-bellied traders, sails snapping sharply in the salty breeze. Eyes wide, Dexterity stared. He seldom needed to visit Kingseat Harbour. Children's toys weren't much in demand as an export, unlike the grain and wine and wool and linens and silks and brocades, the gold and silver and jewelled crafts, the pottery and crockery, the hides and woodwork and metalwork and so forth that poured into Kingseat by river and road, bound for distant lands at fabulous prices. Every so often he'd accompany Ursa to the harbour markets and hold her basket for her as she picked her way around the myriad stalls, hunting for some rare herb or other. On those un-common outings he'd sometimes spy a special piece of timber from the Far East, ebony or foxwood, or a little pot of enamel in a colour not seen so often in Ethrea, and then he'd part with his hard-earned piggets—and maybe, if the wood or colour were fine enough, a talent or two—and endure Ursa's scathing remarks on fools who spent their money as though it were on fire.

"Oh dear," he said to Otto, letting his gaze roam over all those moored ships. "I think we're going to be here for quite a while." Of course if he asked someone for help, a dockhand or a sailor or one of the merchants, he might find what he was looking for more swiftly . . . but he'd also draw attention to himself. And a crawling sensation between his shoulder blades told him that might not be wise.

Not when it's a slave ship I'm looking for.

Instead, he gave himself neck ache swivelling his gaze from side to side, driving Otto at a snail's pace up and down each long pier, searching for a red dragon figure-head. There were bare-breasted ladies and dolphins and horn-headed bulls, seasprites and seahorses and seawolves and even a unicorn, once . . . but no sign of a red dragon. Behind him, the merchant gates were a dot in the distance and there was only one more pier to search.

It was beginning to look as though Hettie had been mistaken after all. Or that the whole thing really could be laid at the door of Ursa's plum duff.

And then the clean salt breeze jinked, and the fresh air was suddenly tainted with the sickly stench of unwashed bodies and the sour sweat of fear, and pain.

Otto threw up his head, snorting, and Dexterity gasped aloud, one hand flying to cover his nose and mouth.

"God save us! What is that?"

At the very end of the harbour's last pier, separated from the other moored ships by three empty berths as though it were a pariah, rocked a deep-bellied boat. Black, without a single wasted line or so much as a brass-sparkle of decoration or brightwork. Even its sails were black, tight furled to the masts like waiting fists, ready at a moment's provocation to strike the wind full in the face.

It had a roaring red dragon figurehead.

The breeze jinked again and another wave of foul stench wafted from the vessel, poisoning the glorious morning. Cold sweat broke on Dexterity's brow and down his back, but he picked up Otto's reins and shook the little donkey into a huffy trot towards the slave ship that Hettie had asked him to find. He attracted a few interested glances from the sailors unloading cargo from the moored ships he passed, but he ignored them.

Oh dear. Oh Hettie. Perhaps this is the dream.

Up close, the red dragon figurehead was a fearsome thing, carved from a scarlet timber he'd never seen before in his life, all scales and teeth, eyes like hot coals glaring over the harbour as though it wanted to burn everything in its sight to ash. Staring at it, one hand still pressed to his nose and mouth, Dexterity felt his scudding pulse stutter.

Movement caught his eye. A sailor, come to look down over the railing, of middle age and sun-burnished skin, lean and long and not to be crossed. He had dark hair clubbed close in a queue, one single green staring eye, and his beard was plaited into three neat tails. If he had to guess, he'd say the man hailed from Slynt.

Heart thudding, he eased Otto and the cart to a standstill. "Good morning, sir," he called up to the slave ship.

"Might I trouble you for a few words?" The sailor with the triple-plaited beard spat. Taking that as sailor speak for "yes", he added, "In private? I've business I'd prefer not to shout at the top of my lungs, if you know what I mean."

The sailor considered him for a moment then put one hand to the slave ship's railing and leapt down to the pier as neatly as a cat. With the supreme indifference of a cat, he proceeded to piss into the softly surging waters of Kingseat Harbour. Finishing his business he tucked himself away inside his baggy blue trousers, hitched his broad leather belt around his narrow, dangerous hips, and turned to take stock of his visitor. The sailor wore no shirt, and his nipples were pierced with small golden rings. The broad sun-browned planes of his chest were tattooed with gory images of harpooned whales.

Dexterity cleared his throat. This close to the ominous black slave ship he was hard put not to gag. More than anything he wanted to fish his handkerchief from his pocket and plug his nostrils to save himself from the eye-watering odour that thickened the air almost past breathing. But something told him the piratical sailor might take offence at that . . . and he didn't look the kind of man who took offence without offering a little bloodshed in return.

"I wonder," he said, "if you don't mind my asking. This fine vessel of yours *is* a slave ship, isn't it?"

The sailor's single green eye burned him up and down. A patch hid the ruination of his other eye, but the long scar that trailed down his sun-leathered cheek like a dribble of candle wax suggested horrors not to be imagined. The man hawked and spat and scraped at his stubbled jaw with the blade of a knife, produced suddenly from the baggy blue trousers.

"And what if it is?" he said, his accent rough and guttural, with daggers in it. Definitely a Slyntian. An unsavoury breed. "You have a complaint?"

"No, no," Dexterity said hastily. "Just making sure, you know. Wouldn't like to think I was bothering the wrong person. Ah . . . where do you hail from, if I might ask?"

"Last port was Insica. You got a problem with *that*?"

Insica. Insica. Oh yes. In Slynt, which made sense. A good two months' sailing distance east, if memory served. "Oh dear, not at all. I was just curious."

The sailor scowled. "Stow your curiosity. What do you want?"

"Ah. Yes," he said, his heart bouncing from rib to rib. "Well, I want to buy a slave. From you. If you have one to spare."

"Buy a slave?" the sailor echoed. His bright blade flashed as he tossed it from hand to hand with casual disregard. It looked sharp enough to shear fingers should he miss . . . but he didn't, nor did he glance once at his lethal toy as he considered the suggestion. "There be no slavery hereabouts. You Ethreans, you disapprove. You got laws."

"Ah," he said. "Indeed. Yes. There are laws. I don't deny some of us do disapprove of slavery, that time-honoured institution." He strayed his fingers to his waist purse. "But not all of us. And you being from foreign lands, and not likely to see me again, I don't expect our laws would trouble you unduly . . . would they?"

The sailor grinned, revealing teeth in good health, if alarmingly orange. "Only if the king's men poke their noses where they be not wanted."

Dexterity smiled back, sweat slicking his spine. "Oh,

I don't see why a private matter of business between two gentlemen should remain anything other than private. Do you? Of course, if there's someone else I should make my request to, someone with more authority . . ." He let his voice trail away suggestively.

The sailor scowled and jutted his jaw, which set his triple-plaited beard bobbing. The wicked knife flashed one last time, then disappeared. "I be as good as captain for now. Boss and crew be at furlough, up in the town. You be speaking to anyone, you be speaking to me."

"Oh, well, that's perfectly fine," Dexterity said, and swung himself down from the cart. Patting Otto, looping the reins about a handy bollard, he whispered, "You stay here, all right? I won't be gone long."

"You wanting to come aboard?" the sailor said.

"Of course," he replied. "Try before you buy, that's my motto. Never settle for a pig in a poke. I'm sure you have excellent taste in slaves but I don't like to part with money without seeing for myself what's on offer."

The sailor grunted and held out his hand, fingers twitching suggestively. "Let's peep the colour of your dosh, then."

For a few coins he'll let you on board, Hettie had said. Dexterity hid a scowl in his unplaited beard, filched two copper piggets from his waist purse and handed them over. At this rate he'd have no money left for buying a three-legged wharf rat, let alone a man, with or without blue hair. "For your time and trouble, kind sir."

The look the sailor gave him was anything but kind. "My time be worth a sight more than that."

Two piggets became four. The sailor hawked and spat again, and the piggets vanished. "Up the gangplank then," he said, nodding at a flimsy piece of timber tying the ship to the shore. It was narrow, and moving, and it had no railings. The sailor's single green eye was maliciously amused.

Dexterity swallowed. This could be unfortunate. Seemed there was a choice here of either drowning or being crushed between hull and pier. But he'd come too far to turn back now, so he took a deep breath, which made him want to vomit, fixed his gaze on the solid railing above his head and scuttled up the gangplank. Behind him, the sailor trod the narrow stretch of timber with the ease of a man sauntering along his own home street.

The smell was even worse on board.

"Where are they?" Dexterity asked, looking about at the trimly coiled ropes, the scrubbed deck, the battened hatches. "The slaves, I mean?"

The sailor stamped his booted foot. "Where do you think? Down below. In the hold."

"Oh." The hold. Naturally. Where else? His eyes were watering from the fumes that breathed upwards from what must surely be a sweltering cesspool of death, if the stench was anything to go by. "I don't suppose you could bring them up on deck for a few moments, could you?" he said hopefully. "Let me have a look at them in daylight?"

The sailor nearly choked to death, laughing. "Bring 'em up? Nay, sir, you'll be going down to shake 'em by the hand, you will. Now or never, for I got no time to mawk about with a jiggirit like you."

Jiggirit. Now there was a word he was glad not to know. "Oh. Well. All right," he said, and watched as the sailor fetched a lamp, lit it, unbolted one of the hatches and stood aside.

"After you," he invited, his careless hand indicating the descending wooden ladder, orange teeth and green eye brilliant in the strengthening sunshine. "Smartly, I'll thank you."

"After me," Dexterity said faintly. "Yes. Of course."

As his head passed deck level and his foot groped unsteadily for the next rung down, the hold's heat and stink smote him like a hammer. He swayed, dizzy, and splintered his hands on the ladder with desperate clutching. It was dark, too, a fuggy lightless gloom leavened only by the sailor's following lamp and the snatches of sunlight filtering through the open hatch above.

"On you go now," the sailor urged. "You want a king's man to come asking of our business?"

No, he most certainly didn't. *Hettie, Hettie, what have you got me into?* His feet touched the hold's floor, then the sailor slid the rest of the way like a monkey down a greased pole and held the flickering lamp high overhead.

Tears of pity burned Dexterity's eyes as he adjusted to the dimness, and could properly see the slave ship's wretched cargo. See the sleeping-pallets stacked floor to ceiling, with barely a foot's space in between them. See the glint of manacles in the lamp's faint glow. See the slaves, rubbing flesh to putrid flesh, packed as tight as fish in a barrel. Some were light-skinned, some were dark. Others were coloured as he'd never seen in his life, puddled white and black . . . or perhaps it was just bruising. The rankness of their unwashed bodies, of bucketed excrement and vomit and urine, of rotting sores and maggoty horsemeat rose up in a wave and crashed upon him, stunning him, leaving him half-robbed of all his senses.

A murmur rose from the noisome crowd as the slaves

realised something out of the ordinary was happening. Dexterity caught a glimpse of countless desperate eyes, gleaming in the near-dark.

'Choose, then," said the sailor, sounding nervous. "Captain'll be back from furlough sometime, and there'll be hell to pay if he finds you here."

"Give me the lamp and I shall," Dexterity said, and held out his hand. "I want to look first."

"Look at what?" the sailor demanded. "One slave's as like another. Choose the nearest and be scarpering off my ship."

"Give me the lamp!" Dexterity snapped, and plucked it from the sailor's surprised fingers. Holding it aloft, he ventured step by unsteady step between the rows of naked, chained men, women and children, heartbreaking as they turned emaciated faces to look at him, stretched bony, begging fingers towards him and whispered in tongues unknown, yet searingly knowable.

Save me, help me, free me. I want to live. Don't let me die.

Speechless, almost blinded by tears, he turned away from them, hurriedly searching for a man with blue hair. He didn't dare call the man's name, call *Zandakar*, for fear of starting a riot or making the sailor even more uneasy.

Hettie, Hettie. Help me, please.

"Come on! Hurry!" the sailor shouted, fear shredding his voice. "Now, else I'll lock you in here with the rest of the vermin and good luck to you at journey's end!"

"One minute, just one minute!" he shouted back. "I'm nearly done."

Hettie, for God's sake. You brought me here, you'd better do something!

Choking on the foetid air, his forearm pressed against his face in a vain attempt to stifle the stench, he forced himself to the back of the hold. There. Up there, on the pallet closest to the ceiling. Was that a glimmer of blue? Was that the man?

Jerkily he clambered one-handed up the side of the bunks, the lamp held high, tearing and kicking himself free of all the reaching, desperate fingers, stopping his ears to the wailing cries for help. He reached the topmost bunk and shone the lamp on its occupant. A man, past his first youth but not old. Desperately thin, a rack of bones draped in dull, coffee-coloured skin. Dirty, stinking, runnelled with sores, daubed with pus and shit and vomit.

Beneath the filth, his tangled hair was blue.

Dexterity felt his heart pound like a hammer. *Hettie, I've found him. Oh, Hettie. What now?* He touched the chained man lightly, afraid his touch might cause more pain.

"Zandakar," he whispered. "Is that you? Is your name Zandakar?"

The man's eyes dragged open. They were blue as well, the clear sharp blue of ice, burning with fever and the stirring of hope. He spoke, a string of foreign, unintelligible words. His voice was a harsh croak.

"No, no, I don't understand you," Dexterity said, still whispering. He hung the lamp on the corner of the pallet and laid his finger like a feather on the man's pustuled lips. "Zandakar? Zan—da—kar?"

The man with blue hair nodded, slowly. Against that feather finger he said, *"Zandakar"*. Then one chained wrist lifted, as though its weight were a torment, and one clawed finger pointed at his xylophone chest. *"Zandakar."*

He patted the slave's bony shoulder. "It's nice to meet you. Don't go away." Turning carefully, he called out to the sailor. "Here! Here I say! I've found the one I want. Bring keys for his manacles and I'll give you gold!" As the sailor stamped and cursed towards them, he turned back to the slave. "Don't be frightened, I'll have you out of here in—oh."

Tears were streaming down Zandakar's sunken cheeks.

"You! You want his chains off?" said the sailor, standing below and brandishing a set of keys. "You unchain him!"

Leaving Zandakar weeping and the lamp hooked in place, Dexterity slithered to the floor. "For gold, my friend, *you'll* unchain him *and* you'll carry him up to the deck and get him safely into my cart!"

The sailor stared. "Me? Carry a slave?" He spat. "You be witless."

He could've torn out the sailor's triple-tailed beard. "Do you want your gold? Gold I'll wager you don't intend sharing with your captain or your shipmates? If the answer's yes, you'll do as I ask!"

More cursing and swearing, but the sailor obeyed. Zandakar cried out as the manacles were torn free of his suppurating flesh, and again as he was dragged off the rough wooden pallet and thrown like a carcass over the sailor's resentful shoulder. Then he fainted, and Dexterity breathed heartfelt thanks for small mercies.

As he took the lamp from the burdened sailor and followed him to the foot of the ladder, the wretches he wasn't able to save realised he was leaving and they were not. They wailed and screeched in more tongues than he could count, battering him with their terror and pain. Weeping himself now, he closed his eyes and scrambled towards freedom as fast as he could climb.

"Batten the hatch, quick," said the sailor as Dexterity flung himself into the sweet fresh air above the hold. "They'll shutten up once it's nice and dark again."

He did as he was told, then discarded the lamp and nodded at Zandakar, still senseless and dangling. In the bright sunshine he could see cooties scurrying through the man's blue hair and on the dark skin. He felt his stomach turn over queasily.

"Now you must put him in my cart."

With a silent snarl the sailor turned and headed for the gangplank. Dexterity followed, and once down on the pier he hurried to Otto and his cart. "Wait, wait a moment," he snapped at the sailor, and shook out the blankets he'd brought just in case. He spread one on the bottom of the cart, then stood back. "Gently, gently!" he cried as the sailor dumped the unconscious slave like an unwanted sack of bones.

"Now pay me and be gone," the sailor said. One hand played with the hilt of his dagger, the other was outstretched, greedy for the kiss of gold. His sharp green gaze darted up and down the pier, alert for the return of his ignorant captain.

Dexterity untied his waist purse from his belt, removed the eight remaining piggets from it, and tossed the purse to the sailor. "There's twenty talents in there, enough to buy ten slaves, I expect. But you've been very helpful, so take it all. And if you're as smart as you think you are you'll never breathe a word of this to another soul."

The sailor laughed, and licked his lips as a stream of

gold poured into his hand. Then his one good eye narrowed and he bit a heavy round coin, to be sure.

"I'll be on my way, then," said Dexterity. He tucked the second blanket around the slave with blue hair, *Zandakar,* dithered a moment, and covered him again with the light canvas he kept stowed in the cart for unexpected rain. Better that casually prying eyes catch no glimpse of this particular passenger. Then he unhitched Otto's reins from the bollard and put his foot on the wheel hub.

The sailor grinned at him. "Come again sometime, and welcome," he said, trickling his gold out of sight. "We'll find you another one, eh, with fine ripe titties!"

"I don't think so," said Dexterity, and hauled himself into the cart. "But I'm sure it's a lovely thought. Good day." With a sharp smack, he slapped the reins against Otto's indignant rump and never once looked back at the sailor, or the black slave ship, or its roaring red dragon figurehead as they made their way back along the pier towards the merchant's gate, heading for help in the only possible place it could be found.

CHAPTER FIVE

Ursa was in her front garden, pruning roses.

"Jones!" she greeted him as Otto and the cart rattled to a halt by her front gate. "You're out and about early."

"Yes, aren't I?" Dexterity agreed, and cleared his throat. "Ursa, I need your help."

"You don't have to tell me," she said, blotting her dirt-smudged face on her sleeve. "I'm always saying it. But why are you saying it, Jones? Should I be worried?"

He looked up and down the quiet street, where one or two other early risers were going about their business, and leaned as close as he could without actually falling off the cart. "It's like this," he began in a confidential whisper.

Behind him, beneath the blanket and canvas coverings, the man with blue hair stirred, groaning.

"What was that?" said Ursa, looking around.

He straightened. "What?"

The man in the cart groaned again, a piteous sound. Ursa planted her hands on her hips. *"That!"*

"Ah . . ." he said. Oh dear. Now that he was at the point of confession he found himself unaccountably nervous. Ursa had firm views on slavery. She had firm views on everything. And she wasn't going to be at all impressed about this.

But that's not important. The poor man needs physicking and that's what he's going to get. And I'm going to get my ears chewed off, I just know it.

"Dexterity Jones, what have you done?" Ursa demanded, dropping her pruning shears into the basket beside her. "Have you gone and run someone down with your donkey cart?"

"No!" he said, offended. "How could I possibly do that? I can walk faster than Otto trots, most days. No. But I do have someone here who's in need of a physick."

Lips thinned, expression grim, Ursa pushed open the garden's front gate. "Jones, what kind of trouble are you landed in now?" she muttered, stamping to the back of the cart.

He swivelled on the driver's seat and tried to look wounded. "Trouble?" he said, as she pulled back the covering canvas and blanket. "Ah—well—none at all." *Trouble is too light a word.*

"Really?" Ursa stared at the groaning naked man with the blue hair. "What do you call him, then?"

"Zandakar," he said, after a heart-pounding moment.

Ursa's eyebrows shot up. *"Zandakar?"*

"Well, it's his name."

"And how do you know?" said Ursa, running her physick's gaze over the unconscious slave's mistreated body and clearly not liking what she saw.

"Ah . . ." He cleared his throat again. "Hettie told me."

"Hettie told—" With a hard-breathing effort, Ursa bit back the rest. "Never mind. You can explain later. For now, help me get this poor wretch into the house."

"No, I don't think so, Ursa. I think he has to stay with me. You can physick him at my place."

"Your place?" Ursa shook her head. "Out of the question. This isn't a simple case of a dab of ointment here and a snippet of gauze there. This man's in a bad way and—"

"I'm sorry, Ursa, but he can't stay here. Your clinic's too busy, someone could notice something's going on. Someone might see him by accident. They'd certainly see me hanging about. And no-one must know this man is in my possession."

She stared at him, incredulous. "Your *possession*? Jones, are you telling me—"

Oh dear. He took a deep breath. "Yes. He's a slave. I

bought him. From a Slyntian." With the money he'd intended spending on new curtains, and more. The enormity of it smote him without warning.

How can it be right that gold can buy new curtains or a man? What kind of a world equates Zandakar with a bolt of cloth? Something to be purchased?

"Please, Ursa," he added. "I will explain later, as much as I can. But for now could you get your pills and potions and come home with me? I don't think this poor fellow should be kept waiting for help any longer, do you?"

"Turn the cart around," said Ursa curtly, pulling the blanket and canvas back over her newest patient. "And wait."

As she marched away he looked at the sick man's shrouded shape. "Don't you worry, Zandakar. Ursa's the best physick in Kingseat. You'll be up and around again in no time, I promise." Which didn't look very likely, in truth, but was the kind of thing Ursa insisted sick people needed to hear.

Except he won't understand me, and I don't understand him, and how we're supposed to make head or tail of each other I'm sure I haven't the first idea.

With an energetic "hup-hup" to Otto he coaxed the cart in the opposite direction. A few moments later Ursa came out of her front door, a bulky, battered leather bag slung over one shoulder and a frown on her face.

"I've left a note for Bamfield," she said, climbing into the cart. "He can manage the clinic on his own for one day. If he can't then I'm not the teacher I think I am."

"Thank you, Ursa," he said quietly. "You won't regret this."

She gave him a look. "Don't be ridiculous, Jones. I'm

regretting it already." She stowed her bag between them and twitched the reins from his fingers. "I'll drive. You're slower than an arthritic hen. Come on, Otto, you lazy thing, get a move on or I'll tan your hide for my winter boots, just see if I don't!"

Otto flailed his long ears and got a move on.

The journey was completed in ominous silence. Glancing often at Ursa's set, uncommunicative face, Dexterity pinned his damp hands between his knees.

Oh dear, she's angry. I knew she would be. But how could I not buy the poor man? Even if Hettie hadn't told me I must, how could I leave him in that hellish slave ship? I only wish I could've bought them all.

They reached home, eventually. Leaving Otto hitched in the cottage's rear yard, Ursa led the way into the small kitchen. She was stringently clear as to how she wanted things to proceed, which involved clearing Hettie's long kitchen table and spreading it with an old, thick blanket, boiling a large pot of water for the scalding of soft cloths she had him fetch from the ragbag, and keeping out from underfoot as she ranged her jars and pots and muslin bags of ointments and salves and possets and so forth along the nearby bench. Rolls of bandages she'd brought with her too, and these she set out from small to large, along with the pins to fasten them. She asked for a tub to be placed on the floor at one end of the table, and an armful of clean towels. Then she set out her scissors, shears, tweezers, razor, needles and threads close to hand, and surveyed all with pleased eagle eyes.

"Right," she said. "Let's fetch in this Zandakar, shall we?"

For all the skin and boniness of him the man with blue

hair was still a weight to carry into the kitchen and lay face-up on the table, where he lolled unconscious, breathing in slow, shallow gasps.

Dexterity uncricked his back. "I must see to Otto. Will you be all right for the while?"

"Of course," Ursa replied absently, staring at the man on the table. "He's in no fit state to be thinking of starting a ruckus. Be off to your donkey but don't dawdle out there, Jones. This is a job for two and no mistake."

So he unharnessed poor long-suffering Otto, and made up for all this early-morning bustle with extra oats and a generous dollop of molasses.

As he stamped back into the kitchen Ursa said, "Water's boiling. Put the rags in it then scrub yourself to the elbows, if you please. Use the soap in the green jar by the sink."

She snapped out orders like a noble but there was no point protesting. It was easier just to do as he was told. "So, Ursa. What do you make of him, then?" he asked, lathering his arms with the yellow paste in the jar. The man with blue hair lay very still, seemingly stuporous, with his eyes half-opened and his hands lax by his sides.

Ursa stood back from the table and balanced her chin on her fingers, frowning gently. "Well, I'd say he's no older than thirty, at the most. Before this he was strong, fit and healthy. He has good bones, good teeth. There used to be muscle, too, before starvation wasted him. He led an active life, but a hard one. There are old scars beneath the new ones. Some look like wounds from a bladed weapon. At least that's my guess. I think others were caused by arrows. One of those has been tattooed. Very odd."

Surprised, Dexterity looked again at the man he'd bought. Bladed weapons? Arrows? "He's a warrior?"

She shrugged. "Perhaps. I've heard there are warrior tribes still in less-civilised lands. Far, far to the east. Of course that could just be romantic rumour. You know what sailors are like."

Finished with his scrubbing, he reached for a towel and dried his arms. "You think he's from the east?"

"I don't know, Jones. All I can tell you is I've not seen another man like him. I've seen races with dark skin before. We all have. Icthians. The Keldrave. But a dark race with blue eyes and blue hair? Never."

An unknown warrior. A man of violence. Lying on Hettie's kitchen table . . . He cleared his throat. "Do you think he might be dangerous?"

Ursa looked at him. "Do you really need me to answer that?"

"I'm sure he's not," he said, feeling anything but sure. Then he was ashamed. *Hettie wouldn't put me in danger. This man won't hurt me even if he is a warrior. Haven't I saved his life? Once he's better I expect we'll become the best of friends. I'll just be certain not to leave any knives lying about.*

Ursa shook her head. "Let's hope you're right, Jones, for your sake. Has he spoken to you?"

"Yes. On the slave ship. But I couldn't understand a word," he said, spreading the damp towel over the sink's edge to dry. "It was a tongue I've never heard before and we hear most foreign tongues these days, in Kingseat."

"We certainly do," she said thoughtfully. "Did you ask the slavers about him?"

"There was no time. The sailor I bought him from had

no business selling me a slave but he was greedy for gold. He couldn't see the back of us fast enough."

"And why exactly did you buy this man?" she demanded, then lifted a hand. "No. Don't tell me, let me guess. Hettie told you."

Helpless, he looked at her. "I'm sorry, Ursa. But you don't want me to lie, do you?"

"Believe me, I'm tempted," she retorted. Then she relented. "But it's done now. We'll talk about it later. All that matters for the moment is physicking the poor wretch." She nodded at the pot of boiling rags. "Empty that."

He glanced over his shoulder as he strained the steaming water out of the pot, leaving the scalded rags to cool. "I've never seen anyone so badly mishandled. The poor fellow's not *dying,* is he?"

"No," sighed Ursa. "But if he'd stayed on that slave ship much longer he'd be more than dying, he'd be stone-cold dead."

Dexterity joined her beside Hettie's table and frowned at the naked man he'd bought. No, rescued. Whoever this Zandakar proved to be, one thing was certain. He was no longer a slave. "So . . . what's wrong with him?"

Ursa snorted. "You'd get a shorter answer if you asked me what was right." She pointed to a round, raised ugly scar on his breast. "See that? It's a brand. About half a year old, I'm guessing. It got badly infected after it was burned into him, see the old pustules? And the way the surrounding muscle has pitted?" Gently she took the blue-haired man by his right shoulder and rolled him towards her. "And these whip marks? Inflicted about the same time, the earliest ones. Some are far more recent, obviously." With enormous care she let him settle onto his back again. "The rest of his troubles are a result of captivity, forced marching, being chained in tight quarters without fresh air, fresh water or decent food. He's running a fever and there's been a blow to the head, too. Bad. It's a wonder his skull wasn't cracked like an egg-shell."

Sickened, Dexterity stared at his unexpected . . . guest. "But you can heal him, Ursa, can't you? It's very important that you heal him." *I know that much, if I don't know anything else.*

"I can try," Ursa said grimly. "But Jones, this is a sick man who's been brutally mishandled. And even if I can heal his body there might be damage to his mind, his soul, that no amount of physicking can repair. You need to brace yourself for that. I know my job but I'm not a miracle worker. Whatever you think you need this Zandakar for, I wouldn't be making any plans just yet."

Oh dear. "Ursa, I'm afraid I don't have the first idea why I need him. All I know is I had to get him off that slave ship. As for the rest . . ." He spread his hands wide. "Your guess is as good as mine."

Ursa just looked at him. "Yet you risked yourself to buy him because Hettie said so?"

"That's right."

"And you're determined to keep him here, in your home, even though he might be dangerous, because Hettie said so?"

He folded his arms. "That's right."

"And you say you've lost your faith. Jones—" She drummed her fingers on the edge of the table. "I'm not sure you understand what you're getting yourself into. This Zandakar will need constant watching, dressings changed every two hours, and medicines he'll not appreciate poured down his throat and slathered over him from head to toe. Suitable food. Water. Bedpans. I'll be honest with you, I don't know whether you're up to this or not. You're a toymaker, not a nurse."

He stiffened. "I nursed Hettie."

She spared him a swift smile. "That you did. And you nursed her well. But we both know this is *entirely* different."

"Ursa . . ." He unfolded his arms and touched his fingers to her wrist. "Please. I *must* be the one to take care of him."

Her expression was a mingling of exasperation, impatience and affection. "Because Hettie said so?"

He nodded. "That's right."

"I don't like it, Jones."

"You don't have to. Just trust me. Please? Zandakar is sick and we have to make him better. Does anything matter more than that?"

"Hmmph," she said, exasperation winning out. "All right, Jones. I'll go along with you . . . for the moment. But don't think that's the end of this conversation. Once my patient here is seen to we'll pick up where we left off. I *will* be getting to the bottom of this nonsense. That's a promise." She smiled, without humour. "And you know me. I keep my promises."

She certainly did. It was one of the best things about her. "And you'll help me to nurse him? I can't do it alone."

She rolled her eyes. "Yes. I'll help you to nurse him."

Dexterity felt a flood of relief. Whatever this mystery meant, he couldn't imagine unravelling it without Ursa's staunch aid and acerbic intelligence. "*Thank you.* Now, what do I do?"

Ursa looked her patient up and down. "For a start we're going to get rid of that disgusting hair so I can see to the head wound and the cooties. Pass me my shears, Jones. I'm going to clip him like a sheep!"

The first touch of the blades startled the man awake. Half rising from the table, he shouted, *"Wei! Wei!"*

"Hold him down, Jones!" said Ursa, stepping back with the shears held high. "The last thing he needs is a finger lopped off!"

Hold him down? Hold him down *how*? There wasn't a square inch of the man's skin that wasn't festering or blistered or slimed with pus. Gingerly he took hold of the former slave's shoulders and tried to restrain him. "Please be still," he begged. "Please don't struggle!"

The man ignored him. Weak and hurting as he was, still he tried to roll himself off Hettie's table. Dexterity let go of his shoulders and seized his forearms instead, doing his best to avoid the open, weeping sores left by wrist manacles fastened too tightly for too long.

"Wei, wei," the former slave repeated, trying to fight free.

"Stop this!" Dexterity shouted. "You'll hurt yourself. Do you hear me? Zandakar, *stop!*"

As though he'd been shot, the man stopped thrashing.

"That's better," he said, and loosened his grip. "We're not going to hurt you. We're trying to *help* you, Zandakar."

"Zandakar," the man whispered. "Zandakar."

The panic had receded in his ice-blue eyes. Dexterity nodded. "Yes. Hello, Zandakar. Remember me?"

"Smile at him, Jones," said Ursa. "I'd say it's been a while since he saw a friendly face."

"Are you sure?" he said, glancing at her. "For all we know, where he comes from smiling is a declaration of war."

"He's unarmed and I've got the shears. *Smile* at him, Jones. Try to make a connection."

Oh dear. Tentatively, Dexterity smiled. "It's all right, Zandakar," he said, in the tone of voice he used to calm overexcited children. "You're perfectly safe here. We're not going to hurt you. *Zandakar*. See? I know your name." He pointed at himself. "Dexterity." He pointed at Ursa. "Ursa." Gently, he touched the man's shoulder. "Zandakar."

It seemed to be working. Responding to the smile, or the unthreatening tone, or maybe to both, the man began to relax. After a moment he nodded. "*Zho*. Zandakar."

"*Zho*. What does that mean?" said Dexterity, with another glance at Ursa.

She shrugged. "Your guess is as good as mine, Jones."

"It sounds like *yes*. Do you think that's what he means?"

"I think I'm getting tired of standing here with these shears," said Ursa. "Shall we press on?"

"Oh. Yes. Of course." He turned back to Zandakar and risked another smile. "All right now? Everything all right?"

Zandakar was frowning. "Dex—Dex—"

"Dexterity. But Dex is fine. It's easier to say." He nodded, still smiling. "*Zho*. Dex."

"Dex," said Zandakar, then looked at Ursa. "Ursa."

He had a deep, musical voice, its timbre rich and dark. There was definitely an accent. Dexterity nodded. "*Zho*, Zandakar. I am Dex, and she is Ursa."

"And Ursa is about to cut your hair," she said, and stepped forward again.

Zandakar saw the shears and shook his head. *"Wei! Wei!"*

"I think it's safe to say that *wei* means no," said Ursa. She raised a warning finger. "Zandakar, *wei*." Swiftly, taking the sick man by surprise, she seized a handful of his filthy matted hair and held it for a moment. When she let it go and held her hand in front of his eyes there were countless parasites crawling over her skin.

Dexterity saw Zandakar shiver with revulsion. He was feeling revolted himself. "Wash them off, Ursa, for pity's sake."

"No point," she said, her fierce gaze not leaving Zandakar's face. "They'll only jump back on me when I start shearing him. Hold up that tub, Jones, and let's get this done with." She gave the shears a little waggle. "*Zho*, Zandakar?"

Holding the tub so the cut hair would fall cleanly into it, Dexterity saw a silent struggle in Zandakar's eyes.

"*Zho*, Zandakar," he said, gently. "You mustn't fret. It's only hair, it will grow back."

Abandoning the last of his resistance, Zandakar closed his eyes. *"Zho."*

"Burn it, Jones," she said when she'd hacked off all the matted blue hair. "Outside, so you don't stink up the kitchen."

When he came back inside, nostrils clogged with the stench of singed hair, she was bent close over Zandakar's ragged skull with a pair of tweezers, plucking fat white wriggling things from the savage wound above his right ear. Zandakar was grinding his teeth, small grunts of pain escaping through his flattened lips.

He stepped closer. "Ursa, what are you—oh! *Maggots!*" His belly heaved and his hand slapped over his bile-scalded mouth.

"Yes, Jones, maggots," said Ursa, sparing him a derisive glance. "And let's thank God for them, shall we? Maggots feast on dead meat only. They eat diseased tissue and prevent rotting. Doubtless we'll find them secreted elsewhere on this poor wretch, so either get used to them or get out. I've not time nor patience for lily-livered fussing."

He took a deep breath and willed his treacherous stomach to behave itself. "Sorry. I'm all right. I want to stay."

Ursa plucked the last maggot free of Zandakar's head wound and dropped it with the rest on the cloth she held in her other hand. "Good. These you can burn in the stove."

As he disposed of the maggots she selected a small glass vial from the bottles arranged along the kitchen bench. After twisting the stoppered plug free she took one of the cooled boiled cloths, dripped some of the vial's pale green contents onto it, re-stoppered and returned it to the bench then slapped the cloth over Zandakar's nose and mouth. His eyes flew open. He struggled once, twice, then sagged into unconsciousness.

"Ursa!" Dexterity protested. "Was that really necessary? I think he was just beginning to trust us!"

"Telling me my job now, Jones?" she said, and tossed the cloth to burn with the maggots.

"No. Well, all right. Yes. I suppose. But—"

She pointed at the somnolent man on Hettie's table.

"*Look* at him, Jones. How likely is it I'm going to be able to help him without hurting him?"

He pulled a face. "Not very."

"Not at *all*. He could barely tolerate me inspecting that head wound and there's a lot worse to come before this is over. Believe me, it was the only decent thing to do."

He sighed, and made himself look at Zandakar's mistreated body. "Yes. Of course. You're right, Ursa. I'm sorry."

She released the rest of her temper in a short, sharp rush of air. "Good. Now let's get to work. Stand beside me, keep your mouth shut and do exactly what I say exactly when I say it."

If she was one of the best physicks in Kingseat it had nothing to do with her bedside manner. "Yes, Ursa," he murmured, and did as he was told.

First she gently washed Zandakar's stubbly skull, softening the scabs and sores and drowning the desperate remaining cooties. Then she examined the head wound, tut-tutting. Trimmed its edges to bleeding and stitched it up. Beneath her skilled, sensitive fingers Zandakar moaned a little, but did not wake.

"Right," she said at last, snipping the final thread. "Now for the rest of him."

Between them, with exquisite care, they washed every inch of Zandakar, scouring him clean of scabs and pus and hidden maggots, dirt and excrement and old dried blood. Pared the nails on his hands and feet, soothed his many hurts with ointment and salve and bandaged the worst of them. Dexterity thought he could have played a tune on the man's ribs, so starkly did they spring beneath the skin. Every scar and weeping wound told a story of depravity and suffering, so that by the end his eyes were burning and he could have hung his head and cried for what the man had endured.

Ursa looked at him. "For all we know he could be a murderer, Jones," she said. "For all we know he could have deserved this and worse."

He shook his head. "No. I won't believe that."

"Why?" She snorted. "Because Hettie told you to save him?"

He met her sceptical gaze squarely. "Think what you like, Ursa. She came to me. She told me to find the ship with the red dragon figurehead, speak to the man with the triple-plaited beard and buy the slave with the blue hair. All three were there as she said they'd be. I can't explain it. I don't need to. Hettie said it, and it was so."

"But Jones . . ." said Ursa, and he could see she was trying very hard to be reasonable.

"I know!" he said raggedly. "Do you think I don't *know,* in my empty bed and my empty house? In all the places where Hettie used to be? But *whatever* it was, dream or vision or ghost from the grave, here am I, and here are you . . . and here is Zandakar. And how would you like to explain that, eh?"

Ursa sighed. "I wouldn't. I don't even begin to have an opinion on what's happening here, Jones."

He was cross enough to be waspish. "Glory be! I'll just run and put a note on the calendar, shall I? Sixth day of spring, Ursa didn't have an opinion!"

She scowled. "Oh, hush up. Keep your mind on the essentials, Jones. Where are you going to put this Zandakar? He certainly can't stay in the kitchen."

"He can sleep in the spare room." The room he and

Hettie had planned for a nursery. "I'll hear him in there if he should stir."

Ursa nodded. "It'll do, to begin with."

Zandakar didn't wake as they settled him into the narrow spare bed. Dexterity lit a lamp and drew the curtains as Ursa straightened her patient's limbs and drew the light blankets over his long, still body. He looked almost respectable, with his clean, sweet-smelling skin and his close-cropped blue hair and the worst of his wounds hidden beneath salve and bandage.

"Well, Jones," she said, folding her arms across her middle. "For better or worse, legal or not, it seems you've got yourself a slave. It even seems he's likely to live. And if he does, what *are* you going to do with him?"

Dexterity gave the curtains a last tug and turned to look at the sleeping Zandakar. "Ursa," he replied, with a sigh. "If you tell me then the both of us will know."

CHAPTER SIX

Basking in the sunshine, Prolate Marlan stood at the royal reception chamber's leadlight windows and watched, with pleasure, the thriving, bustling industry of Kingseat Harbour. Eberg's castle stood on a hilltop overlooking the kingdom's sole remaining port. Every window and casement on this side of the massive stone building afforded a magnificent view of the calm blue waters, the crush of visiting ships with their garishly painted sails and their heathenish carved figureheads, the official harbour skiffs darting like pondskaters about the king's business: checking for overladen vessels, embargoed captains, crews or cargoes, sniffing out any sign of trick or trouble. Even though each visiting ship and boat was inspected before entering the harbour, the royal skiffs were ever-vigilant. Of late even more so, since the deaths of the princes Ranald and Simon, may God rest their careless souls.

Not that he believed in God, of course. But it was the proper sentiment . . . and he was nothing if not a proper man.

For every vessel the tugs guided from their moorings, helping them reach the open ocean beyond the walled harbour's heavily guarded mouth, three more waited to take its place. And each one bound to pay tariffs, taxes and imposts, each one full of sailors and travellers who spent their money freely in the town.

Once, not so long ago, foreign sailors and visitors had been looked at askance. Eberg had changed that, viewing each sailor and visitor as a potential source of information, of news that stirred in the wider world. During his reign such information-gathering had been actively encouraged and widened and had yielded many useful results.

Marlan smiled. *Eberg's legacy is not to be sneezed at. Ethrea is richer now than ever before, its value never greater. Every trading nation supports an ambassador here, every potentate and minor lordling keeps his treasure in our vaults. I wonder if they realise that this small island kingdom without an army or navy is the uncrowned ruler of the civilised world?*

Most of them didn't, he was sure. The lesser nations,

whose influence was minor. To them Ethrea was merely a toothless convenience. Indispensable, certainly, for anyone desiring to sail north to south or east to west, in the same way a belt was required to keep one's breeches from falling. But beyond that?

They are so consumed with their intrigues and wranglings, their petty wars and insignificant alliances, they have failed to notice what we have known for years: that without Ethrea their trading empires would wither and die.

A pity the same could not be said of the three major trading nations: Harbisland, Arbenia and Tzhung-tzhung-chai. For those three principalities he had a healthy respect. If his plans were to ripen as he desired he must tread most carefully around their ambassadors.

Their leaders are not blind. They know full well that without us their personal fortunes would be hostage to fate. The conversations they prefer to keep secret, from each other and their own people, would not be secret any more. We have become as the air to them: essential for continued life.

And at the first sign of a threat to their security he had no doubt they would act to protect themselves.

So I must be careful to ensure they perceive no threat.

Marlan sighed, smoothing a wrinkle in the sleeve of his magnificent black and gold vestments. Soon now he would meet with an anxious delegation of ambassadors from a handful of the minor nations, all of them eager to learn the progress of Eberg's recovery. Their masters knew that much, at least, to be concerned over the question of his successor.

He had kept the truth of Eberg's failing health secret

for as long as he could, but he'd always known it must come out eventually. Even a king was but a man and like every man every king must die. The ambassadors knew that. And provided there was a smooth transition from Eberg to the new king, the fact of his dying would cause no trouble.

Provided there is a smooth transition . . .

And there was the rub. For if Eberg had failed in any way, it was in raising a daughter who refused to accept her womanly place.

With an effort Marlan relaxed his suddenly tensed shoulders. Rhian would not be a problem. She had not attained her legal majority and therefore, in the law's eyes, remained a child. The statutes governing orphaned minors of the nobility were unequivocal and sacrosanct. Her brothers were dead and she had no other living relatives. The moment her father drew his last breath she would be a ward of the Church.

But still that permits her too much leeway. Eberg must make the girl my personal ward, bound in obedience only to me. She will then choose the husband of my choosing. A husband who will rule Ethrea as I see fit, and who will control the girl's waywardness as it should have been from the first. Unlike her soft father I have no intention of indulging Rhian's wilfulness and unpleasing independence. Eberg was a fool to encourage her. A fool to let her think she could be anything more than a woman. When Eberg is dead I shall draw her attention to the error of her ways.

A knock on the door turned him away from the window and thriving harbour to the courtier standing in the open doorway. "The ambassadors are here?"

The courtier bowed. "They are here, Your Eminence."

So the time for careful game-playing had come. Whatever these minor ambassadors might suspect, however inevitable was Eberg's demise, it did not suit him to reveal too much truth just now. Misdirection. Obfuscation. An ungentle reminder that they were supplicants, not lords. These foreign delegates so easily got above themselves if their pretensions were not strictly repressed.

The asking of questions does not guarantee answers.

He crossed to the elaborately carved and gilded mahogany chair—almost a throne, in fact—on its dais against the chamber's short wall. Once seated, with the skirts of his vestments arranged to their best advantage, he nodded to the courtier.

"Admit the ambassadors and their escort."

They came in a gaggle, five of them, herded by three Church scribes, Council Secretary Lord Dester and his ink-stained assistant.

"Gentlemen," he said, favouring the ambassadors with a frosty smile. "I trust God sees you in good health and good spirits?"

They muttered something appropriate, he hardly paid attention. Their religious beliefs did not concern him. Their gold was gold, what and how they worshipped was none of his affair.

"Your Eminence," said the ambassador from Slynt. As usual he was naked to the waist, his short, thick legs encased in deer hide. When it snowed he pulled on a deer hide poncho. An uncouth fellow, with no sense of style. "I give you greetings from my sovereign. He commands me to ask you when he might look to sending his funeral delegation."

My, my, that was subtle. How typically Slynt. "Return the king's greetings to your sovereign, Ambassador," he replied, graciousness personified. "Inform him we have no plans for a funeral." Which of course was a lie, but then that was diplomacy, wasn't it? Lies that smiled and hid their teeth.

"Eminence," said the Icthian ambassador, who at least knew enough to wear velvet and many jewels. "Do you tell us King Eberg is not dying?"

He frowned. "We are all of us dying. But to presume we know the precise moment of our death is to usurp God's manifest omniscience. I, for one, am reluctant to do that."

The Keldravian ambassador tugged one earlobe, pendulous with the weight of its eight wife-rings. They clashed and jangled, much like his household, surely, with so many women in it. "God-matters not the purpose. We come for news of your king."

Marlan lifted his eyebrows. "Then you have spent your time without a purpose, Excellency. I have no news of Eberg to give you."

The ambassadors from Haisun and Dev'karesh exchanged glances. "So we have been misinformed?" Haisun's man enquired, delicately. He had a hard face to read, flat and wide with no betraying frown lines or crow's-feet, or even a suggestion that he knew how to smile. Like his lean body, his emotions were sleekly clothed in silk. "King Eberg is not mortally ill?"

"Your Eminence, you must surely know that is the whispered word on your streets," added the ambassador from Dev'karesh, the words wafting on a cloud of cloves. "King Eberg is dying without an heir to follow him."

Marlan raised his eyebrows. "You place your faith in unsubstantiated lies and rumours, Ambassador? Perhaps that is how your master conducts his affairs of state, but I can assure you that is not the case in Ethrea."

Dev'karesh was a young principality, only recently taking to the high seas in trade. The ambassador's pale skin darkened with blood and his pale fingers tightened by his sides. "Naturally my master does not give credence to gossip. But—"

"Excellencies," said Marlan briskly, "we are all busy men. Therefore allow me to put your minds at ease so we might be about our important business. His Majesty King Eberg is indeed unwell. This is common knowledge, we do not hide it. He has a fever but is physicked daily. As to the question of his succession, you must agree that is something of a delicate matter, an *Ethrean* matter, best left to His Majesty and those of his advisors made privy to his thoughts. Surely you are not suggesting your masters desire you to meddle in our private affairs?"

It was a calculated attack, neat as a stiletto. Nations caught dabbling their fingers in Ethrea's domestic politics faced the severest of sanctions. Huge fines, loss of harbour privileges, confiscation of goods both on board docked ships and in the warehouses given over to their nation's use. Public humiliation, private censure and the weight of every other nation's disapproval—which usually meant more sanctions, trade embargoes and much warlike talk behind closed doors. Sometimes those doors opened . . . and bloodshed resulted. In the past, transgressing nations' entire ruling families and their countries had been bankrupted, changing the course of more than one history.

No. Meddling in Ethrea's private affairs was never wise.

The ambassadors broke out in a babble of protest, denial and eager reassurances. Marlan let them fuss, considering them with a dispassionate gaze. When the noise abated he nodded.

"I am relieved to hear it. Allow me to say again, Excellencies, so you might report the truth to your curious masters: Eberg is king. The House of Havrell rules, and will continue to rule in God's grace until the world is no more. As Prolate of Ethrea, be sure I speak the truth."

"Of course, Your Eminence," said the Icthian ambassador, and sketched a flourish of submission with three graceful fingers. "Your Eminence is a byword for honesty wherever good men gather."

Marlan had little time for Icthians. A sly race, hardly better than grocers. They permitted women in their priesthood. What greater folly could any Church commit? "Wherever bad men gather also, I venture to hope," he said, faintly smiling. "Bad men, after all, are in the greatest need of honesty."

A wave of nervous laughter, too loud and too prolonged. Good. He had unnerved them, turned their busy thoughts to their own welfare, away from the vexed question of Eberg and his unsettled succession.

Not that it will remain unsettled for much longer. Rhian will see reason . . . or suffer the consequences.

The ambassadors were anxiously staring at him, waiting for his next pronouncement. He smiled at them, benevolently.

"Excellencies, His Majesty will be most touched to learn you have come here today out of concern for his wellbeing. Convey to your masters his appreciation for their good wishes."

"We shall," said the ambassador from Keldrave, and was echoed by the men of Slynt, Haisun and Icthia.

"Most certainly," added the pale Dev'kareshi.

He nodded. "Excellencies, I bid you good morning."

It was an abrupt dismissal, lacking the customary invitation to expound on other matters of concern. The five ambassadors hesitated then removed themselves. Doubtless they would congregate somewhere beyond the castle to compare their impressions and seek to sow discord where it might prove most useful. Ah, ambassadors. To a man, the living definition of a necessary evil.

Marlan nodded his dismissal of the Church scribes and Lord Dester, but the council secretary sent off his assistant and remained behind. An irritating minor noble, with a slavering ambition to rise higher than his current post.

"You require further instructions, *Secretary* Dester?" he asked. Pretentious men, like ambassadors, required judicious deflating.

Dester's face flushed with annoyance at the slight. "Eminence, I require no instructions. I understand my duty."

Marlan stared. "Do you imply otherwise of me?"

"Prolate, you play a dangerous game," said Dester, foolhardy. "Those ambassadors—"

"Left here uncertain," he said sharply. "Dester, be guided in this. Diplomacy can best be compared to a chess game, and I have been playing a lot longer than *you*."

"I realise that," said Dester. "But Eminence, you speak not only for the king but for his councillors, too. Would you make of them pawns, that—"

"We are all pawns, Manfrith," he replied, mildly enough. "God's pawns. Perhaps you should pay closer attention in Church. I believe I've spoken on the matter often enough."

Dester flushed again. "You may have thrown those minor ambassadors off the scent, Prolate, but the others won't be so easily duped. Eberg's perilous condition cannot be kept secret for much longer. Ardell tells me—"

"More than he should, I have no doubt. If you are truly his sponsor, my lord, I suggest you educate him on the topic of discretion."

"Eminence," said Dester, through gritted teeth.

"My lord, you allow yourself to be distracted by trifles. Bend your thoughts instead to the tasks of your position. I imagine you have much to do before tomorrow's important council session. I take it you've received the final tally of candidates to be considered for Princess Rhian's hand?"

"Yes," said Dester. "The list is being copied and distributed as we speak, Eminence."

"Excellent." The list wasn't complete, in fact. He had his own candidate to put forward. But that could wait until the council meeting proper. The less time his fellow councillors had to prepare, the better. "Then do not allow me to detain you further, Secretary."

Dester, the blind fool, refused to take the hint. "Do you think the king is well enough to consider the list, Prolate? The decision is a momentous one."

"The question is not relevant. The king will consider it. As a father and a monarch he has no choice but to do so."

Dester nodded slowly. "And if, God forbid, the king should die before he makes his decision?"

God forbid? I don't think so. I can think of nothing more useful. "Then his faithful council will act in his stead. Good morning, my lord. We will meet again in council chambers in due course."

This time, an unambiguous dismissal. Like the ambassadors Dester had no choice but to bow and withdraw. Marlan returned to the audience chamber's leadlight window and rested his satisfied gaze once more on the harbour, and the ships, and the crowded docks and piers.

So matters progress as I would have them progress. Were I in truth a superstitious fool, a man of faith, I might think God and I shared the same ambitions.

But there is no God. There is only me. In the end, it's all one and the same.

According to Helfred, God heard all prayers, all petitions, all whispers in the heart. According to Helfred, God looked with great favour upon a man—yes, yes, all right, and a woman, too—who knelt before him in humble piety and solemn worship, his wonders to proclaim. According to Helfred, it was sinful pride to take up God's time in asking for anything of a personal or worldly nature. Prayer should be reserved for unworldly matters. Or praise. Preferably praise. And abject apology. In large amounts.

Anyone who knew Helfred, Rhian decided, might well believe he followed that last stricture to the letter. Only Helfred, with presumably a better chance than most of being heeded, would resist the temptation to request at the very least a bit of backbone and a face that didn't break out in pimples twice a week.

I could care less about the scripture according to Helfred. If I had a horse to take me there I'd ride right up to God's front door and present my demands to him in person.

And make no mistake about it. They were demands, all right. Not prayers, not petitions, not *Please God, if you'd just take the time to notice such a lowly and worthless woodlouse like myself* . . . God, she decided, hadn't been doing a very good job of late. And if the prolate and the venerables and the chaplains and the devouts were too scared to mention the fact, well . . . she wasn't.

So there.

Beyond the stained-glass panels behind the royal family's private chapel altar, the sun was halfway risen to noon. Rhian shifted a little and winced. Even with a pillow, a day and night vigil before the Living Flame was murder on the knees. But she would suffer a lot more than sore joints, joyfully, to make her father well again.

The long vigil had been Helfred's idea, of course. "Three days without setting foot here, Highness," he'd said, disapproving. "We talked about examples, did we not?" So she'd given in, because she was simply too tired to argue.

And who knew? They hadn't saved her mother, or Ranald, or Simon, but perhaps this time her prayers would make a difference.

Fierce as a hawk she stared up at the enamelled and jewelled gold sconce that held the Living Flame, a symbol of God's presence in the world.

Will they, God? Will my prayers make a difference? I can't say I'm confident. It seems you're determined to take my whole family. I'm a little confused. Was it something I said?

Helfred would be appalled, could he hear her thoughts. Yesterday, once the Litany was thrice repeated, and sensing her unquiet spirit and seething resentment of, oh, so many things, he had presumed—again—to lecture her. God's will was to be accepted with love and humility. It was never to be questioned. Furthermore, to actually imply any *criticism* of God, well, that kind of arrogance was a whipping matter.

"Fine," she'd shouted at him, at long last losing control of her temper. "So whip me, Helfred! See if I care! It can't possibly hurt more than watching His Majesty creep closer to death every day, every hour, and being powerless to save him! God has no *right* to do this. My father has never done anything bad in his life. He's been a good man and a great king. This is wrong, I tell you, wrong, wrong, *wrong*!"

And if arrogance wasn't enough to earn an ecclesiastical beating then blasphemy surely qualified her. Marlan would punish her himself if he knew of her impious outburst. But he couldn't know because she'd not even been summoned to his presence, let alone censured or beaten. That could only mean Helfred hadn't reported her wicked behaviour.

Which, for an ecclesiastical spy, was a very odd way for him to behave.

In the chapel's serene and incense-perfumed silence, her stomach gave a monstrous growl. "Petitions to God," Helfred had told her before he left to pray in solitude, "are oft heeded better when delivered on an empty stomach.

You've eaten once today, Your Highness. Now it's time to fast."

She hated fasting. But so be it, she'd decided. She was desperate. If starvation was what it took to save her father's life she'd reduce herself to skin and bone. Not another morsel would pass her lips until King Eberg was pronounced hale and hearty again.

You have my solemn promise, God. I'll do anything. I'll even forget about Alasdair and marry a man I don't know or love. Just don't let Papa die, I beg you. It's such a small thing I'm asking for. I don't want untold riches. I don't want power beyond the dreams of mortal man. I won't even ask for a handsome husband, although if you could manage to keep him less than twenty years my senior I confess I'd be grateful. Just please, please . . . don't let Papa die.

The Living Flame burned, still as gold.

Perhaps God disapproved of flippancy. She couldn't help it. It was her only armour against the gibbering fear that her prayers would indeed go unanswered, that God was deaf to her or didn't exist. And that when her father died and she was alone she'd be powerless to save herself from—

"Good morning, Your Highness," said a calm, strong voice from the door of the chapel. "Ven'Joscel said I would find you here."

Prolate Marlan, the voice of God in the Kingdom of Ethrea, spiritual father of every soul, Guardian of the Living Flame. The man she would answer to once her father was dead. As a ward of the Church she'd have no other choice.

With a small whimper, for the pain in her muscles and

bones was abominable—it had nothing to do with being afraid or intimidated—she inched around on her pillow to face him.

Marlan was sixty-nine but looked twenty years younger. Nothing about him indicated age or hinted at infirmity. He radiated vitality. He exuded energy and good health. He was immaculate: his bald head was polished, his black and gold vestments spotless and uncreased, his black velvet slippers unmarred by dust. He never shouted: he had no need, for the whisper of God was heard by even the dead. He never apologised: for how could the tongue of God be wrong? In the privacy of his ecclesiastical palace, and with the merest lifting of his little finger, Marlan had sentenced sinning chaplains to death and would have blighted whole villages for disobeying their appointed venerables—if her father had not intervened. It had been the running battle throughout their joint care of the kingdom: how much power should the Church have? Who was answerable to the king?

Her father had always emerged victorious from their encounters . . . and year by year Marlan had grown yet more sour.

And unless there's a miracle he'll own me till I'm twenty. Oh God, God, help me.

She bowed her head. "Your Eminence. You grace me with your presence."

The heavy silk skirts of Marlan's vestments swished against the chapel's mosaiced floor as he approached. When he reached the altar he stopped, pressed his thumb to his heart, his lips, and murmured beneath his breath. Then he looked down on her. "What do you do here, my child?"

She wanted to say, *I'm not your child.* She wanted to say, *What does it look like I'm doing?* She wanted to throw herself in his face and scratch his eyes out for his endless preaching on the holiness of obedient daughters. She said, "I hold vigil for my father the king, Your Eminence."

His long, cool fingers brushed the tangle of her hair. Barely, she repressed a shudder. His touch made her skin crawl. "Dear child. God smiles upon such filial piety. But what of Helfred? Does he not pray with you in your time of trial?"

Damn. Of course he'd notice Helfred's absence. She looked up. "Your Eminence, my chaplain did want to remain with me but I sent him away after some hours. I felt I needed time alone . . . and he suffers from occasional bouts of—that is to say, he was indisposed. I felt it unkind to ask him to kneel with me all night."

"Before God," said Marlan, "what matters the frailty of our flesh? Worship of the divine presence transcends all mortality." The mellow tone of his voice did not alter, but she felt her heart skip. If the glow in the prolate's eyes were any indication, poor Helfred would soon be indisposed in another way altogether.

Poor Helfred? She must be more tired than she realised.

Marlan said, "Have you recited your Litany today, my child?"

"No, Your Eminence." *I've been too busy scolding God.*

"Then let us recite it together." With the oiled ease of an acrobat he sank to the floor beside her. One sideways, disdainful glance took in her pillow, even as his unpadded knees came to rest on the chapel's marble floor. She flushed, waiting for censure, but he did not comment, saying only, "Are you prepared, my child?"

"Yes, Your Eminence," she whispered, and obediently bowed her head.

He raised his arms to the altar and lifted his eyes to the Flame. "O God, who burns unceasing within our hearts, hear now our raised voices, with which we honour you and praise you and give thanks for all thy glory," he intoned, his voice filling the chapel without effort. "Hear us, O God, that do beseech your goodness and mercy, now and unto the very end of days whence cometh the final Flame."

"Hear me, O God," she said, in formal response. Her own voice sounded pale and childish, lacking any kind of strength at all. *It's because I'm tired and grieving. It's not because this man hollows my bones.*

Together, they recited the Litany.

"O God, that did hold back your love from the land and from the people as they did fester and swarm upon the pleasant fields in the fleshly pursuit of power, hear my prayer. O God, that did stop your ears 'gainst the cries of the wicked as they did slay one another in evil war, hear my prayer. O God, who did at last send us Rollin, who opened our hearts to Unification, wherein we dwell in peace, without war, hear my prayer. I beseech you, O God, send wise men to teach me; stern men to love me; wrathful men to chastise me when I err."

Echoing Marlan, Rhian touched her thumb to breast and lips. *Why does the Litany always sound frightening when he says it? It's supposed to bring us closer to God, not make us feel like hiding in a corner.*

Beside her, Marlan inhaled deeply, and then breathed

out. His translucent eyelids lifted, revealing his dark and lightless eyes. "God, I must ask of you one more thing. God, see this child beside me, soon to be orphaned in the world. Bestow upon her the wisdom to recognise her feminine shortcomings and the humility to know that she must yield. God, this child is young and headstrong. Give me the strength to mould her to your will."

Heart beating like a kettle drum, she stared at him. *My feminine shortcomings?* "Your Eminence—"

"There is no need to thank me, Rhian," he said, gently austere. "I have as much care for you as if you were my own. Indeed, when you are made a ward of the Church to all intents and purposes you will be mine."

It was a threat. A promise. A cool reminder of what was to come. "Your Eminence," she said, and lowered her gaze so he wouldn't see the fury in her eyes.

He rose to his feet. "It pleases me to see you so observant in prayer. Continue your devotions. I will send Helfred to you."

"But the king—"

"Is, alas, distressed by your presence. The short time remaining to His Majesty should be spent in spiritual preparation for death, not . . ." Marlan's voice trailed away, suggestively.

Not arguing with me. "Yes, Your Eminence," she whispered, and felt hot tears on her face. "I understand."

Again, Marlan's fingers brushed her hair. "I knew you would. Do not fear, my child. You will see him again, before the end." With a final acknowledgement of the Living Flame, he left the chapel.

Only then, freed from his overwhelming presence, did she realise she was shivering and her teeth chattered and the tears on her cheeks had turned to chips of ice. She lifted her burning eyes to the Flame above her.

"Give me strength God. Show me the way. Save me from that terrible man who'd treat me like a bartered milch cow."

She was exhausted. Hungry. Pain racked her bones. Most likely it was her tired mind playing tricks. But as she closed her eyes and lowered her head, surrendering to her endless vigil, she thought she saw the Living Flame flicker.

CHAPTER SEVEN

With dusk falling fast it was safe to pull back the spare room's faded curtains and let in some fresh air. Dexterity tugged the drapery aside, lifted one window sash a careful four inches then turned to look at Ursa, still sitting beside the occupant of the spare room's bed.

"Well?" he said, feeling his muscles hum with exhaustion. "What do you think? Will Zandakar live?"

Ursa's lips twitched in a brief, fierce smile. "There are no guarantees in this world, Jones . . . but I'll say this. I'm hopeful."

He felt himself sag against the wall. For Ursa, that cautious declaration was almost the same as a wild victory dance. The relief was overwhelming, enough to prick his eyes with tears. The thought of losing Zandakar, when Hettie had given the stranger into his care, was horrifying.

Their restless patient's fever had spiked without warning just before noon. Spiked so high he'd gone into convulsions, long arms and legs thrashing, his ice-blue eyes rolling back, bloodied froth flecking his lips. For nearly five hours he and Ursa had fought to save him, forcing tea and decoctions of feverkill into his ulcerated mouth, sponging him as best they could in cold well-water from the back garden. Grimly they pinned him against the sheets and mattress so he didn't convulse himself out of bed altogether and maybe split his head open again, to make matters worse.

Just as Dexterity was convinced Zandakar would die, must die, a noxious sweat broke out all over the man's thin, abused body. Slimy, stinking, full of poisons, it had stained the bedclothes a belly-churning yellow. Gradually, Zandakar stopped convulsing. His taut muscles relaxed. His eyes unrolled.

"We're doing it, Jones!" Ursa had shouted. "With God's help and the bloody-mindedness of a brindled cow we're doing it. Quick! Fetch me more feverkill. I don't care if we drown the wretch in it, bring me a panful! Hurry! *Run!*"

He'd never seen his astringent friend so agitated. When he brought back the fresh feverkill, a thick green brew that stank almost as badly as Zandakar's sweat, she looked up at him with eyes so implacable he flinched.

"I swear to you, Jones, on my oath as a healer and my faith in God, I will die before this man does," she said, then spooned more of the potion between Zandakar's teeth, stroking his taut throat to make him swallow. Swore at him loud and long that he wouldn't give up, he would not, did he hear her? Was he listening? He had no permission to leave and she'd thank him to obey her or it was over her knee he'd go, grown man or not. It would have been funny if it hadn't been so terrible.

Half an hour later, the sweating stopped.

"Find some fresh sheets and blankets," Ursa whispered, then. "He doesn't need to be catching cold now."

After laying Zandakar carefully on the floor, they'd stripped the bed, turned the mattress damp-side down and remade it with clean linen. In his extremity of distress he'd burst some of his stitches and sweated off his bandages and ointments. Before they put him back into bed Ursa re-sewed his wounds, slathered him with more salves and again bound the worst of his hurts with strips of clean boiled cloth.

"There," she'd said as she tied the last one in place. "That should hold him."

Drawing the blanket up to Zandakar's shoulders, Dexterity had thought he heard him speak. Leaning close he'd caught a few whispered words. Unintelligible still . . . but one repeated, sounding like a name. *Lilit*. The ragged voice had broken, saying it, and he'd felt a stirring of pity.

Now, staring at the silent man in the bed, he pushed away from the window. "I wish I knew who he was," he said, collapsing into the spare room's armchair. His body protested. At the height of the fever Zandakar had punched and kicked. He'd have some spectacular bruises, he was sure. "I wish I could ask him."

Ursa was tidying her bottles and salves into her battered bag. "It's not asking him that's the problem, Jones.

It's understanding his answer. I doubt there's a soul in Kingseat who'd be able to translate his gibberish."

Unfortunately, it was more than likely she was right. "I know," he said, brooding.

She glanced at him slyly. "You could always ask Hettie."

Very funny. "How long before you're certain Zandakar's out of danger?"

"A little while yet. We'll have to sit, and see."

So they sat, in silence, and waited for Zandakar's fever to rise again or his convulsions to return. They waited in vain. Zandakar slept. Not easily, he was still restless, he still muttered his gibberish language under his breath. But his skin remained cool, his temperature low, and that was the main thing.

Dexterity sighed. "You should go home, Ursa. Bamfield will be wondering what's happened to you."

"Bamfield's my apprentice, not my keeper. Are you hungry?"

He was starving, but lacked the energy to stir. "I'm fine."

She snorted. "You're pale as whitewash is what you are. I'll boil you an egg."

"No, no, I can—"

"I've got to make our patient some gruel anyway," she said, pushing to her feet. "I don't trust you to make it, Jones. Sit there quietly and keep an eye on him for me. I shouldn't be too long." With her hand on the doorknob, she paused and added over her shoulder: "You do have the fixings for gruel, Jones, don't you?"

He nodded. "In the pantry."

"Any molasses?"

"Yes. In the pantry."

"Don't be snippy," she told him, and continued on her way.

Beyond the open window, dusk surrendered to evening. The first stars came out, winking as though they shared some private joke. Dexterity closed his eyes and breathed in the last of the day's warm air, laced with perfume from the flower garden Hettie had planted, and tended, and loved so much.

Well, it seems I've saved Zandakar for you, dearest. Now perhaps you'd like to tell me why.

She didn't answer.

Hettie, my darling, you mustn't be so mysterious. Why is this man here? Why did I buy him? What kind of trouble is Ethrea facing?

And still, no answer.

Hettie, what kind of trouble is Rhian in? Hettie? Hettie!

"What's the matter, Jones?" said Ursa, in the doorway. "Having a bout of constipation?"

She was nearly sixty, and looked tired to the bone. Burying resentful exasperation, he levered his aching body out of the armchair. "Ursa, you should go. I'm perfectly capable of making gruel and boiling an egg."

She didn't snap his nose off, which told him precisely how weary she was. Instead she crossed to the sleeping Zandakar and, bending over him, laid her palm on his forehead. "Still cool," she murmured. She checked his pulse. "A little fast, but nothing alarming." With a groan, she straightened. "All right, Jones. If you're tired of my company. But I'll be back after breakfast. If anything should go amiss overnight—"

"I'll bring him straight to you," he promised. "But I think he'll be fine."

"Hmmph," she said. "We'll see. The gruel's on a low simmer and your egg's about to boil. Make sure you have some bread and butter with it. And a good strong cup of tea. I've left you some feverkill, in case you need it. Extra ointments for those wounds I've left uncovered. If he wakes, and you think he's thirsty, offer him water. Nothing else. If he keeps that down you can try him with the gruel. Add a dollop of molasses to it. Just a small one, mind you. And whatever you do, don't let him up. He needs to rest a good while before I'll trust him on his feet. Can you remember all that?"

He smiled. "Yes. Of course. Ursa, I should drive you home."

"Tosh," she said, and picked up her physicking bag. "I don't live that far away. A walk in the fresh air will do me good. Besides, you can't leave the poor wretch. And you'll have to keep yourself awake through the night, in case he has need of you."

He often worked from sunset to dawn. Besides, he had his shepherdess marionette to finish. "At least let me walk you to the gate. I can do that much, after all you've done."

He watched her from the end of his front path, marching down the tree-lined street with her head high and her shoulders square, daring anyone to call her old.

Once she'd gone from his sight he hurried to feed Otto and tidy the donkey's small stable. Those tasks completed, he returned to his cottage. The gruel was cooked so he took it off the hob. The egg had boiled dry, but he ate it anyway with a thick slice of buttered bread, surprised to discover how hungry he was. As he waited for the kettle to boil he put tea-leaves ready in the pot and collected his whittling tools and the unfinished shepherdess marionette. Then, with his hands full of puppet, knives and steaming mug, he returned to his vigil in Zandakar's room.

Zandakar's room. How odd, to think that. Odder still to find he didn't resent this mysterious stranger, thrust upon him so outrageously, who'd cost him quite a lot of money, really. Not to mention his brand-new curtains.

But to resent him would be churlish. What is a little spent gold compared to this poor man's sufferings? How strong must Zandakar be, to have survived that dreadful slave ship, and his brutal mishandling, and that terrible fever . . . and all the misadventures that have brought him to me here. I do hope we can find a way to understand each other. I want to know his story, I'm sure it's quite amazing.

Settled once more in his armchair, with the lamps softly burning and his hot tea in one hand, Dexterity rested his gaze on sleeping Zandakar's drawn face. No tears, now, no whispered muttering. But the man's eyes were restless beneath his closed lids, and a certain tension thrummed through his long, blanket-covered body.

Ah, well. I'm certain we'll come to some arrangement. Clearly he's not a stupid fellow. One way or another we'll learn to communicate, even if it's only with signs.

He let his thoughts drift then, hoping Hettie would return and explain . . . well, everything. She didn't. So he finished his cooling tea, set the empty mug to one side and turned his attention to his shepherdess marionette, who looked like Hettie when she was young, and alive.

*   *   *

Lost in the past, deep in stuporous sleep and burned hollow by fever, Zandakar godhammer dreamed . . . and remembered.

The hardest thing about the journey home to Et-Raklion was the silence. Dimmi refused to speak to him. Refused even to look at him, if he could help it. All their lives they'd been so close. Laughing and affectionate, teasing and together. This terrible coldness, this implacable rage, it was as though he rode with a snakeblade between his ribs, pricking his heart, blood weeping like tears.

He'd long since given up trying to explain.

The thought of Lilit sustained him, growing their son in the warlord's palace. He was riding to his woman, to the woman the god had sent him. Knowing that she waited, knowing how she loved him, knowing she was his future, it made his brother's rejection bearable. Just.

The highsuns passed, and passed, and passed. For the god's glory he wore his gold-and-crystal gauntlet but he never used it, smiting was not his purpose now. One by one the godless lands he'd conquered fell behind them: Na'ha'leima. Harjha. Targa. Drohne. Bryzin. Zree. They did not stop at the Mijaki settlements, where godspeakers would try to interfere. They skirted the ruined cities he'd smitten to rubble and bones, he did not want to go there, they were haunted places echoed with screams. Several times they encountered caravans from Mijak and mounted messengers riding from the Empress or Vortka with questions or commands to be answered and obeyed. He did not stop to speak with them, they of course did not presume to delay him. He was Zandakar warlord, son of the Empress and the god's smiting hammer. He and his silent brother reached the Sand River and cantered into its dry embrace.

There were no accidents this time, no blinding moments of stark terror where it seemed as though he would fail his beloved little brother, lose him to the quicksand, to the demons who everywhere lay in wait. In that first crossing, the knowledge that their mother would not mourn her second son had spurred him on when the strength born of griefstruck terror threatened to fail.

This time they crossed the Sand River as easily as if it had been a soft green meadow in the heart of Et-Raklion.

And the thought of Lilit beckoned, beckoned.

He almost wept at his first sight of Raklion's Pinnacle, that mighty upthrust of the land with Vortka's godhouse at its peak, and Mijak's greatest city spread like bright jewelled skirts about its base.

In the city named for his father there was Lilit, and there was the Empress. Hekat. Yuma. His mother. Who must be pleased, surely, he had at last bedded a virgin and sown her fertile soil with his son. Though doubtless she would be taken aback by the reason for his unheralded return.

As he and Dimmi rode through the city's main gates they were greeted by a panting, sweat-stippled godspeaker.

"Zandakar warlord," he said, his godbraids and the hem of his robes dusty. "The god sees you in Et-Raklion, and every heart must fill with joy. Your arrival has been announced to the Empress. She and Vortka high godspeaker await you in the godtheatre."

The godtheatre? Aieee, his timing was unfortunate. The news he brought home with him deserved a private telling in the palace, without witnesses. But this was not the godspeaker's fault.

He nodded. *"Then my brother and I will ride to the godtheatre with haste, that we might not keep the Empress and high godspeaker waiting. My thanks, godspeaker, for your welcome."*

If the godspeaker noticed Dimmi's ominous silence he did not comment. He only stepped back, so the horses might continue. "Warlord."

Aieee, the sights and sounds and smells of glorious Et-Raklion! City of his childhood, city of his heart. After so long in the godless lands, in forsaken countries among peoples unseen by the god, to hear all around him the pure tongue of Mijak and the dulcet chiming of silver godbells, to taste in his mouth the promise of home.

He turned to Dimmi, his tired eyes blurring. Through a veil of tears he saw his brother's cold, hard face, his hands tight on his stallion's reins, no pleasure in him. Only rage, and pain.

Not for one moment would he relinquish his hate.

"Aieee, little brother. What a wound I have dealt you."

Dimmi did not answer. It seemed more and more likely he never would.

Homecoming's pleasure shrivelled and died.

It was not long before they attracted attention, attracted a crowd on either side of the road. The people threw amulets, threw gold coins, threw copper. They threw silver godbells and long years of godbraids cut from their heads. They had not forgotten him, they knew his blue hair.

"Zandakar! Zandakar! Zandakar warlord!"

No-one called for Dmitrak. Out in the world he'd become a tall man. He looked like a warrior, an obedient attendant. That was all the people saw.

Did Dimmi care? It was impossible to say.

They rode to the godtheatre on waves of acclaim. He entered that sacred space ahead of his brother, hot Mijaki sunshine on his face, in his eyes. The gold-and-crystal gauntlet on his arm drank down the heat, fractured the clean light into prisms of memory.

So many cities, killed in his eye. Killed by his hand. They would haunt him forever.

Ahead was the dais, and the Empress on her scorpion throne. Vortka beside her, aieee, he'd grown an old man. Lilit was on the dais, round as a fat godmoon, bursting with new life. Their child. His son.

Lilit . . . Lilit . . .

Yuma and Vortka faded away.

The laughing shouting pointing crowd of witnessing Mijakis fell silent. They were close enough to see his face, close enough to see the face of his brother. They were not stupid people. They saw something was wrong.

At the foot of the dais's stone steps he drew rein. His horse was weary, it was glad to stop. He slid his feet from the stirrups and vaulted out of his saddle. So was he weary also, his bones shrieked for rest. With the gold-and-crystal gauntlet so heavy on his arm he trod up those stone steps till he stood with Lilit on the dais.

Their eyes met. She smiled, aieee, she smiled. The smile of his dreams was before him in the flesh. The lips he kissed after closing his eyes, the breasts that pillowed him instead of his saddle, his heart's love, his Lilit, his gift from the god.

His appetite for Lilit's face scarcely blunted, he looked at his mother. Six seasons he'd been gone from her, all this time riding home he'd wondered how much she was changed. If she was changed. If time had healed her ravaged body, if it had blunted, just a little, her burning godspark's merciless edge.

She looked no different. She did not smile. She held herself rigid, tormented still by her stone scorpion throne. There was no silver in her hair but there were lines on her face, which was thinner now than it had been before. Vortka moved a little closer beside her, he was silent but his eyes were wide.

Aieee, such a pity they must do this in the godtheatre. He had hoped to speak with Vortka first, tell him of the god's command in his heart, ask him how best to tell the Empress. He had never forgotten Vortka loved his difficult mother. The high godspeaker was a wise man. A good man. A man in whom the god burned gently. The friend of his green days, who softened Hekat's blows.

Looking at Vortka now, he hoped the man was still in the god's eye. That he too had heard its changed message. For if he was not, had not, then how much harder his task would be.

He turned to his mother and pressed his fist to his heart, felt the pounding in his chest. "The god sees you, Empress. Godtouched and precious, it sees you in its merciful eye."

Her eyes were like blue ice, like the frozen water he had seen for the first time in the godless lands. "I did not look to see you here, warlord." Her voice was cold too. She did not sound pleased to see him. "Tell me of your

*prowess in battle. Tell me of the new lands you have con-
quered, making great the god's empire of Mijak."*

He wanted to kiss her cheek, take her hands in his, rest
his head on her shoulder. Instead he removed the gold-
and-crystal gauntlet from his arm and gave it to her.
Though the sun was still shining his fingers were cold.
"Empress, that is not why I am come."

Lilit gasped. She took a step forward, hope blazing in
her face. "Zandakar? You have spared Na'ha'leima?"

He let his eyes answer her, and felt his heart leap to
see the shining joy in her face. Aieee, to know that he
had pleased her. It doused the pain in him, the cold bitter
emptiness of Dimmi's long silence.

Behind him on the stone steps, his angry brother spoke.
"He would not smite that godforsaken city. He says the
god spoke to him. I say he lies."

The god's hammer slid from Yuma's grasp. Vortka
caught it before it hit the dais. "Zandakar?" she demanded; she would never listen to Dimmi or believe a
single word that fell from his tongue.

All his great love for her, he poured into his gaze. "Empress, I tell you, it is no lie. The god spoke in my heart,
it told me conquest was over. It told me to come home. It
has had its fill of blood."

His mother turned to Vortka. "High godspeaker?"

"Empress . . ." Vortka shook his head. "The warlord's
purpose remains unchanged. The god sees him in its con-
quering eye. He is the warlord, the god's smiting hammer. His purpose is to reshape the world."

No. No. That could not be right. Vortka was mistaken,
Mijak's high godspeaker had misheard the god. Crashing
into his back, Dimmi's hard fists. "I knew it! You liar,

you deceiver!" his brother cried. "You sinning betrayer of the god!"

He should never have begun this here, in public. They must return to the palace, to the privacy of home. "Empress. Yuma. I would have words with you alone."

"We are alone," his mother said coldly. "If you have words for me, speak them."

Lilit clasped her hands, let them rest on her belly where his precious son slept. "Zandakar, beloved, tell us what happened. Everything will be all right."

Her beautiful eyes narrow, her lined, scarred face like stone, his mother slid her snakeblade out of its sheath, she held it up so the sunlight flashed on its edge. Her glance flickered sideways. "One more word, you will not speak another."

Aieee, this was madness! He reached out his hand. "Yuma!"

His mother's glare smote him like a blow from the god. "I am not Yuma! I am the Empress!"

He dropped to his knees like a slaughtered bull and bowed his head, trembling. "You are the Empress. Empress, forgive me. I did hear the god. In my heart it told me, enough."

"Hekat . . ." Vortka's voice now, filled with tears. "It was not the god."

Dimmi said, "Tcha. I knew it. He has turned from you, Empress, as he turned from me. All he cares for is that piebald bitch. You should taste her blood, Vortka. I think she is a demon."

He looked up, then, as Hekat caught her breath. Terrible betrayal was in her face, pain as he had never seen, as though he had stabbed her.

Dimmi said, "I tried to reason with him, Empress. I tried to make him listen to the god. He cut me with his snakeblade! He tried to kill me with the hammer!"

Aieee, Dimmi, you are not helping! Dimmi, hold your wicked tongue!

"Is this so, warlord?" his mother whispered. "Did you turn the god's hammer on your brother?"

He was shivering so hard his godbells cried. How could he explain what had happened? How could he make her understand? "Yuma, I swear, I heard the god. I am not meant to make Mijak the world. I am meant for another purpose."

Breathing ragged, his mother the Empress tipped her face towards the hot sky. Around her neck, the scorpion amulet burned. "Aieeeeeeee! The god see me! My son Zandakar is dead!"

Dead? Dead? What did she mean? She meant to disown him, was that her desire? But all he had done was obey the god! How could she disown him for obedience? For doing nothing more than what she had trained him to do since he was born? Stunned, he stared at her.

And as he stared she leapt from her stone throne, she slashed through her scarred face with her cruel snakeblade, she slashed her breasts and her arms and never cried in pain once. Others cried out, though. Lilit. Vortka. The crowd. Even Dimmi protested, he sounded sincere.

Someone else was shouting. He realised it was him. He heard the horror in his voice, saw his hands reaching. "No, Yuma! Yuma, stop! Yuma!"

There was so much noise, his mother could not hear him. Blood filled her eyes, she could not see his hands.

His beloved Lilit was weeping. "Please, Empress, do not do this! Zandakar is your son!"

"Be silent, you patched slut!" his mother raged at Lilit. "Did you not hear me, there is no Zandakar! Zandakar is dead! Dead in the god's eye, dead in mine!"

"No, no, he kneels before you!" Lilit wept. "Do not disown him, forgive him, Empress. Whatever he did, he did for me! For his son in my belly, for the love between us!"

Something terrible happened to his mother's face then. Beneath the blood her blue eyes blazed as though they looked into the coldest pit of hell. Her lips peeled back. The open wounds in her flesh gaped like the screaming mouths of demons. A garbled, choked sound bubbled from her throat. She lifted her snakeblade and spun on her toes.

Lunging forward, he screamed. "Yuma, no!"

With five swift strikes of her snakeblade his mother opened Lilit's bulging belly. As though the god had nailed him in place he saw Lilit's slashed flesh sag. Saw the front of her silk robe turn scarlet. Saw his knifed child slide from the safety of its mother's womb and fall to the stone dais at her feet.

He saw his beautiful son gasp once, and die.

Lilit shrieked, then dropped to the blood-slicked stone dais beside their child, Dimmi's snakeblade plunged into her throat.

Zandakar woke, screaming and weeping, on fire with grief and guilt now as he'd burned with fever before.

"Lilit! Lilit! Aieee, Lilit!"

Strong hands seized his shoulders, held him down as he howled. The dream was familiar, he'd endured it so many times, but the face thrust close to his was not. White skin. Reddish hair. Brown eyes. Cheeks and chin hidden beneath a wiry beard. A light voice, speaking gibberish, except for his name.

"Zandakar. Zandakar."

Slowly, so slowly, the horror of the dream faded. Then he realised he had seen the man before. Memory returned in snatches. The slave ship. A wheeled cart. A stern woman with grey hair. She cut off his godbraids: for that alone, he could weep anew. Lilit had loved them. She had loved his hair.

The white man's lips were still moving, more sounds came out. He could not understand a word being said. But the man's tone was not angry and there were tears in his eyes. In some strange way he could not understand, something about the man reminded him of Vortka.

So. Not an enemy. At least, not yet.

Abruptly, he became aware of pain and crushing weakness. His wasted body was a mass of sores, he knew that already. He tried to look at himself, glimpsed ointment and bandages. Like the godless lands, did this place have no healers, then? Healers who could summon the god's power and knit flesh with a thought? Clearly not.

Aieee, Lilit. Where am I? And why am I brought here? Why am I not allowed to die?

The bearded man stopped talking. Now his face was anxious. He held up one finger, smiled, then withdrew from the room. A few moments later he was back, with water.

His body's demands would not be ignored. He drank the water, thirsty as a camel. Smiling again, the bearded man put aside the emptied cup and said something else.

He shook his head. "You waste your breath. I have more hope of understanding a monkey."

The bearded man blew out air between his lips, frustrated. Then he held one hand under his chin, as though it were a bowl, and with the other mimicked eating with a spoon. Finished with that, he patted his belly. The question was plain. *Are you hungry?*

"No," Zandakar said, and closed his eyes. "I desire no food. I desire nothing from you. Leave me alone. I wish to die."

The last thing he felt as darkness claimed him was the bearded man's warm hand on his shoulder, as though there was caring. As though they were friends.

CHAPTER EIGHT

Majesty," said Marlan, bending low. The man in the high bed scarcely stirred. "*Eberg* . . . attend me. Your time is short. If you would go to God with a clear conscience you must leave behind no unfinished business."

Eberg dragged open his eyes. "*Rhian,*" he muttered. His voice was thin. Depleted. Death approached swiftly, defeating that final rallying of the flesh.

"Yes, Eberg. You must make provision for Rhian, so Ethrea might have its new king."

It was that cold, dark hour between midnight and dawn. Marlan had been roused from his deep sleep by an urgent summons: the king was failing, he must come at once. One look at Eberg's pinched, fallen face told him this was no exaggeration. They were alone in the stifling chamber. Beyond its closed door waited the physick and the chosen witnesses, ready to enter and sign their names to the future.

The future I will bring them. The future they require.

"List," whispered Eberg. "Names. Husband . . . for Rhian."

Marlan shook his head. "Not yet completed."

"Marlan . . ." A meagre tear trickled from the king's right eye. "I was to decide . . . with her."

As if the girl were qualified to have an opinion. "I am sorry, Majesty," he said, not sorry at all. "I fear there'll be no time for that. But I will guide her wisely, you have my word."

Another tear, trickling. "Rhian's decision."

The man was a fool. A soft, indulgent, short-sighted fool. "Of course. Eberg, attend. While you are able you must sign the writ of abdication. Failure to formally create a regency council will lead to unfortunate consequences."

Eberg nodded. "Yes."

"Majesty . . ." He leaned closer, resting his hand on the dying man's shoulder. "By law the princess must become a ward of the Church. But I would suggest to you an alternative arrangement. Still legal, as I am the Church's prolate, but less . . . institutional. Make your daughter my personal ward. I can never replace you as her father, nor would I try. But I have known her since she was born. Indeed, I can tell you in this moment of extremity that in my heart she is the daughter I never had. Grant me that closer bond with your dear child, Eberg. Let the Church be her bulwark, but let me stand a little closer. I would look upon it as a great favour from you."

Eberg's half-lidded eyes glinted. "No."

"No?" Marlan felt his face tighten. "Majesty—"

"You and Rhian . . . do not deal well . . . together," said Eberg, breathing painfully. "She needs . . . light hand. Find . . . wise devout, Marlan. Woman's touch. Misses her . . . mother."

With an effort Marlan relaxed his clenched jaw. *It makes no difference. The man is dying. When he is gone Rhian will still be mine. I will still use her as I see fit. He cannot prevent that. His time of thwarting me is done.* "Yes, Your Majesty. As Your Majesty desires."

"Marlan . . ." Eberg had enough strength left to raise one hand and take feeble hold of his prolate's wrist. "Marriage. Rhian . . . must be . . . happy. Right man for Ethrea . . . but Rhian . . . happy." The hand fell away laxly. "Help my child . . . be happy."

The dregs of Eberg's strength were rapidly dwindling. "I will do my best, Majesty," said Marlan.

"Want . . . to see her."

"Of course, Your Majesty." *Over my own dead body . . .*

Eberg nodded. "Good. Sign writ now."

Marlan went to the door. Opening it, he nodded to the men waiting tensely beyond. "It is time, gentlemen," he said softly. "Let us finish our sad business, then pray for the king."

Dexterity stood in his kitchen, peeling carrots for his planned dinner of mutton stew and keeping one ear cocked for any commotion from the spare room where Ursa was checking on their unlikely patient. The sun was well up, promising a fine, clear day. A pity he'd not be out in it. He'd never liked being cooped up inside.

"He'll do," said Ursa, rejoining him after some ten minutes with Zandakar. She looked less weary this morning, most of her acerbic energy returned. "I've dosed him with a good strong draught of shuteye. It should see him sleep till this time tomorrow."

Dexterity looked up from his peeling. "Sleep without dreaming?"

"That's the idea, Jones."

He set aside the paring knife, reached for his cutting knife and started dicing the carrots. "Good. Because if you'd seen his face, Ursa. If you'd heard him screaming . . ."

Ursa sighed, stowed her physick bag beside the back door and dropped herself into one of the kitchen chairs. "He was a slave, Jones. That's hardly a picnic. I'm sure he's seen any number of horrible sights."

"No," he said, and shook his head. "It was more than that. I'm almost certain it was something personal. Something to do with someone called *Lilit*. And someone else called *Yuma*. He kept saying *Wei, Yuma. Wei, Yuma.* Since we're reasonably sure *wei* means *no,* I think he was telling this Yuma person not to do something. Something dreadful. I think to this Lilit, whoever he or she is. Or was."

"Jones . . ." Ursa sighed again. "Don't get involved."

He stared. "What are you talking about? I'm already involved. He's asleep in my spare room. I paid for him with my gold."

"You know what I mean," she said, glowering. "You're a soft touch, Jones. You always have been. Every time I turn around you've rescued a baby bird that's fallen from its nest or a stray cat with an infected claw or found a sack of abandoned mongrel puppies that didn't drown like they were meant to. And when you're not rescuing the waifs and strays and bringing them to me for healing after, you're giving away toys to children whose folk can't afford them. And don't try to deny it, because you know it's true!"

Yes. It was true. Hadn't Hettie scolded him for his too-tender heart, oh, so many times? But what did they expect him to do, turn a blind eye to suffering when it was right under his nose? "Ursa—"

"Don't you 'Ursa' me!" she said, and rapped her knuckles on the kitchen table. "When I say 'don't get involved' I mean don't go making this man's troubles your own. Don't go breaking your heart over his sad story, whatever it is, because for one thing you can't undo what's been done and for another he might well have brought it on himself!"

Frowning, Dexterity dropped the chopped carrots into the stew pot then swept up the peelings ready for the compost heap. "That's the second time you've suggested Zandakar could be some kind of—of criminal."

"Jones, he could be *anything*. All you know about him is his name!"

No. After last night he knew more than that. Zandakar was a soul in torment. *Is that why I rescued him, Hettie? Have you become a soft touch, too?* He shook his head. "If you're worried I'm in some kind of danger, having him here, you mustn't be. I'm perfectly safe."

Ursa was frowning. "Yes. For now. While he's weak as a kitten and I'm keeping him drugged. But once he's got a bit more meat on his bones, once he's on his feet again and his strength returns, that could be another story. Have you *looked* at him, Jones? *Really* looked at him, I mean, beyond the superficial wounds and emaciation? He's formidable. Or he will be once he's himself again. And the only formidable thing about *you* is your appetite."

Dear Ursa. For some odd reason she was convinced he was helpless. "I don't believe I'm in any danger, Ursa. Once we're a little closer to understanding each other, Zandakar and I will rub along quite well."

She snorted. "Because Hettie said you would?"

Hettie hadn't said that exactly, but he wasn't going to admit it to Ursa. "That's right."

"Then I hope for your sake she's whispered in *his* ear too, Jones! Because if that heathen takes it into his head to swat you like a mosquito how are you going to stop him? Wave a puppet in his face and hope he laughs himself to death?"

"Oh, Ursa, I'll be *fine*. Stop *fussing*. And anyway, as you say, he's too weak at the moment to do anything but sleep. There's plenty of time, isn't there, before he's formidable?"

"Yes," said Ursa, after a reluctant pause. "Several weeks."

"Then I won't worry just yet. When he wakes should I offer him more gruel? Or maybe a little mouthful of stew?"

She got up. "No, not stew. Not unless you want to kill him. You say he refused to eat anything last night?"

Troubled, Dexterity stirred the carrots into the pot with a wooden spoon. "Yes."

"And what else?" said Ursa. She sounded suspicious. "What haven't you told me? I know you, Jones. I know that look."

He glanced up, then busied himself with pinching salt into the pot. "If I tell you, you'll only scold me for *getting involved*."

"Maybe I will, and maybe I won't. But whatever else he is or isn't, this Zandakar is my patient," said Ursa, hands braced firmly on her narrow hips. "It's my business to know everything about him."

Now he added a pinch of pepper to the leeks and carrots and barley and meat. "I don't think he refused because he wasn't hungry. He was thirsty enough. He drank the water I offered him like a drain."

"Why, then?"

He sprinkled some dry herbs into the pot then settled its lid firmly in place. "You'll think I'm imagining things."

"Jones!"

Defiant, he stared at her. "All right then. I thought, when I was looking at him, perhaps he doesn't want to live."

"You think he wants to starve himself to death?"

"Yes. Maybe." He shook his head again. "You didn't see him, waking from that dream. Whatever he's lost—*whoever* he's lost—I tell you plain, there is *agony* in him. The kind of pain that . . ."

"Jones," said Ursa. Not scolding, but kind. "I have no doubt this Zandakar has suffered. I'm sure he has memories that are difficult to bear. But you must realise—"

"No!" he said fiercely. "Ursa, please. I'm not imagin-

ing what I saw. The look in his eyes was the look in my own for a long time after I lost Hettie. Believe me. I understand him."

Now Ursa looked disconcerted. "Are you telling me—"

"No. Even on the worst days I never considered doing away with myself. But I confess, there were times I went to bed hoping I wouldn't wake up."

Ursa cleared her throat. "You never told me."

"You never guessed?"

"No. Jones . . ."

"Ursa, it's all right," he said quickly, sorry that he'd told her. "It's not your fault. I didn't want you to know. Besides, what could you have done? No-one could help me recover from Hettie's death. I had to find a reason to live for myself."

"And you did," said Ursa, with an uncertain smile.

"Yes. I did. Hopefully Zandakar will find a reason too. And if there's the smallest chance I can help him do that, then I must. I'm sorry if you don't approve, but I don't recall asking for your permission."

"No. Just my time and physicking skills," she retorted.

He winced. "True. And I'm grateful."

"So you should be!"

"Ursa . . ." He sighed. "I'm sorry. I don't mean to worry you. But you have to know I've no choice but to do this."

She let out her own gusty sigh. "I do. Just as I've got no choice but to try and save you from yourself. A fool's errand, I admit. So best call me a fool."

He went to her and kissed her cheek. "Never. I call you my dear friend."

Displays of affection never failed to embarrass her. She

swatted his shoulder and retrieved her bag. "I'm off. I'll stop by again this evening to see how Zandakar's getting on."

"Stop by for supper. Mutton stew's still your favourite, isn't it?"

"It is," she said, smiling. "So perhaps I'll see you—if I don't get a better offer in the meantime."

He opened the kitchen door for her. "While you're out and about, would you mind stopping by the shop and letting Tamas know he's on his own today? Tell him I've a belly gripe. And tell him he's to finish painting that farm set by closing or I'll not give him his 'prentice due this week."

She nodded. "All right, Master Jones."

"And mind you keep an ear open for news from the castle. I'm still worried about the princess, and the king. I know in my bones he's much worse than they're saying."

"In your bones?" said Ursa, scoffing. "In your water, more like. Now let me on my way, I've patients to see . . . and your errands to run!"

He stood back from the door. "Till this evening, then. Mind you bring a sharp appetite to match your sharp tongue."

She rolled scornful eyes at him and marched away.

Actuely aware of all the courtiers eavesdropping in plain sight, Rhian took a moment to ensure her voice was calm and composed. "Forgive me, Physick Ardell. Perhaps I'm being stupid but I'm not entirely certain what it is you're saying."

Ardell stroked a thin finger across his moustache, an

irritating habit. More a mannerism, really, designed to give the impression of profound, wise thought. It didn't.

"Stupid, Your Highness? Dear me. Not at all." As always, the physick spoke in a ripe, portentous baritone. It was even more irritating than his incessant moustache-grooming. "I'm sure you're a very clever young lady. But this is a difficult time for you. Grief often clouds the intellect. It is nothing to be shamed by."

They stood in the antechamber to her father's privy room. They'd arrived here together, she and Ardell, but when she'd attempted to accompany him to see her father he'd made her wait outside with the courtiers for company while he went in alone. All right. That wasn't unreasonable, a physick consulting with his patient in private.

But the consultation was over now. And *still* he insisted she couldn't go in.

"Thank you, but my intellect is clear as crystal," she snapped. "I fully comprehend the fragile state of His Majesty's health. What I don't comprehend, since it's been fragile for some time, is why I'm suddenly unable to sit with him."

"Physick Ardell is acting under my instructions," said Lord Dester, sweeping through the open doorway. The attending courtiers hurriedly bowed; unlike herself, the council secretary positively thrived on ostentatious displays of obsequious recognition.

The bow he gave *her* was distinctly . . . reserved.

"*Your* instructions, my Lord Secretary?" she said, and let her voice bite. "Since when do you presume to—"

"Since His Majesty formally relinquished his sovereignty to the council," said Dester. He was positively gloating. His eyes were obscene.

"Relinquished his sovereignty?" No. This had to be a mistake. Or a bluff. "I don't believe you, my lord. Papa would *never*—"

"He did," said Dester. "Before the required five witnesses." His teeth bared in a deprecating smile. "Of which I was one and Prolate Marlan another. The matter is settled, I assure you, quite properly."

Her father's spacious antechamber was suddenly crowded and overwarm. Tilting her chin, because it was fatal to reveal any kind of weakness before men like Dester, Rhian poured every ounce of royalty she had into her voice. "This is unacceptable. I am His Majesty's sole living heir. Why wasn't I sent for? Why wasn't I informed? Consulted? I—"

Exquisitely supercilious, Dester's right eyebrow lifted. "Because, Rhian, such matters are not your concern."

Not her *concern*? With an effort, she managed not to strike him. The omission of her rank was a deliberate slight. *He thinks he no longer needs to worry about things like that. He must discover he's sorely mistaken.* "My dear Lord Dester, you—"

"The king, may God bless him, knew he could no longer perform his duty," said Dester. Clearly, he was determined she should never finish a sentence. "In the early hours of this morning he sent for the prolate who immediately recognised the need for haste and assembled the necessary witnesses and documents. His Majesty signed them, they were duly countersigned and shortly afterwards the king lapsed into a stupor."

The words washed over her like so much bilge water. *No. I don't believe any of it. If Papa's done this thing it's because he was coerced. He would've asked for me, he*

would've wanted to see me first. We're supposed to con-
sider the council's list of my suitors. He promised to sup-
port me in my choice so the councillors couldn't bully me
into a decision that favoured one of them. He wouldn't
want me to face that on my own. He wouldn't want to
leave without saying goodbye.

"Even if what you're saying is true," she said, glaring
at Dester, "that doesn't explain why I can't see him now."

"Now, Your Highness, your presence is required elsewhere. You may rest assured you will be permitted some
time with him before the end. Which won't be long, according to Ardell."

"No," said the physick, just like a trained parrot. "Not
long at all, it saddens me to say."

Permitted? Now the antechamber was gently rocking. Her whole world was rocking, its anchor torn free.
"This is ridiculous. *I am the king's daughter.* Who are
you to—"

"Your Highness," said Ardell, with a glance at Dester.
"Even if his lordship did not need you, I'm afraid the
king's condition cannot allow for any . . . commotion, at
the moment."

She stared at the fool. "You said he was in a stupor."

"A fragile stupor, yes," said the physick. "At long last
His Majesty is free of suffering. But that could change
if the atmosphere in his chamber becomes polluted with
heightened emotions."

"What are you saying? That if I go in there upset he
might wake? Good! Let him wake! I *want* him awake,
I want him to speak to me, we have matters of vital importance to discuss, matters of government that don't

concern *you*, sir." She turned. "Or *you*, Lord Dester, no matter what you like to think."

"What you want is not important," said Dester. "The moment His Majesty relinquished his sovereignty you became a ward of the Church. It is on Marlan's authority I come here to fetch you. And it is to him you will answer if you disobey."

This isn't happening. Rhian clasped her hands behind her back so Dester wouldn't see them trembling. "Before I go anywhere I wish to see the paper my father signed."

"Prolate Marlan anticipated as much," said Dester, and slid his fingers beneath his velvet and brocade coat. When he withdrew them he was holding a square of folded official parchment. "This is your copy. The prolate made certain one was created for you. As you'll see, the signature is genuine."

She took the paper from him, mortified that her hands were still unsteady. Blinking hard, she unfolded the document, then let her eyes rest on the words it contained.

Be it known that I, King Eberg, lawful sovereign of Ethrea, being cognisant of my imminent demise, do hereby and without coercion surrender my sovereignty to the care of my Council, headed by Prolate Marlan, and my daughter Rhian to the Church as its ward. Pray for my soul as I pray that God will guide my good councillors in the best interests of my beloved Ethrea and my daughter, Rhian.

Below the brief declaration, a familiar signature. Erratic, cruelly echoing the illness of its writer, but without any doubt . . . genuine.

Oh, Papa. Papa. What have you done?

The parchment crumpled as she clenched her fist.

"Any questions you have, you may pose them to the council," said Dester. "It awaits you now, Rhian. Among other things there is the matter of your marriage to discuss."

Her eyes were still dry. She lifted them to Dester, making no attempt to disguise her rage and disgust. "My *marriage*? Do you think I care about that, my lord? My father is dying and I am forbidden his side. There will be no talk of marriage until I have seen him and wept for him and settled in my own mind how I feel about the question of a husband."

Dester's expression chilled. "You don't have that luxury. We do not speak of a common husband. We speak of Ethrea's king."

"Ethrea *has* a king!" she shouted, and held up the crumpled abdication. "This paper means *nothing,* you stupid man! Not to me and I promise you not to the people of my father's kingdom! He'll be their king till he draws his last breath and I *won't* betray him by discussing his inferior replacement before he's even *dead*!"

The antechamber's courtiers were goggling. She had no doubt that word of this confrontation would be all over the castle by nightfall.

Good. Let them whisper. My God, let them shout. What's happening here is infamous. Marlan must've gone mad. The thought of so much power at his fingertips has deranged his reason.

Dester stepped close and took her arm in his fingers. He *touched* her. Without permission. As though he had nothing to fear. "It is you who are stupid," he said, his voice low and threatening. "You have *lost,* girl. Eberg has relinquished his crown, for all the power he has now he might as well be dead. You belong to the council, Rhian. Persist in this pointless resistance and you will regret it. That is a promise I am eager to keep."

Oh, he was a bastard, little Astaria's father. Was the rest of the council the same? Would *any* of them stand for her in this mess? Stand for Eberg's daughter, his sole living heir?

They claim to love him. We'll soon see if that's true.

"Come," said Dester. He did not release her arm. "The council is in session and you *will* attend."

She had no choice. At least for the moment. She wrenched herself free of the man, thrust the crumpled proclamation of abdication into her pocket and without another look at Physick Ardell, or the silent, staring courtiers, walked with her head high, away from her father.

But I'll be back, Papa. You have my word. I will be back, with a fine tale to tell.

She entered the council chamber to find the council at war.

"Infamous! Prolate, this is *infamous*!" Lord Porpont of duchy Meercheq shouted, his pale, thin face flushed with temper. His fist smote the council table with a dull thud. "I tell you Duke Damwin will not stand for it!"

"Nor will Rudi," said Lord Volant. His excess of neck chains rattled his outrage. "The Duke of Arbat is a man of God. He attends Church regularly and does all that piety requires, but there is no scripture saying he must countenance *this*."

As the representatives of duchies Morvell and Hartshorn added their raised voices to the protest, Rhian, unnoticed, looked to silent Henrik Linfoi, Alasdair's elderly uncle who now sat on the council in his place. Henrik was a gentle, unambitious soul. She wondered what Alasdair made of him. Linfoi might be Ethrea's least important duchy but when he was a councillor he'd never let that bridle his tongue.

Short of affluence and influence Alasdair might be, but never short of an opinion.

The thought of him warmed her. She felt so alone.

Henrik was the only councillor seemingly not angered by whatever it was Marlan had said. The prolate, unaffected by the shouting, sat at the head of the council table where her father should be—*Oh, Papa*—with his hands neatly folded and his eyes half-lidded, waiting for the objections to abate.

Lord Dester pushed past her and went to his side. Bending, he whispered something in Marlan's ear. The prolate looked at her, his expression unchanging. She felt the air catch in her throat. So did a falcon look, on spying its prey.

Help me, God. I need your help.

Marlan stood, which silenced the council. "Gentlemen, moderate your language. The princess is with us."

As Dester slid into an empty chair and the rest of the council swallowed whatever hot words they'd been ready to say, Marlan inclined his head.

"Your Highness. Welcome to the king's council."

She nodded stiffly in return. "Prolate Marlan." Her heart was beating almost out of control. Her mouth was dry, and it was hard to breathe. She could feel sweat trickling down her spine. If she sweated too much she'd ruin her dress. It was a pale rose silk, her father's favourite. "My lords. You desired to see me?"

There was an extra chair in the chamber, for guests. Marlan did not invite her to take it. *He wants to keep me standing, like a naughty child. He thinks to intimidate me.* Chin tilted again, ignoring the chair, she swept her gaze slowly over each councillor's face. *Six men who think my life is theirs to play with.*

Marlan resumed his seat. "Princess Rhian, you stand before us a ward of the Church. A minor in law, in need of our guidance."

"While my father lives I have all the guidance I need," she said coolly. "What do you want?"

Lord Harley, the Duke of Morvell's blusterful younger brother and his voice on the council, lounged back in his chair. "I think you know, Your Highness. Your father has abdicated. Ethrea's crown is without a head to grace. You must marry and rectify the situation."

"And I shall," she said. "In due course. But I don't even know yet which men of Ethrea this council deems worthy of my hand."

"That hasn't been decided yet," said Lord Porpont, with an evil glance at Marlan. Such a cadaverous man, upon first meeting, people invariably assumed he was the victim of a wasting disease.

Thank God he's married.

"Oh," she said, and let herself show some surprise. "I thought—"

"Lord Porpont is mistaken," said Marlan. "The list is complete."

"The list is *unacceptable*!" said Lord Volant, his fist raised again. "You have no right to put a name upon it, Marlan. You are head of the Church, not ruler of a duchy. You have no business meddling in politics."

Rhian stared at the prolate. *What?* This was what they'd been arguing about? Who did Marlan want added to that list?

"Your argument is as offensive as it is short-sighted, Volant," said Marlan, coldly. "We are not at a horse fair picking out a gelding to ride. We are in the business of choosing a king. Do you suggest we discard a man well suited for the task simply because he and I have a distant connection? He is no blood of mine, which is more than I can say for your duke's candidate. A cousin, isn't he, of the Duke of Arbat? You would reject my lawful suggestion because he does not suit your master's personal and political agenda?"

"It's not my master's agenda we should be concerned with!" said Volant, half rising. "It's *yours,* Prolate Marlan. You are crossing the line! Ethrea has *never* married Church and state and I swear by Rollin's toes it will not do so while *I* am breathing!"

As furious argument erupted again, Rhian edged around the table till she stood behind Henrik Linfoi. The lightest touch to his shoulder turned him round in his chair.

"Highness," he said, under cover of the shouting. "I'm very sorry. Your father has been a great king."

Henrik had such kind eyes. They reminded her of Alasdair. She had to blink hard for a moment before she could speak. "Yes. Henrik, did I hear correctly? Marlan wishes to proffer a candidate? Who?"

Henrik turned back again, but kept his face a little towards her. "His former ward. Lord Rulf. Do you know him?"

His *ward*? A man who must be in his debt, if not his

power? "No," she said. It was hard to speak. "I've never met him. Have you?"

"None of us have. Or else we don't recall him. Apparently he lives on a small estate in the western corner of duchy Kingseat and never comes to court."

A nobody, then, save for his connection to Marlan. And yet Alasdair, soon to be a duke, was deemed unworthy? *I wonder if Papa knows of this.* "How fares your brother, Lord Henrik?"

"Failing," said Henrik. "Alas."

"I'm sorry. When next you write to Alasdair, please tell him he's in my thoughts." She'd write herself, except it wasn't done for unmarried princesses to correspond with unmarried young men. And because since he'd left court Alasdair had never written to her. She missed him like a severed limb . . . and wondered, hurting, if he missed her too.

Henrik nodded. The other councillors were still shouting like fishwives on the docks. Fists thumped the table, spittle dampened the air. They weren't just shouting at Marlan, they harangued each other. They were nearly at blows.

This is ridiculous.

She marched to the ceremonial handbell on its stand beside the prolate and, before he could stop her, picked it up and rang it loudly. *Clang clang clang clang clang.*

The councillors stopped shouting and stared. The looks on their faces were almost comical.

"My lords!" she said stridently, into the abrupt silence. "How can you? For *shame!*"

CHAPTER NINE

The bell was heavy. Rhian plonked it down again, hard. "Were my father here he would send you all packing! You seem to forget, sirs, that *I* am the one who must choose Ethrea's next monarch. It's marriage to *me* that will make a man king. You'd do better speaking sweetly and softly of your candidate's qualifications, rather than brawl like common cowherds in the muck!" She turned on Marlan. "As for this notion that I might marry your former ward, Eminence, I think it ill advised to say the least. There's a connection there that can't be thought comfortable. My father has always done his duty by God, but you know full well his opinion on matters of religion and its place in government."

Marlan's face was smooth and tight, a sure sign that he was inwardly seething. He stood, his black and gold vestments sumptuous in the sunlight filtering through the chamber windows. "You would be wise to moderate your tone, child. Your father, may God bless his memory, has surrendered you to the keeping of the Church and the guidance of this council. Be mindful of that, lest you stray into trouble."

I refuse to pay attention to his threats. "May God bless his memory?" she echoed, incredulous. "Prolate, he's not dead yet!"

Marlan nodded. "True. God has granted us a small

breath of time, that we may secure the succession while His Majesty still lives. If you wish to impress this council with your maturity, Rhian, you should not fritter away the opportunity. Even you, young and female as you are, must recognise it will be better for everyone should Ethrea's new king be declared before Eberg has left us."

Of course she recognised that. Let one whiff of Ethrean instability reach the noses of the world's great trading nations and all hell would break loose. But if Marlan thought she was going to let him trample over her willy-nilly he was sadly mistaken.

Losing her temper, however, would get her nowhere. Somehow she had to hold her ground with this man while not appearing to the rest of the council as a shrill, temperamental, untrustworthy *girl*.

"Prolate Marlan, I fear you do me a disservice," she said, her voice moderate. Her manner more or less deferential. "As a king's daughter I know my duty. And it's *because* I know my duty that I won't rush into any decision as great as this one. The question of my marriage can't be settled hastily. Nor can I be coerced to the altar." She let her hot gaze sweep all the councillors' staring faces. "My lords, it's true I'm now a ward of the Church and subject to the prolate's discipline. But you are His Majesty's council and I know he relies on *every* man upon it. I want to hear your opinions on the matter of my future husband. I want to know who *you* think is the best candidate for king. I've been promised a list of names, gentlemen. I'd like to see it."

It was Henrik Linfoi who broke the strangled silence. He stood, moved round the council table till he reached

Dester's secretarial assistant and removed a sheet of paper from the pile before him.

"Here is the list, Your Highness." Henrik glanced at it. "Lord Rulf's name has yet to be added to it. Indeed, the council is yet to decide whether Prolate Marlan's candidate is—"

She held out her hand. "Thank you, Lord Linfoi, but I don't need the council to deliberate any further. I'll add Lord Rulf's name myself. Our prolate would never put forth a man who was not worthy of a crown. I appreciate my lord's concerns, but as the prolate rightly points out, no man here is indifferent to the outcome of this matter. If you would bar Lord Rulf for his fortunate connections, surely you must also bar your own duke's men."

His eyes warmly approving, Henrik gave her the sheet of paper then returned to his chair. Lord Porpont rose ponderously to his feet. "Your Highness, what you hold in your hands is—"

"Not something I care to read in haste or with an audience," she said. Her temper was beginning to fray. She took a deep breath and brutally subdued her desire to scream. "My lords, you confound me. *My father is dying.* Even if he wasn't Ethrea's king, with every solemn thing implied by that fact, can't you at least show me the common decency any almost-bereaved daughter is owed? Can't you leave me a little while in peace to pray for his soul and for God's guidance in this matter?"

She had shamed them again. *Good. They deserve it. Except for Henrik they're all carrion crows, picking over a carcass with a few breaths left in it. Oh Papa, Papa, what a sorry state we're in.*

Swiftly recovered, Lord Harley snorted. "An ordinary

daughter might be granted that, perhaps. But in this case, Your Highness—"

"My lord, be silent," said Henrik Linfoi. For a shy, retiring man it seemed he could be surprisingly sharp. "Her Highness is correct to chide us. Though she's now a ward of the Church I believe we stand here as her surrogate fathers and brothers. I ask you, my lords: would we wish our own daughters and sisters treated like this?"

Lord Niall, swarthy son-in-law to the Duke of Hartshorn, flicked a glance at Marlan then leaned forward with an ugly sneer. "You're a sloppy sentimentalist, Linfoi. It's a weakness that runs wide in your family. In matters of state such womanish feelings are out of place. As this kingdom's guardians our first and only duty is to secure the succession. And given you have no candidate to offer, you should—"

"It's because duchy Linfoi offers no candidate that I am the only man here who can speak without prejudice," Henrik said calmly. "To which end I suggest we allow the princess to withdraw so she might consider the names upon that list . . . and pray for her father. The matter of Eberg's successor is not the only question we are here to discuss."

Rhian could have kissed him. "Thank you, my lord. It relieves me to know I have one friend at least upon the king's council."

"You are mistaken, Rhian," said Marlan, stirring at last. "Every man here is your friend. Your best interests and the future of Ethrea are intimately entwined. We cannot serve one without serving the other."

The problem with Marlan was he sounded so *plau-*

sible. She met his cool, displeased eyes and nodded. "Of course, Prolate."

He held out his hand. "If I may see the list, Your Highness? Just to be certain Secretary Lord Dester has not made any mistakes?"

He knew damned well Dester had made no errors. She gave him the list anyway, gritting her teeth as he snapped his fingers for a pen, was handed one, and swiftly added his former ward's name to the list. "Thank you," she said, when he gave it back to her. "God forbid I should misspell Lord Rulf's name."

Marlan's eyes flashed. "Be careful," he advised in an undertone. "Clearly you are unfamiliar with the rules governing a ward of the Church. I suggest you rectify that, sooner rather than later."

He could make her skin crawl without even trying. Looking away, she folded the damned list of names and slipped it into her pocket. "Your Eminence." She cleared her throat. "I have your permission to withdraw? I confess I'm feeling somewhat overwhelmed."

Marlan nodded. "By all means, you may leave us. You have until this time tomorrow to ponder the list. As I'm sure your father warned you, no further names may be added to it." He glanced at Henrik Linfoi. "*No* further names, Your Highness. Misplaced romanticism has no business here, and as a minor in law you have no authority in this matter."

She felt herself flush. *Oh, Alasdair. This is so unfair.* "Yes, Your Eminence. I understand."

His elegant finger touched her cheek, lightly. "For your sake I hope so. Be certain to spend some of your time in the chapel, contemplating the obligations of a dutiful child."

She swallowed a retort that would only cause her trouble. "Eminence, when I tried to visit the king I was kept from his side. If he is stuporous I can do him no harm." Her heart was pounding. "*Please.* He's my father. Let me see him. I know you have that power."

How it galled her, being forced to beg. Beg *him,* of all people. But what could she do? She knew enough of what it meant to be a ward of the Church to understand he could blight her smallest asking if it suited his purpose. If he was feeling spiteful. If he wished to punish her.

"Yes, I have that power," said Marlan, after a moment. "I will collect you from your private chapel this evening, after Litany. We will visit the king briefly then."

But I want to sit with him alone! I want to sit with him until he leaves us! Why won't you let me? What harm does it do?

But clearly he was going to deny her that . . . and she lacked the power to overturn him. She nodded. "Thank you, Eminence." She considered the gathered, listening councillors. "And thank you, my lords, for your hard work on my behalf. I'll see you here tomorrow, when we can further discuss the matter of my marriage."

As she closed the chamber door behind her, the councillors again burst into furious debate over Lord Rulf's inclusion.

Good. Let them argue themselves into asphyxiation. The longer they argue, the more time I have to find a way out of this fix.

On returning to her apartments she almost fell over Helfred, lurking in the corridor that led to her privy rooms.

She brandished the list of names in his face. "Did you

know about this, Helfred? Did you know your esteemed uncle wants to wed me to his former ward?"

Helfred gaped. "You mean Lord *Rulf*?"

"I'm told that's his name," she said, and slid the hated list into her pocket.

"Oh, that can't be right," said Helfred, shaking his head. "You must have misheard him, Your Highness. Rulf is—"

"Yes? Rulf's *what*? What do you know of him, Helfred? I've never heard of him until today."

Helfred wouldn't meet her gaze. "Er . . . he's fine."

"That *isn't* what you were going to say, Chaplain."

Helfred muttered something incomprehensible. Rhian looked up and down the corridor. They weren't alone, castle staff bustled in and out of rooms on both sides. She couldn't hustle him into her apartments either, because on the other side of their outer doors lurked her ladies-in-waiting. She could send them away, of course, but that would only give rise to gossip.

And the last thing I need right now is gossip.

She folded her arms. "Helfred, I require spiritual guidance. Walk with me."

"Now, Your Highness?" he said, unhappy. "But it's almost time for lunch."

"Aren't you always telling me fasting's good for the soul? *Walk with me.* You don't want me complaining of you to His Eminence, do you?"

Helfred flinched. "That's unkind."

"I know. I'm desperate."

"Very well," he sighed. "I'll walk with you, Highness. And after we've talked you will kneel one hour in the chapel, contemplating the sin of misusing power."

Well, why not? The chapel was as good a place as any for thinking. She nodded. "Yes, Chaplain. Of course, Chaplain. Now, shall we go?"

The castle's privy gardens had been planted by her mother, when she came to Kingseat from duchy Morvell as a young bride. There'd been gardens there before, of course. Perfunctory things, healthy enough but lacking flair. The previous queen, her father's mother, hadn't really been interested in flowers. But Queen Ilda had adored them, and as she waited for the birth of her first son poured all of that love into creating beautiful bowers, charming grottoes and cunning mazes.

Not even out here were they alone. Three gardeners worked nearby, pulling weeds and clipping blossoms. Rhian led Helfred into the nearest maze. "We don't have long," she said, keeping her voice low. "Someone is bound to wonder where I am. What were you going to say about this Rulf?"

Helfred's fingers found his prayer beads, suspended from his corded belt, and clicked them with agitated fingers. "Your Highness, this is most improper. I am your chaplain. My purpose is to advise you on spiritual matters. Nothing more."

"No, no, no. Helfred, you started this and now you're going to finish it. Tell me what you know about Lord Rulf!"

"Your Highness, it's not for me to say," he said, annoyingly firm. "Marlan is prolate, I can in no way presume to interfere with—"

She dropped to her knees before him. "Helfred, I'm begging you. Haven't you heard? The king has relin-

quished his crown. Until I marry and make my husband
the new king, Ethrea is governed by the council. And as a
ward of the Church *I'm* governed by your uncle."

Helfred was staring. "King Eberg has abdicated? No,
I had not heard. It's not been made common knowledge.
I'm sorry, Your Highness."

To her surprise, his unexpected and genuine sympathy
brought tears to her eyes. "So am I. While my father ruled
I didn't have to consider rushing into marriage. Now, for
Ethrea's sake, I *must* take a husband. The dukes have provided me with a list of names. Your uncle presumes to
involve himself. Please, Helfred. Advise me."

He looked taken aback. "Yes, Your Highness. You
know I will. That is my purpose as your chaplain."

The grass was damp, and ruining her dress. Besides,
she'd made her point. She got to her feet. "Good. Then
tell me of Lord Rulf. Why were you dismayed when I
mentioned his name?"

"Dismayed? Your Highness is mistaken."

"I'm not. You know I'm not. *Please,* Helfred. I've nowhere else to turn."

Agitated, Helfred began pacing the narrow confines of
the maze. "I don't think you realise what you're asking of
me, Highness."

"Oh, Helfred . . . of course I do. You're as subject to
Marlan as I am. But aren't you also subject to God? What
does your conscience tell you, Chaplain? What does *God*
tell you? You must see you have to reveal what you know.
Lord Rulf and I will be bound in wedlock until death—if
he's the man I choose to marry." She felt her breath hitch.
"If he's the man I'm forced to marry."

"Forced?" Helfred spun about. "Nonsense. Scripture

is quite clear on this matter: no man or woman may be pressured to wed against their will or conscience."

She laughed, miserably aware she was starting to sound shrill. "Are you truly that naïve? Of course I'm being pressured." She pulled the council's list out again. "It's been made quite clear to me: I am going to marry someone on this list. Someone I hardly know, or don't know at all." *I have to give him what is rightfully mine: the crown.* But she couldn't tell Helfred that. She'd lose any small sympathy she'd won. "I'm not permitted to follow my heart."

Helfred pursed his lips, looking again like the pompous worm she had come to despise. "No young woman of breeding makes such a decision based on her *heart*, Highness. Nor does she make it unguided by wise counsel. You must restrain your ardent spirit. It is not meet for you, in your tender years, to presume an understanding of these matters. *Especially* when they touch upon the welfare of the realm."

If she smacked him now he'd never tell her anything about Marlan's mysterious former ward. "Yes. Of course," she said, through gritted teeth. "You're right, Chaplain. Forgive me."

He smiled. "You're forgiven."

"Now . . . about Lord Rulf . . ."

His smile vanished. "Highness, I have only met him a handful of times. We've exchanged a few dozen words, perhaps."

"Well, it's more than I've exchanged with him," she said darkly. "Helfred, please. Tell me what you can. Henrik Linfoi said he has estates here in Kingseat."

He sighed. "That's true. They encompass the village of

Arnshill, and some woodland. Lord Rulf is, to the best of my knowledge, a sober, pious gentleman who has never been married."

Well. That sounded exciting. Also . . . brief. "And how old is he, Helfred?"

"I could not say, for certain." Helfred hesitated. "But he's . . . no more than middle-aged."

She felt her nose wrinkle. "You mean he approaches twice my years? He's old enough to be my father?"

Helfred nodded. "At a stretch. Yes, Highness."

But how *awful*. "And what else, Helfred? Tell me, quickly. We can't stay in this maze much longer."

"Rulf is the only son of a distant family connection on my uncle's aunt's side, I believe. When his parents perished he was yet a minor and so was warded to Marlan."

She stared. "Marlan said he was no blood relation."

"He's not. Precisely. It's complicated."

"And why was he warded to Marlan? Surely there was someone else in your family better suited than he."

"I do not know, Highness. Ask my uncle."

No, thank you. The less interest she expressed in Rulf, the better. "And in your opinion, Helfred, would he make a good king?"

Helfred's gaze slid sideways. "Highness, it is not my place to say. The prolate recommends him. Surely that speaks for itself."

"Yes. Of course," she said, biting back anger. "I appreciate the delicacy of your position, Helfred. But—"

He raised a hand. "Highness, forgive me, I cannot speak any further on the matter. I understand this talk of marriage makes you nervous. It is only natural, you're a well-bred virgin. But you must have faith in the council and the prolate. They will not push you willy-nilly into some strange man's arms. I have no doubt you will be given ample time and opportunity to consider each of your suitors in person, and that in the end the choice will be yours."

Did he believe that, or was he just fobbing her off? It didn't matter, really. She was helpless. Powerless. A victim of her father's prejudice.

If only he'd let me betroth myself to Alasdair none of this would be happening now.

He was dying and she was angry. Surely that was some kind of sin.

Helfred said, "Come, Your Highness. We must return to the castle. I have duties to perform . . . and you owe me an hour in the chapel."

Of course he'd remember that. "Very well," she said. "Thank you, Chaplain."

She led him from the maze without having to think about it. The narrow green convolutions held no mysteries for her; she'd played in the garden's mazes with her mother from the time she could walk.

Let's just hope I can find the way out of my current predicament with equal ease.

Dutiful, obedient, the very image of a chaste princess, she walked with Helfred back into her prison.

Marlan occupied a separate establishment in the greater grounds of Kingseat castle, known as the Prolates Palace. There he lived and worked and held his ecclesiastical courts, presiding over his vast network of venerables, chaplains and devouts in their churches and chapels, venerable houses and clericas throughout the kingdom. He was their prolate, the king of their Church.

Helfred waited for a royal audience with his esteemed uncle, wishing he wasn't so prone to sweat.

The venerable who sat guard outside Marlan's inner sanctum, working diligently behind a magnificent desk, had scarcely acknowledged his arrival. Ven'Martin, his name was. A sleekly muscled man a little older than himself, who made him feel unaccountably nervous . . . doubtless because the prolate never spoke of his nephew except to disparage and Venerable Martin obviously knew it. The fact Helfred was the princess's personal chaplain meant nothing, because Rhian had no power of her own to wield.

A bit like me, really. We each have an important relation and precious little else.

After his appallingly awkward conversation with Rhian in the garden maze he'd prayed with her in chapel for just over an hour. To his surprise she'd insisted on staying there afterwards. Perhaps his constant exhortations to piety were finally, *finally,* having an effect.

What a trial she was to him, the princess Rhian. Outspoken. Feisty. So often inappropriate. What in God's name had His Majesty been thinking, filling the girl's head full of knowledge and fire? Did he think he was helping her? Did he think she was happy, grown into a young woman so unfitted for her station?

She will never be happy now. With her family dead and Ethrea's future in her womb, how can she be happy? She is the least domesticated woman I have ever known. God help the man she marries, truly.

It was a great shame with no hope of remedy. God had

decreed a path for Rhian and she must walk it, with pleasure or without.

And if she does marry Rulf almost certainly she'll walk without. Dear God, what is my uncle thinking?

It was why he'd come here, to ascertain the truth. He owed Rhian that much as her spiritual advisor.

A small brass bell affixed to the wall behind Ven'Martin's immaculate desk jangled on its blue and red cord. Without looking up he said, "You may go in now, Chaplain. Do not forget your obeisance."

Did the man think him an utter fool, then? To speak to him as though he were a mere country cleric? Insolent, arrogant, presumptuous . . . *I am the prolate's nephew, after all.*

He nodded. "Yes, Ven'Martin," he said, his voice a deferential whisper. "Thank you, Ven'Martin."

It was never wise to make an unnecessary enemy.

Ven'Martin waved a hand at him and continued with his work. Helfred rapped his knuckles on his uncle's imposing sanctum door, then pushed it open and went inside.

Marlan didn't look up to witness his obeisance, the ritual dropping to one knee, thumb pressed to lips and heart, three times. On his feet again, eyes downcast before the massive desk, he folded his hands and waited to be noticed.

At length, Marlan put down the illuminated manuscript he was reading. "Helfred. Unhealthy looking as ever. It will be a relief when you are finally consecrated a venerable and your lank, greasy hair is removed for good. *If* that day should ever arrive. You have report of the princess for me?"

Oh. Of course. He never came to see Marlan unless it was to tell tales of Rhian. "Not exactly, Prolate."

Marlan's eyebrows lowered. "Then what do you want?"

An explanation. But he couldn't say that, he'd be thrown out on his face. "Your Eminence, I have learned from the princess you wish her to consider your former ward Lord Rulf as a husband. Indeed, as Ethrea's king. I thought I might have misheard her."

"No," said Marlan. His smile was unpleasant. "Though your ears be full of wax, Nephew, yet you have heard her correctly. She will marry Lord Rulf. He will be Ethrea's next king."

"Ah." He shifted a little on the rich, Keldravian carpet. Scented oil lamps warmed the room's timber panelling and struck expensive highlights from the gold-and-jewelled chalices and reliquary boxes displayed around the walls. "I thought she also said she was given an entire list of names to consider, Eminence. Candidates recommended by Ethrea's dukes."

Marlan dismissed the list with a flick of his fingers. "It is nothing, a sop to the other councillors. I have made my choice, Helfred. Rulf will be king."

And that settled the matter? Helfred blinked. "Oh."

"You have an opinion, Chaplain?" Marlan rested his folded hands on his desk and leaned forward. His expression was cordial, his tone gently enquiring.

Helfred thought he might faint on the spot. "No, Prolate. No, I—that's to say, at least, I—" He swallowed, hard. "No."

"I disagree. I think you have come here with a view," said Marlan. "Do enlighten me, Chaplain. I am eager to hear your erudite discourse on the subject."

Oh God. Please help me. "Your Eminence, I implore you, do not mistake my intent. I come to you seeking . . . clarification. I have met Lord Rulf but a handful of times, and that some while ago. I would never go so far as to say I *know* him. But in our rare and brief encounters I did receive an impression of him."

"Yes?"

Rank sweat was coursing beneath his plain robe. He could smell himself, it was a mortification. No matter what he did, what disgusting herbs he swallowed, still his sweat stank like a cow in the byre.

I have to say this. I have to say it. Rollin commands us to be truthful and never parlay with deceit.

"Eminence, forgive me . . . Lord Rulf is a simpleton."

"If by that you mean he is not a sophisticated courtier, you are correct. I count that very much in his favour."

Helfred stared at him. *Say yes, fool. Say that's what you meant. Nod and bow and get out of this room.* His tongue was stuck to the roof of his mouth.

His uncle smiled. "Is that what you meant, Helfred?"

"No," he whispered. "I meant Rulf is an idiot. He would make Rhian miserable. He'd be a disaster as king."

Marlan's cordial expression did not change. "If I hear those assertions repeated beyond this chamber, Helfred, you will regret it. You will know suffering beyond the torments of blessed Rollin. Our blood tie will not save you. *God* will not save you. Am I making myself clear, Nephew Helfred? Do you understand? Or would you like more . . . clarification?"

There was something dreadful in Marlan's eyes. Weak-kneed with horror, Helfred stepped back. "No. That's not necessary. I understand you perfectly, Uncle."

"Good," said Marlan, and returned to his manuscript.

"Uncle—"

Marlan looked up. Helfred stepped back another pace.

"*Your Eminence*. I think I should tell you: the princess is not at all bent towards marriage with Rulf."

"Then I suggest that you bend her, Helfred."

Bend her? Bend her *how*? She wasn't a *tree*. "Eminence . . ." he said helplessly. "She is the *princess*."

With an impatient sigh, Marlan discarded the manuscript. "No, she's a woman. A *young* woman, Helfred. A ward of the Church. She is our responsibility, as is the future of this kingdom."

But what of Rhian's future? "Eminence, I must be candid. I am not comfortable at the thought of—"

"*Comfortable?*" said his uncle. "Have you lost your mind, Helfred? What has your *comfort* to do with anything? The girl is a menace, to herself and to the kingdom. Eberg has spoiled her disgracefully. You know it. He has spoiled her unto the risk of her soul. It is our job to save that soul before she is damned entirely. Before she chooses some fool duke's man who will bring us all to ruin. You will bend Rhian, Chaplain. You will do whatever it takes to see her meek and compliant, obedient to my will and marriage to Lord Rulf. For if you do not . . ."

Helfred felt a wave of icy-cold dread rush through his hot body. He didn't need Marlan to finish his threat.

"Yes, Eminence," he whispered. "I understand, Eminence."

Marlan smiled. "I thought you might. Now get out. You have work to do."

Standing again on the other side of his uncle's sanctum door, Helfred found himself close to tears. Without a word to Ven'Martin, still diligently working, he escaped from the Prolates Palace into its manicured grounds. Gasping for clean air, feeling the foetid sweat dry on his skin, he clasped his trembling hands and stared beseechingly at the blue sky.

Oh God. Oh God. What do I do now?

CHAPTER TEN

Have you heard, Jones?" said Ursa, striding unannounced through his open kitchen door. "King Eberg is dead. Heralds are spreading the news through town. Has it reached here yet? I thought it might not have. Poor man. At least his suffering's over now."

"Dead?" Dexterity took his frying eggs off the hob before they burned. "No. I hadn't heard. I haven't stepped foot past the front gate since you were here yesterday. I've hardly even left the house. I was afraid Zandakar might wake and need me."

She unslung her physicking bag from her shoulder, dropped it to the floor then leaned her hip against the kitchen table. "And did he?"

"No. He hasn't stirred so much as a finger. That concoction of shuteye certainly did the trick." He sighed, panged with sorrow. "Eberg's dead, you say? Well, well. There's an end to an era."

"And a start to trouble," she added, inspecting his pan.

"You've too much butter in there, Jones. Do you want to get fat?"

Suddenly he'd lost his appetite. Eberg dead. That meant Rhian was alone. He put the pan on the bench, heedless of scorch marks. "The poor princess. What a terrible time this is."

Ursa shoved her hands in her blue smock's baggy pockets and started pacing the small kitchen. Dexterity watched her, surprised. He'd never seen her so openly agitated.

"Yes, truly terrible, Jones, and not just for her. A king-less kingdom is ripe for unrest. So for all our sakes she'd best throw a stone out of the nearest window and hope the man it hits is unattached and passably attractive. The quicker she marries, the safer we'll be."

Ursa was right. But even so . . . He moved to stand in the open doorway and let his troubled gaze rest on the cottage's dew-pearled back garden. It was a beautiful morning, sweet smelling and fresh. "She shouldn't be rushed to the altar," he murmured. "She's a young girl with her whole life ahead of her."

"She's nothing of the kind, Jones," Ursa retorted, standing behind him. "She's a princess first, last and always. Her duty's clear: she needs to marry and have a clutch of sons as quickly as nature will allow."

He shook his head. "It's unfair."

"Life's unfair, Jones! Nobody knows that better than you."

No, they didn't. But even so . . . *Poor Rhian. Nearly all hope of happiness snatched away.* But there was nothing he could do about that. The kingdom's great men would see to her welfare now. With an effort he wrenched his thoughts from their melancholy bent and turned.

"Ursa, since you're here, would you mind checking on Zandakar? I should see to Otto. Take him down the lane to his field. The poor chap's been cooped up in his stable since I got back from the harbour."

"All right," said Ursa, rolling her eyes. "Just don't take all day. I've a laundry list of people to physick but I thought you'd want to know about Eberg, so I came here first."

He smiled. "And I appreciate it. Truly." A fresh wave of sorrow washed the smile away. "Eberg dead. I know it was expected, but still . . . He was a good man. A good king. When Queen Ilda died I thought he might remarry. He must have loved her very much. So sad that he outlived his sons. That he died knowing he was leaving behind him such turmoil."

"There'll only be turmoil if the princess doesn't marry," said Ursa. "And the council won't sit still for that. Jones, are you going to eat those eggs?"

He considered the frypan with sour disfavour. "No, I don't think so."

"Then give them to me. Can't abide to see good food go to waste. I'll eat, look in on your Zandakar then be on my merry way."

He handed her the frypan. "Help yourself. I won't be long."

Otto greeted the sound of his footsteps on the flag-stoned path with an ear-shattering bray.

"Yes, yes, I know, I'm sorry," he said as the donkey strained over the stable's half-door, long ears pinned back and top lip curled. "It's not the end of the world, Otto.

You're warm and dry and you've plenty to eat. Now stop complaining. There's donkeys I could show you who'd think themselves in luxury."

Another indignant hee-haw, and a bang as Otto kicked his manger.

Dexterity waggled a finger at him. "Don't you use that language with me!"

Otto shook his head, long tongue poked out derisively.

The donkey's halter was hung up in the lean-to beside the stable, where his hay, oats, harness and little cart lived. As Dexterity reached for it, Hettie said:

"Wait, Dexie love. We need to talk."

Heart pounding, he turned to face his dead wife.

She was sitting on the bench under the flowering hasaba tree. Her favourite spot in the garden, where she used to bring her mending. The pale blue blossoms drooped towards her as though glad of her company after so long.

"Eberg's dead," he said stupidly, dazzled anew by the heart-warming sight of her.

She nodded, not smiling. Sunlight dappled her beautiful face, her golden hair tied up in pink ribbon, her sprigged muslin dress. "I know, Dex. It's why I've come."

"I found that Zandakar," he said, and took a step closer. Would he be able to touch her this time? Hold her? Kiss her? "I've settled him in the nur—the spare room."

Still she did not smile. "I saw," she said. "Take care of him, Dex. He's more important than you know."

Even though this was his beloved Hettie, and he'd been desperate to see her again, he felt a tiny spark of crossness. "I'd know if you'd tell me!"

"Dexie, Dexie . . ." Her sigh was sorrowful. "I tell you what I can."

"Well it isn't enough! You know, you're asking a great deal of me, Hettie. This Zandakar cost me a *fortune*. And do you know something? I think he might be *dangerous*. Ursa thinks he might be dangerous, too. She's convinced he's some kind of heathen warrior. He's certainly got some mysterious scars. And then of course there's the whole question of how he came to be a slave in the first place. I think you owe me an explanation, Hettie."

She didn't answer. Just looked at him sadly. Abandoning the idea of seeing to Otto, he threw himself at her feet.

"Hettie, *please*, you have to tell me. What is *happening*? And why, of all people, is it happening to *me*?"

"Because you've been chosen, Dex," she said. Her hands stayed in her lap. "Now listen to me carefully. I don't have long. Eberg's death spells the beginning of the end. Princess Rhian is in grave peril. Wicked men seek to use her for their own misguided, selfish desires."

"Wicked men? What wicked men? Do you mean the—"

"I mean Prolate Marlan, Dex," said Hettie sternly. "And others like him."

The *prolate*? Surely not. "Now, Hettie—"

"Hush, Dex! Let me finish. If these men succeed, Ethrea is lost . . . and as Ethrea goes so goes the world. And these men *will* succeed . . . unless you do as I say."

He felt his jaw drop. "Me? Hettie, what can *I* do? I'm not important, I'm a *toymaker*!"

"A toymaker who's made a princess his friend," she said. "Now *listen*. You must go to the castle without delay, find Rhian and convince her to run away with you."

"Run *away* with me? *Hettie!* Have you gone quite *mad*?"

"No," she said. Shadows danced, flirting with her hair. "Dex, please. Don't fail me now."

He leapt to his feet. "That's not fair! You know perfectly well I'd do anything for you!"

"Then do this," she said, her voice gently remorseless. "The most important thing I've ever asked. Oh, Dexie, my love. I never said it would be easy. But for countless tens of thousands of innocent souls it will mean the difference between life and death. Surely that's worth a little inconvenience?"

There was a terrible tightness in his chest. He pressed the heel of his hand against his breastbone and rubbed hard, trying to ease it. Oh dear, oh dear. Life and death? Toymakers didn't deal in matters of life and death. Not beyond the safety of a puppet-show, at least.

But Hettie was looking at him, and he loved her so much . . .

"All right," he sighed, almost groaning. "Let's say, for the sake of argument, I go to the castle. Say against all likelihood I'm granted an audience with Princess Rhian and she listens to my suggestion without tossing me out again on my ear. Say she agrees—oh, this is *nonsense*— to run away with me. Where exactly do you suggest we run?"

"The princess will know," said Hettie. "When she realises escape is possible, she'll know where to go, Dex, and what to do next."

"Well, that's a relief!" he retorted. "At least one of us will!"

Hettie ignored that, as she'd always ignored his rare

spats of temper. "There's something else, Dexie. When you do leave Kingseat you have to take Zandakar with you."

"Take *Zandakar*?" He clutched at his beard. "Hettie, you *are* mad. He's a black man with blue hair who doesn't speak a word of Ethrean. How am I supposed to explain him away?"

She stood. All of a sudden he could see hasaba blossoms through the bodice of her dress. "You'll manage it, my love. You must. Zandakar is a vital piece of the puzzle."

"Is he really?" he said, not caring how waspish he sounded. "I don't suppose you'd care to tell me *why*?"

She shook her head. "I can't. Not yet. You'll just have to trust me."

"Of course I *trust* you, Hettie, but—"

"Good!" she said. "Now go to the castle. Rhian needs you." She shooed him with her transparent hands, just as she used to bustle him out of the kitchen before dinner. "*Hurry,* Dexie! There isn't much time!"

A breeze blew through her, and she was gone.

"Well, this is ridiculous," he said, glaring at the empty garden bench. "Do you hear me, Hettie? It's all complete poppycock!"

Except in the cottage behind him slept a man with blue hair. And overlooking the harbour, in the king's castle, was a sweet young girl who'd just lost her father, the last of her kin. Who was all alone now and trammelled about with men who would see her as nothing more than a pawn for the furthering of their grand ambitions.

And if I don't do my best to help her, what kind of a man does that make me?

"Sorry, Otto," he said, turning to his long-suffering donkey. "It seems there's been a change of plans."

Ursa was scrubbing the frypan when he returned to the kitchen. "That was quick," she said over her shoulder. "You must've galloped to Otto's field and back."

"Ah . . ." He cleared his throat and tried to charm her with a smile. "I didn't go, actually. You see—well—Ursa, I need a favour."

"*Another* one?" She frowned. "Jones, this is what's known as stretching the friendship."

The smile wasn't working, so he let it die. "Please. You know I wouldn't ask if it wasn't important. I need you to stay here a little longer. I've an errand to run."

Ursa pulled the plug from the sink then put her soapy hands on her hips. "What kind of errand?"

He couldn't tell her. She'd never believe him. He still wasn't sure he believed it himself. In the kitchen's corner sat an open trunkful of repaired dolls and toys he'd worked on through the night, while keeping an ear out for Zandakar. He gestured at them. "I'm a nodcocky fool. I completely forgot I'm supposed to deliver these back to the castle."

"The *castle*?" Ursa hooted. "Jones, the king just died. What makes you think they'll let you in?"

"Eberg may be dead, Ursa, but life still goes on," he said. "I'll just join the other castle provisioners at the tradesmen's entrance. And you know, I do need to get these toys back. I was supposed to have delivered them the other day but I had to wait for supplies before I could finish the repairs. And truth be told, I need the money. I've Tamas's wages to pay and, well . . . Zandakar didn't exactly come cheap."

"That'll teach you to buy strange men off foreign slave ships," she said, typically unsympathetic. "And what about my patients, Jones? They're waiting for me. I suppose you've forgotten all about *them*!"

Oh. Yes. Her patients. He had forgotten. Embarrassed, he stared at the floor. It needed sweeping, curls of pale pinewood and driftings of sawdust. How Hettie would grumble if she were here to see it. "I won't be gone so *terribly* long," he mumbled. "And I can't leave Zandakar alone. I'm sorry, Ursa. I know I'm a nuisance."

"You're a sight more than a nuisance, Jones," said Ursa. "You're a trial and a 'cumbrance, that's what you are." She shook her head. "So what are you waiting for? Get out of here, would you? The quicker you leave, the quicker you'll be back!"

He nearly kissed her. "Oh, *thank you*, Ursa!"

As he and Otto clopped and rattled through the sleepy streets, heading for Kingseat township and the road up to the castle, he saw the news had finally reached his neighbourhood. People milled on the pavements and gathered around gateways. He could hear muffled weeping, see the wringing of hands.

By this time tomorrow we'll be a kingdom in mourning. And if Hettie's right there's more sorrow on the horizon. And I'm supposed to prevent it? Oh dear, oh dear.

He shook the reins at Otto. "Come on, you. Do get a move on. Ursa will skin us both if we take too long."

Otto flattened his ears and grudgingly picked up the pace. And as the donkey trotted, Dexterity turned his thoughts to Ethrea's current trouble, trying to unravel it like a knot in wool.

*   *   *

"Your Highness. *Please*. You *must* come away. This is *most* unseemly . . . and you don't want the prolate to find you here like this."

Rhian shrugged Helfred's encroaching hand from her shoulder and continued to stroke her father's hair. She hadn't been with him when he died. His face was peaceful now, but what was the truth of his last living moments? Had he suffered? Had he missed her? Had he called her name in vain?

I should've been with him. Marlan should've let me stay.

But Marlan had refused her pleas for more time. He'd granted her a mean half-hour by her father's side, after chapel, then sent her away as though she'd done something wrong.

He's a thief, that Marlan. He stole the last of my father from me. I'll never forgive him. I'll never forget.

"Leave me alone, Helfred," she said, her voice gritty with grief. "I'm a princess in mourning. Have you no respect?"

Helfred stomped to the other side of the bed and glared at her across her father's cooling corpse. "Have *you* no respect, Highness? The king must be taken to the Great Chapel, he must be bathed and oiled and dressed according to his rank, so when he is laid out in state the world will know his great majesty. But so long as you sit here the devouts cannot fulfil their sacred task. Would you leave Eberg in his rumpled bed, Your Highness, soiled and unkempt, in a ruined nightshirt like any common man?"

His sharp words struck like daggers through the fog of anguish surrounding her. *Oh, Papa. Papa.* "Of course not," she muttered. "He must be made beautiful. But I don't wish to leave him. I'll help the devouts, Helfred. I'll escort his body to—"

"Highness, be sensible!" Helfred begged. "You know that's impossible. Prolate Marlan would never permit it. Please. You need some fresh air and time to compose yourself. Let me escort you into the garden. After that you must pray, then dress yourself in mourning. The council wishes to see you at four o'clock."

Her head snapped up. "Today? The council expects me to dance attendance on them *today*? Mere hours after my father's death? Are they deranged, Helfred? Are *you* deranged, to give me such a message *now*? Touch the king's face, you fool! There's a little warmth to him still! My God, you're *outrageous*!"

If her furious accusations hurt him, he didn't show it. "The summons came from the prolate, Highness." Helfred's voice and expression were neutral. "Do you suggest I should've told *him* he was deranged?"

Some venerable or other had mercifully closed her father's eyes. She was grateful for that much. The thought of walking into this chamber to see them empty of his spirit, his soul . . .

She leaned forward and kissed him, kissed each eyelid, his cool lips. His hands. "Forgive me, Papa," she whispered. "They won't let me stay. But I'll see you again soon, I promise."

She could've slapped Helfred, he looked so relieved.

In the antechamber beyond her father's room hovered a gaggle of devouts and four po-faced venerables and a scattering of wet-cheeked, red-eyed courtiers. She swept past them all, her head high, Helfred scuttling at her heels.

As she made her way through the castle's corridors, down the flights of stone stairs leading outside, staff and more courtiers bowed to her, weeping. She nodded but couldn't bring herself to speak.

If I speak, I'll lose control. I can't lose control. I am Rhian, Eberg's daughter. I am Ethrea's rightful queen.

Helfred herded her outside and into the castle's privy gardens, closed the wrought-iron gate behind them and stared at her, uncertain. Then he folded his hands unctuously before him and opened his mouth to deliver a lecture.

"I warn you, Helfred!" she snapped, her voice grating. "Dare to tell me this was *God's will* and I'll beat you to a bloody pulp!"

He gaped in shock. "Your *Highness*! I—"

"You think I won't do it?" Her hands were tight fists, aching to strike him. "You think I can't? I had two brothers, remember? And we all sparred together! I could knock you down with a single blow and you could *never* hope to stop me, Chaplain!"

Helfred took a prudent step back. "Princess Rhian, you are clearly distraught. I will forgive your inappropriate outburst. I must make allowances, for—"

She flung herself away from him. "Oh, Helfred! *Shut up!*"

They were the only two people in the privy garden. Of course, it was a beautiful day. The sky was blue and cloudless, the sun mellow. A light breeze coaxed perfume from the rioting flowers. There were birds in the trees, singing without a care in the world.

Fetch me my bow, someone. I'll shoot them all dead.

Her chest was a vast ice cavern, freezing and hollow.

If she closed her eyes she'd hear the cruel wind, howling through it.

How could you leave me, Papa? How could you go? Don't you realise I'm all alone now? Can't you see I'm at Marlan's mercy? Of no value to him or your precious council, except as a broodmare? Did you know of the prolate's former ward, Lord Rulf? Did you plot with Marlan to see me married to him, this unsophisticated country bumpkin? Did you? Did you? Was I never more than a broodmare to you?

Close behind her, Helfred said, "Perhaps, Your Highness, if you could weep . . ."

She turned on him. "Really? Why? Because it's *womanly*, Helfred? Because weeping is what a weak *female* should do?"

A fresh crop of pimples had broken out on his chin. His hair needed cutting. His habit was limp. "Because you loved him, Highness," he said simply. "And he's gone."

His unexpected words were nearly her undoing. The garden blurred and her throat closed tight. She pressed a fist to her mouth, biting her knuckles hard. When she could trust her voice she clasped her hands behind her back and said, "Yes, Helfred. He's gone. And if the council has its way the shoes I wear to his funeral will do for my wedding as well."

Helfred frowned, censorious. "Highness. Consider your position. It's not seemly to—"

"How much care do you think I have for *seemly*, Helfred?" she demanded, and snapped her fingers under his nose. "*This* much? No, not even so little! Stupid man. If you can't be useful I wish you'd go away."

Again, he refused to react to her temper. "Highness,

you don't know the council wishes to discuss your impending marriage," he said, so reasonable he made her teeth ache. "They could wish only to tender their formal condolences."

She snorted. "You think so? You're generous."

"I try to be," he said, after a moment. "Rollin encourages generosity."

"Why are you a chaplain, Helfred?" she said, considering him closely. "Is it your wish to emulate your uncle and be prolate one day?"

"No!" he said, horrified. "Such a thought has never entered my head, Highness. God called me to serve in the Church, and I answered the summons."

"You had another career in mind?" It was hard to imagine him as anything but a chaplain. Or possibly . . . a swineherd. Lecturing the pigs.

"What I did or did not dream of in my green days, it hardly matters now," he said, pretension returned. "Highness, this conversation is not—seemly. I suggest we return to the castle, where you can collect yourself in your privy chapel before your meeting with the council."

She glared at him, aching anew to punch him silly. *What should I pray for, Helfred? An unexpected fever, to carry me off? Now there's a notion . . .*

"Chaplain—" she began, teeth clenched, then stopped. Over his shoulder she could see a face peering through the wrought-iron garden gate. It was familiar. Completely unexpected. And possibly, oddly, the only face she could bear to look at in the midst of her pain.

"Highness?"

She took a shuddering breath, let it out, and turned her attention intently to her chaplain. *Helfred mustn't see me looking at my visitor. They'll throw him out of the castle and never let him return.* "You're quite right, Helfred. Forgive me. The king's death has—I am—"

"I understand, Highness," he said, nodding.

She let her fingertips rest on his arm. "But I need a little time alone first. The garden is so beautiful. It brings me close to God, and to my parents. My mother in particular. It was her favourite retreat. Please. Leave me. You must have duties, I don't want to keep you from them."

Helfred frowned. "Your spiritual wellbeing is my most important duty, Highness. I'm not sure I should—"

Damn. Why, for once, couldn't he make things easy? "I am, Helfred. You're dismissed."

He had no actual authority to disobey her. She wasn't giving him an unlawful command and she was the king's daughter, after all. That still counted for something, even if to the council it meant as a broodmare.

"Highness," he said, and reluctantly withdrew.

No sooner had the garden gate closed behind him than it opened again and her surprising visitor slipped in.

"Mr *Jones*?" she said as he bowed untidily. "What in Rollin's name are *you* doing here?"

"Oh dear," he said, his expression anxious. "It's a long story, Your Highness."

"You might want to condense it," she advised. "I don't have much time."

"Of course. But first, Your Highness—" Mr Jones bit his lip. "I've heard about King Eberg. I'm so, *so* sorry."

To her complete surprise she burst into tears.

A comforting arm went round her shoulders. A rough hand stroked her aching head. "There, there," said the toymaker, softly. "There, there, you poor young thing."

She didn't weep for long. She'd never been much for crying, it had long since been a point of honour—and an essential survival trait. Tears meant her tormenting brothers had beaten her.

"Mr Jones," she said, embarrassed, stepping out of the warm, safe shelter of his embrace. "Forgive me."

His smile was a benediction. "What's to forgive, Your Highness? If a loving daughter can't grieve for her father what's this world coming to, that's what I'd like to know."

She blotted her face dry with a lace hanky. "And what *I'd* like to know is what you're *doing* here."

His smile vanished. "Princess Rhian, you're in trouble."

She folded her arms, perilously close to hugging herself. "You've come a long way to tell me what I already know."

"But it's not just you," the toymaker added. "It's Ethrea as well. Terrible things are brewing, Your Highness. There's danger on the horizon and it's sweeping in fast."

There was something almost . . . *fevered* . . . in his eyes. Abruptly uneasy, she took another step back. "Mr Jones—"

"Is Prolate Marlan trying to bully you, Highness?" he asked. "Is he . . . I don't know . . . trying to force you to marry against your will?"

The sun was warm but she felt suddenly cold. "How do you know that? How can you *possibly* know—"

"I didn't," he said, a peculiar expression on his face. "At least, not exactly. It's complicated. Let's just say I put two and two together. More or less. And if I guessed right . . ."

He shook himself. "Princess Rhian, do you trust me? Do you believe I'm your man, loyal and true?"

Dreamlike, she nodded. She did believe it. He was an ordinary toymaker, without rank or wealth, but she knew in her bones she could trust him implicitly, her unlikely childhood friend. "Yes."

He looked so relieved it was almost comical. "Your Highness, you can't stay in the castle. You can't even stay in Kingseat. As long as you're here Prolate Marlan and the others will browbeat you until you give in to what they want. And if you do that, I'm here to tell you: Ethrea will be lost."

"Lost?" She shivered. "What do you mean?"

Mr Jones stepped closer. He looked, she realised, very tired. There were shadowed circles beneath his overbright eyes and his gingery hair was more wildly unkempt than ever.

"Princess Rhian, the prolate wants you to marry a man of his choosing. What do *you* want?"

She lifted her chin. *Either I trust him or I don't.* "Mr Jones, I want to be Ethrea's lawful ruling queen."

Mr Jones blinked. "Oh dear. That's awkward."

"Why?"

"Because Ethrea's not in the habit of crowning queens."

"Then Ethrea's going to have to *get* in the habit, isn't it?" she said, belligerent. "I'm the king's true daughter. I'm his sole living heir. I've a right to the crown, Mr Jones. As much of a right as my late brothers ever had. If I'd been born male I'd be a year into my majority and crowned already. I refuse to accept I'm unfit because I'm female. I refuse to have my life run by Prolate Marlan or the council or anyone but myself."

"An admirable ambition, Highness," said Mr Jones. "But, let's be honest, not easily attained. How long before you must choose a husband? Do you know?"

She frowned. "There's the funeral . . . the ambassadorial delegations of condolence . . . the official mourning period lasts one month. I can't think they'd try to force an answer from me before then."

"So we have a month to plan your escape," said Mr Jones. "That's something."

Something, yes. But where could she go? She couldn't flee the kingdom. She couldn't turn to another nation for help. That would surely destroy Ethrea's independence forever. It might even be against the law. And anyway, if she left Ethrea it would be as good as admitting defeat. Marlan would say she'd abandoned her inheritance. He'd say she'd abdicated her right to be the queen consort, never mind ruling monarch. Which meant the ambitious dukes would tear Ethrea apart, like dogs with a sheep.

No. If she was to fight for her inheritance she had to fight for it in Ethrea. So where must she go? Into hiding? Into exile, within her own kingdom? A terrible prospect . . .

But I have no other choice.

"Your Highness?" said Mr Jones, diffident. "Do you know of somewhere you'll be safe, until this business of the succession is settled in your favour?"

Somewhere for certain? No. But . . .

"Duchy Linfoi," she said. "I have a . . . friend . . . there." *I hope. Oh Alasdair . . . Alasdair . . . please God you're still my friend.*

The toymaker swallowed. "I see. That's a long way from Kingseat, Highness. Do you have any idea how we're going to get there?"

She stared. "*We?* Mr Jones—"

"Princess Rhian, you can't do this alone. And even though I know it sounds ridiculous, and I can't explain it just now, I've been tasked with the duty of helping you. So yes. You and I and—" Mr Jones hesitated, and seemed to change his mind. "You and I will be running away to duchy Linfoi."

"You've been *tasked,* Mr Jones?" She frowned. "Tasked by whom? Tell me. I think I'm owed an explan—"

"Of course you are," he said hastily. "But do we have time for explanations right now, Your Highness? I don't think we do."

He was right. She'd stayed out here too long already. Helfred would surely return at any moment, complaining and chiding and herding her indoors.

"All right," she said. "I'll wait. But not forever. And the next time I ask I expect you to answer."

"I will. I promise," said Mr Jones, fervent. "Do you have any idea how we can reach the north safely?"

"Actually," she said slowly, inspiration stirring, "do you know, Mr Jones . . . I think that I might."

"Oh, good," he said. "Because I have no idea whatsoever."

But she did. Oh yes. She had an *excellent* idea . . . one that not even Marlan or the council could protest. Not without laying bare the baseness of their greedy ambitions.

I'll thwart them yet, Papa! And yes, I'll thwart you too. Not because I'm an undutiful daughter . . . but because I'm the daughter you raised me to be.

Despite the grief that devoured her she smiled at the toymaker. "You'd best go, Mr Jones, before you're discovered. I'll find a way for us to stay in touch. Don't come here again. I fear it would be too dangerous, for both of us."

Mr Jones bowed. "Your Highness—Your *Majesty*—I'm yours to command."

Your Majesty. She felt a fresh rush of tears. "God bless you, my friend. I won't forget this. I'll be in your debt the whole of my life."

She watched him slip through the garden gate, torn between relief and terror.

The whole of my life. But if this doesn't work . . . if Alasdair fails me . . . I fear the whole of my life won't last very long.

MIJAK

Hekat stood on her palace balcony, caressed by Et-Raklion's gentle breezes. Aieee, the god see her! Such suffering in her bones. A scorpion lived in her belly, it sank its claws in her gut. Its venom dissolved her. Her eyes were blind with pain.

My eyes are blind because they do not see Zandakar. Aieee, god. My son. My son.

"Empress, I am not to blame for the deserts of this world," said Dmitrak, spawn of Nagarak, spawn of hell. He stood behind her. She cursed the god that he stood at all. "I am not to blame if the god turns its back on us. Speak to Vortka of the god turning its back. He is high godspeaker. Let him swim in the godpool, let him drink the god's blood and tell you why my warhost dies in the desert that keeps us penned in what used to be Harjha."

Not your warhost, you Nagarak spawn. My warhost. My warriors' bleaching bones under the sun.

She turned. "You ride a long way to make excuses for failure."

Dmitrak, his red hair gaudy, his eyes the wrong colour, stepped away from her. "Yuma—"

"Call me that name again and you die!"

On Dmitrak's right forearm the god's gold-and-crystal gauntlet glowed, it surged into life in answer to his rage. He wore it always. He never took it off. She'd been told he fucked women wearing it and if they displeased him he boiled their blood after.

That does not surprise me. He is his father's son.

Unafraid, her snakeblade naked in her fist, she walked towards him. "How many Mijaki warriors have perished since you became the god's hammer? Five thousand? Ten thousand? Will you kill all of Mijak's vast warhost before you are done? With everything I have given you, will you fail the god? Fail *me*?"

Dmitrak's scarlet godbraids were long and heavily weighted. Amulets crowded his hair like ticks on a goat. The ride back from Harjha, that cursed place of patched people, had stripped his meagre flesh to thinness.

"How have I failed you, Empress Hekat?" he demanded. His nose was like Nagarak's, sharp and thrusting. "What you ask for, I give. Harjha is empty, its piebald slaves are no more. Its green lands are Mijak, Mijak's people flow there like a river. Godposts are everywhere. Godhouses worship the god. The demons of Targa are purged at last. Zandakar could not purge them. *I* purged them. With my warhost I rid Targa of demons and Harjha of its piebald slaves. Zandakar did not do that. Zandakar *married* them."

She struck him with her clenched fist. "It is *death* to speak that name in my presence. You think you cannot die, Dmitrak, because you are the hammer?"

He touched his flesh fingers to the thread of blood trickling from his mouth. His ruby-crystal fingers were tight by his side. "I will die when the god kills me, Empress. Are you the god now? Does Vortka know?"

Tcha! He is insolent. His father stares back at me with

*those dark, sunken eyes. In my hot dreams I hear Naga-
rak, laughing.*

"Dmitrak—"

"Empress, the world is more than one desert. Why
must we cross it?" he said, daring to interrupt. "It is sand,
it has no value. We should—"

"If it had no value, demons would not guard it!" she
spat. "You are stupid, Dmitrak, if you are blind to that.
The desert marks the straight way to the world, Vortka
godspeaker says so." She touched the scorpion round her
neck. "*I* say so. But if that were not true, still the desert
must be broken. No nest of demons can be left to thrive.
If we fail to break the desert we fail to serve the god. Is
that your desire?"

His lips pinched. "No, Empress."

"Return to Harjha, warlord," she told him. *Aieee god,
he did not deserve that honour.* "Take the warriors you
need from Et-Raklion's barracks. Tame the great desert
on Harjha's doorstep for the god in the world. That is your
purpose. You are made hammer for *that*. Not to boast
of your power, not to fuck from newsun to lowsun." She
laughed. "You think I would not hear of your boastings,
hear the wailings of the women you plough into dust? I
am Empress of Mijak, godtouched and precious. I hear
whispers in the dead of night. I know what you are made
of, Dmitrak. Nine godmoons you squirmed and seethed
in my belly. Before you drew breath you sought to end
my life. You failed then. You fail now. You think you are
Zandakar. I tell you plainly, *you are not*."

There were scars on his face now, which had not been
there seven godmoons before. Puckered lines. Shiny ci-
catrices. He was a fierce warrior, she could not deny him

that. He had a hunger for killing, a thirst for blood. She knew he used his snakeblade, often, when the hammer would keep him safe. The godspeakers told Vortka this and Vortka told her. The warriors in the warhost told her, when she walked among them.

He is careless with their lives, they do not care, he gives them blood. He gives them blood, he does not give me the desert. He does not give me the world for the god.

Dmitrak sneered. "The man whose name I am not allowed to mention, Empress, is the man who betrayed you. Betrayed me. Betrayed the god. To say to me, *You are not that man,* that is to say a thing pleasing to my ears. Did you intend that? I think you did not."

I think I did not intend for you to be warlord. I did not intend for you to exist. Some hellspawn demon decided that. You suckle at its tit, Dimmi. You are a demon, nourished by hell.

"You will ride back to Harjha after appearing in the godtheatre next sacrifice," she told him. "That is four highsuns from now, warlord. In that time you will choose your warriors wisely. You will seek guidance in the godpool." She smiled, anticipating sweet fear. "You will give yourself to the scorpion wheel for cleansing."

For once, just once, he did not disappoint her. His head came up. Every sinew tightened. The whites of his eyes showed, like a horse shown the whip.

"I do not need the scorpion wheel. My godspark is clean. I am without sin."

She bared her teeth at him. "You are without sin yet the desert is not tamed? *Tcha*. Then you do not know the meaning of that word."

His scars were shinier now. Sweat was on them. "I

know I have done all in my power to tame that desert, Empress. Do not task me that it is untamed, task Vortka's godspeakers, they do not banish its demons. It is demons who break my warhost in the sand, it is demons who suck them dry of life and make of them leather sacks. How is that *my* sin? Godspeakers know the god, I know my snakeblade and this hammer on my arm!" His gold-and-crystal fist came up, flashing fire. "With my snakeblade and this hammer have I given you two nations. I have given you countless cities. I have given you wealth. Ask Vortka for the desert. Task *him,* if he cannot."

Tcha, the god see her. Vortka. *Vortka.*

"Did I tell you to stand here and spit stupid words in my face?" she said coldly. "Dmitrak warlord, I think I did not. Obey my commandments. I am your Empress. I am in the god's eye."

It was in his ugly face how he wanted to strike her. Disobey her. He knew better than to try. He turned on his heel and walked away from her, wordless.

Alone again, she stood on her balcony and stared at the city, spread below Raklion's towering Pinnacle. So big now. So sprawling. But emptier than it was, with the god's people of Mijak pouring into the world. The dry north was almost unpeopled, Jokriel and Mamiklia all but abandoned. The underground rivers had not returned to full flow. Large tracts of Mijak were dead grass and dry dirt.

The rivers will not run again till the god is in the world.

Around her neck, the scorpion amulet throbbed.

Dmitrak fails me. He should never have been born. The god did not want him. I was befuddled by demons.

Demons are responsible for what happened to Zandakar in Harjha. That piebald bitch was a demon. She turned his heart from me. But she is dead now and seven god-moons have passed. His heart must be free of her. His godspark must be reclaimed. He is the true warlord. He is the god's only hammer. He is my only son. What is this Dmitrak?

He is a mistake.

She summoned a slave. "Fetch a litter," she told it. "I go to the godhouse."

Vortka was in the sacrifice chamber when a novice came with a message that Hekat would see him. His hand faltered slightly, cutting the lamb's throat.

"Take the Empress to my private chamber," he said as the lamb's body fell to dust. "Bear her company until I am able to come."

"High godspeaker, I can finish this sacrifice," said Peklia. "If the Empress requires you . . ."

He shook his head. "The god requires me first. Fetch the next sacrifice."

Peklia looked at him. "Vortka . . ."

They had become good friends since he was made the high godspeaker. She was his eyes in the wider world, and travelled frequently beyond Mijak's old borders so he might know first-hand from her how things prospered in their new lands.

They do not prosper as well as they ought. The god whispers in the godpool of an unseen presence, a hell-spawn power like rot beneath firm flesh. When will it tell me more? I cannot defeat what I do not understand . . .

He had not told Hekat of the whispers in the godpool.

She had not told him if the god whispered to her as well. He and Hekat hardly spoke any more.

Zandakar lies like a corpse between us, as though I had not stopped her from slitting his throat.

"Vortka," said Peklia, more insistent. "Please. You should go. I will finish this sacrifice. Do not keep the Empress waiting. She has grown . . . unpredictable, and Mijak has need of you."

Dear Peklia, she was a blessed godspeaker. He nodded. "Very well. I will seek the god in the godpool after highsun sacrifice. See it is prepared for me."

"High gospeaker," she said, bowing.

Hekat, in his private chamber, turned from the window as he closed its door behind him. "I send Dmitrak to you for cleansing on the scorpion wheel. Beat the god into him, Vortka. Nagarak's spawn is a sad disappointment."

Aieee, the god see her. How she had aged since raising Dimmi high. There was skin, there was bone, there was so little flesh.

"Empress," he said. "It is good to see you."

Her lips thinned. "*Tcha.* It is not."

Such a history they had, not easily untangled. "Hekat, it is," he said gently. "Do not stand like some stranger. Take a seat. Tell me more."

"There is nothing to tell you," she said, and did not sit down. "He is here. He wants more warriors, to take the place of those he killed with his incompetence. I do not want him to have them, Vortka."

He would sit, if she would not. "He must have them, Hekat. The god needs warriors to fight for it in the world."

"The god needs a hammer that does not smash the nails that serve it!"

Helpless, he stared at her. "Hekat, if you would only handle him more gently . . ."

"*Tcha!*" she spat, and flung herself into a chair. "I have no desire to handle him at all. He should never have been made the god's hammer. That was a demon's doing, it is time to undo it."

He felt his heart thud once, very hard. His breath hitched. "Hekat?"

"Are you deaf now, Vortka? Has old age stopped your ears?"

I am not old. I am worn down by the god. "No. I heard you."

"Then fetch to me Zandakar. Bring him out of the shadows where you have been keeping him. Let Dmitrak hellspawn take his place there. I never wish to see him again. I wish to see Zandakar. He is my true son. He is the god's own proper hammer."

Aieee, the god see him. The god give him strength.

"Hekat, I cannot," he said. His voice sounded strange. "What you ask for is not possible."

She hissed. "Of course it is possible. Who are you to say it is not? I am Empress of Mijak, Vortka. Not you. If I say he will once more be the god's hammer you will not sit there and say *no* to me." Her fingers seized her scorpion amulet. "I hear the god, Vortka. This is the god's desire."

It has not said so, in the godpool. The god has not told me. Could I have done what I have done if the god still meant him for its hammer?

"Hekat . . ." With an effort, his bones unwilling, he got

to his feet and walked to the window. "Zandakar is not here."

"Then where he is, bring him from there! Are you stupid now, Vortka, as well as gone deaf?"

Aieee, the god see him.

"Hekat, he is not in Mijak," he said. His throat hurt. "I tell you truly, I do not know where he is."

"Not in Mijak?" She sounded uncertain. He did not know what she looked like, he could not bring himself to turn. "What is this, he is not in Mijak? I gave him to you, Vortka. You said you would keep him. Where would you keep him if not in Mijak?"

"Hekat, I kept him for as long as I could. Then I could not keep him, I sent him away."

Her taloned fingers sank into his arm, she pulled him from the window and round to face her. Her eyes were blue fire. She would burn him alive. "Why? Why did you do that? Why did you send him away from me?"

You wanted to kill him. You said you would kill him if you saw him again.

"Hekat, do not ask me," he said, and sighed. "It is done. He is gone."

He felt her nails pierce him. He felt blood on his skin. "I will not ask again, Vortka. *Tell me why you have stolen my son.*"

"I did not steal him. I saved him. Hekat . . ." Aieee, god. He must tell her. "Dmitrak twice attempted his life."

She stepped back, her eyes shocked wide. *"I do not believe you."*

Did she know she was weeping? Hekat never wept. He wanted to hold her. He did not dare. She would kill him if he touched her, he could see it in her eyes.

"I am sorry. I am sorry. Hekat, he is my son too. Would I have sent him away if I had another choice? It broke my heart within me, to send him away. To send him with strangers into the world that is not yet ours, or the god's, though it will be."

Peklia had helped him. As his eyes in the growing empire of Mijak she had found men to take Zandakar to safety beyond its new borders. Half-mad with grief then, not wholly human, Zandakar was taken where his brother could not hurt him.

And if a man could die of weeping, surely I came close to death.

Hekat's shock was passing, swallowed by fury. "Dmitrak will die for this. Dmitrak will die by my hand. And *you,* I should kill *you,* Vortka, for not telling me, for letting Nagarak's foul spawn draw breath one heartbeat after the first time he raised a hand to my son!"

"Aieee, Hekat! Hekat! Why would I do that," he cried, anguished, "when you told me yourself you wanted Zandakar dead? You forbade the whisper of his name, you burned his possessions, his wife and child, you killed his horse, you killed your heart. To you he was already dead, I never thought you would want him back. But Dmitrak did. Dmitrak suspected. He knows you have no love for him. He knew in some little while your heart would come to life again. And so he tried to protect himself. How can you be surprised by this? He is your creation, he is what you made."

"My creation? *My creation?* He is a demon spat out of hell, like his father before him! Dmitrak is no son of mine!"

"Yes, he is. He is your son, Hekat. And more than that,

he was given by the god. You sin if you say otherwise, and you know it. You cannot kill Dmitrak. He is the god's hammer. How will you hammer the world without him?"

Her face was a rictus of fury and despair. *"I would hammer the world with Zandakar!"*

Ignoring the danger, he reached for her. He had not held her for many seasons. She felt like bones draped in expensive cloth. "Aieee, Hekat. Little Hekat. You cannot do that. Zandakar is gone."

She wept against him, and he wept too.

"Nagarak's spawn must be punished, Vortka," she said, her voice muffled against his chest. "When Dmitrak comes to you for tasking on the scorpion wheel, task him for raising his hand to Zandakar. That was not his right, Zandakar is mine. He lives or dies by my hand and no other."

Vortka tightened his arms around her. *Not any more, Hekat, Empress of Mijak. Zandakar is sent far beyond your control. He is in the god's eye, he is gone from our sight.*

He could not say that aloud, to her.

"It is not right to task Dmitrak for the desert. Hekat, I have told you. There are demons at work here. The god's enemies would thwart it, they would hold us back from giving it the world. Dmitrak does what he can. He can do no more."

She pulled free. "You would defend him, Vortka, this hellspawn who raised his hand to my son? How can you do that? You cannot love Zandakar."

A dull pain pierced him. *Even now she cannot admit that he was born of our flesh.* After so many seasons of her denial he should feel nothing, but he was not a man of stone.

"I cannot condemn a man the god has chosen," he told her sternly. "The god intervened when Dmitrak would have hurt Zandakar. Our son is protected, he is in the god's eye. Dmitrak is its hammer. His power is unchanged."

"How can you say so when he does not conquer the desert?"

"Where there are demons it is not his task to conquer," he said. "That is my task, Hekat."

Now her eyes were dry and cold. "Then the failure is yours, Vortka. You have failed the god and you have failed *me*." Her head lifted, godbraids chiming with their profusion of sweet silver bells. *"Twice* you have failed me. We do not cross the desert. Zandakar is not returned to my side."

He met her bitter gaze without flinching. In this, he knew himself safe. "Hekat, I do not answer to you. I am Mijak's high godspeaker. I belong to the god. I do its bidding, always."

"Tcha," she said. "You say *the god* told you to send Zandakar away?"

He nodded. "It did. I do nothing without the god's direction. It wanted Zandakar in the world. In its eye, he was taken to safety."

He knew she knew he would never lie about that. Some of her anger faded, then. Her eyes warmed, moistened, grew haunted. "Why, Vortka?" she whispered. "Why does the god desire me to be alone?"

He cupped his palm against her scarred cheek. "You are not alone, Hekat. I am here. I am always here. Since the slave pen in Et-Nogolor, I am bound to your side."

She jerked her face away from his hand and walked to the chamber door. With her fingertips touching its handle she said, "I want Dmitrak tasked, Vortka. He grows bold. He grows careless. He spends too many warriors, he will not listen to me. If he must be my hammer in the god's eye, so be it. But I am the Empress. *I* wield *him*. I am not *his* instrument. You are high godspeaker. Teach him, Vortka. Show him the error of his ways."

His heart was heavy, he had no choice. He nodded. "Empress, I will."

She nodded, smiling fiercely. Then her smile faded. "Vortka, break the desert. Break its demons. Cast those demons back to hell. If the desert is not broken we cannot give the god the world. You are its high godspeaker. I am its Empress. That is our purpose. Can we fail? I think we cannot."

The door closed behind her and he was alone. Abruptly exhausted, he sank into a chair.

Break the desert, she tells me. As though I have not already tried. As though I do not drown myself in sacrifices, seeking to throw down the demons who fester in that hot place, who have lived there as long as Mijak has lived and have made the shifting sands their own.

His head was throbbing. He pressed his knuckles into his eyes, willing the pain to leave him alone.

She is so sure Zandakar would not fail, as Dmitrak fails. But I am not sure. If he would not fail to break the desert why did the god not wish him kept here?

And where was he now? How was he faring? Was he at long last free of his pain?

I wish I knew. Aieee, god. My lost son Zandakar. Let

him dwell in your eye. Let him find his way in the world. Give us each other when our work for you is done.

A knock on the door and Ritzik novice entered. "High godspeaker, Peklia says highsun sacrifice approaches. The godspeakers gather. The godpool awaits."

"Yes," he said, and waved her away.

Sacrifice. The godpool. And after that, the scorpion wheel. Dmitrak did not love him. He would see his tasking as an act of revenge.

That is not true, Dmitrak will not listen. He hears his own heart only, it is full of Zandakar. And so is my heart. It is full of my son. I love you, Zandakar, wherever you may be.

PART TWO

CHAPTER ELEVEN

Rhian stood back from her full-length dressing-room mirror and considered her reflection. There was no question, scarlet and gold brocade suited her admirably. And the style of this gown, with its severe lines and uncompromising modesty, was unquestionably elegant, while the stiffened collar rising from the neckline shrieked with royal authority. Every inch of her looked like a queen.

She smiled grimly.

Be careful what you wish for, my lords.

The council—led by Marlan, of course—had forbidden her to wear mourning for longer than the traditional month. Sunrise had marked one month exactly since her father's death . . . therefore she could no longer dress in black.

"Once your public grieving is ended you must assume your proper place in the world," Marlan had told her when she met with the council the awful, blurred day that Eberg died. Around the table the councillors had nodded, even Henrik, like a group of Mr Jones' obedient stringed puppets. "The ambassadors will be lining up to see you, Rhian. What they see must not alarm them."

And a daughter mourning her lost father was alarming? Apparently so, if one could believe Marlan.

If he told me water was wet I'd doubt it.

Unfortunately, though she disliked him intensely, he wasn't wrong. Not about this, at least. Until now, protocol had kept the other nations at bay. She'd not been forced to meet with any of their ambassadors except at her father's lavish funeral and during the formal presentations of condolence.

But that was about to change. She was the face of Ethrea; being a minor in law didn't alter that. She knew the great men of the world's trading nations, Ethrea's partners in prosperity and peace, gathered in shadowed corners and speculated on the future. Hers, and theirs: they were inextricably entwined.

If they knew I plan to run away I think they'd be frightened. I know I am . . . but I don't have a choice. Now the push for me to choose a husband will begin in earnest. My official mourning is over and I have no more excuses. Ethrea must have a king.

If she had her way, that king would be Alasdair.

If he's prepared to accept my sovereignty over him. If he still wants me. If he doesn't turn me away from his door . . .

He hadn't even written to her on the death of her father. Just sent a brief message through Henrik. Yes, his own father was dying. That might excuse him . . . or perhaps, with distance and time between them, he'd undergone a change of heart.

Please God, don't let him have changed his heart. If I can't marry Alasdair I'll have to marry one of the others. One of the men named on that damned list.

And so would end the House of Havrell. Not one of those duke's men would let her rule in her own right. She really would become a royal broodmare, good for nothing but birthing sons and keeping silent.

I can't let that happen. Not without a fight, anyway. I wouldn't be my father's daughter if I didn't fight for what was mine. If I must be a queen, and not a duke's duchess, then I'll be a queen on my own terms . . . if I can . . .

Though so much of her life was uncertain at the moment, there was one thing about which she had no doubt. Under no circumstances would she marry Marlan's hope, Lord Rulf. She'd glimpsed the man at her father's funeral. She'd seen most of her potential husbands there, but mercifully hadn't been forced to meet with them. Henrik Linfoi, bless him, had seen to that.

Rulf is an idiot. Nothing more than Marlan's puppet. Put a crown on his head and it's Marlan who'll be king.

The thought churned her belly. A kingdom strong in faith was one thing; a kingdom where the Church poked its nose in everyone's business and its hand in every pocket was another matter entirely. Her father had strenuously resisted it, wherever possible altering the law to ease its grip on Ethrea's people.

"The Church has enough income from its estates, Marlan, and the tithing practices already in existence. It can do without new tithes and unregulated levies and rents not overseen by government clerks. Surely your concern is with spiritual treasures."

Marlan had railed against her father's reforms. Railed without remedy, for the king had prevailed.

I can't let him use me to defeat Papa now. Let Marlan take control of Ethrea through me and Mr Jones' dire prediction will certainly come true.

Her face brooded back at her from the dressing-room

mirror. Thinner than it had been a month ago. Older, too, in some indefinable way. Childhood was firmly thrust behind her. Now she stood on the threshold of adult decisions, bearing with them adult consequences.

If I'm wrong to trust the toymaker . . . if running away proves to be a mistake . . . well, Marlan will have the pleasure of saying "I told you so". But I'm not wrong. I'm not. Crowned or uncrowned I'm the queen of Ethrea. The throne is my birthright, the care of its people my sacred duty. I won't abandon them to the machinations of these men.

In the warm lamplight her gold and scarlet dress shimmered with promise. Clothes, her mother had often said, were as much a suit of armour as any collection of antique breastplates, greaves and gauntlets gathering dust in the kingdom's cellars and museums. While such archaic male battle-wear was now dragged out only for ceremonial parades, women went to war in subtle and unsubtle fashion every day of their lives and it would be a good thing for Rhian never to forget it.

"Don't worry, Mama," she said, in the hope that somewhere her mother may still be listening. "I haven't forgotten."

"Haven't forgotten what, Highness?" said her privy maid Dinsy, bustling back into the dressing-room, her arms laden with jewellery cases.

"Nothing," she said, and turned away from her gold-and-scarlet self to consider the jewellery Dinsy was preparing to show her. "Not the opals," she decided. "Not the emeralds. The pearls? Perhaps . . ."

She took the creamy rope of pearls. It had been her mother's. A gift from the king upon Simon's birth.

"Oooh, Highness, they're ever so pretty," breathed Dinsy. "I love pearls, I do."

A dab of a thing three years her junior, was Dinsy. Traditionally a princess took as her privy maid the loftiest of her noble ladies-in-waiting. But she cared for none of them, stupid creatures forever dangling after the courtiers in hopes of a husband. Choosing Dinsy over them had ruffled a henhouse of feathers, but she didn't care. Princesses were supposed to make friends of nobility's daughters, but since they were children all they'd ever done was laugh at her behind their pampered hands because she'd loved riding and hunting and fencing and learning. Because she'd so often dressed like a boy.

Anyway, it had turned out to be positively providential, with three of them related to her would-be husbands. Dinsy lacked court polish, it was true. She was a plain country lass. But her heart was good and she could be trusted, absolutely. That was more valuable than the noblest of pedigrees.

Rhian smiled at the girl. "So do I love pearls, Dinsy," she said and, turning back to the mirror, held them against her woefully flat chest. "But not this time."

"No," Dinsy agreed. "Them pearls have nothing to say to that dress and that's a fact. Highness, I think it's got to be the rubies, honest I do."

Mama's rubies, a gift from the king upon Ranald's birth. Great carved things fashioned into glowing dragon's eyes, and set in a chain of molten gold. Earrings to match; she could still see her mother taking them out of her ears with a huff of relief after court masquerades and thirty-course dinners for visiting foreign dignitaries.

Marlan wore a ruby ring. He liked to finger it when he thought no-one was watching.

"As usual, Dinsy, you're perfectly right," she said, and tossed the pearls into her privy maid's waiting hands. "The rubies it is." Putting them on, feeling their weight settle in her ears and around her neck, she felt like a knight of old girding for war.

"Oh, Highness," sighed Dinsy, standing back to make sure every last hair on her royal charge's head was settled into place. "You do look like that painting of your blessed mother. The one in the Grand Hall, when she was your age."

Rhian blinked away a prickle of tears. "Really?"

"Oh *yes*, Highness. The spitting image. If the dear king was here he'd say so, I'm sure." Dinsy's hand flew to her mouth. "Your Highness. I'm sorry. My tongue runs away with me, I—"

"Hush," said Rhian. "It's all right. It doesn't matter."

A month since the funeral and the wound was still so raw. She hurt as much this morning as she had the day her father died. More, in fact, because it was impossible to pretend any longer that she could wake, as though from a dream. Her father, her brothers . . . Too much death in too short a time, and she was still angry. No matter what Helfred said it wasn't in her to meekly accept her loss, or the need for the battle she was about to wage because of it.

Dinsy gathered up the rejected jewellery. "Is there anything else you need from me, Highness?"

"Actually . . . yes," she said, feeling her heart thud. "After my meeting with the council I'll have another errand for you to run."

Dinsy nodded. "To Mr Jones, Highness?"

"Yes. You're willing?"

"Always, Highness."

"God bless you, Dinsy," she said, her voice not quite steady. "I'd be in sore straits if it wasn't for you."

"You're the king's true daughter, Highness," said Dinsy, softly. "And a beautiful lady. I'd do anything for you."

Again, she had to blink back tears. "I'll leave the note for you in the usual place. Make sure the ladies don't see you fetch it and be certain not to draw attention to yourself as you leave the castle. Slip out quietly and don't stay away longer than you need."

It was the same warning she gave every time there was a message for Mr Jones. Dinsy, to her credit, didn't sigh or roll her eyes even though she'd heard it five times before.

Instead she nodded, all eager earnestness. "Yes, Your Highness. Must I wait for an answer?"

"Not this time. Just hurry straight back."

Dinsy bobbed a curtsy. "I'll do that, never worry."

Of course she'd worry. The consequences of discovery were too terrible to dwell on. *How I hate you, Marlan, for making me risk this child.* "You've never asked what this is about."

Her privy maid shrugged. "You'd tell me if I needed to know."

Impulsively, she clasped Dinsy's hand. "I wish I could tell you, but I daren't. I can promise you this, though. It's important. It's for the kingdom. For Ethrea. You believe me?"

"I believe you, Highness," said Dinsy. "And I trust you, too. I know you'd never do anything to hurt this land or its people."

The girl's simple declaration of faith was humbling. "I must go. The council is waiting."

"Yes, Highness."

She pulled a face. "Wish me luck." *God knows I need it.*

"Oh yes, Highness. All the luck in the world," said Dinsy, fierce as a tabby cat with one lone kitten. "And mind you don't let them fine lords browbeat you, Princess Rhian. You're King Eberg's daughter and they shouldn't forget it."

"They won't, if I have anything to say about it. Thank you, Dinsy."

With a last glance in the mirror—gracious, she did look like her mother—Rhian swept from her apartments and made her way to the council chamber, head high and chin tilted, with the heavy ruby dragon's eyes swaying regally in her ears.

Marlan sighed, steepling his fingers before him on the council table. "My lords, I was under the impression we had settled the question of Lord Rulf's candidacy."

"Settled? We've barely scratched its surface," said Lord Harley, the intransigent. "Eberg died before we could properly consider your . . . interesting suggestion. Now that the official mourning period is ended and this council *is* meeting again, we need to address the issue before matters progress."

One swift glance around the table showed Marlan that the cursed Lord Harley was not alone in his sentiment. He nodded. "Very well. Though I should remind you that the princess herself accepted Rulf as a potential husband."

"Her father was dying," said Harley. "Grief does

strange things to the mind. Anyway, she's a child. She's not equipped to make that kind of decision. That's what *we're* for."

If he allowed his temper to show, Harley would have a victory. Shuttering his eyes, smoothing his expression, he nodded again. "Very well. Let us settle this once and for all. Am I to understand you dispute my right to nominate *any* candidate?"

"You're not a duke, Prolate," said Harley, his wide smile wolfish. "You don't belong to one of this kingdom's founding families. You—"

"I am a Duke of the Church. My duchy is Ethrea. My concern is for—"

"Yourself," said Harley.

"Do not insult me by suggesting the dukes are not eager to see their fortunes raised with a crown!"

Harley leaned forward. "I don't. But at least the dukes' candidates have breeding to recommend them. This former ward of yours, lord or not he's a *nobody*. An orphaned sprig of an insignificant House fallen into obscurity. How can you think he is worthy to be king?"

"True, Harley," he agreed, nodding. "Unlike you, Rulf cannot claim a duke for his brother. But my former ward is hardly bereft of noble qualities. Enough to satisfy King Eberg of his suit, before his passing."

Harley sat back. "We only have your word for that."

Silence, as the other councillors stared at the man, their mouths hanging open. Doubtless it was what they all were thinking . . . but only Harley was rash enough to say it.

Marlan let his fingertips rest quietly, one against the other. "Perhaps I misheard you, my lord. Or do you indeed imply that I—"

"This is the king's council chamber," said Harley, shoving to his feet. "*We* are the King's Council. You're its titular head, Marlan, but you're not the king. Outside this room, you are God's prolate, with the authority to speak in his name, to chastise your Church subordinates, to lay down his law to them and the people of this kingdom. *Inside* this room we are all the same. God's law is not *Ethrea's* law, and was never designed to be so. Eberg, God bless him, made sure that would remain the case."

Marlan smiled. "Then if we are equal, my lord, you cannot protest if, as a king's councillor, I nominate a candidate for Rhian's hand."

Henrik Linfoi, the old fool, cleared his throat. "Harley, sit down. Remember who we are and the duty laid upon us."

Glowering, Harley sat.

"You're right, Marlan," Linfoi continued, with every civility. "As a councillor you are free to nominate. But let us not forget that Rhian is a ward of the Church and you're the Church's most senior official."

He spread his hands wide. "You're suggesting I would place undue pressure on the girl?"

Lord Niall snorted. "It's not inconceivable."

"It is to me," he said. "Are you saying I *have* tried to influence her?"

"Not yet," said Harley. His face burned a dull red. "Eberg died and threw a caltrop in your path. You've been too busy pulling its points out of your foot to pressure the girl and anyway, she's been shut up in the castle. But she steps back into the world today. A world full of foreign ambassadors eager to know who'll be the next king. I tell you I'm sick to death of falling over them, they want to know who it'll be worse than I do! But until we can trust that you aren't—"

"All we want, Marlan," said Lord Porpont quickly, with a spiked glare at Harley, "is your assurance that as prolate you won't influence the princess's choice of a king."

"It's not an unreasonable request, Marlan," added Lord Volant. "We'd demand the same of each other, should any of us have a similar advantage."

Marlan stared. "Request? Demand? Which is it, my lords?"

Another silence, punctuated by more spiky glares and sneaking glances.

"Stop playing games, Marlan," said Porpont. "Will you agree or won't you?"

"Before I answer that there is still the matter of Lord Harley's outrageous accusation. Am I to let that pass unchallenged?"

Henrik Linfoi raised his hand. "Lord Harley misspoke himself. If you say King Eberg approved in principle of Lord Rulf's inclusion then we of course accept your word on that. Just as we accept your word you'll not pressure Rhian to accept his suit." He looked around the table. "Is that not so, my lords?"

A grudging chorus of murmurs, signifying assent.

"And you, Marlan. You're agreeable to that? And you further agree to abide by Princess Rhian's decision, even if it does not favour your former ward?"

She'll make no decisions I do not approve of. "Yes, my lord. I gladly agree."

"Then the matter's settled," said Linfoi. "Secretary Lord Dester has recorded our deliberations, and they are entered in the official council journal. I think we should move on now. Her Highness will be joining us soon."

Niall said, scowling, "What about his nephew?"

Another chorus of murmurs, this time complaining.

"If you're referring to Chaplain Helfred you have nothing to fear," said Marlan, smiling blandly. "He is bound by his oath before the Living Flame to abjure all worldly desires and ambitions. He has no interest in politics. All he cares for is Rhian's spiritual health."

"And it's no secret the girl barely tolerates him," added Lord Porpont. "You're mad, Niall, if you think she'll pay the least attention to anything that fribble says. Helfred's harmless. He couldn't coerce a dog to scratch fleas."

In silence Marlan watched his fellow councillors smile and nod, as though sneering at the prolate's flesh and blood were nothing to fear.

When Rulf is king in name, and I in fact, we'll see who laughs then . . . and who is chastened.

The chamber doors swung open, admitting a courtier. He bowed. "My lords, Her Highness the Princess Rhian, as requested."

Rhian entered the council room. She looked magnificent. As one man, the other councillors rose to their feet.

Marlan remained seated. She was only a girl. Soon enough she would wear a crown, true. A thing of tin, without any power. In the grand scheme of things she would kneel to him.

"My lords," she said, and swept them an elaborate obeisance. "You desired my presence, so I have come."

Marlan frowned. She was suspiciously meek. He would never trust her, this ill-advisedly educated girl. "Have a seat, Your Highness," he invited, indicating the table's one empty chair. "I think we can discuss state matters in comfort."

She curtsied a second time. "Prolate Marlan," she said, and took her place among the councillors, sitting so straight they could have hung a sail upon her and weighed anchor.

Marlan felt his skin prickle. He deeply mistrusted the glint in her eyes.

"Princess Rhian, in deference to your grief and the protocols of mourning this council has not pressed you in the matter of your marriage," he said. "And were you any ordinary girl still no pressure would be brought to bear. But you are extraordinary, therefore we must put aside delicate considerations and address the needs of the kingdom, which this council holds in trust for God."

She nodded. "Of course, Prolate Marlan." She looked at each face around the table, her eyes wide and guileless, a portrait of sincerity. "A royal princess belongs to herself last . . . and the kingdom first. My father, God bless him, taught me that from the cradle."

"So you accept it's time to choose a husband?" said Lord Linfoi.

"Perfectly," she said, the portrait of compliance. "Indeed, I'm eager to do so. I can think of no better way to honour my father's memory. During my seclusion I have been considering each name on your list. Unfortunately . . ."

Marlan straightened, as the lords exchanged sharp glances. "Unfortunately what, Highness?"

Rhian sighed, her blue eyes cast demurely down. "My lords, I regret to inform you I'm having trouble reaching a decision."

Lord Porpont rapped his knuckles on the table. "And

why is that? I'm told you pride yourself as a young lady of acumen. If that is not vainglorious boasting you must know your choice can be delayed no longer. Do you think to play coy with us? Hold us to ransom for a name more to your liking, though it bring Ethrea into disrepute?"

Marlan watched Henrik Linfoi fold down his mouth in restrained displeasure. Watched Rhian's heavy ruby earrings flash fire as a muscle tightened along her jaw. Watched the heavy ruby necklace prism light blood-red as she brought her breathing under control.

"King Eberg taught me many things, Lord Porpont," she said. "But being coy wasn't one of them. My lords, I ask you to consider my position. Five men—well, four men and a boy—are given me as candidates for my hand. I'm a little familiar with all save Lord Rulf, whom I'd not met before the king's funeral. Indeed, I don't believe I ever knew he existed."

Lord Harley snorted. "You know what you need to know. We have selected them, they are therefore suitable."

"But one must be more suitable than the rest," said the princess. "If the king . . ." Without warning her voice hitched, and her eyes were brighter in the filtering light. Was she play-acting? It was hard to tell . . . "If Papa and I had been granted the time to consider your list together I wouldn't feel so uncertain now. Papa would've helped me make the right choice. With him gone . . ."

Marlan stirred. "God will help you make the right decision. You must pray, Your Highness, until God makes his wishes known." With Helfred's guidance, of course. Prompted by himself.

Rhian clasped her hands. "Oh, Prolate Marlan, God bless you for saying so. You're an answer to my prayers."

It wasn't the response he'd been expecting. He steepled his fingers again and considered her closely. "How so?"

Instead of replying, she turned again to the council. "My lords, I want to do what's right for Ethrea. I want to allay the qualms of the foreign ambassadors so they might tell their own kings and queens and emperors and chieftains that Ethrea continues as safe and untroubled as it ever did. I want to give Ethrea a boy-child to be king. But to do that, I must make the right choice of husband."

"How can we help you, Rhian?" said Linfoi.

"Give me leave to withdraw from Kingseat, my lords. I wish to sequester myself in the clerica at Todding. Such holy surroundings must surely help me hear God clearly. And while I'm there, I can meet with those of you who've presented me with a candidate for king and we can talk of them discreetly, with God as our witness." She smiled. "For while I'm sure your candidates are admirable in their particular ways, no man is perfect. I'd like to know a little of their . . . imperfections, too. And doubtless you'd feel more comfortable disclosing their shortfalls in private."

The princess sat back, hands neatly folded in her lap. Everything about her was meek and mild, sweet as milk, the very essence of gentility. Marlan felt the blood pound in his veins.

I have never known her to be so docile. She is up to something. She seeks to circumvent me.

Of course it was Linfoi who first added his support for the notion. "If it was a short retreat I can't think of a reason to forbid it. As you say, the holy cloisters are conducive to clear thought and receiving guidance from God."

"But hardly helpful in the removal of ambassadors

from my doorstep," complained Lord Harley. "A further delay will see them frothing at the mouth."

"They can froth like mad dogs and harm no-one but themselves," said Linfoi. "This is our business. It is none of theirs. I see no harm done if the princess takes a little longer to choose her king. The harm will come, surely, from a hasty decision. Perhaps, Lord Harley, this has more to do with your candidate's . . . imperfections? Perhaps under closer scrutiny your duke's nephew won't look so appealing. Perhaps he's still in nappies instead of short pants."

Smothered snorts of laughter around the table. Harley was not the most popular of men.

Niall shrugged. "I can't speak for Harley, but my duke's son has nothing to hide. I'd gladly parade him naked before Princess Rhian."

"That will hardly be necessary," Marlan snapped. "Such crudity does you no good service, my lord. As for the question of the princess retreating to a clerica, that's a Church matter. The decision is mine."

The princess allowed herself to look crestfallen. "Prolate Marlan, if I'm not welcome at the clerica . . ."

The little bitch. She sought to manipulate him. What did she hope to achieve by this unlikely display of pious devotion? *If she thinks to hide the reason she is sorely mistaken.* He smothered his fury in bland surprise.

"Did I say so? Any God-fearing subject is welcome in God's sight. There is a long tradition of royal women retiring to a clerica when their days in the public eye are drawn to a close. Yours are just beginning but they could have a worse start. Princess Rhian, you are welcome to a short respite in the clerica at Todding. I will inform Dame

Cecily to expect a guest." He looked round the table. "And to expect certain other visitors, with leave to address you in a private place."

"Oh, Prolate! *Thank* you!" said the princess, her eyes shining. "I know with God's help I'll reach the right decision. May I have a month there? I have a list of five men to consider, after all."

It's a list of one, you silly girl. You'll realise that soon enough with Helfred to teach you.

"I fear a month is overlong," he said. "Let us say instead a fortnight. And not a day longer. Assuming the entire council is in agreement?"

The council was. Already he could see the lords flicking speculative glances at each other from the corners of their eyes. Each man thought this would give him some advantage. Each thought the chance to extol his man's virtues, leaven the bright gilt with the merest hint of plausible tarnish, would leave his duke's son or nephew or cousin or whoever primed to place a crown on his head.

If it keeps them occupied I have no objection. Once she's in the clerica I can at my leisure discover her plan. Whatever it is, she has no hope of succeeding.

King Rulf the First. It has a pleasant ring . . .

"Then it's settled," he said, and rose graciously to his feet. "I will make the arrangements, Highness. Expect to depart for Todding tomorrow."

CHAPTER TWELVE

Smothering temper, Dexterity plastered a bright, encouraging smile on his face. Right now, more than almost anything, what he wanted to do was smack his recalcitrant pupil . . . but aside from making himself feel better, he suspected it wouldn't achieve much.

He's a grown man. I'm a grown man. I don't believe finding common ground is impossible.

Still smiling, he leaned forward and held up his hand. "Cup. Cup. Zandakar, are you listening? Can you say 'cup'? Can you at least try *that* much?"

Apparently not.

He leaned back again, dismayed. "Oh, please, do at least *try*. It's a very small word, you know. It won't break your teeth to say it!"

Listless and unresponsive, Zandakar sat propped against his pillows, hands lax in his blanketed lap, eyes staring at something only he could see.

"You know, this isn't helpful," said Dexterity, dropping the cup on the bed and considering his guest, disgruntled. "I don't see how we're going to get very far if you won't even *try* to learn a little Ethrean."

Still no reaction. He'd get more animation from one of his puppets. Much more of this stubborn unhelpfulness and he was going to get cross with Zandakar. He poked the man in his knee.

"You could at least *look* at me. It's very rude, you know, pretending I'm not even here."

Zandakar stirred and slowly, reluctantly, looked.

"There," he said, and nodded encouragingly. "That's better. See? I'm only trying to help you, Zandakar. You do need help, whether you like it or not."

Zandakar said nothing.

"Who's Lilit? Who's Yuma? If you don't learn to speak Ethrean you'll never be able to tell me who they are." *And I'll never find out what happened to them.*

Zandakar flinched and turned away.

"Lilit," he said again, leaning forward. "Come on, Zandakar. After all I've done for you, the least you can do is make an effort. Lilit, Lilit, Lilit."

Without any warning, swift as a lightning strike, Zandakar snatched up the dropped cup and flung it in his face.

Dexterity touched his lip. Looked at the blood on his finger. Looked at Zandakar, no longer listless. His heart thudded riotously against his ribs.

"Well," he said, breathless. "I suppose that's progress of a sort."

The grief-stricken rage died out of Zandakar's face. He slid down the pillows and pressed one arm across his eyes.

"Right," said Dexterity. "Yes. It might be an idea to leave it there for today. Why don't you rest, Zandakar? I'll bring you some luncheon presently." He stood, stooped to pick up the cup and withdrew from the spare room.

His legs weren't quite steady.

"Hettie darling," he said to the empty kitchen, as he damped a cloth to mop up the blood, "I was right. There's more to Zandakar than meets the eye. I think I'm lucky the only thing he had to throw was a cup."

Hettie didn't answer. Since their last conversation in the garden he'd not heard a peep from her. He had no choice but to believe that no news was good news, that the tentative steps he'd taken towards helping the princess meant he was on the right track and that Hettie approved of what he'd been doing.

"If you *don't* approve, Hettie, you'll just have to say so. I'm not a mind-reader, you know, my love."

Vegetable soup was simmering on the hob. He stirred it with a wooden spoon, feeling his sore, swelling lip with the tip of his tongue.

I wonder if it's safe, letting Zandakar anywhere near Rhian.

It must be. Hettie wouldn't say they had to run away together if the man wasn't safe.

Of course, she said that before he tried to stove my face in with a cup.

"Still," he added, trying to find the bright side while his battered lip hummed with pain. "At least I got through to him. At least I got a reaction."

He'd been starting to think he never would. Thanks to Ursa the man's body was almost recovered from its brutal ordeals. His wounds were nearly healed, the lingering echoes of fever silenced, the hovering fear of death laid to rest. Yes. Physically, Zandakar was as good as mended. But his mind? His mind was another matter entirely.

Every night still, Zandakar dreamed.

Sometimes those dreams woke him screaming and distressed. At other times he didn't wake, but wept and called out for *Lilit*, for *Yuma*. And there were other names, too. At least he thought they were names. *Vortka. Dimmi.*

Every cry was laced with pain.

It was wearing, and a cause for concern. When he wasn't sleeping and dreaming his terrible dreams Zandakar sat silent and motionless under his blankets. The only reason he got out of bed was to use the chamber pot. He showed no desire to leave the small spare room, no interest in the world outside his window. Ursa called it a severe case of *melancholy*. The only reason the man ate was because Ursa had once pinched his nose until his mouth opened then poured soup down his throat. He didn't like that much . . . but at least he fed himself now. Only enough to keep body and soul tethered, though. No more.

So far Ursa had refused to panic. "He may have been through hell, Jones, but it hasn't killed him. If he truly wanted to die he'd be dead. He'll find his smile again, by and by."

If Ursa said so, he was bound to believe it. He just hoped "by and by" meant "very soon" because he was starting to fray around the edges himself. He hadn't slept the night through for a month. When he wasn't rushing into the spare room to make sure Zandakar was all right he tossed and turned in his own bed, worrying about the princess. Worrying about his business, ground almost to a halt these last long weeks. Tamas was doing his best to keep things afloat, but he was still only an apprentice.

And when I'm not worrying about that I'm fretting on how I'll tell Ursa I'm running away with a royal princess and a man with blue hair. Worrying what I'll say and do when Hettie comes again.

Worrying even harder that she wouldn't.

The hearty soup was cooked. Inhaling its robust fragrance, he gave it a final stir, replaced the saucepan's lid and half slid it from the hob. His stomach growled, eager for filling. Well, and why not? An early luncheon was hardly a crime . . .

He turned to fetch himself a bowl from the cupboard, and saw the letter shoved under the back door. Princess Rhian's little privy maid had been and gone, unnoticed.

He cracked the wax seal on the note and read it quickly.

Mr Jones, we come to it at last. Tomorrow I leave for the clerica at Todding, for a two-week retreat so I might finally choose a husband. I'll have some hope of running from there so you must be ready to come and get me at the end of the second week. I can't take Dinsy with me. I'll be alone and relying on you to tell me precisely when and how my escape will be contrived. Godspeed.

"Oh dear," he said, and groped for a chair. "How in God's name do I get you out of a clerica, Rhian?" He looked around his empty kitchen. "I hope you're paying attention, Hettie. You got me into this so you'd best have an idea for getting me safely out of it!"

Hettie didn't answer.

But that made no difference. He'd promised to help the princess. How could he change his mind when she was relying on him? When Hettie was relying on him? When the unaware kingdom of Ethrea was relying on him?

Oh dear. So many people, relying on me . . .

Feeling put upon and hard done by, his appetite routed, he hoisted himself out of the chair and found a bowl for Zandakar's soup. After filling it, he put it on a tray with a spoon, a mug of water and a thickly buttered slice of bread and carried the light meal out to the spare room.

Standing in the doorway, he said, severely, "I've brought you lunch, Zandakar. But I warn you: throw a bowl of hot soup at me and you and I will have *words*."

Zandakar turned his face from the wall and held out his hand; in it was the cup he'd thrown with such frightening force. "Cup," he said. "Dexterity. Cup."

Oh. Surprised to silence, and strangely moved, Dexterity crossed to the bedside table and put down the tray. Then he took the cup from Zandakar's fingers and held it, as though it were precious. Made of gold and jewels.

"Yes, that's right," he said at last. "This is a cup, Zandakar. Very good."

Zandakar touched his own lip, healed of its sores now thanks to Ursa's ointments. "*Yatzhay,* Dexterity."

He stared at his strange guest. He could be imagining things, but he thought Zandakar looked . . . shamefaced. "*Yatzhay*. I don't know that word. Does it mean *sorry*? You're sorry, Zandakar?"

Zandakar shrugged.

"No, I don't know either. But I expect we'll work it out." He put down the cup, picked up the tray again and settled it onto Zandakar's lap. Zandakar looked at his meal.

"Zoop," he said, pointing. "Watta. Brayd."

It was the first time Zandakar had ever started this kind of conversation. Dexterity hid excitement behind his beard. "More or less," he said. "Soup. Water. Bread."

Zandakar frowned. "*Zho*. Zoop. Watta. Brayd."

This was no time for criticism or complaint. "If you say so. Now eat, my friend."

Slowly, still with little appetite even though he'd spent

so long starving, Zandakar ate his simple lunch. When he was finished, Dexterity took the tray back again.

"I have work to do now," he said. "And you should rest." He closed his eyes and pretended to snore. "Rest, yes?" He nodded at the handbell on the bedside table. After some silly miming, Zandakar knew how to use it. "Ring if you need me."

Zandakar nodded.

As he reached the door, Zandakar said, "Dexterity."

He turned. "Yes?"

No more apology in those startling eyes. They were serious. Sorrowful. "*Wei* Lilit, Dexterity. *Wei* Yuma." He spread one hand across his chest, above his heart. Then his fingers clenched tight, as though he suffered a sudden unbearable pain. "*Wei.*"

The message was clear. Dexterity nodded. "*Yatzhay,* Zandakar. I'm sorry. I didn't mean to hurt you, either."

He left the man alone with his terrible memories.

When Ursa came by a few hours later she found him in the kitchen making lists for the journey to Todding, and then Linfoi. Closing the door behind her, she looked at his battered lip and tutted under her breath.

"No need to tell me who gave you *that*. Jones, it's time you—"

"Don't fuss at me, Ursa," he said tersely. His stomach churned with nerves. "I'm fine. It's nothing."

He didn't often snap at her. Her eyes narrowed slightly but she didn't snap back. After a moment she slid her physicking bag off her shoulder then rummaged in it. "Really? Well, don't look now, Jones, but your 'nothing' is bleeding." She held out a small jar. "Put this on it."

He took the jar, pulled out its stopper and dabbed a little brown ointment on his lip. It stung. "Ow."

"That'll teach you to lie to your physick," she said, and took back the jar.

"It really is nothing," he said by way of apology. "Zandakar and I had a little . . . misunderstanding. It's sorted out now. In fact, I'm starting to think there might be hope yet."

"Hope for what?" she demanded. "Getting him out of here? Good. The sooner the better. He's a dangerous man, Jones. Even you have to see that."

Oh, he saw it all right. More clearly now, with his stinging lip, than he ever had before. "Hope that we'll be able to make ourselves known to each other. As for the rest, Ursa . . ."

She held up her hand. "The rest can wait till I've looked in on him. You can make yourself useful and brew me some tea."

When she returned from inspecting Zandakar, her tea was cooling in a mug. A plate of oaten biscuits sat on the table and the incriminating lists were tidied into a pile. He sipped his own tea, kicked a chair out for her and waited until she'd half eaten a biscuit before speaking.

"How is he?"

"A testament to miracles," she said. "And the efficacy of my potions. He'll do, Jones. He needs to get back on his feet, build his stamina again. Stop his brooding inside four walls. He needs fresh air and sunshine. But he'll do."

"So . . . he's strong enough to travel?"

Ursa sat back and considered him, frowning. "I'd say

so. In easy stages at first. Why? Are you sending him on his way?"

"Well—"

She slapped the kitchen table, allowing a rare wide smile. "Excellent, Jones. I'm pleased to hear it. You saved the man's life and that's a good thing. I don't deny it. Now you can see him down to the harbour and onto a free sailing ship. He can go back to wherever he came from, you can get back to *your* business and I can get back to *mine.*"

Oh dear. If only his stomach would unknot itself. "Actually, Ursa . . ."

"Actually, Jones? Actually, there *is* no actually," she said, ferocious. "You can't keep him, slavery's illegal, and if you need someone else to help with the toyshop you can hire another apprentice. That's what young boys are for. This Zandakar's not a lame dog any more, Jones. If he's anything he's a caged wild wolf. The time has come to set him free."

"Ursa . . ." He sighed, and reached across the table to pat her hand. "You've been very patient with me. I'm truly grateful. But this isn't the end, this is only the beginning."

"The beginning of what?"

"Helping Rhian."

"Jones, what are you talking about? Toymakers don't help princesses."

"Not usually, no. It seems I'm the exception."

"*Jones*—"

"Please! Let me explain. Just promise you'll save your questions and shouting until I'm finished. Agreed?"

The look she gave him was almost comical in its outrage. "Shouting? *Shouting?* What are you talking about, Jones? I *never* shout!"

He smiled at her, gently. "All right. Not shouting. Vigorous declamations. How's that?"

"Cheeky rogue," she muttered. "Start talking before I throw a biscuit at you."

He told her almost everything: the visits from Hettie, the cryptic warnings, the meeting with Rhian in the castle privy gardens. Dinsy bringing the letters. Favours asked for. Promises given. The only thing he failed to mention was Zandakar's importance to Ethrea. He didn't want Ursa to know how little *he* knew of that. How large was the leap of faith he took on the man, only for his love of Hettie.

When he was finished he added, "I know it's almost impossible to believe, Ursa. Trust me, there are times I scarcely believe it myself. And then I look at Zandakar . . . and remember it's true."

"It may be true, Jones, but what does it mean?" said Ursa, slowly. "The days of miracles and wonders are long behind us. They died out with Rollin. We're not a kingdom of portents and superstitions. We don't run around being—being *supernatural*. That's for heathenish places like Tzhung-tzhungchai."

He shrugged. "I don't know what it means. All I know is I have to do this, even though it makes no sense."

Ursa's tea had gone stone cold. A half-eaten biscuit was still in her hand. "Because Hettie asked you?"

"Yes."

"Jones . . ." Ursa crammed the rest of the biscuit into her mouth and ground her teeth on it, savagely. "You're right," she said when she could speak again. "It's daft.

And one thing's clear at least—there's no talking you out of it."

"None, I'm afraid," he admitted. *"Yatzhay."*

"Yatzhay? What's that? Are you sneezing?"

"No. I think it means 'sorry'. I learned it from Zandakar when I wasn't dodging thrown cups."

"The two of you had a *conversation*?"

"We had a something," he admitted. "I suppose you could call it a conversation."

Mug in hand, Ursa pushed away from the table and tipped her cold tea into the sink. Then she stared out of the window, breathing quietly. "I don't know what to say, Jones. I'm not even certain how I feel. But it's clear something's going on. Something . . . *bigger* . . . than we are."

She could always surprise him. He'd expected her to shout. Berate. Call him every name under the sun. Some of the tension drained from his muscles. "Yes? But what?"

"How should I know? You're the one being visited by ghosts claiming God's chosen you to save Ethrea." She snorted. "Which only goes to prove what I've always suspected. God's got a dubious sense of humour."

God had *no* sense of humour as far as he was concerned. He took another sip of his own tepid tea. "I can't explain it, either. All I know is I have to help Rhian, just as I helped Zandakar. I can't turn my back on her. It'd be wrong." He cleared his throat, uncomfortable. "A sin."

"You know if you're caught, Jones . . ."

And there was his stomach, once more tied in knots. "I have to trust I won't be. I have to believe Hettie will protect me. If I am doing God's work . . ." He felt ridiculous, saying it aloud. *God's work,* when he and God weren't even nodding acquaintances . . .

Ursa turned to face him. Her expression was guarded, her eyes unconvinced. "You're taking so much on trust, with so little evidence."

He shrugged. "You're the one who says faith spins the world."

"Faith in *God*. Not ghosts from the past."

"I reserve my faith for Hettie," he said stubbornly. "If God should benefit does it matter where my faith lies?"

Her lips thinned but she didn't argue. "I don't suppose the princess mentioned where she intends to run once you've managed to spirit her out of the clerica?"

"North, to duchy Linfoi."

"Hmmm. Even by river-barge that's a long way," she said, frowning. "Five days there, five days back. An extra day or two for unexpected delays."

"I know," he said gloomily. "But there's no help for it, is there?"

"And how do you intend to get the princess out of the clerica?"

"I can't imagine," he said, almost wailing. "It's a cloistered place overrun with devouts. They don't play with dolls there. They've as much need of a toymaker as I have of—of—"

"A wimple," said Ursa, rolling her eyes. "And I don't recommend you masquerade as a chaplain. Your knowledge of scripture is woeful to say the least."

"Don't worry. I already thought of that."

"So it's a good thing, isn't it, that I'm known to Dame Cecily."

"Dame Cecily?" he said, staring. "Who is—"

"Dame of the clerica at Todding," said Ursa, impatient. "The senior devout charged with the running of the house. The woman responsible for keeping her eye on the princess, from under whose nose you'll have to whisk Her Highness without being detected. A mighty feat, I'll add. Cecily's no fool."

He put down his mug, his head spinning. "And you *know* her?"

"We were girls together in Sosset-by-Todding. That's the village where we grew up. I never told you?" Ursa shrugged. "Ah, well. Why would I? It was a long time ago and nothing much happened there. One reason why I left. I wanted adventure."

Dexterity sat back in his chair, confounded. *Hettie, Hettie. Did you arrange this?* "And Dame Cecily?"

Ursa smiled at a memory. "Cecie? She was always the quiet one."

If he believed in miracles . . . "Ursa—it's—it's—"

"Not a coincidence." She was frowning again, her eyes shaded. Displeased. "None of this is, Jones. It's too neat. Too pat. We're part of a pattern, my friend. A complicated jigsaw. I may not like it but I can't deny it."

"Yes. I think you're right." He shivered, suddenly cold. *What will we see when the whole pattern's revealed, I wonder?* "So . . . you can write a letter to this Dame Cecily for me, and I can take it to her, and while I'm in the clerica I can—"

"No," said Ursa. "That won't work. For one thing you can't be sure the letter would reach her. Cecie's an important, busy woman these days. Important, busy women are bristled about with guard dogs. But even if it did work, a letter's quickly read, isn't it? No, you'll need time to sneak a way into conversation with the princess, which means you'll need me with you to keep Cecie occupied for a while. That won't be hard. We've a lot of catching up to do. Once we're within the clerica walls and association with me leaves you free of suspicion, you'll be able to wander about until you accidentally on purpose stumble over Her Highness."

It was so typically Ursa. Snip, snap, problem solved. "And am I likely to do that? Stumble over Rhian accidentally on purpose?"

Ursa's eyebrows shot up, as though he'd said something foolish. "She's not going there for penance, Jones. They won't be keeping her in close confinement."

"I suppose it could work," he said slowly, after a moment. "At least the first time. But after that—when it comes down to helping her escape . . ."

"Then it comes down to faith. If you're meant to do this you'll be shown the way."

"And if I'm not?"

Ursa snorted. "Let's not think about 'if you're not'. Jones, what about Zandakar?"

Oh dear. Yes. Zandakar. He evinced a sudden interest in the plate of oaten biscuits. "What about him?"

"I hope you're not thinking of asking *me* to nursemaid him while you're gone. I can't. I've neglected my physicking for him enough as it is."

"I know you have," he said. "And I'm grateful. Don't worry, Ursa. He won't be your concern."

She nodded, pleased. "So you *are* going to send him on his merry way. Good."

He made himself look at her. "Well . . . no. Not exactly."

"No?"

"Ursa, Hettie didn't task me to nearly beggar myself

rescuing him just so I could watch him sail away to the horizon. She's got something else in mind for Zandakar."

Ursa's eyes were narrowed to slits. "Oh, has she now? Has she indeed? And what would that be, Jones?"

"Of course," he said. "I'd gladly tell you . . . if I knew what it was."

"Jones!" said Ursa, then managed to snatch hold of her temper. "Do you mean to say you're taking him with you?"

"It's what Hettie wants."

"But you don't know why."

"All I know is he's part of the mystery. I trust Hettie'll tell me more when she can."

"If she can. If this isn't some—some—" Ursa pressed her hands to her face, breathing deeply, then let them fall again to her sides. "All right. I can see there's no point arguing."

He gave her an apologetic smile. "None at all. *Yatzhay.*"

"Just tell me this. Does the *princess* know he'll be going with you?"

"The princess doesn't know he exists."

"And if she says she doesn't want him?"

He folded his arms. "She'll have no choice if she wants my help."

Ursa sighed. "Jones, my friend, I hope you know what you're doing . . ."

Don't be silly. I haven't the first idea. And Ursa knew it, too. Worry for him simmered in her eyes. Worry for himself roiled in his belly. *But I mustn't be cowardly. I must have faith.* "I'll be fine, Ursa. I'm sure I'll be fine."

"And what about your toyshop? And your apprentice?"

"Tamas will run the shop while I'm gone. It's not as if he's a first-year indenture. In a few months he'll be making his journey piece and I'll be losing him. Besides. All this responsibility I've given him lately is doing him good."

"Perhaps," said Ursa, dubious. "But how much good is it doing your business? As apprentices go he's not too shabby but he's not *you,* Jones. He lacks your touch."

It wasn't often she complimented his toymaking. Warmed, he smiled at her. "My business will survive. I won't be gone so terribly long."

"Provided nothing goes wrong."

She always did her best to find the rough spot in a plan. "Ursa, *nothing* will go wrong. Hettie will see to that."

"Jones, I swear, if you had two heads I'd bang them together!" she snapped. "Have you stopped to think about what you're doing?"

"I find it's less complicated if I don't do that," he said. *Less complicated and less terrifying.*

Being Ursa, she ignored him. "You, Jones, a harmless, gentle toymaker, are planning to kidnap the last living member of Ethrea's royal family from under the noses of Prolate Marlan and the council and run away with her to the poorest, least regarded duchy in the kingdom, in the company of a black man with blue hair who may or may not be a murderous heathen warrior, all on the say-so of a woman who's been dead for twenty years! I can't *imagine* why I'd think something could go wrong!"

He shook his head. "See? I knew sooner or later we'd get to the shouting."

"Jones—"

"Ursa!" He leapt to his feet. "What's all this? I thought you supported me! I thought you agreed there was a *pur-*

pose here, a *reason* things have fallen out this way. Are you changing your mind now? Are you saying you won't help?"

"No, I'm not saying that!"

"Then what are you saying?"

"I'm saying I'm worried, Jones! I'm saying I'm feared for you!"

A ringing silence as they stared at each other.

"Don't be feared for me, Ursa," he told her. "Just be my friend."

She looked away, blinking. "I'll always be that, Jones. And if I were a better friend I'd do everything in my power to stop this madness before it goes any further." She pushed away from the sink and picked up her physicking bag. "I need to be on my way. You've work to do and so have I. Get Zandakar out of that bed and taking some exercise in the garden. He needs to get moving if he's joining you on the road in two weeks. I'll stop by again this evening with some decent clothes for him and some shoes. He can't travel to duchy Linfoi barefoot in a nightshirt, that's for certain."

Dexterity took a step towards her. "Ursa . . ."

She turned back from the door, physicking satchel slung over her shoulder. She wouldn't meet his eyes. "What?"

He had to blink, to see her clearly. "Thank you," he whispered. "I think you're the best friend a man ever had."

It wasn't often he saw her blush. "Pshaw," she said, and pulled a face. "If that's not an addled thing to say."

He checked on Zandakar again, after she was gone. His mysterious guest was sleeping. Not from weariness or fever, he suspected, but to escape the cruel inexplicable world he found himself in.

He'd done the same thing himself after Hettie died.

"But you can't sleep forever," he told the blanket-covered man. "If you don't die you must live. That's all there is to it."

He closed the door quietly and went back to his lists.

CHAPTER THIRTEEN

Mantled in a fading twilight, Zandakar danced his *hotas* for the first time since Vortka banished him from Mijak. Tears stung his eyes.

I have lost my snakeblade but I am still a warrior. I am naked, without godbraids, but I am still a warrior. The god has abandoned me but I am still a warrior. The god is blind to me, I do not dance for the god. I dance for Lilit and our son who is dead.

It was a good thing his warhost could not see him, the great and gifted warlord of Mijak, creaking and stumbling his way through the set patterns of the knife-dance. How they would point and stare as he forced his thin, protesting body into the pose of the striking falcon, the leaping sandcat, the patient lizard on its rock.

How fortunate I am, they will never see this.

His many wounds were healed, and the hot sickness coursing through him, thanks to the fierce woman who had bullied him back to life even though she had no god-given powers or a crystal to use them. Her name was Ursa and she rarely smiled or spoke. Not like the man

Dexterity. He smiled and smiled and hardly ever stopped talking.

Yuma would have cut his tongue out long ago.

It was a mistake to think of his mother. His bare feet faltered on the uncut grass, his aching muscles refused to support him. He fell, his bones rattling, and breathed in the rich aroma of foreign soil.

"Zandakar!" shouted the man Dexterity. And then something else, some incomprehensible string of words, as he dropped his knife and half-carved piece of wood and left his chair to help Zandakar where he sprawled on the ground.

"Aieee, do not touch me! I am clumsy, I am not hurt!"

But Dexterity could not understand him any more than he could understand the flow of gibberish that fell from the man's lips. He suffered himself to be helped back to his feet. Though he never stopped talking, Dexterity meant well.

Aieee, he is the least cruel man I have met in many godmoons.

His body was full of pain again but it was bearable. Even desirable. This was the clean pain of training, not the filthy miseries of misuse and disease. So long since he'd felt it. He'd been exercising for eight highsuns now, since the woman Ursa had urged him from his bed. First walking in his chamber then walking in the house. Walking, at last, beneath the open sky in the garden. Every highsun getting a little stronger. This was the first time he'd felt strong enough to knife-dance.

I asked the god to let me die but the god does not hear me. I still live.

Strangely, he did not mind so much now. The desire to

die had burned out with his fever, leaving him hollow. Devoid of desires. Emptied of purpose. He was alive and so he would live. Live in this strange land. Live without Lilit. Live with the memory of his murdered son. His murdering mother. His brother the hammer, who had killed his Lilit and twice tried to kill him.

Aieee, how I am punished. My life is a scorpion wheel. I am tasked with every breath.

Dexterity touched his shoulder. "Zandakar. Dinner. Sleep."

When the hairy-faced man spoke slowly it was possible to understand him. Possible to make himself understood, if he spoke slowly, too, the handful of words he'd learned in this new tongue *Ethrean*. A difficult language, with so many strange sounds.

He nodded. "*Zho*, Dexterity. Dinner."

Dexterity smiled. "Yes! Yes! *Zho!*"

He gets so excited when I manage a word or three of his speech. It would be funny, if I could laugh.

But he would never laugh again. Laughter was a dead thing, drowned in hot blood.

With the last of the light drained out of the sky and the unfamiliar stars piercing the dark, Dexterity picked up his knife and half-carved wood and they went into the house.

There were lamps already lit, and dinner cooking. The house smelled good. Closing the door behind them, Dexterity pointed with his blunt knife. "What is that, Zandakar?"

"Chair, Dexterity," he said obediently, because this was their nightly ritual. Repeating the words he'd already learned. Learning new words. Struggling to understand how they all fit together, to understand this kind man's godless world.

If I were still the hammer I would smite this place to ruin. Dexterity has been kind to me. It is good I am not the hammer.

He looked around the room. The *kitchen.* Did the pointing for himself. "Window. Curtain. Wall. Door. Floor. Table. Sink. Hob. Tap."

Dexterity nodded, smiling, as he put away his knife and carving. His teeth were very white in the middle of all that face hair. "Very good. Now. You set the table."

Aieee! Yes. He knew those words. *Set the table.* That meant collecting two *plates,* two *knives,* two *forks,* two *spoons,* two *cups.* He set the table and Dexterity served the meal.

Dinner was *stew* tonight, chunks of meat and vegetable in a thick gravy. It was bland compared to what he was used to, but far better than the maggot-ridden muck he'd eaten on the slave ship. And the drink, the *ale.* Nothing like sadsa but it was bearable. On the slave ship, and before, there'd been little but tainted, brackish water.

He ate because his belly grumbled. He ate because it was something to do.

Soon Dexterity pushed his empty plate aside. He ate quickly, but never belched. "Hello," he said. "My name is Dexterity Jones."

Aieee, back to words again. A greeting. A way of making yourself known to a stranger. It was very odd. All his life he had been known by others. First because he rode with his mother and the warlord, then because he rode as himself. The idea of living without being known, still it took some getting used to. He sighed. Ate the last mouthfuls of *stew* and sat back in his *chair.* "Hello. My name is Zandakar."

"Good!" said Dexterity. "Very good. Zandakar, where are we?"

A question. He must answer. "We are in kitchen."

"*The* kitchen," said Dexterity. "Yes. And?"

And meant Dexterity wanted more words. What words? He was tired. He wanted to sleep. His body ached with the effort of *hotas.* His head ached with the effort of words. "Ethrea."

Dexterity shook his head. "*Wei.* No. Say it properly."

Aieee, he knew what that meant. His answer was wrong. He thought for a moment, then tried again. "We are in the Ethrea."

"No," said Dexterity. "Almost. We are in Ethrea. No *the.*"

Aieee, tcha. First it was the, then it was *no* the. This was a stupid, stupid language. He growled.

"We are in Ethrea."

"Yes! *Zho*! Good!"

The praise warmed him. Dexterity's smile warmed him.

So long since I have been warmed by words.

Dexterity sat back and considered him carefully. "Zandakar. Outside." He pointed at the closed *door.* "In the garden."

Yes. He knew that word. The *garden.* A rambling place full of untidy trees and flowers, bounded by a sagging fence made of wood, not stone. No garden in the palace would ever be so unkempt.

"Zandakar, in the garden," said Dexterity. And then some other words.

He recognised *what,* and *you,* but that was all. Dexterity was asking a question, he had no idea what it might be. He shrugged, a gesture common to both their peoples. "*Wei* understand."

Dexterity made an impatient sound, pushed back his chair and stood, then lifted one knee and hopped up and down. "You, Zandakar. In the garden. What?" He pointed to himself as he continued to hop. "What?"

Now he understood. *"Hotas."*

Puffing a little, Dexterity stopped his stupid hopping. "*Hotas?* What are *hotas*?"

How could he make the man understand? He could not. There were no Ethrean words he knew that could explain. He shrugged again. *"Hotas."*

Defeated, Dexterity sat down. "*Zho,* Zandakar. *Hotas.*" Then he said something else, it sounded like complaining. On his hairy face, an expression of complaining. It looked as though he spoke to someone who wasn't there. It wasn't the first time. And he said a word that was now familiar, *Hettie,* in a way that suggested it could be a name.

"Dexterity," he said, when the man stopped complaining. "Hettie?" He thought hard, wanting to make sure the words were right. "What is Hettie?"

Dexterity stared. "*Who* is Hettie," he said, after a moment. Now he looked shocked. "Say *who,* Zandakar. Not *what.*"

There was a difference? He wished he knew why. "*Zho,* Dexterity. Who is Hettie?"

Dexterity got up and left the *kitchen.* When he returned he was carrying something. He held it up. "This is Hettie. My wife."

A painting of a woman. Young. White skin. Yellow

hair. Brown eyes. Green tunic. Smiling. Happy. She was not beautiful, not to him, but this woman was Ethrean. *Wife.* What was that? A godpromised woman, like Lilit had been?

Dexterity turned the painting to look at it. No more smiling, his face was sad. His fingertips touched the painted woman's cheek, her lips, his eyes were bright in the warm lamplight.

The woman was named Hettie and Dexterity loved her. It was in his sad face, how much he loved her. But she did not live here and she was much younger than him. The painting looked old. Did that mean she was dead?

"Dexterity," he said. "Where Hettie?"

"Where *is* Hettie," said Dexterity, still staring at the painting. He shook his head. "Gone. Hettie is gone."

Gone. Was that the Ethrean word for dead? He felt a tightness in his chest, Dexterity's face was so full of hurt. He knew that look. He knew the feeling that made it. This Hettie was dead, he knew it in his bones.

"*Yatzhay,* Dexterity. *Yatzhay* Hettie is gone." He took a deep breath. Let it out slowly, through the pain in his throat. "Lilit is gone. *Zho?* You understand?"

Dexterity nodded. "*Zho,* Zandakar. I understand. *Yatzhay* Lilit is gone."

They had both loved a woman, they both grieved for their loss. It was hard to believe that he and this strange man could have anything in common. Hard to believe he was here in this strange land, so far from his home.

How did this Dexterity know my name on the slave ship? Why did he buy a half-dead slave? Why does he hide me here, in his house and garden? Why are his eyes afraid when he thinks I do not see him looking? What am I doing here? What is my purpose?

Dexterity frowned. "Zandakar? What is it? Are you in pain?" He made a face, to show hurting.

He knew those words. "*Wei,* Dexterity. *Wei* pain." Not the kind of pain he meant, at least.

"Good. That's good. But you look tired. You should go to bed."

No. If he went to bed he would sleep, if he slept he would dream. He was tired of dreams. He was tired of weeping.

"*Wei.*" He pointed to the chest in the corner, where Dexterity had put his blunt knife and carved wood.

Dexterity stared. "What? You want to try your hand at whittling?"

"Whittling?"

"Yes!" Dexterity mimed carving wood. "Whittling."

Whittling. It was a stupid word. "Aieee! *Zho.* Whittling."

"Well—yes. All right. Why not?" said Dexterity. "I suppose it is too early for bed. We'll clear the table and do the dishes, and then we'll whittle. And while we're whittling we'll talk. I've something to tell you, about a little trip we'll soon be taking."

Zandakar nodded, understanding enough to understand he had his way. Not that he cared very much about *whittling.* But, like eating, it was something to do.

On her knees in the clerica's small privy chapel, hands clasped before the Living Flame, Rhian struggled to empty her tired mind of thought. She failed. Snatches of conversations whirled like autumn leaves in a windstorm, flashing and twisting and scraping her nerves.

Duke Kyrin's brother-in-law has the admiration of many fine ladies, Your Highness.

And yet not one of them had married him. Perhaps she should take the hint.

"My lord the Duke of Arbat bids me tell you how deeply he holds you in affection, Your Highness. His son Adric is a fine, upstanding man—"

With bow legs. Though that wasn't his fault.

"Highness, there is no handsomer man in Meercheq than my duke's cousin Lord Rutger. True, he is a trifle older than Your Highness—"

A trifle? Try fifteen years. Almost as ancient as Marlan's Lord Rulf.

"The proud lineage of my duke of Morvell is beyond dispute, Princess Rhian. Can you even consider these other pretenders when my duke's youthful nephew Shimon—"

Youthful? At eight years her junior he was practically an infant.

"I must be truthful, Highness, in Ethrea you will find wittier men than Lord Rulf. But how much wit is needed to support a crown? Indeed, too much wit can be counted a fault, for—"

And as for Helfred . . . If the dukes and their representatives knew he dared to speak on behalf of the prolate. If only *she* dared to make a complaint . . . but that would only incur Marlan's gross displeasure and jeopardise her chance of escaping this place.

"Why yes, Highness, it is true that Shimon is not quite

bearded yet, but what is a beard? It is no true badge of manhood. I would not be indelicate but—"

Oh, why stumble over scruples now?

"As far as I'm concerned my duke's cousin is a man without fault, but if you insist upon a shortcoming let me say Lord Rutger lacks height and tends toward corpulence, which I hasten to point out is no impediment to—"

Not for Porpont, perhaps, but it surely was for her.

Round and round in her head their voices scurried, deafening her to everything but the scream she held inside.

Of all the voices Helfred's was the worst. She couldn't escape it. She couldn't escape *him*. She'd protested against him being sent to Todding with her but she might as well have saved her breath. He was her personal chaplain. Of course he would go with her. In truth he was her shadow. Marlan's today. Marlan's spy.

"You bear a grave responsibility, Highness. In your hands rest many thousands of souls. These dukes and their candidates, they think only of worldly advantage. They think of their own greatness. You must think of God. You must open your heart to hear God's desires. Lord Rulf is not a man of frivolity, he does not waste good coin on vain show. He is a serious man, a Godly man, in all things he is obedient to God. He knows how far the people of Ethrea have strayed. He knows that a king's first duty is to God. He knows—"

"Oh *shut up*, Helfred! Shut up *all* of you!" cried Rhian, and clapped her hands across her ears. "In Rollin's name would you give me some *peace*!"

The voices fell silent, but she could still feel them gibbering at the edges of her mind. Still hear their echoes, teasing, tormenting.

I never want to see the councillors' greedy faces again. Their eyes devour me. They don't see me, they see their own advancement. I hate their dukes' candidates for no better reason than these eager men praise them. And I hate Lord Rulf because he'd give me to Marlan. He'd give Ethrea to Marlan. I can't let that happen. Papa, Papa. Help me not let that happen.

She sighed, easing herself on the thin kneeling-cushion beneath her. The only duke's man she hadn't seen, the only one she wanted to see, was Henrik Linfoi. But he had no reason to visit except to comfort her and perhaps give her advice. He'd never do it. No matter that duchy Linfoi was out of the running, it would be seen as interference by the other dukes. They'd not tolerate his opinion being given to Ethrea's queen-in-waiting, and she wasn't about to insist. It would only cause trouble for Alasdair and she didn't want that.

I'll be bringing him enough trouble as it is.

Eleven days in the clerica and she still hadn't heard from Mr Jones. Her short time of grace was almost ended. If only she knew what he was planning. It was dreadful, to be so reliant on other people. To be so controlled by other people. By Marlan and by Helfred, his instrument. By the council, who cared little if anything for her happiness.

You never should have given me to them, Papa. Can I ever forgive you? You should've trusted me. I hate that you didn't.

Such a risk she'd taken, trusting Dexterity Jones. Believing him. Thinking a mere toymaker might hold the key to her escape from this nightmare. But what other choice had there been? No-one else had rushed out of the shadows to save her.

Maybe he's had second thoughts. Maybe he won't come for me at all.

No. She mustn't think like that. He'd come. He'd *promised*. He was a man of his word, and he never cheated a customer.

He won't cheat me. I'm a prin—the Queen of Ethrea.

She was. She *was*. No matter what the council or Marlan said. She was.

Oh, God. I wish I was older. If you had to die, Papa, why couldn't you have waited seven more months?

Soft footsteps sounded behind her. She opened her eyes, feeling every muscle seize with rage. Beyond the chapel's stained-glass windows, with their pious little pictures of the martyred Rollin and earnest Kingseat venerables, night was freshly fallen. The devouts in residence were gathered in their meeting hall, exchanging news of the day's doings in hushed, restrained voices. For this small time only she could be by herself, in a quiet place, with her thoughts and her fears and her prayers to a God she wasn't sure was listening.

Wasn't sure was there *to* listen.

"I *told* you, Helfred, I wish to be left *alone!*" she said without turning. "Must you plague me every minute of every hour? How many more times do I have to say it? I don't *want* to marry Rulf and you can't *make* me! I wouldn't care if he was *God's* former ward. Is that plain enough for you? Do you understand *now*?"

"Perfectly, child," said Dame Cecily's cool voice. "But do *you* understand the penalty for blasphemy before the Flame?"

Rhian scrambled to her feet and turned, her face hot. "Dame Cecily! I thought—I'm sorry—I believed—"

"You spoke to your chaplain. I gathered that," said the Dame. She was a tall, thin woman with hazel eyes and straight grey eyebrows. Her dark blue habit and intricate head-dress made her look even taller, even more lightly fleshed. There was about her the severity of winter, the purity of ice. She never smiled. At least, Rhian hadn't seen it. She never raised her voice, either, but was seldom disobeyed.

She and the prolate were a match made in heaven.

"Dame Cecily . . ." It seemed prudent to kneel again, so she dropped once more to the inadequate cushion. "I didn't mean to blaspheme. I—"

"Yes, you did," said Dame Cecily and lowered her hand. "You wanted to shock Helfred, and discomfort him. You dislike your chaplain. You consider him an imposition and a nuisance. You very much wish to kick him down the stairs."

Damn. The woman was a mind-reader. "Dame Cecily, I'm sorry. I—"

"Another lie," said the dame. "Your second sin in a handful of minutes."

Rhian gritted her teeth. "Forgive me. It's been a trying day. That's why I wanted time alone, Dame Cecily. I needed solitude, to order my thoughts and calm my heart." *Because otherwise I was going to do more than kick Helfred, I was going to kill him.* "I really didn't want to be disturbed."

Dame Cecily considered her. "Yet here I am, disturbing you. Perhaps you'd like to kick me down the stairs instead?"

"Dame *Cecily,* I—"

"Peace, child. I'm teasing." The dame indicated the nearest of the chapel's plain wooden pews. "Be seated, Rhian. I would talk with you."

Teasing? Since when did an icicle know how to *tease?* But then, looking closer, Rhian thought she saw a hint of warmth in those cool hazel eyes. Perhaps even a touch of sympathy in their frosty, measured gaze.

Oh, no. Don't be nice to me. If you're nice to me I might start crying. I can't afford to cry. I have to stay strong.

She got off her knees and sat in the pew. Dame Cecily sat beside her. "Child," she said, "did you come here this evening to ask for God's guidance or to instruct him on how to act in this matter?"

She opened her mouth to answer, reconsidered, then closed it again. After a moment, with her fingers linked in her lap, she sighed. "I suppose that makes three sins, Dame Cecily."

Dame Cecily nodded. "If you were one of my devouts it would go hard with you, child. But you are a guest here and the future Queen of Ethrea, so I will overlook it. To a point. I draw the line at chaplains rolling down the stairs."

"Of course, Dame Cecily," she murmured. Then added, encouraged by the unexpected humanity, "It's just—Helfred—he's so *infuriating.*"

"Men frequently are. But God made them that way for his purpose and it's not for us to complain, but endure."

"I'm sorry, but I'm at the end of my endurance," she retorted. "Ever since I got here, Dame Cecily, I've been *plagued* by men pretending to care for me when all they care about is winning the prize. I'm not a *prize*! I'm their *queen*, it's not fair that—"

"You were expecting life to be fair? How exceedingly foolish of you, child."

Rhian stared at her gilded slippers. "Yes. I'm a fool. But fool or not I won't be forced to the altar. I won't be *bullied* into making a choice."

"Are you saying Helfred bullies you?" asked Dame Cecily softly, into the silence.

Rhian lifted her gaze to the Living Flame, burning serenely on the chapel's altar. "You know who he is, Dame Cecily. You know who he answers to."

"I know a man cannot choose his relations."

"No, but he can choose what he does and what he says! And if Helfred had any backbone he'd choose to mind his own business. But a snail's got more backbone than Chaplain Helfred. Prolate Marlan is determined that I marry Lord Rulf. Helfred, the obedient nephew, harps on about him every day. He's even quoting scripture to support the suit. It's *wrong*, Dame Cecily. Prolate Marlan said he wouldn't use his position to influence my choice."

"You've not laid eyes on the prolate since you left Kingseat, child," said Dame Cecily. She sounded reproving.

"No, but Helfred is Marlan's mouthpiece. They may as well have the one tongue between them. I don't need a chaplain while I'm here, I have you to guide me in spiritual matters. But the prolate refused to let me leave Helfred behind. My chaplain has one purpose only: to wear me down on his uncle's behalf."

Dame Cecily was frowning. "It disturbs me to hear you level such accusations."

"I'm sorry!" said Rhian. "But this is your clerica. You

should know what's going on beneath your roof. Helfred is abusing his power as my chaplain on behalf of Prolate Marlan, who has plans to wed the Crown and the Church by wedding me to his former ward! He wants Church law and state law to be indivisible so he can become the supreme authority in the kingdom."

"No, child, that can't be," said the dame. "Blessed Rollin himself makes it clear in Second Admonitions that the spheres of Church and state are not to be—"

Oh, God. Please, make her hear me. If she really is blind please open her eyes. "I don't wish to be rude, but it doesn't matter what Rollin says. Rollin is centuries dead and Marlan is prolate. He wants to join Church and state law throughout the land. He argued about it with the king many times. Papa always defeated him. But now with Papa dead he thinks to have his way through me." She took in a deep, shuddering breath and lost the fight against emotion. "Well, he *won't,* I tell you! I *won't* betray my father or Ethrea like that. Not so Marlan can feed his greedy ambitions."

Dame Cecily stood and stared down at her. "You are speaking of God's supreme representative," she said, her voice ice again. "Moderate your language and your tone or I will disregard your royal blood and punish you as I would any common sinner within these walls."

Flinching, Rhian bowed her head. *Stupid, stupid! How can you forget where you are?* "Forgive me," she whispered. "I've been overwhelmed. I never imagined we'd lose Ranald *and* Simon, and that *I'd* have to choose who'd be Ethrea's king."

"I know," said Dame Cecily more kindly. "But this is what God has chosen for you, child. Therefore you must shoulder your God-given burden with courage and grace."

Rhian looked up. Dame Cecily's face swam before her, muddled through a prism of tears. "I don't know if I can. I don't know if I'm strong enough." Strong enough to run away. Strong enough to fight the battles that running away would bring. Strong enough to stand against Marlan, the council . . . against Alasdair, if he refused to do what had to be done for the good of the kingdom and its people.

"You have no choice, Rhian," said Dame Cecily, relentless. "What you imagined your life would be does not matter. *This* is your life now. What can you do but live it, with God's love to guide you through the years?"

She blinked and blinked until the dame's face resolved itself. "Yes. I know. I'm sorry. I'm . . . tired."

Dame Cecily nodded. "Then you must seek your bed, child. Prolate Marlan will be here in the morning."

Marlan? God, *no.* She shifted on the pew, heart thudding painfully. "Why? I've three days yet before I have to decide. The council agreed to that, he can't just come here and—"

"Of course he can come here. He is the prolate. This clerica is under his authority."

"Under *your* authority," she said daringly. "You're its dame."

Dame Cecily breathed in and breathed out. Her lips were pinched tight. "And like every dame of every clerica in the kingdom I am subordinate to the prolate's will, after God. As *you* are subordinate to him, being a ward of the Church." She stepped back. "The prolate will arrive shortly after Morning Litany. You will hold yourself

in readiness and conduct yourself with the humility that
befits a child of scant experience."

Rhian stared after the dame as she swept from the
chapel. Her heart still pounded like a runaway horse, her
hands fisted so tightly her fingernails threatened to punc-
ture her palms.

*I'll conduct myself as befits a queen of Ethrea, Dame
Cecily. It's what Papa would want of me . . . and what
our people deserve.*

CHAPTER FOURTEEN

Hettie said briskly, "Come along now, my love. Time's
a-wasting and the princess needs you to rescue her."

Dexterity looked around, at the meadow and the spring
lambs flirting with the flowers. "I'm dreaming, aren't I?"

Hettie nodded. She was dressed in yellow poplin, and
the sweet breeze rippled the fabric about her legs. "I can't
always come to you in the world, Dex. Sometimes I can
only reach you through dreams. What matters is that you
listen to me and do what I say. Everything depends on
it."

The spring sunshine was gentle on his face. He looked
down at himself and saw he was garbed in his favourite
trousers and shirt. The last ones she'd made for him so
long ago, that he'd kept together with mending and love.
His feet were bare, the grass cool between his toes.

"Help me, Hettie. How am I to get Rhian out of the

clerica? I've only got a plan to get in there and with luck pass her a message. But I might not even see her. What if—"

"I can't tell you," said Hettie, with regret. "So much depends on things I don't control. You'll find a way, my love. Father never wanted us to marry, remember? But you slipped under his guard and got his permission. You found the way then." Her eyes were bright in the sunshine. "You'll find it this time, I know."

Her faith in him was like expensive wine in his veins. He felt light-headed and slightly drunk. "All right. Say I do rescue the princess. Then what?"

"Then you get on the road to duchy Linfoi and no matter what happens you don't look back."

The breeze smelled like freesias. He smiled at the scent. "And then?"

"And then things will unfold. Remember this and you won't go wrong: Rhian is meant to be the true queen of Ethrea. To rule in her own right and defend her kingdom against harm. Especially from those who claim they have God's authority to throw her down. But it won't be easy. You must be brave and strong, Dex. You must prevail no matter the cost. And there will be a cost, my love. I can't save you from that."

Her words were dire. He should be afraid. But in this pleasant dreaming place it was hard to feel fear. Hard to feel anything but warm and safe. He wagged a finger at her.

"Hettie, sweetheart. You keep forgetting. I can't fight for the princess, I'm a toymaker. All my soldiers are painted wood."

"You have Zandakar."

"Yes. About Zandakar . . ."

She shook her head. "I'm sorry, Dexie. I have to go. You've made a good start with him but you've further to travel along that road. Whatever happens *don't* cast him aside. You're going to need him, no matter how much he frightens you." She raised her hand in a gesture of farewell. "You've black days ahead, Dexie. Turn to God when you're feeling bleak. I'll come again to you when I can."

A lamb leapt through her, and he sat upright in his bed.

"Hettie!" he called into the darkness. "Hettie, come back!"

She didn't. With a shivering sigh he curled himself under his blankets. The warm deliciousness of the dream meadow was vanished. Now all he could think of was the danger Hettie had hinted at. Dark days. Zandakar.

For all he's been behaving himself, no more thrown cups or any such nonsense, there's a tiny part of me afraid of him. Beneath his docile surface lurks something wild . . . something untamed and brutal. He's not a safe man. I just hope I can control him if . . .

But that was nonsense. He was being ridiculous. Hettie would never put him or Rhian in danger.

Beyond the loosely drawn curtains it was still night. There was nothing he could do until dawn broke. When the sun rose he'd put his rescue plan in motion. It wasn't perfect, there were risks involved, but it was the best he could do. He was a toymaker, not a military strategist. He didn't even play chess very well . . . though he did make a splendid chess set.

I hope Otto forgives me for leaving him behind. I hope he doesn't forget me. But I can't take him with me, he can't

*possibly pull a peddler's van. And Tamas'll take grand
care of him while I'm gone. He won't have to work any
harder for the apprentice than he does for the master.*

Tamas had been thrilled to learn he'd be put in charge
of the toymaking business while his master went on holi-
day for the first time in years. A good lad, Tamas, with a
promising eye for carving puppets. He'd be sorry to lose
the boy once his apprenticeship was done.

*As for the rest, I'll just have to trust that once Ursa
and I are in the clerica things will fall out to our advantage. For if they don't . . .*

Smothering nerves, Dexterity closed his eyes and
dozed fitfully until the sky beyond his bedroom window
lightened and it was time to get up.

Standing in the kitchen, drinking tea and keeping one
eye on a panful of sizzling bacon, he stared into the back
garden and watched Zandakar dance his *hotas* for the rising sun. The man was much stronger now, far steadier
on his feet. He didn't look precisely *well* yet, but at least
his face was no longer a death's-head and his emaciated
frame was beginning to fill out.

When he reached full strength, he'd definitely be
formidable.

*His hair's growing back. I'm not sure that's wise. Bad
enough he's got dark skin to make him stand out, but at
least that's explainable. I've got no hope of explaining
away blue hair.*

With the bacon nearly cooked he set a second pan on
the hob, dropped in a chunk of butter to melt and fetched
six eggs from the pantry ready to fry. Zandakar came
in through the back door, sheened in sweat and lightly
panting.

"Good morning, Dexterity," he said with care. His Ethrean was improving. He had a lightning-fast mind. Looking at the hob's two frypans, he thought for a moment then added, "Eggs and bacon for breakfast."

Dexterity nodded. "Good morning. Yes, eggs and bacon. Well said. And tea. But bathe first." He mimed scrubbing with a sponge. "Bathe. *Zho?*"

Zandakar gave him a look. "Zho. Bathe." He muttered something else in his own incomprehensible, tongue-twisting language. Whatever it was, Dexterity doubted it was flattering.

While Zandakar made himself presentable for the table, Dexterity cooked the eggs and served the meal on two plates. Zandakar returned and they ate in companionable silence.

"I clean kitchen," said Zandakar when they were finished.

He nodded. "Good. And I'll send a message to Ursa."

"Ursa," said Zandakar. His expression was wary. "*Wei* Ursa. Zandakar *wei—wei—*" He slapped the table. "Aieee! Tcha!" Then he pulled a face of extreme pain and pretended to retch.

"Sick," Dexterity said. "Zandakar *wei* sick." He nodded reassuringly. "*Zho.* Yes. I know. It's all right."

Zandakar considered him suspiciously for a moment then relaxed. "All right."

"Yes. *Zho.*"

"Tcha," said Zandakar, with another look, and got up to clear the table and do the breakfast dishes.

Dexterity fetched pen and paper and scribbled a quick note to Ursa. *Must see you urgently. Come at once.* Then he sealed it with a drop of wax, addressed it and fetched a pigget for the messenger.

After he'd put coin and note in the message box on his front gate and lifted its red flag so the next passing runner-boy would know to stop, he took a moment to look up and down his quiet lane. No-one was stirring yet, it was still too early.

If my neighbours knew what I was planning they'd never believe it. I hardly believe it myself.

But he only had to look at Zandakar to be reminded it was all too real. He went back inside, to wait for Ursa and soothe his jangled nerves with carving.

Helfred paced Dame Cecily's privy chamber, wiping his damp palms down the front of his habit. Unlike his uncle's opulent office, the dame's official retreat was spare of decoration. A small Flame burned in its holder on one wall. That was it. She didn't even have a portrait of Rollin anywhere. Her copy of his Admonitions, leather-bound without a hint of gilt, sat on the oak table before the window. The window was plain glass, not a stained picturesque pane to be seen. A severe woman, Dame Cecily. Strict in her faith. Strict in her oversight of this devout community. Revered and respected, it was unlikely she was loved.

Perhaps I should've asked her to speak with the princess. Perhaps she might've had better luck.

His wretched palms were damp again, and sweat trickled its short way down his spine. His uncle would be here soon. An outrider had arrived half an hour ago as he took morning tea with the dame, to warn of the prolate's imminent arrival and request on his behalf private conversation with Her Highness's chaplain. Dame Cecily had nodded, dismissed the outrider and left Helfred in her chamber to stew in apprehension and solitary silence.

Marlan's going to be furious. He's going to blame me.

Princess Rhian, despite every argument and appeal he could think of, steadfastly refused to accept Lord Rulf's suit. She steadfastly refused to accept *any* suit, the dreadful girl, insisting that she needed more time.

Marlan will never agree to that. He knows what he wants and he expects to get it. Now that Eberg is dead he thinks to get everything he wants. He can't begin to imagine she might stand in his way as did her father for nearly twenty years.

Besides, who was he to question a prolate? To decide Lord Rulf wasn't fit to be king? What was Helfred but a lowly, powerless chaplain? If God didn't want Rhian to marry the man surely he'd do something to prevent it. Nothing happened in the world without God's desiring, even events as tragic and inexplicable as the deaths of Eberg and his sons.

Whimpering, he turned to the Living Flame burning in its sconce and fell face-down in extreme supplication.

"Dear God, please help me. I've done my best to persuade the princess but she's not a biddable girl. Her father raised her unwisely. He put mad ideas in her head. She is far too educated for her sex. I've done my best to counter what she's been taught, I swear it, but I fear the damage is done, her womanliness ruined." He sat up and wiped his moist hands yet again down the front of his habit. "Please, God, make that clear to my uncle."

As though words might conjure flesh he turned to the

door. It remained blessedly closed. A little time yet, then, before the storm broke over his head.

Marlan won't understand. He doesn't seem to realise what Rhian's like. Proud. Wilful. Stubborn. Every inch her father's daughter. If he wanted me to have any real authority over her he should've made me a venerable.

The door opened without warning and his uncle entered. "Well, Helfred? What have you to say?"

He scrambled awkwardly to his feet. "Prolate Marlan," he said, his thumb pressed to his thudding heart and then his dry lips. "God save Your Eminence."

The devout acting as escort bowed her head and withdrew, closing the door. Marlan, his eyes cool and calculating, clasped his hands before him. "God save you, Helfred, if you disappoint me."

Helfred swallowed. *I just have to tell him. There's no pretty bow to tie around this harsh truth.* "Forgive me, Your Eminence. The princess remains . . . unpersuaded."

"I see," said his uncle. Todding was well over an hour's ride from the capital on a fit, fast horse but he looked unweary. Immaculate. His robust travelling vestments were untouched by sweat or dust or any sign of the road. Despite his age he never seemed to feel fatigue. His body was lean, unblemished by fat. He had ten times the energy of any younger man. He liked to say, *God's strength is mine. The divine power moves me. How can I falter when his will runs through my veins?*

Helfred stepped back. "Please. You must believe me. I have toiled ceaselessly on your behalf, extolling Lord Rulf's virtues for hours at a time." And in doing so had he perjured himself? He was so afraid he had. *Dear God, forgive me.* "Armed with your privy information, Eminence, I have pointed out to the princess the true flaws and shortcomings of the dukes' candidates, making sure to paint them in the most unflattering light. I have reminded the princess more times than I can count of her duty to you, Ethrea's supreme spiritual advisor. In short I have used every method of persuasion I can think of. Still she is not moved."

Marlan smiled. "Not every method, Helfred." He opened the door. "Come."

Uncertain, Helfred followed his uncle through the halls of the clerica. Every devout they passed dropped in a deep curtsy. Marlan nodded but never once looked at a face.

The only face he sees is God's. The rest of us are just . . . scenery, I think.

He risked a question. "Eminence, do we go to the princess? Do you know where she is?"

"She waits in the privy chapel," said Marlan. "Dame Cecily has advised me."

And where was the dame now? Marlan strode through this place as though it were the Prolates Palace, as though every brick and tile and pane of stained glass were his personal possession.

I suppose they are, really. He is the prolate after all.

The dame had given excellent directions. His uncle found the privy chapel without a single wrong turn. Rhian was in there . . . and so was Dame Cecily. Both women shifted round on their knees as he and his uncle entered the quiet, incensed chamber.

"Leave us, Dame," said Marlan at his most austere.

Dame Cecily bowed her head. "Your Eminence," she murmured, and withdrew from the chapel with her gaze downcast. It was astonishing to see. Marlan's crackling aura of power had extinguished her entirely.

Princess Rhian did not wait to be commanded onto her feet. As the privy chapel's door closed behind Dame Cecily she rose in a single smooth motion, letting her simple linen skirts fall around her as they may. Her riotous black hair was contained within a modest, unjewelled net, baring her fine facial bones for admiration. Her dark blue gaze was steady, her pointed chin lifted high. She was the epitome of beautiful, self-contained royalty . . . but Helfred could see the throttled fear behind her haughty mask.

"I was praying," she said, her tone curt. "You've disturbed me, Eminence. I hope for a good reason."

Helfred bit the inside of his cheek, and tasted blood. *You stupid child. Don't bait him like that. Can't you see the dangerous mood he's in?* He tried to warn her with a glaring stare but she wasn't looking at him. She never looked at him if she could help it. She never hid, either, her impatient contempt. Once it had hurt him but he was used to it now. And he never let it interfere with his battle for her soul. What kind of a chaplain would he be if the personal were permitted to dictate duty?

Marlan considered Rhian coldly. "If your late father had listened to me, girl, we would not now be in this invidious position. You may thank Eberg for what is about to transpire."

"I see." Rhian's eyes glittered. "Helfred has told you I will never marry Lord Rulf."

"Helfred has told me of your impious intransigence, yes."

"And you think where he's failed to persuade me you

can succeed?" Unwisely, she laughed. "Then you've ridden a long way for naught, Eminence. Nothing you say will change my mind. I'm not interested in putting your puppet on the throne. And let's not pretend any more, Prolate. This Lord Rulf would be your puppet."

In the light shining through the chapel's pretty windows, Marlan's jewelled chain of office, containing a piece of the arrow that had slain Blessed Rollin, flashed emerald fire. His face was tranquil. His eyes were ice.

"As a minor in law and a ward of the Church you are bound to obey me, Your Highness. I stand before you in the place of your father. As you owed obedience to him while he lived, now he is dead you owe it to me."

Helfred saw his uncle's words strike Rhian like arrows as deadly as any that had slain a saint. She blinked. "You are not my father, Eminence. My father respected me. He loved me. He—"

"Is dead," said Marlan. "You are mine in law. Body and soul."

Rhian stepped back. "I belong to myself, we have no slavery in Ethrea. But if I *am* owned by something, I'm owned by the Crown. By my duty as the last living Havrell. This kingdom owns me, Eminence. And I won't sell myself elsewhere because *you* say I must. I tell you again, I'll never marry Lord Rulf. Have you forgotten there is more than one candidate for king?"

Marlan laughed. "You can marry no-one without the Church's release. You are its ward, girl. How often must you be told?"

For the first time the princess looked uncertain. "Are you saying you'll refuse me permission to wed any man but Lord Rulf? The council won't permit that."

Marlan shrugged. "The council has no say in spiritual matters. Whoever you choose, girl, will have his soul examined most closely. I think I can say with surety that only Rulf's soul is clean enough to be crowned."

Helfred flinched. *That is a misuse of power. Can God desire this? I find it hard to believe . . .*

"Marlan, you're perfidious," said Rhian, pale with temper. "You're an insult to the God you claim to revere. You make me want to vomit, you—"

"Be silent!" hissed Marlan, seizing her jaw between his fingers, forcing her face up so she looked into his. "You impious slut. You say you were *praying* when I entered this room of God? I doubt you know the meaning of the word. You are a prideful sinner, puffed up with conceit. You think you know more of God's will than his chosen prolate? God forgive you. How far you have strayed."

A pulse beat frantically at the base of Rhian's throat. "This has nothing to do with religion, *Eminence*. You—"

"Nothing?" roared Marlan, and flung her away from him. "You ignorant girl, every breath you take has to do with religion! You breathe the air God sends you to breathe! *Helfred . . .*"

He swallowed a shriek. "Your Eminence?"

"I thought your duty lay in guiding this girl? In teaching her to more perfectly understand God's will? Are you her chaplain or are you *not*?"

"Don't blame Helfred!" said Rhian, before he could answer. "He's done *everything* you told him to, Prolate. He's nagged and nattered and hounded and harassed till I thought I'd be driven to distraction. When he doesn't bore me to sobs with prosing lectures he bleats on and on about your precious Lord Rulf and denigrates the dukes' choices as though they were spittled degenerates. If I were a weaker woman I'd have surrendered by now. But I'm *not* weak, Marlan. I'm my father's daughter. He didn't raise me to simper and sigh."

"Nor did he raise you to respect authority as you should," said Marlan. His sibilant voice was loud in the chapel's hush. "It is past time, girl, that I remedied the lack. On your knees before the Living Flame."

Some madness seemed to have possessed the princess. She threw her head back and met Marlan's glare with her own, her fair skin still marked from the cruel pressure of his fingers. "The Flame's behind me, Prolate. Don't you mean on my knees before *you*?"

Marlan raised a clenched fist. "*Kneel, you proud bitch!* Kneel before I knock you to the floor!"

She dropped to her knees but kept her head lifted. "You'd best be careful. The dukes won't tolerate your interference. You've no business meddling in matters of state. You should concern yourself with the Church and let me worry about the Crown."

"God never did a better thing than take your father from the world," Marlan whispered. "He made of you a rank unfit monstrosity, devoid of common virtues the meanest woman counts as her own. As for the dukes . . ." He bared his teeth. "An assembly of straw men. God's fire will consume them. It will consume you too unless you mend your wicked ways." He reached inside his vestment tunic and withdrew a short-handled whip with many thongs. "Helfred. What is this?"

He had to wet his lips before he could speak. "Eminence? It's—it's a whip."

"Commonly known as?"

Oh, God save the unfortunate princess. "Eminence, it's known as the penitent's friend." Every Church novice in the kingdom, male and female, was familiar with it. Friend by name, most unfriendly by nature.

"I think it time Her Highness made its acquaintance," said Marlan, gently. "Take it. Introduce them."

Horrified, he stared at the whip Marlan held out to him, then looked up. "Your Eminence? You—you want me to beat the princess?"

Marlan nodded. There was no pity in him. "Blessed Rollin in his Twelfth Admonition speaks at length of a child's duty to God through instant obedience to the will of his parents. Kneeling on this chapel floor, Helfred, is a manifest sinner. She rages, she rails, she refuses obedience. She must be corrected for the good of her soul."

And in the same breath I'm punished too, for failing to convert her to your desire. Oh God. Helfred took the whip. His hand was trembling. "Prolate Marlan—"

"Make her weep, Helfred," said his uncle, immoveable. "Only her tears can purge her of sin."

Beneath his plain habit, his entire body ran with sweat. He dragged his sickened gaze away from his uncle and stared at the princess. The fresh colour had fled from her cheeks and her eyes were wide, like a startled horse. He thought it was pride alone that kept her from breaking.

"Well, Helfred?" she said, her voice thin and tight. "You heard your uncle. Beat me, for all the good it'll do. All you'll achieve is an aching arm and a stain on your soul. You know this is wrong."

Dear God, it is. King Eberg would never beat his child. Not to make her marry a man like Rulf.

This is wrong . . . and I can't prevent it.

Rhian's steady gaze was taunting. "Come along, Chaplain. What are you waiting for? You've been dying to do this from the first day we met."

What? No! All right, yes, he'd wanted to slap her. He'd yearned to slap her, and more than once. But *beat* her? *Whip* her? No, he'd never wanted that.

"Helfred," said his uncle. His eyes were terrible. "Would *you* disobey me? I don't advise it. I make a bad enemy. Blood stretches so far and no further."

Oh God. He looked at Rhian. "Your Highness . . . please. Submit to the prolate. Admit his authority over you. Acknowledge your sin and be guided by your betters. Say you'll marry Lord Rulf. After all . . ." He tried to smile. "You must marry someone."

Rhian closed her eyes. "I've told you and told you, Helfred. I won't marry *him*."

Sweet Rollin, the foolish girl. Did she really think she could defy his uncle? No-one defied Marlan. At least not for long or more than once.

"Helfred," said his dead mother's brother. "I'm waiting."

Sweating profusely, he did as he was told. The first blow across Rhian's back was as light as he could make it. If he stung her a little she'd realise the trouble she was in, surely, and save them both a lot of grief. She must have felt it, even through her linen bodice, but pride wouldn't let her make a sound.

"Harder," said his uncle. His eyes were narrowed, his gaze trained on Rhian's face. "Again."

Teeth sunk into his lower lip, he struck the princess a second time. Thank God Marlan hadn't told him to rip her dress open. If he'd had to whip her on naked skin . . . well. Thank God he didn't, that was all.

"*Harder,* Helfred," said his uncle, his gaze incendiary. "Are you capable or should I demonstrate? On you?"

Helfred stared back at him over the top of Rhian's head, feeling the sweat on his skin turn to ice. *Oh God. Princess, I'm sorry.* He hit her again and this time was rewarded—punished—with a flinch and a gasp.

"Better," said his uncle. "Continue, Chaplain Helfred."

He hit Rhian as slowly as he dared, with his own gaze fixed on her lovely, netted hair. Once he looked up into his uncle's face. What he saw turned his stomach. He almost wept.

He made sure not to look up again.

Rhian was a strong girl. Too strong for her own good. If she wasn't so stubborn she'd let herself break. Give Marlan what he wanted, some tears, some sign of weakness. Penitence. But even though she was in pain, even though she rocked on her heels with it, her cries remained trapped inside her throat. The only sound that escaped her was a small, choked moan. It wasn't enough to satisfy Marlan.

"*Harder!*" said his uncle. "I will break this bitch if it takes all day."

Please, Rhian, stop trying to win! You'll never win, you don't know him like I do! His arm was aching now, rising and falling. *For the love of God, girl! Give him what he wants!*

With the next blow he saw a thin line of crimson spring through the pale blue linen covering the princess's bowed, shaking back.

He looked up. "Prolate. She's bleeding."

"*Good*," said Marlan. "Strike her again."

The whip dropped from his fingers. "I—I can't. Eminence, she's the *princess*. She'll be Ethrea's *queen*. What if I damage her, what if I—"

"You pimpled *fool*!" snarled Marlan, striding forward and snatching up the whip. "It doesn't matter if you beat her to pulp. She can remain in this clerica until her flesh is mended. This is Church business, it will stay between us."

"You think so?" said Rhian, her voice tight with pain. "I don't. I'll shout this from the rooftops. I'll strip naked in the street so the people can see—"

Marlan snatched her hair in its plain net and wrenched her head back. "The only words you'll be shouting are *Yes, I'll marry Rulf.*" He released her and turned, the whip outheld. "Helfred, continue."

The look on his uncle's face was frightening. "Eminence, this isn't right," he whispered, the words rising unbidden and escaping his tongue. Something deep inside him was breaking, some cherished belief was tearing apart. "Please. Let us withdraw a time and pray together. Once you've mastered your temper and the princess has had time to reflect, perhaps then—"

With a wordless cry of rage his uncle lashed the whip over his face. Helfred felt the skin split. Felt the blood burst forth. Felt the dreadful pain a heartbeat later.

"*Get out!*" cried Marlan. "Before you join her on the floor, you cowardly turd!"

As he reached the chapel door he heard the whip descend again. Heard his uncle's joyful exhalation. Heard Rhian scream at last.

He made it three staggering paces down the corridor

before he lost his breakfast onto the clerica's cool stone
tiles.

God forgive me. I'm a wicked cowardly wretch.

CHAPTER FIFTEEN

Marlan returned to the capital from Dame Cecily's
clerica in a filthy temper.

*The little bitch. Defying me. Thwarting me. If this in-
transigence continues I'll do more than welt her back.*

His mood wasn't improved by Ven'Martin's delivery
of a message from the council: he was summoned to an
extraordinary session in the castle.

"By God, gentlemen, you risk your very souls!" he declared, storming into the council chamber. "Am I some
servant, to be sent for on your whim?"

Of course it was Harley who answered, the arrogant
boor. "No. You're a charlatan whose word is worth less
than a Dev'kareshi sailor's."

All the dukes' men were glaring at him, even Henrik
Linfoi, their fists knuckled on the council table. Dester,
his head down, recorded the comment, sharpened quill
skittering across his paper.

With an effort Marlan kept his fists to himself. "In the
interests of good government I shall overlook that man-
nerless outburst. This time."

Henrik Linfoi raised a restraining hand in Harley's direction. "The choice of words was ill considered, Prolate,

but our concerns are not. Reliable sources tell us you have been to the clerica at Todding. Is that true?"

He stood his ground before them. "Am I answerable to you for Church business, Linfoi?"

"Marlan, you *swore* to us you'd not use your position to pressure the princess," said Linfoi, his face grave. "Do you deny it? Dester can read back the record of that meeting if, for some reason, memory plays you false."

Reliable sources? *When I find the traitor in my staff I will make him sorry. God knows I will.*

"Gentlemen, you astound me," he said, letting a little of his deep contempt show. "Your confidence in your dukes' candidates must be slight indeed if you have convinced yourselves they stand so little hope of success after all your wheedling and finagling into Princess Rhian's ear. I wonder, do your dukes know how precarious is your faith?"

"Our dukes know you have a vested interest in the outcome of this matter," retorted Volant. "My lord Duke of Arbat has expressed himself most forcefully, *Eminence.*" His tone made the honorific an insult. "But you also have a vested interest in not overstepping your bounds. Perhaps it's time you remembered that."

Around the table the other councillors nodded, eyes meeting briefly and sliding away. The room stank, suddenly, of unspoken threats.

Overproud fools. When Rulf is king I will see them on their knees. This council will be disbanded, it is an echo chamber for idiots.

He fixed his stare on Arbat's toothless lapdog. "You may tell your ducal brother-in-law, Volant, that any attempt to withhold or divert the pittance of tithes owed to my churches and chapels in his duchy will be met with the severest ecclesiastic recriminations. I doubt Rudi would care to explain to his people why they can no longer marry or be buried or hear the Litany or receive spiritual comfort of *any* kind for so long as said tithes are not promptly paid."

"Dear God, you are *shameless*!" cried Lord Niall, as Volant spluttered incoherently at his side. "I knew we would come to this, sooner or later. I *knew* you would abuse your position, Marlan, and so I've told Duke Kyrin. The princess must be brought back from Todding. Today. She must stand before us and declare her choice, she's had enough time to make up her mind. As long as she stays in the clerica she's in your power and duchy Hartshorn will not support that."

A groundswell of muttering. Dester was writing so fast his paper was practically smoking.

"My lords, you astound me," Marlan said, sweeping them with an icy glare. "Are you truly simpletons? Or so afraid for your positions you would imperil your souls with blusterings against a man of God? I have done *nothing* untoward or outside the bounds of my authority. If you say otherwise then show proof of my misdoings. Take it to the Court Ecclesiastica, that its Most Venerables can see how their prolate acts against the interests of God and this kingdom. Can you do that? I say you cannot."

Silence. Uneasy, sideways, slipshod glances. Cleared throats. White knuckles.

Henrik Linfoi released a sigh. "Your Eminence . . . Marlan . . . these are testing times. We face a crisis that with better management we need never have faced at all. Eberg, God rest him, accepted the truth of his mortality, his imminent demise, too late. It has left us uncertain and quick to fear the worst."

Eberg, the pliant fool, had let himself be cozened into believing there was a chance he'd recover. Battered by grief at the loss of not one son but both, tormented by guilt that he'd let his heirs romp around the world, weakened by flux and fever and pain, it had been easy enough to help him delude himself. *No man is so blind as one afraid to see.*

Marlan kept his face strict, but smiled behind it. *This council will not blow me from my course. These councillors are nothing. Gusts of hot air in bags of skin.*

"Gentlemen, you have raised a sweat for little purpose. Perhaps if you bothered to ask my reason for travelling to the clerica, instead of leaping to unfounded conclusions, you would look far less ridiculous. Dame Cecily sent word to me that the princess seemed distressed by the energetic importuning of her many eager visitors. She asked me as a matter of urgency to see for myself Princess Rhian's distress. As prolate it is my duty to ensure she is not unduly worn down by the momentous burden God has seen fit to place upon her frail, female shoulders."

It wasn't a lie. Not entirely. Cecily *had* sent urgent word. The wilful spoilt brat *was* in a pelter over being harassed but it wasn't the dukes' men who'd driven her hardest to distraction. Helfred, the stupid clod, had bungled his task.

"And how did you find Her Highness?" said Linfoi. "Was she distressed, as Dame Cecily claimed?"

Not as distressed as how I left her.

Remembering the stubborn overproud bitch's weeping, he felt himself smile. Henrik Linfoi misread him entirely.

"Our concerns *amuse* you, Prolate? I find that alarming! Our current predicament is without precedent," said Linfoi, scandalised. "Since the days of Rollin this kingdom has never lacked a clear line of succession. In the last week every councillor here has fobbed off a clutch of ambassadors or been made aware of whispers on the street. This continued uncertainty is doing great damage, it *must* be resolved. The three great nations *cannot* be given a reason to question the accord."

"I know that, Linfoi," he said. "Am I a fool?"

Linfoi sighed. "Of course not. And nor am I. Please, Marlan, answer my question. Did you find the princess distressed?"

"I did."

"Were you able to calm her?"

"She is reconciled to her duty."

"Has she made her decision?"

He smiled. "I expect it forthwith."

Around the table the councillors stirred, exchanging glances. Linfoi folded his hands. "Did she give any indication—"

"My lord, I did not ask her if she'd formed a partiality," he said. "That might be perceived as me unfairly using my influence."

"You showing your face in the clerica was unfairly using influence!" said Harley. "You know it, and we know it. I've no doubt you left the poor girl in tatters."

Time to put an end to this nonsense. "My lords, you do me a grave disservice. I am a man of God, my oaths sworn before the Living Flame. I say I went to Todding with the purest intentions. Do you say I would perjure my soul? If that's what you think, gentlemen, I tell you declare it! Say to my face: you think me God's enemy, and the kingdom's too."

A sharp silence. Their bluff was called. They might think and think, but brought to the point they would never accuse him outright. He was Prolate of Ethrea. They were mere dukes' men, barking on command.

"Then be told by me and trust I tell you the truth," he said, when the silence had stretched long enough. "Princess Rhian is aware of her duty and fully capable of carrying it out. She knows the time has come to make her choice."

Harley snorted. Of them all, he was the most resilient. "Her choice, Marlan? Or yours?"

"Lord Harley, it seems to me that unless the girl selects your brother's nephew—*your* nephew—as Ethrea's next king you will *never* be satisfied that I kept my hands clean of her choice."

"You're right," said Harley, leaning forward. His florid face was ugly with suspicion and dislike. "I won't. You never should've had a man in this race, Prolate. I said it at the start. I still say it now."

"And I say it's irrelevant," he replied. "Even without Lord Rulf in the running, if Rhian doesn't choose your man you'll find a way to call the outcome into question. You'll accuse me of taking bribes to steer her towards Meercheq, or Hartshorn, or Arbat, or claim some other duke's man applied undue influence."

And that was no lie. The other councillors knew it. Lord Harley was a troublemaker and always had been. He had no friends in this chamber, only convenient, temporary allies. The councillors looked at each other and then at Harley, their lips pursed and their eyes chilled with calculation.

Harley surged to his feet. "This isn't about *me*! Don't try and make this about *me*!" He glared at the other men seated at the table. "Niall—Volant—Porpont—you *idiots*! Don't you see what he's doing? Intimidating—bullying—don't let him do it. We've already agreed he's just a councillor in here."

Marlan swallowed a smile. *True. But the moment I set foot outside this chamber I am the prolate once again. And no duke with a spoonful of self-preservation is stupid enough to forget it.*

"Gentlemen," he said. "I find this uproar ridiculous. The girl will reach her decision in the next day or two. Until then I suggest we adjourn. We are all busy men, with busy lives and much work to do. Dame Cecily will send word when the princess has made her choice."

What could they do but agree and obey? The meeting broke up. Preparing to withdraw, Marlan felt a touch on his elbow and turned. It was Linfoi.

"Your Eminence, perhaps it might be useful if I visited Her Highness," the old man said. "I have no reason to harass her, no need to harangue. As far as anyone can be, I'm a neutral party in this matter. I could—"

Cause trouble. When I left her the girl was in no state to receive visitors.

"Lord Linfoi, it's a kind thought. But the princess made her feelings quite clear. She wishes to be left alone to pray. Given everything that's happened I think we owe her that much, don't you?"

Linfoi's lined face creased further. "Of course. But

you're sure she's all right? She's a good girl, despite her . . . unusual ways. I don't like to think of her being unhappy."

Sentimental old fool. "Henrik, I assure you," he said, dulcet as a dove, "there is no cause for alarm. As you say, the child is somewhat wild. I fear Eberg did not always discipline her as he might have." He sighed, smiling. "A danger for every doting father, I fear. But she benefits from her time in the clerica. If she is unhappy it will soon pass. When she is a wife and a mother she'll have no time to brood. Indeed, I feel her unhappiness springs from her lack of womanly pursuits. That will be remedied soon enough."

"Yes," said Linfoi, slowly nodding. "Yes, I expect you're right. Once she's married and settled things must improve. Very well. I'll not trouble her any further."

He clasped Linfoi's shoulder. "A wise decision. Indeed, Henrik, you've impressed me throughout this difficult time. It can't be easy, speaking for a duchy without any suitable man to put forth as our next king."

Linfoi considered him. "As to that, Prolate, while I'm flattered by your observation, I must say I cannot agree with your assessment. I bowed to the late king's wishes to exclude Alasdair from consideration because they were the late king's wishes. As Rhian's father it was his right to decide who was eligible for her hand. But fathers can be wrong. And so can kings." He nodded sharply. "And now, excuse me. As you say, we are all busy men."

He watched Linfoi leave. The only person left in the council chamber was Dester, hovering in the background, hoping to be noticed.

He turned on his heel and walked away.

*   *   *

Dexterity was mired in late-night book-keeping when Ursa finally came in answer to his note. To his surprise she let him lead her into the kitchen and tell her what he wanted without interrupting him, for once. When he was finished she stared with her eyebrows high.

"Leave for Todding tomorrow morning?" she echoed, her spine like iron and her arms intransigently folded. She stood in the doorway, having refused a chair. "Jones, that's very short notice. I've a clinic in the morning. I don't think I can get away. Really, you're the *most* exasperating man." Not waiting for his reply, she fixed her sharp gaze on Zandakar. "And what have you to say for yourself? How are you feeling, my mysterious friend, hmm? Zandakar?"

Seated at the kitchen table, paying no attention to their conversation, Zandakar looked up from his fledgling attempts to whittle a piece of soft yellow pine. "Ursa?"

"How—are—you—feeling?" she repeated, with exaggerated care.

He shrugged. "Good, Ursa."

"Yes, you're looking much better," she agreed, pleased. "There's some meat on your bones now and your eyes aren't so sunken. All thanks to me."

Dexterity straightened from his slouch against the sink. "And me! I did quite a lot of the nursing myself!"

Ursa sniffed. "I'm not inclined to give you any credit, Jones. You're trying to bustle me, and I don't like being bustled."

Tcha. And she called *him* exasperating. "Well, I'm sorry but I'm not the one doing the bustling. I told you. It's Hettie."

Ursa unfolded her arms and frowned at her herb-stained fingertips. "Yes. You told me."

And what was *that* supposed to mean? "Ursa . . ." He stepped forward, little prickles of foreboding dancing over his skin. "You said you'd help. Have you changed your mind?" *Hettie, don't let her do that! I'm sunk without Ursa.*

"Jones, Jones . . ." Ursa let out a gusty sigh. "If I have, can you blame me? In the cold light of day can you wonder if I'm wondering whether this isn't all a terrible mistake?"

He flung out his hand and pointed at Zandakar. "After everything that's happened?" he demanded, not trying to hide his angry dismay. "With *him* sitting in my kitchen? Yes, Ursa, I can!"

Zandakar looked up from his carving. From the expression on his face he didn't care for raised voices. His pale eyes narrowed and his fingers tightened on the small, almost blunt whittling knife. Not the best tool for carving even soft wood . . . but it had seemed prudent. Abruptly, for the first time since the business with the thrown cup, he looked dangerous.

"It's all right, Zandakar," he said quickly, softening his voice, and raised a placating hand. "All right. *Zho?*"

Zandakar's sharp gaze shifted between them then settled on Ursa. "Ursa? All right?"

If she said no, what would Zandakar do? From the look on her face she was wondering the same thing. After a moment she nodded, though she was far from happy. "Yes, Zandakar. All right."

"Tcha," he said, then added something in his own tongue. Not a word of it was familiar, but his tone was

easy to read. *Behave yourselves. Act like adults.* A strict authority echoed in his voice. Scarred and diminished and reduced as he was, still he seemed for a moment formidable.

Unexpectedly embarrassed, Dexterity felt his face heat beneath its unruly beard. "Ursa. Please," he said, making his voice reflect entreaty, not temper. "I can't do this without you. I don't understand. What's made you change your mind?"

"Oh, *Jones*," she said, goaded, and stamped around the kitchen. Zandakar looked up again, frowning, but she paid him no mind. "Why do you have to be a such a *dreamer*?" She stopped stamping and fisted her hands on her narrow hips. "Sometimes I think there's never more of you in the real world than a toe and two fingers. I was in town this morning. There's a nasty feeling in the air and it's got nothing to do with a breeze from the fish markets. I swear I could cut the tension with a knife. The sun's shining, birds are singing. Folk are out and about, as always. On the surface everything looks fine. But underneath it all? Jones, it's *not* fine."

He scrubbed his fingers through his hair. "No? Well, I suppose people are still grieving for Eberg. The funeral wasn't that long ago and he was our king for a good many years. It's only natural that—"

"There's nothing natural about it!" said Ursa. "I wish you'd listen to what I'm saying. The mood is tense. Every person I spoke to had just one thing on his mind: how long before the princess marries and gives us a king? Everyone's *worried*, Jones."

"Yes, perhaps they are," he agreed. "But shopkeepers

and carters and the like, they can't be expected to understand how these matters are—"

"No, but it's not only the working folk dancing on their
toes!" she retorted. "It's the muckety-mucks as well. I'm
a physick, I treat rich and poor alike. Silk and velvet's
no protection against gripe. You'd best believe me, *everyone's* fretting. And it's not just us Ethreans either. The
foreigners are rattled too."

"What? How do you know?"

"How do you *think* I know?" she said, exasperated.
"The harbour's full of ships, those ships are full of sailors,
and when they drink one rum too many and trip over in
the gutter they need stitching up, don't they? And they're
not like Zandakar, here, gabbling gibberish no soul can
understand. *They've* got the decency to speak Ethrean!"

He gaped at her. "Ursa, I'm sorry—what are you talking about?"

"I'm talking about trouble, Jones! Stop wittering and
listen! As a favour to another physick I stitched up more
than my share of split skulls today and whether you like
it or not, here is the truth. Kingseat's a tinderbox looking
for a spark."

He'd never seen her like this. Never heard such rancour
and fear in her voice, or seen her eyes look so accusing.
"What—and you think *I'm* a spark?"

"I think you could be!" she snapped. "I think if you
run away with that girl you could set fire to the whole
blessed kingdom!"

"But Ursa . . ." He clutched at his beard. "If I don't
run away with her, if I don't find a way to stop Rhian
being forced into marriage with the wrong man, the king-

dom's going to go up in flames anyway! And not just the kingdom!"

Ursa sniffed. "So *Hettie* says."

"Yes! She does!" He saw the scepticism in her face and crossed his arms, fighting to keep hold of his temper. "Oh, I see. We're back to that again, are we? Me being overworked and imagining things? *Ursa*—"

"Don't you *Ursa* me, Jones!" his friend said fiercely. "I'm trying to look out for you, can't you *see* that? If I help you and that girl run away and you get caught—what do you think will happen, eh? How do you think the lords and dukes will react? Not to mention Prolate Marlan. What do you think they'll do to a toymaker found meddling in affairs of state?"

"Nothing!" he said hotly. "*If* I'm caught, which I won't be, Rhian will speak up for me and *they'll* have to listen, she's the rightful queen of Ethrea and—"

"And she's a *girl,* you stupid man! *They* won't listen to a word she says! If they listened to her, Jones, she wouldn't have to run away in the first place, would she? She'd be handing out royal decrees and commandments like cupcakes at afternoon tea and *they'd* be covered in crumbs, wouldn't they?"

He opened his mouth to argue, then closed it again. Ursa had a point. *But it doesn't matter. I know what I have to do and I'm going to do it.* With a sideways glance at Zandakar, who was glaring again, he took a deep breath and made himself calm down before the man did something unfortunate with his blunt whittling knife.

"Ursa, I understand you're uncertain. If you've had second thoughts and you'd rather not be involved, of course that's your right. I won't say another word. All I'll ask is that you keep this a secret and don't try to stop me, even though you disagree."

She dropped into an empty kitchen chair, her face half hidden by salt and pepper hair escaped from the knot on top of her head. "Oh, Jones," she sighed. "You haven't heard a word I said."

He took the third chair at the table and covered her hand with his. "Yes, I heard every one of them. I still have to do this. I promised Hettie and I promised Rhian. At dawn tomorrow, Zandakar and I are leaving for Todding. I'd much prefer you left with us but I will understand if you decide you can't. I'll just have to think of another way into the clerica while we're on the road."

"There is no other way, you silly man," she said, and pulled her fingers free. "If I don't go with you, you'll never get in."

He shrugged. "Then the future's in your hands, Ursa, isn't it?"

"I don't want that." She looked away. "I'm frightened, Jones. The mood in town, it scared me. I've never felt anything like it before. I don't think you realise what you've got yourself into. What Hettie's got you into. If it's Hettie, of course."

"Ursa," he said gently, and took her hand again. "Look at me." Reluctantly, she looked. There were tears in her eyes. He felt a breath catch in his throat. *I don't believe it. Ursa never cries.* "Of course it's Hettie. Who else could it be?"

Her cheeks flushed. "Some malevolent spirit. Some wicked thing bent on mischief."

"And you rail at *me* for being impractical?" he said, and laughed. "Oh, Ursa. That's superstitious nonsense!

Foreign sailors who don't know any better, they believe in demons and sprites. But you?"

Her chin shot up. "There's good in the world, Jones. Why can't there be evil?"

"Of course there's evil. People do bad things every day. But it's *people* doing them, not—not invisible agents of darkness."

"I see." She glared. "You'll believe in a ghost but not malevolent spirits? Or God?"

Now they were straying far from the purpose. "If I am going in the morning I've a lot to do between now and then. So let's settle this once and for all, shall we? Are you coming or are you staying behind? I promise I won't nag if you decide not to come. I just need to know."

"I can't tell you, Jones!" said Ursa. "I'm sorry, but I can't. After the fracas I saw in town, I'm going to need the night to think on this."

Dismayed, he stared at her. "But Ursa—"

"I know! It's not what you want to hear. I can't help that, I'm afraid. I'm asking you to give me the night. I think I've earned a few hours of space, Jones, after all I've done for you these last few weeks."

Of course she had. But it wasn't like her to say a thing like that . . . which meant she really must be unnerved. He sighed. "Yes."

"If, come sunrise, I'm standing in this kitchen with a packed bag in my hand you'll know I've taken leave of my senses," she muttered. "If not, well . . . I'll give you a letter to give to Cecily."

He nodded, trying to hide his disappointment. "I'd appreciate it." Then he looked at Zandakar. The man with the blue-stubbled skull had finished his tentative whittling and stared at them now, his expression guarded.

"All right, Dexterity?" he asked slowly. He still had trouble getting his tongue around the words. "All right, Ursa?"

Not really. Not now. But what could he say? "Zho. All right." He reached out and patted Zandakar's arm. "We worried you. Yatzhay, Zandakar."

The tension went out of the tall man's face. "Yatzhay. All right."

Dexterity looked at the wood Zandakar had carved. "Gracious. What's this?" He picked it up and examined it. "Some kind of creature? Ursa, have you ever seen anything like this before?"

"No," said Ursa. She still sounded cross. "Must be from his own lands, wherever they are."

The crudely carved creature was some three inches long. It had eight legs, four on each side. The front two were large and fearsome, ending in wicked-looking pincers. It had a tail curved over its back. The carving was clumsy, hardly refined. Zandakar had talent but no practised skill. And yet . . . and yet . . . there was something powerful about the thing.

Something menacing.

He held it up. "Zandakar? What is this?"

The strangest look crossed Zandakar's thin, scarred face. In his eyes, a tangle of emotions. Fear. Respect. Longing. Despair.

"Chalava," he said. His voice was hushed. Tinged with awe.

"I see," he said, not seeing at all. "Chalava. That's . . . very nice." He handed back the carved wooden creature.

"But you need to put it away. There's a lot to do before we leave at dawn to rescue the princess."

Zandakar handed the carved creature back again. "You."

"Me? You mean you want me to have this? Well, Zandakar, that's kind of you but—"

"You!" said Zandakar. His face was fierce, his eyes cold and uncompromising. *"Chalava.* You."

"Keep it, Jones," said Ursa. "Why upset him if you don't have to?"

Why indeed? Dexterity looked again at the crude pinewood carving. Definitely, it was menacing. It made his skin crawl. But it was important to Zandakar . . . and the giving of it might mean they were, at last, forging a bond.

He slipped the carved creature into his pocket. "Thank you, Zandakar. Thank you very much."

Zandakar nodded. *"Chalava.* You."

He smiled, bemused. "Yes. *Chalava.* Me. Now, what say we get started on the packing?"

CHAPTER SIXTEEN

I beseech you, O God, send wise men to teach me; stern men to love me; wrathful men to chastise me when I err."

On her knees before the Living Flame, Rhian watched her fingers tighten into fists. She couldn't not say the

words, she was in the chapel with Helfred, but while her
tongue was obedient her heart was wicked. A riot of rebellion. It seethed with resentment as her beaten flesh
burned and throbbed.

*I hate you, Helfred. I hate your uncle. And if God is on
your side then I hate God too.*

Litany concluded, Helfred kissed his thumb, touched
his breast and stood. After Marlan had departed the clerica yesterday, leaving inviolate instructions that she be
confined to constant prayer until she saw the *error of her
ways,* the chaplain had returned to her in the privy chapel. If he felt any shame or remorse for what he'd done to
her, she hadn't seen it. He'd shown no more emotion than
a painting. Nearly a full day later that hadn't changed.
Looking at his stiff back, at the rigid set of his shoulders,
she knew she'd never hear a word of regret from him.

"Helfred . . ." She cleared her throat. The thought of
begging a favour from him hurt as much as her abused
body but . . . *What can I do? Marlan's made him my
guard dog. I have to go through him no matter how galling that is.* "I need to see the infirmarian."

Still he didn't turn from the altar. "You can't. The
prolate's orders are clear. You must remain in the chapel
praying until you bow to God's will."

"You mean *Marlan's* will."

"They are one and the same," said Helfred, toneless.
"Cease your sinful defiance of the prolate, Your Highness. You are a ward of the Church. You must bow to the
inevitable sooner or later."

No. Never. *Mr Jones will send word to me. He has to.
He promised.* The thought of that plain, kind man's ear-

nest support was the only thing keeping her from violent hysterics. She took a deep breath, feeling vilely ill.

"Helfred, please. You don't understand. I'm faint. Exhausted. I think I'm fevered. I'm not made of *stone*. How can I stay here forever, praying?"

"If you bow to God's will you won't have to, Highness," said Helfred. "Accept Lord Rulf as your husband and king and you will be free to seek remedy from the infirmarian."

She felt a heaving sickness roil through her. *This is my own stupid fault. I never should've come here. I was mad to think I'd be safe from Marlan in a clerica.*

"Helfred. I'm begging you. I'm unwell. How is God served if—if—" She let her voice fade away. Played up her fragile condition . . . but not by very much.

Helfred turned. His pallor suggested he felt no more robust than she. The broad welt marring his cheek was swollen, and looked painful. *Good.*

"God is served by obeying Marlan! You unnatural, wretched girl. It's your duty to obey him. Do as he tells you and we will *both* go home!"

So. He showed emotion now, but of course it was selfserving. Helfred was a toad. A hateful, cowardly, spineless sycophant. A witless puppet dancing on the end of his uncle's strings.

To think I felt sorry for you. How stupid was that? You and Marlan deserve each other. I hope he makes you miserable for the rest of your life. I hope that welt on your cheek is the first of thousands.

It hurt her so much she nearly shrieked with the pain, but she made herself stand and face Helfred on her feet. Waves of hot and cold washed over her skin.

"I think you must have maggots in your brain. Do you think you can go on abusing and mistreating me without consequence? I am *Eberg's daughter.* I am *Ethrea's queen.*"

"You're a ward of the Church before you're anything, Highness," said Helfred. "If you don't remember that you will continue to suffer."

I'll never forget it. Nor forget my father.

If she didn't sit down again she'd sprawl at Helfred's feet. Teeth gritted, she lowered herself into a pew. "Chaplain. Surely, as a man of God you must have compassion. I've had no respite since Marlan left. I haven't even been permitted to change my dress!" The dried blood on it chafed her. What her back must look like she didn't care to think. "I haven't slept or eaten or drunk or even taken my privy ease. There are slaves on ships in Kingseat Harbour who are treated less harshly than you're treating me. My God! Are *you* stone? I doubt you'd treat a dog like this! How can you be so cruel to *me?* What have I ever done to *you,* Helfred, to deserve such misery at your hands?"

Helfred's eyes were wide, his cheeks chalky-white. "I am bound to obey the prolate," he whispered.

"And does he want his precious broodmare sick, or dying?" she retorted. "You *hurt* me, Helfred. Will you stand there and pretend you didn't?"

His head jerked, as though she'd struck him. "You hurt yourself," he said, his voice low and hard. "Your disobedience hurt you. And Marlan. He beat you too. It wasn't just me."

"Yes! You both hurt me! And you'll both be responsible if I succumb to your beating. But if you think *Mar-*

lan will take any responsibility you *are* as stupid as you look."

Again, Helfred flinched. "I am only a chaplain. These matters sit high above my head."

Oh, for God's *sake*. "Then go to the dame! Ask Cecily if she wants my blood on her conscience, my suffering to blot out the light of her clerica."

Helfred dithered a moment, shifting to stare at the Flame as though it would tell him what to do. By his sides, his fingers clenched and unclenched.

"You stay in this privy chapel," he said at last, heated. "Step one foot beyond it and not even God will save you from Marlan. Do you understand me? Do you understand how precarious you are?"

If she hadn't before yesterday, she certainly did now. She nodded. "I'm not well enough to go anywhere, Helfred," she said tiredly. There were tears inside her, desperate for release. "Please. Just see Dame Cecily. Bring her here to me if she has any doubts. I'll pray while I'm waiting."

"Highness, the time for prayer is passed," said Helfred. "What you must do is choose between your possible futures: life as Ethrea's queen . . . or Marlan's prisoner."

What? "Helfred, are you witless? Your uncle can't hold me a *prisoner*."

The look on her unwanted chaplain's face was a muddle of pity and contempt. "Highness, you have been spoiled beyond redemption. Your old world, where your kingly father made the rules, where you and he could choose how strictly was followed the creed of Rollin and most often chose an ill-advised path—it's dead and buried just like Eberg. Can't you grasp you're in *my* world, now? Until your majority Marlan can beat you daily if he likes. He can lock you in a clerica cell and feed you stale bread and brackish water but three times a week. He can have you declared imbecile, unfit for the crown."

"Oh, don't be ridiculous! The council would *never*—"

"The council?" said Helfred. His face was red now, the welt on his cheek bright scarlet. "You think the dukes' puppets can save you? God have mercy. If you think that you *are* too naïve to rule."

She'd never before seen Helfred so passionate. It was a bit like being savaged by one of Mr Jones' stuffed toys. "Helfred—"

"*Submit to the prolate*. It's your only hope."

He stamped out of the chapel, leaving her shaken and unsure.

My only hope is Mr Jones. And if he fails me . . .

The crowding tears in her breast and throat escaped in a sob. Sliding to her knees, she rested her arms on the back of the pew in front of her and let her forehead fall on them as she wept.

Oh Papa, Papa. How could you do this to me? How could you leave me at the mercy of that terrible man? Marlan is a monster, how did you not see it?

A tentative hand touched her shoulder. "Your Highness? Princess Rhian?"

"*Mr Jones!*" She was so startled she lost her balance. The effort required not to slide between the pews made her cry out in pain.

"Your Highness!" he said, alarmed, and helped her to sit on the hard wooden bench again. "What's wrong? What's happened?"

She found it difficult to meet his worried eyes. "Oh—well—"

But he wasn't looking at her now. He was staring at the back of her dress. "That's dried blood," he said, his voice harsh and cold. "Rhian, what happened?"

He had no leave to use her untitled name but she didn't care. "What do you think happened?"

"I think—" He shook his head, as though struggling to believe. "I think it looks like you've been beaten. But how could—"

As fever chills shook her, she heard herself laugh. "Prolate Marlan and I had a difference of opinion."

"And *this* is how he would win the argument?" said Mr Jones, incredulous. "He beat you bloody? The Queen of Ethrea?"

"He and Helfred. My personal chaplain. He's Marlan's nephew. They're determined I'll marry the prolate's man, Lord Rulf." Tears were sliding down her cheeks again. "Mr Jones, what are you *doing* here? I was expecting to receive some kind of message . . ."

He dropped to a crouch beside her, fished a blue kerchief from his coat pocket and handed it to her. "It's a long story, Your Highness. I'll explain later. First we have to find a way to get you out of here, tonight."

Tonight? *Oh, yes, please, God.* Grateful for the kerchief, she wiped her cheeks dry and handed it back. Then she frowned. "I'm sorry. Did you say *we*? I don't—"

He pressed his fingers to her lips. "Either you trust me, Highness, or you don't. If you don't then I'd best leave now."

"Yes, I trust you," she said, pulling away. "But—"

"And you can trust my friends." His smile was warm, and reassuring. "We're here to help you."

Did she have a choice? Unless she freed herself from this place soon, freed herself from Marlan's clutches, she was desperately afraid Helfred would be proven right.

I've always believed that as a princess I was inviolate. But it seems I've lived my life sadly mistaken. Any power I had came from my father and brothers. Without their protection I've no more power than—than a slave.

A sobering thought. Cold enough to freeze her, if she hadn't been so hot . . .

"Highness?" said Mr Jones. "Are you all right?"

She shook her head. "Not really."

He took her hands in his, another serious breach of protocol. But it felt so good, a friend's kind touch. His face was thunderous. "If Prolate Marlan's a true man of God then *I'm* an Icthian."

She managed a watery smile. "You're far too handsome to be an Icthian, Mr Jones. Tell me, how do you and your friends intend to—"

"I don't know yet. But never you fear, I'll find a way. In the meantime—"

"Hush!" she said, and turned towards the chapel's open doors, wincing. "That's Helfred's voice. Mr Jones—"

But he was already diving across the aisle to conceal himself on the floor between the most distant pews.

God, don't let Helfred see him. Do that much for me at least.

Helfred re-entered the chapel with Dame Cecily by his side. She faced them on her unsteady feet, one hand holding the end of the pew to forestall any embarrassing collapse, and fought the insane desire to look where Mr Jones was hiding.

Dame Cecily swept her head to toe with a single glance and said, "Chaplain, I can only think that you are blind. Princess Rhian is *sick*. Why did you wait before coming to me?"

"I was under strict instruction from Prolate Marlan," said Helfred, muted. "She—she is wilful and disobedient, she must be brought to an understanding of her duty to God."

"An understanding you wish her to demonstrate for him face to face?" said the Dame tartly. "This is *my* clerica, Chaplain. *Nothing* is done here without my authority."

Helfred flushed. "Prolate Marlan—"

"Is not the one who will have to explain to the council how it is that Ethrea's queen looks to follow her father and brothers into the grave!"

"She's not queen yet, Dame Cecily," said Helfred.

"Nor will she ever be if you have your way! *I* am not blind, I can see that much! Do you presume to dispute with me, Helfred? *You, a chaplain,* without even the authority to walk a mile unless you are granted leave and a direction?" She turned her back on him. "Your Highness—"

Rhian, torn between satisfaction at seeing Helfred so chastised and feeling as though she might faint with her next heartbeat, perilously released her grip on the pew. "Yes, Dame Cecily?"

"You will accompany me to the infirmary, where your discomforts shall be eased overnight."

She felt a surge of triumph. *Yes, they will be . . . but not in the way you think.* Bowing her head, she said, "Thank you, Dame Cecily."

The dame nodded. "But do not imagine it means you'll be excused your penances for defying the prolate. Chaplain Helfred is right in one thing, at least: you must be brought to an understanding of your duty to God and Ethrea. Those born to high estate are not free to please themselves like common men are free. If that is something you have failed to learn, then shame on your father. But you will learn it now, child. God has sent you here that you may be taught."

I know. But what he wanted to teach me was the truth about Marlan . . . and I've learned that lesson well, I promise you.

"Dame Cecily," she murmured, outwardly obedient, inwardly seething, and followed her and Helfred out of the privy chapel. Walking was a torment. Every soft step jarred her shrieking flesh, made her vile headache worse, made her think she would retch her stomach onto the floor. She kept on walking, head low, hands demurely clasped before her.

I'm the queen of Ethrea. I can do this. I must. And tonight will see me out of this prison, out of Marlan's clutches, on the road to Alasdair and the future I make, for myself and for my kingdom.

Dexterity waited a full quarter hour before daring to slip out of the small, beautiful chapel. He'd hardly taken ten steps along the corridor before he was accosted by a devout.

"You there! Stop! What are you doing here?" the woman demanded.

He turned. "Oh, forgive me, forgive me!" he whined, cringing. "I'm looking for my mistress, she's here seeing

Dame Cecily. She and the dame are dear friends, bosom companions from childhood."

The angry devout hesitated, some of her ire fading in the face of such a pedigree. "Indeed? Well, neither Dame Cecily nor your mistress is here, man. And you should not be here either, this is a privy place. Be off with you at once."

He knuckled his forehead. "Yes, devout. God forgive me for a sinner."

The devout sniffed, still suspicious, and watched him out of sight round a bend in the corridor. He ducked through the same door that he'd entered by, out into the afternoon sunshine and the clerica's well-tended gardens.

Breathing more easily, he made his way back to the extensive herb-beds where Zandakar still toiled. It was their excuse for being here, Ursa's need for particular leaves and buds for her physicking for which the clerica at Todding was particularly famous.

Of course she had pots and pots of the wretched things growing in her greenhouse at home, but Dame Cecily wasn't to know that, was she?

Zandakar turned at the sound of his name. His freshly shaved head gleamed in the warm light and his still-thin frame was disguised by a fresh set of clothes: roughspun wool trousers, a heavy cotton shirt, stout leather half-boots laced firmly round his ankles. He didn't look quite so out of place dressed like that. Not quite so foreign, despite his brown skin.

"Dexterity," he said, dropping fuzzy red-leaf herbs into the woven reed basket at his feet. "All right?"

Oh dear, oh dear! That betraying accent! *"Hush!"* he said, alarmed, and waved a finger under Zandakar's nose.

"No *talking*, Zandakar. Remember?" He pressed the finger to Zandakar's lips. *"Wei. Wei."*

Zandakar rolled his eyes, and pushed aside the finger. "Tcha."

"Wei tcha!" he snapped, and looked around to make sure they were still alone. They were, but for how much longer there was no way to know. He put the finger again to Zandakar's lips. *"Shhh! Shhh!"*

Something of his urgency at last made an impression. Zandakar nodded. His eyes were resigned.

Poor chap. How hard this must be for him, living at the mercy of strangers, barely understanding a word we say, bullied and prodded into following us about.

He sighed, his conscience pricking, and patted the man's shoulder. *"Yatzhay,* Zandakar. I hope soon we'll share enough words so I can explain."

Zandakar pointed. It was Ursa, threading her way through the herb-beds and trellises.

"Well?" she said, reaching them. "How did you go, Jones?"

"I found the princess," he said. "How about you?"

"Cecily and I were having a fine old chinwag until some gormless little chaplain interrupted us and dragged her away."

"That was Helfred. He's Marlan's nephew." Remembering, he felt the rage stir again. "Ursa, they've beaten Rhian. They've beaten her *bloody.* When I found her she was weeping as though her heart would break. She's so unwell from her mistreatment she's been taken to the infirmary."

"Who's beaten her? What are you—"

On a deep, ragged breath he caught hold of his temper.

"Who do you think? The prolate and this Chaplain Helfred."

Ursa stared. "What? Oh Jones, that's nonsense."

"It's not nonsense! Rhian told me herself. And your friend, Dame Cecily, she's in on it too! I had to hide in the chapel when they came for the princess. I *heard* them talking."

"But Jones—"

"No!" he said fiercely. "It's the truth. We have to get Rhian out of here tonight, before they hurt her again. And they're going to, Ursa. All they care about is that she does what Marlan wants, because he's the prolate and she's just a girl. I was nearly *sick,* listening to them. No wonder she was weeping. No wonder she's so desperate to run away. *I'd* run away from them and I'm a man grown!"

Now Ursa looked distressed. "It's hard to think Cecily could be like that," she murmured. "She was always so gentle when we were girls."

"Power changes people, Ursa. And let a man get it into his head that his power comes from God, *well.* Will there be any stopping him? Or her, for that matter? Only with a great deal of difficulty." He sighed, not indifferent to the pain in her eyes. "I'm sorry if your friend's become a disappointment. That must be hard. But hard or not—"

"I *know,* Jones! Don't try teaching your grandmother to suck eggs."

That was better. Ursa all prickly was an Ursa he could recognise, and manage. "The princess will be in the infirmary all night. It's probably our best chance to get her out of here. Has the dame invited you to dinner, like we hoped?"

"Yes. A private supper. You and Zandakar are to eat with the lay servants in their hall."

He thought about that. "So . . . you can slip the sleeping potion into the dame's dinner and I can take care of the servants, but what about the devouts? We can't have them wide awake and prowling the corridors while we're trying to steal Rhian out of the infirmary."

"No," said Ursa, eyebrows pinched in a frown. "We can't." She shook herself. "I'll just have to wangle my way into the kitchens. I can dose the devouts' supper when the cook's back is turned."

It sounded tricky. "Wangle how?"

She smiled, briefly. "I'm an old friend of Cecily's. Leave that to me."

Dinner in the clerica was eaten after the evening Litany. Dexterity, with Zandakar wide-eyed and uncomprehending beside him, sat at the back of the main chapel as Chaplain Helfred led the gathering in worship.

It was the first time he'd set foot in church or recited the sacred words since Hettie's funeral.

Ursa, a privileged guest, sat right up in the front of the chapel with Dame Cecily and the clerica's resident chaplain who'd been demoted to make way for the prolate's nephew. Dexterity smouldered at Helfred, his guts tied into knots.

Call yourself a man of God? God should strike you dead for what you're doing to Rhian. Hettie, can you see him? Can you send him some boils to keep his pimples company? You knave. You gribbet. I'd like to beat you bloody, I'd like to do that.

On and on the nasty little man maundered, but at last

the service came to an end. Dexterity waited respectfully at the rear of the chapel as the devouts filed out, led by the chaplains, with Zandakar beside him and remembering not to speak. He knuckled his forehead as Ursa and the dame approached.

"Mistress," he said ingratiatingly.

"My servants," said Ursa to the Dame, her tone dismissive. "Useless lumps the pair of them, but I'm not rich enough to pay for better wits." She turned. "You, Doggell. When you've eaten in the servants' hall—and mind you don't gobble a mouthful more than your share—see the horses hitched to the van and wait in it for me at the front gates."

"You're certain you can't stay the night, Ursa?" said Dame Cecily. She almost sounded wistful. "Your servants can sleep with mine, there are pallets to spare."

Ursa's expression folded into regret. "Oh, I wish I could, Cecie. Alas, duty calls me back to Kingseat. I shouldn't really be staying for supper but how could I refuse your kind invitation?"

"You'll be travelling nigh three hours in pitch darkness," the dame protested. "It won't be comfortable."

"No, but I'll survive it," said Ursa. "God didn't put us here for our comfort, did he?"

Dame Cecily nodded. "Very well. If you're sure. Perhaps another time. You could come for a short retreat, a few days of worship and peaceful reflection."

"I'd like that," said Ursa. "We've let too many years slide away from us, haven't we? Doggell!"

Dexterity jumped. "Mistress?"

"Do you understand my orders?"

He knuckled his forehead again. "Yes, Mistress."

"Then obey them," she said, and left with the dame.

Smothering a smile, he tugged at Zandakar's sleeve. "Come along!" he said, loudly and slowly as though to a man as thick as a tree. "Food now. Come along!"

Zandakar nodded and followed him out.

As servants of an important guest he and Zandakar were invited to serve themselves first from the cauldron on the servants' hall sideboard. Gesturing Zandakar to stay on the bench at the long wooden table, Dexterity ladled a modest helping of the fragrant leek and mutton stew into their bowls then, his heart thudding, emptied the vial of Ursa's strong sleeping powder into the rest. A quick stir with the ladle and the deed was done.

"It's not any kind of potion that'll raise suspicions in the morning," Ursa had promised. "They won't wake late or any such nonsense. But it'll keep them soundly snoring while we're about our business."

If she said so, he believed her. Nobody knew herb lore better than Ursa.

When he and Zandakar had finished eating, Dexterity made their excuses with thanks and a smile. They returned in silence to the stables and hitched the two muscular brown cobs to the cosy peddler's van he'd purchased—oh dear, all that gold!—and they trundled out of the clerica to sit in silence beyond its front gates.

It was a cool night, with clouds drifting across the moons. Rain tomorrow, most likely. A mixed blessing. It was always a misery travelling in rain, but it meant folk would be preoccupied with their own discomforts and less likely to pay attention to others on the road.

With Zandakar stowed in the back of the van among the bits and pieces they'd brought with them for the long trip to duchy Linfoi, Dexterity huddled in a blanket on the driver's seat and tried not to let his imagination run away with him.

We won't get caught. Hettie won't let us. There'd be no point in us coming in the first place if we were going to get caught. Oh dear, hurry up, Ursa. Eat quickly for once. All this waiting is upsetting my stomach.

Since she wasn't coming with them they'd have to drive most of the way back to Kingseat before turning again for the closest river-station so they could take a barge north all the way up the Eth river.

The van was supplied with things to help them disguise themselves as best they could. Of course disguising Zandakar might prove something of a problem, but then he could spend most of his time hidden in the back. If they made sure he only came out late at night the chances were good he'd not attract undue attention. And the further they travelled from Kingseat the easier it would be for Rhian. Outside of the capital few people knew what she looked like.

If I could keep her hidden in the van I'd be much happier . . . but I'll need another pair of hands. And I don't think too many people will question a man and his daughter, humble travelling peddlers, quietly going about their business. I doubt even a duke's soldiers would think of stopping us.

"Jones!" said Ursa in a piercing whisper, appearing without warning out of the dark. "What are you doing, sitting there muttering to yourself? Help me up, I've eaten so much I'm going to burst!"

"What are *you* doing, sneaking up like that?" he whispered back, taking her wrist and hauling her beside him. "You nearly scared me out of my wits!"

"What wits?" she said, settling under his blanket. "Now hush up, voices carry at night, and drive on a bit. We'll have to wait somewhere inconspicuous till it's time to do the deed."

She was right but he still felt annoyed. The way she went on sometimes you'd think she was the only one who knew *anything* and that was a fact.

He picked up the reins and chirruped to the brown cobs. The horses grunted, leaning into their harness. The single lit torch on the peddler's van stuttered and flared, throwing a little light on the road before them.

"This'll do," said Ursa as they reached a rutted laneway some minutes from the clerica's gates. "Let's wait here."

It was as good a place to stop as any. Dexterity halted the horses and extinguished the van's torch. They plunged into darkness, the night damp on their skin. Overhead the starry sky streamed with clouds.

Dexterity pulled his share of the blanket closer.

Well, then, Hettie. Here I am, just as you wanted. So you make sure things go exactly to plan.

CHAPTER SEVENTEEN

Mantled in night, the clerica slept.

Rhian shifted beneath her light blanket, wincing as movement stirred her pains from slumber. Was it her imagination or did the place seem even more silent than usual? She was the infirmary's only patient but the devout in charge of the pills and potions, Agitha, had assured her that she or her assistant always remained awake between dusk and dawn, in case of trouble. But Agitha hadn't returned to check on her since supper, and that was hours ago. No-one else had checked on her either. Not even Helfred, and she'd been sure he'd come to stand over her and gloat.

Something's going on.

The clerica's deep silence—did it have to do with Mr Jones? She thought it must have. She didn't really believe in coincidences. He was here. He'd come to help her escape. Though how he expected to spirit her out from under Dame Cecily's nose she couldn't begin to imagine . . .

A lamp burned on a table by the window, shedding enough light so she could comfortably see. She sat up, cautiously, swallowing a whimper. Whatever was in the foul concoction Agitha had forced upon her earlier had eased the alternating heat and shivers . . . but done nothing to alleviate her acute discomfort.

They want me to suffer, they just don't want me to die.

Her ruined blue dress had been taken away. For rags, most likely. It was fit for nothing else now. In its place she'd been given a plain brown clerica robe. On edge, skin prickling with premonition, she slid off her narrow cot and slipped the robe over the cotton shift she wore for modesty since her various underthings had been taken away too. The rough wool was heavy enough to hurt, and the room swung around her in a dizzy swoop. She staggered sideways a few paces and groped for the wall.

"Your Highness!" a voice whispered from the door.

She turned, and was swamped by a crashing wave of relief. "Mr Jones!"

His teeth appeared in a smile, which was genuine but a trifle strained. "We have to hurry. I don't know how much longer we can trust the clerica to remain asleep."

So he *was* responsible for the silence. God bless the man. She took a step towards him and gasped. Oh, it *hurt*. She could grit her teeth and keep walking if she had to, but as for *hurrying* . . .

She felt her eyes burn. "Mr Jones . . ."

His smile disappeared and his face turned grim. "It's all right. Don't worry." He looked away, into the corridor. "Zandakar! Come!" His hand beckoned urgently. *"Come."*

Zandakar? What an outlandish name. Who was—

"Oh," she said faintly. "Mr Jones?"

The tallest man she'd ever seen in her life stood in the doorway behind the toymaker. His skin was dark. His head was bald, like a venerable's. His eyes were the most incredible blue, and so exquisitely beautiful she felt her heart thud. *He* was beautiful. He was—he was—

"Zandakar," said Mr Jones, and tugged the man by his plain sleeve into the room. The man Zandakar looked down at him enquiringly but didn't speak. Mr Jones mimed picking something up and holding it like a baby, then pointed.

What? Did he mean *her*? Oh no. Oh no. Oh—

"Forgive me, Your Highness," whispered Mr Jones as the tall dark man Zandakar swept her easily off her feet. "But we really are in a terrible hurry."

"Mr Jones, who *is* this?" she demanded, keeping her voice low.

"It's a long story. I'll explain on the road. He won't hurt you, though. I can promise you that. And he doesn't speak much Ethrean, either. Best let me do the talking." He looked up at the tall man holding her. "Good, Zandakar. Now come."

Cradled against the man's broad chest, feeling his heart thumping steadily beneath her ear, Rhian was surprised by a sensation she'd not experienced for years.

Safe. I feel safe. I don't know this man, and yet . . . I feel safe.

She also felt pain. His strong arms were pressed against her battered back, but that didn't matter. They were getting her out. She'd endure more than this to escape Marlan's clutches.

In silence they made their swift way along the infirmary corridor. As they passed one open door she glanced in, to see Devout Agitha sleeping face-down at a desk. She wanted to ask Mr Jones how exactly he'd accomplished this miracle, but satisfying her curiosity would have to wait.

The corridor they travelled joined with another, running across it. Mr Jones turned left and Zandakar followed. Incredibly, he wasn't even breathing hard. Carrying a strong young woman at a fast walk was no burden to him.

Who is this man? Where does he come from? And what is he doing with Mr Jones?

A door stood open at the end of this corridor. She felt the night air caress her face and caught a glimpse of the moons, half shrouded by cloud. Then they were outside the clerica, on tended lawn. Freedom was only moments away.

Mr Jones touched her shoulder. "Not long now, Your Highness. It's nearly done."

They rounded the corner of the building . . . and came face to face with Helfred, prowling the grounds.

"Your Highness?" said her chaplain, his voice squeaky with shock. The prayer beads he was counting fell from his hands. "What are you *doing*? Who are these *men*?"

It was like being doused with a tubful of iced water. She couldn't speak. Could barely breathe. Mr Jones was silent too, his mouth open, his eyes wide with dismay.

Helfred snatched up his prayer beads then took a step closer. It was hard to see his face clearly in the clerica grounds' guttering torchlight but she could easily imagine the expression her chaplain wore. As she stared, and he stared, she felt a spit of rain on her cheek. A breeze sprang up abruptly, sighing with the cold.

"You're running away," said Helfred. He sounded accusing. "You've found some accomplices and you're *running away*."

She'd have preferred to confront him on her own two feet but she wasn't strong enough to stand, thanks to him and Marlan. There was tension in Zandakar now, she could feel it in his arms, in his whole body. She knew, without being told, without knowing how she knew, that he was poised on the brink of violence. She eased one hand free and pressed her palm to his breast, hoping he'd understand the gesture.

He stared down at her, a question in those amazing eyes. She smiled at him, nodding, and felt a little of the tension leave him. Relieved, she looked at her chaplain.

"Yes, Helfred. I'm running," she said, and was amazed by how calm she sounded. "What choice have you given me, you and your uncle? You're trying to steal the kingdom—my birthright—from me. Worse, you're trying to steal the people's future. If you have your way Ethrea will be plunged into misery. I won't let that happen. I'll fight to prevent it with my dying breath, I swear."

Helfred groaned. "Your Highness—"

"You can let me go, Helfred, or you can stand in my way and pay the price. Your choice."

"You'd accost me?" he demanded. "You'd lay hands on a man of God?"

She met his outrage with leashed fury of her own. "Why not? You laid hands on a queen of Ethrea."

Mr Jones stirred. "Your Highness . . ." His voice was a warning.

She glanced at him. "I know." Then she fixed her gaze on Helfred again. "Make up your mind, Chaplain. And know that God will judge you for your decision."

"God has judged me already, Highness," said Helfred after a short and difficult silence. "I have spent hours praying, and my prayers have been answered."

To her surprise he sounded . . . different. The outrage had left him, and the self-righteous pomposity. Now he seemed resigned. Almost afraid. Or humble.

Helfred, humble? The world must be ending.

"Princess Rhian, I won't stop you from running," her chaplain added. "In fact . . ." He took a deep breath and released it tremulously. "I'm going to run with you."

For a moment she couldn't speak. *"What?"* she said, when her voice returned. *"No.* I don't want you. After I leave here I never want to lay eyes on you again! I *hate* you, Helfred. I *despise* you. I *loathe* you."

"I know you do, Highness," said Helfred simply. "But you also need me."

"*Need* you?" She could've spat. "Helfred, I need *you* like a case of the plague."

"Your *Highness*!" said Mr Jones. "Please! We mustn't linger!"

"Let me come with you," said Helfred, defiant, "or I'll raise the alarm. Then you'll never escape this place, Your Highness. And Marlan will descend on you like the wrath of heaven."

Oh dear *God*. The pustuled slimy little *toad*.

I'll get you for this, Helfred. I swear I'll get you.

"We've no choice, Mr Jones," she said to the toymaker. "Helfred comes with us . . . at least for now."

As the clerica slept behind them they hurried through the darkness and more spitting rain, to the gates of the devouts' house and onto the road.

"Hurry! Hurry!" panted Mr Jones, and broke into a jog-trot. "For all we know someone's woken up by now!" Zandakar loped beside him, untroubled by his burden or the increased speed. Helfred wheezed several paces behind, his sandals slopping on the increasingly wet road.

Rhian bit her lip to stop herself from crying out. There was fire in her flesh, threatening to consume her. As they ran she prayed with all the strength left in her.

God, don't let them catch me. Don't send me back to that place. If you let them catch me I'll never talk to you again.

They ran and ran. A long way down the empty road there was a lane, and a peddler's van. A woman sat in it, leaning forward to greet them in the gloom. "Have you got her, Jones? What *took* you so long?"

"Yes, Ursa, I've got her!" said Mr Jones, almost breathless. "At least Zandakar has."

The woman Ursa rummaged at her feet and held up a small, smoked lamp. The dim light fell over Helfred, bent double and gasping. "*Jones?* Who's *this*?"

"A complication," said Mr Jones, briefly. "Ursa, we have to go."

"Yes, yes," said the woman Ursa. "You get up here and drive the van. The rest of us will climb inside. I hope we can fit. This girl needs physicking or we'll all be in the suds."

This girl. Well. It certainly wasn't a respectful way to describe the Queen of Ethrea. It lacked deference and a recognition of protocol, but somehow it was reassuring. Or perhaps it was the woman's voice that reassured. Tart. Brisk. Used to being obeyed. But with a rough compassion that was of more comfort than the soft-spoken murmurings she'd received in the infirmary.

There was a certain amount of grunting and heaving as Mr Jones clambered up on the van's seat and the woman Ursa clambered down. Rhian felt cool fingers on her cheek, a gentle pressure against the scudding pulse in her throat.

"Don't just stand there, Zandakar!" snapped Ursa. "Get her in the back!"

When Zandakar hesitated, the woman made a hissing sound of impatience, grabbed his rain-dampened sleeve and dragged him along to the rear of the van. There were steps attached there, and two wide half-doors hinged like the doors on a stable. Ursa wrenched them open, stood back and pointed.

"*In!*"

As Zandakar followed the curt instruction Rhian heard Ursa say, just as curtly, "And you, Chaplain Complication! Get in after them. Hurry! Quick!"

Helfred staggered up the steps into the van's cramped, lamplit interior and the woman Ursa leapt up then after him. She was remarkably spry for a woman with so much grey in her hair. Swinging the doors shut, she shouted, "Off you go, Jones! What are you waiting for?"

The van lurched, the wheels creaked, horses' hooves scraped against stone and mud, and they were on the move.

"Right!" said Ursa. "You, chaplain, on the bench there, and I'll thank you to keep quiet even though you're a man of God. If you want to pray on the inside, that'll be fine with me. Zandakar, put the girl down. Last thing I need is for *you* to fall over."

Zandakar fall over? Why would he do that? Rhian stared into his face and saw he hadn't completely understood what the woman Ursa meant. Saw too, for the first time, beneath the man's beauty and realised he'd been gravely ill, not too long ago. She knew the signs, had seen them written on her brothers and her father.

It was a language she'd never forget.

She patted the tall man's chest again. "Zandakar." When he looked down at her she pushed away from him. Wriggled, in what she hoped was some kind of common gesture. He nodded and eased her gently to her feet.

"Good, Zandakar," said the woman Ursa, pointing

to the small space of bench left beside Helfred. "You sit down too. I'll see to the princess."

Helfred looked horrified. Despite the pain and faintness, Rhian felt herself smile. Zandakar was still holding her arm. She looked up at him again, standing hunched and patient beneath the van's low ceiling. "Zandakar. Thank you."

He smiled, so he must know what those words meant. Then he said something in a tongue she'd never heard before. It sounded harsh but oddly compelling. She turned to Ursa.

"Don't ask me," said the woman, shrugging. "We don't even know where he comes from, let alone how to make head-or-tail of his heathen speech."

How extraordinary. "Then—"

"Never mind that," said Ursa. "There's plenty of time ahead of us for questions and answers. Just you come and lie down. Jones said you'd been poorly dealt with and for once I can see he's not letting his rackety imagination run away with him." She shifted her sharp gaze. "Zandakar! Sit!"

If the tall man minded she spoke to him as though he were a dog, he didn't show it. He just nodded and sat beside the appalled, staring Helfred.

"Right," said Ursa. "You sit down too, Your Highness. There."

Guided by the brusque woman's pointing finger Rhian shuffled painfully to the other side of the van, where two sleeping-shelves had been attached to the wall, one above the other. They looked cramped and hardly comfortable. But there was nowhere else to put herself and at any moment she was going to fall flat on her face, so . . .

"What now?" she said faintly.

"Now we undo a little of the damage," said Ursa, then reached out and pulled a curtain, rattling along its rail to shut out the sight of Helfred and Zandakar sitting side by unlikely side. "I'm a physick," she added, rummaging under the bottom sleeping-shelf and pulling out a battered leather bag. "A good one. You needn't fear I'll make matters worse. Just you shrug out of that robe and lie belly-down on the mattress so I can see what mischief you've got yourself in."

"Why are you doing this?" Rhian asked, shedding her clerica clothes with much wincing and hissing.

"Why do you think?" said Ursa, helping her. "You're the Queen of Ethrea and I'm a loyal subject."

"Yes. Of course. I mean, how did you—"

"It doesn't matter," said Ursa. "I told you, didn't I? Questions and answers can wait."

After a lifetime of having every whim obeyed, of being surrounded by bowing, scraping courtiers and servants, it felt most odd to be spoken to like that. Even though her parents had impressed upon her from the time she could talk how important it was not to abuse her position, still . . . she'd never been dealt with so abruptly before. Well, except by Marlan, and even then it was different.

This woman Ursa treats everyone the same. She snaps at Mr Jones, she snaps at Zandakar. She snaps at me, even though I'm her queen and she knows it. It's reassuring. It's honest. I think it means I can trust her.

And in the days to come, trust would be something in short supply.

With a groan partly of pain, and partly relief, she let Ursa help her lie down on the sleeping-shelf. Tried not to groan again as the woman's competent fingers investigated her whip-scored back. There was more pain as a strong-smelling ointment was smeared on her cuts and welts. It stung abominably, far more than the salve Devout Agitha had used. She trapped a whimper in her throat but couldn't stop hot tears escaping her eyes. Her fingers tightened on the thin mattress and her heart thudded hard.

A gentle hand came to rest on her head and began stroking her damp, tangled hair. No-one had stroked her hair like that since her mother, so many years ago when she was still a little girl. The tears came faster, pouring like the rain now drumming on the van's wooden roof.

If Marlan had been kind to her, she might never have stood against him.

"There, there," said Ursa. "Poor child. It's been a hard road and it'll get even harder before it comes to an end. You try to sleep now, Rhian. You're safe with us, at least for now."

She couldn't speak so she nodded, her eyes tightly closed. Ursa's gentle hand kept stroking, stroking.

After a while it lulled her to sleep.

When she woke it was to the sound of a heated discussion. The van had stopped moving but she had no idea if daylight had broken yet or not. Lamplight still danced shadows across the thin curtain drawn across her makeshift bed.

Ursa was saying: "—your decision, Jones, it's mine. *I'm* the physick. You're just the driver. So why don't you drive and leave the physicking to me?"

"But Ursa," Mr Jones protested. "It's not my decision, it's Princess Rhian's. You'll have to wake her so I can—"

"I'm not going to wake her! The poor girl's in desperate need of her rest!"

"All right then, I'll take you closer to Kingseat so it's less distance for you to walk home in the rain," said Mr Jones, being stubborn. "Maybe by that time Rhian will have woken and—"

"I'm awake now, Mr Jones," she said, lifting her head from the pillow.

"There! *Now* see what you've done!" said Ursa, aggravated. The curtain twitched, revealing two inches of cross face. "You've scarcely been asleep for an hour, Your Highness. Never you mind what Jones and I are saying, just you—"

She sat up. "Thank you but no. Mr Jones is right. Any decisions that need to be made here will be made by me. I'd like to know what you're arguing about." She reached to the floor and picked up the rough wool clerica robe, pulled it over her head and rolled a little unsteadily to her feet. Once she was sure of her balance she arranged the robe properly, making sure all her bare skin was covered, then looked at Ursa expectantly.

Ursa's lips pinched in deep disapproval but she shuffled backwards to make some room and pulled the makeshift curtain aside. Beyond it, Helfred and Zandakar still sat on their bench. The dark man's eyes were closed, it seemed he was sleeping. Helfred was squashed in the corner as far away as he could get, a greenish cast to his pasty pimpled face.

"Your chaplain's road-sick," said Ursa, seeing her stare.

"I've given him a lozenge to suck but it doesn't seem to be helping."

I couldn't care less about Helfred's queasy insides.

She nodded. "How were you speaking to Mr Jones?"

Ursa shifted sideways, revealing a little hatch in the van's rear wall. It was open, and Mr Jones was peering worriedly inside. "Your Highness," he said. "I'm so pleased you're awake. Perhaps you can talk some sense into Ursa."

"Jones, she could make it a royal decree and I still wouldn't pay a blind bit of difference," said Ursa. "When it comes to physicking *I'm* the queen here."

Rhian lifted a hand to silence her and looked at Mr Jones. "What's the trouble?"

"Ursa wants to change the plan," he said, plaintive. "She says you're not well enough to travel without a physick attending you. She says Zandakar isn't either, though that's *not* what she said before we left Kingseat."

She looked at Ursa. "So, you want to continue travelling with us?"

"'Want' has nothing to do with it," said Ursa. "This is about 'need'. This kingdom needs a strong queen, a healthy queen, to stand up to those who'd see you stripped of your birthright."

"You could leave your salves and ointments with me," said Mr Jones. "I could—"

"What?" said Ursa, scathing. "Muck about in the back of this van with a half-naked girl young enough to be your daughter who just happens to be the next ruler of Ethrea?"

Even through the little hatch it was easy to see Mr

Jones blush. "Well—well—there's the chaplain there, he could stand as a chaperone! He—"

"Oh no, he couldn't," said Rhian, grimly. "He's a disgrace to the Church. As soon as the matter of my succession is settled I intend to see him stripped of his divinity."

In the corner, Helfred stirred. "You can't," he said feebly. "That's not your prerogative."

She turned on him. "I'll *make* it my prerogative, Helfred! And unless you want me to see you're arrested for gross assault on a royal personage I suggest you shut your mouth *now*."

Helfred subsided, looking greener than ever.

Ursa was staring at her, salt-and-pepper eyebrows raised. "Are you going to tell me I'm wrong, Your Highness?"

More than anything, she wanted to say yes. But she knew she couldn't. It *was* more than just her mistreatment by Marlan and Helfred. She felt fragile. Battered. Grief was an illness, an accumulation of pains. They were lodged deep in her chest, in an aching hollowness of loss. She felt sick with grief. Infected with grief. Prey to the cruel depredations of grief.

There must be a pill she could take for that.

She looked at Mr Jones. "Why are you so set on not letting Ursa come with us?"

"Because it's *dangerous*!" he said, anguished, his face pressed against the hatchway. "You of all people know the men we stand against, Highness. Ursa has devoted her whole life to helping others. She could lose *everything* if this goes wrong."

"So could you, Jones," said Ursa. "Danger doesn't play

favourites. Besides. Who's going to save you from yourself if I don't?"

"Oh . . . well . . ."

Clearly Mr Jones was used to losing arguments with Ursa. Hiding a smile, Rhian turned to consider Zandakar, who was awake again and closely watching. "How sick has he been?"

"Very sick," said Ursa promptly. "Rattling death's doorknocker. It's a miracle the door stayed closed. He's on the mend now, I won't deny it, but that might change. I can't in conscience leave him, Your Highness. Or you. I'd be betraying my physick's oath."

"Well, we can't have that. Mr Jones . . ."

He sighed. "Yes, Your Highness?"

"I'd feel better if Ursa stayed, at least for a while. She's right. I'm not well. And I must *be* well if I'm to triumph over the forces ranged against me."

Another sigh and a slow resigned nod. "Of course, Your Highness. If it's what you want . . ."

"It's what I want for the moment," she said, then looked at Ursa. "But if that should change for any reason I expect you to accede without question. I stand barefoot before you, beaten and laid low, a fugitive in my own realm. But I *am* Ethrea's queen, whether I wear a crown or not. Today you are my royal physick, Ursa. Tomorrow? Who knows?"

Ursa nodded. "Your Highness," she said mildly. "I can live with that."

"Well, if that's how it must be," said Mr Jones, still unhappy, "we should get on our way. I think the nearest river-station to here is—"

"River-station?" said Helfred, rousing. "Where are we going?"

Rhian had to sit again, even her bones were on fire. "North," she said, dropping stiffly to the sleeping-shelf. "To duchy Linfoi and the duke's son Alasdair."

Or he could be the duke by now. His father was as ill as mine when he left . . .

Helfred squawked and flailed to his feet. *"Linfoi?"* he demanded, incredulous. "Princess, are you demented? You would run to Alasdair Linfoi after the council—*your father*—forbade you *expressly* to—"

"Zandakar!" said Mr Jones. *"Wei! Wei!"*

Breathless, Rhian stared at Zandakar. He towered over Helfred, who was forced to his knees with his neck bent impossibly sideways. A fraction more pressure from those dark, steady hands and Helfred's neck would surely snap. Her chaplain was sobbing, his greenish face drained chalky-white. The welt on his cheek burned starkly livid. Zandakar's face was calm, his expression sternly disapproving.

Dear God, who is he?

"Jones, do something!" said Ursa, harshly. Her eyes were wide, her breathing rapid.

"No. I will," said Rhian. She glanced at Mr Jones. "What did you tell him?"

"Wei. It means no." His fingers were bloodless on the edge of the hatchway. "Your Highness . . ."

Though it hurt almost beyond bearing she made herself stand. Reached a hand out to Zandakar and touched his arm. *"Wei,* Zandakar. Let go of him. He can't hurt me. You understand? *Let him go."*

Zandakar looked at her, then took his hands from

Helfred and returned to the bench. Helfred dropped to the floor and curled into himself, gasping. Biting back a groan, she knelt beside him.

"Never raise your voice to me again, Helfred. Your days of authority over me are ended. The council's authority over me is ended. I will travel to duchy Linfoi. I will meet with Alasdair. And after that I'll do what I must to make Ethrea safe from your uncle the prolate and all men of his ilk. Is that clear?"

Helfred nodded. "It's clear, Your Highness." His voice was meagre, a soft puff of sound.

Ursa had to help her back on her feet, then help her some more to lie down again as Mr Jones roused the horses and the van creaked forward again through the night and the rain. Oblivion descended to the sound of the physick and Mr Jones arguing once more, this time about the best road to take them up to the river. As darkness claimed her she thought:

Please, God, don't let them kill each other. I've the feeling I'll need them before I'm done.

CHAPTER EIGHTEEN

Rhian woke to the tantalising aroma and sound of frying sausages. She sat up cautiously, relieved to discover her pains much muted. Peering around the edge of the curtain, she found herself alone within the stationary peddler's van. The top half of its hinged door stood open, letting in shafts of early light and a sense of space unfettered by street or buildings. Voices murmured indistinctly somewhere close by.

Someone had laid out clothes for her at the foot of the sleeping-shelf. Dark blue woollen hose, a heavy green cotton shirt, lighter cotton underthings. Thick woollen socks. A wide brown leather belt and brown leather half-boots. Boys' clothing. A piercing reminder of happier days, and her brothers. But before she could think about making herself presentable she had more urgent matters to consider . . .

Someone, thank God, had left a chamber pot under the sleeping-shelf. She used it hurriedly, in case one of the others returned, then shed her clerica robe and shift and pulled on her new clothes. They fit remarkably well. Her hair was a disaster but she couldn't see a brush or comb anywhere. Ah, well.

No-one noticed her standing on the van's top step. She looked around, breathing in the fresh air. They were in a lush field, near a trickle of stream. The unhitched horses had been safely hobbled and were snatching enormous mouthfuls of grass. It seemed as though the rain had passed. The few patches of cloud in the sky were high and filmy, blowing west. Birds sang lustily in the field's lone oak tree. Early bluebells added colour to the peaceful scene.

Her unlikely travelling companions were all accounted for. Mr Jones cooked the sausages over a small fire ringed with stones. Ursa had the contents of her physicker's bag spread on a cloth before her and was closely inspecting them. At a small distance Helfred was on his knees, oblivious to the wet grass, his back to the others and his head bowed low in prayer. She could hear his prayer beads clicking. And at another distance was the foreigner, Zandakar.

"Mr Jones?" she said, her gaze fixed on the stranger. "What is he doing?"

"Highness!" He scrambled to his feet. "You're awake."

She rolled her eyes. "Obviously."

He came forward to help her down the van's steps but she waved his hand away, still looking at Zandakar. Rebuffed, he looked too.

"He calls them *hotas,* Highness."

Memory assaulted her. *Helfred on his knees, neck bent, one heartbeat away from a broken neck and death. Zandakar standing over him, unmoved.*

"Who is he, Mr Jones?"

"A friend."

She spared him a pointed glance. "Who speaks hardly any Ethrean, looks like no man I've ever seen and who, on the surface at least, doesn't seem quite *safe.* How well do you know him?"

An uncomfortable silence. "Your Highness, do you trust me?" said Mr Jones, at last.

Dear God. *What have I stumbled into?* But she'd come this far on faith and hope . . . "Would I be here if I didn't?"

"Then—if I said he was needed, no matter how strange he might appear?"

"Does that mean you trust him?"

"Highness!" Mr Jones sounded shocked, and hurt. "Would I let him so close to you if I thought he'd do harm?"

The graceful dark man leaping and spinning across the green grass was naked to the waist, his skin terribly marked with fresh scars and old ones. They suggested a barbaric past. Violence and suffering on a scale she'd never known.

"He seemed willing enough to harm Helfred, last night."

"He thought Helfred was a danger. He wanted to protect you."

She felt her lips curve into a smile. "Yes. He did."

"*Is* Helfred a danger?"

"I doubt it," she said, dragging her gaze away from the lithe, fluid Zandakar to consider her praying chaplain. "Not so long as we keep him close-watched."

"I'll do that," said Mr Jones. "He'll not betray us."

But could the same be said of his strange friend? "So you vouch for Zandakar?"

He nodded. "Highness, I do."

"Very well." She took a deep breath and considered again the morning's restful beauty. "Mr Jones, I don't wish to sound ungrateful but this all seems terribly . . . *relaxed* . . . to me. I thought running away would have a greater sense of urgency."

Mr Jones shrugged. "The horses can't keep going forever, Highness. And neither can we."

She looked at him more closely, and felt a sudden pang of remorse. After a long night of driving he was clearly weary to the bone. He still wore the same clothes, rumpled and grass-stained now about the knees. His hair was a bird's-nest, his beard sadly in need of comb and scissors.

"No. Of course not," she said, gently. "Have you had any rest, Mr Jones?"

"Never mind about me, Highness. How are *you* feeling?"

Lost. Adrift. Overwhelmed. Uncertain. "I'm fine. Where are we?"

"A little ways past a village called Finchbreak. A good lot of miles away from Todding and the clerica."

"But still in duchy Kingseat. If only just. Whose field is this?"

"I don't know, Highness," he said, shaking his head. "But the gate stood wide and there are no animals pastured here. If someone comes to enquire we can pay them a few piggets, or move along if they insist."

"Yes. We mustn't cause trouble. So you have money with you, Mr Jones?"

"Of course."

She felt her face heat. *I've never carried money. People just give me things ... or they appear when I need them, as if by magic.* She'd never thought about it before. Never had to. *Does that make me spoilt? I think it does. How ... uncomfortable.* "I have no money, Mr Jones."

He smiled. "I know. Not to worry, Highness."

Yes, but I do worry. "Mr Jones, you are not the Royal Treasury."

"He is today," said Ursa, looking up at last. "Jones, aren't those sausages cooked yet?"

"Cooked enough, I expect," he said cheerfully. "And the tea's brewed too."

"Then we'll eat," said Ursa. "And then we'll decide what to do next. The princess is right, we must get a move on."

Rhian frowned. If she wasn't careful this masterful woman would take over completely. "I told you last night what we're doing next. We're going to duchy Linfoi." And before the physick could say something argumentative she marched over to Helfred, who was still on his knees. "Chaplain. Breakfast."

Helfred's lips stopped moving. He opened his eyes. "Thank you, no. I am fasting, Highness. A penance for my soul."

"You can't fast, Helfred. You're going to need all your strength on this journey."

His complexion was still pasty, his chin richly pimpled. The whip-cut on his cheek had been daubed with green ointment. Without his customary air of self-assured condescension he seemed strangely younger. "I must."

"You can't," she insisted. "You're going to have to do your fair share of the work. Driving the van, grooming the horses, cleaning their harness—"

"What?" he said, and for a moment was his old self again. "I am a chaplain, I don't—"

"Helfred, you'll do what I tell you," she said, leaning close. "Give me any trouble and I'll bind you and gag you and tie you to the van's roof."

His eyes widened. "You *wouldn't*."

"Try me," she said, and stepped back. "Now come and eat breakfast with us. I won't invite you again."

He wasn't a stupid man. He stood and stalked over to Mr Jones and Ursa, who were organising plates and a canvas cloth for them to sit on while they ate.

Feeling suddenly shy, she approached Zandakar, who paid no attention to anything save the rhythms of his mysterious *hotas*. A faint sheen of sweat glistened on his face and scarred chest. His eyes were closed, his expression serene.

"Zandakar," she said softly. "Zandakar, breakfast."

He kept on dancing, spinning in place with one knee raised, one arm straight above his head, the other bent, fingers extended as though poised to strike.

"Zandakar."

This time he heard her. His eyes opened. He stopped spinning in a heartbeat to stand tall and still and lightly breathing. His physical control was complete. Absolute. He inclined his head, briefly.

"Rhian."

"Breakfast," she said again, heart pounding beneath her borrowed cotton shirt. "You understand?"

He smiled. *"Zho."*

Dear God, scarred or not the man was shockingly handsome. Who *was* he? What was he *doing* here? It was a mystery she would solve, sooner or later. She beckoned. "Come, then. Come and eat."

There was bread to go with the sausages, and a crock of butter. Honey for the tea and a splash of milk.

"Not that it'll go far with two extra mouths to feed," said Ursa. "And I know I'm one of them. I'm just saying. We'll have to tighten our belts between here and Linfoi."

Rhian nodded. "But not for long. It's quite a fast trip by river-barge."

"True," said Ursa. "And the sooner we make it the sooner we'll be home again with this rumpty-tumpty put behind us. But before we tidy ourselves up and head for the nearest river-station there's the small matter of appearances to deal with."

"Appearances, Ursa?" said Mr Jones, around a mouthful of sausage.

"Yes. We have to change them as much as we're able.

Hair's got to come off, and beards too. There'll be eyes out looking for us soon, if they're not looking already. We've got to do our best to fool them."

Mr Jones swallowed. "My beard? But Ursa, I've worn my beard for nearly twenty-five years!"

"Exactly! Shave it off and cut that mop of hair close to your skull, I doubt even Hettie would recognise you, Jones." Ursa turned. "And we'll have to get rid of your fine tresses too, Your Highness. Pity you're not a blonde. If you were I could dye your hair dark to boot. But I've no hope of dying that black hair gold. As for you, Chaplain Helfred—"

Helfred, who'd barely touched his food, shrank from her. "Out of the question. You cannot—"

"Oh, but I can," said Ursa, grey eyes glinting with a touch of ice. "For a start I can get you out of that habit. Last thing we need to do is advertise we've got a man of God in the van. Peddlers don't traipse about the country-side with their own personal chaplain. So it's into plain clothes for you. And while I've got the shears and razor out I should probably—"

"No!" said Helfred. "You cannot take my hair, woman. Only venerables bare their skulls to God. I am not a venerable, I will not smirch the—"

Ursa bared her teeth. "You've already smirched, Chaplain. You used God to intimidate a young girl in your charge. So we'll hear no more of *smirching* from you. But since you are a man of God I'll just cut your hair short like Jones."

Helfred still looked appalled. Rhian sighed. "Stop being precious, Helfred. It's only hair. It'll grow again."

"You do not understand," said Helfred, in a low voice.

"I understand completely," she contradicted. "I just don't care. And finish your breakfast! Unless you want me to have Zandakar hold you down so I can force it down your throat?"

At the sound of his name, Zandakar looked at her enquiringly. Helfred stared at him, eyes popping. "This heathen? You'd allow this—this—"

"Helfred, I'd *help* him."

"But he's a *heathen*!" Helfred protested. "He's barely civilised, he speaks almost no Ethrean! Your *Highness* . . ." Amazingly, words seemed to fail him.

On the brink of commanding Helfred to choke on his own tongue she stopped, and smiled. *Now, that's a good idea . . .* She turned to Mr Jones. "I think I know what to do with Helfred."

"Yes?" said Mr Jones. He was still fingering his riotous beard, his expression mournful.

"Whatever else he might be he's a well-educated scholar. He can teach Zandakar to speak fluent Ethrean, far more swiftly than the rest of us combined. He might even be able to teach him to write it a little. If that would be helpful. Would it?"

Mr Jones laughed. "I think that's a fine idea, Your Highness. They can sit all nice and inconspicuous in the van while you, me and Ursa ride up on the seat. Nobody need ever know they're travelling with us."

"Which *is* a good idea," Ursa added. "Because the further north we go the harder it's going to be, explaining away a big bald dark-skinned man who looks like he could break any one of us in half without blinking."

Silence, as they all considered Zandakar.

"Yes," said Mr Jones. "It's a very good idea. Provided

it's just everyday Ethrean and not scripture. There's no need to confuse the man. Chaplain?"

Helfred swallowed. "I suppose it's better than grooming the horses." He sounded surly. Looked sulky.

"No, that'll be Her Highness' task," said Ursa. "Grooming, feeding, taking care of the harness. And cooking our meals too. Cleaning up after. I doubt anyone'll look twice at a roustabout young lass with dirt on her face and under her fingernails."

She snorted. "They will if you keep on calling me 'Your Highness'. Best you all start calling me by some other name."

"Such as?"

"Becky," she said, after a moment. "And Mr Jones is Pa. And you're Tant, Pa's older sister. A peddling family on its way north, minding its own business and finding no trouble. That'll be us when we're with other folk. Agreed?"

"Agreed," said Mr Jones. "Now let's get ourselves clipped and shaved and dressed how we should be. We need to be on the road before someone stumbles over us."

Marlan sat behind his library desk, fingers steepled before him, and stared at Dame Cecily in blank astonishment.

"The princess is *gone*? What are you saying, Dame? How can she be *gone*?"

Dame Cecily's cheeks were parchment pale. Her rich overdress was travel-stained, her habitual air of calm authority stripped away by this calamity.

I will strip her of more than that before I'm done with her!

"Well, woman? *Answer me!* How can Princess Rhian be gone from your clerica?"

"Eminence, I am at a loss to explain what's happened," said the dame, her gaze downcast. "When the clerica retired after supper last evening she was in the infirmary, recovering from her chastisement. The night passed without event. When we woke for dawn Litany she was . . . gone." Her hands clasped each other tightly. "And so was her chaplain. Your nephew. Helfred."

Helfred? "That is not possible."

Dame Cecily looked up. Was that a gleam of malice in her eyes? "Eminence, I am accustomed to telling the truth. Chaplain Helfred is nowhere in the clerica. We have searched the grounds and buildings to the last half-inch. He is not in residence. He and the princess absconded through the night."

Yes. Malice in her eyes, a faint triumph in her voice. *She thinks to escape punishment because Helfred is somehow involved. She is mistaken . . . but that can wait.* "What happened yesterday? What untoward events occurred that might help to explain this mystery?"

"Nothing, Eminence."

"No strangers loitering at the gates? None of the dukes' men come to press their suit again?" Because he wouldn't put it past them. They were venal, snatching men.

"No, Eminence."

"*Nothing* beyond what you were expecting?"

Dame Cecily shook her head. "No, Prolate Marlan. Only a brief visit from a childhood friend. She desired some rare physicking herbs from our gardens. She ate supper with me and left soon after."

A childhood friend? That meant the woman was old. Old women were not his concern. "No other visitors?"

"No, Your Eminence."

He leaned forward. "Are you *quite* certain? Dame Cecily, you cannot hope to save yourself from retribution. The girl was in your care and you have failed to keep her. If there is something more to tell, then tell it. Mincing words now is pointless."

"I mince nothing, Prolate," said Dame Cecily, stung. The malice was gone, replaced by fear. "I am as eager to learn where she is as you are."

I doubt that. "And tell me, Dame, how did the princess spirit herself away? On foot? On horseback? Did she take a clerica cart?"

"They left on foot, I think. No horse or mule or cart is missing."

They. *Helfred, when I find you . . .* "In which case she cannot have travelled far." He unsteepled his fingers and laid his palms flat to the desk. "You did right in coming to tell me yourself," he said, his voice cool and even. "Return to the clerica. You and your devouts are henceforth under Writ of Seclusion. Until I have lifted it, *personally* lifted it, you will admit no visitor save myself to the clerica grounds. You will speak of this matter to no-one save myself. You will not set foot past the clerica gates unless you are summoned by my express wish. Disobedience will be met with dire consequences."

The dame curtsied. "Yes, Your Eminence."

"You are dismissed." He permitted himself a cold, cruel smile. "When this matter is dealt with I will turn my attention to your punishment, Dame Cecily. Until then I suggest you and your devouts make prayer your life."

"Eminence," the dame whispered, and wisely withdrew from his sight.

When he was alone and did not need to guard himself, he released his rage in a shout and pounded his fists on his desk.

Gone? The bitch is gone and Helfred with her? What mischief is this? Who is responsible?

Someone had to be responsible. The girl wasn't able to do this alone. One of the councillors was involved, he was sure of it. During a visit to the clerica a plot had been hatched. Rhian and one of the poppycock dukes' men, huddled together scheming against him.

I curse their black souls. I will see them pay.

But how to deal with this? If he called a council meeting, if he let them know Rhian was gone . . . Imagining the furore that would erupt, he shuddered. No. Impossible. This news must be kept secret from the council. He would find Rhian and Helfred too. Return them to the clerica and act as though nothing had happened.

And I will make them regret the day they were born. Them, and the councillor who would dare cross my purpose. Do they take me for a fool, these pathetic dukes' men?

Breathing heavily, he yanked on the bell rope beside his desk. A moment later Ven'Martin opened the door and slipped inside.

"Prolate?"

Martin was his man through and through. Reliable, dependable and utterly discreet. He could trust Ven'Martin as he trusted himself. Even his firebrand piety was useful, when properly guided. "Get word to our chaplains in the councillors' establishments, Martin. They must increase their vigilance for any whisper of . . . unusual occurrences. And send for Commander Idson."

The other thing that made Martin invaluable was his lack of curiosity. He nodded. "Eminence."

The door closed behind him. Marlan pushed away from his desk and moved to the window, to glare into the wide world where Rhian and Helfred now hid. The sun was on the point of tipping towards the horizon. The day slipped away . . .

I expect nothing but treachery from Eberg's bitch of a daughter. But how could Helfred betray me? My own flesh and blood. After the advantages I have pressed upon him . . .

Unless there had been no betrayal. His disappearance could be foul play. He could be in a ditch, somewhere, beaten. Or dead.

If harm has come to you, Helfred, woe betide the miscreant responsible. But if it has not. If you left the clerica willingly. If you have truly betrayed me . . . there is nowhere in the world you can safely hide.

Kingseat Garrison Commander Idson arrived some twenty minutes later. By international treaty Ethrea had no standing army or navy but that didn't mean it lacked the means to discipline itself. Each duchy had its own small force of arms, sufficient to patrol its section of the island's encompassing wall and keep the peace when tempers ran high and foolish citizens failed to heed Ethrean Church and Crown law.

"Eminence," said Idson, with suitable obeisance.

Marlan sat at his desk again and kept the man standing. "What I am about to tell you is a state secret. On peril of your life and your soul's damnation you will not repeat it to *anyone,* not even a duke's man or his sworn representative. Is that understood?"

Eyes wide, Idson nodded. Short and broad, he wore his command sash and uniform with ease. "Eminence."

"Princess Rhian has been taken from the clerica at Todding where she was in retreat. You and a handpicked band of guards, no more than five of your most trusted men, must find her. You're looking for a small group of people travelling without fanfare. Doubtless hastily disguised. The princess, perhaps one or two other men, and possibly a chaplain."

"A chaplain?" said Idson, startled out of his horrified silence. "You think she was stolen by *Ethreans,* Your Eminence? Not by a foreigner seeking to take advantage of the king's recent death?"

"No foreign power would risk breaking any treaties. This is a domestic matter, Idson," he said, impatient. "And its politics are none of your concern. Now be gone. Start your search at the river-station nearest to the clerica. Wherever the princess is headed, the fastest and most direct route is by river-barge, at least at first. Go about your business circumspectly and *find* her, Commander. Before sunset would be preferable."

"Yes, Eminence," said Idson, but he hesitated. "As Kingseat's garrison commander I have jurisdiction along the length of the river. But if she's been taken into one of the other duchies where I hold no authority . . ."

It was a good point. Marlan rummaged in a drawer and withdrew one of his gold seals. "Here," he said, tossing it to Idson. "That will silence any obstinate objectors." At least temporarily. Long enough to achieve his ends.

The commander slipped the seal into a pocket. "Eminence. Rest easy, I'll have her home before supper."

He raised his eyebrows. "See that you do, Idson. The kingdom's welfare depends on it."

Alone again, Marlan paced his library and wrestled with the urge to fling himself upon a horse and gallop madly about the countryside searching for Rhian and his nephew.

I can hold off the dukes' men for a week, perhaps two. But the councillors are right about one thing, damn their eyes: the foreign ambassadors are like underfed dogs, and none more slavering than the men of Harbisland, Arbenia and Tzhung-tzhungchai. I will see them again next Grand Litany in the High Church. Twelve days. If I cannot produce the little bitch for them then . . .

He felt his stomach turn over.

I will have her by then. I will. I must.

For the hundredth time since driving away from the field in Finchbreak, Dexterity fingered his naked chin. His face felt so *wrong* without its beard. And his head felt cold, even in the warm spring sunshine, so closely had Ursa cropped it. He was practically *bald*.

"Stop fretting, Jones," said Ursa, riding on the driving seat beside him. "It'll grow back by and by. And you have to admit, not a soul in your street would recognise you if they could see you now."

He grunted. "I know." He'd nearly fallen over when he'd looked at himself in the hand-mirror Ursa had brought. So many years since he'd seen himself beardless. How disconcerting, to be surprised by his own reflection.

As though I were another man entirely. And perhaps I

am. The Dexterity Jones I know would never be found on
the road in a peddler's van with a chaplain, a freed slave
and a runaway princess hiding in the back.

He glanced at Ursa. "I'm not sure you should've slipped
that sleeping potion into Rhian's tea."

"I am," she said. "Are you blind, Jones, to see how
she's exhausted? Running on raw nerves? Beaten down,
not just by the prolate and the council but by life? The
poor lass needs all the sleep she can get. Rollin himself
knows she'll have precious little rest once she reaches
Linfoi. I say let her sleep all day every day between now
and then if she needs to."

He nodded. She was right again. *Poor Rhian. Poor*
child. Will she ever be strong enough to face what awaits
her?

The Kingseat countryside unrolled around them,
green fields and hedgerows and overhead the wide blue
sky. After the night's rain the air smelled washed clean.
Behind, in the van, the sound of muffled voices as reluctant Helfred led obliging Zandakar in a language lesson.
The brown cobs, friendly beasts with strong legs and stout
hearts, flicked their ears and didn't seem unduly burdened
by the weight of the van. Dexterity stared at their broad
rumps and brooded.

"Ursa . . ." he said eventually, sliding his stare sideways. "Why did you change your mind and come? I'd
convinced myself I'd have to rescue Rhian without you."

Ursa rubbed her nose and rested her grey gaze on
the flitting birds in the hedgerows. "Why does it matter,
Jones? I came."

A loaded hay cart was approaching. Dexterity guided
the brown horses hard against the left-hand hedgerow and

tipped his head to the carter, who sang out *Good morning* but didn't slow his draughthorse's plodding pace.

"I'd like to know," he said, when the hay cart was safely behind them. His heart thudded. "Was it—was it Hettie?"

"No. I've not seen or spoken to Hettie since the day she died."

"Then *why*?"

Ursa's fingers scrubbed at a stain on her old woollen skirt. "Jones . . ."

She was blushing. She *never* blushed. "*Please,* Ursa. *Tell* me."

"I couldn't abandon you," she muttered. "I couldn't let you do this on your own."

"Because I'm a dreamer?" he said, stung. *When will she stop treating me as though I were daft?* "Because you can't trust me out of your sight?"

"No!" she said, goaded. "Because I owe you a *debt,* Jones, and here's my chance to pay it back! God knows I've waited long enough."

A debt? What debt? Then he realised. "Oh, Ursa. *No.* It wasn't your fault. You did everything in your power to save her."

She stared hard at the passing countryside. "It wasn't enough, though. Your wife still died."

"Not because of *you.* You were wonderful. She couldn't have had a more devoted physick. Anyone would've thought she was your own flesh and blood."

Ursa sniffed. "If only she'd asked for help sooner. If I'd had more *time* . . ."

"Don't," he said, and covered her hand with his.

"What's done is done and you owe me nothing. I'm just glad you're here. I'm glad I don't have to do this alone."

"Alone?" She managed a watery chuckle. "Jones, have you counted how many we've got in the back of this van?"

"You know what I mean." He tightened his fingers, surprised she hadn't pulled away. "Ursa . . . I'm sorry for the trouble your friend will face because we've spirited away Princess Rhian."

"Cecily?" Her voice was cold. "Don't waste pity on her. She had no business conniving with Marlan the way she did. Standing by and letting him abuse the girl like that. That's not the behaviour of a God-guided woman. I don't know who Cecie is now if she could do that."

Beneath the habitual briskness, a strong thread of pain. "Perhaps she was only obeying the prolate," he said gently. "He's a powerful man and she answers to him."

"He's supposed to be a man of God," said Ursa, almost to herself. "But what man of God beats a young girl senseless to make her marry where he'd have her wed, claiming all the while he does God's will? That's not the God I grew up worshipping, Jones."

He'd never heard her sound so lost. Poor Ursa. Her life was turned upside down now, just like his. Time to distract her from unhappy thoughts . . .

"Do you know I've not the first idea of where we are?" he said. "You're the one who knows duchy Kingseat's countryside like the back of your hand. How far away is the river-station at Grumley?"

She gave him a look. "Jones, you're *hopeless*."

"I know," he said, and swallowed a smile.

"We've been on the road an hour, give or take," she

said briskly. "Another half-hour will see us at Lower Grumley. Grumley proper and the river-station lie a half-hour or so beyond that. But I've been thinking. It might serve us better not to take a barge at Grumley, but travel on to Pipslock instead."

"You think Grumley's too quiet?"

"I think Pipslock is a conveniently bustling place. Less chance of us being noticed in a station where so many barges and wagons and travellers abound. Not that I think we're anything to notice," she added. "Just one more peddler family eking a livelihood on the highways and byways of jolly old Ethrea. But why stick out like a sore thumb when we don't have to? That's what I'm thinking, Jones. What do you think?"

He pretended to have a spasm. "You're asking me? Not telling me? Ursa, are you feeling well? Perhaps *you're* touched with a fever!"

She swatted him. "You're only half as funny as you think you are, Jones. I hope you know that."

"I know you think so," he said, grinning, then considered her suggestion. "I suppose it's better to be safe than sorry. Even though I'll be nervous as a cat in a roomful of rocking chairs until we're safely on the river. All right. We'll travel to Pipslock. I hope you know the way."

"Of course," said Ursa, scornful. "We'll get there just on sunset. Another good reason to take that road. We'll be even less noticeable on a barge at night while we're still so close to Kingseat capital."

And that was a good thing, he had no doubt.

Please, Hettie. If you're listening. Don't let us be noticed. Let us get away unseen.

CHAPTER NINETEEN

There were Kingseat guards at Pipslock river-station.

Rhian took one look at them through the little hatch behind the driver's seat and sucked in a sharp breath.

"The man in charge? That's Commander Idson," she hissed. "He's garrison leader of the whole Kingseat guard. Damn. The man's like a terrier on the scent of a rat. If he even *suspects* I'm here . . ."

Dexterity sighed. *Hettie, Hettie, I asked for your help.* The guards, led by this Idson fellow, were questioning the folk who'd passed through the river-station barrier and were waiting for clearance to load onto the next waiting barge. They were inspecting the carts, wagons and carriages too. They didn't seem rude, just briskly determined. The many lamps lit to hold back dusk's shadows threw their sharp faces into relief.

"But does he suspect it?" he said, hoping against hope. "Maybe he's not looking for you at all. It could be some other matter that's brought him to Pipslock."

Ursa snorted. "And if you believe that, Jones, I've some swampland going cheap to sell you." She shook her head. "It doesn't matter anyway. Even if he's not looking for our runaway princess, if we join the line to get onto a barge here he's going to poke his nose into the back of this van and see her. Even with her hair cut off and dressed like a lad he'll know who she is. She's not safe from being recognised till we're out of this duchy."

Dexterity glanced over his shoulder at Rhian's frowning face, framed in the hatchway. "If Idson and his men are after you, Highness, who's sent them, do you think?"

"Marlan. The clerica will have got word to him once they realised I was missing."

He looked again at the garrison guards. "There aren't very many of them. If the prolate really is searching for you, surely—"

"No," said Rhian. "Marlan won't want to raise any public alarm. He can't afford the council discovering he's lost me. If he can find me quickly and spirit me back to the clerica with no-one the wiser . . . Mr Jones, we can't stay here. We have to move on."

Their van was halted on the side of the road, just before the sloping side-street that led down to the Pipslock river-station where the bustle and disruption of the unexpected inspections kept everyone preoccupied.

But anonymity wouldn't last forever. Once the final cart was inspected and passed onto the waiting barge, the guards would notice the peddler's van at the top of the street . . .

"You're right," said Dexterity, picking up the reins. He looked at Ursa. "Perhaps if we take a barge from Grumley after all? Surely they've already been to Grumley."

"No," said Rhian, before Ursa could answer. "Grumley's behind us. We have to move *forwards*. I must reach duchy Linfoi as soon as possible."

"Your Highness," he began, but she cut him off with a hard slap of her hand against the wooden wall between them.

"*No*, Mr Jones! You rescued me and I'm grateful but don't let it go to your head. I'm not asking for your advice or permission. I'm your queen and I'm telling you plainly, *we don't turn back*."

"She's right, Jones," said Ursa, softly. "The sooner we get out of Kingseat the better. It may slow us down a bit, travelling by road for a while, but better that than ending up in Commander Idson's custody. If we stay on the byroads, keep away from the towns, we can higgledy-piggledy across country into duchy Meercheq and keep on moving north until Idson loses heart along the river. Then we can get a barge. At Chaffing, if we've reached that far. Or maybe Rippington. That's a plan as should keep us out of trouble."

"Yes," said Rhian. "Idson might be able to throw his weight around along the river but he has no authority to hunt for us in Meercheq itself. In *any* duchy. To get it he'll have to ask permission from the duke in question and that'll mean awkward explanations. By the time Marlan's forced to that point I should be safely in duchy Linfoi. Now let's get out of here before someone thinks to ask why we're loitering."

Dexterity roused the brown cobs and eased the van back onto Pipslock's torchlit main street. Dusk was surrendering to the onset of night, and the last shops were closing their doors and shuttering their windows. Lamps bloomed into life behind curtains in the dwellings above. Townsfolk hurried home along the sidewalks, laughing and chattering in pairs or groups, and silently alone.

Nobody bothered to wonder about a single peddler's van, drawn by plain brown horses clip-clopping on the cobbles.

As they reached the end of Pipslock's main thoroughfare and came upon the open countryside beyond the small township, Dexterity glanced behind him at Rhian's hatch-framed face, exchanged a look with Ursa, then voiced what he knew they'd both been mulling over.

"You seem to be placing an awful lot of faith in Linfoi's duke, Highness."

"Not its duke," she said, her voice distant and calm now. "The duke's son. Alasdair. We're friends. He'll help me."

"You're sure of that?"

"Of course," she said, and slammed the little hatch shut between them. A heartbeat later it opened again, and she added, "As sure as you are of Ursa's help, Mr Jones. And by the way . . ." Her voice had dropped several chilly degrees. "Drug me again without my knowledge or permission, Ursa, and when this is over you and I will have *words*."

The hatch shut again, just as firmly.

Dexterity winced. Oh dear. "I'm sure she didn't mean it. She's just feeling disappointed and upset. The sight of those Kingseat guards. They'd put anyone off."

Ursa snorted. "Of course she meant it, Jones. Didn't you hear her? She's the *queen*. Or she will be, provided we can get her to duchy Linfoi in one piece and this friend of hers can perform some kind of miracle that'll get her crowned and on the throne despite the opposition of both council and Church."

That made him stare. In the wagon's burning torchlight, Ursa's face was flickered with doubt. "You don't think we can do this?"

"I don't know, Jones." She sounded tired. "What I do

know is I *don't* like to think about what she's up against. What *we're* up against. Gives me the heebies."

Shaken, he looked back to the road. "Hettie said—"

"A lot of things, apparently. But not a word about how we're going to *win*." She sniffed. "When are you going to tell Rhian, anyway?"

"About Hettie?" He shook his head. "I don't think that's wise, Ursa. She's wound tightly enough as it is."

"You'll have to sooner or later. When she asks you how you know what you know. And she will. You'll have to tell her about Zandakar, too."

"I'm hoping Zandakar can tell us about himself. Provided that wretched chaplain really can teach him to speak Ethrean properly."

"Hmmph," said Ursa, and folded her arms. "I think he can, Jones. He seems powerfully motivated *not* to touch the horses. I just wonder . . ." Her voice trailed away.

"Wonder what?"

"What kind of story Zandakar has to tell," she murmured. "Because you know what they say, Jones. Curiosity killed the cat."

Yes, they did say that. It was most disconcerting. "Ursa, where should we head now? This road out of Pipslock, where will it take us?"

"To the river-station at Jabsford, which straddles the duchy line with Meercheq and Morvell. We don't want to go anywhere near it. We'll turn off before then and head towards Foscote."

She never ceased to amaze him. "How is it you know so many places?"

"Because I'm an old wicked woman, Jones. And when I was young no matter how hard I scratched my itchy feet they wouldn't let me stay in one place for long." She closed her eyes then, which meant she didn't want to talk any more.

He took the hint and kept on driving.

Some two hours after turning at the sign for Foscote he'd had enough of travelling and so had the horses. He'd found water for them at a carters' stop an hour ago but they were tired and hungry, their heads drooping, ears flat. He guided them off the wide country road, down a rutted laneway with verges broad enough to hold the van and the tethered cobs.

I'll have to buy more oats for them, next village we come to. And supplies for us too. It's bread and cheese for supper tonight.

After settling the horses he joined the others. It was too dark to find wood for starting a fire, so they were crammed into the back of the van. A single lamp burned, they were saving the lamp oil, and Chaplain Helfred's face was a shadowed patchwork of discontent.

"No decent hot food?" he demanded as Ursa handed him his share of the night's meagre meal. "How is a man meant to live on such pitiful rations?"

"Hold your tongue, Helfred," said Rhian, tearing her bread into small, crumby pieces. "At least it's something to put in your belly."

He glowered at her. "This was a mistake. After sober consideration I've decided it's wrong for us to travel any further. If we repent now, God will forgive us."

Rhian swallowed a mouthful of cheese. "Your uncle won't."

"Prolate Marlan—"

"Is a power-hungry despot. You're wasting your breath, Helfred. We're not going back."

Helfred put his plate aside. "You cannot keep me here against my will! That would be kidnapping a man of God! Your soul will be blackened beyond redemption if you don't release me!"

Rhian seared him with a look of contempt. "Release you? So you can run squealing back to Kingseat, make things up with your uncle and tell him my plans and where we are?" She dusted her hands together. "I don't think so."

"Princess Rhian—"

Cross-legged on the floor, with his back to the hinged doors, Zandakar lifted his head at the new tone in Helfred's voice. Dexterity held his breath. The look in the dark man's eyes was frightening. Cold and pitiless, it was like staring into the face of death.

"No, Zandakar," said Rhian, her hand raised. "Helfred can't hurt me."

Zandakar frowned. "Rhian is all right?"

She smiled at him, her cheeks tinted delicately pink. "I'm fine."

Dexterity cleared his throat. He didn't dare look at Ursa, but knew they shared the same thought: *Oh dear.*

"Chaplain, this isn't easy for any of us," said Ursa briskly. "But Princess Rhian is right. You can't change your mind now. If it's any consolation we'll make sure to tell the prolate you were kept against your will, should the need arise."

Helfred's back was pressed so hard against the wooden wall his shoulder blades were in danger of cracking. Ignoring Ursa, he pointed a shaking finger at Zandakar.

"He wants to *kill* me! That heathen has *murder* in his heart!"

"Oh, don't be ridiculous," snapped Rhian. "He just doesn't like it when you raise your voice to me." She gifted Zandakar with another radiant smile. "And I appreciate it. He's a heathen foreigner who hardly speaks my language and he has more respect for me than one of my own subjects." Her smile vanished. "How do you think that makes me feel, Helfred?"

Helfred shook his head. "You're a fool to trust him. All of you, fools. There's a malevolence in him. Can't you feel it? Are you all so blind?"

"Oh, Helfred," said Rhian, breaking the tautly uncomfortable silence. "You do make me tired. Another word out of you and I'll push a sock in your mouth."

"Now, Highness," said Ursa, reproving. "He's your chaplain. A man of God. And until God discards him you'd be wise to remember that."

Rhian flushed again, but not with pleasure. "You take it upon yourself to task me?"

"Please!" Dexterity said, lifting both hands placatingly. "Everyone! It's late, and we've had a very trying day. Let's not say or do anything we can't mend. I'm going to check the horses, and then I think we should all just . . . go to sleep."

No-one disagreed with him.

By virtue of rank and age, Rhian and Ursa had been granted the two sleeping-shelves. Dexterity left them rummaging about behind their curtain while Helfred and Zandakar eyed each other warily and cleared space on the floor. Carrying a second lamp, he went out to make sure the horses weren't tangled in their tether lines. They were fine, dozing hipshot and not pleased to be woken. He patted them briefly then took advantage of the moment to relieve himself against a handy tree.

"Dexie," said Hettie, appearing without warning beside him.

"Hettie!" His heart was threatening to pound through his chest. "Do you mind? I nearly had a nasty accident, then!"

She glowed in the lamplight, dressed in pink. "I don't have long, Dex. Let me speak, quickly."

He pulled a face as he rearranged his clothing. "You never have long, Hettie. Where do you rush to? What's more important than telling me what's going on?"

Her smile was full of sorrow. "I can't explain that. I don't have time."

He felt a prickle of temper. "Hettie, you're asking a great deal of—"

"I know I am. Now hush. I've come to let you know you're not forgotten. And to tell you not to travel north by river. It's too risky. You'll be discovered if you get on a barge."

"But Hettie, it'll take us *days* if we go by road. We don't have days."

"You'll have the number of days that you need," she said. "That much I can promise. And there are things that must happen while you're on the road."

He stared. "What things? *Hettie*—"

But she was gone again.

"This is *ridiculous*," he grumbled, snatching up the lamp. Holding it high, he threw the light in a circle as far it could reach. "Hettie, come back here! Hettie, I need *answers*!"

She didn't return. The brown cobs stared at him in amazement, eyes liquid in the lamplight, nostrils flared wide, ears sharply pricked.

"Oh, *Hettie*," he groaned, and let the lamp drop to his side. "What kind of trouble are you getting me in *now*?"

He stamped back to the van, pulled both halves of its hinged door shut behind him and doused the lamp he'd taken outside. The inside lamp had been turned down low. Helfred huddled beneath a blanket on the bench. Zandakar sat in the opposite corner, far too tall to lie down comfortably. He'd put a cushion behind his head and draped a blanket over his legs. His hands were quiescent in his lap.

"Hello, Dexterity," he said, his voice quiet. All traces of killing rage were gone from his face. His blue eyes were warm again, and sleepily lidded.

"Hello, Zandakar," he replied just as softly, and settled himself on the floor against the hinged door. Someone had left him a blanket and a cushion. He stretched out on his side with his knees tucked close to his chest. No sound came from behind the drawn curtain. Either Rhian and Ursa were asleep or they wanted everyone to think so.

"Are you all right, Dexterity?"

Goodness. In one short day Rhian's chaplain had worked a miracle. Or perhaps Zandakar was working things out for himself.

He nodded. "*Zho*. I'm fine, Zandakar. You?"

Zandakar shrugged. Said something in his own tongue. It sounded . . . derisive. Perhaps: *What do you think?*

It was a good question. *What do I think, Zandakar? I think Helfred was right. You did want to kill him. You*

*want to kill anyone you see as a threat. And what that will
mean for us . . . I'm not sure. Not yet.*

Zandakar tipped his head to one side. The faintest of
blue sheens gleamed on his skull. He'd need to shave his
head again soon or risk looking more outlandish than he
did already. "Dexterity?"

He looked up. "Yes?"

Vivid thoughts and feelings paraded across Zandakar's
face. For the first time Dexterity thought he could read the
ex-slave's inner self. Fear. Caution. Exhausted patience
and a growing frustration. *Aieee, I want to speak with
him!*

"I know, Zandakar," he said, and smiled. "I want to
speak properly with you, too." *I want to know who you
are and if, after everything, we should be afraid.*

"Tcha!" said Zandakar, rolling his eyes.

"Sleep now, my strange friend." He reached for the
lamp and turned its wick down. The van's interior plunged
into darkness. "We'll talk more tomorrow."

Five minutes later, Helfred started to snore.

They woke to a pink dawn gauzed with cloud. After a
breakfast of more bread and cheese, Dexterity gave the
others the news he'd been dreading to share.

"What do you mean, *not* go by river?" said Rhian,
staring. Her face looked subtly older with her hair cut so
short. Curls crowded closely, outlining the elegant shape
of her head. Her eyes stood out sharply, and her high
cheekbones. She'd been beautiful before. Now she looked
exotic, a young queen out of myth and legend, slender as
whipcord . . . and about as yielding.

"Jones," sighed Ursa. "I think it's time you told her."

"Told me *what*?" demanded Rhian. "What's going on here? I want to know. I *won't* have secrets kept from me. Not any more."

The interior of the peddler's van really was too small for so many people. Standing with his back to the hinged door, Dexterity bit his lip. "I understand, Highness. It's just . . . well . . . there's no way I can explain without sounding like a madman."

"Try," said Rhian grimly. "Because I'm losing my temper. And as Helfred will tell you it's not a pretty sight."

Seated beside her on the bottom sleeping-shelf Ursa shrugged, her eyebrows high. "What have you got to lose, Jones?"

More things than he cared to think about. *Oh, Hettie, Hettie. You should be explaining this instead of me!* Tentatively, he cleared his throat. "Your Highness, do you remember when I came to you in the privy palace gardens?"

She nodded. "Of course."

"And you were amazed by how I knew what I knew when by all rights I should've known nothing?"

"I'm still amazed."

"Yes. Well." He took a deep breath and let it out in a whoosh. Let his gaze drift to Helfred, still crammed in his corner and pretending not to listen. Then he looked at Zandakar, leaning against the wall. The man's expression was intent, as though he could understand every word. "I used to be married a long time ago. To a woman named Hettie. I loved her very much . . . but she died."

Rhian's severe expression softened. "I'm sorry. I never knew that."

"Of course you didn't. Why would you? You weren't born when I lost her."

"I'm still sorry. But—and forgive me—what does her death have to do with us not travelling to duchy Linfoi by river?"

He felt his insides strangle tight. "Hettie said not to."

"*Hettie* said . . ." Rhian stood, hands fisted at her sides. "Mr Jones, is this some kind of *joke*?"

"No, Your Highness. Not unless it's being played on me. Hettie tells me things. Things that turn out to be true. Last night she said we can't travel by river, that we should stay on the road."

From the look on her face Rhian didn't know whether to laugh, cry or scream. "Mr Jones, do you *hear* yourself?"

He nodded. "Sadly, I do."

In his sulky corner Helfred stirred. His eyes were alight with renewed vigour. "It's a demonic visitation," he pronounced, standing. "Princess Rhian, we must depart. To stay in this place is to imperil our souls."

For the first time Rhian looked at her chaplain without thinly veiled anger and deep dislike. "Demonic?"

"Absolutely!" said Helfred promptly, and pointed at Zandakar. "That—that—*man*—is its fleshly incarnation!"

"Oh, bilge!" said Ursa in disgust. "That man is a man, nothing more, nothing less. I dragged him kicking and screaming from death's threshold, Chaplain, so I think I should know. And there's nothing demonic about what's happening here. I'll lay you good money Hettie is *God's* messenger in this." She turned. "Come along, Jones! Don't just stand there like one of your puppets! Tell the girl what else Hettie said!"

He focused on the princess, trying to blot out the

sight of Helfred's appalled, self-righteous face and the watchful wariness in Zandakar's eyes. "Rhian, it was Hettie who told me that Ethrea is in danger. About the prolate trying to marry you to the wrong man for the wrong reasons. I came to see you, to offer you my help, because she said I must. I don't begin to understand what's going on but I know she's not a *demon*." He flicked Helfred a hot glance. "There's no such thing as demons. That's just superstitious nonsense to frighten children."

"Blasphemy!" gasped Helfred. "You are an unbeliever!"

"I don't know what I am," he said crossly. "I only know that when Hettie lived she was the sweetest, kindest, gentlest woman in the world . . . and all she cares about now is protecting Ethrea and saving the princess."

"This is very confusing," Rhian muttered, and rubbed a hand across her eyes. "I'm not in the habit of taking counsel from men who talk to ghosts."

"And I assure you, Highness, I'm not in the habit of talking to them," he said. "If it hadn't been Hettie I'd have called it indigestion. But denying what's happened since the first time she came to me would be like going outside and saying the sky isn't blue."

The faintest of smiles touched Rhian's face. "Put my fears at ease, Mr Jones. Poke your head out of the van and look up, would you? Just to make sure?"

He smiled back at her as the knots in his chest began to ease. "It was blue ten minutes ago. I don't think it's changed since."

"Then I envy the sky," she said. "My life has changed so much I can scarcely recognise it . . ."

"I know. I'm sorry."

"Did Hettie say why we mustn't travel by barge?"

"Your Highness!" said Helfred, scandalised. "You can't give this blasphemy credence! You can't mean to remain with these—these—*people*!"

Rhian scorched him with a look. "Be quiet, Helfred. Mr Jones?"

The knots tightened again. "No, she didn't, Your Highness. But I believe her. She's my wife."

"Your wife is dead, Mr Jones," said Helfred. "And this is *outrageous*. You endanger our souls by—"

"I said *be quiet*, Helfred!" Rhian snapped. "Mr Jones endangers nothing. He *saved* me. How could he do that without divine guidance? Are you denying the existence of miracles?"

"Of course not!" said Helfred, hotly. "But this toymaker is no Rollin!"

"You don't know that! You don't know anything! You're nothing but a toady for your precious uncle! Do you even *believe* in God?"

Helfred spluttered incoherently, his face so red he looked in danger of his life. Dexterity exchanged a look with Ursa, who reached out and patted Rhian on the arm.

"That's enough, Your Highness. You've made your point."

"I don't think I have," Rhian said. "From the moment he was forced on me this *horrible* little man has thrown God in my face at every opportunity. And yet, when you get right down to it, how can any of us be certain God even exists? Has anyone seen him? Spoken to him? Heard his voice?"

"No," said Ursa. "That's where faith comes in."

"*Exactly!* And Mr Jones has faith in Hettie. Faith that's been borne out because she was right. Do *we* have to see her to believe she's on our side? Isn't it enough that Mr Jones can see her?"

"No!" declared Helfred. "Faith in God cannot be compared to faith in an apparition whose provenance is unproved!"

"*You* say!" spat Rhian. "But *I* say you're wrong and God's sent us a miracle. What a good thing you weren't around in Rollin's day, Helfred! Given the chance I bet you'd have shot the first arrow!"

Helfred was shaking. "That is a *monstrous* accusation! You *wicked* girl, how *dare* you—"

Zandakar stepped forward, his expression menacing. Rhian pointed at him. "You stay where you are! This is between me and my chaplain!"

As Zandakar stopped, understanding Rhian's tone and gesture at least, Dexterity cleared his throat. *If I don't do something we'll tear ourselves to pieces, and what will happen to Ethrea then?* "Chaplain Helfred, I'd like to ask you a question. If you don't mind."

A moment of silence, as Helfred and Rhian battled for self-control. Then Helfred nodded. "Of course, Mr Jones."

"Why did you leave the clerica with us? Why not stay behind and raise the alarm?"

Helfred laughed, an angry sound. He looked nothing like a chaplain, not out of his habit. In plain trousers and shirt he looked more like a ledger keeper or some other breed of persnickety indoors man.

"As if you and your tame heathen would have let me! If I'd tried to call out you'd have—you'd have—"

"We wouldn't have hurt you," said Rhian, contemptuous.

"Perhaps not," said Helfred, glaring. "But you'd have dragged me off with you against my will. Do you deny it?"

Rhian stared at the floor. "No."

"But the point is we didn't have to," said Dexterity, quickly. "You came with us of your own accord, Chaplain. Because you know the prolate is wrong. You know something is gravely awry in Ethrea. And you know Princess Rhian is the only one who can put it right."

"And if I'd known you consort with apparitions I'd have shouted till the clerica fell down around our ears!"

"Why are you so convinced Hettie's evil, Helfred?" said Rhian. "Can it only be a miracle if God speaks to *you*?"

The question seemed to knock the wind right out of him. He sat down, slowly. The silence stretched on. Dexterity opened his mouth but Ursa shook her head at him, so he looked at Zandakar instead. The menace was gone, sunk back beneath his surface. He was watchful again. How much did he understand?

I wish I could ask him. I wish I knew who he was.

Rhian was staring at Helfred. The fury had died out of her face. She looked almost . . . *sympathetic*. "Chaplain, you were right about one thing last night, at least. If you don't wish to stay with us I can't compel you. I'm your queen, I'm not a gaoler. I'm not Marlan, ruling by coercion. If you truly believe I'm tainted by evil, that we are God's sworn enemies, then return to your uncle. Tell him everything that's happened. Help him track me down, drag me back to Kingseat and force me into marriage with Lord Rulf, whom he would make his puppet. If you think that's God's will, Helfred . . . who am I to thwart it?" She flicked a glance sideways. "Mr Jones?"

Heart pounding, sweat trickling even though it was a cool morning, Dexterity stepped away from the hinged door, flipped up its latches and swung both halves wide.

Beyond the van freedom beckoned. Disaster taunted. The waking world held its pale, cool breath. Groaning, Helfred turned his face to the wall. "I am a wretched, tormented creature! You *know* I can't leave you, Highness. I took an oath to succour your soul. Would you have me forsworn? Would you have me forsake you? Is that your low opinion of me?"

As Rhian went to him, Dexterity shook his head at Ursa then looked at Zandakar. "Come on," he said. "This isn't our business. You can help me with the horses. It's time this van returned to the road."

CHAPTER TWENTY

She wants *more* time?" Lord Harley looked around the council table, incredulous. "What's wrong with the girl? It's not as though she's got one hundred men to choose from. Is she losing her wits?"

Henrik Linfoi cleared his throat. "Mind now, Harley. Remember you're speaking of our future queen."

"She's not our queen until she marries!" retorted Harley, his face florid. "And if this nonsense is allowed to go on much longer my infant grand-daughter will be wedded before Rhian takes her vows!"

Marlan kept his expression blandly neutral as his fellow councillors shifted and muttered and nodded in agreement.

Niall drummed his fingers on the table. "I'm sure we're all sensitive to the princess' feelings. But I agree, there is a limit to our forbearance. The foreign ambassadors are—"

"Not a part of this government," said Marlan pleasantly. "They are guests of the realm granted certain patents and privileges . . . *at our discretion.* My lords, in the midst of our grief and concern for the kingdom I think we've allowed ourselves to lose sight of an important fact. These ambassadors' masters need us far more than we need them. If we closed our harbour to their ships tomorrow international trade as we know it would cease. This is why they agitate so strenuously. They don't care a whit for us, they care only for their own positions. I think it's time they remembered we're aware of that."

"And I think you've stayed out in the sun too long!" snapped Porpont. "Marlan, we are bound by international treaties. We can't just dismiss the ambassadors' concerns as though—"

"Of course we can. The treaties have to do with access to the harbour, with secure confidential banking facilities, with guaranteed neutrality in the case of external conflicts and other matters of a similar nature. *How* the kingdom functions is none of their business. All that matters is that it does. And I think you'll agree, gentlemen, that under our guidance it is functioning perfectly. Yes, there was a short time where feelings ran high in the streets of Kingseat, when fear and uncertainty threatened self-control, but that time has passed. Thanks to the efforts of my chaplains and venerables, with God's grace the populace's confidence has been restored."

Around the table, acknowledging nods.

"And now what do we see?" he continued. "We see that life has returned to normal. Ships come and ships go. The harbour is never empty. Tariffs flow into the Treasury. Merchants' purses fill with coin. Ethrea's many and varied exportable commodities continue to be exported without restraint. Civil order is maintained. With the shock of Eberg's death largely passed, the people go about their lives cheerfully and in good order." He smiled. "Indeed, I think this council is to be congratulated."

It was Linfoi, inevitably, who couldn't leave well enough alone. The other councillors were nodding again, struck by the truth of his salient observations. Linfoi frowned. "But still, the kingdom needs a king."

Marlan made himself smile. "Of course it does. And it will have one, Linfoi. But I for one am not eager to see Her Highness wedded solely to please a smattering of foreigners who do not have *her* best interests at heart. She will choose her husband when God sees fit to guide her to the right man. Who am I to hurry God, gentlemen? Who are any of us to act with such impudence?"

"No, no, you're right, of course," said Volant. "But I wonder—if we were to speak with her again . . ."

Marlan sighed, a portrait of regret. "I'm afraid that's not possible. Princess Rhian is in seclusion. She's asked to be left alone so she might pray more deeply upon the merits and flaws of the men presented to her."

"And we're sure she *asked* for this seclusion, are we?" said Harley, glowering.

"Harley, be reasonable!" said Henrik Linfoi. "In one breath you're accusing Marlan of having too much influence over her, of possibly forcing her to choose his man Rulf. In the next, when it's clear she's having difficulty making a choice, which demonstrates he *hasn't* forced her, you're *still* trying to point a finger at the prolate. Make up your mind, man. You cannot have it both ways."

Marlan smiled inwardly as Harley launched into an impassioned diatribe. It seemed Henrik Linfoi had his uses after all. It was certainly convenient having a decent man of conscience fighting his battles for him.

Much better this way. No-one could accuse Linfoi of being in my sway. And if any one of these men should discover the bitch is gone, before I've found her and dragged her back . . .

A week, and still no sign of her. Either she'd slipped past that incompetent idiot Idson and escaped Kingseat by river . . . or she was somewhere on the roads of Ethrea. His discreet enquiries had satisfied him she was not in league with Hartshorn, Arbat, Meercheq or Morvell. Which left only one possibility.

She's heading towards duchy Linfoi, I would wager my palace on it. There's nowhere else in the kingdom for her to run. Does she think to save herself by marrying impoverished Alasdair? Stupid girl. Even if she reaches him she's a ward of the Church. She cannot wed without clerical dispensation and she'll never get it. I'll see her deposed—or dead—first. So there's yet time . . .

Time to find her. Time to bring her back and show her the error of her ways. If she'd thought she knew what pain was before he'd be pleased to show her she was mistaken. He'd re-called Idson and his men, the useless sots. Now he'd send Ven'Martin swiftly north, to inspect the venerable house and clerica of duchy Linfoi and conduct a general audit of every parish. It was a plausible visitation. He regularly sent venerables to the religious houses of the kingdom, to bring him reports of their conduct and the conduct of their districts. No-one would remark on Ven'Martin's presence. And when Rhian arrived in duchy Linfoi, Ven'Martin would tell him and then he'd have her.

It occurred to him to wonder, briefly, as Harley brangled on and on, whether Henrik Linfoi knew about any of this and in keeping it secret played some devious game of his own. Was that possible?

No . . . upon consideration, he didn't think so. The man was a sheet of glass, easily seen through. He could never keep such momentous news secret. It was doubtful he'd try, he was such an honourable man. But even men of honour could succumb to divided loyalties. If his brother the duke commanded him to hold his tongue, for instance . . . there was an excellent chance Henrik Linfoi would hold it. It wasn't the kind of information he'd share with a chaplain, either. *I need a privy clerk in Henrik's Kingseat household. One who I can control.* A tricky task, but not insurmountable. He'd accomplish it within a few days.

Emerging from introspection, he saw that the disagreement between Linfoi and Harley had spilled over on the rest of the council. Now they were all shouting, their nerves perilously on edge at the continued delay in learning whose choice would be king. Dester had given up trying to record the session. Doubtless the rumpus would be covered by a brief: *and there followed an animated discussion*. It wouldn't be the first time.

He stood. "*Gentlemen!* You are rowdy, and to no useful purpose!"

Like a class of chastised novice devouts they turned to face him, jaws dropped and eyes wide. He let his disdain show as he stared back.

"My lords, instead of this profitless and self-indulgent bickering I suggest we discuss how we intend to deal with our gaggle of troublesome ambassadors. Speaking for myself, I am sorely offended that these foreign mouthpieces would presume to intrude themselves upon our sovereign jurisdiction. It must be made clear to them that our domestic governance is none of their affair and that we will take grave exception to any further harassment and demands for information. If we do not they will see it as a sign of weakness or indecision on our part and presume to interfere with more than words."

"They wouldn't dare," said Niall, blustering. "By God, they wouldn't! Not even the Emperor of Tzhung-tzhung-chai would presume so far."

Marlan raised an eyebrow. "You think not, my lord? Your confidence surprises me. Every man in this chamber recalls what happened last year between Barbruish and Haisun. Two treatied trading partners whom we now cannot permit the same window of landfall. And then, of course, there was the Arbenian incursion into Dev'kareshi waters, and the attempts by the Potentate of Harbisland to involve our merchants in the dispute and thus turn the matter to their advantage. Truly, Niall, are you so naïve as to think that given the chance these lofty rulers *would not presume*?"

They were useful memories to resurrect. Blood had run in Kingseat's gutters after the Barbruish and Haisun unpleasantness.

Niall grimaced. "That was different, surely."

"To some degree, perhaps," he allowed, and let his gaze linger on their thoughtful faces. "But at the nub of it, gentlemen, let us not forget: the Grand Convocate of Barbruish allowed the Little Emperor of Haisun to imagine he had a say in their internal affairs . . . a lapse of judgement with unfortunate results. Are we so careless of our own dignity that we would make the same mistake?"

His fellow councillors said nothing. Bloated silence was its own assent.

"Then we are agreed," he announced, and smiled. Far from being irritated, he could have kissed the ambassadors. Their persistent haranguing gave the councillors something useful and distracting to focus on. Encourage them to believe Ethrea's independence was being trampled and their jealous pride could be trusted to thrust aside concerns over Rhian. He sat down again. "Now . . . I suggest we spend the rest of our time today deciding upon the language with which we shall remind our presumptuous guests of their . . . limitations."

"Jones! Jones! Stop the wagon!"

Startled out of reverie, Dexterity sat up straight then rolled his eyes. "Again? Ursa, we've already stopped six times since sunrise. What is it *now*? At this rate we'll never reach the border with duchy Arbat!"

"Tcha! Of course we will. We'll reach it by sunset,"

said Ursa, sitting beside him, and snatching the reins from his loose grasp. "And I'm not driving past the best crop of liverberries I've ever seen in my life!"

Liverberries. He'd never heard of them. But then he'd never heard of foxfoot, wormslime, toadflax or puffed jilty before, either, and they'd had to rush about collecting them too. "And that's good, is it?"

She withered him with a look. "Would I be stopping the wagon if it wasn't?"

It was on the tip of his tongue to say something pointed, but he thought better of it and didn't take his reins back. It was far easier in the long run just to give Ursa her head.

The brown cobs slowed, the van creaked to a stop. Ursa threw the reins at him and, with more agility than was decent in a woman of her years, clambered off the driving seat down to the puddled ground. Zandakar, striding ahead, heedless of mud and splashes, realised the van no longer followed him and turned. Ursa waved an impatient hand.

"Come along, Zandakar, you can make yourself useful! Get my basket from the back of the wagon then help me pick these berries! You never know, they could save your life."

"Berries?" said Zandakar. "What are berries?"

"Little fruits," said Ursa, wading into the tangled undergrowth along the side of the narrow grass and dirt road. "In this case liverberries. Guaranteed to cure a case of jaundice in two shakes of a duck's tail!"

"Shakes of a duck's tail?" Zandakar echoed, bewildered. His Ethrean had come along remarkably with Helfred's intensive tutelage, but even so . . . "*Yatzhay,* Ursa. I do not un—"

"Oh, never mind," she said, grubbing amongst the riotous thorny vines. If she wasn't careful she'd end up scratched to pieces. "Just fetch my basket!"

"He's doing his best, Ursa," Dexterity reminded her, then raised his voice. "It's all right, Zandakar. I'll fetch the basket."

"Fine!" said Ursa. "So long as *somebody* fetches it!"

Shaking his head at her impatience, Dexterity hauled on the van's brake and looped the reins around its handle. Not that the brown cobs were flighty types but it was his habit and he didn't like to take chances. Not with Rhian sleeping behind him.

But when he stepped round to the rear of the van she was awake and swinging open its hinged door, Ursa's basket held in one hand. "I wasn't sleeping, I was thinking," she said when he'd finished apologising for waking her. "And even if I was, who could stay asleep with all the shouting? Except Helfred, of course. I think he could sleep through the end of the world."

"He might have stayed with us but our chaplain remains a troubled man," he said. "Highness, perhaps it's time we let him start saying the Litany. At least on those days we're alone and camping in a field or on the side of the road, with no-one nearby to hear and ask questions. Not saying it chafes him."

"He can say what he likes," she muttered, looking rebellious. "Just so long as *I* don't have to listen."

"So now you're blaming God for Helfred's shortcomings?"

The look she gave him was hot blue fire. "I blame God for a lot of things, Mr Jones."

She was still so angry. So full of grief. "Oh dear, you shouldn't do that."

"Why not?" she countered. "You do."

And then she leapt from the steps to the grass and slipped past him, Ursa's basket hooked over her arm, slender and swift in her boy's rough clothing. Feeling eyes upon him, he turned to see Helfred, hovering in the van's open doorway. The chaplain's pasty cheeks were pink.

"I should be reciting the Litany *every* day, Mr Jones," he said, his pimpled chin unsteady. His prayer beads dangled from one hand. "Regardless of where we are or who can see us. Your souls are in danger if you turn your back on God."

Dexterity had no intention of miring himself in a debate on theology. "You should be taking fresh air every day, Chaplain. It's not good for you to spend most of your time cooped up in the back of this van. You can teach Zandakar under blue skies just as well."

Helfred nodded reluctantly, his eyebrows pinched. "I suppose."

Honesty prompted Dexterity to add, "You've done a fine job with him. I never dreamed he could progress so well."

Despite the frown, a little gleam of pleasure touched Helfred's eyes. "He is learning at a goodly pace, isn't he? Perhaps I missed my true calling." The gleam died. "Perhaps I should've been a teacher." He slipped the prayer beads into his pocket. "I'm not a very good chaplain. If I were, the princess would have a better care for her duty."

"I doubt you need worry about Her Highness' sense of duty. There's more duty in her veins than blood."

Helfred's chin tucked in. "And there is more to duty

than claiming a crown. She has an obligation to set a spiritual example. I fear her father did not always do so. He was often careless of appearances, and frequently contradicted the prolate. In *public*."

"From what I can gather, Chaplain, the prolate could do with contradicting," Dexterity said sourly. "Besides, who are you to talk? You're contradicting Marlan just by standing there."

Deeper colour flooded Helfred's cheeks. "That's quite different and it's certainly not the point. Rhian is to be our queen. She *should* be hearing Litany daily. The fact that she refuses my request that she do so raises questions about her fitness for a crown. She—"

Dexterity stepped closer. "For an obviously bright and well-educated man, Helfred, you certainly know how to spout nonsense! Whatever else she is, thanks to her birth. Rhian is a young proud woman *you* treated disgracefully. Her stripes and bruises may have healed but her pride will take longer. Can't you see you *wronged* her? You'd have better luck if you went down on your knees and begged her forgiveness. Because the more you pontificate and sulk, the more you justify her dislike."

"*Sulk?*" Helfred looked outraged. "I do not sulk, I—I—contemplate matters of grave spiritual importance!"

"With a look on your face that could curdle cream! Truly, Helfred—" He softened his tone. "I'm not saying you're entirely wrong. As Ethrea's queen, Rhian does have certain obligations. But she's not a novice devout under your jurisdiction."

"Actually, she is," said Helfred. "In a manner of speaking. She's a ward of the Church and I'm the only Church representative here."

You pompous prat. Life was so much easier when it was just dolls and puppets . . . "A Church representative on the run from his prolate. No better than the rest of us, Chaplain. We're all in the same small peddler's van and you know it."

Helfred seemed to deflate. The self-righteous zeal leached out of his face, leaving only misery behind. "Yes. I do."

"But that doesn't matter," Dexterity added. "Because we're doing the right thing."

The prayer beads appeared again. Helfred fingered them, then heaved a tremulous sigh. "Yes."

Dexterity swallowed a groan. He didn't like Helfred. Who could like Helfred? Even Ursa had doubts and she was predisposed to liking the clergy. Still, he had to feel sorry for him. It couldn't be easy with Marlan as his uncle. And it had taken courage to defy the prolate like this. Perhaps it was a damp, self-righteous courage . . . but Helfred had taken a stand, even if it was wobbly.

"Rhian is our queen, Chaplain. Remember that and I'm sure everything will be fine." He glanced at the sky, where pale clouds flirted coyly with the sun. "The rain's passed. We've a few hours more before we'll need to stop for the night. Why don't you walk and talk with Zandakar for a while? You're looking peaky. Definitely out of sorts. If you don't remedy the situation Ursa will dose you with one of her concoctions—and I wouldn't wish that on the worst of my enemies."

Helfred shifted in the van's doorway, uncomfortable as a man with a pebble in his shoe. "About Zandakar, Mr Jones . . ."

Oh dear. Why did I embroil myself in conversation with this man? "Yes?"

The prayer beads clicked again, a nervous habit. "I'm feeling . . . concerned."

"Why? Zandakar seems fine to me. Ursa says he's made a complete recovery."

"It's not his health that worries me," said Helfred. He came down one step, his expression earnestly fretful. "How well do you know him?"

With a heart-thumping effort, Dexterity kept his face and voice calm. *I can't tell him the truth. Anything I say will be twisted to the sinister. Lying in a good cause means it's not really a lie.* "Well enough to know that *I'm* not worried, Chaplain."

Helfred chewed his lip. "Would that I could share your confidence. Alas, I cannot. I believe your friend *studies* us, Mr Jones. To what purpose . . ." He shrugged. "I fear it can be nothing good."

Oh, the wretched, *wretched* man. "Now why would you say that? He's done nothing to harm us."

"Is your memory so short?" said Helfred, offended. "He's twice threatened *me*!"

"Because he thought you were threatening the princess. I'd say that's reassuring."

Helfred reddened. "Hardly! He's a stranger, a foreigner, from a land none of us know. And given how cosmopolitan Kingseat is, well . . . I find that frightening, if you want the truth."

Dexterity fixed his gaze on the van's steps. The chaplain wasn't the only one unnerved by Zandakar. "He's too quiet, Jones," Ursa kept on saying in private. "I don't like it."

Loathe as he was to agree with her, he had to admit there was something to what she said. There was about Zandakar the skin-crawling impression of a lidded cauldron on the fire, and beneath his placid surface the water was simmering.

But being quiet isn't a crime. Being a man of complexity isn't against the law. He shook his head and looked up. "You're imagining things, Chaplain."

Click click click went Helfred's prayer beads, sliding through his fingers. His face was troubled. "Am I, Mr Jones? Only time will tell. But I pray when we learn the truth, it's nothing to our detriment."

And if I prayed, I'd pray for the same thing. Hettie, my love, solve this puzzle for me soon.

Dexterity left Marlan's nephew to the finding of his sandals and returned to the front of the van where he stood with the placid horses and watched as Ursa, oblivious to scratches, feverishly continued to fill her basket with liverberries assisted by a more cautious Zandakar and Rhian.

Their Hettie-inspired decision to travel by road to Linfoi had meant a serious rethink of how they'd best conduct themselves. He'd brought money with him, certainly, but nowhere near enough to feed five adult bellies on the long road north.

So it seemed only commonsensical that they should make use of what skills they had between them to eke out his purse of coins. They were pretending to be peddlers, after all.

He'd brought his whittling tools and a trunkful of half-finished dolls and puppets with him, worried he'd be bored witless on the barge ride up the river. A fortunate bit of foresight, that. He'd finished six stringed puppets and three dolls already and sold them for decent prices, considering. As for Ursa, she was like a lamb in clover with all the wild herbs and roots she was collecting. Some she sold, some she kept, though there wasn't much room in the back of the van. She'd done a little paid physicking too, on outlying farms and in a handful of villages.

They were the only ones who could earn any money. It was far too risky for Rhian to be seen odd-jobbing . . . although she did help paint the toys' faces and fashion their fancy little clothes. She was a neat artist and handy with a needle and scissors. For some reason he'd not expected that. Helfred had nothing to recommend him but a strong grasp of scripture and anyway, they didn't want any passing chaplain or venerable to recognise him. And Zandakar . . .

Yes. Well. Zandakar.

I won't believe he could harm us. Just because he's a mystery doesn't mean he's evil. And why should he trust us? Yes, Ursa and I nursed him, but for all he knows we could have done it to sell him again later.

There was nothing to do but wait and watch and in the meantime keep forging onward to duchy Linfoi, doing what he could to supplement their meagre money supply and keep them out of trouble.

With a creaking groan Ursa straightened amongst the tangled liverberry vines, pressing her scratched and juice-stained hands into the small of her back.

"All right!" she announced. "That's enough. We'd best be rolling on again, before Jones drops to the ground in a frothing conniption."

"I never said a word!" he protested as the berry-pickers

picked their way out of the undergrowth. Rhian's woollen leggings got caught on a bramble. Before she could free herself Zandakar was there, kneeling, tenderly loosing her from confinement.

Oh dear.

Ursa, joining him, pretended not to notice. "Jones, you *sighed*. You've got the most eloquent sigh in all of Ethrea."

"Well, if I did sigh I think I've got cause. Every second meadow or copse or bush has something *you* say we can't do without!"

She poked her elbow into his side. "And so we can't. Liverberries are *rare*, Jones. They fruit once a year only, for a handful of days. It's a miracle to have found them. Once they've dried they'll sell for a fortune." She looked at Rhian, freed now from the bramble. "Come along, Your Highness. Your bones are decades younger than mine. Pretend you're a monkey and climb up on the van's roof, will you? That's the best place for drying berries."

Rhian nodded, good-naturedly resigned to being ordered about. "All right."

Helfred appeared from around the back of the van. "And Zandakar can walk with me as we revise what I taught him before lunch. Zandakar?"

Zandakar nodded. So agreeable, so unprotesting. *And under the surface, the water seethes . . .* "Zho, Helfred."

"It's *yes*. Not *zho*. How many times do I have to tell you?"

"Come along then, Highness," said Ursa, watching Rhian watch Zandakar stroke the horses as he passed. "Didn't you hear Mr Jones? Time's a-wasting!"

Rhian rolled her eyes as Ursa bustled away. "She's very . . . organised . . . isn't she?"

Dexterity grinned. "That's one word for it. But she's a good woman. And we owe her a lot."

"I know," sighed Rhian. "But you're right about one thing. We need to hurry. Marlan can't keep my flight secret forever. By the time a general alarm is raised I *must* be in duchy Linfoi." Her wry smile faded. "I must have one ducal supporter . . . or I don't see how I'll triumph against him."

More than anything their greatest enemy was despair. "Of course you'll triumph!" he told her robustly. "Aren't you Ethrea's rightful queen? When the truth comes out about what the prolate was up to you'll have more ducal supporters than you'll know what to do with!"

"I pray you're right," she whispered. "For if we've misjudged this . . ."

"We haven't!" he said, and gave her shoulder a squeeze. "Now onto the roof, quickly, or Ursa will scold."

Rhian smiled and did as she was bade.

Such a good lass. She'd make a fine queen . . . provided the prolate didn't win.

Are you listening, Hettie? Don't you dare let him win.

CHAPTER TWENTY-ONE

A finger before lowsun, Dexterity guided the van off the rutted grassy track they followed and into an open space ringed by tall, lushly leafed trees. A stream ran close by. So many trees and streams in this far-away place *Ethrea*. It was as green as Harjha. Damp, and growing, and full of sweet rain.

Unharnessing the horses, Zandakar felt the random thought pierce him, sharp as a snakeblade.

Stupid Zandakar, do not think of Harjha. Do not think of Lilit. You will dream again.

Since his strength had returned his nights were not haunted. Not by Lilit or his mother or memories of the slave ship and what had come before. Not by Dmitrak, little Dimmi, his murderous brother. Or, if he did still dream of them, the memories no longer woke him to pain and screaming.

I think that is a good thing. Remembering is too hard.

Now that his body was mended, recovered from its wounds and fever, now he was strong again dancing the *hotas,* he at last could think beyond the mere physical. He was more than a dying husk now. More than suppurating flesh bound tenuously to life. He could look further beyond survival. He could start to ask questions.

Is this wet green Ethrea to be my home? Do I have a purpose here or am I nothing in the world? The god does not speak to me, I do not live in its eye. Am I dead to the god now, as I am dead to my people?

The plain brown horses fluttered their nostrils as he exchanged their bridles for halters. He petted them, aware of a waiting darkness, a yawning chasm of doubt when his whole life till now had been stone-hard certain.

I was angry, god. I closed my heart to you. It is open now, I have opened my heart so I will hear you. Tell me my purpose. Show me my path.

His heart stayed silent, the god did not answer.

I am alone.

Even as despair rose, threatening to destroy him, the voice of his saner self spoke in his mind. *Was* it his failing that the god did not answer? Or could the god only exist where its godspeakers were? Did the godspeakers summon it with their rituals and blood?

If that is so I will not hear it again until Dimmi and the warhost and the godspeakers come. They will come and burn green Ethrea to ash, they will drown the land scarlet and I will hear the god.

Leaving the harness for later, he led the horses to the stream so they could drink. The water was shallow, they pawed at it playfully. "Tchut, tchut," he told them. They flicked their ears and obeyed.

See me, god. I am a warlord of horses.

"Zandakar!"

He looked up, turning. It was the girl, Rhian. Her hair and eyes reminded him of Lilit. She was beautiful, as beautiful in her way as he remembered his mother, when he was a boy and she was still young. Before Dimmi's hard birth had made her old and bitter. Before constant pain and disappointment had sunk their claws in her godspark, left scars in her flesh and wrung her heart dry of joy.

"Zandakar," said Rhian a second time, and beckoned him to join her under the trees.

Rhian was beautiful and she was in trouble. He did not understand everything but he understood that. The man Helfred, who every day gave him more and more words, that man had hurt her.

I know these people are wicked sinners, god, Ethrea does not live in your eye. But I am who I am. I am who you made me. I did not protect Lilit, I must protect Rhian. I will kill Helfred for her if she asks. I will kill him if she does not ask and he hurts her again.

He was a strange man, Helfred. Not a man he would have tolerated in his warhost. But Helfred was giving him words, and that did count for something.

If he gives me words and he does not hurt Rhian I will have no reason to kill.

The horses had drunk enough. He led them to Rhian, and she held them as he fetched their hobbles. "Helfred's insisting on holding Litany," she said. "I'll have to let him. Ursa's very keen."

Keen. Litany. So many words, new ones every highsun. If the Ethreans spoke slowly he could make some sense of their speech. Of course, not often with Ursa. Ursa's tongue ran like a lizard across hot desert sand. But with Rhian, yes. And with Dexterity. Helfred did not talk to him unless it was in a lesson.

I miss Vortka's teaching. I miss Vortka.

Another thought he must push away. It was likely he would never see the high godspeaker again. Vortka had saved his life three times. He wondered if his mother was angry for that, his mother who had wanted him dead.

Aieee, the god see me, do not think of that either!

Rhian touched his arm, briefly. "Zandakar?"

He made himself breathe like a shadow, and wrenched his thoughts from the bloodsoaked past. "Litany?"

She sighed. "I can't begin to think how I'd explain it. Just come. Do what we do. I promise, it's painless. More or less."

Leaving the horses to graze, he walked with Rhian to Dexterity and Ursa who waited beside the van. Dexterity's face said he did not want to do this. A moment later Helfred came down the wooden steps, no longer wearing his plain shirt and baggy Ethrean leggings. Now he wore his blue robe that covered him from neck to ankle.

He stood before them, his face said he was important. He raised his hands and Rhian knelt on the ground. So did Ursa and Dexterity. Helfred frowned at him, so he knelt too. Helfred kissed his thumb and pressed it to his heart then held his arms wide, his palms cupped towards the sky, and started talking. On and on Helfred droned, so many strange words. It was like listening to Dexterity's donkey. He kept on looking at the sky. What was he looking at? Who was he looking for?

Then the cadence of Helfred's voice changed and the others spoke with him. Rhian and Ursa recited the words easily, but Dexterity's face said he was having trouble remembering. His tongue stumbled often. Helfred's face was transformed, fierce and fearless, he looked older and stronger, all petulance wiped away.

Zandakar frowned. In Helfred's changed face was something familiar, a teasing remembrance from his lost

Mijak life. In a startling moment memory showed him Nagarak, showed him Vortka, showed him godspeaker faces as they communed with the god.

Aieee, the god see him! Helfred was a *godspeaker*.

So there is a god in Ethrea and godspeakers to serve it. But it demands no blood, no sacrifice, no suffering. There are no scorpions here to punish wicked men. Ethrea's god is a god like Harjha's, a soft thing, a weak thing. A thing of sighing breezes and pretty flowers, it does not show its face. It will never stand against the god of Mijak. When my mother the Empress brings the god here, Ethrea will drown in blood. Rhian will drown. And Dexterity. And Ursa. Helfred will drown, his unseen god will not save him.

A terrible thought, all that drowning blood. If he closed his eyes now he would see the ruined cities . . . hear the screams of the dying thousands as he sent them to hell . . .

I do not want that to happen here. I am tired of slaughter, it sickens my bones. The god told me to stop slaughtering, I know I heard that in my heart. I need Vortka to help me hear it again. I need to swim in the godpool and ask the god's guidance in the sacred blood!

"Zandakar?" said Rhian. Helfred had stopped praying, so had Dexterity and Ursa. He had spoken aloud, the echoes of his anguish hummed in the air.

"Zandakar," said Dexterity, staring. "Are you all right?"

Helfred's face was red and shiny with temper. He said something loudly, his eyes were narrow and hard. He waved a clenched fist at the sky then kissed his thumb and pressed it to his breast.

Rhian turned on him. "No, Helfred! He didn't mean anything! He doesn't understand what the Litany is!"

Helfred said something else, too many unknown words spoken too quickly, in anger. Zandakar did not care that the man was angry with him. After Nagarak other men's anger was nothing. Helfred wore no scorpion pectoral, he had no power of smiting to death. He was weak, like his god of flowers and sunshine.

There is no sacred blood here. I must find blood, I must make it sacred. Only with blood will I hear the god speak.

Helfred had no doves, no lambs, no goatkids. There were the horses but they were needed to pull the wagon. Then he remembered. In Mijak the godspeakers gave their own blood sometimes.

But I have no knife. I am a warlord without a weapon.

There were stones in the stream. A sharp stone would cut him. He would have blood and the god would speak in his heart. He turned from the Ethreans and ran to the trickling stream, plunged into it on his hands and knees and began searching desperately for a sharp enough stone.

The Ethreans were shouting, they followed him to the water.

"Zandakar, stop!" Dexterity cried. "What are you doing?"

"I told you, Jones!" said Ursa. "I said he was too quiet!"

"Mr Jones, get him out! Before he hurts himself!"

That was Rhian. He looked up. Her beautiful blue eyes were worried for him. He had never seen worry like that in his mother's blue eyes. Lilit had looked like that the last time he saw her, before she was murdered, before their son died butchered at her feet. She had looked at him like that with such tender concern. And then she had died, her belly slashed open, their son cut to pieces, his mother's rage unstoppable—

His fingers closed on a small sharp stone. He snatched it up and slashed at his arms.

"Aieee, god, are they dead for my sins? Must I see Ethrea weep blood so you are appeased? Here is my blood! See? I bleed for you, god! Speak to me, I beg you! I am deaf in this place. I am blind in your eye!"

"What is he saying?" Helfred godspeaker demanded. "Is he summoning a curse?"

"I don't know!" said Dexterity, and jumped into the stream. "Don't stand there, Chaplain! Help me get him out!"

His flesh was cut open, his blood was flowing. It dripped into the water and swirled away. He had no sacred cup, on his bruised knees he sucked the blood from his wounds and listened desperately for the god.

Dexterity and Helfred godspeaker tried to drag him from the stream.

"Wei! Wei!" he cried, shaking them loose.

They took hold of him again, he did not break their bones. He did not want to hurt kind Dexterity or Helfred godspeaker. All he wanted was the god. Dexterity and Helfred pushed and pulled him towards the stream's edge. He freed himself a second time and opened more bleeding wounds in his flesh.

Where are you, god? Let me hear your voice!

The god was silent, it was too far away. In his head he heard himself screaming.

I am here, god! I am Zandakar! Why will you not speak?

"Get him *out* of there, Jones!"

That was Ursa, shouting. Dexterity and Helfred god-speaker seized him again, he could not defeat them, the god's cruel silence had swallowed his strength. They hauled him from the water and flung him to the cold, damp grass. Then Ursa was there, kneeling astride him. Her hands framed his face, she was staring at him with her fierce healer's eyes. He tried to throw her clear but her knees clamped round his heaving ribs. Her strong fingers pried his mouth open, something thick and sour poured over his tongue. Pressure on his throat meant he had to swallow.

"*Lilit . . . Lilit . . . Yuma . . . wei . . .*" His voice was a whisper, its strength lost to despair. Behind Ursa stood Rhian, with tears on her face.

The blue sky dimmed and the world went away.

"All right, Mr Jones," said Rhian severely. "I've been patient long enough. I want the truth now. *All* of it. *Who is Zandakar?*"

Mr Jones stared at her, still shaken, and managed a helpless little shrug. "Your Highness, I can't tell you."

She felt her precarious temper stir. "Mr Jones, are you under the impression I'm giving you a choice? I assure you I'm *not*!"

Sitting on the van's bench, where she'd ordered him, Mr Jones winced. "No, Your Highness."

She stood with her back to the van's closed hinged door,

arms folded tightly across her chest. Zandakar lay on the bottom sleeping-shelf, breathing slowly and heavily thanks to Ursa's potion. The ragged slashes on his arms had been smeared with green ointment and neatly bandaged. Ursa and Helfred were outside, making smoked bacon and vegetable soup. The faintest aroma seeped inside. It smelled wonderful. A pity her belly was too knotted to appreciate the thought of food.

For the love of Rollin, how can I hope to rule this kingdom if people are forever trying to protect me? Monarchs can't be protected! We live in the harsh glare of judgement and difficult decisions. That's what it means to be a monarch!

Or so her father had taught her. And he was right.

Mr Jones was looking apologetic. "The thing is, Highness, I honestly don't know."

"You said he was your friend! How can you be friends with a man you don't know?"

"It's . . . oh dear. It's complicated."

"I don't care! Tell me!"

Hesitantly at first, and then with more confidence, he began to speak. She listened intently.

It was indeed an incredible story. His first visit from Hettie. The slave ship. The unspeakable filth and misery of the poor wretches it contained. The look on his face, remembering, told her more than she wanted to know about their plight.

After I'm crowned I shall revisit the matter of slave ships in my harbour. What hypocrites we are. No slavery in Ethrea, we tell ourselves proudly, as we grow fat on the profits from those nations with less particular morals.

"I'm sorry, Your Highness," said Mr Jones, when his

tale was finished. "I had to buy him. Save him. I had to bring him with me."

"Because Hettie said so."

"Yes. She says he's important to Ethrea and I believe her."

Of course you do. But must I believe her too? "Important how?"

"She wouldn't tell me. I don't know why, but she'll have a good reason."

"Oh, do you think so?"

He winced at her sarcasm. "Please, Highness. Don't lose faith now. She's been right at every step. You wouldn't be safely away from the prolate without her."

She gave him a look. "I'm not safe yet."

"No . . ." he admitted, reluctant. "But you are safer."

Brooding on Zandakar's sleeping face, she said, "It's not a question of faith, Mr Jones. I hold the kingdom's future in my hands. This man . . . this extraordinary, mysterious man . . . Am I expected to trust Ethrea's future to *him*? Without explanation? Without knowing who he *is*?"

"Hettie says you must."

"Oh, *Hettie*." It would feel so good, to stamp her foot. Releasing a harsh breath, she let her head rest against the closed door behind her. "Zandakar's command of Ethrean improves markedly every day. If your precious Hettie won't tell me about him, he can tell me about himself."

Mr Jones made a small, dubious sound. "Yes, he might."

She stared. "*Might?* Why wouldn't he? If he has nothing sinister to hide . . ."

"It's not about being sinister, Your Highness," he protested, uncomfortable. "It's about trust. After all, we're strangers to Zandakar."

"Strangers who saved him from slavery and healed his hurts," she pointed out. "He's not stupid, Mr Jones. He knows we're good people. If I were him I'd want to tell us everything so we could help me find my way home!"

"And so would I," Mr Jones agreed. "But I'm not Zandakar."

She pushed away from the door, suddenly suspicious. Something in the tone of his voice . . . "You know more of him than you've told me. *No more secrets,* Mr Jones! How can I make wise decisions if I don't have all the facts?"

"I don't know if I'd call them *facts,*" he muttered.

"Well, whatever they are I want to hear them!"

Mr Jones sighed. "When Zandakar was still so very sick, after I rescued him from the slave ship, he suffered terrible dreams. Ursa had to keep him heavily stupored, like now, so he could rest. Otherwise he just dreamed and screamed . . ." He shuddered. "Or wept. Raved on and on, reliving something . . . *dreadful.* You've never heard a man in such torment."

But she had. Ranald and Simon had suffered as they died. Once the first stage of the plague passed, and they were no longer infectious, she'd returned to the castle and helped to nurse them. Dreaming and screaming . . .

Yes. I know what that's like.

"What did you *learn,* Mr Jones?"

"He was married, to a woman named Lilit. And I think she was murdered by someone called Yuma."

"Murdered!" Shocked, she looked again at the sleeping Zandakar, folded onto his side, his knees pulled close to his chest. "Why?"

"I don't know," said Mr Jones, shaking his head. "But I have been thinking about how he could've ended up here, in Ethrea. What if he ran away to escape being murdered himself and—and—fell into hardship and was taken by slavers!"

"Perhaps," she sighed. "It's a plausible story, but I can think of three other explanations without even trying. The truth is we don't *know*, Mr Jones. What if he was involved in killing his wife?"

Mr Jones sat up, offended. "Oh, no. Hettie wouldn't have me rescue a murderer."

He was so blindly certain. In his own way, as frustrating as Helfred. "Mr Jones, you don't seem to understand my dilemma." She pointed. "For all I know this strange man could bring Ethrea to ruin! Perhaps not on purpose but—"

"Surely not, Highness!" Mr Jones protested. "How could one man endanger a kingdom?"

"How can I answer that? *I don't know who he is!*"

"No, but you know Hettie says he's important. And I trust Hettie and you trust me! So . . ."

So this is the way you want me to rule? A friend of a friend says you can trust this tall dark stranger so turn him loose, Rhian! What could go wrong?

"Mr Jones . . ."

"I know, Your Highness," he said, slumping. "I'm sorry. I only wanted to help."

He sounded so forlorn. His face was woebegone, oddly vulnerable without its beard. "You have helped," she said, taking pity. "Enormously. And I don't mean to scold or imply that I doubt you. It's just . . . Zandakar gave me a fright. Seeing him hurt himself like that, it was very disconcerting. And these last long weeks . . ."

Mr Jones nodded. "Of course, Your Highness. They'd try a man twice your age."

"Oh . . . call me Rhian," she sighed. "Given our current circumstances an excess of formality seems ridiculous."

Taken aback, he stared at her. "That's—why, I—Your Highness—"

"Rhian," she insisted, and blinked tears away. "With my father and brothers dead I've no-one left to say my name." *No-one but Alasdair, and I'm a long way from Linfoi.* "Shall I make it a royal command?"

"No, no, of course not," he said, flustered. "I'm honoured. And you'll call me Dexterity?"

"I will," she said, smiling. "I'd like that."

"Well . . . Rhian," said Dexterity. "I know it seems addled to be trusting Zandakar's no danger to us, just on the word of a dead woman. If it wasn't Hettie . . ."

"But it is."

He nodded. "Yes. And that's everything. At least, it's everything to me."

And without him she'd still be a prisoner in the clerica. Maybe even married to Rulf by now. Pregnant, and breeding a dynasty for Marlan.

One way or another this keeps coming back to faith.

"Very well," she said. "I'll accept Hettie's word, for now, that Zandakar's not sinister. But when she comes to you again, Dexterity, tell her I expect to be told what's going on, sooner rather than later!"

"Well, Rhian . . ." he said cautiously, "I'll certainly mention it. Though it's only fair to warn you, even when she was alive Hettie never was a biddable woman, bless her." He cleared his throat. "I wonder. Since we're having a chinwag . . ."

"Say it," she said. "Only a foolish queen ignores advice from her councillors." Another lesson she'd learned from her father. *See, Papa? I remember. I'll do you proud yet.*

Dexterity took a deep breath and huffed it out. "All right, since we're speaking of trust. It seems to me you're putting a lot of faith in this Alasdair Linfoi. If he's not the man you think he is . . ."

No letters since he'd left the capital. No attendance at her father's funeral; just a brief message through his uncle, Henrik. Had her father forbidden him or had she slipped from his heart?

I don't know. I mustn't think it. Alasdair will help me. He's the only hope I have.

"I put no more faith in him than you're putting in Hettie. And at least we'll all be able to *see* Alasdair when we reach him." Just a few days from now. Lord, she was nervous.

"True," Dexterity conceded, rueful. "If I might ask, Highness. What do you intend to ask of the duke when we do reach duchy Linfoi?"

There was no easy way to say it. "Alasdair, marry me."

He choked. *"What?"*

"I need a husband," she said baldly. Beneath his blanket Zandakar stirred, muttered, then slid back into sleep. "Without one I can't rule in my own right. Alasdair's a legal man, he doesn't need anyone's permission to wed."

"But Rhian, you're not a legal woman! As a ward of the Church you—"

Folding her arms against his dismay, she met his worried gaze unflinching. "I have Chaplain Helfred. He can release me from Church wardship and marry me to Alasdair in five minutes. And if he knows what's good for him that's exactly what he'll do."

Dexterity gaped like a goldfish. "But the prolate—the prolate—"

"Won't be able to *un*marry me. Not without rewriting his own precious Church laws. And if he tries that he only plays into my hands. I have no choice, Dexterity. And neither will Alasdair. I'd rather not marry anyone right now, but I must. And he's the only man I can think of that I'd like to see as king."

"Well, you've taken my breath away," said Dexterity. "I never—"

But she never learned what he'd never, because the wagon's hinged doors opened and in came Ursa and Helfred, with dinner.

"Suppertime!" said Ursa, with a sharp, assessing glance at Zandakar. "Don't sit there, Jones, with that look on your face. Get the bowls and the spoons, man. Rollin protect me, anyone'd think you'd never seen a pot of soup before!"

When the sun rose next morning, Zandakar rose with it and left the van to dance his *hotas*. Rhian heard the hinged door's soft closing, lay under her blanket on the wagon's bench for a few moments fiercely arguing with herself, then got up, dressed with held breath, and followed him. No-one tried to stop her. On the floor, Helfred and Dexterity snored in harmony, while Ursa was an unmoving mound beneath her blankets on the top sleeping-shelf.

This early in spring there was a nip in the air. She sat

on the van's bottom step to pull her shoes on over her socks, then hesitated. Zandakar always danced his *hotas* barefoot. She put the boots on the ground, stripped off her socks and tucked them safe and dry inside. Then she rolled her woollen leggings up to her knees, stood, and marched across the dewy grass to where Zandakar leapt and cartwheeled and spun on his hips. He'd taken the bandages off his wounded arms. Ursa's green ointment had worked its magic, the stone-slashes in his flesh were already knitted closed.

He was stripped to the waist, as usual. The thin, dawn light burnished his skin, sliding over the marring scars on his chest and back and belly and shoulders. Sculpted with muscle, he was aesthetically perfect. He looked like a statue by pagan Icthian artists brought miraculously to life.

I shouldn't be noticing that. I'm travelling north to marry Alasdair.

But it was impossible to ignore Zandakar's physicality. Not even her brothers or their friends, riders and fencers every one, could touch him for breathtaking elegance of movement. For the implicit violence that was his *hota* dance. Set beside Zandakar, Ranald and Simon and the men of their acquaintance were merely children playing at war.

If every warrior where Zandakar comes from is as perfect and deadly as he . . .

He was a warrior, of course. She didn't need Dexterity or Zandakar to tell her that. She'd trained in swordplay with her father and brothers enough times to recognise a war dance when she saw one. Thrust and feint and disembowel with a stroke. Zandakar held no knife but still she could see one. See it severing limbs, slashing throats, spilling guts. Watering the ground with fountains of blood.

Thousands of Zandakars . . .

The thought came to her unbidden, enough to dry her mouth with fear. Ethrea had no warriors. Kingseat's garrison, the dukes' soldiers charged to keep their local peace, they weren't warriors. Ethrea held the upper hand against other, warlike nations because of the treaties that bound them and because gold could blunt the sharpest sword. But against an enemy who recognised no treaty . . .

And then she shook herself, because she was being silly.

A month ago I never knew a race like Zandakar's existed. Now I'm imagining them on the rampage. I must be overtired. Even if it's true, which it's not, it doesn't affect us. We don't need our own army or a fleet of warships. Our treated foreign friends are pledged to defend us. We are their bankers. They'd die for us gladly. Well, they'd die to save their fortunes but it's the same thing. Ten thousand Zandakars couldn't stand against their might . . . or determined, greedy self-interest.

Ethrea was safe.

Provided I defeat Marlan.

On that cheerful thought she shook her head and folded her arms. "Zandakar."

He must have known she was there, but hadn't so much as looked at her. Now he did look, and ended a sequence mid-step. His face was calm. No outward sign of exertion, no echo of the anguished man she'd seen yesterday in the stream.

"Good morning, Rhian," he said. His voice was calm too, tranquil as a pond. "You want?"

"Good morning. Yes. I want you to teach me *hotas*."

In silence he considered her, his clear blue eyes grave. "*Hotas?*" he said at last. "Why?"

"Because."

"Because why?"

She shrugged. "Because why not?"

"Tcha," he said, unimpressed. Because he understood her, or because he didn't? She couldn't tell. But just in case . . .

"Because I am a queen, and a queen should know how to defend herself." *And because I will know you in my own time, not Hettie's.*

"Queen," he said slowly.

"Do you know that word?"

He nodded. "Queen. *Hushla*." His expression changed. "Yuma." The word was scarcely more than a whisper.

Yuma? The name Dexterity had mentioned last night. So, if he was right, Zandakar's wife Lilit was murdered by his queen. But then . . . who did that make Zandakar?

Dammit, I want this mystery solved!

"Zandakar, these *hotas*." She raised her hand as though it held a weapon, mimed slashing and stabbing an invisible foe. "They are for fighting. Yes?"

Again he nodded. "*Zho. Hotas* for fighting."

"Then I want you to teach me."

He glanced at the quiet peddler's van, where nobody stirred. "Dexterity . . ."

"Does not command me. *I* am queen here, Zandakar. *I* decide."

His ice-blue eyes didn't blink at her tone. "Rhian queen. Rhian decide."

She nodded. "Exactly."

"*Hotas . . . wei* easy. *Hotas . . .* hard. *Zho?*"

"I'm used to hard work," she said, shrugging. "You won't frighten me with that." His expression said he didn't follow her comments. She tried again. "*Hotas* hard is all right. *Zho? Zho* hard."

His turn to shrug. "*Zho,*" he said, and cut her feet out from beneath her with a lightning-fast scything of one leg. She hit the grass rump-first, her teeth nearly closing on her tongue.

Outraged, she glared up at him. "*What was that?*"

His face was calm but his ice eyes were laughing. "*Hotas,*" he answered, and held out his hand.

She let him help her up. His response was to whip her in a fast circle around her shrieking shoulder-joint, plunging her back to the grass again. This time she landed face-first, which was good. Duchy Arbat's greenery swallowed her shriek as he slapped her behind.

"*Hotas,*" he said again, as she rolled over. His hands beckoned her. "Stand, queen. Lesson now."

She stood, fiercely smiling.

Think you're clever, don't you? Well, fool me once, shame on you. Fool me twice, shame on me. Fool me a third time? Don't get your hopes up.

CHAPTER TWENTY-TWO

Zandakar was right about one thing. *Hotas* were hard work. They made her years of training with a foil seem like a giddy romp for infants. By the end of her first lesson she was panting like a bellows and running sweat as though she'd stood beneath a waterfall. Even her bones ached. He'd pushed her unmercifully. Shown no respect for her person. Swatted her behind so many times she'd lost count.

She didn't mind. He took her seriously. It had become obvious, very quickly, that the fact she was female meant nothing to him. In his eyes, if they weren't equal it was because she was a student—not because she wasn't a man.

I like that. I like it a lot.

By the time they were finished she could tell she'd impressed him. His exclamations of *tcha* had started out impatient, scornful, but his last one had contained a note of reserved approval.

I wasn't imagining it. I wasn't. He thinks I'm not . . . bad.

And that was something else to like. A lot.

Afterwards, as they stood calf-deep in the cold stream drinking in great gulps and splashing water on their sweaty faces, she glanced at him and said, "All right. It's time to talk. Who are you?"

He didn't look at her. "Zandakar."

"Don't play games with me. Who are your people? Where is your country? Why were you a slave when Dexterity found you?"

Probably he wouldn't understand all the questions but the words tumbled out of her before she could stop them. Not that she tried. She needed the answers. Before she reached Alasdair she had to know who Zandakar was.

"Zandakar?" she prompted. "Please. Tell me who you are."

Now he did look at her, his face impassive again. The approval she'd seen there, and the restrained humour, were hidden away behind his mask. He shook his head. *"Wei."*

She let out a hard breath. *"Zandakar—"*

"Wei," he said again, and held up a silencing hand. "Rhian. I know name. I know *hotas.*"

It hurt, that he'd deny her. "And your wife was Lilit. Yuma killed her. You know that. Dexterity told me."

A flash of searing pain in the clear blue eyes. *"Zho."* He shrugged. *"Wei* more."

She stared. "You can't remember where you came from? Who your people are? *Nothing* else?"

He met her gaze squarely. *"Wei. Yatzhay."*

Odd, to think that while he'd been learning her language, she'd been learning his. *No. Sorry.*

But was that true? Or was he lying?

And if he's lying . . . what has he to hide?

God protect her, there was too much here unknown. Suddenly aware of his closeness, his overwhelming physical presence, suddenly feeling not quite so safe, she took a step back. Put some space between them.

"*Yatzhay*, Zandakar. I'm sorry, too. I'm very sorry you don't remember."

From the direction of the van came a plaintive shout. "Highness? Where are you? Zandakár? Are you near?"

Ursa. She looked at Zandakar and he looked back. For a moment she knew her expression mirrored his: guilty apprehension. "Oops," she said. "We're caught out. I think we'd better go."

Zandakar grinned. It was so unexpected. So vivid and mischievous. She felt her heart thud. "*Zho,* Rhian," he said. "We go."

Turning her back on that blinding smile, she stumbled over the running stream's uneven stone bed and onto dry land. Zandakar leapt out beside her, flashing her another swift smile. The dry land shifted beneath her feet and her blood became a waterfall, thundering through her veins. She pressed a hand against her thudding heart and made herself breathe normally.

It's nothing. It doesn't matter. I'm going north, to Alasdair.

They were greeted back at the van by outrage. Helfred, of course, led the chorus of dismay.

"Your Highness, what were you thinking, disappearing like that?" he demanded, thrusting himself at her with his hands fisted on his hips. "What were you *doing*?"

She looked quickly at Zandakar, whose blue eyes had kindled. "*Wei.* I'll deal with this." Turning back to Helfred, she stood her ground before him. "I was taking exercise, Helfred. Zandakar was teaching me his *hotas*."

"His *hotas*?" Helfred's eyes popped wide with shock. "Whatever possessed you? You've no need for his heathenish dances!"

"I disagree," she said coolly. "Helfred—"

He shook a pointed finger in her face. "Princess Rhian, you will listen to *me*! You are an unmarried minor, a ward of the Church! You *cannot* traipse about the countryside unsupervised with a man of no character, a man not your father, a man of dubious antecedents! Good God have *mercy,* think of your *reputation*! If you—"

"Helfred," she said, her voice coated with ice. "One more word and I'll unleash Zandakar."

As Helfred gobbled, Dexterity cleared his throat. "Rhian, really, he's not being unrea—"

She turned on him. "Did I ask for your opinion? I don't believe I did. Or yours, Ursa! Hold your tongues, both of you!"

They pursed their lips, but stayed silent. Rhian shifted her glare back to Helfred.

"You are my chaplain, Helfred. Not my father, my brother or my keeper. I don't require you to lecture me on proper conduct. Whatever I do is proper, because *I* do it. Can you honestly think you have more care for my name than *I* do?"

The colour had drained from his face. He looked pinched and older and bitterly hurt. "Your Highness—"

Hurt? Why hurt? I'm the injured party here. "Oh, you make me tired," she snapped. "I was *perfectly safe*."

"Not necessarily," said Ursa, irrepressible. "Zandakar is a powerful man. He might have injured you. Perhaps not deliberately, but by accident."

She rolled her eyes. "*Tcha*. I'm not injured. And I'm not discussing it any further. I'll be learning the *hotas* until I decide I've learned enough. Now if you'll excuse me, I'm sweaty. I'd like to bathe. Can someone please cook breakfast? We need to get on the road."

No-one dared contradict her, which was just as well for them.

After a silent, uncomfortable meal they continued their journey northwards through duchy Arbat. Zandakar drove the van alone. Ursa asked Helfred to sit on its roof with her and talk to her of scripture as she winnowed her dried liverberries and strung them on waxed thread. Dexterity asked Rhian to help him with his toys. She'd nodded, unsmiling, and they climbed in the back.

Two hours later he put down his whittling knife and held at arm's length the puppet's head he'd carved. Even though its features weren't painted yet the puppet looked back at him with a pirate leer that was quite engaging.

"There," he said, almost to himself. "I think you're done, my bold friend. And your name is . . ."

Sitting cross-legged opposite, on her sleeping-shelf, Rhian looked up from stitching the puppet's scarlet jerkin. "Ranald."

"Ranald?" he said doubtfully. "Are you sure? It doesn't seem proper, somehow."

She smiled for the first time since her furious display of temper. "Yes. Ranald loved playing pirates when we were young. That's the reason he and Simon went on that stupid sea voyage. Well." She pulled a face. "One reason. *'It was our childhood dream, Rhee! Sailing the mysterious oceans to adventure! What a shame you're a girl or you could come too!'*"

"Did you want to go?"

"Quite desperately. But Papa wouldn't hear of it. Adventuring is for princes, not their well-behaved sisters. Silly boys and their silly games."

"I'm sorry," he said. "You must miss them dreadfully. And your father."

She nodded, keeping her head down. "Yes. Dreadfully."

And he knew what that pain felt like. Long sharp nails hammered through the heart and soul. Hammered through the lungs so that breathing was hard. But there was no point talking about it. Talking didn't make the grief go away. Sometimes not even time could do that, and for her the loss was still too close. So, change the subject. He put the finished puppet's head aside.

"Rhian . . . what possessed you to have Zandakar teach you his *hotas*?"

She shrugged. "I don't know. I thought perhaps they might come in useful." She stretched a little, wincing. "They're certainly good exercise. I've found muscles I'd forgotten I had."

"You were awfully sharp with Helfred," he added, taking a chance. But he had to say something. She was fatherless, now. Someone older and wiser had to guide her.

Her needle flashed in and out of the puppet's jerkin, making tiny stitches. "Was I?"

You were, and you know it, and it was painful to see. But he couldn't say that to her. High-mettled and brimful of temperament, that was Rhian. "I know his manner's unfortunate but his only concern is for you. And he's taken a terrible risk supporting you instead of his uncle. If things don't work out the way we hope . . ."

"But they will," she said, still stitching. "They must. You know that better than anyone, Dexterity."

Yes. But there are no guarantees. "You say you intend to marry Alasdair Linfoi. You say Helfred can marry you, if he grants you dispensation from your wardship. But if you keep treating him so roughly, Rhian, what makes you think he'll oblige? There's no law says he must. You're dependent upon his good will. Would you fritter that away with harsh words and rough handling?"

Her busy fingers faltered. "Everything I do, I do for Ethrea," she said, her voice tight. "Helfred says he serves the kingdom. If that's true of course he'll oblige. What other choice will he have?"

There were so many arguments he could make. So many ways to show her she was wrong. But he could see, looking at her, she wasn't ready to hear them. Perhaps when they reached duchy Linfoi she'd be ready to listen.

If she's to be queen she'll have to learn how to listen. Not even a queen is right all the time.

Rhian reached for the scissors, snipped her scarlet thread then picked up the jerkin's little gold fringe. "Zandakar's so solitary," she said, rummaging in the tin for a reel of yellow cotton. "He needs a friend. Someone to share his thoughts with, as far as he's able."

Ah. "And you thought that if you shared his *hotas* first, if you got him to trust you while he taught you their patterns . . ."

"Then perhaps he'd share his thoughts with me, too. Share his past, and I could learn if he is a possible threat to Ethrea." She glanced at him. "Yes. It's my duty. Or should I have suggested *you* learn his *hotas* instead?"

He shuddered. *His* middle-aged bones dance those impossible steps? *God forbid.* "No. It was clever. Clearly he likes you. He may have given me his *chalava* but beyond that he's shown no desire to be friends."

"His *chalava*?"

Dexterity fished under his shirt and pulled out the crudely carved wooden creature Zandakar had pressed on him back in Kingseat. He'd hung it around his neck on some twine. "He was very insistent I keep it with me, always. I didn't want to upset him. This seemed the simplest solution."

"Chalava?" said Rhian, staring. "What's that?"

He shrugged, fingering the odd carving. "I've no idea. Something important, though. Probably superstitious. Perhaps you could ask him the next time you dance the *hotas.*"

"Yes. Perhaps." She was frowning. "Dexterity . . . he says he's lost his memory."

Startled, he looked up from tucking the *chalava* back under his shirt. "Really? Do you believe him?"

She pulled the remnant of red cotton from her needle's eye and rethreaded it with a length of yellow. "I don't know," she said, tying a knot at the end of the cotton. "You said he had dreams from his past."

"I . . . well, I suppose there might be a difference between dreaming something and remembering it when you're awake. We could ask Ursa. She'd know."

Rhian looked up. "I don't think so. I think we'll keep this between us, Dexterity. At least for now. As you said, it could just be he's as wary of us as we are of him."

"Yes. It could be."

"And can you blame him?"

"No. I can't."

She laid the threaded needle aside, took pins from the

tin box and pinned the gold fringe to the scarlet jerkin. "Of course he *could* be lying. Men dissemble all the time. Women, too. I grew up watching that at court."

Of course she did. *Stop seeing her as a girl, you fool. She's been raised a princess and fate's made her a queen. There are things she could teach you, for all you're old enough to be her father. Best not forget it.*

She added, "But you know, even if Zandakar hasn't told the full truth about himself I can't help but like him. There's a gentleness, a—a—decency there. I can feel it." She pulled a face. "Does that sound silly?"

"No. It doesn't. I've felt it myself."

"And he was sent by Hettie."

She was almost teasing, but he didn't smile. "Yes. He was."

"She must've been quite a woman, Dexterity."

"Indeed," he said softly, his smile unsteady. "She was my sun and my moons and every star in the sky."

And I miss her more now, for seeing her, than I have in many years.

"Would you do me a favour, Dexterity?" asked Rhian, gently. "Would you climb up on the roof and tell Helfred I'd like to see him?"

So . . . she was reconsidering her hasty words, was she? *Proud, but not too proud if an apology is needed. I think she'll make a fine queen, Hettie . . . if she's given the chance.*

"Of course, Your Highness," he said, standing. "I'll fetch him directly."

The journey through duchy Arbat continued.

In the township of Whistling Grove they sold Ursa's

dried liverberries for enough coin to see them safely the rest of the way to duchy Linfoi. Helfred proposed they complete their trek by river-barge but Rhian wouldn't hear of it. There was still a chance of men posted to watch for her. They must stay on the byroads, the laneways, the cart tracks. How foolish to come so close then throw victory away.

Helfred, mollified by her private apology, proffered the princess no argument. Everyone breathed a sigh of relief.

Every day, twice a day, she danced the *hotas* with Zandakar. His training was merciless. She asked for no mercy. The time she spent learning emptied her mind of fret and care. It was escape, of a kind, from the cruel memories of all she'd lost and the fear of her uncertain future. When she was sweating, exhausted, humming with pain, it was harder to hear the clamouring voices of doubt.

Helfred, still disapproving but powerless to prevent her, assuaged his conscience by insisting on his presence at the training sessions. Rhian sighed and gave into him that far. It was easier, in the long run. She did snap at him, though, when he complained Zandakar was not treating her with the deference she was due.

"Helfred, I'm his *pupil*. This is how it works."

"Your Highness, he *strikes* you!" Helfred turned pink. "On your—on the—it's not *seemly*. I must protest."

"I'm the one he's striking, Helfred. If I'm not protesting then you can hold your tongue."

Defeated, displeased, Helfred surrendered. Zandakar taught her the *hotas* and was taught in turn by Helfred, who was just as merciless in his way. Dexterity drove the wagon. Ursa made copious notes in her journal and gathered what healing plants she could find when time allowed.

The journey continued. They were anxious to end it.

Zandakar strode through the slow-falling night with the peddler's van following and his heart empty of the god.

He was slowly becoming accustomed to its silence, becoming accustomed to the grinding ache of loneliness that had taken residence in his bones.

I am a clay man, with nothing inside me.

Behind him, Dexterity drove the horses and spoke of toymaking with Rhian. He was teaching her whittling. She was a woman who liked to learn. Her *hotas* were progressing, though she had come to them too late. Dexterity had lit the van's torches, their pitchy smoke stank up the clean air and drifted among the branches of the close-growing trees.

I miss the open spaces of Mijak, the desolate plains and the hot red sands. This place is too wet, too green, too crowded. This place is not Mijak. I want to go home.

An evening breeze danced across his naked head, making him shiver. He wanted to grow his godbraids back, he did not like that his head was bare. Perhaps that was why the god was silent, because his godbraids had been cut off and burned and every three highsuns he shaved his head. No godbraids . . . no sacrifices . . . no blood for the god.

If Vortka could see me, aieee, it would be the scorpion wheel.

He had many words now, thanks to Helfred. He could explain to Dexterity that he must grow back his godbraids . . . except Dexterity would ask why and he was not ready to say. He was not ready to tell these people of the god, of Yuma, of Dmitrak with his smiting hand. Dexterity and Ursa and also Rhian, they smiled and they smiled but he was not safe here. Helfred never smiled, but Helfred did not count.

If I tell them my truth they might seek my life for it. Nor do I know what the god requires. I do not know if it wants me to tell them or if it wants me to hold my tongue.

Why it still mattered, he could not say. If the god had abandoned him why should he care for its desires? Why should he strive to work its will in the world? The god had his mother. The god had Dimmi. It had thrown away Zandakar. Why should he care?

It is something to care for. Without it I have nothing. I will be a clay man forever, with nothing inside me.

The breeze swirled around him. As well as pitchy smoke he smelled standing water and unknown flowers and something dead and decaying, some animal in the undergrowth. The breeze jinked into his face and he smelled something else.

Men. Unwashed men. They stink of danger. They stand in the shadows and wait for prey.

As he spun around, shouting, "Dexterity! Stop!" a rock soared out of the lowering gloom and took the horse Priddy hard in its face. The horse screamed and reared, throwing its harness-mate Star into panic. "Dexterity! Down! Down!" he shouted, and ran towards them.

Aieee, the god see me! No snakeblade, no slingshot, no bow and arrow of my own!

But Dexterity was clutching a stout wooden club. Where had it come from? "What is it? What's happening, Zandakar? Good God, are they footpads?"

Footpads? Not a word he knew. That did not matter. He

snatched a torch from the corner of the wagon and held out his hand. "Dexterity. Give!"

Dexterity looked at the wooden club, hesitated, then handed it over. "But Zandakar, there's only one of you! Oh dear—" He pointed. "We'll have to try running!"

Zandakar spun round again. Six men on foot, four held flaming torches, each one armed with a knife or sword. The two without torches held knives in both hands. Rough men, walking swiftly. Greed in their eyes.

Death in my eyes. They will not touch the god's knife-dancer.

He heard Rhian say, "What is it? What—oh, Rollin save us!"

They will not touch Rhian. They will not touch anyone. These sinning wicked men will die.

"Zandakar, no! Zandakar, what are you—Jones, don't just *stand* there, *stop* him!"

And of course that was Ursa, tumbled out of the van to tell everyone what to do. He paid no heed to her. Light on his feet he danced towards the rough men, the *footpads,* torch in one hand, club raised in the other. He did not say a word to them, he did not warn them or tell them to leave. They laughed to see him dance towards them. He was one man and they were six, why would they fear him?

You will fear me soon enough.

Without breaking stride he threw the club hard overarm, and the strongest man in the warband collapsed to the ground, his face bloody and pulped. The first one dead, he would not be the last. For three pounding heartbeats his five living enemies stared in shock. Three heartbeats was long enough to dance the dead man's knife into his free hand, then into the throats of two more rough men.

Three dead . . . three to die.

They ran at him, howling. He dropped his own torch and showed them the striking falcon, the spinning blade, the stinging scorpion. He lost himself in the glory of the dance, he bathed himself in the blood of wicked men.

I am made flesh again! I am full of killing!

Hot blood dripped down his face, from his hands, soaked his arms and the front of his brown cotton shirt. Blood slathered the blades of the knives he held. At his feet sprawled the bodies of his defeated enemies, slashed and sundered. None of them breathing. Every godspark sent to hell.

He threw back his head and screamed to the godmoon and the godmoon's shy wife, screamed to the strange stars they strode among.

"Aieee, the god see me! I am Zandakar, its warlord! I have slain its enemies. The god see me in its eye!"

Dear God. There's so much blood . . .

Staring at the slaughtered robbers, Rhian felt her empty belly turn over. She'd never enjoyed the killing part of hunting. Fast riding cross-country on a good horse, that was exhilarating. But the actual blood and death of it? No, she'd hated that. Wrenching her sickened gaze from the gaping wounds, the tangle of entrails, the bloody gleam of shattered bone, she looked at Zandakar instead.

Zandakar, who did this.

He wasn't even breathing heavily. And he was calm again now, after that savage cry of triumph. He stood in the road so self-contained, with a blood-clotted knife in each bloodsoaked hand. Completely and supremely self-possessed. He'd killed them so *fast*. They hadn't stood a chance. Simple, stupid footpads thinking to prey on un-suspecting peddlers.

Prey on my people and take their safety from them.

She realised then, with a cold stab of surprise, she wasn't sorry the men were dead. Not knowing who she was they would have stolen from her. Maybe raped her. Maybe even killed her, and Dexterity and Ursa and Helfred.

What is Rudi of Arbat doing with his time and sol-diery, that men like this can wander the byways of his duchy in freedom? My duchy, for he only holds it in trust for me . . . and my people. A trust that's been shattered if this is allowed.

"Thank you, Zandakar," she said. "You've done the Crown a great service."

"A service?" Helfred's voice behind her sounded thin and frightened. "Are you mad? This is *murder.*"

She turned. "Don't be ridiculous. Murder was doubt-less what *they* had in mind. This was justice. Rough. I'll grant you. But if they'd not raised their hands to us they'd still be breathing."

The sight of so much blood had leached the colour from Helfred's face. In dying, the footpads had soiled themselves. The stink of it hung on the cool evening air.

"I am not ridiculous," he protested. "Zandakar could have saved us without killing them! Without spilling their insides over the road!"

"Could he?" Her nerves still thrummed from what she'd witnessed. *His speed . . . his pure mastery . . . the perfection of his violence . . .* "I'm afraid I don't see how, given he was outnumbered six to one. Perhaps you could instruct him, Helfred. Give him a few pointers from your vast store of experience."

Helfred closed his mouth with a snap.

"Well," said Ursa, breaking the tense silence, "at least we know now what his *hotas* are for."

They certainly did. *If I study them for long enough will I be able to do this too?* She looked at Helfred again.

"Chaplain, I don't revel in bloodshed any more than you. But these men had no good intentions. If they had not attacked us they would've attacked someone else. Perhaps they already have. We were lucky, we had Zandakar to defend us. Other peddlers, other innocent travellers, they're not so fortunate. These footpads had to be stopped."

"As you say," said Helfred woodenly.

She turned away from him, afraid her temper would get the better of prudence. "Mr Jones? Dexterity?"

He'd not said a word, just stood with the frightened horses, his kerchief pressed to Priddy's stone-wound. His gaze was fixed on Zandakar as though he'd never seen him before.

In a way he hasn't. None of us have. And now that he's revealed to us . . . what does it mean?

CHAPTER TWENTY-THREE

As though waking from a dream, Dexterity stirred. Tucked the bloodied kerchief into his pocket and left the horses, walking towards Zandakar as though they were alone.

"Jones!" said Ursa.

Rhian took the physick's arm. "No. It's all right. Dexterity is safe, I'm sure of it."

"Really? I'm not!"

"Ursa," she said, and tightened her fingers. "He's safe."

"And if he's not," said Helfred under his breath, "how do you imagine you'll be able to help him?"

Zandakar was watching Dexterity approach, his face as calm now as it had been while he was killing. "Dexterity. Priddy all right?"

Halting in front of him, Dexterity stared up into his peaceful blue eyes. "Priddy is fine. Are you? Were you hurt?"

Zandakar shook his head. *"Wei."*

"Good. Zandakar, I don't see—did you have to kill *all* of them?"

Now Zandakar looked baffled. He said something in his own tongue, then frowned. "Tcha. *Wei* words." He nodded at the corpses strewn at his feet. "Bad men. *Zho?"*

"Zho. They were bad."

Zandakar shrugged. "Bad men die."

"Perhaps where you come from," said Dexterity. His voice sounded ragged. "Wherever that is. But in Ethrea, Zandakar, we have a rule of law. We don't kill bad men out of hand. We give them to the duke's soldiers and they are put in prison. They're not—not butchered like hogs. They were bad, but they were men."

Zandakar was looking at Dexterity so intently. "You are angry."

"No!" said Dexterity, and pressed a hand to his head. "Not angry. Not exactly. But Zandakar . . ."

Rhian stepped forward. *Time to remember who is*

queen, I think. "No one is angry, Zandakar. You did the right thing." She swept the others with a cold hard look. "No more complaints or criticisms, thank you. If you must say anything, make it a grateful prayer that Zandakar was here. We'd be dead in the ditch, else."

"Prayer is a good idea," said Helfred, subdued. "I must speak for the souls of these poor misguided—"

"Not now," she said. "We have to put some distance between us and this place before we settle for the night."

"You mean to leave them?" said Helfred. "Lying in their gore, unsanctified?"

"I suppose you'd like to put them in the van?"

"No, but we should bury them at least! They may have been wicked but—"

"We can't bury them, Chaplain," said Ursa, tiredly. "Someone will have to see their faces. They may have families needing to be told. And we can't take them with us."

"She's right," Rhian said flatly. "Let someone local find them and send word to this district's sheriff. We can't get involved. We have to go."

Helfred looked close to tears. "Your Highness—"

She touched his shoulder. "I've made my decision. Abide by it, Chaplain."

"Yes, Your Highness," he whispered.

Against her will she felt a wave of compassion for him. *Poor Helfred. You should've stayed in the clerica. Or better yet in Kingseat. See what you get for meddling in my life?*

"Please allow me a moment, Your Highness," he added. "A few words . . . it won't take long. I cannot leave these poor souls without—"

"Yes, yes, all right. But quickly!"

"Ursa—" Dexterity turned to the physick. "Do you have some ointment for Priddy's face? It's a nasty cut, that rock caught him just below the eye."

As Helfred prayed over the bodies and Dexterity and Ursa saw to the injured horse, Zandakar retrieved the rest of the slain footpads' weapons and wiped the worst of the blood off them on the damp grass beside the road. The last dusklight had faded completely. The glow from the torches burnished his dark skin and gleamed on the scarlet splashes on his face, arms and clothes.

Watching him, Rhian shook her head. *He doesn't even notice. If I had that much blood on me I'd be screaming for a bathtub.*

Zandakar finished cleaning the knives and swords. One of each he set aside for himself. Then he selected a second knife, a wickedly sharp dagger, and held it out to her.

"Take. For *hotas*. Rhian is ready to dance with a knife."

She hesitated, staring at it. The dead sprawled around them, rebuked in their sin. *Ready to do this? Oh Zandakar, I don't think so . . .*

She'd held fencing foils before and, laughing, tried to stab her father through the heart. But that was frivolous swordplay. That was exercise, it wasn't war. A heart touch meant winning a contest, not washing yourself free of someone else's blood. Not watching them die because you'd killed them.

"Rhian," said Zandakar. His pale blue eyes were serious. "Take knife. For *hotas*."

She took the dagger. Her hand was shaking. "I've never thought of killing anyone," she whispered. "I've never had to. There are no warriors in Ethrea, Zandakar. We have no wars. We're a kingdom of peace."

Now his eyes were derisive. "Tcha. *Zho* warriors. Rhian warrior. Rhian dance *hotas*."

If I keep this dagger . . . if I learn to dance his hotas with it . . . will I stay the person I am now? I'm not a warrior queen. I'm not any kind of queen, not yet. Not ever if Marlan has his way. How far must I travel from myself, to put a crown on my head? Must I kill to make myself queen? Oh, Papa. What would you say? What would you do?

Her fingers closed tight around the dagger's bone hilt. Staring at its clean, sharp edge she took a deep breath, and another. Then she looked at the dead men lying at her feet.

"Zandakar . . . how many men have you killed like this?"

He shook his head. "*Wei* remember. *Yatzhay.*"

Yatzhay, yatzhay. Always *yatzhay.* She thought he was lying. She thought he didn't want to say. *All right. Let him keep that secret, for now. But I'll ask him again. I will have an answer. I must have an answer. I need to know.*

Helfred, his prayers done with, joined them. He wouldn't look at Zandakar. "Highness, he should bathe and change his clothes before we go. He can't sit around covered in blood like that."

She nodded. "He will. And you can help me with these weapons."

"What?" Helfred stepped back. "You mean to *keep*—"

"We've a distance to travel yet before we reach duchy Linfoi!" Rollin give her patience, the man could rile her like no-one else. "And we can't assume these are the only footpads we'll meet. Perhaps we can avoid further bloodshed if we show the world we're not to be trifled with!"

"Oh," said Helfred. "I see. Perhaps that's not an unreasonable viewpoint."

"Well *thank you,* Chaplain. I'm sure I'll sleep perfectly tonight knowing you approve."

"Highness—"

She stabbed him with a look, not a dagger, even though the thought was wickedly tempting. "Oh, no more, Helfred! I've endured enough for one night!"

Wisely he held his tongue after that, even when she slid her new dagger through her belt. Leaving Zandakar to wash in water from the supply barrel, she and Helfred carried the booty of weapons back to the van. He left her alone, then, to take clean clothes to Zandakar, and she stowed the knives and swords safely out of sight.

"There you are," said Ursa, and closed the hinged door behind her. "You all right?"

"I'm fine. How's Priddy?"

"He's a horse. He'll live," said Ursa, perching on the bench. "You're quite certain you're all right? That's a lot of blood to see in one place if you're not used to it."

Rhian retreated to her sleeping-shelf. Slid the dagger out of her belt, to avoid an accident, and pretended to be terribly interested in its hilt. "And you are?"

"I've patched up my share of brawls down at the harbour. Foreign sailors don't always play nice."

"I'm sure they don't." She waited for Ursa to say something about the dagger. When she didn't, she held it up. "Zandakar says I should start training with this."

"And what do you say?"

She slid the dagger under her pillow. "I say he's probably right. There might be more footpads between here and duchy Linfoi."

"And that's what you're upset about, isn't it? Bad men in your realm," said Ursa. She settled herself more comfortably on the bench. "You're wondering if it's your fault. If they only dare to attack innocent folk because there's no king in Ethrea. Because instead of marrying to make one you've decided to crown yourself queen."

Yes, but how does she know that? Can she read minds as well as pick herbs and dry liverberries? "You think I shouldn't concern myself?"

Ursa snorted. "Of course you should. That's what being queen means, girl. Always wondering. Always worrying. You accuse Helfred of being sheltered and maybe he is. Was. But the same thing can be said of you. Growing up in your castle. Spoilt darling of a king and two princes."

That hurt. "I'm *not* spoilt! If you want to see spoilt I'll introduce you to some of the court ladies! Vacuous, empty-headed, caring for nothing but their jewels and their sweeties and giving orders to servants! Violetta Dester, and the rest of her ilk! All right, it's true, I never wanted for anything, but that doesn't make me *spoilt*. I'll have you know I worked hard to be educated. I hosted important dinners and parties for the king three times a week at least! I—"

"I'm not saying you never lifted a finger," said Ursa. "I'm sure you worked very hard to be a princess your father and brothers could be proud of. But it's not the same."

"Do you think I don't know that?" she demanded, still stinging. "Do you think I don't know how ignorant I am

of the world? I've never left Ethrea. Of course I'm ignorant. And I tried to remedy that, I *begged* to be let go with
Ranald and Simon!"

"Then it's a good thing your papa said no, isn't it?" said
Ursa quietly. "Or you'd likely be buried beside him and
your brothers, and what kind of a pickle would Ethrea be
in then?"

Suddenly exhausted, Rhian lay down. "What kind are
we in now?" She stifled a shiver. "Those footpads . . ."

"Made their choices," said Ursa, shrugging. "Just like
you've made yours. Rhian, Ethrea's our home and we
love it and that's proper. But that's not to say the place is
perfect. It's got good folk and bad folk like everywhere
else. And the only reason the bad folk don't get the upper
hand is because the good folk don't let them. They see a
weed, they pluck it out. They don't let it grow and seed
and spread itself further till all the flowers are choked
and dead."

She smiled, despite herself. "So if I want to be queen I
should think like a gardener?"

"Or a physick," said Ursa. "To keep the body healthy
sometimes you have to lose a little flesh."

The van's hinged doors swung open again and Helfred
climbed inside, carrying the empty water bucket and Zandakar's stained clothes. He dropped them in a corner then
took his customary place on the far end of the bench. He
looked distressed. The van creaked, moving again. The
little hatch in the wall slid open.

"We're on our way," said Dexterity. "I say we travel
another hour then find somewhere to stop for the night.
An hour should put enough distance between us and those
bodies."

Rhian sat up. "Agreed. Where's Zandakar?"

"He's walking ahead again . . . just in case."

With a knife and a sword, for their protection. "Good." She pulled her knees to her chest, and wrapped her arms around them. "That's good."

The hatch in the wall slid shut and they continued in silence.

They met no more footpads. Nearly an hour and a half later they stopped for the night, in a small clearing by the side of the road. At dawn Rhian woke and joined Zandakar for their *hotas*.

It felt dangerous to be dancing them with a knife. Trying to mimic him, she dropped the dagger many times. From the corner of her eye she saw him smiling. His eyes were laughing at her. He thought her amusing. She couldn't believe how deftly he handled his blade. It was like part of his body, silver flesh and edged bone. It didn't look deadly, it looked beautiful as he danced.

But then she remembered. The dagger slipped from her fingers. Panting, sweating, she stood beneath the slow-climbing sun.

Blood spurting. Men screaming. Men howling as they died.

She didn't realise she was weeping until she felt Zandakar's fingertip touch her cheek. She struck his hand aside and turned away.

"I'm all right, Zandakar! I'm perfectly fine!"

"Not fine," he said, behind her. So close she could feel his breath on her bare neck, no longer covered by coils of long hair. "Rhian is sad."

"No. No, I'm just . . ."

Pathetic. A spoilt child. Want to be queen, do you? Want to dress up for the crowd? Fool. You fool. It's going to take more than a pretty dress to put you on the throne. Just like those footpads, there are men in this kingdom who'll take what's yours if you let them. If you're weak. It's not enough just to say you're the queen. If you want to be queen, Rhian, you'll have to fight.

She picked up her dagger. Turned and stared into Zandakar's concerned face. "Well? Don't stand there, Zandakar. Teach me my *hotas*. Make me a warrior so I can fight for my crown." She lifted her chin, making her stare a challenge. "No more playing. No more pretend. Don't indulge me. Don't *smile*. You understand?"

He understood. She could see it in his eyes. The concern in them slowly faded, and he looked her up and down in a new way. A cold way. A way that said he found her wanting. For a moment it stung her, his cold dismissal. Who was he to look at her like that? He was an ex-slave and she was a queen!

Don't be stupid, Rhian. Whoever he is, he's a lot more than that.

"Rhian is sure?" His tone was arrogant. Disbelieving. "She want to learn hard?"

Learn hard? That sounded . . . daunting. Especially if up till now she'd learned *soft*. But once she reached duchy Linfoi she'd be fighting for her life. Even with Alasdair to help her . . . if he agreed to help her . . . still, in the end, she'd be on her own. She needed to be stronger. Tougher. Fiercer. She needed to shed spoilt sheltered Rhian, who hadn't seen Marlan coming for her from the moment her brothers died.

I need to remake myself in the image of this man.

"Yes, Zandakar," she said, though her heart was pounding. "That's exactly what I want. I want to learn hard."

"Good God," said Dexterity as he came down the van's steps. "What is she doing? What is *he* doing? Ursa, what's going on? Has Rhian lost her *mind*?"

"No!" said Ursa, cooking sausages over a small fire. She caught his arm as he blundered past her. "Keep your nose out of it, Jones. The princess is fine."

Across the road, in another cleared patch of countryside, Zandakar's slashing knife skimmed a hairsbreadth past Rhian's cheek.

"Fine?" he demanded. "Ursa, he's *assaulting* her! One mistake and he'll *kill* her!"

"Assaulting her?" echoed Ursa, and pushed to her feet. "You fool, Jones, he's *training* her. Properly training, not that soft prancing like before. And of course he won't kill her. You saw him last night. Do you think he's capable of making a mistake? These *hotas* are like breathing to him. You might as well say he could make a mistake walking."

"But—but—" He held his breath as Rhian tried to match Zandakar's mastery of the knife. The blade flew from her fingers and landed on the ground.

"Tcha!" said Zandakar, and slapped the side of her head. Not gently. Not kindly, like a teasing friend. This blow was hard and impatient. It snapped Rhian's head back. His eyes blazed contempt. *"Rhian adzuk chu'hota! Adzuk. Tcha!"*

Rage and shame and embarrassment turned her sweat-streaked cheeks scarlet. Too furious to speak she shoved her way past him, snatched up the fallen dagger, took four angry paces . . .

. . . and stopped. And turned.

"*Adzuk?* What is *adzuk?*"

Zandakar thought for a moment. "You say—I think—*stupid.*"

She nodded. "I see. So I'm stupid?"

"*Zho.* Stupid." He thought again. "Clumsy. Slow. *Wei* warrior."

"*Wei* warrior?" she demanded. Her knuckles were white on the dagger's dark hilt. "You arrogant *bastard!* Who are *you* to—" Then she laughed. "Oh. I see. Very clever, Zandakar." She slapped her own head. "You're right. I'm *adzuk*. To fall for that trick? *Adzuk, adzuk, adzuk.*"

Zandakar nodded. "Good. Again."

As their sparring continued, Dexterity looked at Ursa. "Trick?"

"He was trying to provoke her," said Ursa. "To break her focus." She nodded. "He did a good job."

"Oh," he said faintly. *My heart's not strong enough for this.* "Oh—oh dear!" he added, as Rhian misjudged a cartwheel and crashed to the ground.

"I think," said Ursa, "I'd best make up a poultice. Keep an eye on the sausages, Jones. They're almost done."

She clambered back into the van. A moment later Helfred came out, his blue chaplain's robe pulled over his plain trousers and shirt. "We should say Litany, Mr Jones. We must—oh. In Rollin's name. *What* is she *doing?*"

Dexterity sighed. "Being Rhian, Chaplain. What do you think?"

Helfred ground his teeth. "I think I am the only sane one amongst us."

The sausages were starting to char round the edges. Ursa would skin Dexterity alive if he let them burn through. Hastily averting disaster, he glanced at Rhian and Zandakar then back up at Helfred. "Pass me that plate there, Chaplain."

Helfred passed him the plate. "Don't tell me you approve of this, Dexterity. Don't tell me you think she's not in mortal danger."

"Of course she's in danger," he said, stabbing the sausages with a fork and putting them on the plate. "But not from Zandakar. She could've died last night, Helfred. We all could've died. Without Zandakar and his *hotas* I think we would be dead." He put down the heavy plate, rose from his crouch and watched for a moment as Rhian executed a perfect cartwheel, her dagger held firmly in her hand. "It's only sensible, that she learns how to protect herself."

Helfred squared his shoulders. "God will defend us! If our cause is just."

Dexterity sighed. "Perhaps God *is* defending us. Perhaps God sent us Zandakar. Did you never consider that?"

And leaving Helfred to splutter incoherent protests behind him, he went to tell Rhian and Zandakar that breakfast was cooked.

"I hope you don't intend to scold me," she told him, frowning. "Because—"

"No," he said. "I'm not that presumptuous. I've come to tell you it's time to eat."

She nodded. "Excellent. I'm starving." She glanced at Zandakar. "Thank you. I'll do better tomorrow."

"Do better tonight," Zandakar suggested.

"*Wei,*" she said. "Tonight we'll be on the river."

"The river?" said Dexterity, startled. "You mean—"

"Yes, Dexterity. It's time this journey ended," she said. Beneath the mud and sweat her face was older. Determined. "I'm not prepared to risk any more footpads. As soon as we've eaten we'll head for the nearest river-station, and charter a barge to duchy Linfoi. Ethrea is in dire need of its queen."

Alasdair, Duke of Linfoi, sat in the overstuffed leather armchair that had been his father's and stared through the library windows out into the gardens in front of Linfoi Manor. Someone was in the rose beds, pruning. Or possibly collecting buds for forced blooming. He should tell them to stop. Bright scented roses seemed wrong, somehow, in a house dank with mourning.

And anyway, Father hated them.

Roses. Lapdogs. Chestnut horses. Roan bulls. All hated by Duke Berin with the same strength of passion he'd lavished on every part of his life.

Dear God, I miss him. It's not right that he's gone.

Wrenching his thoughts from that unprofitable avenue, for his dead father had hated maudlin men as much as roan bulls, he turned away from the windows and looked again at the letter clasped loosely in his hand. It was from Henrik, who stayed in Kingseat while the current discreetly contained crisis continued.

I can't believe Rhian hasn't chosen someone. Since when was she unable to make up her mind?

Rhian. Another unprofitable avenue. He refused to think of the wretched girl. Refused to let his vivid imagination run riot, seeing her wedding another man. Bedding another man. *Oh, God.* He'd done very well these past four months, not thinking of Rhian. Not remembering her blue eyes. Her black hair. Her soft skin. Her sweet smile. The feel of her shy lips pressed against his own.

You have to marry someone, my love. You can't rule alone.

His uncle's letter, brought by messenger, was typically circumspect and constrained. Handwritten by Henrik, with his clear, precise penmanship. Only someone who knew him very well, like a nephew, would notice a certain . . . tremor . . . in the pen strokes.

Her Highness Princess Rhian has entrenched herself in the clerica at Todding, refusing to depart or declare her candidate for king. Marlan puts a good face on it but I think he is furious. My fellow councillors are torn between temper and hope. So long as she delays choosing there is still a chance for them. We must pray she knows what she is about. This kingdom needs a crowned head. I like not the whispers I'm hearing from Tzhung-tzhung-chai and Arbenia. Alasdair, I am sorry I cannot return home for the funeral. But I dare not leave the capital with matters so delicately poised.

It was the third time he'd read the letter and the pain in it still hurt him. Henrik and his father had been close all their lives. Writing to tell his uncle of his only brother's death had been a cruel thing.

But I am the duke now. It's my job to do cruel things. Like stand in the shadows watching the woman I love more than my life being bartered off to the highest bidder.

The thought could stop his breathing. It was a knife thrust through his heart. A miracle, surely, the damned thing kept on beating.

A deferential tap on the library door was a welcome distraction. He turned. "Yes, Sardre?"

"Lord Henrik's man is preparing for his return to Kingseat, Your Grace," his houseman informed him. "Is there any reply to this morning's missive?"

This morning's missive. Sardre was always so exquisitely correct. "Ah—yes. Yes. Tell the man to wait. I'll bring it out directly."

Sardre nodded. "Your Grace."

Alasdair reached for the inkpot and quill and a fresh sheet of paper. *Uncle, your news would be alarming if I did not know Rhian. But I'm certain she knows what she's doing. Her first, last and only thought will be for Ethrea. I'm sure she'll make the right choice at the right time.* He looked up from the paper, undecided, then slowly continued. *If you should chance to speak with her again, please tell her I have faith that she'll do the right thing. If you think that is helpful. I trust you'll know what's best. What are these whispers you mention? Can you elaborate? I am far removed from Kingseat but what happens there affects me here. Tell me what you can. I would not be in the dark.* The letter concluded, he signed it, folded it, snatched up the stick of sealing wax, melted its end in the candle-flame and sealed the note with his father's signet ring. His signet ring. The ducal crest of Linfoi.

How ridiculous. I'm a duke.

Grief lashed out then, that barbed emotion, thudding his heart fast and catching him unawares. Lips pressed tight he stared at his father's forbidding portrait, hung above the library mantelpiece. Not a very good artist, Hansyn. He'd caught all of the bluster and none of the smile.

His uncle's man waited in the manor house forecourt, mounted on a swift horse that would take him the first stage of the journey back to the capital.

"Directly to Lord Henrik, mind," he instructed, handing over the letter. "No other hand but yours and his must touch it, you understand?"

The man tugged his green velvet cap's flat brim. "Yes, Your Grace." Then, with a light touch of spurs, he spun and galloped away down the long, oak-lined driveway leading to the manor's wrought-iron gates.

Alasdair watched him go. *I wish it was me riding back to Kingseat. I'd like to stare Marlan full in the face and ask him myself why Rhian feels the need to hide. He hasn't a whit of care for her. A man of God? There's more piety in a tomcat.*

As he turned to retreat into the manor house, movement at the very end of the driveway caught his eye. He turned back. Shaded his face with one hand. What was that? A *peddler's van*?

His late father had never had time for ceremony. He was a bluff man, a forthright man, duke of the stoniest, poorest duchy in Ethrea. Oh, there'd been mining, once. Some gold. A little tin. But the earth had yielded up its treasures many dukes ago. Duchy Linfoi had no riches the world wanted to buy. It had stone quarries. It had timber. It produced a thin, sour ale. And labour, of course. That was Linfoi's primary produce. Sons and daughters who couldn't wait to flee south.

The wrought-iron gates at the end of the driveway always stood open. There was no-one worth keeping out. Hardly anyone visited. Certainly no-one important. He couldn't remember the last time *peddlers* had stopped here.

Perhaps they were lost.

He waited, curious, prepared to be gracious. The dukes of Linfoi prided themselves on their egalitarian approach to the citizenry. It was one of many reasons why Rhian's marriage to him had been deemed unsuitable. But peddlers were people, too. And who knew? They might have something interesting to sell.

The brown cobs pulling the weather-beaten van looked weary. As though they'd travelled a very long way. The man driving the van—Alasdair stared. *Good God.* Dark skin. Bald head with—yes, a sheen of blue hair. Where was he from? *I've never seen anyone like him before.*

The long driveway ended in a gravel circle at the manor's wide front doors. The van stopped. Its extraordinary driver just sat there, unspeaking.

Alasdair stepped forward. "Ah . . . can I help you?"

The sound of wood banging against wood, then of feet crunching on the gravel. A moment later four people stepped out from behind the van. An elderly woman with liberally grey-streaked hair. A middle-aged man, clean-shaven and close-cropped. A younger man, closer to his own age, also close-cropped, wearing an expression of sour discontent. And a young lad—no—young *woman*—but dressed like a lad. With short curly black hair, and amazing blue eyes, and—

Alasdair stared. *"Rhian?"* He walked forward, the ground not quite solid beneath his feet. How was this possible? Rhian was in the clerica at Todding. "Is that you?"

The girl's chin came up defiantly.

Oh, yes. It's her.

Heedless of the others he closed his arms about her in one hard, convulsive embrace. Then he let go and stepped back, tangled equally in foreboding and joy.

"Rhian—what's going on?" He folded his arms to stop himself from holding her again. Touching her. "What are you *doing* here? Henrik's just sent me word you're safe in a clerica. For the love of Rollin, why *aren't* you safe in a clerica? What are you doing traipsing about Ethrea in a peddler's van? Well, don't just *stand* there! *Say* something!"

She bared her teeth in a glittering smile. "I would, Alasdair, if you'd just bite your tongue."

He took a deep breath and let it out, hard and fast. "Rhian. Please. What's going on? Why have you come here?"

She put her hands on her slim hips and tipped her cropped head to one side. *Her hair, her hair, her beautiful hair.* He felt his pulse quicken: he mistrusted that look.

"Actually, it's quite simple," she said. Behind the smile, he thought she was frightened. "I've come to get married."

"Married." He felt his heart stutter. "You mean . . . to *me*?"

"No, Alasdair. To your kennel-boy. Of *course* to you."

God, he wanted to kiss her. Instead he shook his head. "Rhian . . . it's impossible. You know it's impossible. Your father—"

"My father is dead."

"So is mine, as it happens," he heard himself say. "Three days ago. I'm Linfoi's new duke."

"Oh, Alasdair," she whispered, and came to him, and

pressed her palm to his cheek. Her eyes understood completely. "I'm so sorry."

He covered her hand with his. Her fingers were cold. "I know. So am I." His voice broke. "I loved the old bastard."

"And I love the old bastard's son," she said softly. "I love him so much I want to make him my king. King Alasdair of Ethrea. Has a nice ring to it, don't you think?"

The power of speech had deserted him. So he did kiss her, and be damned to the world.

Rhian . . . Rhian . . . what have you done?

MIJAK

Hekat sat on the couch in the godhouse healing chamber, her fingers holding tight to her scorpion amulet. It had not whispered to her for many highsuns, now. So many highsuns she'd lost all count. The god had not spoken to her in the godpool, either, though she had trod down its stone steps six times since the last fat godmoon.

I do not care, it does not matter. I am Hekat, godtouched and precious. I know the god, the god is in me.

Vortka was staring. "Hekat, no. Are you demonstruck? You cannot ride out of Et-Raklion with the warhost. You are not strong. You are not well. If you try to do this I fear we will lose you. We cannot lose you. What is an empire without its Empress?"

Tcha. He was timid. When had Vortka high godspeaker grown to be timid? He was old, too, and shrunken. His beauty was gone.

"It is what the god wants, Vortka."

"The god has not told me so! Has it told you? I think it has not! If you say it has, you lie!"

He was frightened for her. She would not smite him for that. She closed her eyes and turned away from him, which was for him a kind of smiting.

I am Hekat, chosen of the god. I am not timid. My beauty remains. The god has not ceased speaking to me. There are demons at work still. They thwart the god's will. They stop my ears against its voice, they muffle its desires in my heart. Not even Vortka can turn them aside. Vortka has grown old and soft. No . . . he was always soft. His softness is a sin. Dmitrak too is helpless against these demons. He throws warriors at the desert like stones at a sandcat, the desert does not fall before him. He is not the god's Empress. He is nothing.

Only I can prevail in the world.

She released the scorpion amulet and, opening her eyes, made herself stand even though her bones were aching. "Vortka. Hear me. If we do not throw down the demons in that desert and cross the hot sands to the godless lands on the other side then we are no empire. If we fail the god in this, the god will abandon us. We will earn its smiting wrath as the sinning people of Mijak earned its wrath once before. Do you desire that? I think you do not."

"No, I do not," said Vortka. "But Hekat, be reasonable. I heal you as best as I can, all my healing power I pour into your body. Does this make you young again? Can you knife-dance as you did the night we met on the barracks field? Can you ride with your warriors as you once rode through Mijak?"

No. She could not. She rode rarely now. She was carried from place to place by slaves, in a litter. The people still bowed to her, they threw themselves on the ground as she passed, chanting *"The Empress! The Empress! The god sees Empress Hekat!"* They did not care she passed by in a litter instead of riding a horse. They did not know the pain in her, they would never know, it was not their business.

She bent on Vortka her sternest gaze. "I will knife-dance again, high godspeaker. I will ride a horse. I am the god's Empress. What I say will come to pass."

"Tcha!" he said, exasperated. "You are the same wilful stubborn she-brat riding Abajai's camel. Then you told yourself you were not a slave when I knew you were. Will you make the same mistake now, Hekat? Will you tell yourself you are not feeble when I tell you your health is frail? Would you kill yourself to prove I am wrong when you *know* I am right? When your mirror tells you I am right?"

Soft, foolish, timid Vortka. "The god will not let me die, high godspeaker. What is my body? It is a living thing I command, as I command every living thing in my empire. I command you to make my body stronger. You must find new ways to heal me, you must keep me alive. That is your purpose. I will ride to Harjha with a warhost. I will do what Dmitrak cannot. I will destroy the demons in that desert and lead my warriors beyond it into the world. You will ride with me. You will pour your healing power into my bones. If you must sacrifice one thousand bulls a day to keep me strong, you will. Or you will fail the god. You will fail me."

Vortka stared at the healing crystal in his hand, his silver-turning godbraids limp and silent. The stone scorpion pectoral hung heavy upon him. "Hekat . . ."

"If you had not sent Zandakar away I would not need to ride with a warhost," she said. She would never forgive him that sin. He was the high godspeaker, he should have known she would need her son. "So you will do this, Vortka. You will do this or you will be thrown down."

"That is not your business," he said, his eyes hostile, angry. "Only the god can throw me down."

Her fingers returned to the scorpion amulet. "Am I not the god's chosen? What I ask for I receive."

"Hekat, how can I leave Mijak? I have work here, the godhouses need me, the god needs me to—"

"I need you more, Vortka, whatever I need it is the god's need also. What the god needs most is the world tamed in its eye. No demon has ever stood against me. Abajai and Yagji could not have me killed. Nagarak could not kill me in the godhouse scorpion pit. His hellspawn brat could not kill me in its birthing. Demonstruck Hanochek could not kill me in war. The demons in the desert will not defeat me, Vortka. I will destroy them. I am in the god's eye."

He nodded, sighing. "I know that you are."

She stepped away from the healing couch and rested her hand on him, even though she would never forgive him for sending Zandakar away. "Vortka, we are old friends, we dwell in the god's eye together. Peklia will stay behind in Mijak, she will rule the godhouses in your absence. You are more than high godspeaker of the Mijak-that-was, you are high godspeaker of the god's reborn empire. You have not seen it. It is time that you did."

He knew who she was. He knew the god was in her. He nodded, obedient. "Empress, I am yours."

Yes. You are mine, you betrayed me over Zandakar but you are still mine. You will do as I tell you, so the god will be served.

She returned to the couch and lay down upon it. "Heal me, Vortka, pour your strength into my bones. It is a long way to Harjha and I must be strong to fight with demons."

"Empress," said Vortka, and began his healing work.

It pained her, aieee god, it woke every last pain in her embattled body. She endured. She was Hekat. Precious and chosen.

The warhost cheered when she told them they rode to Harjha. They wept when she told them she would lead them there herself. The people of Et-Raklion wept when they learned she was leaving them. They wailed, they threw amulets, they begged the god to see her in its eye.

She rode from Et-Raklion at the head of her warhost, she rode highsun to lowsun and only Vortka, riding with her, knew the cost of her riding. Every lowsun he healed her, she distended her belly with cups and cups of sacred blood, she slept with her scorpion amulet pressed to her heart.

They passed without incident across the tamed Sand River. She rode through the conquered lands of Drohne and Targa and Bryzin and Zree, where the resettled people of Mijak-that-was wept to see her and to see Vortka also.

She rode to Harjha where Dmitrak waited. He did not smile to see her. He was not a happy man.

"Empress," he said. "You sent no word that you were coming."

They stood alone in his warlord's dwelling where all the slaves were women, and young, and for his taking. She could see that, she was not surprised. She said, "Do I answer to you, Dmitrak? I think I do not."

"Empress—"

She silenced him with a raised hand. "You have not defeated the demons in the desert."

He could not look at her, he looked at the floor. "No."

"You are the god's hammer, yet you fail the god."

Now he looked up. "Where there are sinners to smite and cities to raze I do not fail, Empress! I could build you a new city of bones, that is how many sinners I have thrown down." He raised his clenched ruby-and-gold fist, let the power shimmer with its promise of death. "These demons in the desert have no form, they are not seen. No godspeaker can find them and show them to me. I cannot destroy what I cannot see, Empress. If you do not believe me, go there yourself."

"I will," she told him.

Vortka tried to stop her, he wasted his breath. He insisted on riding to the desert's doorstep with her, she did not say he must stay behind. Dmitrak rode too, the three of them rode there together.

"Stay here," she said, and slid from her horse. Pain woke within her, she clasped her scorpion amulet and walked on alone, across the burning sand, beneath the burning sun, into the heat of the demons' defiance. The sky above her was vast and still. The silence was vast, it swallowed her godbells' silver chiming.

She could feel the demons around her, pressing her to turn back.

I will not turn. I will not turn. You cannot defeat me. I am Empress of Mijak.

She walked until she could walk no more and then she folded to her knees. The hot sand scorched her through her horsehide leggings, she did not pay attention to the pain.

I am here, god, among your bitter enemies. I am Hekat, your one true Empress. Do not let these demons silence you in my heart. My heart is open, it is listening for you. Speak to me. I will do what you ask.

When the god's voice came it was the thinnest whisper. The demons fought hard to keep it from her heart. But she was Hekat, she would not be defeated. She heard the god's whisper. She learned its desire.

When she opened her eyes a single scorpion was before her. Silver-white and stunted and missing three legs.

"I hear you, god," she told it. "I will do as you ask. This defiant desert will be thrown down. I will break it."

She drowned the hot sands in human blood.

When the sacrifice was ended five thousand slaves lay dead around her, their naked bodies baking in the sun. The desert had turned from gold to scarlet and rivers ran where they had not run before.

Vortka, praying, opened his eyes. "It is done," he whispered. "The demons are destroyed."

She knew that already. *I am the god's Empress, nothing hides from me.* She laughed, though she was weary and her body shrieked with pain. "Did I not tell you, Vortka high godspeaker? Am I not Hekat, godchosen and precious? No demon spawned can stand against me." She looked at Dmitrak. "Assemble your warhost, warlord of Mijak. I will lead it across this tamed, docile desert. You will ride behind me. That is your place."

He was not pleased to hear it. He did not dare protest. His fisted hand thudded over his heart. "Empress."

She turned and stared across the wet, red expanse of

sand that seemed to lead all the way to the horizon. The air was thick with the stench of death.

"How did you know?" said Vortka, standing close. "How did you know only human blood could break the demons' hold on this desert?"

She smiled. "How do I know anything? The god told me, Vortka."

For I am Empress of Mijak . . . and the world will be mine.

PART THREE

CHAPTER TWENTY-FOUR

Alasdair stood at the library window and stared into the gardens below, where Rhian and the strange dark man who'd driven the peddler's van leapt and spun and cheated death on the lawn. The sun was sinking, trailing dusk behind it with cool, shadowed fingers. A beautiful evening for dancing with knives.

"Tell me, Mr Jones," he said. He'd been standing and watching for some time now. In the end an angry curiosity had overcome him and he'd sent for Rhian's unlikely chaperone. "What exactly is Her Highness doing?"

"Ah," said the toymaker. A pleasant fellow, it seemed. Earnest. Harmless. He stood ten deferential paces from the window, obedient to his summons but reluctant as well. "Yes. They're called *hotas,* Your Grace." He came hesitantly to the window. "Rhian—I'm sorry, forgive me, Her Highness—performs them morning and night, if she can."

"Dare I ask why?"

"Why? Oh dear. Your Grace, perhaps it would be better if you asked Her Highness that."

I would, if she'd stand still long enough for me to talk to. But since her startling marriage proposal they'd not managed a private word. She and her travelling companions were weary, they needed to bathe and change their clothes and eat something that wasn't bread and cheese, Alasdair, they'd been on the road for days and days, if they didn't soon sit down on something that wasn't moving she swore every one of them would burst into tears.

He knew what she was saying, beneath the spate of words. *I need time, Alasdair. I need space. Don't crowd me. Stay back.*

Because he loved her he'd listened and obeyed. He'd said nothing as she bustled and fussed, ordering the van and horses be housed in his stables, seeing the old woman and the toymaker and the dark man and the other man, the sulky one, the old woman's apprentice, assigned rooms and servants in his largely empty manor. He understood she needed to recapture her calm. What she'd done was momentous, beyond imagining when her father was alive. But Eberg was dead and her world in disarray.

Still. He wasn't prepared to wait forever. With her arrival on his doorstep his life was topsy-turvied too. His life. His duchy. His people, now he was their duke.

She wants me to be king? Father, can you believe it?

He'd taken Sardre aside, swiftly. "Word of the princess' presence here must not spread. It must be as though she never came. If word should leave the manor grounds before the best time, the consequences will be dire for all of us."

Sardre had served the House of Linfoi for three decades. "Your Grace," he said. And that was enough.

Thank God for Sardre. I'd be lost without him.

On the close-clipped grass beyond the window Rhian flirted with death. Turning somersaults and cartwheels, leaping forward, darting back, swinging beneath her opponent's slashing arm—and seemingly fearless—she looked like some fairytale warrior-queen. The tip of the dark man's knife missed her shoulder by a whisper. Vivid as lightning, triumph lit her face. But it didn't last long. She was shorter by two hands, he was superior in reach and speed. Dear God, he was fast. And focused. *He's frightening.* Even as he watched, the man's leg took Rhian's out from under her, mid-spin. She crashed to the ground, her knife flying from her fingers.

The dark man smacked her hard on the side of the head.

"It's all right, Your Grace!" said Mr Jones, stepping closer. "It's just Zandakar's way. He'd never hurt her. I know it's alarming but this is how they train. I promise, you get used to it. More or less."

Zandakar. What kind of a name was that?

Alasdair watched his fists relax. "More or less? I see. And who exactly is this Zandakar? Or is that another question best asked of Her Highness?"

"Yes, I think it is, Your Grace," said Mr Jones. "I think you should definitely ask the princess."

He turned. "Believe me, I will. But I'm interested in hearing what you have to say first."

The toymaker bit his lip. "Forgive me, it's not my place to—"

"I'm making it your place. Who is he, Mr Jones? How does he come here? Why does Rhian trust him with a knife—with her *life*? Black skin, blue eyes, blue hair if his skull wasn't shaved. I've not seen a man like him before."

"I believe nobody has, Your Grace."

"Nobody? Where does he come from?"

"Originally? I'm afraid I don't know. But . . . I found him on a slave ship. In Kingseat Harbour."

This was getting more ridiculous by the moment. "A *slave ship*? Are you telling me you *bought* him?"

"Perhaps *rescued* him would be a better word," said Mr Jones hastily. "Your Grace, I understand this is most disconcerting. It's natural you should have a lot of questions. I wish I could answer them. But I beg you, ask the princess. It's not right for me to tell you the little I know unless she gives me leave."

He admired loyalty, so he didn't press the man. Instead he turned back to the window and stared at the woman who would be his wife. His queen. Beyond the gardens and the manor's fringe of woodland the languid sun was sinking in a haze of pink and violet. Rhian and Zandakar danced with their knives. There was an intimacy between them he could feel even at this distance, with glass and stone and air between them.

When I lived in Kingseat she and I would fence together. We hunted together. We stood at the butts and shot arrows together. If anyone is to teach her knife-play it should be me.

Except he'd never seen knife-play like these *hotas*. Never seen such speed and power. Such lethal combinations of cut and thrust. Rhian was a talented, natural athlete but compared to this Zandakar she was a clumsy dolt.

Where in God's name does he come from?

Dragging his gaze away from Rhian, he looked at Mr Jones. "You're a *toymaker*?"

A glimmer of amusement touched the older man's tired eyes. "By Royal Appointment, as my father was before me. I've known Her Highness since she was born. I made her first rattle. I made toys for the princes, too, may their souls be at peace."

Grief for his friends, blunted now by his more recent, dearer loss, scraped his raw nerves. *Ranald. Simon. What would you say if you were here now?* What would they think of him marrying their sister?

"I see," he said, thrusting aside the thought and the pain. "I suppose that explains how it is you know the princess. But how in God's name did you get embroiled in *this* mess? In my experience toymakers don't often truck with the politics of royal succession."

Mr Jones snorted. Easy to see why Rhian trusted this plain, inconspicuous man. He had the kindest face . . . and an innate gentleness that couldn't be denied. "We assuredly do not, Your Grace. But if I told you how I happen to have stumbled into it I fear you'd say I was moonstruck."

"Perhaps. Perhaps not. But I do want to know."

"Your Grace . . ." Mr Jones sighed. "Please. I mean no disrespect. But I must decline to answer until—"

"The princess gives you leave." He waved a hand, accepting the refusal. "Very well, Mr Jones. You may go. But consider this conversation postponed, not abandoned."

The toymaker bowed. "Your Grace."

He turned back to the window as Mr Jones withdrew, to see that Rhian and Zandakar had finished their lethal training. They were stretching now, easing the kinks out of their muscles. Letting the sweat cool on their skins.

He went downstairs to join them.

"Alasdair!" said Rhian, and untwined herself from around her leg. Her knife was slid into her belt. "Is something the matter?"

Suddenly he felt shy. How ridiculous. *Shy?* He could feel the dark man's gaze, considering him. Assessing him. "No. I just . . . I saw you from the library window."

"And?"

"And I was most impressed," he said lightly, warned by the dangerous light in her eyes. "Your Mr Jones tells me they're called *hotas*."

"*Dexterity* told you—" She breathed hard for a moment, her lips pressed tight. Then she turned to the dark man. "Zandakar. Thank you." She punched her fist to her breast. "Again in the morning, *zho?*"

"*Zho*. In the morning," the man said, returning her salute. "Here. At dawn." He turned. Nodded. "Your Grace."

At least he thought it was "Your Grace". The man's accent was guttural. The words sounded more like "Yur Grarz". He nodded back. "Zandakar."

The tall dark man left them, heading for the stables. Rhian watched him for a moment then shifted her gaze. "What you want to know you ask me, Alasdair."

She was *rebuking* him? "You were busy."

"You've no right questioning my people. It's not fair on them. If you want to know something, *ask* me. I'll tell you."

All right, then. "What does *zho* mean?"

"It means *yes*."

"And what language would that be?"

She hesitated. Shrugged. "I don't know what it's called. It's Zandakar's language."

"And who *is* Zandakar, Rhian?"

Her eyes were glinting again. He saw temper, and unease. "A friend."

"A friend you know nothing about. Who came off a *slave ship,* from an unknown country."

She frowned. "Dexterity's got a busy tongue."

"He hardly told me anything," he said, close to temper himself. "He said to ask you. So I'm asking, Rhian. Why is Zandakar with you? What is going on?"

Hands fisted on her hips, she shifted away from him. In the swift-fading light it was hard to read her face. "It's a long story, and it's complicated."

"Which I want to hear," he said, trying desperately to sound reasonable. But he knew he was failing . . . and realised he didn't care. "I want to know who he is, Rhian! He spent the last hour waving a *knife* in your face! He nearly cut your throat three times that I saw. Nearly stabbed you to death five times, at least! And you don't even know what *country* he's from?"

"What does it matter where he comes from, Alasdair?" she retorted. "What does it matter if his speech is strange? He saved my *life.* I'd be *dead* without him. What does *anything* matter compared to that?"

Did she even know the knife was back in her hand? Did she know how fierce she looked, how suddenly foreign? With her short hair and her boy's clothes and a killing light ignited in her eyes?

She saw his shock, and the fury fled her. "I'm sorry. I'm sorry. I'm tired, Alasdair." She let the knife fall to the grass. "I'm so tired . . . and I'm so alone."

He opened his arms to her, and held her tight to his chest. "Idiot. You're not alone. You've got me. You're here, safe in Linfoi. What do you mean, he saved your life?"

"In duchy Arbat," she said, muffled against velvet. "There were footpads. They attacked us. Zandakar . . ."

"He killed them?"

She nodded. "They had swords and knives. They weren't intending to ask for directions."

Could she feel his heart pounding? Surely she had to. "How many?"

"Six. And he was unarmed. Well, except for a club. At first, anyway."

And you wonder why I'm worried? "I'm glad he saved you," he said. "Of course I'm glad. But—"

She pulled free of him, stepping back. "What's going on in duchy Arbat, Alasdair? Armed footpads roaming the country roads? Setting upon innocent travellers with *swords*? What are Rudi's soldiers about, letting ruffians like that run loose about the place?"

He shrugged. His arms were empty. "I don't know. But you can ask him yourself soon enough. He's coming here for Father's funeral and my investiture as duke."

"Coming *here*?" she echoed, dismayed. "Well, yes. Of course he is. *All* the dukes are coming? Edward and Damwin and Kyrin?"

"That's right."

"How soon will they arrive?"

"Three days from now. After Father's buried and I'm made the next duke we're supposed to travel south to Kingseat, so I can be confirmed in the High Chapel by the prolate and my king. Except . . ."

"Yes," she sighed. "I know. Except." She pressed a hand to her eyes, then let it fall away. "You haven't said if you'll marry me."

"Rhian . . ."

The only light now came from the rising moons. It

wasn't much. "What happens next, Alasdair, depends on your answer."

He wanted to call for someone to bring flaming torches. This wasn't a conversation to be held in the dark. "I *know* that. But Rhian—the implications—the consequences—have you thought of—"

"Since leaving the clerica I've thought of little else!" Her voice sounded bleak. "It's you or one of the others. I don't want them. Do you want me?"

"Do I *want* you? Rhian, how can you—"

She rested her hand against his chest. Her expression was solemn. Resolute. "I don't care that my father forbade a match between us. His opinion no longer carries weight. If you want me you can have me. But you can't have the crown."

He knocked her hand away, furious. "You think I want you for the *crown*?"

"Why not? Everyone else does."

"I'm not everyone else! I wanted you *before* there was a crown, remember? I wanted you before Ranald and Simon died, before *Eberg* died. Even when I knew it was hopeless I wanted you. I wanted you when I was twelve and you were six!"

"You did?" She sounded surprised. "You never told me."

He wasn't going to be distracted. She might as well have cut him with her knife. "How can you stand there and accuse me of being like those others? Why come here to marry me if you think I'm like *them*?"

"I don't," she said, quickly. "Alasdair, I don't."

"You just said—"

"Forget what I said. I didn't mean it. I'm sorry. I told you, I'm exhausted. I've come a long way from Todding."

"You certainly have." She'd come so far he wasn't certain he knew her. "Who else in Kingseat knows you've fled the clerica? Anyone?"

"The clerica's dame. And Marlan. Cecily must have told him, she'd have had no choice. And there were Kingseat guards looking for someone at the Pipslock riverstation. That's why it took so long to reach you. We came by road most of the way."

"Marlan," he said, feeling sick. "Rhian, you can't mean to stand against the Prolate of Ethrea. He's as powerful as a king. And you're his ward, you—"

Her chin came up, sharply. "No. I'm the Church's ward. There's a difference."

By a hairsbreadth, maybe. But it was an argument that could wait for later. He took her hands. They felt small and cold. "Rhian . . . when you say I can't have the crown . . ."

In the faint light, her eyes were shining. "It's my birthright, Alasdair. I'm Eberg's legitimate offspring, his only living heir. No man in this kingdom, not even you, has a greater claim to the throne. I won't give it away just because I'm a woman. I won't give it away because *Marlan* says I must. I won't give it to *him*. I'll go to hell first."

He wasn't surprised. How could he be surprised? She was Eberg's daughter. "So if I marry you . . ."

"You'll be my king consort. My chief advisor. Ethrea's monarch after me. You'll be a king, and the father of kings. Is that enough for you? I can't—I *won't*—give you more."

To be made Alasdair, King Consort? He'd never

dreamed so high. "And what happens to Linfoi? The duchy needs a duke."

She slid her hands free of his and folded her arms. "Well . . . who'd become duke if you dropped dead in your sleep? Henrik?"

"Ludo. Henrik renounced his claim in my cousin's favour when I came home and he took my place on the council."

"Did he?" She pulled a face. "No-one told me. Then Ludo would be duke. Is that acceptable to you?"

He nodded. "Ludo's a good man. I'd thought to name him to the council once Henrik stepped down."

"Then we're agreed, at least in principle?" Her lips curved in a tiny smile. She was trying to flirt with him but her eyes were too anxious. "You'll marry me, and be my king?"

He felt like a tree branch torn loose in a storm and flung pell-mell into a raging torrent. "In principle? Yes. I suppose. But it's more complicated, surely! Aside from Marlan you're still a minor in law, we can't—"

"Hush," she said, her fingers pressed against his lips. "We're agreed in principle. Let's leave it there for tonight. I'm tired and I'm hungry and I'm desperate for another bath. But first . . . will you take me to see your father?"

His father? "Yes. Of course. He's in the chapel."

He didn't need torches to help him find his way to the free-standing stone chapel that had held services for the manor's people for over five hundred years. As they walked through the darkness she slid her hand into his, he thought to seek comfort as well as offer it.

"Is there someone in there?" she said, seeing the lamp-glow through the ancient stained-glass windows.

"One of the chaplains from the venerable house," he said. "There's a vigil between now and the funeral. I'll ask him to leave his praying for a while so he won't see you."

She stopped. "Send him away altogether. Tell him you want to stand the rest of the vigil yourself. It's important," she added, when he opened his mouth to argue. "I'll explain later, I promise."

"All right," he said, and let go of her hand. "Wait here. I'll dismiss him. Assuming he'll let me."

"Assuming *nothing,* Alasdair. You're the Duke of Linfoi. Send him away."

The chaplain departed with a walking-lamp, protesting but acquiescent in the end to his ducal authority. Once the man was gone Rhian entered the chapel and knelt by the bier supporting Alasdair's father's heavy, lead-lined coffin. It was draped in the Linfoi standard, seeming too small to contain such a larger-than-life man. Alasdair knelt beside her, his bones achingly familiar with the cushions placed before the bier.

They prayed in silence, and he remembered love and laughter and a life lived in duty.

"My father always said a man was more than the coins piled high in his coffers," Rhian said eventually, lifting her head. "Yet he used your father's lack of affluence as an excuse to deny us and refused to explain himself. I came close to hating him for it." Her voice broke. "What kind of daughter hates her father on his deathbed?"

He rested his gaze on her profile, on the sweet curve of her cheek. "An angry one."

"As if that's an excuse."

"Our fathers liked each other well enough, Rhian, before they both fell in love with the same woman."

She looked at him, startled. *"What?"*

Oh. So even at the end, no-one had told her. "My father once had his eye on your mother. It was before she was Queen Ilda, of course. When she was still plain Lady Ilda of Morvell and your father was Prince of Kingseat. Mine had just become Duke of Linfoi."

"I never knew that," she said, scowling. "Probably the *boys* knew." She jabbed him with her elbow. "Why did *you* never tell me?"

He stared at the coffin. "My father asked me not to. He thought it a sleeping dog best left to snore undisturbed."

"Well, I want it woken. What happened, Alasdair?"

"Nothing good," he said, pulling a face. "At first their rivalry was . . . playful. Then they realised they both were deadly serious and the games turned nasty. Things were said and couldn't be unsaid. Their friendship was poisoned, and never recovered. Father withdrew his suit. He knew he couldn't afford to offend the future king. He chose my mother soon after and they were happy enough."

But then she died birthing his brother, and the baby died with her, and somehow his father had never remarried. *I've got my heir*, he'd always said. *More than one leads to trouble. You'll do as the next duke. I don't need another wife*.

Rhian shook her head. *"Men."* Her breath hitched. "What a *stupid* reason to keep us apart. Why were *we* to pay for the foolishness of our fathers?"

"Some hurts don't heal," he said. "Anyway. It's over now."

"No, it's *not* over! Don't you see? I'm still paying. If

Papa hadn't been so petty *none* of this would be happening! We could have married before he died and I never would've been made Marlan's prisoner. So much awfulness avoided, if only—if only—"

He put his arm around her shoulders. "I know. I'm sorry."

"Don't be sorry!" she said, shrugging free of him. "Be *angry*! How can you be so *calm*?"

"I don't see the point of being anything else. Anger won't change what happened. It's the past. It's done."

She got to her feet and went to stand before the Living Flame flickering gently in its sconce. "How admirable. Clearly you're a better man than I."

With her hair cut short the nape of her neck was exposed. Slender. Vulnerable. Desire stirred. "Rhian, whether you're here or in a clerica or even in your castle, until you turn twenty you're still Marlan's prisoner. I don't see how we can marry when—"

She glanced over her shoulder. "Ursa doesn't have an assistant, Alasdair. That man is my personal chaplain. His name is Helfred and he's Marlan's nephew. He was forced on me the day after you left court."

Swearing and cursing in a chapel was a sin. He sinned anyway, scrambling to his feet. "Rollin's wounds, Rhian! What were you *thinking,* bringing him here with you? Marlan's *nephew*? When the prolate finds out he'll put the duchy under *interdict*. I'll have the people in arms against me for imperilling their souls!"

"Marlan won't find out," she said, turning. "Not until it's too late for him to do anything so foolish as to interdict Linfoi. Helfred has no intention of telling his uncle where he is. He's broken with the prolate, Alasdair. He's with me, not against me."

He couldn't stand still. Pacing round his father's coffin, hands tucked into his armpits so he didn't shake Rhian, he said, "And this Helfred's how you plan to get around your Church wardship?"

She smiled, a thinly dangerous curve of her lips. "As a divine chaplain he has the power to release me from it and marry us."

"Why would he do that? Marlan will destroy him when he finds out!"

"Why? Because it's the right thing to do . . . and because he owes me a debt. Marlan is venal and Helfred knows it," said Rhian. Her smile vanished. Her eyes were bleak. "When we are married and naked together, Alasdair, you'll see the mementos from my sojourn in the clerica. Marlan claims to love me like a daughter but he has a poor way of showing it."

He stopped pacing. "The prolate beat you?"

"Till I fainted. Twice."

"Rhian . . ." No wonder she was different. No wonder she had run.

"It doesn't matter," she said. "He did me a good turn. Helfred never would've sided with me otherwise and without him I'd be lost and so would Ethrea." Sighing, she turned back to the Flame. "It might still be lost. I don't know. Too much is still uncertain."

The thought of Marlan hurting her made him sick to vomiting. Quelling nausea, stifling rage, he joined her at the Flame. "What does that mean?"

"There's more I have to tell you, Alasdair." Her sideways glance was . . . complicated. "I doubt you'll like it overmuch. Or even understand. I don't understand it all myself. I'm travelling on blind faith. On the faith of a toy-maker. On whispers and rumours and promises from the grave."

What? "Rhian—"

"Not here," she said tiredly. "Let's go back to the manor. I'll bathe. We'll eat. Then we'll sit down and talk."

Dexterity perched on the edge of a beautiful tapestried library chair with his hands tucked between his knees and his heart lodged in his throat.

Oh dear. Oh Hettie. Please do what you can. For if the duke rejects us . . .

He wasn't alone. Rhian, Duke Alasdair, Ursa, Helfred and Zandakar, they all sat in the library with him. Dinner was eaten, the servants largely gone to bed. The library door was closed tight and the time for spilling secrets had come. Again.

"I think, Alasdair," said Rhian, breaking the silence, "it would be easier if Dexterity explained things. All I ask is that you hold your questions till he's done."

Alasdair Linfoi wasn't a handsome man. He wasn't ugly, but he was certainly . . . plain. His eyes were a pale brown, his hair a few shades darker. Straight and untidy. Unfashionably short. His face was bony. There were cal-luses on his hands. His body was well knit but his car-riage lacked elegance. He looked more like a farmer than he looked like a duke.

He doesn't look like a king at all. But Rhian loves him, and we must believe she has cause.

The duke nodded. "All right. I'll hold my questions. Mr Jones, your explanation."

Dexterity glanced at Ursa, who nodded once in support. Helfred was staring at the faded carpet. No help there. Zandakar stood in a corner, his hands clasped before him and his extraordinary eyes half closed. With them but not with them. As usual, apart.

"Go on, Dexterity," said Rhian. Her expression was serious but her eyes were warm. "Just tell him. You'll be fine."

So he told his ridiculous, unbelievable story. True to his word Duke Alasdair stayed silent. When the tale was told he sat quietly behind the library's desk, his brown eyes staring at his folded hands.

"You believe him, Rhian?" he asked at last, looking up.

"I do, Alasdair," she said firmly.

He looked at Ursa. "And you, Madam? You believe this?"

"Yes, Your Grace."

"And you, Chaplain Helfred? How does the prolate's nephew feel about this?"

"I told His Grace the truth," said Rhian. "It was needful. Say what you like, Helfred. Let conscience be your only constraint."

Helfred released a cautious breath. "My feelings are divided, Your Grace. To all outward appearances Mr Jones is an honest upright man, though his carelessness of scripture must be a cause for concern. I do not doubt his care for Her Highness. I do not doubt he believes what he says. Nor can I deny that some of what he says has come to pass. I am *less* convinced, however, that we deal with benign forces."

Duke Alasdair nodded. "And what do you make of Zandakar?"

"What *can* I make of him?" said Helfred, his face pinched. "He is mysterious and dangerous, Your Grace. An unsavoury combination. To be blunt, I have deplored Princess Rhian's easy acceptance of the man. He is a brute, from what I suspect must be a brute race. If you had seen his killing of those unfortunate men . . ."

"Unfortunate?" said Rhian, temper kindling. "They were footpads set on violence, Helfred! Would you rather now be lying dead in a ditch?"

"I would rather not have witnessed such a casual slaughter!" Helfred retorted. "I do not say the men shouldn't have been stopped. But there are ways of stopping men short of death, Highness! And if, God save us, there must be death, do you call it seemly to *revel* in it after? And Zandakar *revelled* in it! You were there! You saw him! You *know* he did!"

"I know nothing of the sort," said Rhian, her voice tight in her throat. "You're letting your dislike of him colour your opinion. Hardly scriptural, Chaplain. Doesn't Rollin say in Eighth Admonitions that no man is perfect, therefore can render no perfect judgement? Or have you conveniently forgotten what transpired in the clerica?"

Helfred pushed to his feet. "You would throw the shame of Todding at me *again*? When will that business be laid to rest between us, Highness?"

"I have no idea, Helfred!" said Rhian, leaping to face him. "I suggest you ask me this time *next* year!"

The duke sighed. "Rhian—"

"Zandakar can't remember where he comes from!" she said, searing them all with her blazing stare. "He was sold like an animal, chained on board a stinking, filthy slave ship surrounded by disease and slow death, carried across countless leagues of ocean, and somehow, *somehow,* did not go mad or die. And we are told in no uncertain terms, by ways that are surely miraculous, that he is the key to Ethrea's safety. And let us not forget *he saved our lives.* Would you have me throw Ethrea's key away, would you have me question the miracle, all because he is strange to our eyes? Tell me! *Would you?*"

Dexterity watched as Helfred slowly sat down. "I do not know," the chaplain sighed. "I can only speak what is in my heart. Zandakar frightens me. I fear he is not safe."

"Your shadow frightens you, Helfred," said Rhian. "You must learn not to fear."

The duke looked at Ursa. "Madam? What are your thoughts on this foreign man?"

"Contradictory," said Ursa, after a moment. "For he's a living contradiction. But the princess is right about one thing, at least. He surely saved our lives."

"Do you believe him a miracle, sent to us by God?"

She frowned. "I believe God can send us miracles, Your Grace, often unawares. I don't know if Zandakar is one. In my experience God is usually more . . . subtle."

"And you, Mr Jones?" said the duke, shifting his regard. "It seems you and Zandakar are the most intricately linked. You rescued him. You nursed him to health. Who is right, here? Her Highness or the chaplain?"

"No disrespect intended, Your Grace," he said, sitting straighter, "but I'm guided by Hettie. She says we need Zandakar. She says we're doing God's work."

"I say so too," said Rhian. "And if you oppose me . . ."

Dexterity held his breath. The princess and the duke were staring at each other, so many complications in their eyes. Zandakar said nothing. It seemed he was content to stand in his corner and let them argue without him.

If he even understands what we're saying. He might not . . . but I think he does.

The duke drummed his fingers on the library desk, thinking, then nodded sharply. "Very well. We trust . . . for now. Chaplain Helfred . . ."

"Your Grace?" Helfred looked and sounded exhausted.

"Princess Rhian has asked me to be her king consort. I've accepted the honour. But without dispensation of her wardship she cannot wed. If she does not wed she cannot be queen. And if she is not queen, Ethrea falls into darkness . . . or so we are told. Chaplain, our fate is in your hands."

Helfred stood. "Your Grace, I could wed you and still not save Ethrea from darkness. The prolate will not accept the marriage. He will never accept a woman as ruling queen."

"I understand we would earn Prolate Marlan's enmity," said the duke. "But am I mistaken to think it would be a marriage sound in law?"

"No, Your Grace. You are not mistaken," said Helfred heavily. "I have the power to make Princess Rhian our queen."

"And will you do it, Helfred?" asked Rhian. "Though we share bitter memories. Though we anger each other almost beyond reason. Will you wed us for Ethrea's sake?"

Dexterity held his breath. *Oh Hettie, give him a nudge, would you? For if he says no we're wrecked upon the rocks!*

Helfred nodded. "Your Highness, I will."

CHAPTER TWENTY-FIVE

The first dawn after they reached the home of Alasdair Linfoi, Zandakar danced his *hotas* alone.

After rising and dressing and going downstairs he'd waited a little time for Rhian to join him in the manor house garden. When she did not come he shrugged, and danced without her.

See me dancing with my knife for you, god. See me in your silent eye. Here am I in another strange place, surrounded by more strange people of Ethrea. Why am I here, god? What is my purpose?

The god did not answer. An empty man, he danced for no-one.

The sun climbed higher, cresting the tops of the distant trees. His *hotas* flowed like a river, deep and strong. He felt strong. He felt rested. Last night he'd eaten his fill of rich meat for the first time since being sent away from Mijak. He'd drunk wine with the rich meat, it was not as good as Et-Raklion wine. When the talking was over he'd been shown to a solitary room, no snoring Helfred. He'd smiled at that and slept the night through in a bed so soft it almost killed his memories of the slave ship. But only almost.

I think I will not forget that ship until I die.

After the cramped peddler's van, his bones and muscles in the soft bed almost wept with relief. His eyes almost wept. It was good to be still. Good to be silent. Good to be apart from the others, away from tension and unhappiness and glowering Helfred.

He does not trust me. He is afraid. He should be afraid. He is a small soft man.

Hot blood pounded through his veins. He leapt, he spun, he watched the rising sun flash crimson on his knife. A straight blade, no sinuous curve, but it had killed wicked sinners just the same.

I have kept that much purpose. I slay wicked sinners.

Without Rhian to teach in the *hotas* he could dance much faster and harder, the way he used to dance when training with Dimmi and his warhost. When training with his mother when she could still dance. It felt good in his body to knife-dance hard and fast. Sometimes he was afraid he would never be a true warrior again, after his time on the slave ship and his time in chains before that, and fever, and woundings, and so long spent in this soft green land.

Soft lands breed soft people. Mijak's warriors will devour Ethrea. It will fall, their God will not save it.

The thought dismayed him. Was that a sin?

Tell me what you want, god. Do you want Ethrea thrown down? Am I here to help its falling? Dexterity does not think so. He thinks I am here to save his country, save his people. What do you want, god? Why am I here?

Silence. Silence. Nothing but silence.

I am tired, god. I am tired and alone. If I have no great purpose you must let me die.

Prickling skin told him someone was watching. He turned in his dancing but it was not the princess come late to her *hotas*. It was Alasdair duke, ruler of this land. This *duchy*. The duke stood in the archway leading into the gardens and watched in silence as the *hotas* flowed.

Dexterity had told him a duke was an important man. Below the king, the most important. So a duke was like a warlord in Mijak. But this Alasdair duke looked nothing like a warlord. He looked young and uncertain. Dexterity had told him the man had twenty-five seasons. If that was true he was the same age as Dimmi.

Aieee, the god see him. Dimmi will eat this Alasdair alive.

Dexterity had also told him Rhian loved this young, uncertain duke. He did not see that. Love was what he'd felt for Lilit, slender and beautiful in the sunshine, in his bed. Love was the light in her eyes for him, love was the painful pleasure of her touch. Love was her sweet smile, her soft laugh, her brave heart beating in time with his. That was love, he did not see it between Rhian and this duke.

A sharp pain pierced him. *Aieee, Lilit. Lilit.*

He stumbled, then, and missed his footing. If his mother had been here she would have shouted and slapped him. His warhost would have pointed and scoffed. Dimmi would have scoffed loudest of all.

Stupid, Zandakar. Do not be stupid. They are the dead past, do not think of them. Do not think.

His naked chest was running with sweat. His muscles

ached, they begged for rest. He had danced enough. It was time to stop and bathe and eat.

And wait to be told what I can do, like a slave.

After dancing it was important to stretch, warriors must have limber muscles. So he breathed deeply and stretched and thrust the dead past behind him.

Seeing the *hotas* were finished, Alasdair duke stirred from the archway and came forward, slowly.

"Is it true you've lost your memory?"

Sweating, breathing, he pressed his forehead to his knees. *"Zho."*

"And yet you recall these *hotas* of yours. Curious."

He straightened. *"Zho."*

The duke looked at him closely, arms folded. "A man of few words, I see. Because you don't know them? Or because you prefer to remain unknown . . ."

Ah. Like Helfred, this Alasdair duke suspected him of hiding truths. Breathing lies. On the surface his voice was pleasant. Underneath, it had sharp teeth. So perhaps he was not quite as young and uncertain as he seemed.

"So . . ." The duke folded his arms. "You recall your *hotas* . . . and that you had a wife. She died?"

Like all the men he had seen in Ethrea, this Alasdair duke was pale of skin. He had mud eyes and mud hair. His nose was crooked, with a bump in the middle. His face was long and narrow, he had a pointed chin. His clothes were plain, there were muscles beneath them. Was he counted beautiful in this soft land? In Mijak he would not be beautiful. In Mijak he would be a slave.

He is warlord here, I must not anger him. I must not strike him. I must lie down before him like a dog. Aieee, this dog's life, where no man lies down before me.

With a conscious effort he loosened his muscles. His blade was in his belt, he must leave it there. "*Zhò*. Lilit." He felt his heart hitch. "Lilit is dead."

Something flickered in the duke's mud eyes. "I'm sorry."

In his own tongue he said, "Do I care for your sorry? I think I do not."

Alasdair duke raised his eyebrows. "I didn't quite catch that. Your language is strange to me."

"*Zho. Yatzhay.* You want of me, duke?"

"You didn't defend or explain yourself last night. In the library," the duke said. "When we were talking about you to your face. Why is that? Did you not understand?"

He'd understood enough. "*Zho.*"

"Yes, you understood, or yes, you didn't?"

What? "I hear words. I know Ethrean now. Some Ethrean."

"Obviously," said Alasdair duke. "But do you know enough to know *why* we were discussing you?"

"*Zho.* Dexterity friend. Rhian friend. Ursa friend. Helfred *wei* friend."

"Yes. That sums it up," said the duke. "If I understand you correctly. But what about Zandakar? Is Zandakar friend?"

If he said *no* he was a dead man. If he said *yes* he'd live, for now. *Yes* would be a lie if the god's purpose for him was to smite Ethrea. This Alasdair duke was looking for lies.

What do I say, god? What do you want?

Alasdair duke stepped back, his arms unfolding. "You don't answer. That's an answer in itself."

Aieee! "I am friend to Rhian, duke. I am friend to Dexterity. Ursa." *And if I sin for that, god, tcha. I sin.*

"I see," said the duke. He was poised like a sandcat, ready to strike. "But not friend to Helfred?"

Helfred was a godspeaker. Helfred sensed things the others did not. Helfred was dangerous. *"Wei Helfred."*

Muscle by muscle, the duke relaxed. "Hmm. Well. If you understood what he said last night I don't suppose I can blame you. But hear this, Zandakar. Likeable or not, Chaplain Helfred is a man of God, a guest in this duchy and under my protection. I give you fair warning: harm him at your peril. Do you understand *that*?"

He nodded. *"Zho.* I understand."

"Yes." The duke smiled thinly. "I thought you might."

This man was a warlord. A kind of warlord. A warlord without weapons but still, he had power. *I am alone. I do not need a warlord enemy.* "Question, Alasdair duke."

The duke looked at him. "Ask it."

"Is Alasdair duke friend?"

Birds warbled in the woodland. Voices on the breeze, belonging to the manor's farm-workers going about their business. Not *slaves,* but *servants.* A stupid Ethrean difference.

Alasdair duke looked at the distant trees. "I wed Rhian today. Did you know?"

This highsun? So soon. *"Wei."*

"But you do know what 'wed' means? To become man and wife?"

"Zho. I know wed." *Laughter and loving and a heart so full.*

"That's why she's not down here, dancing your *hotas.*

Women's business. Dresses and so forth." The duke almost smiled. "If you've been married you must know."

He had no idea what the man meant. It was safest not to say so. *"Zho."*

"Once the marriage is done, Rhian becomes Ethrea's queen," said the duke, his brief amusement fled. His stare was a challenge. "I become its king. Did you know *that*?"

Queen was like Empress. "I know queen."

Alasdair duke frowned. "She says when she is married she will still dance your *hotas*. She says Ethrea has need of a warrior queen. She says you are a warrior, the only man who can teach her."

He nodded. "I teach Rhian *hotas*. Queen must be strong."

Alasdair duke stepped close. "I wish to *God* you'd never come here. You can't help keep Ethrea together, it's a matter for Rhian and me and the dukes and the Church to resolve. It's Ethrea's business, it's not the provenance of foreigners. Especially foreigners who don't even know where they come from!"

He held his ground against the duke. He would not step backwards for this man. "I teach Rhian *hotas*."

The duke's eyes were hot, his bony face savage. "She is more than Rhian, Zandakar. After today she'll be my *wife*. And I will have a care for her, I promise. Now. Tell me you understand."

"Zho," he said quietly. "I understand."

"Rhian believes in you," said Alasdair duke. "You saved her life, stood up to Helfred for her. Whatever you tell her, she believes. You and your sad story, they've touched her tender heart. She thinks you're . . . *romantic*.

Trust me, Zandakar. I don't. If you endanger Rhian, if you hurt her, believe *this:* your *hotas* won't save you. Rhian won't save you. I'll see you dead if knowing you brings her harm. Tell me you know *those* words, Zandakar. Show me you understand *that.*"

I understand I have no place here. I understand I am lost in the god's eye. I understand I must find my purpose or I will go mad in this green, godless place.

"*Zho,*" he told the man who would wed with Rhian. "*Zho,* Alasdair duke. I understand."

Rhian looked at herself in the full-length mirror. It felt peculiar to be in a dress again. After so long in boys' garb the skirts were cloying. A hindrance. The dress was too heavy. An anchor, weighing her down.

It's also some twenty years out of fashion . . . but I suppose it's churlish of me to even consider that.

The gown had belonged to Alasdair's late mother Arlys, the last Duchess of Linfoi. His father's second-best choice. This meant there was a certain breeziness beneath the jewel-encrusted brocade, since Duchess Arlys had been more generously endowed. But that didn't matter either. It was a dress, it fitted her well enough for the purpose, and once she was married she could take it off again.

She watched her pale cheeks flush pink.

I'm not going to think about clothes coming off. I've enough to worry about without thinking of that.

In the mirror, Ursa's wrinkled reflection smiled. "You look lovely, Your Highness," she said, a most unlikely new Dinsy. "That blue really becomes you."

"Thank you, Ursa. Ursa—"

"Your Highness?"

She sighed, and turned away from her overdressed image. "Nothing. It doesn't matter."

"The duke seems a fine man," said Ursa, after the smallest hesitation. "As far as I can tell on so short an acquaintance."

"Oh he is. He is." *I know he is. Even if he does seem oddly like a stranger.* "He's a splendid man, Ursa. And he'll make a fine king."

Ursa nodded. "He will. There's not so many men I know who'd willingly stand behind a woman so she could rule as queen in her own right."

"Dexterity would."

"Yes, well, *Jones,*" said Ursa, and shook her head. "He's another rare one. Which is probably for the best. Too many men in the world like your duke and that Jones, we'd never know whether to laugh or cry."

Rhian looked at the softly ticking clock on the bedroom mantel. Twenty minutes to go. Twenty minutes until her life changed forever. Again.

Every time I turn around it seems my life changes. Will it ever be settled? Will I ever just . . . be?

Ursa unboxed the diamond tiara that had come with the dress. "The servants have polished it as best they could," she said. "It should've gone to a jeweller for cleaning, but of course there's no time for that. Or a jeweller, as it happens. Your duke's very *rural.* I expected he'd live in the duchy's capital."

"There's a ducal residence in town, but the late duke hardly went there," she said. "He loved the country. Alasdair's the same."

She took the tiara from Ursa, blinking away a sting

of tears. At home in the castle were her mother's wedding jewels. She'd always planned on wearing them, as her mother had the day she and Papa stood before God in Kingseat's grandest Church.

Mama's jewels. A cloth-of-gold wedding dress made especially for me. Papa at my side, proud enough to burst. Ranald and Simon pulling faces. Poking fun. Pretending they didn't think I was beautiful. And a grand party afterwards with dancing in the streets. That was how my wedding was supposed to be. Not this cobbled-together, clandestine affair.

Without the slightest warning she was swamped by a dreadful wave of fear.

Oh, God. Am I doing the right thing? What if Alasdair's changed his mind and doesn't love me any more? What if he's only doing this because he thinks he should? Because he said he would? Because he's tired of being duke of the poorest duchy in Ethrea?

"All brides are nervous," said Ursa, gently. "Being a princess doesn't save you from that."

Speechless, she stared at the old woman. Then she found her voice. "It's not just the wedding, Ursa. It's—it's *everything.* What am I starting? When Marlan learns what I've done—when the other dukes arrive and find out—"

"There'll be a ruction," said Ursa. "We might hear the prolate's bellowing all the way from Kingseat. And the dukes? They'll likely kick up their heels too. But you knew that, Rhian. When you ran from the clerica and set your course for duchy Linfoi, you *knew* there'd be serious repercussions. Married or not you must know you wouldn't be *handed* the crown, that you'd have to fight for it. Are you trying to tell me you've changed your mind?"

"No!" She took a deep breath, seeking her balance. "No, I haven't changed my mind. How can I? An entire kingdom's depending on me. It's just—since my brothers came home sick, nothing's seemed real. Too much awfulness too quickly. It's like I'm living someone else's life and it's a terrible mistake but I can't escape it. And now—"

"Your Highness," said Helfred, entering without announcement or even a knock on the door. "A few words, if you please."

'I'll leave you,' said Ursa, and closed the bedroom door behind her.

Helfred's official robe was looking the worse for wear. *He* was looking the worse for wear, with dark circles imprinted under his eyes, his cheeks pale and hollow, his shoulders tense.

Swallowing a sigh, Rhian put down the tiara. *Oh Helfred, Helfred. This would be much easier if I liked you.*

"Don't tell me, Chaplain. Let me guess. You've changed your mind and the wedding is off."

Helfred's set expression didn't change. "No, Your Highness."

She felt her heart stutter. *"Alasdair's* changed his mind?"

"No-one has changed their mind, Princess Rhian," said Helfred, close to snapping. "Unless—"

"No," she said, and shook her head. "I'm determined to do this. I don't have a choice. But there is still time for you to change your mind. I'm completely—"

"Please, Your Highness, I—"

"*No.* Let me finish." She smoothed down her borrowed, ill-fitting dress, waiting until she could trust her voice.

"You mustn't think I don't know what this is costing you. I doubt there's another chaplain in Ethrea who'd dare to thwart the prolate's will."

"That's not your concern, Highness."

"Of *course* it's my concern! Without you I remain an unmarried princess. I'm in your power, Chaplain. Let's not pretend we don't know that."

Helfred nodded. "Very well."

"I don't want you to think I'm doing this lightly, or taking your sacrifice for granted. I'm not a reckless child, Helfred, chasing a pretty bauble. I know there'll be consequences, for both of us. But if I hadn't run from the clerica . . ."

"My uncle would have won," said Helfred. "He would have seen you beaten daily until you conformed to his will . . . or married you off to Lord Rulf by proxy and had you locked away as mentally infirm. Prostrated to madness by the loss of your father and brothers. He would have given the council documents in which you bade them accept Rulf as king. Forged, if he couldn't coerce you into signing them."

"He would have, wouldn't he?" she whispered. "Helfred, he's your *family*. You must have known what he is!"

Helfred turned away and stared out of the chamber window. "I knew him as arrogant. I believe even as a small boy he expected instant obedience to his demands. He was raised for the Church. A brilliant scholar. An energetic chaplain. The youngest venerable ever consecrated. A most venerable at thirty. At thirty-eight he headed the Court Ecclesiastica. And at fifty-six he became the kingdom's prolate. How could he do any of that if God weren't on his side?" He swallowed. "No. I never questioned. I wondered, when he suggested you marry Rulf. But it wasn't until the clerica . . ."

"That you realised he was evil?"

Helfred turned back. "Evil? It's not my place or yours to judge him so. But I will stand against him, because I believe he's wrong."

Damn. And now he'd humbled her. "Helfred—"

He raised his hand. "I know you find me a prosing bore, Your Highness. Pretentious. Condescending. In the way. Perhaps you're right, perhaps I am all those things. But I am also a dedicated man of God. I have faith in divine guidance. And no matter my reservations about Zandakar—which are grave—I cannot deny there is some power at work here."

"You said last night you feared it wasn't benign. Have you changed that opinion?"

"No. But neither am I sure. If it is malign I must fight for God. If God is in this I must fight for him. I will not desert you, Rhian. I will not permit myself to be such a man."

Rhian. He had never called her by her first name before.

She took a step towards him, thoughts and feelings an uncomfortable jumble. "Helfred—thank you. I'm sorry I'm so impatient. I'm sorry for being rude. I swear on my father's tomb, I won't let any harm come to you. I won't let Marlan punish you for helping me."

Surprisingly, Helfred managed a small smile. "The sentiment is appreciated, Highness. But I suspect that God alone is capable of protecting me from my uncle. So I shall leave that in his hands if it's all the same to you.

Now . . . we should take a moment to pray before I wed you to Duke Alasdair."

Awkwardly, she knelt. Helfred stood over her and let his palm rest on her close-cropped hair.

"God, whose infinite wisdom and kindness we can never deny, look upon this proud child and see into her heart," he intoned. "God, who sees all and knows all and forgives when we are penitent, hear now your daughter's heartfelt admission of wrong-doing that she might meet her ordained husband with no stain upon her soul . . ."

The manor-house chapel was small and spare. The Living Flame burned in an ungilded sconce. The ceiling was white, with no elaborate frescoes proclaiming Rollin and his miracles. Serviceable rugs, threadbare in places, covered the polished timber floor. The windows were stained-glass, but plain in design. The late duke's bier still occupied a goodly space, which was unfortunate but couldn't be helped.

"Are you sure Rhian's all right?" Dexterity whispered to Ursa, sitting beside him on the leading pew. "I can't imagine she won't be nervous. I was, the day of my wedding."

"She's fine, Jones," Ursa whispered in reply.

He sighed and took another look around the chapel. Some of the other pews were occupied by manor-house staff. The cook. Some housemaids. The housemaster, Sardre. They sat in stiff silence. It was hard to tell if they approved or not.

If we were in Kingseat we'd be in the High Chapel. The gilded pews would be overflowing with nobles and ambassadors from every great nation in the world. Ursa and I would never have been invited. Like the rest of the populace we'd have heard about it from the heralds.

He turned again to Ursa. "Not the wedding a girl dreams of, is it? Not the wedding you think of for a princess who's about to become queen. Do you think she minds? She's such a practical girl, I thought perhaps she might not mind but . . . it's her wedding. I remember how excited Hettie was."

Ursa shrugged. "I don't know, Jones. I didn't ask. Whatever she did or didn't dream of, this is the wedding God's seen fit to give her. And it's more of a wedding than some people get."

That made him stare. "Ursa . . . did *you* ever—"

"No," she said shortly. "Besides, we're not talking about me."

He knew so little about the life of young Ursa. She told him what she wanted him to know and bit his head off if he touched on memories she'd decided were none of his affair. He'd long since made his peace with that.

He turned to Zandakar, seated on his other side. "How were you married, Zandakar? Do you remember?"

A wary look came into Zandakar's eyes. *"Wei."*

"Oh. That's a shame," he said . . . and tried to ignore a stab of doubt.

Stop being so suspicious, Jones. Most likely he just doesn't want to talk of it. The screaming dreams have stopped but that doesn't mean he's not still grieving. When he thinks no-one's looking I see such sadness in his face . . .

Footsteps sounded outside the chapel. Dexterity looked behind them and saw the duke enter. Dressed in black velvet with pearls and rubies sewn sparsely on his sleeves and collar, his bony face was pale and set.

I was nervous on my wedding day but I was pleased as well. Duke Alasdair doesn't look pleased, he looks cornered. Oh Hettie. Are we making a terrible mistake?

The duke made his silent way to the front of the chapel and stood with his back to his guests and his manor staff, head lowered, perhaps praying.

A few moments later Rhian and Helfred arrived. She was pale too, weighed down by an old-fashioned blue dress sewn with sapphires the size of a small child's fist and edged with lozenges of heavy solid gold. A tarnished tiara graced her short curling black hair. Dexterity smiled up at her as she softly walked by. She spared him a single glance and his heart seized in his breast.

Oh Hettie, she's frightened. If you can, won't you comfort her? Send her a dream and let her know she'll be all right.

Helfred led Rhian to Duke Alasdair then stood before them, the Living Flame at his back. As they knelt he spread his arms wide, palms upturned.

"God, in your presence, let what we do here be sanctified," he said, his head lowered. "As a son of your Church, ordained and codified by the laws of that same Church which holds Princess Rhian in wardship, I surrender her safekeeping to Duke Alasdair Linfoi. Henceforth let him hold her guardianship until she reaches a legal age." He looked up. "Duke Alasdair, in the presence of God before his Living Flame, do you accept this child's guardianship until she turns twenty?"

The duke nodded. "I do."

Helfred swept his stern gaze around his small congregation. "I call upon you witnesses. Can any one here say this man is not fit to guard this child?"

No-one answered.

"So be it," said Helfred. "Princess Rhian is surrendered to the duke. Henceforth the Church holds no authority over her."

Dexterity, watching closely, thought he saw Rhian's shoulders slump as though some terrible weight had been lifted from her.

At last she's out of Marlan's clutches. Helfred has done a good thing this day.

"God," said Helfred. "Look upon this man. Look upon this woman. They desire to handfast in wedlock until death. Look upon these witnesses, gathered in your presence. Hear the words of these witnesses if they should object."

The chapel was silent. No-one moved. No-one spoke.

Dexterity felt his hand creep sideways and hold on tight to Ursa's hand. Her fingers closed around his, warm and strong.

"So be it," said Helfred, and looked at the duke. "Alasdair, Duke of Linfoi, do I handfast you willingly to this woman?"

"You do," said the duke.

"Rhian, Princess of Ethrea, do I handfast you willingly to this man?"

Rhian nodded. "You do."

"In the presence of God, without regret or coercion, you are handfast together," said Helfred. "Until death claims one or both of you, your flesh is as one."

Rhian and the duke stood and turned to face their witnesses in the chapel. Neither was smiling. Both appeared stunned.

Dexterity swallowed tears. *It's done, Hettie. It's done.*

Rhian lifted her chin. Her eyes were sparkling. "Friends, you have witnessed my marriage. Now witness this: no longer am I styled *Rhian, Her Highness, a princess of Ethrea.* Now you will know me as Rhian, your queen." She took Alasdair's hand. "And here is my husband. Once a duke, now king consort. In God's presence I declare this, before his sacred Flame."

Dexterity took a deep breath and slid from the pew onto his knees. "God bless Queen Rhian," he declared, his voice ringing out. "God bless her king."

One by one the others in the chapel followed his example. Even Zandakar knelt, though he stayed silent.

"Know this," said Rhian, tears standing in her eyes, once the echoes of the joyful shouting had died. "You are my people and I will defend you unto death. I will defend my kingdom from all who'd seek to harm it or steal it or stain it with blood. In God's presence, before his sacred Living Flame, this I swear. This I swear. This I solemnly swear."

"And as Ethrea's king consort," said Alasdair, "in God's presence, before his sacred Living Flame, I solemnly swear also."

Rhian smiled at him, almost shyly. Then her expression hardened again.

"Now let the word go out to the people of Linfoi. Let it go out to every duchy in the land. Rhian is married and she is the queen. And let any man who would stand against her beware . . . for she will hold on to what is rightfully hers."

CHAPTER TWENTY-SIX

The next day Dexterity came downstairs for breakfast to find Ursa had eaten already.

"I'm off physicking, Jones," she said, all bustling impatience. "There's been an outbreak of scaleytoe the next village over and the local physick has sent to the duke—the king—for aid. I've treated my share of scaleytoe in the past so I'm lending a hand."

"Oh," he said. "Do you need help? I've nothing to do here. In fact, when we finally see her again I was thinking of asking Rhian for leave to go home."

"Before the dukes come, and learn how their world's been rearranged without them?" Ursa shook her head. "You can't do that, Jones."

"Why not? I've done what I said I'd do, I've got Rhian to safety. She's the queen now. She's married. She doesn't need me."

"Zandakar needs you," said Ursa, lowering her voice, mindful of servants who could enter the dining room at any moment. "And we need you keeping an eye on *him* till we find out what's what. That man's a mystery yet to be unravelled, Jones. And he's *your* responsibility. Just you stay put."

She was right, of course, but he still felt like wailing. "And what about my toyshop? For all I know Tamas has taken leave of his senses and it's burned to the ground!"

"If that's the case, Jones, you can't unburn it from here," said Ursa. "Stop fussing and eat some bacon. I'll see you again at dinner, I expect."

"Wait. Can you use another pair of hands or not? If people are ailing . . ."

She considered him, hands on hips. "Have you ever had scaleytoe?"

"I'm not even certain what it is."

Ursa sighed crossly. "Tcha. Then you're no use to me. It's nasty, and catchable if you've not survived a tussle with it. We don't need it spreading any further. Now let me go, Jones. I've sick folk waiting."

He stepped back, gloomily. "All right. Be careful. I'll see you at supper."

She hurried away, full of purpose, leaving him to enjoy a solitary breakfast. He ate bacon and mushrooms and drank good Kingseat cider. Replete, with no sign of Rhian or the new king—and not surprised, considering—he took himself back to his room to collect his whittling tools and his latest half-finished puppet then wandered outside to find an out-of-the-way patch of sunshine in the gardens where he could work undisturbed. He didn't know where Zandakar was, or Helfred, and for the moment he didn't care. He'd not been alone with his thoughts since leaving home for the clerica. It would be a relief, to sit quietly and whittle.

Time drifted by, and no-one bothered him. The manor buzzed worse than a beehive with preparations for the dukes' imminent arrival. Servants rushed about, chattering and laughing. Smoke from the breadhouse ovens floated on the breeze, mingling with the aroma of baking bread. Alarmed cackles from the poultry-shed beyond the neat hedges suggested chicken would be part of the funeral and investiture day's feasting. From where he sat, idly carving, he could see a steady procession of wagons trundling up and down the manor drive, loaded with wine casks and ale barrels and extra servants to cope with the dukes' retinues. Striped tents went up on the wide lawns beside the manor house. Pipers and lutists and a harpist arrived. Their determined practising added motley music to the mix.

Sighing, content for the first time in many long days, Dexterity used the tip of his knife to gouge out an eye for his new puppet, which bore a passing resemblance to Zandakar. Reminded, he paused in his whittling to frown across the manor garden's fragrant flower beds.

You know, Hettie, when I rescued Zandakar I didn't expect him to become a permanent part of my life. I never imagined he'd be my responsibility . . .

"I know you didn't, Dexie," said Hettie, apologetic. "I'm sorry I wasn't more truthful with you."

"Hettie!" Startled, he ran the whittling knife into his finger. *"Ow!"*

Conjured out of thin air, she sat beside him on the garden's worn wooden bench. "Oh, Dex." She took his hurt hand and kissed away the blood-drop welling from the small wound. The pain ceased. The wound healed.

He stared at her. "How did you do that?"

"Magic," she said, smiling. But the smile was strained, and something about her looked wrong . . .

"Hettie, what's the matter? You look *exhausted*. How can that be? You're not—you're a—" He fumbled to a halt, uncertain. Suddenly afraid. "Hettie?"

She patted his knee. "Don't worry about me, Dex. You've worries of your own."

"I know," he said, and looked around, but none of the passing manor servants seemed to notice he was sitting with a strange woman who hadn't been there a moment before.

"It's all right," said Hettie. Her face was pale. Almost translucent. Was he imagining things or did the faint shapes of flowers show right through her? "They can't see or hear me."

"But they can see and hear *me*! They'll think I've gone mad, sitting here talking to myself."

"No. All they see is you whittling your puppet."

"Good." He shifted a little so her hand fell from his knee. "So why have you come this time, then? Is there someone else for me to rescue? Or do I get an explanation at last? Better yet, you could say hello to Rhian and the du—the king. You could put Helfred's mind at rest. I'm starting to weary of folk looking sideways at me."

"Dexie . . ." She sounded hurt. "You're not pleased to see me?"

"I'm not pleased my life is such a rambunction," he retorted, reckless with dismay. "I thought I'd be safely back home by now, rousing on Tamas and being condescended to by Lady Dester. Instead I'm stuck here waiting for the dukes to arrive. It's the last place in Ethrea I want to be. When they find out what's happened there'll be a terrible ruckus. I'm a toymaker, Hettie. I'm not cut out for terrible ruckuses."

"I know," she whispered. "I'm sorry."

He felt horrible, railing at her, but he couldn't help it.

*My life was so peaceful. I just want things back the way
they were. Is that too much to ask?*

He sighed. "What do you need?"

Hettie smoothed her blue dress over her knees. For the
first time he noticed the cotton was faded and patched in
places. The lace on its hem was stained. Torn. It wasn't
like Hettie to be unkempt. Despite his crossness he felt a
clutch of fear.

"Not me, Dex. It's Zandakar. He needs you."

"Why? What do you mean?"

"His heart is troubled, my love. He carries a burden of
secrets. It's time he shared that burden before it destroys
him."

A burden of secrets. His guts roiled in protest. Sweat
dampened his skin.

*I knew that. I knew Zandakar was hiding from us. And
still I defended him. Was that a mistake?*

"Is he dangerous, Hettie? Have I put Rhian in—"

"Every man is dangerous, Dex. In his own way."

"Have I endangered Rhian? *Tell me!*"

Hettie took his hand. Her fingers were cold, as though
she were sickening with something. He remembered her
cold fingers. Their touch chilled his heart.

*You're a ghost already, Hettie. You can't die twice . . .
can you?*

"You've saved Rhian, Dexie," she said, holding tight.
"Don't ever doubt that. You can save Zandakar, too. You
have to."

He tugged his hand free. "Save him from what? Hettie,
do *you* know his secrets?"

She wouldn't meet his eyes, which was answer
enough.

"*Tell* me! What's the good of you keeping secrets too? Tell me what you know of him and—"

"I can't," she said. There were tears in her eyes. "I've done all I can, Dex. This is your battle and you have to fight it."

"And how can I fight it if I don't know what's going on?"

"Zandakar can tell you. You have to make him tell you."

He stared. "Hettie, I can't *make* Zandakar do anything and to be honest with you, I'm not inclined to try. In case you haven't noticed he's a bit handy with a knife."

"You must try," she said. "Zandakar needs you, Dex. He's alone and grieving and he's lost his way. You can help him by being his friend. You *have* to help him. He's the key to everything . . . and you're the key to him."

The half-finished puppet was still in his other hand. He looked at its rough face, an echo of Zandakar. "Well . . ."

"Please, Dex. Go now. He's faltering. He's about to do something that can't be undone." She leapt up. "Hurry, Dexie! He's in the farmyard. *Run!*"

The fear in her eyes was the most frightening thing he'd ever seen. He dropped the puppet's head and stood. Since the first day they met, he'd never been able to say no to her. "All right. I'm going."

She snatched at his sleeve. "And Dex—whatever he tells you . . . it must remain secret."

"*Secret?* Hettie—"

"Rhian's not ready. Neither is Ethrea. There's strife here to settle before she can know the truth. *Trust* me, Dexterity. You can't tell a soul. If you don't keep the truth of Zandakar to yourself we'll be worse off than ever. Promise me you'll do that. *Promise* me, Dex!"

Hettie . . . Hettie . . . the things you ask of me. "All right," he said. "I promise."

Her smile was a pale thing, as pale as her skin. "Thank you. Now go."

Churning with fear, with love and trepidation, he turned his back on her and started to run.

Hettie was right. He found Zandakar in the manor's farm-yard. In the slaughter pens, where the eviscerated carcasses of calves and sheep hung from hooks draining out their blood, ready to be roasted for the investiture feast. The morning had slipped away. It was the working men's dinner hour, and Zandakar was the only soul there.

When Dexterity saw him, he nearly cried out. The man he'd saved from the slave ship was on his knees before one of the draining-tubs set under the butchered beasts. Oblivious to everything around him, in one breath he poured cupped handfuls of blood over his head . . . and in the next he poured it into his mouth. Choking, swallowing, he drank the clotting stuff. He was bloody to the elbows, his neat Ethrean shirt and trousers soaked scarlet. In profile he looked as Helfred had described him: a brutal man from a brutal race.

Hettie . . . Hettie . . . who is this—this creature?

Apparently sated, Zandakar started chanting, a singsong litany in his own strange tongue. He was lost in his ritual, and there were tears in his voice. Such grief. Such sorrow. Such despair beneath the sun.

The knife he danced with, the one he'd taken from the

footpads, was slipped through his belt. He pulled it out and held it before his face.

"Chalava!" he said, his tear-fractured voice knotting in his throat. *"Azai azai chalava wei Zandakar. Wei navnaki, wei jokoribi, Zandakar wei, aieee, chalava, Zandakar zho huknuza!"*

What was the knife for? What did it mean? Was it part of this dreadful ritual? Or was Zandakar planning something worse . . .

"Chalava! Huknuza zho Zandakar!"

Dexterity reached under his shirt and touched the crude wooden carving he still wore around his neck, that Zandakar had given him—it seemed a lifetime ago, now—back in Kingseat. *Chalava.*

Could that be a *god*?

He knew some nations worshipped animals as gods. He knew the people of Haisun worshipped no god at all. And in Tzhung-tzhungchai it was thought God was the wind. Men listened to windchimes, to hear his voice.

Did Zandakar drink blood to learn his god's desires?

Rollin have mercy, Hettie! What manner of man have you brought to us here?

And then he did cry out, because Zandakar slashed himself with the knife, slicing through sleeve and flesh on his left forearm, cutting more deeply and dangerously than he ever could with a stone.

"Zandakar! *No!*"

It was madness, of course, to accost a man like Zandakar. He was thrown aside as easily as a dog tossed by a bull. He felt a sharp burning as the knife's edge caught him and opened a shallow cut down his cheek. Ignoring the pain and the swift spurt of blood, he threw himself for a second time at the ex-slave because yes, he clearly was mad, and heard Zandakar let out a startled grunt and a whoosh of air as his elbow connected hard with the man's belly. Remembering the way Zandakar had put Rhian on her back in the *hotas* he swung his leg round in a clumsy arc and was rewarded with another grunt.

Zandakar hit the ground on his back. Sickened, recalling Ursa's tales of knife-fights by the harbour, knowing he had only a heartbeat of time, Dexterity dropped to his knees and with all his strength banged his fist onto the cut in Zandakar's arm. Zandakar shouted. The knife fell from his fingers. Puffing, groaning, Dexterity tossed the blade aside and flung himself across Zandakar's ribcage.

"Stay down! Stay down, you fool of a man! What are you doing? What were you *thinking*?"

A stream of foreign words was his only reply. They didn't sound cordial. Nor was the look on Zandakar's blood-slicked face the smile of a friend. His lips were peeled back in a snarl of fury as he cursed the interference that had likely saved his life.

Abruptly aware of the pain in his cheek, Dexterity eased himself off prone Zandakar's ribcage to sit on the ground, and pressed his fingers to the shallow cut in his flesh. "I'm sorry," he said. "*Yatzhay*, Zandakar. But if you think I'm going to stand idly by while you slice yourself to ribbons you're very much mistaken. I lost far too much sleep over you in Kingseat, my friend."

Silence. In the distance a rooster crowed. Dexterity looked at the blood on his fingertips.

How will I explain this to Ursa, I wonder?

"Dexterity *wei* understand," said Zandakar. The anger was gone from him. He sounded lost, and empty. He didn't sit up, he just sprawled like a dropped puppet and stared at the sky.

"No, I certainly don't!" he snapped, wiping his fingers down the front of his shirt. "But you're going to explain. You're going to explain *everything*."

Zandakar shook his head. "*Wei,* Dexterity. *Wei* remember."

Dexterity poked Zandakar's shoulder. "Oh yes you do. You remember it *all*."

"*Wei,* Dexterity. *Wei* remem—"

"*Don't lie to me!*"

Shocked, Zandakar stared at him, his pale blue eyes wide.

Dexterity leaned close, his heart drubbing his ribs. "Don't lie," he said again, close to a whisper. "You remember well enough. You've been keeping secrets."

"Secrets?" Zandakar shook his head. "*Wei* understand word *secrets*."

"Truths, Zandakar," he said sternly. "Things about yourself you remember, and say you don't. *Zho?*"

Zandakar said nothing, but his eyes showed he understood.

"I *know* you've been keeping secrets, Zandakar. Hettie told me."

"Hettie," said Zandakar. He sounded . . . resigned.

"Yes," he said. "She told me you were about to do something stupid, too, and she was right." Without asking, he snatched up Zandakar's left arm and looked at the bleeding knife-wound in it. "Look what you've done, you foolish man! You might've severed an artery! You might've bled to death. Can you wriggle your fingers?

Can you make a fist?" He wriggled his own fingers, to explain, then clenched them tightly.

If the wound still hurt him, Zandakar didn't show it. He wriggled his fingers. He made a fist.

Dexterity sighed. "Well, that's something at least. You didn't slice through a tendon. And of course Ursa's not here, is she? The one time she's needed she's off saving folk from scaleytoe!" He reached for Zandakar's knife, tugged his shirt out and slashed off a length of it from around the hem. "So a rough bandage will have to hold you until she gets back."

"Dexterity . . ."

"You be quiet!" he said fiercely. "And sit up. I need to bind this wound."

Obedient as a puppet now, Zandakar sat up.

"We'll have to invent another reason for this cut, you know," he added, swiftly wrapping Zandakar's hurt forearm. "We don't dare tell Ursa the truth. She'll go spare if she hears you did it on purpose and believe me, Ursa going spare isn't something you take lightly. There. How's that? I think it's tight enough to stop the bleeding."

Zandakar looked at the rough bandage and shrugged.

"You're welcome," Dexterity said, glowering. *You troublesome man.* "Next time I think I *will* let you bleed to death."

Zandakar lowered his head, his skull glinting blue in the sunshine where his hair had started growing back. Flakes of dried animal blood fell from his face and spiralled to the ground. "*Yatzhay,* Dexterity."

Oh dear. Oh Hettie. He clambered to his feet and stuck the knife through his own belt. "Come on. We can't stay here. The men's dinner hour will be over soon. They can't come back and find us like this." He looked around. "There's a pump and scrubbing brush there," he added, pointing. "Wash as much blood off as you can, quickly. Then you and I are going for a little walk in the manor woodland, Zandakar, and you're going to tell me who you are and where you're from and what you know about this great danger Ethrea faces. Do you understand? *No more secrets.* The time for secrets has *passed*."

For a moment he thought Zandakar was going to refuse, or fight him. Every muscle in him was tensed, and his pale blue eyes were rebellious. Then he let out a long, slow sigh. Bone by bone, he got to his feet. "*Zho,* Dexterity. We will talk." His eyes glinted, strangely. "But Dexterity *wei* like what Zandakar says."

The first workers were returning to the farmyard when he and Zandakar made their escape, abandoning the cultivated manor grounds and slipping into the dappled woodland edging the ducal estate. Well-worn paths wound through the trees, with old hoofprints showing this was a popular place for the duke and his people to ride. It was pleasantly cool in the shade. Sunlight filtered through to the soft damp ground. Birds and squirrels danced and chattered in the leafy branches overhead.

Despite the green tang of wildflower and fresh air, Dexterity could still smell the rank stench of death. If he closed his eyes he could see the knife, slashing, the butchered animal carcasses, the blood pouring into Zandakar's open mouth.

A fallen tree, bearded with lichen and cushioned with moss, barred their path a few paces ahead. They were deep in the woodland now. It was unlikely they'd be discovered or overheard.

"Here," he said, stopping. "We'll talk here."

Zandakar slowed. Halted. His expression was guarded. If his cut arm pained him he gave no sign.

Dexterity perched himself on the fallen tree. *Just two friends chatting, that's what we are. And if I'm sitting perhaps he won't get confrontational.* Even with the knife in his own belt he didn't feel entirely safe. *You'd better be watching, Hettie. If he gets confrontational you'd better be ready to save me. In my world knives are for whittling, not killing.*

There was little purpose to beating around the bush. "Who are you, Zandakar? Where are you from?"

Zandakar leaned his shoulder against the bole of the nearest standing tree. Washed clean of the animal blood, emptied of that dreadful killing despair, he seemed his calm self again . . . at least on the surface. But Dexterity thought an echo of that madness still lurked in his eyes.

"Listen," he persisted. "I understand you're wary. You're alone here. You're frightened and you don't know who to trust. But you can trust *me,* Zandakar. Haven't I shown that? Haven't I proven that you can trust me?"

Zandakar didn't answer. From his lack of reaction a man might think he was deaf.

Come on, Hettie. A little help, please. "Zandakar, we've reached a crossroads. There are things that *must* be said now, because you and I didn't meet by accident. Tens and tens of thousands of lives depend on what we do next. *Trust* me. I won't betray you. Do you understand?"

Zandakar nodded. *"Zho."*

"And do you believe me when I say I mean you no harm?"

"You *wei* mean harm." Zandakar *shrugged*. "Harm still come."

And there was the voice of bitter experience. "Not if I can help it. Zandakar, this is *important*."

Zandakar frowned. "Hettie say?"

"Yes. She did. She also said these secrets of yours are hurting you. And since you were cutting yourself open with a *knife* I think it's safe to say she's right. And I won't have it."

Zandakar's blue gaze touched him and slid away. "Hettie dead."

Oh dear. "It's complicated. Do you understand complicated? Did you understand what I told Duke Alasdair—the king—in the manor library?"

"Dead Hettie speak to Dexterity."

"Yes. She does. Today she told me to learn your secrets. She told me to keep them, and keep them I will. And please, Zandakar—" He held up a hand. "Don't insult me by saying you can't remember. We both know that's not true. You remember just fine."

Zandakar exhaled in a long, slow sigh. Let his blue-stubbled head rest against the tree's smooth bark. *"Zho."*

It came as an odd kind of relief to hear him say it. "Very well, then. We understand each other. So who are you, Zandakar? Where are you from?"

"My land is Mijak," said Zandakar. His eyes lost their focus, staring into the woodland. Staring at memories.

Mijak. No, he'd never heard of it. "Is it a long way from Ethrea?"

Such a sadness in Zandakar's face. *"Zho.* Mijak far.

Travel many moons on land, with slaves. More moons in slave ship. Mijak far."

"And who are you in Mijak, Zandakar?"

Again it seemed Zandakar struggled to answer. Not with remembering, but with his willingness to trust. *"Chotzu,"* he said eventually, with reluctance.

"Chotzu? I'm sorry, I don't know that—"

"Chotzu!" Zandakar banged a fist on the tree. "Like Rhian."

Like *Rhian*? "Zandakar, in Mijak . . . are you a *king*?"

"Wei. Wei. Rhian before queen."

"Oh! You're a *prince*?"

Zandakar shrugged. *"Chotzu."*

Well. That certainly explained a few things. No wonder he carried himself like royalty. He *was* royalty. A warrior prince from an unknown land.

Who drinks animal blood and can kill six men without blinking.

"If you're a prince—a *chotzu*—how is it you were sold as a slave?"

Zandakar said nothing. It was in his face, how much he hated to be questioned. How much he didn't want to talk about his past.

Damn you, Zandakar. Don't make me say what we'll both regret . . . "Zandakar. *Tell* me."

Zandakar's fingers tightened to fists, his eyes full of anguish.

Dexterity stood. *I have to do this. I have no choice.* "If you don't tell me I'll tell Rhian you're dangerous," he threatened, his voice unsteady. *I don't want to be this man.* "I'll tell her Hettie told me to send you away. She'll believe me. You know she will. You'll be all alone, Zandakar. No friends. No home. No money to live. Is that what you want? It's not what I want, but I swear I'll do it. I'm your friend but I'll do it."

"Tcha!" said Zandakar. "Dexterity *wei gajka!*"

He stepped forward, heart pounding so hard. *"How is it you became a slave?"*

"Dmitrak!" said Zandakar, as though the word were cut from him with a knife.

He knew that name. He'd heard that name in Zandakar's dreamings. "Who is Dmitrak?"

"Dimmi is—is—" Zandakar growled in frustration. "Helfred give word. *Zho!* Dimmi is brother."

"Your *brother* sold you into slavery?" Dexterity said, horrified. "Why? So he could become *chotzu*?" It was a popular theme, brothers usurping brothers for the sake of a crown.

"Wei."

Oh. "Then who?"

"Vortka," said Zandakar, still reluctant. "Dmitrak want to kill Zandakar. Vortka send Zandakar away."

Another name from his delirious ramblings. "Who is Vortka?"

"Vortka—" Zandakar thought for a moment, his face softening. "Vortka *gajka*."

He nodded. "I see. No, actually, I don't. Your friend saved your life by making you a slave?"

"Wei!" said Zandakar. "Vortka send Zandakar away. Slave-men find. Slave-men take."

Good God. I was right? How amazing. "Zandakar. Who is Yuma?"

Zandakar's face clenched in a spasm of pain. *"Wei. Wei* talk more, Dexterity."

"*Zho!* We must."

"Why?" Zandakar demanded. "Lilit gone. *Wei* talk Lilit alive."

"I know," he said. "I know it won't bring her back. But not talking is killing you, Zandakar. Your secrets are killing you and I can't let you die. I promised Hettie I wouldn't. Don't be afraid. You're not alone. Whatever the truth is, we can face it together."

Zandakar shoved away from the tree. "*Wei,* Dexterity!"

"*Zho,* Zandakar." He grabbed the man's arm, breathless. "Zandakar, *zho.*"

Stillness. Silence. A squirrel chattered, scolding. Close by a fox barked, derisive in the hush. Zandakar stood tall and straight and braced, as though he was the last living man on a battlefield . . . and the enemy rode towards him with his death in their eyes.

Dexterity let go of him. "Zandakar. Please."

Something seemed to break in Zandakar, then. His mask slipped. Behind it, the face of the man who had dreamed. "Yuma is mother," he whispered. "Hekat. *Hushla.* Mijak queen."

It took him a moment to make sense of the words. "Your *mother* killed Lilit?" He knew he sounded disbelieving but he couldn't help that. Mothers didn't murder the women married to their sons. At least, not in his world.

I've left my world behind. I wonder if I'll ever find it again?

Zandakar, his eyes dreadful, rounded his hands over his belly as though he was pregnant. Then he mimed slicing himself open with a knife. "*Wei.* Yuma cut, son die. Dimmi kill Lilit. Zandakar *wei* save."

Dear God, what a family. Oh Hettie. Hettie. No wonder he was dreaming. No wonder he screamed. Sickened, Dexterity put a hand on Zandakar's shoulder. "*Yatzhay. Yatzhay*, Zandakar . . ."

Perhaps it was the genuine sorrow in his voice. Perhaps it was the relief of telling someone, even a stranger, the terrible truth that had festered for so long. Zandakar pressed a hand to his face and sobbed, a dreadful mourning for all that he'd lost.

Dexterity waited for the storm of grief to pass. Eventually Zandakar lowered his hand and stood there, exhausted, as though he'd wept out all his strength.

"That's terrible, Zandakar," said Dexterity, quietly. "But it's not everything. Hettie says Ethrea's in danger. Your wife and child dying can't put this kingdom in harm's way. There's something else. Something worse. You have more secrets and I need to know them all."

CHAPTER TWENTY-SEVEN

Zandakar said nothing. The woodland silence deepened.

Dexterity, watching him, felt his heart thud like a drum. *If I didn't know better I'd say he was afraid. I do know better . . . and yes. He reeks of fear.*

Zandakar afraid was a frightening thing.

"Dexterity *wei* understand," Zandakar said at last.

"Then *help* me! I'll understand if you explain."

"Dexterity . . ." Zandakar looked at the bound cut on his arm. *"Chalava."*

That word again. He fished out the carving from under his shirt. "This is *chalava, zho*? What is *chalava*? Is it— is it your god?"

Zandakar looked at the crude carving. *"Chalava,"* he whispered, his face chased with awe and longing and despair. *"Zho.* I think . . . *god."*

"Good! See? I understand. *Chalava* is the god of Mijak."

"Wei," said Zandakar, frowning. *"Chalava* is *chalava."* He made a sweeping gesture with his arm.

God is god . . . everywhere? "No, Zandakar. *Chalava* is not god everywhere. There is no *chalava* in Ethrea. Or Slynt, or Barbruish, or Dev'karesh or Arbenia. *Chalava* is *chalava* in Mijak."

Zandakar shook his head. *"Chalava* is *chalava."*

There was no point arguing. "You can discuss that with Helfred. He's the chaplain, scriptural philosophy is his meat and ale. What I want to know is—"

"Dexterity," said Zandakar. *"Chalava* is *chalava*. God of Ethrea *wei chalava*. God of Ethrea—*tcha."*

The contempt in his face was unmistakable. A good thing Helfred wasn't here to see it. Dexterity, despite his own troubles with the Church, felt an uncomfortable sting of resentment. "I'm sure you're free to think so," he said. "But you'll not find a soul in Ethrea who'll agree. And I don't suggest you voice that opinion, at least not while we're travelling with Rhian, or we'll have a nasty fight on our hands. Several ugly wars have been fought over who's got the best god. Religious folk take their beliefs . . . very . . . seriously . . ." His voice trailed away. He felt sweat on his skin.

Zandakar in the farmyard, drinking clotted blood. Calling for *chalava*. Calling for help? Zandakar insistent: his god was everywhere.

Oh, Hettie. Hettie. Surely not . . .

Zandakar's gaze was fixed on the carving. "*Chalava* is *chalava*."

The urge to sit down again was almost overwhelming. His knees had gone all wobbly. His head was light, his mouth dry. "And what does *chalava* want, Zandakar? Do you know? Can you tell me?"

Zandakar looked away. "*Chalava* is *chalava*."

He bit back a frustrated oath. "Yes, so you've said. I do understand that much. What I *don't* understand is what that means to Ethrea." He snatched up the wooden carving dangled round his neck. "You wanted me to have this. Why? For protection? Do you think this carving will *save* me from your god?"

Zandakar said nothing. His face had gone tight, with a small muscle leaping along his jaw.

He does. He does. Oh, Hettie. This is dreadful. "Your god is god of Mijak. Does it want to be god of other places, too? Does it want you to conquer for it?"

"Conquer?" said Zandakar. He was braced again, and wary. "*Wei* understand."

"Conquer. It means . . . take," said Dexterity, and mimed snatching something precious to himself. "Take. *Zho?*"

A long, dreadful silence. Then Zandakar nodded. "*Zho.*"

Oh, Hettie. He was suddenly cold. "You're a warrior of

Mijak, Zandakar. You're *chotzu*. Mijak's prince. Are you *chotzu* for *chalava*? Some kind of *holy* warrior?"

"*Wei. Wei.*"

He didn't believe that. "Perhaps not now. But you were, Zandakar. Before."

Another slow, reluctant nod. "*Zho*. Before."

Before his mother killed his unborn son and his brother killed his wife. God have mercy. Here was the truth Hettie had charged him to find. Here was the danger that Ethrea faced.

"When you were *chotzu*, Zandakar. When you fought for your god. Did you conquer other countries?"

Zandakar understood that. It showed in his eyes that he understood. But he didn't want to answer. He turned his head away.

"Zandakar! *Did you?*"

"*Zho*," said Zandakar, almost too softly to hear.

"How many? Who were they? Can you even remember? Or don't their names matter?"

Zandakar flinched. "Targa. Zree. Drohne. Bryzin. Har—"

"And the people in those places?" he demanded, cutting short the list. *So many names, Hettie. So many lost.* "What happened to them when you came?"

Zandakar looked at him. His eyes were cold. Derisive. "What does Dexterity think?"

He felt sick. So sick. "I think you killed them."

"*Zho.*"

"*All* of them?"

"*Wei*. Some slaves."

It was like looking at a stranger. *Did I nurse this man? Did I succour him? Was there pity in my heart?*

"How many, Zandakar? How many killed? How many enslaved?"

Zandakar sat on the fallen tree. Suddenly he looked tired. Abandoned. As though living was too hard. "I think you say . . . thousands."

Dexterity felt his hands clench. His chest was hurting. It was hard to breathe through the piercing pain.

Thousands. Thousands. Hettie, he's murdered thousands.

He was a peaceable man. He'd never liked ructions and raised voices. He liked his life quiet, and not stirred about. He'd never enjoyed cockfighting, or any sports made of blood and death. Never been drunk in an alehouse and found himself in a brawl. He was a plain man. A staid man. He was gentle. He made toys.

Drenched in scarlet fury he rushed at Zandakar, fists raised. "And I thought *six* men dead was a slaughter? You should've *told* me! How dare you not *tell* me?" He shoved Zandakar so the man half tumbled from the fallen tree. "*I let you close to the princess of Ethrea!* I told her to *trust* you. I promised her you were *safe*! But you're a *murderer*! A *conquerer*! You've destroyed entire *countries*! God save me, you want to destroy *my* country! You and your *chalava,* you want to conquer *Ethrea*!"

Zandakar raised a hand. "*Yatzhay—yatzhay—*"

"And was it *yatzhay* to the thousands you butchered and enslaved? *Yatzhay* to Targa, Zandakar? *Yatzhay* to Zree?"

Zandakar pushed himself up from his knees. "*Wei,* Dexterity. Listen. Listen."

So angry he was fearless, he shoved Zandakar down again. "Listen to a murderer? No, I don't think so! I think

Hettie must be *mad* to have me rescue you. I should've left you on that slave ship to rot! I should have left you there to *die*!"

A breeze sighed through the sweet green woodland. He heard a voice sigh with it: *Dexie, love. Have faith. We need him.*

He spun around. "Hettie?"

The breeze died away. Hettie was silent, if she'd even been there. He turned back to Zandakar, who sat splayed on the damp ground staring up at him, his pale blue eyes wide. Almost child-like. The animal blood had dried rust-red on his clothes.

"And what am I to do with you now?" he demanded, his voice ragged. "Do I pretend I never learned this? Do I pretend I don't know you're this *chotzu* for your god?"

Wearily Zandakar shook his head. "*Wei chotzu*, Dexterity."

"Then what are you now? Besides a murderer."

"I am—I am—*tcha*." Zandakar made a sharp, slashing gesture. His face twisted in disgust.

I am nothing.

More silence. Dexterity stared at him, flayed with doubt. Then Hettie's words sounded again, an echo in his heart. *We need him.* Slowly the scarlet tide of fury receded, taking with it the impulse to batter, to hurt. He stepped back.

"What happened, Zandakar? Why are you no longer *chotzu* in Mijak? Why did your mother and brother kill your wife and son?"

Zandakar let his head thud against the fallen tree. "Yuma hate Lilit," he said dully. "Lilit people Harjha. Slave people, Yuma say." He spat on the ground. "Animal."

Well, how charming. "But you didn't think so. You loved her. You *married* her."

The pain in Zandakar's face was almost too great to look at. "*Zho*. I loved Lilit."

"And because of Lilit your mother turned away from you?"

"*Wei*. Because I did not conquer Na'ha'leima."

Na'ha'leima? *Oh, Hettie. All these lands I've never heard of.* "You *didn't* conquer . . ." He shook his head, confused. "Why not? After all those other countries, why stop there?"

Zandakar punched a fist against his heart. "I hear *chalava. Chalava* say *wei* conquer. Dimmi is angry. I go to Et-Raklion with Dimmi. Vortka say I *wei* hear *chalava.*"

Dexterity sat on the far end of the fallen tree. His legs felt like they were stuffed with cotton. His head was aching. His throat was tight. "How would Vortka know?"

"Vortka is *chalava-chaka*. Like Helfred, *zho?*"

"A holy man? Ah. I see."

"Vortka hears *chalava*. He say *chalava* wants conquer. Yuma—Yuma—" Zandakar's face twisted again. "Yuma want conquer. Yuma want to kill Zandakar. Vortka say *wei.*"

"So Vortka saved you twice. A friend, indeed," he murmured. "And what happened then?"

"Yuma say Dimmi is *chalava-hagra.*"

"What is *chalava-hagra*?"

Zandakar shrugged. "*Wei* words. *Chalava-hagra* . . ." He held up both hands. Fisted one, and smashed it into his other palm. Again. Again. Again. "*Chalava-hagra.*"

A weapon. Like a hammer, for his bloodthirsty god. *I feel sick.* "So it's Dimmi who comes to Ethrea? Dimmi who conquers the world for your god?"

"*Zho.* Dimmi comes. With *chotzaka.* I think you say army."

"But . . . you said your god told you to *stop* the killing. Who was right? You or Vortka?"

Zandakar's face reflected his torment. "*Wei* know, Dexterity. *Wei* know."

Dexterity jumped up from the fallen tree and stamped a few paces up and down the woodland path. "Well I do, Zandakar. *You* were right. Your people have no business thinking to conquer the rest of us. You should have stayed in Mijak where you belong."

I thought he was gentle. I thought I sensed something good in him. And now I find he's slaughtered thousands. Enslaved thousands more. Helfred was right. He's a brute, from a brute race. A race of people who are coming to kill us in the name of their dreadful god.

Unbidden, his fingers found the carved *chalava* hanging round his neck. They tightened on it, and he went to tear it off its twine so he could throw it away.

"*Wei!*" shouted Zandakar, lurching to his feet. "Dexterity, *wei. Chalava* for you."

"I don't want it! I want nothing to do with this god of yours."

"*Wei,* Dexterity," said Zandakar, looming over him. "Keep *chalava.* Please." He touched his eye. "*Chalava* see Dexterity. *Chalava wei* kill."

Dexterity stared at him. *He said please. He's never said please before. And if I say no he might turn uncooperative.* He let his hand drop. "All right. I'll wear it."

Zandakar nodded. He seemed relieved. Then he pressed his fist to his heart. "*Yatzhay,* Dexterity. *Yatzhay* for Targa. *Yatzhay* for Drohne, and Harjha, and Bryzin, and Zree. *Yatzhay* for Ethrea if Dmitrak comes."

Against all commonsense he believed Zandakar's sorrow. Something in the tone of his voice . . . the pain in his eyes . . . a shadow of memory darkening his face. But he couldn't forgive the man. At least not yet. He jabbed his finger into Zandakar's chest.

I think I know now why you had me save him, Hettie . . .

"If Dmitrak comes, Zandakar, *you're* going to stop him. You're going to be *chalava-hagra* for Ethrea. Understand?"

"*Zho.* Understand."

"And you *never* speak of what you've told me today. This is *our secret.* If anyone learns who you are, where you're from, what you've done and what your people plan to do . . . I think they'll kill you outright. And that's not what Hettie has planned. You're here to save Ethrea and that's *exactly* what you'll do."

Zandakar frowned. "*Wei* tell Rhian?"

Dexterity jabbed him again. "Especially *wei* Rhian! She can't know this, Zandakar. She's about to face a terrible trial, she's about to fight for her right to the Crown! God alone knows the kind of powers she'll be up against. She might even have to fight the whole Church. She can't be distracted with tidings like *this.* We'll tell her when it's over and she's safe on the throne. Not a minute before."

Did Zandakar understand? It was hard to say. But he nodded, as though he did. "*Zho,* Dexterity. Secret."

"Good," he said, stepping back. "Now we'd best make

our way home to the manor. Else they'll be sending out someone to look for us and I'd rather not be found here. Let's go."

Zandakar held out his hand. "Knife, Dexterity."

The knife. Yes. It was still stuck through his belt. He pulled it out and looked at it, then at Zandakar. It would seem odd, after all this time, if Zandakar didn't carry it. Odder still if a toymaker did.

"If I give this back to you, I want your promise," he said sternly. "*No more cutting yourself.* And no more *blood*! It's *disgusting*."

Zandakar nodded. "*Zho*. No more blood."

"All right then," he muttered, and gave the knife back.

On returning to the manor house, Zandakar went to the stables. Dexterity, pleased to see him go for the moment, fetched his abandoned whittling tools and carving from the garden and took them inside. He found Ursa in the dining room, safely back from her physicking and enjoying a bowl of soup. The day had slipped away from him. It was late afternoon and the air was cooling.

"You'll spoil your appetite," he said, smiling briefly.

"Tcha!" she scoffed, and swallowed another spoonful. "Sixty years of living and it hasn't happened yet."

In need of support, he leaned against the wall. "Things go all right today then, did they?"

Another spoonful of soup. "They went fine. The outbreak wasn't as bad as first thought. Which is a mercy, considering." She sat back, her eyebrows lowered. "What's wrong, Jones? You look like your donkey just died."

The urge to tell her was overwhelming.

Funny you should ask, Ursa. As it happens, I've just

discovered Zandakar's an exiled warrior prince from a land full of marauding warriors. He's slaughtered thousands of innocents. He's conquered entire countries. He's got a mother and brother twice as bad as he is and apparently they're on their way here to kill or enslave every last breathing one of us. Apart from that, everything's fine.

He wanted to tell her, oh, he wanted to share the news. To let her carry some of its burden. To make himself not so *alone*. Except he'd promised Hettie he'd say nothing. He'd promised Zandakar too. The thought of keeping his promise to a man like Zandakar struck him as odd in the extreme, but that couldn't be helped.

Besides, if I tell her she'll have a conniption. It'll be the end of Zandakar. Hettie's trusting me to keep him safe. So I'll hold my tongue no matter the cost.

And there would be a cost. He could feel that in his hollowed bones.

Forcing a smile, he shook his head. "Nothing's wrong. I'm fine. A touch of megrim, perhaps. I fell asleep in the sun, whittling." The lie stung. Never before had he told an untruth to Ursa. It felt like a betrayal. As though he'd broken something that might never be mended.

"Fool of a man," Ursa scolded, and put down her spoon. "I've a potion for that. You come with me."

She led him upstairs to her room where she handed him a vial of something horrible and watched him drink it.

"Thank you," he said, his mouth shrivelled, and handed the empty vial back.

"Don't suppose you've seen the prin—the queen today,

have you?" said Ursa, washing the vial clean in the privy basin on its stand under the window.

"No. But then I was outside and—and sleeping a good few hours." The lie stung him a second time. He thrust the pain aside. "Besides, they are newly married, Ursa. They'll want a day to themselves, I'm thinking."

She sniffed. "A day, perhaps. But no longer. We've a kingdom in crisis and dukes arriving soon. This is no time for dalliance, Jones. She's a long, rocky road ahead of her. She needs her wits sharp."

"I think she knows what's ahead of her, Ursa." Some of it, anyway. "It's because of what's ahead of her she needs this one day."

"I know," said Ursa. She put the cleaned vial aside to dry then perched on the end of her enormous four-poster bed. "And I don't mind telling you, Jones . . . what's ahead of her's got me nervous. It's all very well her standing up in that tiny manor-house chapel in front of a handful of servants and nobodies and declaring herself queen, but a queen's only queen when the dukes and the Church say she is. And Prolate Marlan's not going to say so. Helfred might've had the law on his side when he married the girl to Alasdair but he's not got the power to declare her queen."

Dexterity perched on the bed beside her. "He doesn't need it, Ursa. There's no law that says Rhian can't rule. She's Eberg's heir, that's the start and finish of it."

"Tcha. *Law*. What's the law when you've tradition behind you, Jones? What's the law when the Church says you've done the wrong thing? I tell you, we've landed ourselves in an ugly business. I don't like it. I wish we were home."

He put his arm around her shoulders. "And if we were home, Ursa, who'd've saved those poor villagers from a nasty case of scaleytoe?"

"Stop humouring me," she said, and shrugged his arm away. "I won't be humoured, Jones. I'm right to be worried."

He sighed. "What's going to happen will happen. We just have to have faith."

"Hark at him!" said Ursa, snorting. "Have faith, he says, a man who's not set foot in Church for twenty years!"

"What are you talking about? I was in a church yesterday."

She glowered. "You know what I mean, Jones."

He rarely saw her this upset. Putting his arm around her again, he let his cheek rest on the top of her head. "Yes. I know. But that doesn't mean I'm wrong. Things are stirring here, grand things, frightening things, that we don't understand, or aren't meant to know of yet. But we're on the right side of them, Ursa. We're fighting for good, you and me. We're fighting for Ethrea. We must hold on to that."

"You're getting philosophical in your old age, Jones," said Ursa. She didn't shrug him away this time. "I don't like it. Next thing I know you'll be on your knees in a church properly, and then I'll have to take to my bed."

He kissed her hair. He'd never done that before. *It's because I feel guilty.* "You should take to your bed anyway. You look tired. Why not sleep awhile, before the servants call us for dinner?"

"Do you know, Jones? I think I might," she said. "Treating scaleytoe is no simple business. And what's more, I'll say the same to you. Get some rest. Potion or no potion you still look like your donkey died."

He took her advice. In his own room, with the door closed, he sagged onto his bed, aching as though he'd just tumbled down a hill. The weight of what he knew, now, was enough to grind his bones to dust. The weight of his promises. The weight of Zandakar's terrible secret . . .

Oh, Hettie, my darling. I hope I've done the right thing.

"Alasdair . . . Alasdair, tell me I'm doing the right thing," whispered Rhian.

In the bed Alasdair shifted, mumbling. In her chair by the window, dressed again in her boy's clothes, Rhian stared at the plain, bony lines of his face and wished she could lay her cheek against his. Wished his bed was hers so when she opened her eyes tomorrow morning the first thing she'd see was his sleeping face.

But that couldn't be. Not yet. The marriage had been consummated, as was only prudent. A fumbling affair with much awkwardness on both sides. Not . . . unpleasant, however. At least not entirely. And there'd been certain hints that things might improve upon practice.

Though when we'll get to that practice I've no idea.

Because from tonight she and her new husband would sleep apart until the matter of her right to rule was settled. They had to. The last thing she needed was to fall pregnant when she could be facing civil war. There were herbs, Ursa said, and had given some to her, but herbs weren't always reliable. She needed reliable. She didn't need complications.

My life is complicated enough as it is.

The dukes would be arriving tomorrow, and she would face them as Ethrea's uncrowned queen. If they supported her, if they recognised her right to rule as Eberg's legitimate heir, she might just manage to keep the kingdom together in the face of Marlan's certain opposition and the rallied opposition of his widespread Church. If they didn't . . .

It will be civil war. Ethrean turned against Ethrean. Blood will be spilled.

"Alasdair," she whispered. "Please. I need to know. Am I being unreasonable? Greedy? Spoilt? Should I stop this now before it truly begins?" Renounce her right to rule. Let the House of Havrell's time come to a quiet end. Live out her days in duchy Linfoi as a simple duchess and let the dukes fight it out amongst themselves to make a new king.

Would that even be possible? Or would I just be a lightning rod for trouble? I don't know, I don't know.

"You're my husband, Alasdair. Tell me what to do!"

Alasdair snuffled, and pulled the blankets over his head.

Right. Yes. Thank you. That's enormously helpful.

Except . . . he was right. She was Ethrea's queen. It wasn't his place to tell her what to do. And if he tried he'd only make her angry. He knew that. In many ways he knew her better than anyone ever had. Knew her. Loved her. And she loved him. Even if things were strained between them . . .

Everything's happening too fast, that's the problem. And there's too much trouble brewing that he wasn't prepared for. And with his father newly dead . . .

Beyond the curtained windows the light was slowly

fading. Restless, lost, she unfolded herself from the deep velvet chair and slipped from the chamber. Manor servants about their business curtsied as she passed. Nodding brief acknowledgement, she trounced lightly down the staircase to the ground-floor reception hall then outside into the approaching dusk.

Zandakar was in the gardens, dancing, the slow, steady limbering steps that warmed the body so it could tolerate the more energetic *hotas* without injury. He turned, hearing her approach, and stopped. Acknowledged her with a brief dip of his head. He'd stopped shaving it, so now a blue sheen shimmered. So odd. She wondered if she should order him to shave it again, to make him less conspicuous.

Perhaps she would. But not yet. In truth she was curious to see what it would look like, grown . . .

"Rhian," he said, one eyebrow lifted.

"Zandakar." She frowned. "Is something the matter? You look . . ." Wrong. Somehow upset. Beneath his familiar composure she could sense a deep unquiet. And there was something in his eyes . . . "Are you all right?"

"*Zho.* All right."

"You're sure?" she said, unconvinced. "No-one's been bothering you, have they? No-one's made you feel unwelcome? Because you're part of my retinue. I won't have you made to feel unwelcome just because you're . . . different."

"*Wei.* Zandakar all right."

Relieved, she smiled at him. "Good. That's good." She slid her knife from its sheath on her belt and pressed her fist to her heart in the ritual of pupil to master. "May I join you?"

"Where is king?"

"Asleep. Why? What does Alasdair have to do with the *hotas*?"

The look he gave her was gently derisive. *What do you think?*

She lifted her chin. "I do what I will, Zandakar. I do what I *must,* to prepare myself for the struggle ahead. The *hotas* make me strong. They help me focus. When I dance the *hotas* I'm not a woman. I am Ethrea's queen. Do you understand?"

He almost smiled. *"Zho."*

"Good. Then may I join you?"

Instead of answering he flowed once more into the first set pattern, an easy gliding sidestep and stretching of arm. She followed his lead. Tried to let the now-familiar steps take control of her body and calm her unquiet, doubt-plagued mind.

Her mind refused to be calmed.

"Zandakar," she murmured, sweeping her knife in a slow, smooth arc, "how does it feel to kill a man?"

He spared her a single disapproving glance. "You want *hotas*? Dance *hotas*. You want to talk? Talk another place."

"Zandakar, please. I need to know."

"Why?"

She abandoned the *hotas* and stood before him. "Because I'm afraid if I can't convince the dukes who are coming here that I am the rightful Queen of Ethrea, there will be fighting. Not just with words, but with knives. With other weapons. I might have to fight, Zandakar, to keep what is rightfully mine. I might have to kill. I have never killed. Do you understand?"

With a sigh, he stopped dancing. "Rhian . . ."

"It doesn't seem to trouble you. Killing," she persisted. "Is that because you're a warrior? Have you killed so many you can't feel any more? If I kill, will *I* stop feeling? And if I do can I still be a good queen? What *is* a good queen? If I truly love Ethrea should I even be doing this? Should I be risking civil breakdown, putting our treaties with the trading nations at risk? Putting Ethrea's future and sovereignty at risk? And do you have any idea what I'm saying? Or would I be better off asking these questions of a tree?"

Zandakar frowned. "Trees talk in Ethrea?"

Despite her rising distress, she had to laugh. "No. Of course not." She shook herself. "I'm sorry. Never mind me. You're just a warrior, how could you possibly understand?" She held up her knife. "Let's continue, shall we?"

But he didn't resume the *hotas*. Instead he considered her with his pale, piercing eyes. "Rhian . . . not easy, be queen. You want queen, you fight." His clenched fist struck his chest, above his heart. "You hard here. You afraid to fight, you afraid to kill, you no queen. You die. Ethrea die. You want to die?"

"No. Of course not!"

He shrugged. "Then fight. Kill. That is queen."

"Where *you* come from, perhaps! Wherever that is. But not *here*! Not in *Ethrea*!"

Another shrug. "All places, Rhian. All places men are men. Men want, men take. You want stop?" He raised his knife. "This stop."

She stared at him, appalled. *Dear God, is he right? There's been peace in this kingdom for so long . . . The*

*treatied nations, they fight all the time. Small squabbles,
bloody conflicts. Battles over land, religion, over trading routes, over husbands and wives, over who sells what
thing of value to whom and for how much. But not here.
Here we've been spared that for hundreds of years.*

Until now, perhaps. Because of me.

"Zandakar," she whispered. "*Tell me.* What does it feel
like to kill?"

He sighed. "Kill bad, Rhian."

She shivered as a chill skittered over her skin. The look
in his eyes . . . "Even when there's no other choice? When
it's an enemy who wants to destroy you? Even when you're
killing for the greater good?"

"Always bad, Rhian," said Zandakar. "For you."

"Why for me?" she said, stung. "Because I'm a
woman?"

The strangest look came into his eyes, then. Sorrow
and shadows. A memory? Perhaps. Something unpleasant
if it was. He shook his head, his lips curved in a sad smile.
"*Wei.* Because you Rhian."

Strangely she found his comment comforting. The idea
that anyone could get used to killing . . . or worse still,
could en*joy* it . . . "I don't want killing to be good, Zandakar," she whispered. "I don't want to kill at all. But I'm
afraid that to save Ethrea I might have to."

"Kill bad, *zho,*" he agreed. Then he shrugged, with a
cold, resigned fatalism. "Rhian . . . die worse."

And that was it, wasn't it? Really, when all was said
and done? Sometimes, in the end, it was desperately simple. *Kill or be killed.* There was nothing else.

She looked at the dagger in her hand. Felt its weight.
Its promise. "Come on, then," she said, and turned to face

him. "What are we doing, standing here talking? Let's dance our *hotas*. Let's prepare for death."

CHAPTER TWENTY-EIGHT

Alasdair was in the library, going through the manor-house ledger a final time, when his cousin was ushered into the room.

"Ludo!" He shoved back his chair and went to greet him. "It's grand to see you."

"And you, Alasdair," said Ludo. "Though the occasion lacks joy."

They embraced, then Alasdair looked to Sardre, still standing in the doorway. "You have need of me?"

"Word from the venerable house, Your Grace," said Sardre. "The venerables and chaplains will be arriving within the hour to make preparations."

He nodded. "Very good. See that all is ready for them." *And make certain our unusual guests are safely tucked away in their rooms, out of sight.*

Sardre nodded, hearing perfectly the unspoken command. "I shall see to everything, Your Grace."

And he would. It was, as ever, *thank God for Sardre.* As the door closed behind him, Alasdair turned back to his cousin. Tall, lean and elegantly attired, the jest between them had always been that Ludo had inherited the Linfoi charm and good looks, leaving nothing but the title for poor old Alasdair. *And now he'll have everything. If he wants it. If he stands by me.* "I appreciate you coming early, Ludo."

"Nonsense! I'd've come days ago, if you'd asked for me," said Ludo, throwing himself into one of the two chairs by the window. "But you always were one to lick your wounds alone."

Alasdair took the other chair. "Yes. Ludo, have you heard from your father recently?"

"Yesterday," said Ludo, nodding. "He's sorely distressed at not being here, Alasdair. You don't bear him ill will for staying in Kingseat, do you?"

"Of course not. I need him in Kingseat. I need his voice on the council. His eyes and ears. My uncle is a canny bird."

"A canny bird who's squawking about the princess," said Ludo, torn between amusement and concern. "She's still refusing to leave the clerica. He says the council's about at daggers-drawn over it. Marlan's defending her right to religious retreat for all he's worth." Ludo pulled a face. "It'd be easier to believe in his protestations if he didn't have a man he wanted her to marry."

Alasdair stared at his hands. "Yes."

"I'm sorry," said Ludo. "You've not erased Rhian from your heart yet, have you?"

It was an astute observation, surprising from Ludo. Though he was two years older, Ludo oftentimes seemed the younger of them. He had a roving eye and a rollicking sense of humour. He was unmarried and showed no sign of repenting. Like a bee taking pollen he supped from this blossom, then from that. But never so deeply as to mire himself in scandal, he was too wily to get caught compromised in the wrong bed. His father Henrik was old-fashioned, and so was duchy Linfoi. Not even a ranking noble could flout moral convention with impunity.

"Don't fret on her, Alasdair," Ludo added. "If you loved once, you'll love again. And even if you don't you still must marry. A duke must have a duchess, at least in the beginning."

Alasdair nodded. "Yes. I'm glad you can see that." He looked up. "Ludo, I am married. I've married Rhian."

Ludo's jaw dropped, the look on his face comical.

I might even laugh at it if this were not so serious.

"But you can't have, Alasdair," Ludo protested. "Eberg forbade it. And anyway, she's in a clerica at Todding."

"No, she's upstairs actually. Taking a morning bath."

His cousin nearly fell out of his chair. "She's *here*?"

"Yes."

"And you've *married* her?"

"Yes."

With an effort Ludo regained his composure. "Does my father know?"

"We thought it safest not to tell him. Secret letters don't always remain secret."

"No," said Ludo. He sounded dazed. "Well, you always did love the wench." He shook himself. "And the council doesn't know? What about Marlan?"

"We're sure he knows she's escaped the clerica and for his own reasons is keeping the news to himself. He knows Rhian will have no choice but to show herself, sooner or later. He'll make his move against her then."

"But—but *Alasdair*," said Ludo, torn between astonishment and shouting. "How can you have *married* her? She's a ward of the Church!"

"We received a dispensation. Ludo—"

But Ludo wasn't listening. Shoving out of the comfortable armchair, he ranged about the library, the heel of one hand pressed to his brow. "Good *God*! Do you know what this means? If you've married Rhian that makes you the—"

"King," said Alasdair. "Yes. I do realise."

Ludo spun around. *"Alasdair!"*

He felt himself smile. "Ridiculous, isn't it?"

"Ridiculous?" Ludo flung his arms in the air. "It's—it's—is it *legal*?"

"I'm told it is, yes."

"Told?" Ludo stared. "Told by whom?"

Ludo had to know all of it. He and Rhian had agreed on that yesterday, as they'd talked through the implications and consequences of their marriage. If Ludo was to take his place as duke he had to know it all and support their decisions. "Chaplain Helfred. He's the divine who dispensed with the Church wardship and married us. Ludo . . . he's Marlan's nephew."

Ludo collapsed once more in his chair. "I am speechless," he announced. "Shocked beyond words. How in Rollin's name did you convince the prolate's nephew to do such a madcap thing? He'll be stripped of his divinity and thrown into a Church prison for the rest of his days. And the council will declare the marriage invalid. It'll have you arrested and likely executed for the rape of a royal princess!" He cleared his throat. "Ah—I take it there are grounds for a charge of—"

"There are," Alasdair said, coolly. "But you're assuming Rhian will allow the council any such leeway. I promise you she won't."

"Rhian won't allow—" Ludo's jaw dropped again.

"Alasdair—you don't mean—you're not telling me she's—"

"I do. She is. She intends to rule in her own right."

Ludo slumped, amazed. "A *queen* ruling Ethrea? It's never been done!"

"Thank you, Ludo," he said, his voice dry as dust. "We hadn't considered that."

Ludo wagged a finger at him. "There's no point raising hackles at *me,* Alasdair. *I'm* not the one taken leave of his senses. Do you have the faintest notion what will happen when word of this spills out?"

"Surprisingly we do. Ludo, we haven't acted on a whim. We know there will be loud opposition from men who have only their own best interests at heart. But their opposition can be no more than empty posturing. There's no question of Rhian's breeding, she *is* Eberg's heir and I'm of undisputed noble blood. The marriage was contracted lawfully . . . and, being married, Rhian is lawfully queen."

"Which makes you what, cousin? If you're not to rule?"

"It makes me king consort," he said quietly. "And if you think to sit there and suggest I am somehow *unmanned* by that, Ludo, then shame on you."

Ludo's cheeks flushed. "I—I—*don't,* I *never*—Alasdair, you're being unfair!"

"Many will say it. I just don't want you to be one of them."

"Well, I *won't*!" said Ludo hotly, and pushed again to his feet. "And shame on *you* for thinking I'd be so base! We've been friends all our lives, Alasdair. Is this to be our first quarrel?"

"No, our sixth," he retorted. "At the very least. Or have you conveniently forgotten the others since you lost them all to me?"

Ludo waved their previous arguments away. "I concede not a one of them. Nor will I argue with you now. You say you're happy to be the king consort, who am I to gainsay that? You're a man who knows his mind."

"I'm a man who needs a duke," he said. "Now that I'm king, duchy Linfoi's in want of governance."

"Me? You'll make *me* duke?"

"You're already the heir presumptive."

"Yes, but I never thought—I never *imagined*—I imagined you married and siring a baby duke of your own."

"And so I am married, Ludo. But I'll be siring a king." He smiled. "Or a queen, perhaps. That's for God to decide. My concern is this duchy of Linfoi. Will you accept it from me, cousin? Will you be my loyal duke?"

All indignation and comical dismay vanished from Ludo's face. He went down on one knee, his wide-fingered right hand pressed hard to his heart. "I will, Alasdair," he said solemnly. "I'll be yours until death. Only . . ."

"Yes, Ludo. You will have to get married."

Ludo mimed himself arrow-shot. "God have mercy! Pierced to the heart!"

Alasdair stood and extended his hand. "You'll survive the experience, cousin," he said, pulling Ludo to his feet. "I hope. Though I must give you fair warning . . . Rhian is making a list."

"A list?" echoed Ludo. "Of suitable damsels? You mean I can't choose my own bride?"

He pulled a face. "It seems unlikely. I'm sorry."

"Politics?" said Ludo, scowling. "Of course. Always politics. I should've married when I had the chance."

"Yes, you should've. Truly, I am sorry," he added, sincerely. "So is Rhian. She knows how it feels to be used in this way. But—"

"Don't fret," said Ludo. "My heart's not given to anyone."

"A blessing." He stepped back. "You'll be invested as Linfoi's duke after the funeral. That's when Rhian and I will tell the other dukes how things now stand."

Ludo shook his head. "I fear we're in for an interesting afternoon, Your Majesty." His eyes opened wide, then. "Your Majesty," he murmured. "Truly, it hardly feels real."

"Not to me, either. And if we fail in placing Rhian on the throne most likely it won't be. Not beyond these four walls."

"Marlan will oppose you. He'll instruct the Church to oppose you. Alasdair, I fear life will become monstrous ugly."

"Nothing is more certain. *But* . . . I'm told I must have faith, that we proceed upon divine counsel."

"Divine counsel?" Ludo stared. "Who told you that? This foolhardy Chaplain Helfred?"

"No. Another man. You'll meet him presently."

"And when do I meet your bride, Alasdair? When do I meet Rhian, Ethrea's queen?"

"After the funeral. She'll witness your investiture and give her seal to your elevation."

"Which, along with your kingship, might not last beyond these four walls," said Ludo, grimacing. "Alasdair, what will you do if the dukes refuse to recognise her? Or you? What will you do if you find yourselves alone in this?"

"With God on my side?" he said, striving for lightness. "I'd hardly call that *alone*."

"Alasdair—"

"I know, Ludo. I know," he said, his hands raised placatingly. "But even without God, I'm not alone. I have you. I trust I'll have your father too. And I trust the other dukes, once they recognise it's a choice between Rhian and Marlan's puppet, will not stand against us. At least, not for long."

"And if Marlan threatens them with the power of the Church? If he declares God is on *his* side? Do you trust the other dukes will stand with you then?"

Alasdair sighed. "Ludo, not counting you there are currently four dukes of Ethrea. Four men among the many thousands who live in this kingdom. Rhian is Eberg's daughter and he was *loved* by the people. They will love her too. She'll make a magnificent queen. If the people see she is persecuted by Marlan when her right to the Crown cannot be disputed they will turn against him."

"Even if he says that turning against him is to turn against God?" Ludo chewed his lip. "Alasdair, it's a fearsome gamble."

"Yes, it is. But what choice do we have? Rhian is Ethrea's rightful queen. The rest of it is nothing but greed and ambition. What kind of man would I be if I allowed myself to be intimidated out of acting for the truth?"

"You wouldn't be yourself, I know that much," said Ludo. "And I'd not be *myself* if I didn't stand with you. And the people of duchy Linfoi will stand with you too. We're loyal to our own, Alasdair. And we're loyal to the king—or queen. That's as important as our loyalty to God. We've always been stubborn, cross-grained and independent. Comes of being despised by Ethrea's spoilt south. If Marlan forces us to choose sides, I think I know whose side we'll choose."

Moved almost to tears, Alasdair embraced his cousin. "God bless you, Ludo," he whispered. "And God keep you safe. I must go now. The venerables and chaplains will soon arrive and I must greet them with the proper face. The dukes too. I expect them here by noon. Stay here. Rest and read a while. The most recent manor ledger is on the desk, there. You'll need to make yourself familiar with the estates and their business. I'll have Sardre bring you refreshments."

Ludo had never been one for books and study. He eyed the open ledger with despair. "Are you sure there's nothing else I can do for you? Perhaps there's a window or two that need washing . . ."

Alasdair laughed. "Read the ledger, Ludo. I'll come for you when it's time."

"Tyrant," muttered Ludo, and sat himself behind the desk.

As his fingers touched the library door's handle, Alasdair turned. "Ludo."

Ludo looked up. "Hmmm?"

Alasdair's vision blurred for a moment, an excess of emotion that for once he didn't try to hide. "Thank you. I won't forget this. Neither will Rhian."

"Just make sure my bride will be beautiful, Alasdair," said Ludo. His eyes were tear-bright too but his smile was unrepentantly wicked. "All things considered, it's the least you can do."

*   *   *

Most Venerable Artemis greeted Alasdair in the manor chapel, where a host of venerables and chaplains gathered ready for his father's solemn farewell. Artemis was a gracious elderly man who'd never quite forgiven Alasdair's father for refusing to remarry. *A tempting of God,* Artemis had called it, and professed permanent astonishment that God had found the strength to resist.

"Your Grace," he said, splendid in his elaborate vestments. "God give you mercy on this sad day."

He nodded. "Ven'Artemis. It eases my sorrow to know you'll preside over the ceremony. And I know my father would be equally pleased."

"Indeed, Your Grace," said Ven'Artemis. "And it would give me great pleasure to perform the office for him. However . . ." Turning, he crooked a finger at a venerable who was standing a small distance away. The man was of medium height, lithe and alert beneath his sober religious garb, and his light green eyes had an oddly wolfish look. Seeing the summons he joined them before the Living Flame.

"Most Venerable?"

His tone and manner were suitably deferential but Alasdair felt his spine stiffen. *This man is not safe.*

Seemingly oblivious, Most Venerable Artemis was benignly smiling. "Your Grace, I present to you Venerable Martin of Kingseat. Ven'Martin, behold Alasdair, Duke of Linfoi. Strictly speaking not until his investiture, of course, but I think we need hardly stand upon ceremony."

Odd, that Artemis would so single out a venerable.

"Welcome to duchy Linfoi, Ven'Martin," Alasdair said, nodding slightly.

Ven'Martin considered him with his odd, light green eyes. "Your Grace. My sympathy for your loss."

"Ven'Martin is the prolate's personal assistant," Artemis added. There was the slightest hint of strain beneath his temperate smile. "He has come north to visit duchy Linfoi's venerable house and its parishes. I have asked him to conduct your late father's obsequies and he has kindly accepted in Prolate Marlan's name. Provided you do not object, of course."

Well . . . damn. "How could I object?" he said, punctiliously correct. "I am honoured that so important a divine as Vèn'Martin would consent to this task."

"The loss of a duke is no small matter," said Ven'Martin. "Only the loss of a king ranks more highly, Your Grace. We did not see you at Eberg's funeral."

This man must not see his temper. "My father's brother Henrik represented duchy Linfoi, Ven'Martin. I was at the time concerned with my late father's declining health."

Ven'Martin nodded. "Of course."

Turning to Artemis, Alasdair dismissed Ven'Martin from his attention. The man was too much danced upon already. "Most Venerable, are your preparations completed?"

"They are, Your Grace. We will be ready to proceed once your fellow dukes arrive."

"I doubt they'll be much longer, Most Venerable. Can I have a simple repast prepared for you and your brethren, which you can partake of while you wait?"

"Thank you, no," said Artemis, after a glance at

Ven'Martin. "Prayer will sustain us until the appropriate time for feasting."

"Very well, then. I will see you again in due course."

"God bless Your Grace," said Artemis, kissing his thumb and touching it to his heart.

"God bless," murmured Ven'Martin.

"And you, sirs," he replied, and made sure to walk with unstudied confidence away from the Living Flame and their regard.

Sardre met him as he entered the manor house's main doors. "Your Majesty, the runner reports the dukes are approaching."

"All of them?" he said, surprised.

Sardre never betrayed unbecoming hilarity, but there was a gleam of amusement in his eyes. "Yes, Your Majesty. It would seem they have met at some predetermined destination so they might arrive together with no loss of precedence."

"Of course they have," he said, rolling his eyes. "Doubtless they've drawn straws to see who enters the gates first." Sighing, he added, "Welcome them in my name when they arrive, Sardre. Show them into the Great Hall and see their retinues settled in the pavilion and their horses in the stables. When that's done, come to fetch me. I'll be upstairs with the queen."

"Yes, Your Majesty."

"And it's Your *Grace,* remember?"

"Certainly, Your Grace."

"And don't forget Ludo's in the library. Send him in to the other dukes when they're settled. But *don't* call him Your Grace. He's still Lord Ludo for the moment."

"As you say, Your Grace."

He let his hand rest briefly on Sardre's immaculate velvet sleeve. "Thank you, Sardre."

"Not at all, Your Grace."

Leaving his impeccable servant to his duties, he took the stairs up to Rhian three at a time.

"Alasdair!" she said, standing as he entered their private salon. "Is it nearly time? I'm going mad cooped up in here."

"It's nearly time," he said, and kissed her. "The dukes have been seen. They'll reach us soon."

She was so beautiful. She wore another dress that had been his mother's, a concoction of gold and green silk taffeta. The manor seamstress had altered it to fit as though it had been meant for her all along. She wore his mother's pearl necklace and earbobs and her fat pearl ring.

"Look at us," she said, striving for gaiety. "Don't we make a fine pair?"

He was wearing his Kingseat court attire, which his father had paid for even though Linfoi's coffers were nearly bare. Silk and velvet in varying autumn shades, russet and gold and tangerine.

He kissed her again. This time she kissed back. His blood stirred, heating. Her eyes gleamed, colour high in her cheeks. "Perfect," he said, smiling. Then he turned to the window. "Don't you agree, Helfred?"

Chaplain Helfred stood by the curtains, his gaze downcast before such displays of physical lust.

A good thing he didn't see us on our wedding night. He'd have burst into flames from embarrassment, I swear.

"Your Majesty," said Helfred. Agreement? Warning? Who could say?

"Alasdair? What's wrong?" said Rhian. She knew him too well.

He cleared his throat. "It seems we have a slight . . . dilemma. Chaplain Helfred—"

Helfred looked up. "Majesty?"

"What do you know of a venerable named Martin?"

"Ven'Martin?" said Helfred. It seemed he stopped breathing. "He is Marlan's palace assistant . . . but I suspect more my uncle's eyes and ears about the kingdom. Certainly trouble follows wherever he goes. He enjoys my uncle's complete confidence. Why?"

"Because he's in the manor chapel, preparing to lead the funeral service."

"Ven'Martin's *here*?" Helfred kissed his thumb then clutched at the Rollin medallion round his neck. "God save us. Marlan's sent him. He knows we're in Linfoi."

Rhian's hands were fisted by her sides. She looked like a doe cornered by the hounds, ready to fight for her life. "If he knows, he'd have sent Commander Idson and some men. Or at least he'd have tried."

Alasdair shook his head. "I don't think so. He knows the other dukes would object, and he needs their support. That's why he's sent Ven'Martin. He guessed you'd run here—it's the obvious place—and he's been waiting for you to reveal yourself. Once you do that, Ven'Martin will send word to Kingseat. Then the battle will truly begin."

"It was going to begin today, regardless," said Rhian. Her face was pale, her eyes wide and brilliant. "We know it's too much to hope that all the dukes will support me. Whoever refuses to accept me as queen will doubtless turn to Marlan for some kind of alliance. Whether that man tells Marlan or Ven'Martin does, the result is the same."

"Can we not delay?" said Helfred. He was pale too, and sweating. "I tell you, the later my uncle learns of what we've done, the better. We could travel clandestinely back to Kingseat and—"

"No. We can't delay," said Rhian. "I need to know *now* which dukes support me. And I *won't* hide myself again, Helfred, like a common criminal. When I start my royal progress back to Kingseat I'll show my face to Ethrea unashamed. I'll greet my people as their queen and then we'll see how much hold Marlan has over them."

Alasdair felt his heart lift. *My wife. She is my wife. My fierce, my glorious warrior queen.* "I agree," he said quietly. "What does skulking in shadows say but that we are not sure? Or that we are ashamed? We *are* sure and by God there is no shame. We have the right. Rhian is queen. She will not hide."

The smile she gave him was more radiant than the sun. "No. She will not."

He moved to the window so he could look down into the forecourt. "Ludo's here," he said, as Helfred stepped aside to pretend interest in a painting "He's reading in the library."

"You've told him?"

The forecourt remained empty of dukes, but they could not be far away by now. "Yes." He flicked an amused glance over his shoulder. "He asks that you find him a beautiful wife."

"He's pledged his loyalty?"

She sounded . . . sharp. He turned, staring. "Without hesitation. Why? Did you think he wouldn't?"

Her steady gaze unsteadied, just for a heartbeat. "No. No, of course not." She sat again, and arranged her skirts around her on the chamber's straight-backed wooden chair. "Tell him I'll do my best in the matter of his bride but I can't make him a promise."

"I did already. He understands your position. He's ours, Rhian. Or are you in doubt?"

She folded her hands in her lap. "I hardly know him, Alasdair. He rarely came to court."

"He's my *cousin*. *I* know him. Do you say that's not enough?"

"No, no—"

"Rollin have mercy!" he swore, heedless of Helfred's sharp indrawn breath. "The people *you* brought here, Rhian, not even related. The toymaker, that physick woman, and Zandakar. *Zandakar.* You expect me to trust *them* and then you look sideways at *my cousin*?"

"You're right, Alasdair. You're right. I'm sorry," said Rhian. "Of course I trust Ludo. I'm feeling fractious. Forgive me."

"I'm feeling fractious too," he muttered, after a moment. "I'll be glad when this is over." The funeral . . . the revelations . . . *I'm burying my father today, yet somehow his death has been pushed aside. Made less important.*

Rhian joined him at the window. "I'm sorry," she whispered, and laid her palm on his cheek. "This day should be about your father, and instead I've made it about me. I promise you'll have time to mourn him, Alasdair. He won't be forgotten."

He pulled her to him, not caring about the fine dress. Not caring about anything save the feel of her skin against his and the pounding of her heart against his chest. She could undo him with a glance.

"We'll survive this, Rhian," he said, his lips pressed to her short curling hair. "We'll survive Marlan and every obstacle he raises against us. You were born to be Ethrea's queen." A sound from beyond the window turned him. "Ah."

"The dukes," she said. Her arm was tight around him, where it belonged. "They've arrived."

All four of them together, as Sardre had said, complete with an excess of soldier escorts for vanity and show, and mounted servants and expensive, gilt-chased carriages pulled by the glossiest plumed and caparisoned horses. Each duke's extravagant retinue was badged with his duchy's personal device: a leaping red lion for Morvell, a bugling silver swan for Meercheq, a stag for Hartshorn and a snarling deerhound for Arbat. Sardre moved among the jostling throng leaving calm and order in his wake.

Look at them all, it'll cost a fortune to feed them. Ah, the dubious honour of being a duke.

"You'd best go down there," said Rhian. "They'll be expecting to see Linfoi's new duke."

He turned his back to the window. Held her again. "Sardre will come for me once he's sorted them out. I can wait until then. I'd like a moment with my wife . . ."

He felt her soften within his embrace. Her arms tightened around him, making it hard to breathe. He didn't care. If he died like this he would die content.

"The storm's come, Alasdair," she whispered against him. "It's breaking over our heads. Tell me one more time we're strong enough to prevail."

His eyes met Helfred's over the top of her head. The chaplain's gaze was steady, and bleak. He looked away.

"We're strong enough, Rhian. We will prevail."

CHAPTER TWENTY-NINE

It's not fair. I should be at the funeral. Alasdair needs someone to stand with him as he buries his father."

Seated on a plain wooden stool, as befitted a chaplain, Helfred looked up from his well-worn Book of Admonitions, his sole source of comfort in these difficult times. The princess—the queen—*Rhian*—mindful of accidental notice, stood to one side of the salon window staring into the empty sky. She looked remote, and beautiful, and too young for strife.

He marked his place with the tip of one finger. "The king is not alone, Majesty. He has Lord Ludo."

"It's not the same. Ludo's a man. I'm his wife. A good wife supports her husband in these things."

Wife. Husband. The words touched colour to her pale cheeks. She was indeed young. "And a good queen knows the value of discretion. He knows your thoughts are with him, Majesty."

She nodded. "He does."

He waited for her to speak again. When she didn't, he returned his attention to Rollin's advice. "*. . . insomuch as any man can seek to know the heart of God, then in his own heart should he—*"

"You still think I'm misguided, Helfred. Don't you."

With the smallest of sighs, he closed the book. "What I think is of no consequence, Majesty. You've chosen your course and now you must run it."

"*Our* course, you mean. That *we* must run, because I have said so."

"As you say, Majesty. But now that it's chosen there's no turning back. Therefore I see little advantage in having second thoughts."

She rounded on him, her eyes bright with temper. "A good ruler always reconsiders decisions to make doubly certain the right choice was made. My father taught me that, Helfred. Are you saying he was wrong?"

"No, Your Majesty. Are you saying *you* were?"

"No, I am *not.*"

She was nervous. How could he fault her? He was nervous too. Beneath his chaplain robe his skin was moist with sweat. Not even the soothing familiarity of Rollin's Admonitions had succeeded in calming his erratic heart.

Moving from the window, Rhian sat once more on the straight-backed chair that best accommodated her elaborate dress. Her gaze upon him was fixed and uncompromising.

"Are you afraid of meeting Ven'Martin, if he's still here? Are you afraid of what will happen when your uncle hears what you've done?"

"Yes," he said baldly. "You've no idea what he's like when his anger is riled."

"No idea?" she echoed. Her face twisted, scornful. "You've a short memory, Helfred."

The crack of the whip thongs on her welted, bleeding back. His uncle's grunts of satisfaction as she cried out in pain. His memory was not short. Those sounds would sear him till the day he died. "Tcha," he said. "The clerica was nothing. He was irritated then, Your Majesty. Just irritated. Nothing more."

"Then why did you help me, if his wrath is so much to be feared?"

He smoothed his fingers over the cracked leather cover of his Admonitions. "It was the right thing to do."

"Does that mean we'll be victorious, Helfred?"

He shrugged. "The future is in God's hands, Your Majesty. All we can do is pray."

Her lips quirked in a tiny smile. "Is that a hint, Chaplain?"

"Well . . ." He resisted the temptation to smile back. "It cannot hurt."

She slid from the chair onto her knees before him. Clasped her hands and bowed her head, demurely. "Then by all means, Chaplain, let us take a moment to pray. I don't mind confessing it—I need all the help I can get."

"Majesty . . ." He sighed. "You must abandon this unfortunate tendency towards levity. These men who've gathered here, these dukes who you must sway to your cause . . . you require them to take you seriously. They must see you as queen. How will they do either if you cannot?"

She looked at him, sharply. "Don't be stupid, Helfred. I take this so seriously I've risked *everything* to achieve it. My life. My liberty. Perhaps even my soul. I have risked Mr Jones and his friend Ursa. I've risked Zandakar. You. And I've risked Alasdair." Her voice broke on the duke's name. It was a moment before she spoke again. "Helfred, I've risked *Ethrea*. My father's greatest legacy. The brightest jewel in the world, a beacon of peace and hope and prosperity to countless thousands in lands I'll never see. No matter what strife there may be in their lives they know *we* are here. A safe port in any storm, one nation in all the world that will *never* succumb to violence. And yet here am I pushing us to the brink of bloodshed because I believe it's the only way. Because I believe I am meant to be Ethrea's sovereign. Because I have listened to a dead woman's voice." She brushed tears from her cheeks. "And you say I don't take this matter *seriously*? Oh, Helfred . . ."

He felt his own eyes prickle. She so easily, so swiftly, drove him to distraction, offended him and frustrated him and made him question his actions and sanity both. But how could he doubt the truth of her beliefs when she laid them before him with such conviction? Such passion?

"I do not doubt your heart, Majesty," he said, resting his hand upon her bent head. "If I doubted, if I did not believe in your claim to the Crown, I would never have allowed you to escape the clerica at Todding. I would never have run with you or married you to Alasdair."

"I thank God you did, Helfred. Without your help . . ."

"My helpfulness is most likely at an end," he admitted, withdrawing his hand. "I have no influence over the dukes. But I would make an observation . . ."

"Speak your mind," she said, looking up at him. "No queen can count herself higher than well-meant counsel."

"Another lesson from King Eberg?"

She nodded. "He was very wise."

And were he alive he would be proud of his daughter. *And if he was not proud, then shame upon him.* "Majesty, I know you better now than ever I did in Kingseat. But the dukes, they knew your father. They do *not* know you. They saw you here and there as a child, growing up. They saw you at Eberg's funeral, where they paid their brief respects. But you are not a real person to them. You are a symbol of the power they believe they can accrue through you. When they see that power lost they will be most displeased."

She pulled a face. "True. But there is power yet to be had, if they're willing to look a little lower than a crown. With no surviving male in my family I must still create a Duke of Kingseat. The dukes have sons and nephews whose noble blood qualifies them for notice. And of course there's the question of Ludo's marriage. I've made a list of eligible girls. The next Duchess of Linfoi will be related to a duke of Ethrea and married to the cousin of Ethrea's king. No small prize, I think you'll agree. There is every reason for the dukes to mind their manners."

"Certainly," he murmured. "But when tempers run hot, Majesty, common-sense runs out the doorway."

"Then I'll just have to cool them down, won't I? And I will cool them, Helfred. I will sway them to my cause. I am my father's daughter . . . and I intend to have my way."

"God willing," said Helfred. "Now, Majesty. Let us pray."

The king's man Sardre came to the salon almost an hour later. With their prayer concluded, Rhian had lapsed into pensive silence. Helfred had returned with gratitude to the solace and sanctuary of Rollin's Admonitions. When the rap on the door came, he answered it.

"Chaplain," said Sardre, austere and discreet as was his habit. "The dukes are gathered in the Great Hall, in the expectation of the Linfoi investiture. His Majesty suggests Her Majesty join him there at this time."

Rhian stood. "Thank you, Sardre. Chaplain Helfred and I will be downstairs directly."

Sardre bowed. "Your Majesty."

"Sardre . . ."

"Majesty?"

"Would you know if a divine by the name of Ven'Martin is also downstairs?"

"I believe he is, Majesty. Also Most Venerable Artemis, from the Linfoi venerable house."

"I see. Thank you." As the door closed, she smoothed down her dress and favoured Helfred with a challenging stare. "Are you ready, Helfred? Is your courage high? We're about to walk into a storm, you know. Ven'Martin is your superior as well as being your uncle's trusted man. Can you stand against him? If you doubt yourself, stay here. I won't think any less of you."

"Because your opinion is already sunk low?" he said. "Majesty, I will not shrink from what I have done. What I have done has been for God, and Ethrea."

"And me," she said, her eyes glinting. "I'm in your debt, Helfred. Never think I don't know it. My opinion of you is not so low as that."

"Majesty," he said, bowing, then opened the door for her and stood aside. She swept past him as regal as any monarch born and he fell into trembling step behind her.

Dear God . . . Blessed Rollin . . . I beg you give me strength.

*   *   *

Trestle tables had been erected in the manor house's Great Hall, ready for the feasting that would follow the funeral and investiture. Neatly clad servants, their tabards badged with duchy Linfoi's exuberant salmon, moved among the dukes and their retainers proffering goblets of ale and spiced wine to quench thirst and pass the time till the ceremonies commenced.

Helfred stood behind Rhian, who stood in the Great Hall's open double-doorway, and watched as the dukes failed to notice her arrival. Then he looked past them to find Ven'Martin. Ah . . . there he was. Standing silent in a corner, his raised hand refusing an offer of drink. The divine standing with him must be Most Venerable Artemis. The older man's vestments proclaimed his seniority but his demeanour was less assured. The divines of duchy Linfoi were not counted high in Marlan's estimation. Tainted by their duke's lack of prestige they were largely left to fend for themselves. Never had one of their brethren risen to prominence in the Prolates Palace.

The poor man must have lost his continence on the day Ven'Martin darkened his venerable house door.

The dukes continud talking, still oblivious to Rhian's presence. Then the king saw her . . . and his face lit up. Beside him Ludo realised that his cousin's wife—his queen—had joined them, and he too smiled . . . though there was anxiety in his eyes.

Rhian stepped forward. "God's grace upon you, my lords," she announced above the hum of conversations. "You are welcome to my temporary court."

Silence fell, as though God had stolen every tongue.

"Rollin's arrow!" cried Damwin, Duke of Meercheq, the first released from stupefaction. "Princess Rhian!"

A tinkling smash and a splatter as his dropped glass goblet hit the floor.

Ven'Martin came forward, pushing between the dukes and their retainers and King Alasdair's servants, his broad face suffused with anger. "*Chaplain Helfred?* In the name of the Prolate explain your presence here!"

"Helfred's presence is not your concern," said Rhian, her tone icy. "Control yourself, divine. You are not recognised in this court."

"Court? Court? What are you talking about, *court*? What are you *doing* here?" demanded Duke Edward of duchy Morvell, his blond whiskers bristling with outrage. "You're supposed to be in Todding!"

"And so I was, Duke Edward," Rhian replied, calmly. "But despite our prolate's unorthodox opinion a clerica is not a prison. I was free to leave, and so I left."

"As a ward of the Church you are free to do *nothing* that is not sanctioned by its prolate!" snapped Ven'Martin. "You are in gross breach of conduct, Your Highness. You will be brought to task. Gather your belongings if you have any. We will depart this place for Kingseat immediately, where on your wicked knees you will explain your disobedience to His Eminence."

The king moved to speak, but Rhian silenced him with a gently raised hand. "Your name, Venerable? I believe we are not formally introduced."

"This is Ven'Martin, Your Highness," said Most Venerable Artemis, hesitantly approaching. "Prolate Marlan's representative and a guest of duchy Linfoi's venerable house. I am Most Venerable Artemis, its preceptor. Welcome to duchy Linfoi. My sympathies for the loss of your great father, Princess Rhian. You must know all of Ethrea grieves with you."

"Your sentiment is appreciated," said Rhian, with a gracious nod. "But I must correct your form of address, Most Venerable. I am no longer Her Highness Princess Rhian. I am now Queen Rhian, monarch of Ethrea."

A second stunned silence. Then Kyrin of Hartshorn leapt at the king. "You *bastard*, Linfoi! What have you done?"

As Lord Ludo caught the duke before violence was committed Ven'Martin marched across the Great Hall, through the goggling dukes and their retainers, marched past Rhian as though she were a chair, and fetched up short.

"Helfred," he said. His voice was shaking with fury. "Explain yourself on pain of dire retribution!"

"You must!" added Most Venerable Artemis. "If indeed, as it seems, you have involved yourself in secular matters beyond the limits of your authority."

Helfred had never cared for being the centre of attention. Sweat trickled down his skin beneath his plain chaplain robe. Ven'Martin's green eyes were venomous. All the dukes were glaring too, their baffled rage scorching him like the heat of a monstrous bonfire. Kyrin had wrenched himself free of Lord Ludo. A vinegar-faced barrel of a man, his chest was heaving with the depth of his ire.

"Most Venerable, Ven'Martin, you lack my leave to question Chaplain Helfred," said Rhian, quietly. "He did not exceed his authority. He is a good son of the Church."

Ven'Martin turned on her. "The Church does not

recognise your right to an opinion! You are female and a minor. *You* will hold your tongue!"

"That is not the accepted way of addressing a queen, Ven'Martin," said Rhian. Temper echoed through her voice. "I advise you to mind your manners."

"How are you a queen?" demanded Duke Rudi of Arbat. "To be a queen you must be—"

"Married," said Rhian. "And so I am. To Alasdair of Linfoi, King Consort of Ethrea. Chaplain Helfred granted dispensation of my wardship—a lawful act—and wed us in God's sight the day before last. As Eberg's heir I have claimed my birthright. I *am* Queen Rhian, Ethrea's sovereign ruler."

Duke Damwin of Meercheq took a step forward, his pointed finger shaking. "You—you deceitful, conniving, upstart *miscreant,* Linfoi! You were forbidden to marry her! Eberg expressly excluded you from marriage consideration! You accepted the decree. Henrik Linfoi said so! Or is the man a liar just like—"

"Call my father a liar at your peril, Damwin!" said Ludo, glowering.

"My peril?" snarled Damwin. "You would threaten me, you gadabout upstart, you—"

"Forget him!" said Kyrin, and spat on the floor. "He's a cur pup not worth your notice. Henrik Linfoi's gone back on his word. What else would you expect from a Linfoi? *Honour?*"

"*No,* Ludo," said the king, and threw out a barring arm. "These are empty words, they have no meaning. I won't brook bloodshed under my roof."

Lord Ludo gave ground, reluctant and resentful.

"For shame, Alasdair!" Rudi chimed in, hotly. "To

marry the princess out of hand like this! It's not the conduct expected of a duke! Your father's rattling his coffin, he's pounding on the doors of heaven! Shame on you for a disreputable tyke!"

"When Marlan hears of this," said Damwin, face thunderous, "you can expect a full Church censure! In fact you can expect questions as to your fitness to inherit duchy Linfoi! You've invited us here for your investiture but after *this* act of arrant recklessness and impropriety I won't—"

"My cousin Lord Ludo will be the next duke of Linfoi," said the king, standing ground. "With you or without you he'll be invested this day and confirmed by Queen Rhian. You're here by courtesy, not necessity. As for Eberg . . . he is dead, God rest him. And Rhian—Her Majesty—was in danger from the prolate." One by one, he looked at the dukes. "As Ethrea's premier nobles you should've had a care for her. As Eberg's declared friends you should've been more concerned for his daughter than for yourselves. But your representatives on the King's Council, those little men who dance to your tunes, all they did was harangue her and torment her with word of who *you* wanted to see made king. And while you sat safely in your duchies, gloating yourselves to fatness, dreaming of the power that you would make your own, Marlan was free to persecute her at his leisure. Or have you forgotten he wanted her to marry his former ward, Lord Rulf?"

The dukes exchanged hasty glances, momentarily put to shame. Ven'Martin took advantage of the hush. "You shameless hussy, you'd dare impugn His Eminence in this fashion? You Godless defier, woe to you and all your kind. This duchy will fall to interdict! Prolate Marlan—"

"Is not Ethrea's king!" said the king. "Though he thought to make himself one, through Lord Rulf." He turned back to the discomfited dukes. "And thanks to you, my lords, he nearly succeeded. Marlan had the chance to persecute Rhian and he took it. *I have seen the scars.*"

Ven'Martin's voice rose above the flurry of protests. "You are a liar! A liar, a lawbreaker, and a blasphemer! Prolate Marlan—"

"Tried to flog me into submission!" cried Rhian. "Chaplain Helfred assisted him until God softened his heart! King Alasdair is right. Shame on you for putting your own ambitions before the welfare of Ethrea!"

"Don't waste your breath trying to turn us from the prolate!" roared Damwin. "We do not confuse politics and God. Ven'Martin is right in this. We are not come here to be lectured by disobedient little girls. This is a mockery. A tarradiddle. A *disgrace*! Is this how you think to honour your father, Highness? Lies and deception and wilful malfeasance, a reckless disregard for—"

Rhian scorched him with a glare. "Do not presume to raise your voice to *me,* Damwin! I am Eberg's daughter and beyond your petty censure! Good *God!* If you thought I'd meekly abandon Ethrea to your ambitions, my lords, you were sorely mistaken. If you thought I was pliable and malleable and easily cowed, you were wrong. Were I born Eberg's third son there would be no thought of dissent. I—"

"But you were not born his son!" said Rudi, seething. "You were born his daughter. Your duty is to marry and make your husband King of Ethrea!"

Rhian smiled. Holding out her hand she said, softly, "And I have, Your Grace."

"King *Consort*," spat Rudi. "No better than a eunuch!"

King Alasdair took the queen's outstretched hand. "If by that insulting epithet you mean to remind us that Rhian is the true monarch here, Your Grace, then yes. By blood and by right she now rules over Ethrea. Your royal ambitions are ended. There remains a place for dukes in the governance of this land . . . but the crown has slipped forever from your grasps. Best make your peace with that and bend your stiff knees."

"To *her?*" said Edward. Within its whiskers his face was so red he looked to Helfred in danger of his life. "A girl young enough to be my granddaughter? *Never!*"

"Yet you'd yield to your nephew Shimon, a boy young enough to be your grandson?" said Rhian, releasing the king's hand and letting her fingers fist by her sides. Her voice dripped with contempt. "For your ambition's sake you'd deny me my birthright, our most sacred tradition. To slake your greed for power you'd see Ethrea pulled apart in bloody violence rather than accept God's will in the matter of its rule?"

"God's will? God's will?" Ven'Martin was close to choking. "There is nothing *Godlike* in this travesty, girl! You flout Church law with these wild declamations. Prolate Marlan will *never* confirm you as queen, he wil denounce you and chastise you and—"

Helfred stepped forward. "Do not presume, Venerable, to pronounce on God's will. Would he have permitted vows between Queen Rhian and King Alasdair to be exchanged before his Living Flame if his will was not done in this?"

"*Silence, clod!*" snarled Ven'Martin. "You're a forsworn man. You've disobeyed your prolate and smirched your soul as a result. You're a chaplain with no standing, you have acted without authority! You are a man of mud, Helfred, and in the mud you will be thrown!" He turned on Rhian. "Do you think you sit above judgement, girl? A child unlawfully married, her maidenhood squandered to fornication and lust? Do you think all you need do is blow hot air in God's face and God will fall meekly at your dainty feet?"

At long last Ven'Artemis found his tongue. "Please, Ven'Martin, have a care. Such intemperate language is—"

"Shut up, old fool!" said Ven'Martin, spittle flying. "Never presume to lecture *me*, Prolate Marlan's most trusted man, for I—"

"Should beware, Ven'Martin," said a gentle voice from the hall's open doorway. "God sees all and hears all . . . and does not take kindly to the thwarting ambitions of greedy men."

Helfred, with Rhian and the king, turned to the doors. Everyone else in the Great Hall gasped, even Ven'Martin.

It was Mr Jones the toymaker, glowing like a lantern filled with God's Living Flame. His arms were outstretched, and in the centre of each upturned palm danced a bright red tongue of fire. Slowly he entered the manor house's Great Hall, scattering servants and ducal retainers like a cat strolling through mice.

Helfred closed his fingers around his Rollin medallion. *God help me, I am witness to miracles. The age of Rollin has come to us again. Forgive me, God, if ever I doubted.*

"What's this? It's a trick! A blasphemous trick!" said Kyrin as the toymaker halted between two bare trestle tables, burning without pain or sound or any sign his flesh was being consumed. The duke's face had drained sickly pale. "Get him out of here, Linfoi! Would you call God's wrath upon all of us?"

Rhian shook her head, slowly. Her eyes were wide, her expression stunned. It seemed clear she had not expected this. "God's not wrathful, Kyrin. And Mr Jones has guided me from the start. Now . . . I think . . . he is made a prophet."

"A *prophet*?" said timid Most Venerable Artemis before Ven'Martin could protest. "My child—"

Ignoring him, Rhian shifted her astonished gaze away from the toymaker. "*Helfred?* What do you think?"

He thought he might easily burst into tears. "I am a lowly chaplain, Your Majesty. But it seems to me this is indeed a miracle, and Rollin tells us miracles are the province of prophets. So you might well be correct. Mr Jones could be our very own Rollin."

"*Never say it again!*" said Ven'Martin, convulsed with rage. "This is darkest blasphemy! I tell you in the Prolate's name that any man supporting it will be cast down beyond redemption!"

"You are wrong, Ven'Martin," said Mr Jones, serene. There was a curious blankness in his face, as though his personality had been smoothed away . . . like a footprint on a sandy beach washed to nothing by a wave. On his upturned palms the red tongues of fire danced. Under his skin God's power glowed. "The blasphemy is in denying Rhian's birthright. She is Ethrea's queen, born in this time and place to rule. Let no man dispute it lest he imperil his soul."

"What?" said Kyrin. He seemed torn between awed fear and disbelieving fury. "Who is this—this *man*? From his clothing he's not noble. He's not *anything*. Who is *he* to—"

Helfred felt the words well up inside him, their truth unstoppable. "He's a messenger from God, Your Grace. If you're displeased with God's selection I suggest you task him directly."

"Helfred!" said Ven'Martin. Even Ven'Artemis looked shocked.

Helfred pulled his prayer beads from his robe's belt and wrapped them round his hand. Smooth from years of fingering, their comfort was immense.

"How can you stand there denying God's presence?" he asked Ven'Martin. "Can it only be a miracle if it's performed through *you*?"

A shocked silence fell. Helfred avoided Rhian's gaze. Around the hall the first panicked reaction was settling. Some of the dukes' people were praying, others huddled in corners and whispered or stared, waiting for their masters and the venerables to tell them what to do. As for the dukes . . .

Rudi exchanged glances with Edward. Then, with a last askance look at Mr Jones, he turned to Rhian. "Your Highness—Majesty—*Rhian* . . . you are asking us to accept a great deal on faith! *Miracles,* in your name? Not even your father claimed such favour from God!"

"I don't claim it either, Rudi," she said, hushed, staring at serene Mr Jones. "I swear on my father's soul I did *not* know this would happen. I can't explain it. All I can tell you is I've been guided by this man and he's never been wrong. I believe with all my heart he cares only for Ethrea."

"And so do *we* care for Ethrea!" said Edward. A riot of uncertainty was in his face and eyes. "You're gravely unjust to say we do not. It's *because* we care that we are so alarmed. You claim a ruling birthright but you are a *woman*. You're practically a *girl*! How can we trust you'll not rule Ethrea to ruin? You're not trained for kingship. You understand embroidery, not—not—international treaties and trade negotiations and foreign relations and taxation and law and currency and—"

"Your Graces—" Rhian began, but she got no further. The flames dancing on Mr Jones' upturned palms flared higher, joining over his head in a rainbow of fire. His skin grew incandescent so it was hard to look at him.

Every man and woman in the Great Hall cried out. King Alasdair moved to Rhian's side and put his arm around her shoulders, holding her close. Lord Ludo joined them. His face was resolute.

Helfred kissed his thumb and pressed it to his heart, hand shaking. *Dear God. Dear God. That I live to see such things!*

"On your feet!" cried Ven'Martin to those ducal retainers who had dropped to their knees. "How *dare* you pay homage to this *trickster,* this tool of evil!"

None of them obeyed him. They hid their faces and sobbed.

The fiery rainbow arcing from palm to palm over the toymaker's head burned in eerie silence, no crackling, no smoke. But the air in the manor house's Great Hall smelled suddenly sweet, tinged with freesias and roses and ladalia blossom.

"Woe upon you, proud dukes of Ethrea!" he cried, his voice ringing to the rafters. *"Heed not this warning and see your kingdom fall to ruin! See your children slain upon its streets! See your green fields blighted, see your churches pulled down, see your freedoms ground to bloody mud beneath your foolish feet! Kneel to Rhian, your rightful, blessed and God-given queen! Let her lead you in God's name! For if you do not there will be no more Ethrea."*

"No more Ethrea?" said Edward, incredulous. "How can that be? Ethrea is the safest kingdom in the world!"

"It has been the safest," said Rhian, her gaze not shifting from the toymaker's face as he stood before them soundlessly burning.

"But not any more?" said Rudi.

She shrugged. "Perhaps. If we do not heed our new prophet's warning. We—"

"Are only in danger if *you* are on the throne!" said Damwin, nearly spitting in his rage. "No woman is capable of ruling a kingdom! Women bear children. *That* is their domain. This—this—*nonsense* is nothing but your desperate attempt to overthrow the natural order! This is trickery, this so-called *prophet* is your puppet, a fool and a knave. Throw a bucket of water over him and his miracle would soon be quenched!"

"No," said Helfred. "His words come from God. What consumes him is God's Living Flame."

"What consumes him is *evil*!" shouted Ven'Martin. "What you smell in this hall is the stink of *hell*! Whosoever heeds this blasphemy I declare him tainted, corrupted, the *enemy of God*!"

"And *I* declare *you* a blind fool, Venerable Martin!" retorted Rhian. "In thrall to Marlan who is no friend to God or Ethrea or me, its queen. I've done *nothing* unlawful. I'm not tainted or corrupt. The corruption is yours, that you'd use God as a weapon to silence honest men. Tell Marlan this from me when you run to him with your tail between your legs, as I know full well you will. I won't be silenced or intimidated by the Church. I *am* the rightful queen of Ethrea and to deny me fealty *is* to break the law. Tell the prolate to consider that, Venerable. Tell him to have a care for *his* soul, should he oppose me."

Ven'Martin shuddered with an anger so violent, Helfred thought the man would drop where he stood. "You wicked woman, God's Flame will—"

She turned her back on him, leaving Ven'Artemis to silence his ranting, and glared instead at her horrified dukes.

"Your Graces, attend me. The people of my duchies look to you for leadership as much as they look to the Church for solace. I need you standing with me, your disappointments set aside. If you don't want to see this kingdom destroyed you'll—"

"Ethrea will only be destroyed if we allow this nonsense to continue!" said Kyrin. "Are you mad, girl, to think we would side with you against the prolate? You'd have us take the word of a disgraced chaplain and this—this *charlatan* in a matter so vital to the kingdom's interests?"

"Kyrin's right," added Damwin. "And so is Ven'Martin. Aiding you is blasphemy, Your Highness. Clearly grief has unhinged your mind. For the kingdom's safety you must be put away."

King Alasdair stepped forward. "Lay one hand on her and you'll answer to me."

"And God, Your Grace," said Helfred, frowning. "Do not imperil your soul."

Damwin sneered. "A blasphemer lectures *me* on the health of my soul. If I were not so close to vomiting, I tell you I would laugh. Men of Meercheq, to me!"

As Duke Damwin's hangers-on stepped forward uncertainly, Kyrin snapped his fingers. "Hartshorn, to me!" Then he glowered at Rhian. "Like the Duke of Meercheq I am no credulous fool. I will not risk myself or my duchy by supporting your lost, unlawful cause."

Side by side, ignoring the miracle of Mr Jones, Damwin and Kyrin made for the Great Hall's doors, their hangers-on obedient at their heels.

"This blasphemous treachery will not go unpunished," said Ven'Martin, retreating with them. "The wrath of God and the prolate shall descend without mercy. Artemis! With me!"

The Most Venerable hesitated, looking to the king.

"Go, Artemis," said King Alasdair softly. "Don't cause trouble for you and yours." He gestured at the ceaselessly burning Mr Jones. "We have nothing to fear from Ven'Martin or the prolate."

"Artemis!" shouted Ven'Martin, waiting at the doors.

The Most Venerable departed with tears in his eyes.

Rhian looked to the remaining dukes. "Well, Edward. Rudi. Does this mean you're with me?"

Before they could answer, Mr Jones released a sigh.

The holy fire in him extinguished . . . and he slumped unconscious to the floor.

CHAPTER THIRTY

Dexterity stood in a charnel-house, surrounded by death. Everywhere he looked he saw burnt sundered bodies. Men. Women. Children. Infants. Dogs. Horses. He'd never seen so much death in his life. Never imagined it could look like this. Curdled with smoke, the air smeared his skin. The stench of charred flesh coated his tongue, his throat. His stomach heaved, gushing bile into his mouth. He spat it out, sickened by the taste. Underfoot, the rubble of this strange city. Something had destroyed it, smashed the brick and timber buildings to pieces like a vengeful god's angry hand. The sun was a sullen eye, red and glaring.

His eyes burned. There were tears on his cheeks.

"Hettie!" he shouted. "Hettie, where are you? Hettie, where am I? Hettie, please, *answer*!"

And she was beside him, dress tattered, hair wild. So little colour to her that for the first time she looked truly a ghost. "Here I am, Dex."

He staggered back from her, nearly stumbling over a dead woman and her son. What looked like her son. The monstrously burned child was clasped in her spasmed arms. "Where are we, Hettie? What is this place? Why have you brought me here?"

The sorrow in her face was as stark as a wound. "This city is . . . *was* . . . called Garabatsas."

"Garabatsas?" He shook his head. "I've never heard of it."

"It was a small place. Unimportant. There's no reason you would."

"What country, Hettie? What country are we in?"

She looked at him, sadly. "Sharvay."

"Sharvay?" He felt a nasty jolt under his ribs. "I've heard of Sharvay."

"I know you have, Dex. That's why we're here."

"Sharvian beadwork! It's prized by the court ladies. You can spend a fortune on one little—"

"Dexie, I know," she said, and clasped her hands together. They were pale and trembling. "My love, let me speak."

But he couldn't. Not yet. Memory was returning, sharp enough to blot out the dreadful sight of Garabatsas, destroyed. "Hettie—in the manor house. Something happened to me—something—" He shuddered. "I was *glowing*! And walking and talking but somehow it wasn't *me*! Hettie, was it *you*?"

She nodded. "Yes."

Rolling through him, a terrible sense of betrayal. A feeling he'd never known her at all. "Without *asking* me? Without *warning*? Hettie, how could you?"

"Oh, Dex . . ." She tried to smile but her eyes were bleak with sorrow. "If I had asked . . . if I had warned . . . would you have helped me?"

"I don't know! Most likely! But—"

"Then it's all right, isn't it? Dex, I'm sorry. I was in a

hurry, I had no time. And you weren't harmed, were you? You have to know I'd never harm you."

Such love in her face. How could he doubt her? "Yes—of course—I know you wouldn't—but really, Hettie, that's not the point! It was very frightening and—and—" He stopped. "Where am I, really? While I'm having this dream? Am I still in the Great—"

"You're tucked up in bed, my love, with Ursa counting every breath and eye-twitch."

Well, at least that was something. "But what happened? Has Rhian managed to convince the dukes? Have they—"

"You'll find out shortly," said Hettie. "Right now I have to show you something else. Take my hand."

"Why?" he asked, ashamed of his suspicion. "I don't want to see any more dead people, Hettie." He looked around at the slaughtered Garabatsas and felt a fresh burning in his eyes. "I've seen enough. I'd like to go now, please. I'd like to wake up."

"You will soon. I promise."

He took her hand, reluctant, and looked again at the dead. "All these poor people . . ." he whispered. Dear God, her fingers were so cold. "Who could do such a terrible thing?"

"You already know, Dex."

"No. Not *Zandakar*!"

Hettie raised her other hand and waved it slowly across the face of the red, sullen sun. Garabatsas the charnel-house rippled and was remade around them. Now the air was free of smoke, sweet-smelling and fresh. The buildings stood intact, brick and timber painted yellow, orange and blue. Bright colours. Bright, cheerful faces of the people in Garabatsas, a short race with olive skin and light hair. This was a marketplace. Chickens squawked in wooden cages, luscious fruits piled high under canvas awnings. Horses hitched to spindly carts swished their tails at biting flies and dogs hunted among the market-goers for scraps and attention. Men and women bought and sold their wares. Squealing children chased the dogs and each other.

Dexterity glanced at Hettie. "They can't see us?"

"No."

"Then why—"

She squeezed his hand. "Hush, my love. Watch . . . and wait."

So he stood unseen in the marketplace of Garabatsas and smiled to see the people so unafraid.

And then someone screamed, a shrill shriek of fear. Above the marketplace sounds, a dreadful deep chanting. Coming closer. Growing in strength.

"Chalava! Chalava! Chalava zho!"

The warriors came on horseback, their long curved knives unsheathed and shining in the sun. Thousands and thousands of them, too many to count, rank upon rank in a slow, steady jog. Their hair was tightly braided, sewn with amulets and silver bells. Their horses' hides were blue and black and striped and spotted, not like any horse he'd ever seen.

The warrior who led them had braids as red as blood.

"Not Zandakar," he whispered, and could have wept with the relief.

"No," said Hettie. "His brother."

"Dmitrak." Dexterity felt sick again, fresh bile in his mouth. "Hettie, can't you stop this?"

"It's the past, Dex. It's already happened."

Dmitrak didn't carry an unsheathed knife. On his right arm he wore some kind of gauntlet, made of red crystal and gold. He raised his arm above his head. Closed his eyes. Cried out to his god. To *chalava*. His fingers clenched tight . . . and the gauntlet caught fire. A bright scarlet stream of it, surging towards the sun.

"Oh, Hettie!" he sobbed, as Dmitrak's arm came down, fire streaming from his fist, and the people died and the buildings burned and Dmitrak's warriors slaughtered whoever the killing flames didn't touch. *"No . . . no . . . no . . ."*

Hettie snapped her fingers and Garabatsas disappeared.

Now they stood beside a tranquil pond in the heart of a forest. Deer grazed all around them, spotted fawns and liquid-eyed does and a magnificent stag with its many-pointed antlers. Pale pink butterflies floated over the grass. But its beauty wasn't real to him. All he could see was the death of Garabatsas. All he could hear was the sound of agonised screaming . . . the terrible chanting as Mijak's warriors rode through blood.

"Chalava! Chalava! Chalava zho!"

He fell to his knees and wept without restraint.

"Why did you show me that?" he demanded, when he could speak.

"Because seeing is believing, Dex. I needed you to know."

"Zandakar told me. I knew already!"

"It's not the same."

No, it wasn't the same. "Those people! Those poor people!"

"I know, Dex," said Hettie. She was kneeling beside him, her cold hand on his shoulder. "But it's over. The people of Sharvay are beyond our help."

"Then *why*—"

"Because there are others we *can* help. God needs us to help them."

He pulled away from her. "God? You show me that then talk to me of *God*? There is no God, Hettie! Or if there is he's not a God I can believe in! What is God *for* if not to stop things like that? How can God love us and allow such brutal slaughter?"

She caught his face between her hands. Pressed her forehead against his. Her tears fell on his skin, warm and swift. "I know it seems like that. It's complicated, Dexie. One day you'll understand. For now, can you believe *me* when I say God does what he can? That's why I'm here. And why you're here with me."

He took her hands in his and gently tugged them from his cheeks. "Hettie, I have to know this. Is *chalava* God?"

Her face twisted, the gentle Hettie he knew almost lost in revulsion. *"No."*

"Then what—"

"They think it is," she said, shivering even though the meadow was warm. "The people of Mijak. Their priests believe they commune with God. But what they touch is an ancient pool of dark power. It feeds and replenishes itself and them on endless offerings of blood and death. Drunk on that power the priests perform miracles. Abominations. The priests and their warriors live only that they might kill. And the more they kill the more powerful they become."

It sounded . . . *appalling.* "I have to tell Zandakar. He has to know the truth. If he—"

"*No,* Dex! He won't understand. He'll think you're trying to destroy him. And we need Zandakar's help. We won't save Ethrea without him. *Promise* you won't tell him, Dex."

Slowly, he nodded. "All right. I promise." After all, what was one more secret? He closed his eyes and saw again the terrible streams of fire from the red-crystal gauntlet. "This blood power. That's how Dmitrak was able to—"

"Yes. And Zandakar too, before he . . . stopped."

"And their mother? This Hekat?"

"She's mad, Dexterity. Mad and convinced she does her god's will."

"And you think *I* can stop them?" He stood and turned his back to her. The deer kept grazing, undismayed. "A toymaker from Kingseat? Hettie, *you're* mad."

"Not by yourself, Dex," she said. "That's why you need Zandakar. That's why you have to protect his secret. And why you have to make sure Rhian is not defeated by Marlan and his petty dukes. She's so important, my love. She has the power to unite the untouched nations against the warhost of Mijak. Not just because Ethrea alone holds no allegiances, and can be trusted by all the rest, but because she is *special.* God's grace is in her. She was born to do this . . . but she needs help."

The forest's heart was safe and beautiful. Her words had left him cold and afraid. He turned. "Hettie . . . you've never told me this much before."

She was standing now, too. Her sad smile was translucent. "It wasn't time, before. But the blood of slain innocents broke through the barrier that kept Hekat's warhost at bay. She has crossed the great desert. Sharvay has fallen and more lands will fall after it. The world is in peril, Dex . . . I have no more time."

She was talking in riddles. "Hettie—"

"I've said all I can, my love. Now I must ask a favour. And I am *asking* this time. It's too big a thing not to ask first . . ."

"What?" He folded his arms, uncertain. "Are you talking about more glowing, Hettie? And walking about like one of my own puppets come to life?"

"A little like that."

"Why?"

"For Rhian. She must become queen." Hettie's eyes filled with tears. "Please say you'll do it, Dex. It's ever so important."

How could he refuse her when she looked at him like that? "Yes. All right. I'll do it. For you and for Rhian, but—"

"Thank you," she whispered. "Make sure Rhian goes by road back to Kingseat. By road, not by river."

"Oh, but—"

She kissed him to silence, stealing his breath. His heart broke all over again, feeling her lips on his. Searing heat rushed through him . . . suns burst into life behind his closed eyes . . .

And he was alone.

"Hettie!" He spun in a circle, the world spinning with him. The startled deer scattered. "Hettie, come back here! Hettie? Come *back*!"

"Hettie's not here, Jones," said Ursa, tartly. "You're dreaming again. Time to open your eyes."

He sat up, unsurprised to find himself in the manor house. His lips still tingled from Hettie's kiss. It was a kind of torture, to feel that again. His chamber's curtains weren't quite drawn properly. Beyond the window it was night. He was in bed and he'd been dressed in a nightshirt.

He plucked at it. "Ursa, did you do this?"

"I did, Jones," she answered, unperturbed. "And I didn't see anything I've not seen before. Although I'm curious to know why you wear that carved monstrosity under your shirt."

He slapped his hand to his chest but the *chalava* was still there. More than ever he wanted to tear if off, throw it away, but he didn't dare. "As a favour to Zandakar. Ursa, what's happening?"

"Hush," she said. "How are you feeling?"

"Do you want me to hush or answer the question?"

"*Jones* . . ."

"I'm fine."

Ursa sat back in her chair and considered him. "For a man who burst into flames but doesn't have a mark on him, yes, you certainly *look* fine."

"I burst into flames? I don't remember that. I remember I was glowing . . ."

"Glowing was just the start of it, Jones. You glowed, you burned, you delivered messages from God. It was miraculous. I didn't know you had it in you."

"It wasn't me, it was Hettie," he said, and rubbed his hands across his face.

"I gathered that much," said Ursa, dryly. "When you woke up shouting for her to come back. Well?"

He looked at her, cautiously. "Well what?"

"Well what did she have to say this time?"

Nothing I can tell you, Ursa. At least almost nothing.
With an effort he thrust aside the dreadful memory of Garabatsas and settled himself onto his pillows again. "You should prepare yourself for . . . more miracles."

The wry amusement died out of Ursa's eyes. "I don't think that's wise, Jones. You're not a saint, you're a flesh and blood man. Humans weren't meant to glow and burn with holy fire. If you could've seen Helfred after you collapsed. I had to pour half a goblet of brandy down his throat before I could get one sensible word from him!"

"But I'm not harmed, Ursa. You said so yourself. And this is important. It's for Rhian. After everything else I've done, how can I stop helping her now?"

"Driving her from Todding to Linfoi is one thing," snapped Ursa. "Bursting into flames at the drop of a hat is something else entirely! You weren't harmed this time, it's true, but what about next time? What does Hettie expect you to do? Burn from here to Kingseat proclaiming Rhian queen?"

It was a fair question. "I don't know," he said tiredly. "I just know I said I'd do it, so carping at me isn't much use. Hettie's gone. Until I see her again we'll just have to trust she knows what she's doing."

"Jones!" said Ursa, her fingers knotted in her lap. "If you're not the most *infuriating* man!"

He dredged up a smile for her. "I know. I'm sorry." He rubbed his face again, then considered her. "You're taking this very calmly, I must say. I thought you were convinced I couldn't be a new Rollin."

She shrugged. "I was wrong. I've always believed in miracles, Jones. I'm a woman of faith. You think I go to church for fun? Besides, physicking is full of wonders. I must see three a week, at least."

How could he have expected another answer? He shook his head. "Of course. Now, tell me what's happened since I was carted up here."

"The dukes of Arbat and Morvell have agreed it's God's will they support Rhian. But Damwin of Meercheq and Kyrin of Hartshorn stormed off, swearing bloody vengeance and God's wrath. So did Marlan's spy, the lovely Ven'Martin. Rhian, King Alasdair, the newly invested Duke Ludo and Helfred, along with Dukes Rudi and Edward, are meeting in the library to decide what we'll do next."

"I see. And Zandakar?"

"I've no idea, Jones," said Ursa, with another shrug. "I've been here with you since you collapsed."

"I need to speak to him. And to Rhian. I'm going to get up now . . ."

She took hold of his wrist before he could throw back the blankets. "I don't advise it. Miracle or not, what you did wasn't natural. You need to rest. You can gad about, come the morning."

Gently, he freed himself. "Sorry, Ursa. The morning might be too late. I feel fine, I promise. And if that changes I'll come straight back to bed. My word as toymaker by Royal Appointment. Or as a miraculous burning man . . . whichever carries more weight."

Ursa stood. "I can see there's no stopping you, so I shan't waste my breath. But when you fall flat on your face, Jones, you can send for someone else to pick up the pieces!"

*   *   *

Sardre stood sentinel outside the manor-house library. Dexterity, re-dressed in his least-worn clothes, gave him a friendly nod.

"I must speak with the queen."

King Alasdair's man was too well trained to betray emotion but he couldn't quite keep the awed respect from his eyes.

Oh dear. Is everyone going to look at me like that now?

"Mr Jones," said Sardre, and tapped on the library door. A voice commanded it to open and Sardre looked in. "Your Majesty, Mr Jones requests an audience."

"Admit him," said an unseen Rhian. She sounded weary, but relieved.

He stepped past Sardre, who closed the door behind him, and faced the unnerving stares of the people gathered in the library. Rhian sat alone behind its elegant desk. King Alasdair stood behind her on the right, Helfred on the left. The young man he hadn't met must be Ludo, King Alasdair's cousin. He stood by the window. The other two men, seated before the desk, were the Dukes Edward and Rudi. The jewelled devices pinned to their chests told him which was which.

With Kingseat that's four duchies out of six on Rhian's side. The odds could be worse . . . except that there's Marlan.

The three dukes were staring as though they expected him to burn again any moment. King Alasdair's expression was circumspect. Helfred was fingering his prayer beads, their clicking loud in the hush.

Rhian smiled. "Dexterity. It's good to see you're unharmed by your adventure."

"Thank you, Your Majesty," he said, bowing. "Quite unharmed, it seems. Although I've no memory of what I said or did in the Great Hall. Ursa seems to think it was . . . miraculous."

"Miraculous indeed," said Helfred. Like Sardre, awed respect shone in his eyes. "A harbinger of God sent softly among us."

"Was there something you wanted?" asked Rhian.

She looked different. He'd grown used to her in rough boy's clothing, woollen hose and a hardspun shirt. He knew how to speak easily with that Rhian. But *this* one . . . grander even than the Rhian in Kingseat . . . by far more royal and infinitely less approachable . . .

He felt his cheeks heat. "Ah. Yes. Well. Ursa mentioned you were discussing what happens next . . ."

"Yes?" she prompted. "You have a suggestion?" The question earned her sharp looks but she paid no attention. "Speak your mind, Dexterity. Your counsel is invaluable."

"That's very good of you, Your Majesty. Can I ask if you've decided how soon you intend returning to Kingseat?"

"As soon as we can," she said. "Before Marlan has a chance to turn the whole Church against me. There are some attendant matters to deal with first but when they're concluded we'll take a river-barge and—"

"No, Your Majesty," he said.

King Alasdair's eyebrows rose. "*No?* Mr Jones—"

Heart pounding, he nodded. "That's right. I'm sorry. No. We have to go by road again."

"Dexterity, we can't," said Rhian gently. "It would take too long. I can't give Marlan time to—"

"We must," he said, and stepped closer. "Hettie said."

She exchanged a glance with the king. "Hettie. I see."

Duke Edward leaned forward. "I don't. Who's this Hettie and why should we care what she has to say?"

"Edward," said Rhian, one hand lifted in warning. "It's sufficient that I say we should." She nodded. "Very well. We go by road."

The dukes gaped at her. Then Rudi of Arbat banged his fist on his knee. "I can't accept this. It's far too high-handed. If we're to be your council you must consult with us before—"

"Gentlemen," said Rhian, coldly. "'Council' is *not* another word for 'men who tell me what I shall and shan't do'. Is that understood?"

The affronted silence was broken by a snort of laughter from the window. "Well, Alasdair, you always said she was Eberg's daughter," said Duke Ludo. "And God knows she'll need strength if we're to bring this mad business to a good end."

"Strength, yes," said Rhian. She wasn't smiling. "And faith. And unbending resolve. I can't waver from my purpose, gentlemen, and neither can you. God knows we'll have enemies enough ranged against us." One by one she looked at them, and one by one they nodded.

Dexterity felt his spirits lift. *You were right, Hettie. She's special, is Rhian. So you use me however you see fit if that means it puts her on the throne.*

"Was there anything else, Mr Jones?" said Rhian, politely dismissive.

He bowed. "No, Your Majesty. With your permission I'll leave you to your privy business."

"You have it," she said, her eyes warm with affection.

"We'll talk again tomorrow. I hope you pass a restful night."

"And you, Majesty." He bowed again. "King Alasdair. Your Graces. Chaplain. Good night."

Escaping the royal presence, he nodded his way past Sardre then stopped and turned back. His belly was grumbling but before he sought the kitchen to assuage its complaints . . .

"Sardre, would you know where Zandakar might be?"

Sardre frowned. "The last I saw of him he was in the garden performing his . . ."

"*Hotas.* Are you saying he's not come in? Because it's dark, you know."

"I'm saying I've not seen him," said Sardre, ruthlessly correct.

Which, since this was Sardre, was the same as saying Zandakar had remained outside.

Odd. Most odd.

"Thank you," Dexterity said, and went off to find him.

The manor's godhouse was small and clean. No tang of blood. No sign of devotion with knife and sacred beast. How did these people summon their god to them without blood? Without sacrifice? Why would their god believe in them when all they did was kneel and talk? How could they believe in their god when it never revealed itself in the world?

Zandakar frowned. *Except Ursa says it did reveal itself this highsun. Through Dexterity, who is made a true godspeaker. I wish I had seen that. I would like to see this*

Ethrean god. I would like to know if it has more power than mine.

On the chapel's wall the Ethrean god's flame burned. It burned because there was a wick in a pot of oil, secreted inside the wall. Dexterity had told him when he asked. *Pots of oil.* That was a human thing. That was no godly sign. No stinging scorpions. No godspeakers with their smiting hands. No sacrificed lambs that puffed into dust. Nothing in this soft green Ethrea said a god was here with its power and rage.

And yet in this small clean room he felt at peace. More at peace than anywhere in Mijak. The peace of Harjha, that was in this place. Still and quiet so his godspark might rest.

I feel so weary. I do not know who I am.

Since that time in the woodland, when he had told Dexterity about Yuma and the god and the warhost of Mijak he had held his breath, he had waited for death. Dexterity said, *I will keep your secret,* but why would he do that? He was a soft man, he wept for dead people, the truth had angered him. Such anger in his eyes.

He says I must be warlord for Ethrea. The god's hammer for Ethrea. But what does the god want? I still do not know . . .

He heard the chapel door open behind him, and turned on the wooden seat Helfred said was called a *pew.*

Dexterity.

"You're in *here*?" said the toymaker. "I've been looking for you *everywhere*. What are you doing in *here*?"

He got to his feet, slowly. Since the woodland, Dexterity had not wanted to see him, had not wanted to speak with him. Since the woodland, Dexterity had been cold.

He shrugged. "Chapel quiet. Quiet good, *zho?*"

"*Zho*. Quiet good." Dexterity walked towards him, his face was a frown. "Zandakar, I saw Dmitrak."

Dimmi? He saw Dimmi? How could he see Dimmi? Was the warhost here, was it come to Ethrea already?

"*Wei*, Zandakar!" said Dexterity, alarmed, and reached a hand to his arm. "*Wei* here. In a dream. Hettie showed me."

"*Wei* here?"

"In a dream," said Dexterity. "Put the knife away."

Heart pounding, he slid the knife back through his belt. "What dream? Why?"

Dexterity slumped into the nearest pew. "I think she wanted me to know exactly what we're facing. I think she wanted to remind me . . . how important you are."

"You saw Dimmi?"

"*Zho.*" Dexterity nodded. There were tears in his eyes. "Your brother. He has red hair, *zho?* In braids, down his back?" Dexterity patted his own hair to show what he meant.

Red. He knew red. "*Zho*. Dimmi has red hair."

"And he wore this strange gauntlet . . ."

Gauntlet. He did not know that word. But then Dexterity raised his right arm, fingers fisted, and he held it in front of him and his face was fierce.

The god's hammer. Dexterity has seen its power.

"The people, Zandakar," Dexterity whispered, his arm dropping to his lap. "Good God, the poor people. Burned. All burned. And cut open, by his warriors. And the buildings, his power struck them and they flew apart, like—like *sand*! Who can stand against that? Hettie says *you* can . . . but how? You don't have a gauntlet. *We* don't have a gauntlet. There are *thousands* of them, Zandakar. Your brother and his warriors. Thousands and thousands. They're like *locusts*. They're a *plague*."

Locusts. Plague. He did not know those words. But he could see in Dexterity's face they were bad things. "*Yatzhay*, Dexterity."

"Dmitrak wasn't *yatzhay*," said Dexterity, growling. "He was pleased. He praised his warriors. And they chanted. They chanted. *Chalava! Chalava! Chalava zho!*" He shuddered, then dragged his hand hard down his face. "A little town called Garabatsas. Destroyed. Smoke and ash. Nothing left. All dead."

The chant was unknown to Zandakar, Dimmi must have made it. It sounded like Dimmi, all bravado and rage. He did not know Garabatsas. Dimmi was making his way in the world. He was riding closer . . .

"How far Garabatsas?"

"Not far enough." Another shudder. "I've seen what will happen to Ethrea if we can't stop Dimmi. Stop your mother. *Hekat*."

He felt his heart constrict. "Dexterity saw Yuma?"

Dexterity shoved to his feet and wandered restless round the chapel. "No. I saw enough without seeing her too." He made a sound like a laugh, except it was full of pain. "God help me, Zandakar. Your brother. If you told me you loved him I—I think I'd—" He covered his eyes with one hand. "It doesn't matter. What's done is done." But then he stopped and took his hand from his face. "That was you once, wasn't it? Mijak's *chotzu*? The *chalava-hagra*? What I saw Dimmi do to Garabatsas . . . that's what you did to Targa? To Zree? To those other places?"

There was scorpion pain in Dexterity's voice, his face, his eyes. Dexterity was a hurting man.

Slowly, Zandakar nodded. "*Zho*. Those places. But *wei* Na'ha'leima."

Dexterity flinched. "And that makes a difference, does it?" Then he sighed. "Yes. I suppose it does. Dear God. I'm a *toymaker*. I'm not meant to know these things . . ."

Zandakar owed this small sad man his life, but what was there he could say or do that would ease his pain? "Dexterity . . ."

Dexterity looked up. *"Zho?"*

"*Yatzhay,* Garabatsas."

For many heartbeats Dexterity stood there, silent. "I know you are, Zandakar," he said at last. "God help me, so am I." Then he straightened his spine, he put on his strong face and showed the world he was a man. "I'm *yatzhay,* and I'm so hungry my stomach thinks my throat's been—" He stopped. "No. Perhaps not." He crooked a finger. "Come on. We should go. They'll be wondering where we are."

Not moving, Zandakar watched him start for the chapel door. "Dexterity. Garabatsas. You tell Rhian? You tell king?"

"Wei," said Dexterity, pausing, and shaking his head. "It's not time. Garabatsas is our secret. What's one more after all, with so many held between us?"

Dexterity kept on walking, and this time Zandakar followed.

CHAPTER THIRTY-ONE

Marlan's chamber-servant woke him in the early hours before dawn, whispering: "Eminence? Your Eminence? A letter has come."

All his life he'd been a light sleeper. During his novitiate it had earned him an unwarranted reputation for piety; driven to distraction by the dreaming snores and snorts of fourteen other boys he'd often be found studying his Admonitions by candlelight. It never occurred to the venerables it was because the novices were permitted nothing else to read.

Wrapped in a silk robe, the servant dismissed, he sat pooled in lamplight and stared at the folded message. He didn't need to open it to know it was from Ven'Martin. The swift, spiky penstrokes directing the letter to Prolate Marlan's attention belonged to no other man and the outside of the paper, spoiled a little from its journey by carrier pigeon, was imprinted with the Linfoi venerable house's mark, a salmon leaping over the Living Flame.

He broke the letter's cracked wax seal.

Eminence, you are betrayed. Helfred has released Eberg's brat from her wardship and married her to Alasdair Linfoi. She styles herself queen and is claiming miracles in God's name. The dukes of Hartshorn and Meercheq stand strong for God, the others are corrupted. I will do whatever you command. Advise me, I beg you, that I might serve God and you. Martin.

He watched as his fingers crushed the letter to ruin. Red spots of rage danced before his eyes. He felt empty, light-headed, his bones made friable and his blood turned to acid.

I will destroy Helfred for this. I will destroy them both.

He wrote a reply to Ven'Martin.

She will attempt a return to Kingseat. Finance yourself from the Linfoi house Treasury and follow her. Inform me daily of her progress. Do not alert her to your presence— and leave Helfred to me. He shall be chastised. What do you mean, she is claiming miracles?

Next he wrote instructions to the Most Venerable Artemis, then summoned his chamber-servant with a shout.

"Have these letters dispatched immediately to the Linfoi venerable house. And send for Ven'Barto. I would see him at once."

The chamber-servant bowed and took the letters. "Yes, Your Eminence."

While he waited for Martin's barely adequate replacement to arrive, he dressed himself in his most severely sumptuous vestments. These heinous crimes were not mere personal attacks. Helfred and Rhian had assaulted the Church . . . and the Church's physical embodiment would meet their perfidy dressed in splendour from head to toe. Silk and pearls and gold and rubies: this was the armour of God's chosen Prolate.

A bleary Ven'Barto arrived in due course and was sent smartly on his way to rouse the sleeping members of the Court Ecclesiastica. Helfred must be judged and tried and condemned. Then would come Rhian's turn, in the Court Ecclesiastica *and* the King's Council chamber.

Challenge me, would you? Think to strike me down? Fools. You shall not escape me. There is no corner of Ethrea that will hide you from my wrath.

The Court Ecclesiastica comprised the kingdom's prolate and ten learned Most Venerables. The venerables' outcry when he sorrowfully informed them of Helfred and Rhian's blasphemy was something of a balm to his lacerated pride. Standing in the court's chamber on the highest floor of his palace, surrounded by oak and velvet and gilt, he waited for their shocked protests to subside.

"Imagine my dismay, brothers," he said, and let his voice tremble. "My nephew, my own flesh and blood, corrupted in this hideous fashion. Indeed I must wonder if I am still fit to lead you, so deceived as I am. My judgement must be suspect."

Most Venerable Thomas creaked to his feet. An old man, and doddering, with a touching faith in his prolate's unimpeachable pronouncements. "God forbid such words on your lips again, Eminence! You are our prolate, the Father of our Church. Was not Rollin himself deceived by wicked men? The fault lies not in you but in the perfidy of Helfred's stained soul, and in the wretched arrogance of a girl ruined in her childhood."

Fervent murmurings as the other most venerables agreed.

Marlan pressed his hand to his heart. "Brothers, you move me to displays of unseemly emotion. Can I take it we are agreed: there is no question of innocence in this? Helfred is guilty beyond shadow of doubt?"

"Yes! He is guilty!" said Thomas, resuming his seat. Nods and echoing voices greeted his declaration.

He clasped his hands lightly before him, bowing his head lest the light of vengeful triumph burn too brightly in his eyes. "Then it is the will and pronouncement of this holy court that Helfred, a chaplain, be stripped of his divinity. He is cast down from God's sight and lies naked and sinful in the mud. He is banned from Church office. He is denied the Living Flame. Let no man's hand be stretched towards him. Let no man's smile be seen on his approach. He is anathema . . . and so he is declared."

"And so he is declared," echoed the Court Ecclesiastica.

"Now . . ." said Marlan, rage partly assuaged. "With regards to our wayward princess . . ."

Rhian was just as easily dealt with, although, since she was of the blood royal, different rules applied. The Court Ecclesiastica reproved her rash actions. It did not recognise her marriage. It reinstated her wardship and called upon her immediate presence that she might answer for her sins.

The duchy of Linfoi was placed under interdict.

"And also the duchies of Morvell and Arbat, by reason of their dukes' grave misconduct," Marlan added. "So shall fall all persons, parishes, districts and duchies to dire interdiction, should any support this disobedient child Rhian. Support for the princess is anathema . . . and so it is declared."

"And so it is declared," echoed the Court Ecclesiastica.

"Finally there remains the matter of the King's Council," he said. "And the supporters of the malfeasant dukes. I shall deal with that business myself, come morning.

You, my brothers, I leave to the business of spreading word of interdict and anathema to our brethren throughout Ethrea. The smallest parish can be left in no doubt. This blasphemy must be nipped in the bud lest chaos wreak calamity and see us forever lost to God's mercy. When the proclamations are ready bring them to me for my signature and seal. I want them nailed to every chapel door and shouted from every pulpit within the week. Is that clear?"

The venerables nodded, muttering and kissing their thumbs. Satisfied, he left them and returned to his rooms.

After an austere breakfast of bread and figs he sent word to his fellow councillors, calling for an urgent meeting in one hour's time. They wouldn't refuse him, they clamoured daily for Rhian's return with a decision on her marriage. He neglected to inform Secretary Lord Dester of the summons, however. Some meetings were better recorded in hindsight. Then he ordered Idson to his study.

"Commander," he said, his fingers steepled before him. "As the man in charge of Kingseat's peace you will be grieved to learn of great imminent unrest."

Idson tensed. "Your Eminence?"

"Your men must be placed on the highest alert. I want soldiers throughout the duchy riding day and night. In the capital your men will proceed on horseback, no more foot patrols. They must make it clear, Idson, that civil disobedience will not be tolerated. Nor will we tolerate the unruliness of foreigners. In fact . . ." He pretended to be struck by a new thought. "Arrange for the immediate withdrawal of shore passes to all visiting ships in the harbour. I fear it likely we will need to keep foreigners from our streets until the crisis is passed."

"Eminence . . ." Idson frowned. "What crisis?"

"The crisis you allowed to fester by failing to apprehend Princess Rhian!"

Idson stepped back, his face losing colour. "Your Eminence, I—"

"It is too late for apologies!" he snapped. "The damage is done. However . . ." He gentled his voice. First the stick, then the carrot. "I have faith in your determination to expunge your failure, Commander. Indeed it's in your best interests that you do."

Sweat stippled the man's brow. "Eminence."

"It grieves me to tell you, Idson, that Princess Rhian has acted disgracefully. Unlawfully. With the connivance of certain members of the King's Council she seeks to undermine the stability of the kingdom. She must be stopped. She *will* be stopped. But I fear for the people until that is accomplished. That is why we must take control before panic sets in and there are . . . unfortunate consequences."

"Eminence, I assure you, I will not fail a second time," said Idson. His voice was unsteady.

Marlan smiled. "Be sure you don't."

"Eminence," said Idson, bowing. "Was there anything else?"

"Indeed. You will report to the council chamber with a skein of guards—" he glanced at his clock "—half an hour from now. Wait outside. Do not enter until I summon you. Understood?"

"Understood, Your Eminence."

"Then you are dismissed."

Alone again he let himself sit, just sit, and wait for his freshly stirred rage to subside before making his way to the castle and the council chamber.

That bitch and my whey-faced nephew and the rabble from Linfoi. That they would dare to thwart me . . .

They had dared and they would fail. And soon would pay . . . and pay . . . and pay.

"Married?" said Henrik Linfoi, blankly. "You claim Rhian and my nephew Alasdair are *married*? How can they be married? She's in the clerica and he's in duchy Linfoi."

Marlan, on his feet, favoured duchy Linfoi's representative with his coldest stare. "My source of information is beyond question, Henrik. Ven'Martin, my assistant. He stumbled across this gross deception while attending your brother's funeral. Rhian is with your nephew on the ducal estate."

Uproar in the chamber. Marlan let it run, unchecked, watching the faces of the dukes' men for signs of complicity. He didn't see any but that did not mean complicity was absent. He would trust not a one of them.

"How is this possible, Marlan?" Porpont shouted, fist pounding the table. "She was in your care, she was under your protection! How in God's name did she—"

"We contend with enough blasphemy already without you adding to the tally, Porpont! Hold your tongue. All of you, be silent! I have not finished speaking!"

They stammered to silence.

"Rhian escaped the clerica with help from agents outside," he said, chilling them with his voice and eyes.

"Employed by men seeking to advance themselves at the expense of Ethrea's best interests."

"Ridiculous," said Niall, faintly. "Why would we—or our dukes—connive to put a turd like Linfoi on the throne?"

Before Henrik could respond, Marlan bared his teeth in a smile. "Linfoi *isn't* on the throne. Rhian styles *herself* queen."

More uproar. He silenced it with a single word.

"Enough!"

"I tell you, *all* of you," said Henrik Linfoi, vehemently, "I had no knowledge of any such plan!" He swept his fellow councillors with a hot, frightened stare. "If someone helped Her Highness escape the clerica it was one of *you*, my lords, or one of your dukes. *It was not me*. I am *innocent* of—"

"Why should we believe you?" sneered Volant, his fists clenched. "When you stand to benefit from—"

"And why should we believe *you're* not involved, Volant?" said Marlan. "When your duke aligns himself with the princess and her turd?"

"My duke?" Volant goggled. "*Rudi* supports this? It's a lie, Marlan. I don't believe you. You're lying."

Marlan sat back. "Don't compound calumny with blasphemy, my lord. That cannot end well. Rudi of Arbat and Edward of Morvell have declared themselves for this traitorous queen and the disloyal upstart she married against our will. That makes them traitors. Their duchies are interdicted until they repent."

Harley leapt to his feet. "Edward is no traitor! My brother is a true and loyal servant of the Crown! If the little bitch has married let that be upon her own head. I'll not stand by while you destroy my family!"

"Or mine!" added Volant. "Rudi's married to my sister. What touches her touches me! If you think I'll let you tear us down in your attempt to rule by default you're mistaken, Marlan!"

"How did she marry Linfoi, anyway?" demanded Harley. "She'd need a Church dispensation. Who would—" And then he stopped, mingled understanding and delight dawning in his piggy eyes. "*Helfred?* Her *chaplain?* Your *nephew,* Marlan? Your own flesh and blood thwarted your ambitions and wed Rhian to Linfoi? *Ha!*"

He could not deny it and did not try. "My nephew is not your concern, Lord Harley. He has been dealt with by the Court Ecclesiastica. Now you must be dealt with by secular means."

The malicious delight in Harley's face extinguished. "Dealt with? What are you saying, *dealt with*? I'm innocent of this debacle, Marlan. This is *your* calamity! You and your nephew's! I've nothing to gain from Rhian's disastrous marriage and neither has Edward. Find your scapegoats somewhere else."

"Nothing to gain?" said Niall, glaring. "Are you a fool, Harley, or do you take Porpont and me for lackwits? *Nothing to gain.* You seek influence in a new court, you seek royal largesse. Your brother fawns at the feet of this girl, at the feet of the nobody she's chosen to marry, hoping to see Ethrea rewrit in his favour! And what then the fate of my duchy? What do you plan for Hartshorn and Kyrin? Do you intend to see him thrown down and his lands plundered for your gain?" He swung about. "For

I'll wager my estates my wife's father does not support Rhian!"

"Duke Kyrin is loyal," said Marlan. "And so is Damwin of Meercheq. As for the others . . ." He spread his hands wide.

Henrik Linfoi shoved his chair back, his face the colour of cold ash. "Before God and his Living Flame I swear to you, I *swear,* I had *no* knowledge of this matter! Alasdair has said *nothing* to me. Send to my home, search all my correspondence! You'll find no evidence of treachery there."

That much was true. The clerk he'd insinuated into Linfoi's residence had already confirmed it. "Of course not," Marlan said smoothly. "You are many things, Henrik, but a fool is not among them. Whatever plans you hatched with usurping Alasdair you hatched in direst secrecy."

"I hatched no plans!" Linfoi shouted. "And you will never prove I did. From the outset I accepted Linfoi would *not* be considered for the crown. My dying brother accepted it, God rest his departed soul, and so did my nephew."

Marlan smiled, sorrowful. "Yes, that is the complaisant face you showed to this council. You told us your brother and nephew were reconciled to their irrelevance. But the moment your brother died your nephew wed with Rhian, thus betraying his true heart. And so Ethrea is betrayed—by you and your fellow conspirators."

"I've betrayed no-one!" said Linfoi. Sweat trickled down his face. "I am *ignorant* of this marriage. If Alasdair had told me his intention I'd have *discouraged* him, heartily. This kingdom cannot be torn apart by dissension. At the first hint of instability we are laid open to the

attentions of those nations who would seek to exploit our unique standing. I would *never* put us in such an invidious position!"

"Nor would I!" protested Harley.

"Nor I!" added Volant.

"And yet," said Marlan, dulcet, "it is your dukes who support this insupportable marriage. Curious, is it not, to consider your duchies share common borders with each other and Linfoi?"

A heartbeat of staring then the chamber filled with shouting. Marlan raised his voice above it. *"Commander Idson! To me!"*

The uproar fell into silence as though cleaved with an axe. The chamber door opened and Idson entered with his armed guards.

"Commander, escort lords Linfoi, Harley and Volant to a castle cell," Marlan instructed. "There to await a more leisurely interrogation."

"A *cell*?" said Linfoi, as the commander advanced. "Marlan, are you *addled*? You have no standing to order any such *thing,* we are council representatives, you are—"

"Prolate of Ethrea," said Marlan. "The only uncorrupted power in the land, given what has happened to the King's Council. Go with the guards quietly, Linfoi . . . or we shall read resistance as your confession. We will take it as a declaration it was always your plan to put Rhian on the throne."

Linfoi's face blanched from grey to white. "No. I do not support Rhian ruling in her own right. She's not even a woman, she's still a child. You must not forget that.

Whatever she's done, Marlan, she's acted out of grief and a misguided fear she had no-one else to turn to."

He smiled. *Thank you, Henrik.* "So you defend her wicked actions. At least we now know for certain where you stand."

"I stand for the rule of law!" retorted Linfoi. "There is *no* law placing you at Ethrea's head!"

"Lord Linfoi, we are in crisis. When this news reaches the foreign ambassadors, can you not imagine their consternation? If they for *one moment* fear Ethrea is ungoverned what will they tell their eager masters, do you think? What do you suppose will happen next?"

There were agitated mutterings as Niall and Porpont considered the unwholesome future.

Marlan clasped his hands before him, presenting the perfect image of calm control, and swept Idson and his guards and the councillors with his coldest, clearest gaze. "It is shown to us without a doubt this kingdom cannot proceed rudderless any longer. Not without inviting the kind of interference we have sought to prevent since Eberg's demise. Only the Church, with its divine protections, its infallible teachings, its God-inspired network of ordained divines, can keep us afloat now. Our times have become turbulent, gentlemen. Or would you disagree?"

His audience said nothing. Even Linfoi was silent. Even Harley and Volant.

"Take them, Idson," he commanded, wielding his voice like a penitent's friend. "But do not think to accost them save they give you strict cause."

"No, Your Eminence," said Idson. A curt nod to his guards saw Linfoi, Harley and Volant taken in hand.

Marlan smiled to see it. "And when these parlous men

are disposed of, as their conduct dictates, see to the securing of this castle," he added. "Nobility related to these miserable miscreants shall be held in comfortable but close confinement. So too the servants. All others to be dismissed from the grounds but not permitted to leave the capital. Is that clear?"

Idson bowed. "Eminence, quite clear."

Stunned and no longer protesting, the troublesome councillors were removed. Marlan waited for the chamber door to close behind them and once more looked to Porpont and Niall.

"Have no fear, gentlemen," he said. "For I will subdue this riotous disarray. God will not be mocked in Ethrea. Go about your business never hinting of your dismay. Should any ambassador accost you, direct him to me. What has been revealed in this chamber will not be spoken of beyond it, on pain of my extreme displeasure. Trust in me, as you trust in God. For am I not God's chosen man in Ethrea?"

They were sheep in dire need of a shepherd. Fools who could no longer be trusted with so much as a thimbleful of power. Behind their anger and resentment, a bleating of fear.

"Your Eminence," they muttered, and withdrew with all haste.

Blessedly alone, it was all he could do not to laugh out loud as he was struck by a new and welcome realisation.

Eberg's bitch of a daughter and her lovestruck swain have, without meaning to, done me a favour. No-one will accept her as queen in her own right. No-one will accept Alasdair, that pauper of the north. Arbat and Morvell have damned themselves by association. Hartshom and

Meercheq will fall over themselves to prove their loyalty. I will move to have meek, untroublesome Rulf declared the new Duke of Kingseat and thus what I have dreamed for will come to pass. It's a scant distance from a duchy to a Crown . . .

Rhian sat in the manor-house library's windowseat, dressed in her boy's clothes, knees pulled to her chest. She'd danced her morning *hotas* with a Zandakar still distracted by something he refused to share, and had meant to go upstairs to bathe and change into a more seemly dress . . . but she'd heard Edward and Rudi's rumbly voices as the dukes came down the wide staircase and ducked for safety into the library. She wasn't ready to face them yet, after a late night in debate that had solved so little. She'd sat in the windowseat, intending to wait only a moment to be sure it was safe to venture upstairs . . .

. . . and somehow more than an hour had passed and she was still here, the sweat dried on her skin, and even though she was hungry and thirsty she felt no inclination to stir.

Too much has happened too quickly. I don't know who I am any more. When I look in the mirror I don't recognise myself. Who does Alasdair see when he looks at me now?

Alasdair. Her husband. The king at her right hand.

Is he truly content to stand one pace behind me? Does he truly believe I am strong enough to rule? Ludo thinks he's suntouched, I can see the disbelief in his eyes. The dukes are humouring me, I'm sure they think that once the dust has settled and we're all safe in Kingseat Alas-

dair will step forward and I'll retreat to the nursery where I belong.

Assuming, of course, they reached Kingseat safely.

She shook herself. There was no reward in thinking like that. Of course she'd see her home again. She'd see the castle and her people. She'd see Dinsy. She'd ride waving through the streets and laugh to hear her name called. The people would accept her. Hadn't Dexterity said they would?

And who am I to argue with God's harbinger?

She shivered, even though she sat full in sunshine. The sight of Dexterity, bursting into flames . . . the sound of his voice: his, and yet not . . . the public declaration that she was the chosen of God . . .

I never asked to be chosen. I never asked for this. I'd have been perfectly happy to die Duchess of Linfoi. Now it seems I must die as a queen . . . please, God. When that time comes let me be old and frail and surrounded by my children.

The library door opened and Alasdair came in.

She felt her heartbeat quicken to see him. He wasn't a handsome man. Next to Zandakar he was dreadfully plain. But she remembered his kisses and the way her breast fit so neatly in his hand.

He looked over and saw her. "Rhian! There you are!"

"I was thinking," she said, sliding to her feet. "A moment's solitude. Are you going to scold?"

"No," he said, frowning. "Were you outside before? With Zandakar?"

"I was dancing my *hotas*," she said, the knife heavy at her hip. "I'm not going to argue over them any more."

"Did I say I wished to argue? Rhian—" His lips tightened and he returned to the open door. "Sardre!" he called through it. "The queen is here. Tell the dukes to come, would you? No—wait—" He glanced back at her. "You're ready to meet with them?"

She nodded. "I can bathe later. And ask Sardre to bring me ale and some bread and soft cheese, would you? I'm famished."

"Breakfast for the queen, Sardre," he said. "Then send for the dukes."

The dukes' eyes widened when they saw her, dressed like a boy and quaffing ale like a sailor in the meanest Kingseat Harbour tavern.

"Be seated, gentlemen," she told them with a wave of her goblet. She'd already eaten coddled eggs and felt much better for them. "I'm in no mood to stand on ceremony. We've decisions to make and little time in which to make them. The longer we stay here the more advantage we grant to Marlan."

Cautiously, they sat. Edward cleared his throat. "Nevertheless, Majesty, I wonder if we might revisit the question of how we'll travel to—"

"No, we might *not*!" she said, thudding her goblet on the desk. "I've made my decision. We ride to Kingseat by road."

"Yes, Your Majesty," said Edward. "I know. This is about the manner of our travel. It's a question of your security."

"I am perfectly secure! This is *Ethrea,* not *Icthia,* where rulers succeed through assassination. Edward—"

"Is right to be concerned," said Rudi. His broad, fleshy fingers were laced across his soft paunch. "All four of us are concerned, Majesty. The king and your dukes."

She flicked a wounded glance at Alasdair. *You're supposed to be on my side, not discussing me behind my back.* Standing at the fireplace, the echo of his portraited father, he caught the glance but his face didn't change.

Fine.

"Gentlemen," she said, temper rigidly controlled, "I will say this once and then I tell you the subject is *closed.* I won't take to the roads of my kingdom surrounded by a garrison's worth of soldiers. What kind of message does *that* send to the people?"

"A less messy one than the sight of your bleeding, broken body in the dirt," said Ludo, who'd taken her place on the sun-painted windowseat.

"Ludo!"

He raised his hands in surrender. "Forgive me. But I think we must face facts. Violence against you is a distinct possibility if Marlan incites the people to act in peril of their souls."

"He has a point, Rhian," Alasdair murmured. Of course he'd agree with his volatile cousin. "The people are Marlan's most potent weapon. If they won't accept you . . ."

But Dexterity said they will. "They surely won't if they think I *fear* them."

"No-one's suggesting you give that impression," said Ludo. "But neither can you travel to Kingseat unprotected. Not with such a tenuous grasp on authority."

"I won't *be* unprotected," she retorted. "I'll have Zandakar at my back."

Ludo and Alasdair exchanged guarded looks. Rudi and Edward's expressions were far less self-contained.

She narrowed her eyes. "What? You think he can't protect me?"

"It's not a matter of *can't*," Alasdair said quickly. "I don't doubt his skill for a moment. I've seen his *hotas*. I've seen how fast he moves, and his strength. Rhian, I know he's saved your life once already but—"

"What?" said Rudi, sitting up. "When was this?"

"Are you keeping secrets, cousin?" said Ludo, displeased.

Rhian thumped the table. "*I* decide who knows what and when, gentlemen. If you have a complaint you may direct it to me. Ludo?"

He stared at the carpet. "No, Your Majesty."

"Excellent." She looked at Rudi. "As I travelled through Arbat I was attacked by six armed footpads. It seems, Your Grace, that your soldiers have better things to do than keep your duchy safe. Zandakar killed the men. Do you wish to object?"

Rudi flushed a dull red. "Majesty, I apologise. I—"

"Oh, it doesn't matter now," she said, impatient. "What matters is Zandakar's proved himself. And I do have my *own* knife, you know. I'm not completely *helpless*."

"Of course not, Majesty," said Edward. "But do you truly desire a foreign mercenary—for that's what this Zandakar will be, to all intents and purposes—to ride alone at your back with a knife in his hand? At a time when you'll be fighting to convince the ambassadors in Kingseat that their interference in our affairs is unwelcome? Is *that* a message you wish to send? Is it the message you should send to your people, that you don't trust your own kind to keep you safe?"

Damn. It was an excellent point and she should've

seen it. "You're right, Edward. Very well, a compromise. I will ride with a personal bodyguard. A *small* one. Two soldiers each from Linfoi, Arbat and Morvell. Zandakar shall choose the men and lead them."

The men exchanged looks, but wisely refrained from argument. "Fine. But we need more general soldiery than that," said Rudi. "If Damwin and Kyrin should offer arms to Marlan . . ."

"They won't," she said firmly. *They can't. Dear God, they can't.* "Ethrean against Ethrean? You're talking civil war."

"If it looks like he's losing, Marlan might not care," said Edward. "And he'll find a way to blame you for spilled blood."

Rudi cleared his throat. "Majesty, if you're not willing to risk confrontation you'd best abandon the crown now."

She bit her lip. *This isn't what I wanted. I never looked for war.*

"Her Majesty prefers to be safe, not sorry," said Alasdair. "The rest of Edward and Rudi's men will ride with us, plus twenty more from Linfoi—if Ludo permits?"

"Of course," said Ludo. "The garrison's best men are yours."

Alasdair looked at her. "Rhian?"

"Agreed," she said, something breaking inside her. "Now, as to the question of Kingseat's new duke. Rudi, I have in mind your younger son, Adric." As Rudi spluttered incoherent thanks she turned to Edward. "You have an unmarried daughter, Your Grace? I seem to recall meeting her at last summer's revels . . . Very shy and pretty."

Edward's whiskered jaw sagged. "Yes, Majesty. Dimelza."

"Is her heart unspoken for?"

"Her heart is my affair. If you mean what I think you mean she will—"

Rhian leaned over the desk, fingers drumming a warning. "My recent rough wooings, Edward, have left an indelible impression. You'd do well to believe me when I say I'll have no unwilling girl broken on the back of your ambitions. If Dimelza is amenable she shall marry Adric of Arbat, whom I name Duke of Kingseat. You'll be a duke and goodfather to a duke and grandfather to the *next* duke . . . *if* Dimelza accepts. If she declines, you will remain a duke for as long as it pleases me . . . and she is left undisturbed for her choice. I trust you understand me?"

After a brief, startled silence Edward nodded. "Perfectly, Majesty. The choice will be hers."

She bared her teeth in a smile and sat back. "Yes. I thought it would."

Reluctant admiration warmed Edward's eyes. "You're Eberg's daughter right enough."

"Yes, I am. Rudi—"

"Majesty?"

"You've no objection?"

"None at all! I am deeply honoured!"

She sighed. "It's a small thing, gentlemen. And I know what you've risked by standing with me."

It was important that they know she knew it. Their pleased smiles eased, a little, the burgeoning pain in her head.

See Papa? I can be diplomatic as well as warlike. I'm not going to fail you. I'm going to make you proud.

For another four hours nearly they thrashed out the details of the imminent journey south. Which were the best roads to take. Which townships and villages they should visit and which they should avoid. Should they sleep rough, on common land, or risk the complications of commandeering public inns? They debated provisions and proclamations, speculated on how the Church might react and how they could best show the people that their lives would be enhanced, not harmed, by the crowning of a queen.

And then they were interrupted by a knock on the door. Saldre, his face disciplined but his eyes perturbed.

"Forgive me, Your Majesty, but a message has come from Lord Henrik's people. By pigeon. I fear it is . . . urgent."

She held out her hand. "Very well. Present it."

With the merest shift of his gaze to his master and back again, Sardre crossed the room and gave her the note.

She read it, and the room reeled.

"Rhian! What is it!"

She looked at Alasdair, dizzy and sick. "It's Henrik," she whispered. "He's been arrested."

CHAPTER THIRTY-TWO

It was a sombre procession that four days later departed the Linfoi ducal estate, bound for Kingseat and confrontation with Marlan.

Most Venerable Artemis had brought the announcement of interdict himself as Rhian and her council sat stunned by the news of Henrik Linfoi's arrest. Shown into the library, Ven'Artemis had spared one uncomfortable glance for Alasdair and the dukes then focused on her.

"I'm grieved to bring you such dreadful tidings," he said, his voice unsteady. "Your Highness, I *beg* you—"

"Your Majesty," said Alasdair, standing at her back. "You are addressing Ethrea's queen."

Ven'Artemis wrung his thin hands. "Forgive me, I can't. I am instructed not to recognise Princess Rhian's claimed estate."

"Who told you that?" said Rhian. "The Venerable Martin?"

"Ven'Martin has returned to Kingseat, Your Highness. My instructions come from the prolate himself."

Rhian sighed. *Of course they did.* "I appreciate you're in a difficult position, Ven'Artemis. But I would remind you that Rollin was quite clear on this matter: Church and state are two separate institutions. You may not use Church powers to achieve a political end. Marlan has no right to interdict this duchy or any other, just because he'd prefer I wasn't queen."

"I'm a simple country divine at heart, Your Highness," said Ven'Artemis. "These matters are above me. All I wish to do is tend the needs of my people."

"As do I, Artemis! As queen I wish to tend the needs of everyone in Ethrea. And I'll not allow a creature like Marlan to stand in my way!"

"Please . . . you must not refer to His Eminence in that fashion!" Ven'Artemis protested. "I have come here to implore you, Highness, to reconsider your rash actions. There is yet hope of reconciliation. I would be pleased to act as arbiter. I'm sure if you did but throw yourself upon the mercy of the Court Ecclesiastica then—"

"*Mercy* from a group of old men who'd punish the innocent because Marlan tells them not to recognise my lawful accession?" She stood. "That's not mercy, Ven'Artemis, that's arrogant caprice. I will *never* bow my head before your Court Ecclesiastica. Those old men have no authority over *me*."

Ven'Artemis sighed. "You will do as you must, Your Highness . . . as will I. Where can I find Chaplain Helfred?"

Helfred? "Why?"

"I am charged to take him into my custody."

"Your *custody*?"

"Helfred is judged by the Court Ecclesiastica which you must agree has authority over *him*. He is declared anathema and must surrender to the venerable house and thence the prolate."

Anathema? Oh, that Marlan . . . his own *nephew* . . . Rhian glanced at Alasdair, then the dukes. In their faces she saw dismay and support. She looked again at Ven'Artemis. "Helfred is my chaplain. He remains with me. It is distressing enough that Marlan has seized a good man like Henrik Linfoi. I'll not willingly give him another, for God alone knows what abuse he has in mind."

"It would be in your best interests to leave now, Most Venerable," said Alasdair. "With no ill will on either side. You've always been a champion of Linfoi's people. Continue as their champion. These troubled times will pass."

After the most venerable's defeated departure, Rhian excused Alasdair, Edward and Rudi and offered Ludo what comfort she could.

It wasn't much.

"I must ride to Kingseat with you and Alasdair, Rhian," he said. His eyes were dry, but horribly bleak. "I have to rescue my father. He's an old man. He's not well. The shock of this—it could—" He closed his lips, tight.

She'd given him leave to use her name in private. "Ludo, I understand—and I share your distress. But I can't believe Marlan will raise a hand against Henrik, the nobility won't tolerate it. He'd lose his moral authority in a heartbeat. He's done this to frighten us. Frighten *me*. Nothing will happen to your father. He's too valuable alive."

Ludo paced the library. "You can't be certain of that."

"No, but it's likely," she said. "Ludo, I know this is awful. But you're Linfoi's duke. Your place is here."

"My place is with my father!" He turned. "Alasdair understands that. If you refuse me then—"

"It's not Alasdair's decision." Her heart was racing as though she danced her *hotas*. "You're staying behind."

The look on Ludo's face was worse than a mortal wound.

He hardly spoke to her again after that. Only when he had to, and with the fewest curt words. The hasty preparations for the royal progress continued. Every seamstress in the ducal village and from the outlying farmsteads had been pressed into service, making royal liveries and procession banners and pennants in the Havrell colours—peacock blue, royal purple and gold—with the Havrell device on each piece, subtly altered: still the traditional three-pointed gold crown, but now bordered with silver-white snowdrops, the flower of Linfoi, and a single blood-red rose, Rhian's personal device. Dexterity and

Ursa sewed alongside them. With nobody ill and Hettie stubbornly silent there was nothing else they could do to help. As for Helfred . . . kept in ignorance, he lived in the chapel and wore his knees out praying.

Word came for Rudi and Edward that their councillor kinsmen were taken with Henrik Linfoi and their duchies placed under the same interdict. Rudi's son Adric arrived at the manor house and Rhian invested him Duke of Kingseat . . . but there was no celebration after. Who could laugh and smile when good men were taken hostage? When whole duchies and their people were denied the Living Flame?

Though her council was doubtful she wrote to every foreign ambassador.

"There's no point pretending we're not in some degree of chaos," she'd told her dukes sharply. "They know what's going on. And you can be sure Marlan's whispering in their ears as fast as he can, lying until he's blue in the face. They must hear from the rightful Queen of Ethrea. I can't allow Marlan's to be the only voice in this kingdom."

"She's right," said Alasdair. "As king, I concur."

So she wrote her careful letters, to be sent south to the capital with trusted couriers. Most particular were her words for the ambassadors of Harbisland, Arbenia and Tzhung-tzhungchai. Win the confidence of those countries and half her battle would be won.

She decided she'd ride home to Kingsear, not travel in a carriage. Since no horse in Alasdair's stables pleased her sufficiently the duchy was hastily scoured for an animal she'd accept. A silver-grey stallion with a mane down to its knees appealed. She named it Invincible and gave

Zandakar the black stallion she'd liked almost as much. Alasdair made no outward objection but his eyes were brooding. Zandakar, smiling, named the horse *Didijik*.

Despite the long meetings and the frantic preparations she made time to dance the *hotas* with him morning and afternoon, lingering a little while after each session to watch him with the ducal soldiers he'd chosen as her personal bodyguards. They were competent men already . . . but Zandakar, knowing time was short, schooled them without mercy in all the hours they had left.

"I know you hate to hear this but you must. He frightens me, Rhian," Alasdair said in a low voice, walking back to the manor with her the afternoon before they departed. He'd come to watch her *hotas* in the worn and grass-trampled gardens, and stayed with her as the bodyguards returned to their relentless training. "He has skills I've never dreamed of."

A familiar, unwelcome throbbing started up at her temples. "Skills we need, Alasdair. You can't deny that."

He couldn't, but it was clear he wanted to. "I have to say, Rhian, *you* frighten me a little too. You look so fierce doing those *hotas* with your knife."

She made herself smile at him. "You've seen me fence before. We used to fence each other back in Kingseat. Were you afraid then?"

"That was different," he said, shaking his head. "It was fencing and it was . . . a game. You're not playing now." He touched the knife belted at her hip. "And that's no button-tipped foil."

He was right. Dear God, how much she hated that. "I know. But I don't have a choice, Alasdair."

A complication of pains darkened his eyes. "You could choose to let me defend you."

She sighed. "No, I can't. Alasdair—"

"I'm your *husband,* Rhian!" he said violently, taking her arms in a biting grip. "God help me, I'm your *king.* Have you no use for me now wedding me and briefly bedding me have put a crown on your head?"

"That's not fair!" she hissed, pulling herself free. They were still a small distance from the manor and alone, for the moment. "That's your wounded pride talking! *Think,* Alasdair. I'm Ethrea's first queen. How can I *ever* hope to rule if it's seen that my own husband doesn't trust me! I *must* stand alone. I can't be overshadowed by you!"

"But you can be overshadowed by Zandakar?"

She could easily pummel her fists against his broad, stubborn chest. "Zandakar doesn't count! Why won't you *see* that? Why do you insist on letting jealousy blind you?"

He looked away. "I'm not jealous. I'm worried. We've a long way to travel from Linfoi to Kingseat. We both know a lot can go wrong between here and there."

"Which is why I need to know how to use this knife! I need to be more than a royal decoration. If I'm not more than a royal decoration I'll never win this fight. Unless . . ." She looked at him, her eyes pricking. "Is that what you want? Would that make you happy?"

He released a harsh breath. "I don't think you want to know what would make me happy, Rhian."

Now he was wounding her, his words as cruel as any knife. She stepped back. "No more, Alasdair. I'm too tired. I know you're unhappy. I know you're disappointed in me. In what your life has become. You dreamed of a duchess not—not a warrior queen. I'm sorry. This isn't what I wanted, either. And if you think it is then you never knew me."

"That's the trouble, Rhian," he whispered. "I *do* know you. Better than you know yourself, though you'll never admit that. I can see what this is costing you . . . and it's killing me that you won't let me help."

"You want to help me, Alasdair?" She blinked hard, her throat tight. "Then stop nagging me about Zandakar. Don't carry on because I must put myself first. You want to *help* me, husband? Then remember *I'm your queen!*"

She spun on her heel and walked away. Before she said something else, something worse. Before he did.

First Ludo angry with me, now Alasdair. And though the dukes aren't angry I can tell they're afraid. Of course they're afraid, their families are in danger, their duchies are indicted. They've put their faith and their futures in the hands of an untried girl.

Dear God. Dear God. Don't let this be a mistake . . .

The royal procession departed the following dawn.

Rhian, astride Invincible, still dressed like a boy but in fabrics more feminine, watched as Alasdair embraced his cousin.

"The duchy's yours now, Ludo," he said, his voice not quite controlled. "There's no other man breathing I'd lief entrust it to. Be visible among the people. Let them know you're here and that you care. Give them no cause to doubt you'll fight their battles to the death."

Ludo nodded. "I will. I swear it. But Alasdair—"

"Hush," he said, and rested his hand against Ludo's

face. "This is right, and you know it. I'll rescue your father. You have my word."

"Your Majesty," Ludo whispered. He turned. "Queen Rhian. God speed your journey south and may he keep you safe and see you on your throne where you belong. Duchy Linfoi is yours until the end of time."

For a moment she wasn't sure if she could trust herself to speak. Then she nodded. "Duke Ludo, the Crown holds you in the highest regard. What you give up will be returned to you tenfold. Do not fear for your father or the people whose lives are trusted to you. I will see them safe . . . or perish in the attempt."

Somehow, Ludo managed to smile. Managed to release his burden of hurt anger. "Please don't perish, Your Majesty. You owe me a wife."

Which made her smile too, and lightened her heart for a moment.

The manor-house staff and the ducal estate workers lined the long driveway to see them leave. If their loyalty was tested by Marlan's interdict they didn't show it. They waved and shouted and called "God bless Queen Rhian! God bless our King Alasdair!"

She waved and smiled at them, Alasdair at her right hand. Edward, Rudi and Adric rode directly behind them, side by side, her loyal dukes. Then came Zandakar on Didijik, and the handpicked soldiers, who had swiftly come to respect him for his fluency with a blade. Next the peddler's van, driven by Dexterity, with Ursa and Helfred riding in the back.

Rhian felt a prickle of pain. She still hadn't told Helfred that Most Venerable Artemis had come for him. He knew about the interdictions and that was enough. He'd

wept at the thought of all the people denied God. To keep
him safe she'd ordered he not set foot from the van in daylight and stay close to the royal camp at night.

He'd tried to argue. Ruthless, she'd shouted him
down.

After the peddler's van came a handful of ducal retainers, three supply wagons and the rest of the armed escort.
Not the most inconspicuous assemblage.

But her purpose wasn't to be inconspicuous. Her purpose was to declare herself to the kingdom. There was
risk involved, she would be open to challenge by chaplains
and venerables and the people whose lives her existence
upset . . . but it was a risk she knew she had to take.

The people must see her, and know her, and accept her.
Showing fear or hesitation would doom her . . . and make
everything she'd done for naught.

"What do you think, Jones?" said Ursa, riding beside him
on the van's driving seat for a while. "Do you think we'll
reach Kingseat unscathed? Or will one of Marlan's ranting chaplains see us pulled from this van and drubbed for
our sins?"

Dexterity put the reins in one hand and scratched his
nose. "There'll be no drubbing of any kind. Not so long as
Zandakar's with us."

Since leaving the manor house they'd passed through
three large villages. Each time the villagers had spilled
into the streets and each time the royal procession was met
by the local chaplain, who attempted to bar their progress
and waved a Book of Admonitions in their faces.

"For shame! Repent! Ask for God's mercy!"

That was the cry from Marlan's chaplains, to a man.

Rhian had commanded them to stand aside for the Crown.

"I am Rhian, Eberg's daughter. Do not listen to the lies of unGodly men. God has granted me my birthright. I am your true and loving queen. Beside me rides Alasdair of Linfoi, son of your late duke. I have made him your king. Have faith, people of Linfoi, and don't despair. God has not been taken from you. Only God can take God from the world, and he will never do that. His Flame lives in your hearts. Trust in him and rejoice."

So young, and so regal. The villagers cheered to hear her words and the chaplains were hushed. It was possible God held their tongues . . . but it was more likely they saw Zandakar and the bodyguards and realised their best safety lay in silence.

"Zandakar," Ursa mused. "You know, it seems to me he's been keeping very quiet."

"He was never talkative, Ursa. And he's been kept busy training the soldiers and Rhian."

She nodded. "True. But something's changed in him. He seems sadder than usual . . . or afraid. But what could frighten a man like him? What's got *you* frightened, Jones? More than the rest of us, I mean. More than what's sensible."

The trouble with Ursa was that her wits were too sharp. "Frightened? I'm not frightened. If anything I'm pleased. We're going home to Kingseat, Ursa, and not before time. I miss my toyshop and I miss my little donkey. I even miss Tamas, but never tell him I said so."

After a long silence, broken by the creaking of cartwheels and the steady clopping of horses' hooves, Ursa sighed. "We've been friends a long time, Jones, unlikely as that seems. So why you'd think to start lying to me now . . ."

The hurt in her voice pained him like a knife thrust. *Oh, Hettie. If this business costs me Ursa* . . . "You're imagining things. I'm not lying to you."

"Being old doesn't make me stupid, Jones. And being my friend doesn't give you leave to be insulting."

Before he could stop her she'd climbed down off the peddler's van, even though it was moving, and gone round the back again to travel inside.

I'm sorry, Ursa. I know I've upset you . . . but it's better this way. You don't want to know the things I've been told. You never want to see the horrors I've been shown.

How he wished he didn't know them. How he wished he'd never seen.

Please, Hettie. Get us safe to Kingseat and help Rhian to her throne so I can pass this burden of secrets to her and be a simple toymaker again.

Hettie's reply was to send another miracle.

It happened the next morning, in a village called Heddonvale. The royal procession had spent the night in common woodland and at first light, after a brief service conducted by Helfred, started travelling again. They reached Heddonvale mid-morning, where they were greeted by a chaplain who railed against Rhian as an unnatural woman led astray by the forces of evil, and declared anathema on any who would aid her. Rhian defended herself vigorously and soon they found themselves in the centre of a shouting crowd in the high street. Some villagers sided with the chaplain, others with their new queen.

Dexterity stood up on the driving seat to get a better

look at the commotion. Behind him, the van's wooden hatch slid open.

"What's all that shouting, Jones?" Ursa demanded. "Since the chaplain can't come out and I'm keeping him company you'll have to tell us what's going on."

"Another chaplain," he said, shading his eyes with one hand. "Stirring the crowd against us."

"It seems to be working," said Ursa. "They sound irate."

"It's not his fault," Helfred chimed in. "He's got no choice but to follow my uncle's commands. If he disobeys *he'll* face interdict . . . or worse."

Which may have been true but it didn't much help matters. If Rhian had misjudged the people's love of Eberg and his daughter . . .

Before that unsettling thought had time to bloom further Dexterity heard another shouting voice. He turned.

A man was running towards them. "Help! Help! I need Physick Graythorne, help!"

"What's that?" said Ursa. "Is someone calling for a physick?"

"Yes. Ursa—"

She slammed the hatchway shut and a moment later appeared with her physicking bag beside the van. The shouting man passed her, his face shiny with sweat and maybe tears, running as though a fiend was at his heels.

"Physick Graythorne! Physick Graythorne! Are you gathered here? I need you!"

"I'm here!" a man replied, stepping clear of the villagers ranged around Rhian. He was younger than Ursa by some thirty years. "Joby!" he exclaimed as the shouting man staggered to a halt. "What's happened?"

The man Joby bent over, heaving for air, seemingly oblivious to the gathered crowd. "Rogue swarm. Got Walder." He straightened and pointed back down the street. "His father's bringing him."

"Did I hear that right, Jones? Rogue swarm?" said Ursa. "Is he talking about bees?"

"I don't know," said Dexterity. "I'm not a beekeeper, Ursa."

"Tcha!" said Ursa. "Much good *you* are!" Hefting her physick's bag, she marched past the bodyguards and the dukes, the ranting chaplain, Rhian and Alasdair, and presented herself to the other physick. "I'm Ursa. Are we talking bees?"

The man stared at her, bemused. "Yes. Bees. I'm sorry, who are—"

"I'm the queen's physick," said Ursa, planting her bag on the ground. "We can swap entertaining flux stories later. Now I've heard of bees swarming but what's this *rogue* business mean?"

"Means there's been a mistake," said Joby, breathing easier now as he stared back along the street, his face pinched in a worried frown. "Worker bees aren't supplied proper with doings for the new hive. Makes them angry. They don't go peaceful-like, looking for a new home. Walder couldn't hear the difference in the swarm's voice." A choked sob escaped him. "Poor little chap, he got in the way."

Ursa took his arm. "And who's Walder?"

"The beeman's son. He's nine," said Physick Graythorne, and shook his head. "A bad age for swarm-sting."

"I'm telling you, Physick, he's mortal sick," added Joby.

"Can you use a second pair of hands?" said Ursa. "Not that I've had much doings with rogue bees, but—"

"Yes. Yes. It might take two of us," said Graythorne. "If you can spare the time . . . if the queen permits—"

"Permits?" Ursa gave him a look to blister skin. "You think I'd ask permission to do my healing work? What kind of a physick are you? What kind of a queen do you think Rhian is if you think she'd expect me to ask her permission to heal a child—or that if I did she'd have the nerve to say no!"

"Graythorne!" said the village chaplain. "I forbid you to take any help from this woman. She is under interdict by association and—"

"You hold your tongue!" said Ursa, furious. "You'd let a boy die and call yourself a man of God?" She looked at Graythorne. "Is your clinic close? There must be supplies you need."

The physick nodded. "Yes. Of course. I'll be back in a moment."

As he shoved his way through the crowd, Ursa turned. "Jones!"

"Yes, Ursa?"

"Back of the van, under the bench. Green pouch tied with blue cord. Bring it!"

"I'll take it to her," said Helfred, through the open hatch.

"The queen said you were to stay in there," Dexterity answered, tying off the horses' reins. "Best obey her, Chaplain."

Helfred, scowling, handed him the pouch Ursa wanted through the hatchway. "If there's a child in need, Mr Jones, then I—"

"The village chaplain can see to his soul. Please, Helfred. Her Majesty doesn't need anyone else to worry about."

"Tcha," said Helfred and banged shut the hatch.

"That's it, Jones," said Ursa as he handed her the green leather pouch. "Now just you stand back. This is physicking business."

Seated on her magnificent stallion, the king beside her on his restive blood bay, Rhian leaned down. Her eyes were anxious. "Ursa . . . can you save the child?"

Ursa looked up from unknotting the pouch's laces. "I won't know till I've seen him, Majesty. And even then . . . well. Some folk are struck funny when it comes to a beesting. But I'll do my best, God knows I will."

"Here they come!" shouted someone in the crowd. "Beeman Loryn and Walder!"

Everyone looked. Puffing and panting his way up the village street, a grizzled man with a small lolling boy in his arms. Toiling in his wake, a weeping woman. The boy's mother, surely. Such terror in her face.

The sour chaplain pushed forward, daring to lay a hand on Rhian's bridle. "I tell you this is forbidden by the Church! You are a hussy and your marriage is unlawful! Get you and your rabble gone from our streets or by Rollin I shall—"

"You little man," said Zandakar. "Get back from her . . . or die."

Gasps from the crowd as Zandakar nudged his black stallion closer. Bright morning light glinted on his knife.

"No, Zandakar!" said Rhian. "I'm in no danger. Put your blade away."

Zandakar's blue hair, much longer now, shone like sapphire in the sun. *"Wei.* He threatens you. He is not safe."

Wei. The watching dukes could guess that word. Rhian flicked a glance at their shocked faces, knowing too well how this appeared. Dexterity felt his skin crawl.

Zandakar, obey her. The trouble you'll cause us if you don't!

Rhian lifted her chin. Her eyes were coldly angry. "Zandakar. I am *hushla.* Do as I say."

A muscle leapt along Zandakar's jaw. Then he nodded. *"Zho. Hushla."* He sheathed his blade.

More protests and babbling from the chaplain and the crowd. Then everything went silent: the beeman and his son and the weeping woman were in their midst.

"Where's Graythorne?" said Loryn and laid his child on the hard ground. The woman knelt beside him, keening with fear.

"I'm here," said the physick, shoving his way back through the crowd, burdened with a physicking bag and two corked jugs. "Let me see him. Physick Ursa, you'll look with me?"

"I will," said Ursa, and with a grunt crouched beside him in the street.

The swarm-stung boy Walder sprawled insensible, his naked body a mass of swollen, weeping boils. Dead bees tangled in his curly yellow hair. His father and mother clutched each other, stricken.

"It's not promising," said Ursa.

"No," said Physick Graythorne.

"Save him. Please save him," sobbed Beeman Loryn. "My poor Walder!"

Graythorne uncorked one jug and poured something

brown and sticky down the boy's swollen throat. Ursa pulled her mortar from her physicking bag, slopped in a splash of oil then added some dried plant from the green leather pouch.

Graythorne stared. "What's that?"

"Yadder-root," said Ursa, grinding hard with the pestle.

"Yadder-root? I don't know—"

"It's a Dev'kareshi plant. Strong blood purgative."

"Foreign?" said the physick, doubtful. "Can I trust—"

"You can try," said Ursa fiercely. "Can it hurt the boy now?"

Walder's mother wailed, hearing that. Her husband, his arm around her shoulders, pressed his cheek to hers and groaned.

"All right," said Graythorne, his face drawn and defeated. "As you say. I doubt it could hurt him now."

A terrible hush descended, broken only by the harsh, dry sobs of Walder's mother. Somewhere in the distance a dog barked. A cow lowed. Comfortable, familiar sounds made ugly by this looming tragedy.

As Ursa carefully trickled more pinchfuls of the powdered yadder-root into her mortar and Physick Graythorne watched anxiously to see if his brown elixir was taking any effect, Dexterity let his gaze roam the weeping, watching crowd. Fresh young girls, worry-worn women. Farmers and shopkeepers. Cheeky boys and their sober older brothers. Villages were small places where every face was known, if not loved. Where joy was shared joyfully and one broken heart broke all.

"Don't just stand there gawking, Jones!" said Ursa. "Help us get this paste on the child!"

Kneeling, he joined her and Graythorne in smearing the stinking concoction over the boy's hot, lumpy skin. The child whimpered pitifully as the greeny paste touched him, but there was no fighting strength in the sound of protest.

Walder was dying.

"How quickly does this yadder-root work?" asked Graythorne. His eyes were hollow with despair.

"Quick enough as a rule," said Ursa. "But this time . . ." She flicked a look at the boy's distraught parents. "I've never seen so many bee-stings before."

Rhian looked to the village chaplain. "A prayer," she said. "Walder's one of your own. Don't abandon him because of me."

"Chaplain Mede?" said Walder's mother, her voice catching on a sob. "Call for God's grace! Please ask God to save my boy!"

"I will not!" spat the chaplain. "Duchy Linfoi is under interdict! A prayer for the dying will perjure my soul!"

His refusal sparked more furious outcry. Rhian, the king, Ursa and the nearest villagers, they all shouted at the recalcitrant man. Letting the protests wash over him, Dexterity again wandered his gaze across the tear-streaked faces of Heddonvale's people.

Hettie stood among them, her fair hair bedraggled and covered in an unravelling gossamer shawl, her hands folded before her, her brown eyes haunted and brimful of tears. They met his, and held his, and she slowly shook her head.

No, Hettie! Do something! Don't let this little boy die!

Physick Graythorne pressed his fingers to the boy

Walder's throat. Let them rest there a moment then sighed, and looked up.

"Listen to me! *Listen!*"

The shouting stopped.

"I'm sorry. So sorry. But Walder is dead."

CHAPTER THIRTY-THREE

*N**o!"* screamed Walder's mother. *"No, not dead, not my little boy!"*

"It's God's will!" said Chaplain Mede, lifting his voice above the crowd's wailing and the terrible weeping of the dead boy's parents. "This is a judgement. We allowed this wicked woman and her blasphemous followers into our village and God has judged us for our sin!"

"How dare you say so!" King Alasdair shouted, as Rhian choked back a sob and the dukes sat straighter in their saddles, hands hovering above the hilts of their swords. "You think God makes his point on the bodies of *children?* If anyone in this place has lost sight of God it's you, Chaplain Mede. Not Her Majesty. She's the Church's true daughter and unlike *you* she grieves for Walder. He was her subject and as her subject she loved him." He stared at the villagers. "She loves every one of you. She is your *queen*!"

Chaplain Mede started ranting again. Still kneeling with Ursa, Dexterity looked at her face. It was still and sad. She'd seen a great deal of death in her time. He took her hand in his and squeezed, then looked for Hettie.

Yes. She was still here, in the crowd, weeping.

Do something, Hettie! Don't just stand there in tears.

She shook her head. *I can't, Dexie love. But you can. You can save him.*

Her lips hadn't moved but he heard her voice anyway. A whisper, a breeze of words, sighing through his heart.

Me? I can't save him!

She smiled. *Yes you can, my love. Trust me. Trust God. Have faith . . . and save the child.*

Before the last echo of her words faded he felt a wave of scorching heat rush through his body. He stared at his hands. beneath the dried smears of Ursa's ointment his skin began to glow.

Ursa noticed. "Jones?" she said, alarmed, letting go of him. "What's that? Good God have mercy. Are you doing it *again*?"

He couldn't answer. There was a roaring in his head as though his skull were full of flames. Memory returned.

Oh dear. Yes, Ursa. I'm doing it again.

He looked for Hettie . . . but Hettie was gone.

Everyone scrambled to get away from him, even Walder's distraught parents. The villagers were shouting and pointing. Chaplain Mede gobbled, incoherent. Ursa kept hold of Physick Graythorne, keeping him safely at a distance. King Alasdair's arm slid around Rhian. A terrible hope was burning in her eyes.

The heat in his body was so intense now. He couldn't see properly, the air had taken on a fuzzy reddish-gold glow. It blurred all the faces around him, they looked like they were made of wax and melting. With dreamlike surprise he saw his shining hands drift towards dead Walder and lay themselves palm-down on his motionless bee-stung chest. Through the roaring in his head he heard voices cry out. Then he heard another voice . . . and realised it was his. He was a puppet again, his body used by someone . . . something . . . else.

"Rise, Walder! Breathe again! In the name of Rhian, Eberg's daughter, Ethrea's true and noble queen, awake from your cold sleep and live with joy!"

Walder, the dead boy, opened his eyes.

"Rise, Walder! Stand and embrace your loving family! Praise Ethrea's Queen Rhian who with God's blessing has been raised so high!"

Walder, the dead boy, got to his feet.

"Mama?" he whispered, confused and afraid. "Mama, what happened?"

"Walder!" his mother cried, and flung herself upon him. His father was only a heartbeat behind. Beneath Ursa's ointment the boy's previously swollen, pustuled skin was flawless.

Still snared in his dream-state like a bee in its honey, Dexterity lifted his hands in front of his eyes. As he watched, the shining light faded from them. They became his ordinary whittling hands again, stained with ointment, marked with pale scars. His burning blood cooled and the world cooled with it, the air fading slowly from reddish-gold to gone. As though someone had magically vanished his bones he felt himself slip sideways to slump on the ground.

"Jones!"

That was Ursa. He'd know her voice anywhere.

"Don't stand there, Graythorne! Help me get him on his feet!"

Strong arms slid around him and he was hauled to the vertical. Muzzily he blinked and blinked. His head felt empty, his body light as thistledown.

Silence. Everyone was staring at him. Walder. Walder's parents. Chaplain Mede. The villagers. Rhian and Alasdair. Zandakar. The dukes.

"Are you all right, Dexterity?" said Rhian, her voice hushed. "Can you speak?"

He cleared his throat. "I—I think so, Your Majesty."

Walder's mother said, "Thank you. *God bless you*."

"Oh . . ." He blinked. His empty head was spinning. If he wasn't careful a breeze would blow him away. *Is this what you meant, Hettie, when you asked for that favour? I'm not sure I like it. I'm not sure at all!* "Er . . . yes . . . you're welcome . . ."

"And God bless Queen Rhian!" Beeman Loryn cried loudly. His arms were tight around his son, now wrapped in someone's hastily donated shirt for decency. "With God's intervention she gave my son back to me!"

Chaplain Mede clenched his fists. "Loryn, you damn yourself! The prolate has declared this woman anathema. This was not the work of God, it is evil, God will disown you if—"

"Be silent, you foolish man. God will do nothing of the sort."

Helfred.

Chaplain Mede turned on him. "And who are you?" he demanded. Spittle flecked his lips and his eyes were wide with zeal.

"I'm a brother chaplain," said Helfred. His hands were

clasped quietly before him, his travel-worn robes edged with dust from the street. "Whatever you've been told by the prolate, disregard it. Prolate Marlan is . . . mistaken."

"*Mistaken?* God's *prolate*?" Chaplain Mede growled in his throat. "What kind of a chaplain are *you,* to make such a pronouncement?"

Helfred smiled, thinly. "The kind who knows more of the prolate than a village divine who's doubtless never seen him in the flesh. Prolate Marlan is—."

"Your superior," said Rhian. "Helfred, you forget yourself. Return to the van."

Shocked, Helfred stared at her. "Your Majesty—"

"*Do not call her that!*" cried Chaplain Mede. "Every soul here is interdict because of her!"

"You fool," said Helfred. "The interdict is nothing but an attempt to steal power. God has chosen Queen Rhian to lead Ethrea out of danger. The child Walder lives to show you a sign! Do you deny what has happened here? Do you say there was no miracle?" He flung a challenging glare at the crowd. "Well, you people? Do *you* deny it?"

The villagers looked at each other then slowly shook their heads. How could they deny it with Walder standing before them, alive when moments before he'd been dead?

"Evil can hide itself in miracles!" said Chaplain Mede. "Evil can—it can—"

Ignoring him, and Rhian, Helfred turned again to the crowd. "Good people of Heddonvale, do not despair!" His expression was transformed into a peaceful serenity, all past peevishness washed away. "Clouds cover the sun's face, the land is darkened . . . but briefly. In God's name, as his divinely ordained chaplain, I tell you to celebrate the miracle you have seen. Keep it not secret but spread the joyful word: Rhian is God's chosen queen of Ethrea. She is the light. Let her light shine!"

"God save Queen Rhian!" cried King Alasdair. "God's mercy on Ethrea and Rhian, our queen!"

The people of Heddonvale took up the cry. Under its cover, Rhian nudged her horse forward. "Thank you, Helfred. *Now get back in the van.*"

Dexterity watched startled Helfred flinch. Then the chaplain nodded. "Your Majesty," he murmured, and did as he was told.

They left Heddonvale soon after, with Chaplain Mede vanquished and the villagers' shouting as great a benediction as any reading of the Litany. Ursa, insistent, put Dexterity in with Helfred to sleep and drove the peddler's van herself. They did not stop again until twilight fell.

Once the royal party was settled for the night, Dexterity was summoned before Rhian.

"All right, Mr Jones," she said, seated on a fox-pelt travelling stool in her small pavilion. Behind her stood the king, the dukes and a pensive Helfred. "I'd like an explanation."

Oh, Hettie. Hettie. I could do with you now . . .

"Your Majesty, I'm not certain I can give you one."

Rhian leaned forward, her hands fisted on her knees. "I don't wish to hear that! The child was *dead* and you brought him back to life. *How did you do it?* I want to know, *now!*"

"That's just it," he said, helpless. "I didn't do it, Majesty. It was Hettie. She saved him. I was just . . . there."

"I see," said Rhian, after a moment. "And you're all

right? You look all right. Certainly you don't look any *different*."

I'm shaken to pieces but aside from that . . . "Perfectly fine, Majesty. Thank you for asking."

"I think it's time you told us about this *Hettie*," said Duke Edward, his whiskered face grim. "I think it's time you told us everything, Your Majesty."

"I agree," said Duke Rudi. "I want to know all there is to know of this woman. And how it comes to pass that a foreign mercenary seems willing to kill a chaplain of Ethrea for you without bothering to wait for an invitation. Or how that foreign mercenary fell in with a simple toy-maker in the first place. There are many such mysteries here, Your Majesty. Edward and I have risked our duchies and kinsmen for you. I think you owe us more than half-truths and excuses."

Rhian looked at him, her eyes hot. "I've made your son Duke of Kingseat, Rudi. Are you certain you wish to be speaking of debts?"

"And I'm honoured and humbled by that, Your Majesty," said Duke Adric, a handsome young man with dark hair and eyes and his father's hookish nose. "However, if I may be so bold as to speak, like my father and Duke Edward . . . I am curious and concerned."

"Rhian," the king said quietly. "It's time. And if you didn't think so you wouldn't have called Mr Jones before your full council."

Rhian's lips thinned for a moment, then she nodded. "Perhaps. Helfred. Who is Hettie?"

Dexterity nearly bit his tongue. *Helfred?* Why ask *Helfred?*

From the look on his face the chaplain was wondering the same thing. "Your Majesty?"

"You're the chaplain here, aren't you?" said Rhian, impatient. "And we've witnessed our second miracle, this one even more miraculous than the first. Surely this is the provenance of our Church."

"Your Majesty," said Helfred faintly. Then he collected himself and looked at the dukes. His face now held an echo of his former lecturing pomposity. "Hettie, Your Graces, is a messenger from God who appears to Mr Jones in the guise of his dead wife."

"Rollin save me," said Duke Edward. "I've never heard of such a thing. Not outside of scripture, and these aren't scriptural times."

Dexterity cleared his throat. "You can't be more surprised than I am, Your Grace."

"Hmmph," said the duke, then turned to Helfred. "Have *you* seen this—this messenger, Chaplain?"

"I have seen its manifestation in miracle, Your Grace," said Helfred. "As have we all. I suggest doubt at this point is . . . pointless. And displeasing to God."

"But why *him*?" said Duke Rudi. He sounded almost offended. "Why is he singled out for God's favour? He's a toymaker. He's—he's—"

"Loyal, brave and wise," said Rhian, sharply. "He risked *everything* for me with no thought for himself. If I live to be a thousand I'll never be able to repay him."

"Nor will I," said King Alasdair. "I'd not be wed to Her Majesty if this man hadn't saved her from the clerica, and Marlan. We are *all* in his debt, Your Graces. This kingdom most deeply of all."

"Blessed Rollin was a humble man," added Helfred.

"It seems God has a fondness for those unspoiled by high station."

The dukes exchanged affronted looks, but forbore protest.

"Very well," said Duke Edward. "You're the chaplain. If you're satisfied then so must we be."

"What about Zandakar?" said Duke Adric. "A fierce man, and most . . . unusual. Have we seen his race in Ethrea before?"

Rhian said, "I'm not certain. So many foreigners set foot on our shores these days. His is a sad tale, Your Graces. The physick, Ursa, patched him up after he was brought to her in a terrible state. A harbour-tavern brawl, you know what sailors are like. His ship sailed without him. Abandoned him without a care. Mr Jones took pity on him, offered him work and a roof over his head till he could find his way home again. He's a generous soul. Isn't that so, Mr Jones?"

Dexterity held his breath, not daring to look at the king or Helfred. *Why is she lying? Does she not trust her own dukes?* He swallowed. "I don't know about generous, Your Majesty. It seemed the right thing to do. And then of course the king died and—well—things got complicated. And he's been very helpful, one way or another."

"Very," said King Alasdair, stony-faced. "Indeed. A sad tale."

"But where's he *from*?" said Duke Rudi. "I've never met a sailor so skilled in deadly knife-play. And the way he trains our soldiers . . . amazing. You'd swear he spent his life giving orders, not taking them."

"I believe he hails from somewhere in the east," said Dexterity vaguely.

"And it doesn't matter," said Rhian. "Like our humble toymaker Mr Jones, Zandakar has proved a friend. I suggest you cease fretting on him. We have more important things to think of, wouldn't you say?"

The dukes muttered agreement. Rhian let her gaze touch the king's face then slide away.

"Mr Jones," she said. "Can we expect more miracles as we travel to Kingseat?"

Everyone stared at him. He stared back, feeling like a trapped butterfly confronted by pins. "I—I really don't know, Your Majesty. I wasn't expecting the first two. They just . . . well . . . they *happened*."

"There've been no more messages from Hettie? You've had no more dreams?"

Oh dear. More lying . . . "I'm sorry, Your Majesty."

There. Not *exactly* a lie.

Helfred made a diffident sound. "If I may interject, Your Majesty?"

Rhian nodded. "You may."

"It was Mr Jones—at God's insistence—who said we must return to Kingseat by road, not the river. Given what happened in Heddonvale I think it most likely we *will* be visited by more miracles. Miracles are God's way of showing us what is true. So it was with Blessed Rollin, and is again in this, our time. We travel by road so you might be seen by your people, Majesty. We travel by road so they will know you are God's chosen queen of Ethrea."

"I believe he's right," said King Alasdair. "We are queen and king and dukes and chaplains in trust. Our sacred duty has always been to safeguard the people of Ethrea. Marlan and Kyrin and Damwin have *forgotten* this. They've forgotten no-one rules without the people's consent . . . or God's blessing. These miracles will remind them."

Dexterity considered him, impressed. *There speaks a true king. No wonder Rhian loves him.* The Dukes Edward and Rudi didn't look quite so sure . . . but young Adric's expression was thoughtful. As though the king's words had been spoken at just the right time.

The trouble is, though, I don't want to do more miracles. At least, I want to support Rhian—but raising folk from the dead? Oh Hettie, please, no more raising from the dead.

"Dexterity," Rhian said gently. "I can see you're dismayed. I'm sorry. I can only imagine how you must feel. But if God had to choose someone . . . I won't regret he chose you."

He bowed. "And I won't regret being used in your cause, Majesty. I may not understand the hows and whys but I do know this much: we're doing the right thing. That's all I *need* to know. As for the rest, I'll leave that to Hettie."

"And God," said Helfred, with lifted eyebrows.

He nodded. "Of course."

"Thank you, Mr Jones," said Rhian, her tone a warm dismissal. "Be sure to eat a good meal and rest well tonight." She glanced at her dukes and Helfred. "You may all retire, gentlemen. His Majesty and I would have some small time in private."

As the dukes nodded and shifted, stamping their blood into movement after standing for so long, Helfred stepped close. "Forgive me, Majesty. I have a question."

From her expression it seemed Rhian knew already what he wanted to ask. "Yes, Helfred?" She sounded . . . resigned.

"Why do you not permit me to travel openly in your retinue? Why must I spend each day cooped up in that stuffy peddler's van? Am I being punished? Have I somehow offended you?"

"Offended me? No. Helfred—"

"It's enough that the queen has decreed it, Chaplain," said King Alasdair, frowning. "I'm disappointed. Your sermons place great emphasis on the Second Admonition. 'Be Thou Obedient to Authority, lest unrest be your harvest.' Do you see yourself *above* the—"

"Alasdair," said Rhian, her hand raised. "It's all right." She looked at Helfred. "I've asked you to remain hidden, Chaplain, because I don't wish to run the risk of you being recognised on the road."

"Recognised?" said Helfred. "Why would it matter if I am—oh. I see." His voice wasn't quite steady. "My uncle."

Rhian's eyes were full of compassion. "Yes. Before we left the manor house Ven'Artemis came for you. I'm sorry."

"He *came* for me? What—and you sent him away?"

"I did."

Shocked, Helfred clasped and unclasped his hands. "You shouldn't have done that, Majesty. Marlan will be furious. What did the most venerable say? Am I censured? Am I summoned before the Court Ecclesiastica? Am I—" His voice broke. "Am I still a chaplain?"

Dexterity didn't like him overmuch, even now, but a statue would be moved by the grief in Helfred's voice.

"I don't know," said Rhian, her gaze too steady. Dexterity, watching her closely, felt his skin prickle. *She does, and fears to tell him.* "I don't want to know," she added.

"That's why I refused Ven'Artemis's request for your person. You're my chaplain, Helfred, until *I* say otherwise."

"Majesty," whispered Helfred. "I—you—"

"You're welcome, Helfred," Rhian said with brisk kindness. "Now everyone leave us."

Dismissed a second and final time, Dexterity stood back to let the dukes and Helfred depart the queen's pavilion before him.

"Oh. And Helfred?" added Rhian, as the chaplain was about to disappear through the tent-flap.

"Majesty?"

"I'll have no repeat of Heddonvale," she said, voice and eyes stern. "*Stay in the van.* Or I might change my mind."

Outside the pavilion, as the dukes withdrew to fill their bellies, Helfred stood like a man transfixed.

"Chaplain?" said Dexterity. "Are you all right?"

"I might not *be* a chaplain," said Helfred, stricken. "I might be sinning to wear these holy robes and conduct the Litany for the queen's company."

Oh, Hettie. Dexterity touched the man's shoulder. "Helfred, what have you been saying since we left Linfoi manor? Interdict does not come from God so it can't part us from his loving mercy. You're not a chaplain because Marlan says so and you won't *stop* being one because he says you're not. If you're a chaplain it's because *God* says you are . . . and only God can take that away."

Helfred looked at him, a little of the despair fading from his face. "Yes. That's true."

And now I sound like a chaplain. Oh dear. "Of course it's true. Now are you coming to eat or not? Because

I'll tell you, I'm famished. Working miracles is hungry business!"

"Now *that's* close to blasphemy!" snapped Helfred, falling into step beside him. "Shame on you, Mr Jones!"

Dexterity smiled, and let him scold.

Marlan met with the dukes of Meercheq and Hartshorn two days after their mudstained arrival in Kingseat's capital.

It was important to keep them waiting. Damwin and Kyrin were ambitious men whose temporary alliance in the face of Rhian's bold move strengthened their positions as defenders of Ethrea. As the only dukes whose duchies were free of interdict they enjoyed the favour of their ducal subjects. That favour would bolster their confidence, lead them to believe they were selected of God. Let the first flush of outrage and uproar pass, let them see the throne empty . . . and ducal ambitions would soon begin to stir.

Rhian is lost to them . . . No need now to give a relative the crown and enjoy power second-hand. Now they can dream of placing it on their own heads and wielding royal power for themselves.

So would Damwin and Kyrin eventually conclude, if they weren't thinking such things already. Soon enough they would see each other as rivals, not allies. Enemies, not friends. Which meant that instead of troubling him they would simply trouble each other . . . to his satisfaction and ultimate reward. If that happened too quickly, though, before Rulf was established, Ethrea's fragile stability would be further threatened.

So, for the moment, he needed them smiling and eager, engaged in the fight to bring Rhian to heel. Let them console each other as the prolate kept them waiting. Mutual condolence could prove a useful tool.

"Your Graces!" he greeted them, as they were shown into the late king's audience chamber in the castle. "Can you forgive me this sorry delay? I am consumed with Church business. Interdict is a fearsome thing."

Damwin, imposing still for all he was near to sixty and had lived a vigorous life, stamped up to the dais. Feet wide, fisted hands on his hips, he thrust out his chin and narrowed his eyes to slits.

"Kingseat's streets are full of soldiery and empty of foreigners, Marlan. How much is that costing the Royal Treasury?"

He smiled, fingers caressing the audience chair's carved wooden arms. "You'd prefer Commander Idson's men amuse themselves dicing in the garrison while frightened citizens raise ruckus unrestrained and spies for the ambassadors milk every tavern for gossip they can pass to their masters?"

"Ha!" said Kyrin, his bearish body swathed in red velvet, precisely the wrong fabric for a man of his bulk and hue. "We'd prefer you end this nonsense, or better yet let us end it for you! Where's Eberg's misbegotten brat now, do you know?"

"She is still in duchy Linfoi. She's travelling by road." Or so Ven'Artemis had informed him. He was yet to hear from faithful Ven'Martin. Getting word to his prolate as he trailed Rhian discreetly might tax even Ven'Martin's resourceful ingenuity.

"Then we'll have her!" said Kyrin. "What a fool she is not to come down by river. My soldiery's ready and so is

Damwin's. The minute that sly bitch sets foot in Hartshorn or Meercheq she'll be arrested and that will be *that*."

"You'll do no such thing," said Marlan. "Your Grace, are you mad? Rhian is Eberg's daughter, newly bereaved and beloved of the people. Would you make of her a public object of pity, to drag her through Ethrea in chains like a criminal?"

"She *is* a criminal!" said Damwin. "As for the people, why would they care? Outside of this city they don't even know what she looks like. They don't love her, Marlan. They love the *idea* of her, if that."

"Precisely. Which makes her even more dangerous. I will not make of her a martyr, a Rollin for our times."

"You can't let her run free about the kingdom, either!" said Kyrin. "We must drag her down, her and Linfoi and the rest of the bastards with her. They threaten *everything*, Marlan. She must be stopped, now!"

Marlan stood, using the advantage of the dais's superior height to intimidate. "She will be stopped, Your Graces. When she reaches Kingseat she will assuredly be stopped. Let her parade among the people, gentlemen. Let her spread the despair of interdict and anathema in her wake. The misguided of Ethrea will cease loving her soon enough when they learn from my clergy what their loving has cost. And when she has crossed the border into duchy Kingseat, then will your soldiers, Damwin, and yours, Kyrin, line twenty-deep behind her. Once she is caught in Kingseat there'll be no second escape north, for her or any miscreant riding at her side. Her calamitous rebellion against God's authority will end and the peace of Ethrea shall be safeguarded once more."

The dukes exchanged glances. "And the ambassadors

will be silenced?" said Kyrin. "I tell you, Marlan, Niall is plagued hourly by their demands and requests. So is Damwin's Porpont. They don't like the port restrictions you've imposed. Your safety measures put our treaties to the test!"

"Have no fear," said Marlan. "Our treaties have withstood the passing of centuries. One disobedient girl-child shall hardly imperil them. Thank you for coming, Your Graces. We'll speak again, soon. In the meantime, I suggest you urge the people of your duchies to remain strong in faith. Alas, should any succumb to Rhian's allure, interdict must surely follow."

They didn't care for the reminder or the abrupt dismissal, but nor did they seek to test this alliance just yet. They departed with promises and flowery compliments.

No sooner had he rid himself of them than Ven'Barto entered, his eyes filled with alarm. "Eminence, the ambassador from Tzhung-tzhungchai awaits you in the antechamber. I did encourage him to leave and return upon your summons. He declined to do so. He says he'll see you now."

Still standing on the chamber dais, Marlan felt the warm glow from his audience with the dukes chill. "Declined how, Ven'Barto?"

Ven'Barto swallowed, convulsively. "Eminence, he declined with a smile."

The courtesy of Tzhung-tzhungchai could not be taken lightly. "I see. Then by all means tell the ambassador I am pleased to receive him."

Ven'Barto bowed. His forehead was damp with the sweat of relief. "At once, Eminence."

Slowly, Marlan sat down in the ornate audience chair.

Damn Tzhung-tzhungchai and its unseen emperor! If he did not tread carefully, if he did not allay this inconvenient ambassador's suspicions, Ethrea's independence could come under real threat.

"Ambassador Lai!" he said, genially, as Ven'Barto ushered in the emperor's man. "My apologies for keeping you waiting. I was collecting my thoughts after meeting with the dukes of Meercheq and Hartshorn. Was I expecting your visit? I do not recall the appointment . . ."

Ambassador Lai of Tzhung-tzhungchai was a splendid example of his race. Tall, elegant, with amber skin and long, straight black hair. He wore his national costume like a second skin, silk pants and jewelled silk tunic. His brown eyes expressed nothing but gentle pleasure . . . but beneath the urbanity cold dark currents swirled.

"Eminence," he said, mellifluous, and offered a meticulous bow. "Surely friends might visit without first making an appointment."

God save us from the friendship of Tzhung-tzhungchai. "Indeed, Ambassador. And you're heartily welcome. How may I help you?"

Lai clasped his hands tranquilly before him. The movement sparked fire in his ruby-and-emerald collar. "My emperor is, as always, touched by your concern for our welfare. If ever the antique and glorious empire of Tzhung-tzhungchai should require assistance we will know where to turn. But I am here to offer our help to *you*, Eminence. Whispers have reached us of . . . internal discord. Unsettling rumours that all is not well in the royal House of Havrell and therefore in your precious kingdom."

Dissembling popinjay. He knew perfectly well what Rhian had done. His spies were everywhere, they couldn't be rooted out. They were all alike, these great sneering nations: Tzhung-tzhungchai, Harbisland and Arbenia. The three great trading nations of the world who carved it up to suit themselves and let the smaller, weaker countries gather crumbs as they may. They treated Ethrea like their personal property, as nothing more than an outpost of their wealth and influence.

"Ambassador, it is sadly true Eberg's untimely death has left us somewhat disarrayed. But you can assure your emperor there is no need for dismay. If he has heard whispers that say otherwise he has been . . . misinformed."

The people of Tzhung-tzhungchai did not age as other men. This Ambassador Lai could be a stripling of thirty or he could carry thrice that many years. There was no way to tell. His graceful eyebrows lifted. "These whispers come from Princess Rhian herself. Or should I say *Queen* Rhian? For so she signed her letter to my imperial master."

With an effort that threatened his heart, Marlan kept his fingers unclenched on the chair. That bitch wrote to the *emperor*? Who else did she write to? Did she write to them *all*?

He never dreamed of such boldness. *I will throw her down . . .*

"Alas, these young unmarried women," he said, forcing a smile. "Flighty and wanting a wise man's advice. I urge you, pay no heed to the princess' letter. She is mistaken. She is not yet crowned queen and lacks lawful authority to speak for Ethrea to your master. Grief has disordered her. I know you understand."

"Yes," said the ambassador. "What good fortune I came to you. I am so pleased to learn the truth."

"And I am pleased you are pleased to learn it," he said, still smiling. "Extend my warmest regards to your honoured emperor. Ethrea is moved to know he is our loyal friend."

Ambassador Lai bestowed a smile of his own. "Always, Your Eminence. And as a true friend should, he will continue his concerned regard for your welfare."

It was a warning. The unwelcome eyes of Tzhung-tzhungchai would be watching.

The ambassador departed, with more smiles and meaningless platitudes. Marlan stood alone in the audience chamber and let the hot rage warm his bones.

You'll be sorry for this, Rhian. By God, I'll make you sorry. You'll weep tears of blood before I'm done with you.

CHAPTER THIRTY-FOUR

Like fire running through a wheatfield, word of Rhian's progress leapt ahead of her retinue. There was no time to stop in every township and village in duchy Linfoi, but everywhere they did stop Dexterity found the injured and ailing and healed them. Glowing with the power of God's Living Flame, he proclaimed Rhian queen as the healed shouted with joy . . . and in those places the chaplains and venerables who tried to silence him were silenced.

"Seems to me you're looking to change professions, Jones," said Ursa, trying to make light of what none of them truly understood. "Should I take up toymaking? I think I'd be quite good."

"Don't be silly, Ursa," Dexterity told her, and kept himself to himself. The miracles were draining, he slept more and more. He had to believe Hettie wouldn't let them destroy him . . . but sometimes, in the dead of night, he woke startled and afraid.

Five days after leaving Linfoi manor the company crossed the border into duchy Arbat. By this time life had settled into a routine. At first light Rhian danced her *hotas* with Zandakar, then he trained her bodyguards while Helfred held a swift service. She met with her council over a hasty breakfast and then the company moved on, continuing its circuitous road south. At nightfall they stopped and she danced with Zandakar again.

Dancing the *hotas* was her only respite from thought.

Not every village and township in Arbat welcomed them, even though Duke Rudi, now riding with Rhian, told his people to ignore the prolate's interdict and cleave to Eberg's daughter, their lawful queen. In those places, faced with hostility that not even Dexterity and his miracles could overcome, for the chaplains called him "*sorcerer*" and the people heeded them, the company rode on and did not dwell on what might have been.

Elsewhere riots broke out between those who sided with Rhian and those whose obedience to Marlan and the clergy was greater than any loyalty to a duke or a girl who'd married the wrong man. The first time that happened, in the wool town of Nyngdon, Rhian wanted to intervene. Alasdair prevailed.

"A single drop of blood spilled in your name will *end* this," he said, voice low and urgent, his hand on her stallion's reins. "The best we can do is ride on, swiftly, and let this turbulence die down. Things will be settled when we reach Kingseat."

It broke her heart to see the people fighting because of her. With a last plea for calm and a promise to serve them faithfully she led the company out of the town and did not weep until that night, in the dark and alone.

But not everyone rejected them. Other towns and villages in Arbat welcomed her. So did many people in the duchy of Morvell, encouraged by the sight of their Duke Edward riding by her side and the miracles they witnessed with their own eyes.

Rhian found comfort in that, and her progress continued.

"Prolate, when will you put a *stop* to this madness?" demanded Duke Damwin. "The air is thick with tales of miracles, they've reached my people in Meercheq and now me. Listen to *this*!" He fumbled within his sleeve for a piece of folded paper, unfolded it, and read aloud.

"'. . . *and the burning man said "Queen Rhian is God's chosen monarch of Ethrea"*' . . . and this—this— '. . . *put his hands upon the stricken babe, and the babe recovered, and the man said, "I have done this in Queen Rhian's name, that she might be known as the true queen of Ethrea"* . . .' And this, also! '*I prayed God would throw down this wicked girl but instead a man I do not know burst into flames which did not consume him, and he said "Here is Rhian, your lawful queen"*'."

As Damwin crumpled the paper, Kyrin added, "I've received word too. Marlan, I thought miracles were *your* business! By God, it seems to me *we're* in need of one now!"

Marlan stood with his back to them, staring out of the window in his palace library. In the desk drawer behind him sat the latest missive from Ven'Martin, who continued to follow Rhian through the countryside, documenting her every move and sending the reports by the swiftest messengers he could find. A ruinously expensive undertaking, but worth it. These carping dukes told him nothing new.

"Prolate!" said Kyrin, perilously close to a shout. "Are you listening? The girl builds herself a following and many of your chaplains and venerables seem powerless to stop her. Indeed from what I can gather, chaplains and venerables are flocking to her cause! You must *crush* this rebellion against our authority! We don't want this upheaval in either of our duchies! The garrisons of Hartshorn and Meercheq stand ready, as do Commander Idson and his men, and yet you do *nothing*. You owe us an explanation!"

His shoulders tightened. *I am your prolate, I owe you nothing. Have a care, Your Graces. The ice you tread is thin.* He turned, his face schooled.

"If you believe we can settle this with violence you are as beef-witted as you look, Your Grace."

"Beef-witted!" Kyrin surged forward. "I don't take that kind of insult from anyone, not even a prolate. You—"

"Step back."

Breathing heavily, Kyrin retreated one pace. "I'm warning you, Marlan, I'll not stand idle while that bitch sets my duchy upon its ear! You may lack the courage to act but *I don't.* I will—"

"Hold your tongue before God shrivels it!"

As Kyrin spluttered, Damwin cleared his throat. "Marlan, you must see our position. Rhian and her rabble lie a stone's throw from our borders and interdict has not tamed the traitors hanging from her skirts. Your chaplains—your venerables . . ." He shook his head. "She has somehow *suborned* them."

I am betrayed by the very people I placed into power, by the venerables and chaplains who owe their pastoral authority to me, who owe me the silk vestments on their backs.

"They will be dealt with," he said coldly. *"As I see fit."*

"I suppose the reports of miracles could be exaggerated," said Damwin, pathetically hopeful. "Country folk are notoriously simple. They see signs and omens in a bird's nest. In a spill of grain."

Marlan nodded. "That is true."

Except he'd received word from horrified venerables in some townships also claiming to have witnessed miracles. They confirmed what Ven'Martin had already told him.

But miracles are not real, they are fables and allegories. They are tales told to frighten children and keep weak fools in their place. A man on fire must burn to ash. The dead do not rise because God says they must. God is nothing but a superstitious need for safety in an unsafe world. These miracles are clever trickery on Rhian's part, nothing more.

He could not say so to these credulous dukes.

"Your Graces, you have allowed emotion to cloud your wits. Indeed you stand in danger of being suborned yourselves. These things are not *miracles,* they are manifestations of evil."

"What are you saying?" demanded Kyrin.

"Rhian has made an unholy alliance. She has bargained with men who are unknown by God. Not all countries of the world are pure in spirit, gentlemen. You must know, as I do, of lands with . . . unsavoury practices."

Kyrin's cheeks paled. *"Sorcery?"*

He shrugged. "It exists. God forbids it here, but God can be thwarted. In Tzhung-tzhungchai, for example . . ."

"Rumours," said Damwin, shuddering. "Sailors' gossip. Nothing more."

He smiled. "You think so? I do not. The Tzhung emperor is an acquisitive man. It runs in his family. Since I was a boy the empire has doubled in size. And now I must tell you, Rhian has written to him . . ."

The news struck them like an axe-blow. "She did *what*?" said Kyrin. "When? And how long have you known?"

Damwin's colour was dangerously high. "Who else has she written to?"

"I can't answer that," he told Damwin. "But the emperor's ambassador has been my only visitor. The others seem content to wait and watch."

"And Lai told you she'd contacted Emperor Han? What game is she playing?" Kyrin fretted. "Good God, is she *mad*?"

No. She thinks to bring the great trading nations to her side. She thinks their sympathy will somehow make a difference.

"Marlan, do you suggest Eberg's brat has allied herself with the heathen Tzhung?" said Damwin. "Do you think she intends to surrender Ethrea to the emperor in return for his assistance in gaining her the throne?"

Marlan opened the desk drawer, sifted through Ven'Martin's letters, and withdrew one. " *'Eminence, there is a man in the princess's party'*," he read aloud. " *'Dark-skinned and pale-eyed with hair inhuman blue. He seems most deeply in Princess Rhian's trust. There is about him an air of danger.' "*

"The Tzhung have brown eyes," said Damwin. "And their hair is black. No race of men has blue hair. It's a mistake, or deliberate mischief."

He replaced the report in its drawer. "Neither. Rest assured the report is true. As for this man's origins, who can say what they are? Have you travelled to Tzhung-tzhungchai? Do you know what mysteries lie in the heart of that land? Sorcery is powerful. Who knows the ravages it might wreak on human flesh."

"But the treaties," Kyrin protested. "Emperor Han won't risk the treaties. Or war with the other nations. Arbenia—Harbisland—they would *never* permit—"

"We talk of conquest, Your Graces," he pointed out. "There is little a greedy man won't risk if he believes the prize rich enough."

Damwin thudded his fist on the back of a nearby chair. "We need proof so we can take action, Marlan. What does Henrik Linfoi say? Has he made a full confession yet? What does he know of Alasdair's dealings with Rhian? Our self-made king might have been a go-between for her and Emperor Han while residing in Kingseat. The bitch could've been planning this for *months*."

"That's true," said Kyrin. Then his eyes opened wide. "Good God! If sorcery's involved Eberg and his sons might not have died naturally! *She* might have arranged it with help from duchy Linfoi and the Tzhung."

Marlan swallowed a sigh. These superstitious fools. Duchy Linfoi had plotted nothing, he knew that much from Henrik. No man hid the truth with his limbs pulled apart. Nor were Harley and Volant party to their dukes' betrayal. As for Rhian, she was too weak to consider such direct action. *But it cannot hurt my cause if Damwin and Kyrin continue to see conspiracy and demons in every shadowed corner.*

"God knows, Your Graces, Eberg's brat seems capable of anything."

"We can't let Rhian rampage about the countryside spreading heretical sorcery unchecked!" asked Damwin. "God will condemn us for it. We should have arrested her when we had the chance, before these blasphemous *miracles* began. We *must* ride against her now with our soldiers! Between the three of us we can raise some ten thousand swords. She has no hope of standing against such a force!"

"And when *she* is dealt with we must deal with Emperor Han!" added Kyrin.

Marlan felt his guts twist with frustration. *Prating, windblown, short-sighted idiots. They each want the crown so badly they cannot think past its golden lustre.*

"God have mercy, Damwin. Have you forgotten every word I've said? Would you turn Rhian into a martyr? Lay hands on her in sight of the common people whose childish wits are so easily addled and who have not blood in their veins, but rivers of sticky sentiment?" He shifted his contemptuous stare. "And you, Kyrin. You would have us break treaty with Tzhung-tzhungchai by offering them violence, or denying them the ship-rights and other concessions they've enjoyed for centuries? If so you'd bring down on our heads the wrath of every treated nation, merely because we *suspect* their interference!"

"But we can't do nothing!" cried Damwin, incensed. "You are Prolate of Ethrea and caretaker of the kingdom. This business touches upon both sacred authorities. Eberg's brat is not only undermining the Crown, she challenges the very foundations of the Church whose powers her father diminished in his rule! How can you stand there and not wish to see her broken?"

Marlan bared his teeth in a smile. "Did I say I don't wish to see her broken? I wish to see her broken into one hundred bleeding pieces. *And I will*. In the time and place and manner of *my* choosing."

"How?" said Damwin, standing his ground. "If you won't permit us to send soldiers against her? How do you hope to throw this bitch down?"

He laid light fingers upon the back of his tall chair. "By letting her believe I cannot stand against her. You must have heard the saying: 'Give a man sufficient rope and he will helpfully hang himself'? I feel it can be applied equally to a woman."

"What does that mean?" said Kyrin. "You're going to let her ride freely into duchy Kingseat? Her family's stronghold where even the rocks and stones would sing her praises if God was foolish enough to give them tongues?"

He nodded. "I am."

"Then you're a fool, Marlan!"

"Careful, Kyrin," Marlan said softly. "Or do you think a duke is above reprisal?"

Kyrin flushed. "I only meant—"

"I know what you meant. You're wrong. In duchy King-seat Rhian will feel herself safe. In your duchies, gentle-men, she will be on her guard, *if* she elects even to set foot in them. She might yet finish her journey by river. Either way her guard will relax when she comes into Kingseat and finds not a single hand raised against her. It is then I will strike."

"Strike?" said Damwin. "Strike when? Strike how? Marlan, we are the only two dukes who've stood beside you. You owe us—"

"*Nothing.* The debt is yours. Your duchies will be raised high in Ethrea as the true supporters of God's Liv-ing Flame." Marlan tightened his grip on the chair and fixed the dukes with his coldest stare. "Be satisfied with that. Or God will turn his face from you and darkness will claim you as it claimed those who stood against Rol-lin in those bleak times we thought were left behind."

"Very well," said Damwin curtly, after a moment.

Was he truly cowed, Marlan wondered, or only bid-ing his time? It didn't matter, so long as his stupidity was contained until it could damage only himself.

"It's not that we doubt you," said Kyrin. "You are God's prolate. But as dukes of Ethrea, men whose families are entrusted with so much, it would ease our concerns if you could share—"

"No," said Marlan. "This is my burden, not yours. Do you think I take lightly the thought of disciplining a prin-cess? I loved her father. I have known her since she was born. The thought that she likely now consorts with sor-cerers, has perhaps sold Ethrea to a nation like Tzhung-tzhungchai, my heart bleeds within my breast. I have failed her somehow. It can only be that. This matter is between us. The dukes of Ethrea will stand aside."

Defeated, neatly whipped to heel, Kyrin nodded. "Very well, Eminence. We will follow your lead."

"And in so doing earn God's love," said Marlan. "Now I feel the time has come for you both to return to your duchies. I will send word to you once Rhian has crossed into Kingseat. Then you can raise your garrisons against her by cutting off her means of escape." He smiled. "And we shall have her . . . and you shall see her thrown down."

But his smile faded soon enough after the dukes had withdrawn. Turning again to the window, his gaze fixed unseeing upon the gardens below and the criss-crossing of chaplains and venerables about their divine business, the conversation just past played and replayed in his mind.

Rhian proves more troublesome than ever I anticipated. This business of miracles . . . she is ingenious in her deceits. Whether she works alone or with the Tzhung Emperor, could it be possible Damwin and Kyrin are right? Could I be mistaken, letting her journey continue?

Or should I find a swifter, simpler solution . . .

For Zandakar, the journey back to Kingseat woke memories of the time he rode with his mother and Raklion warlord across the wild face of Mijak with the chastened warlords who had dared to defy the god in Mijak's Heart, and paid a terrible price for their wicked disobedience. The people of Mijak had shouted to see their warlord and their warlord's son. They did not shout to see Hekat for she was not the empress then. But he remembered the shouting of the people when she was, and rode so proud and bold among them.

Rhian is an empress. She is Empress of Ethrea.

In those dead days it was the godspeakers and their sacrifices that showed Mijak's people they were in the god's eye. Here in Ethrea that was Dexterity's doing.

He said their god is silent but it is shouting now. Their god shouts in the sunshine, it shouts with healing miracles, Dexterity is in his god's eye even though he sheds no blood.

It was very strange. Mijak's god did not speak through healing but through death. Mijak's god did not speak to him, his heart stayed silent. He had promised Dexterity no more blood.

If I break my promise he will tell my secret.

Like the time before Raklion warlord, when Mijak's seven warlords fought and killed among themselves, so was Ethrea in danger of tearing itself to pieces. If Rhian knew the truth of him, if Alasdair king and her council of dukes knew Mijak was coming, they would kill him without a thought. When Dexterity first found him he had wanted to die. Would he care now if life was taken from him?

Yes. I would care.

Even with Lilit dead, even though he was banished, even though the god was stone silent in his heart, he did not wish to lose his life.

Why this is true the god must tell me. I do not know. I wish I wished to die.

He worried for Dexterity, the toymaker was not born a godspeaker. His golden god's power scoured him so he had to sleep in the peddler's van when he was not making miracles. One of the dukes' men drove it then, or Ursa if she did not need to sit with Dexterity and pour strengthening elixirs into his mouth.

He was not able to sit with Dexterity, he was warlord of Rhian's bodyguards. No. Not warlord, he was their shell-leader. Rhian's bodyguards were his shell. Every highsun he trained them, they were not warriors, these soldiers chosen by the dukes. The least of his warhost would have killed them in a heartbeat but they were improving. Too slowly ever to save themselves from Mijak's warhost, but if a man of Ethrea thought to bare a blade near Rhian that man would soon die screaming in his blood.

For safety they did not sleep in buildings, they camped on open ground or by the side of rough roads. Each new-sun and lowsun he danced the *hotas* with Rhian. She was skilful now, she was sleek and quick. If she had learned them as a child she would be as fierce as Yuma, if she'd had as fierce a heart. Rhian was not fierce, like Lilit she was gentle. He worried she did not have a fierce, killing heart.

Their training sessions were his favourite part of the day. Dancing *hotas* with Rhian he felt at peace. Rhian had danced into his hollow heart, where there had been Lilit now there was Rhian.

But he must never tell her that.

In between the *hotas* there was the travelling. He loved his horse he had called Didijik. He felt like himself again, riding a horse. He felt like a warrior, like a warlord, like Zandakar.

The lowsun before they crossed the border into duchy Hartshorn they camped at the edge of a tangled woodland. He trained his shell even harder than other times. Rhian was nervous crossing into that place. Alasdair king was nervous, the dukes were nervous also. Hartshorn's duke was an enemy. So was the Duke of Meercheq.

He knew how it felt, to have enemies wanting you dead.

When he finished training his shell they were sweating and exhausted. He was sweating also but his strength was not gone. Rhian came to dance with him, Alasdair king and the loyal dukes came to watch.

"Do you mind?" said Rhian as she stretched her body slowly in the first *hotas,* her blue eyes gazing at her sharp straight blade.

"Wei," he said. "Do you?"

"Well . . ." She sighed. "A little. Dancing the *hotas* is time for myself. Time I needn't worry about being watched. And now . . ."

He snorted. "You queen, Rhian. You sun in sky for your people. You always watched. You *wei* like?" He shrugged. "You *wei* be queen."

"Don't be ridiculous," she said, warming her muscles, making them fluid. "Of course I'm the queen."

"Then you be watched."

"I *know* that!" she said, her eyes angry. "I was a princess before I was a queen. I grew up being watched, Zandakar. But at least in Kingseat I had the castle, I had my own room where I could be alone. I haven't been alone and unwatched since I set foot in the clerica. All I want now is a little time for myself when I can take off my mask. *Tcha.* Anyone would think I was asking for the world."

He frowned. "Mask?"

"It's the face you wear when people are watching." Abandoning her *hotas,* she stood up straight, head high, shoulders back, and her expression changed from frustration to pride and confidence and strength. "The face you wear when you want other people to believe in you. *Zho?*"

Yuma had always loved being watched. She loved dancing in the god's eye and where the people could see her. She was never truly happy unless she was seen. As the warlord's son, and then the warlord, he had been watched too and he had enjoyed it. Rhian was strange, not to like being watched.

"*Zho*. But face not make people believe, Rhian," he said, and turned a slow cartwheel. Upright again, he looked at her. "They believe when you smite enemies."

"How often must I tell you?" she said, and turned her own slow cartwheel, hand . . . hand . . . foot . . . foot, she did not drop her knife as once she always did. He had not slapped her in training for many highsuns now. When the cartwheel was finished she pressed her forehead to her knees. "I'm not smiting *anyone*."

Alasdair king and the loyal dukes stood at a distance, talking softly, waiting for the fast *hotas* to start. "Enough stretching. Striking snake," he instructed. They were here for dancing, they could not talk until night.

"Bully," she said, and positioned herself opposite him for the *hotas* that strengthened legs and back and heart.

As she raised and lowered her arms above her head, focusing her concentration, he said, "Then they are not your enemies? Marlan? Damwin? Kyrin?"

"No. Well, Marlan is," she said, and began her first long, slow lunges, knife extended in her hand as though she would pierce him through the heart. "And Damwin and Kyrin certainly don't support me. But I don't believe they're truly enemies. They're just misguided. They've let themselves be blinded by Marlan and foolish ambitions they have to know will never come to anything." Limber now, she began to lunge and thrust more swiftly, demanding greater effort from herself. "They may try to bluster me, but they know the law. They know they've no basis to challenge my accession."

"Alasdair king thinks this?" he said, lunging in time with her now, letting her set the pace, letting his knife-tip stop a whisper from her breast.

"*Alasdair*?" Sweat was beading on her brow. "Alasdair thinks I'm being naïve. Alasdair says I can never trust them. He wants me to tear down their Houses, to disinherit their sons, to—" She breathed out hard. "And I won't do it. I won't be that kind of queen."

"What if Alasdair king is right?"

"He's not," she insisted, eyes narrowed with concentration. "Why? Do you think he is?"

"I think Rhian is stupid to trust enemies. Dukes must die if not loyal to Rhian."

"There's a word for people who rule with fear and brutality. I'm a queen, not a tyrant. I'm not killing *anyone*!"

He shifted the angle of his blade, and its tip scored a shallow groove across the back of her hand. "Then Rhian not be *hushla* for long."

"*Zandakar*—" Snatching her hand back, she pulled out of her lunge and sucked the welling blood from the cut. Then she turned and waved to Alasdair king, who was staring. "It's all right!" she called out. "I'm not hurt! I just wasn't paying attention!" Turning back, she stabbed him with a glare. "You did that on purpose!"

Shifting into a deep sideways lunge, he absorbed her anger without flinching. "You not kill, you not queen. You think enemies listen to weak word *please?* Rams fighting *hotas, zho?*"

"I think any ruler who rules by fear and bloodshed is a wicked tyrant who should be thrown down," she said, the new *hotas* flowing from her like sweet breath. "My father never ruled with violence, nor his father before him, nor *his* father before him. Not since the time of Rollin has a king ruled Ethrea by the sword. I *won't* be a queen who rules with blood and terror, Zandakar. I won't shame the House of Havrell like that."

He knew enough Ethrean words to understand she still did not grasp what it meant to be a ruler. She thought her proud face was enough to stop her people's wicked defiance. She was wrong.

Without a god like Mijak's god, and godspeakers who can hurt as well as heal, the people of Ethrea can defy her if they want to and she is powerless to stop them. They will defy her if she pretends she has no knife.

It made his heart hurt to think of her pretending.

"I know our ways seem strange to you," she said, as they danced the pattern of the *hotas*. "I can only imagine how harsh life must be where you come from if you believe I must rule with fear. But if it's the only way to keep my crown, then . . . I'm not sure I want it."

Aieee, the god see him. She was so like his Lilit! Gentle and compassionate, overflowing with love.

She stumbled out of the *hotas,* he did not correct her. Her eyes were distressed, her pain was his. "Marlan wants to rule with fear," she said, standing straight and catching her breath. "He wants to terrify the people with the threat of God's anger if they don't do what he tells them. He wants to use God as a whip and beat them with his mean interpretations of scripture. I have to be different. I have to be strong, I know that, but I can't be like *him*. And I won't kill in God's name, just for a crown." She shook her head. "I may not be the most devout person in the kingdom but if I did *that* I'd lose my soul for sure."

And if you do not fight to keep your kingdom you will lose it to this Marlan or someone like him and then what will happen when Yuma and Dimmi come with the god?

The thought terrified him, and terror edged his tongue. "Then why you dance *hotas*?" he demanded. "*Hotas* teach Rhian how to kill."

She looked away again to where Alasdair king and the dukes watched them. Were they admiring her? Or did they disapprove? She should not care for them. She was queen. They were beneath her.

"They teach more than that, Zandakar," she said. "And they help keep me fit. Now shall we continue? Or is it your opinion that I'm wasting your time?"

She was angry, she was hurt. He was sorry for that. He was afraid she would learn he was right too late.

He nodded, sharply. "*Zho,* Rhian. We dance."

And in the *hotas* they lost themselves. They forgot their disagreement. They danced with their knives like two halves of one shadow . . . and no-one was watching. They danced alone.

CHAPTER THIRTY-FIVE

Late that evening, private in her royal pavilion, Rhian sat cross-legged on an overstuffed cushion and dabbed more of Ursa's ointment on the cut from Zandakar's knife-blade. Alasdair was hunched on a leather stool, staring at the letter from Ludo he'd received that morning.

"My love, rest your eyes," she said. "That's the tenth time you've read it. The words won't change. Nothing will change until we reach Kingseat."

"I know," he grunted, but kept on staring.

She wished she could pluck the letter from his fingers and fling it in the campfire, but that would only upset him. He'd been so tense since they left Linfoi. So curt and swift to snap.

"No news doesn't mean bad news, Alasdair. There's no reason to think harm's come to Henrik."

He nodded. "I know."

"Your uncle *will* be all right," she said, for what felt like the thousandth time. "Marlan won't dare—"

"A cornered animal will dare almost anything," said Alasdair. "He dared beating you and that was *before* you made yourself queen."

She stared, her heart thumping. *"Made myself queen?* Alasdair—"

"I didn't mean it like that." In the lamplight his face

was shadowed. She couldn't see its expression. "You know what I mean."

She knew he was angry and frightened for Henrik. She knew he was overwhelmed by what they'd started. *What I've started. He was prepared to let me go without a protest so I could be married to another man. If I hadn't forced things he wouldn't be king.* Was he wishing she hadn't forced them? Was he sorry she'd run to him? *I can't ask him. Not now. Perhaps not ever. What's done is done. It's too late to turn back.*

He stood, shoving the stool aside, and restlessly paced around the small space. "Your Zandakar worries me."

"He's not my Zandakar," she said, feeling her spine stiffen.

"Well he's certainly not *mine*. All that talk of killing . . . that's not our way. Is it your way now? Is that why you train with him, to learn the art of slaughter?"

She pressed her fingers to her temples where pain throbbed like a drum.

I shouldn't have told him what Zandakar said. I thought it would reassure him, to know Zandakar thought Damwin and Kyrin were enemies too. Instead . . .

"No. Of course that's not why," she said, striving for patience. "I've told you why, must I explain it again? I agreed with you about Nyngdon, didn't I?"

"You agreed then," he said. "Perhaps you've changed your mind."

She took a deep breath and forced back the tears. "I haven't, Alasdair. I think you're right and that's what I told Zandakar. *No killing.* Please, let's not fight. We're both weary, we're both worried for Henrik and the others Marlan's imprisoned. Tomorrow we cross into Hartshorn and anything could happen. Can't we just sit quietly to-night? Hold hands and pretend just for a little time our world is at peace?"

He stopped pacing. "How can we pretend that? It's *not* at peace. Despite Mr Jones' miracles not all the people are rushing to support you. For every chaplain who's renounced Marlan's interdicts we've met three others who scream 'anathema' and curse your name."

"I know, but many *do* support me," she said. "And those who haven't yet *will*, once I'm confirmed on the throne. They're ignorant and backward and they're listening to lies. Once Marlan is silenced—"

"And how will you do *that*?"

She watched her fingers clench, feeling her hand sting beneath Ursa's green ointment. "I don't know," she said. There was iron in her voice. "But I will."

He shook his head. "You've changed, Rhian. You're not the girl I—" he looked away "—knew, in Kingseat."

He'd been going to say *the girl I fell in love with*. She'd seen it in his eyes. Her heart hurt her so badly, as though Zandakar's knife had plunged right through it. Blinking away the weak tears, she lifted her chin.

"Of course I'm not. A lot's happened since we were last in Kingseat. I'm not that carefree princess any more."

"No," he said, softly. "No, she's gone."

"Go on. You can say it. I've become hard." She scrambled off the cushion to face him, her own anger kindling. "And I think that's not so bad. You might not like Zandakar, Alasdair, but you can't deny he's right about one thing: if I want to defeat Marlan and the others I can't be soft. Being soft with Marlan would be fatal and you know it."

"I'm not saying you should be *soft!*" he protested. "I'm saying I don't like his careless talk of killing. And I don't like how easily you trust him. He's good with a knife and that's all you know. You don't know how many men he's killed or why he killed them. Rhian, there are *questions* about Zandakar that haven't been answered. If there weren't you'd have told your dukes the truth of him, not made up that story about tavern brawls and—"

"Keep your voice down!" she hissed. "I told the dukes what they needed to hear. And you agreed with me!"

"I didn't contradict you," said Alasdair. "That's not the same thing. God save me, Rhian. For all you know, Zandakar could've killed *innocents!* Why won't you accept that he might not be—"

"Oh, Alasdair. Please. I'm not asking you to trust *him,* I'm asking you to trust *me.* Are you saying you can't do that?" She stared at him, stricken. "Are you saying you *won't?*"

Alasdair had a royal face he could put on at will. He wore it all day, every day, but it was discarded now. Now he looked exhausted and hurt and overwhelmed.

Just like me.

"Rhian . . ." He folded his arms across his chest. "Be fair. See this from my side. One minute I'm sitting with my dying father, preparing to be duke of a poor, disregarded duchy, and the next you're on my doorstep, running from the Church, ordering me to marry you so you can be queen, and your new best friends are some old physick, a foreigner who thinks of nothing but bloodshed and a toymaker who bursts into flames and heals the dying on a whim! It's not that I don't trust you, it's—well, can't you see how this *looks?*"

"You selfish bastard," she whispered, as the tears she couldn't hide spilled down her cheeks. "You think I *wanted* this? My father dead, my brothers dead, the welfare of a kingdom thrust into my hands? You think I wanted to be given into Marlan's cruel keeping? Should I have accepted *that,* Alasdair? Married his former ward and put the crown on his head? Thrown away everything my father fought for throughout his reign? Is *that* what you'd prefer? Is that the kind of woman you think you married?"

His face flushed a dull red, all its plain lines turned ugly. "I'm not sure who I married, Rhian. What I know is you don't smile at me the way you smile at Zandakar. Perhaps if *I'd* killed six men on the road, perhaps if *I* could show you a dozen dances of death, show you how to gut a man ten times over with a blade . . . would that make you smile at me? Would that stir your blood?"

His attack was so unexpected, so ludicrous, she could only stare, her heart pounding out of control. *"Alasdair . . ."*

"I've seen how he looks at you, too. When he thinks no-one's watching."

She almost laughed. "Oh, that's *nonsense*! We're friendly, I don't deny that. But I'm not in *love* with him. He's not in love with me! I told you, he was married, he lost his wife in tragic circumstances! He still mourns for her. And he's alone. Would you begrudge him a harmless smile? Are you so mean? How could I not know you were so mean?"

"Mean?" Slowly, Alasdair unfolded his arms. "You think I'm *mean*?"

And now she'd hurt him. Part of her was glad, he was

being so childish, so jealous, so *hateful*. Most of her was sorry, though. She held up her hands.

"No. Of course I don't. Please, Alasdair. We're tired. We're worried. And we're saying things we know aren't true. Everything's a mess. It's such a mess. And it's going to get messier before it's over. Let's not quarrel. Not over Zandakar. Not over *anything*. It's late. We should get some sleep. I know we didn't marry under ideal circumstances but we *did* marry. You're my king. I'm your queen. And Ethrea needs us. Can we leave it at that, at least for tonight?"

His eyes were so wounded. He stood close enough to touch her yet he seemed far away. He offered her a horrible, stiff little bow. "Certainly, Your Majesty."

"Oh, Alasdair, *no—don't—*"

But he was walking away from her, walking to the pavilion's unlaced door. He was walking through it, and she was alone.

Numb and despairing, she dropped again to the cushion on the floor.

Oh, Papa. Papa. What do I do now?

Blessedly solitary, Dexterity sat on the bench in the back of the peddler's van with a cooling bowl of stew beside him and no appetite to eat it. He had no appetite for anything now save the tainted oblivion of sleep.

Did I ask to be turned into a miraculous human bonfire? Let me think for a moment. No, I don't believe I did. I didn't ask for any of this. I was press-ganged. And I want to stop. Hettie, are you listening? I've had enough. If God wants this mess fixed he can fix it himself.

She didn't answer. He'd not seen or heard from her

since Heddonvale and the miracle of Walder. There'd been so many more miracles since then, they'd all blurred together. All he could remember clearly were the flames. And even though they never hurt him, still he was in pain. He was desperately exhausted . . . and his soul was in despair.

So many frightened people. So many Ethreans torn and confused. Who should they believe? Me or their chaplains? Marlan tells them they'll be interdicted if they follow Rhian, I tell them God says Marlan is wrong. Then I frighten them witless by bursting into flames. And all the sick people . . . for every one I cure five more are turned away. Ursa does her best to help them but she's one physick. She can't save them all. I can't save them all.

I can't even save myself.

He realised, then, there were tears on his cheeks. He was weeping, silently. Dear God, he was so weary.

Without warning, the van's hinged doors pushed open.

"Dexterity," said Zandakar, ducking inside. "What is wrong? You need Ursa?"

Hastily he dragged his sleeve over his face. "No. I'm fine. What's happened? Is Rhian—"

Zandakar closed the van's doors and perched on the sleeping-shelf opposite. "Rhian fine. I come see you."

"Oh." Although he was exhausted, he felt his muscles tense. "Why?"

"We *wei* speak many days," said Zandakar. "You doing your god's work. I training soldiers and Rhian. We speak now." He looked around the van's cramped interior. "Where is Ursa? Where is Helfred?"

"The king sent for Helfred. He and the dukes want

to talk of Marlan. Since we're about to cross into what will surely be hostile territory, with Kyrin of Hartshorn standing against us, they want to know what the prolate will likely do. And Ursa's seeing to one of Duke Edward's men. He has a belly gripe. She should be back by and by."

Zandakar nodded. "Dexterity look bad."

I don't want to talk about it. "I told you. I'm fine."

"Zho?" said Zandakar. His tone was disbelieving. "You burn for your god three times this day."

"Really?" he said, waspish. "I wasn't counting."

There was no trace remaining of the mortally sick man he'd rescued from the slave ship. Zandakar's strength had returned in full. He moved like a cat from the jungles of Haisun. Rhian's bodyguards held him in mixed fear and respect. His stamina seemed endless, he never tired of riding or training or dancing *hotas* with Rhian. As Ursa had foretold, he was formidable. Half-lidded, his startling eyes stared steadily.

"You *wei* like burning. You *wei* like your god, make you burn three times one day."

Dexterity grimaced. "Believe me, Zandakar, I *wei* like my God long before the burning started. That's just the latest in a long list of reasons not to like my God." Still not hungry, but needing something to hide behind, he picked up the bowl of stew and forced himself to take a mouthful. "You like *chalava*, do you? After every terrible thing your god has made you do?"

"Like?" Zandakar shrugged. "What is like? *Chalava* is *chalava*."

Ah, yes. That familiar refrain. "And what if you don't want to? What if, like me, you have no interest in God?"

Zandakar looked baffled. "Want? *Wei* want, Dexterity. All obey *chalava*."

Lowering the spoon, he considered that for a moment. Considered what Hettie had told him about the god of Mijak. *I wish I could tell him. He believes in a lie.* "Zandakar, does *everyone* in Mijak believe in your god? I mean, is there no-one in Mijak who thinks there *is* no god?"

From the look on Zandakar's face it was a stupid question. "You *wei* believe sky, Dexterity? You *wei* believe sun? Moons? Stars? *Chalava* like that. Every day Mijak people see *chalava* in *chalava-chaka*. They see, they obey. *Wei* obey, *chalava* smites."

Chalava and Marlan seem to have much in common. Thinking about it, he supposed it made sense that Zandakar and his people never questioned their god's existence. *If I'd grown up seeing miracles on a daily basis . . .*

He nodded. "I understand."

"Like people of Ethrea now," Zandakar persisted, anxious to make his point. "Dexterity is *chalava-chaka* for Ethrea god, *zho?*"

"*Zho.* I am." *Unfortunately.* "But my God is not a god of smiting, Zandakar. God doesn't kill those who disobey."

Clearly Zandakar wasn't impressed. He muttered something under his breath in his own mysterious tongue.

"What was that?" he said.

Zandakar scowled. "Ethrea god like Rhian. Soft. *Wei* smiting. You want Zandakar be *chalava-hagra*? How be *chalava-hagra* Zandakar *wei* smite?"

Dexterity's head was pounding unmercifully again. He'd have to ask Ursa for another posset when she returned. She'd nag him and nag him and most likely rail at

Rhian . . . "I don't know. We mustn't speak of that, Zandakar. Someone might hear. Let's worry about what we're facing at the moment, shall we? That's enough to be going on with, there's no need to borrow—"

The van's doors pushed open again, revealing Ursa. "Well, well," she said, staring at Zandakar. "Look who the cat dragged in."

"Ursa," said Zandakar, and stood.

"Oh, you remember?" she said, sniffing. "I suppose I should be flattered."

"*Yatzhay,*" said Zandakar. "Must go." He pressed a fist to his heart. "Dexterity."

"*Zho.* You be careful. Remember what I said."

"What was that about?" asked Ursa as Zandakar closed the doors behind him, leaving them alone.

"Nothing. He stopped by to chat."

She snorted. "Zandakar? Chatting? That'll be the day." Then she poked at his abandoned stew bowl. "Jones, what's this? Haven't I told you enough times? You have to *eat.*"

"I did eat. I just didn't finish it."

"Jones, you barely *touched* it!" She straightened, fists on her hips. "And you've another megrim brewing, haven't you? I swear it's a good thing Hettie hasn't shown herself to me, for I'd be giving her the rough side of my tongue!"

"As opposed to the smooth side? Are you sure there's a difference?"

"Tcha!" she said, and rummaged in her physicking bag. "Don't try to be clever, you'll sprain something." She tossed him a small glass vial. "Here. Trickle that under your tongue."

He stared at the bottle's unsavoury-looking contents. "What, no posset?"

"You've had too many possets, Jones," she said, sitting on the bench beside him. "Herbs can harm as well as heal. That'll dull the worst of the pain. The rest you'll have to take care of with sleep."

Ah. Yes. Sleep. Where he kept revisiting slaughtered Garabatsas. "All right. Thank you."

As he unstoppered the bottle and tipped the vile stuff into his mouth, she asked, "So . . . what were you and Zandakar chatting about?"

He disguised his dismay in a grimace over the bottle's foul contents. "I don't remember. It was nothing. Just . . . talk."

Ursa sat back, her hands folded tightly in her lap. "You're lying again, Jones. And if you deny it something precious will be broken."

It was already broken. He was broken. His soul was bleeding. Hettie's miracles had crushed him till he was little more than paste. "Ursa . . . I'm sorry . . ."

"It's to do with Zandakar, isn't it? Zandakar and Rhian and these wretched miracles."

He nodded. "Yes."

"And you can't talk about it. Because Hettie said not to?"

"I'm sorry," he said again, helpless.

She sighed. "So am I. For it's not just the miracles giving you megrims, is it? It's what you know that you're not allowed to speak of. There's a look in your eyes, Jones. I've never seen you so afraid. Not even when Hettie was slipping away from us."

He was holding the small vial as though it could save

his life. A fraction more pressure and he'd have glass slivers in his hand. He loosened his fingers and put it carefully on the bench between them.

"Ursa . . ."

"It's all right," she said. "I know about keeping secrets. Every physick does. Just tell me this *one* thing. Do you know what you're doing?"

He pressed his hands to his face. "Hettie does," he said, muffled. *At least, I think so. I hope so. For if she doesn't . . .*

"In other words I'm to trust you. No proof or questions asked."

His hands dropped. "You've trusted me so far. Are you having doubts?"

She picked up the empty vial and brooded over it. "Things are different since we left Kingseat. I'm more involved in this business than I ever asked to be. We're fighting the *Church,* Jones!" Her voice caught. Her eyes were too bright. "Some say we're fighting God."

She was his best friend and he'd hurt her. Not on purpose, but still. "We're not," he whispered, his throat hurting and tight. "You *know* we're not. We're fighting *for* God, Ursa. We're fighting for Rhian and for Ethrea. Don't lose your faith now. I can't do this without you."

"I just wish I knew why we needed Zandakar," she murmured. "I wish I understood where he fits in."

Oh, Ursa. I'm so sorry. I'd tell you if I could.

And then a knock sounded on the van's double-door and a voice called out, "Mr Jones! Are you in there, Mr Jones?"

Relieved, and searingly ashamed at the relief, he pushed off the bench and looked to see who wanted him. It was one of the duchy Linfoi soldiers who made up the larger company escort. What was his name? Oh yes. Maxwil.

"Mr Jones, I know it's late. I'm sorry to disturb you," said guardsman Maxwil. "But there's this woman with a baby. We tried to explain you couldn't come but she's powerful upset and—"

"Oh, for the love of Rollin," said Ursa. She pushed to her feet and joined him at the doorway. "Jones is *not* coming out to do a healing! He's done enough healing for one day. *Go* tell the woman a physick will be with her directly."

Maxwil shifted uncomfortably at the foot of the van's steps. "I'd say this baby's too far gone for physicking. Looks three-quarters dead to me. And the mother's walked more than two hours in the pitch dark to find us. She's nearly dropping herself."

"And I'm sorry to hear it," said Ursa. "Sorrier still that a clumsy soldier like yourself thinks he knows more of physicking than—"

"It's all right, Ursa," Dexterity said, his bones aching. "I'll go."

She glared at him, dismay and displeasure mingled. Despite their differences, as always so concerned. *"Jones!"*

"No." Surprising them both, he kissed her wrinkled cheek. "It's what I'm here for. It's what Hettie would want."

Walking by torchlight beside guardsman Maxwil, feeling the vicious headache battering his skull, he cast a look upwards at the twin moons and the night sky.

Somewhere out there Dmitrak and his mother Hekat are looking at those same stars. Somewhere out there

*they are planning our doom. Somewhere out there an-
other Garabatsas is weeping.*

What was a headache compared to that?

The next morning, before they rode out to cross the Morvell border into Hartshorn, Rhian cautioned her sombre
dukes.

"Gentlemen, from this moment we must maintain a
constant vigilance. You know Kyrin as well as my father
did. He is hotheaded and foolish enough to try taking us
with soldiers. If that should happen—"

"We won't let it," said Adric, bolstered by youth.

Alasdair shook his head. "No. We must let it."

It hurt her so much that they could be at such sharp
odds yet so deeply in sympathy. "The king's right, Adric,"
she said, as her newest duke would have argued. "Blood
spilled in my name will be our undoing. Let's just pray
that Kyrin thinks before he acts, for once."

Adric's father grunted. "If he does it'll be for the first
time."

She smiled at Rudi, though she didn't feel amused.
"God has favoured us so far. We must trust his favour will
last a little longer."

"We could still go by river," said Edward. "Make haste
to Kingseat without ever tempting Kyrin to attack. Or
Damwin after him."

"And prove ourselves cowards in our own kingdom,"
muttered Adric, just loudly enough to be heard.

Rhian closed her eyes. *If this is how Adric and Edward
rub along, perhaps I should reconsider Edward's daughter for his wife.* "Adric," she said, "that was unseemly.
Edward thinks of my safety. Season your courage with

caution, Your Grace. You're no use to me dead or maimed by bravado."

"What of Edward's suggestion?" said Alasdair quietly. "Abandon the wooing of Hartshorn and Meercheq and take the fight to Marlan in Kingseat sooner rather than later?"

She was desperate to show him his value to her, that his thoughts mattered even though they were at odds. "You think the notion has merit?"

His eyes remained opaque. "It's not my place to comment. You're the queen."

He was hurt, she understood that, but oh, she could have slapped him. As the dukes pretended not to notice something was amiss, she gritted her teeth. "I'm asking your opinion."

He shrugged. "Very well. Then, *in my opinion*, you risk more unrest in those duchies than can be justified. With their dukes and their chaplains ranged firm against you, the chances of violence are too high. I think Edward's right. We should finish our journey by river."

"Except Hettie said not to," she answered, after a moment. *Another rejection. Will he ever forgive me?* "And if I avoid both duchies I'll embolden Marlan and those rebellious dukes. They'll think I'm afraid. I can't afford to give those men a false scent of blood."

"What do you suggest, then?" said Edward. "We fling caution to the winds and beard both dukes in their dens?"

She took a deep breath. "No. I suggest a compromise. We'll travel fast through Hartshorn, gaining whatever support we can find, and from there cross into Kingseat and ride as hard as we can for the capital. Once I'm back in the castle with my standard flying from the battlements, the people will see I am here to stay."

"And Meercheq?" asked Rudi.

She tugged her riding gloves from her belt and pulled them on slowly, finger by finger. "Meercheq I leave for my procession of triumph. Gentlemen, to horse."

She walked away from her husband, his following stare hot on her skin.

I'm sorry, Alasdair. But you were wrong and I'm right.

It took them three days by the shortest route to reach Hartshorn's border with Kingseat. In that time they saw not a single Hartshorn soldier. Not wishing to stir trouble, they steered clear of towns and villages as much as they were able. When they did meet up with Kyrin's people there were miracles and healings and the inevitable clashes of belief and loyalties. Duke Kyrin held his duchy in a tight, relentless grasp. Marlan's clergy also stood firm for the most part. They made few converts to the queen's cause in Hartshorn.

It was a piercing relief to reach the duchy Kingseat border.

"And there it is," said Rhian. "Kingseat." Her eyes prickled with tears. So much had happened since she'd fled her home duchy. She was another person entirely. The world around her had been remade, and not in ways entirely to her pleasing.

But I can't worry about that. At least I still have a world. At least I'm not married to Lord Rulf and imprisoned in the castle, or on his estate. Things could be a lot, lot worse . . .

She sat astride her stallion Invincible, on the top of a rise overlooking a placid expanse of wheat and flax. The crops were planted chequerboard style, great bold splashes of green and gold. A living tablecloth covering the fertile soil. Breathtaking. Heartstopping.

Beside her, Alasdair looked without comment. The fresh dawn light rested in the hollows of his cheeks and lightened slightly the dark shadows beneath his eyes. He was exhausted, and so was she. Exhausted already and their fight had barely begun. For there was Kingseat, the heart of Ethrea, containing Marlan and all the foreign ambassadors who were surely uneasy now, and clamouring for answers.

Perhaps I shouldn't have written them those letters. But how could I stay silent? I had to tell them I am queen.

"We should keep on," said Alasdair. "Travel swiftly, while we still can. You know what'll happen once we strike the first village."

She nodded. "Yes. I just wanted a quiet moment."

Behind them waited the rest of her retinue. The dukes. The soldiers. Her bodyguards, and Zandakar. Ursa, Helfred and Dexterity.

Dexterity. What would I have done without him? He is the one who has truly crowned me queen. Without his miracles I might as well have surrendered myself to Marlan and been done with it.

Her quest for a crown had cost him dearly. Pale and so thin, now, he was rarely glimpsed when not proclaiming her name. Ursa came close to looking at her with dislike.

I'm sorry but there's no help for it. I'll make it up to him after.

"Rhian . . ." said Alasdair. He sounded curt. Out of patience.

Oh, God. Is our marriage over before it's begun?

She tore her gaze away from the lush crops and looked at him. "Are you ready for what awaits us down there?"

"Does it matter if I'm ready?" said Alasdair, indifferent. "We must face Marlan regardless. And Damwin, and Kyrin."

She shivered, even though her clothes were more than warm enough to withstand a touch of early-morning chill. "I have the law on my side, Alasdair. They *have* to acknowledge me. If they don't they'll push Ethrea into civil war!"

"You've pushed us halfway there already. We've left nothing but arguments and upset in our wake."

I won't cry. I won't cry. I will not weep before him. "We've left more than that. We left Walder behind us. We left scores of healed people. We left entire towns and villages with hope. Alasdair, why are you doing this? Are you wishing you'd sided with Damwin and Kyrin, now?"

His face was remote. He'd gone so far away. "No. Of course not. I'm worried for Henrik."

"So am I," she whispered. "Alasdair, I told you we'd save him. If Marlan has hurt him then Marlan will pay."

He nodded, as though he couldn't trust himself to speak. But she could see the thought in his face. It echoed in her own heart, tearing with taloned claws.

Henrik's paid already. Because I insisted on a crown.

"If Henrik were . . . all right . . ." said Alasdair, carefully, "He'd have sent word long since to Ludo and Ludo would've found a way to tell me. There's been nothing, Rhian. What can I do but fear the worst?"

He'd nearly said *alive*. He thought his uncle was dead. She couldn't afford to let him despair. He was the King of Ethrea and she needed him beside her.

"There are lots of reasons why you've not heard from Ludo," she said, softly. "One messenger trying to reach us could've encountered many delays."

He nodded. "I know."

"I *swear* to you, Alasdair, if Marlan has harmed him I *will* make him pay. My word as queen. But for now you have to banish Henrik from your thoughts. What has happened *has happened*. And you can't change that or help him. Not until we've won."

The bleakest of smiles touched his lips. "As if I need you to tell me that."

Oh, Alasdair. She shifted in her saddle and beckoned to Adric.

"Majesty?" he said, riding up to her other side.

She nodded ahead. "So here is your duchy, Duke Adric of Kingseat. Does it please you?"

Adric surveyed the landscape with avid, glowing eyes. "Your Majesty, it does."

Even after Volant's proxy wooing for him and these long days on the road, she hardly knew Duke Rudi's son. When duty had called him to Kingseat in the past he'd spent his time with Ranald and Simon and any other young noblemen who'd been at court at the time. Simon had quite liked him but they'd never been boon companions.

"Prince Ranald was loved in Kingseat," she said. "He made a fine duke. He would've been a great king. It's a precious gift I've given you, Adric. I pray you don't lose sight of that."

He nodded. "I won't, Your Majesty. How I'll repay you I don't—"

"You can repay me by not twisting your future good-father's tail," she said. "And by continuing your loyalty to the House of Havrell."

"I will," said Adric. "Your Majesty . . . about Lord Volant . . ."

"I have promised Rudi and I promise you no less: if Lord Volant is hurt by Marlan on my behalf, then he and your family shall be avenged."

"Thank you," Adric whispered. "My father has been most distressed."

She led her retinue forward then, with Alasdair by her right hand and Adric by her left. She led them in silence, not because Adric wished to stop speaking but because she did.

So many small powers, when one is a queen. When I was a princess I did not have so many. I was a princess but still I was outranked. Now no-one outranks me. I stand above all. How easy it would be to abuse my position. Perhaps I should be grateful for Helfred. Little chance of abuse with him harping in my ear.

"Something amuses?" said Alasdair.

She shook her head. "No."

"But you were smiling," he insisted. "What—"

"It was nothing. I told you."

She used her voice like a whip. Adric stared at the fields, uncomfortable, as Alasdair closed his mouth tight and rested his gaze on his horse's ears.

See, Adric? This is what being married to a queen is like. I'll bet you're hardly disappointed now . . .

On they rode, as the sun shone brightly and climbed behind them.

CHAPTER THIRTY-SIX

Of all the duchies, Kingseat knew Rhian best. Loved her best. Opened its arms widest and took her the deepest into its heart. Although word of Dexterity's miracles had reached Kingseat long before her arrival, they weren't required to sway the people to her cause. Love of Eberg's daughter burned as hot as any flame.

Which was just as well, as it turned out. After two more days of miracles Mr Jones was so poorly Ursa forbade him setting foot beyond the van.

"He's burned to the socket for you, Majesty," the physick said, with no great deference. "Three-quarters killed himself. I don't know who's got me angrier: you or his dead wife. Now you'd best reconcile yourself. Jones' miracles are over. He won't be doing any more."

Rhian went to see him. "I'm so sorry," he whispered, his sunken eyes too bright. "Forgive me. I've failed you. I just—I can't—"

"*No*," she said, and kissed him. "The failure's mine, Dexterity, not to see how ill you are. You've done more than I asked for. More than I deserve. You rest now. It's time I did this on my own." She kissed him again. "Just listen to Ursa and get well. Don't worry about me, I'll—"

But he'd fallen asleep, so thin, so pale. Terrified, she

kissed him a third time and left to sweat her fears out with the *hotas*.

And continued the next day without Dexterity's miracles.

Undeterred, the people of her duchy's towns and villages thronged their streets, lined the country laneways, shouted and shouted and shouted her name. Their wild acclaim lifted her, bore her gently aloft.

"Rhian! Rhian! God bless Queen Rhian and her king, Alasdair!"

A few stubborn venerables and chaplains tried to denounce her. They were roughly cast aside. The handful of citizens who spoke against her quickly regretted it. Emboldened by her people's welcome, Rhian grasped every chance to speak to them herself. In village marketplaces, in larger town squares, in crowded thoroughfares and from horseback on common grazing lands, she raised her voice in thanks for their devotion. Reminded them of their duty to the Crown. Gave them their new duke, Adric, who would love them and speak for them at court. Encouraged their resistance against false authorities.

"Revere God," she instructed, "and live by Rollin's teachings. As your lawful queen I insist upon that. But don't think to set the Church *above* Ethrea's law. That way lies calamity. Obey the law in your lives and God in your hearts. That is the recipe for a peaceful, prosperous kingdom. Eberg knew that and aren't I Eberg's daughter?"

She halted her party and spoke so often that a journey of four days stretched to eight. She spoke to so many excited crowds she would have lost her voice but for Ursa's foul-tasting concoctions and her protective council's insistence upon rest.

The last township they stopped at was historic Old Scooton, the birthplace of Rollin. It lay a scant two hours from Kingseat capital. There, after another rousing address and a reception from the people that made her laugh with joy, she was invited to sleep the night in rough splendour at Old Scooton's best inn, a guest of the town council. What she ached for was peace and quiet, a chance to collect herself without an eager audience. But she was queen now. Solitude was a luxury she might never again afford. So she accepted the invitation and resigned herself to noise and crowding and a magnificent banquet she could barely bring herself to touch.

Afterwards, having eaten too little and drunk too much of the inn's oak-aged red wine, she sat in her guest chamber's armchair by the window and stared through the glass at the waxing twin moons.

"We'll reach the capital tomorrow," said Alasdair. "It will be a momentous day. You should sleep."

He was already in bed, propped up with pillows. Now they were in Kingseat there was no reason for them to sleep apart. Indeed the sooner she gave Ethrea an heir the happier, it seemed, her council would be. She agreed. It would certainly be prudent.

But for her to fall pregnant she and Alasdair must make love . . . and since their quarrel over Zandakar he'd not even kissed her lips.

Inexperienced as I am, even I know that's a problem.

She didn't look at him. "I'm not tired."

"Not tired? You're exhausted."

"I meant I'm not sleepy. I've a thousand worries playing hide-and-seek in my head."

"Forget them. Come and play hide-and-seek with me, instead."

Now she looked at him. "What?"

"I miss you," he said simply. In the lamplight he looked grave. Almost a stranger. "I know there is much still to say, to forgive, for both of us, but for tonight, Rhian . . . please. Be my wife."

How could she refuse him? If she let hurt feelings threaten their future surely she didn't deserve to be queen.

He loved her tenderly. Gently. His care made her weep. Cradled in his arms afterwards, his hand stroking her growing hair and their quarrel a memory, she felt safe and at peace for the first time since her father had told her he was dying. A lifetime ago, now. The pain of a Rhian who no longer existed.

Papa. Ranald. Simon. Until this quiet moment the most important men in my life. I wonder what they'd think of me if they were here. I wonder if Papa imagined their deaths would wreak such change.

"You're thinking again," said Alasdair, his voice drowsy.

She spread her fingers against his warm chest. "I can't help it."

"Still sorry you married me?"

"*Sorry?* Alasdair, I was never *sorry.* I only ever wanted to marry you."

His hand stroked her hair, but there was tension in it. "You didn't fight for me, Rhian."

She pulled back to stare at him. "Papa was dying! Every minute we shared was precious. How could I spoil that time with arguments, how could I exhaust what was left of his strength? What if I'd killed him, fighting for you?"

He tightened his arms until she laid against him again. "You'd never have forgiven yourself. Or me."

"And what about you?" she said, still stung. "You didn't fight for me, did you? You didn't even write. You passed that message of condolence through Henrik and after that, nothing."

He flinched at her mention of his uncle's name. "Your father forbade me contacting you again when I formally requested permission to leave court and return home. He said my suit would never prosper. *'Linfois make adequate dukes but as husbands they leave a great deal to be desired.'* He said it would be unwise to dispute him so I didn't. We both knew what he meant by that."

So did she, but . . . "I can't believe Papa would've stripped you of the dukedom."

He sighed. "You say. The dukedom was my father's legacy. I had no right to risk it, not even for you. For all I knew Eberg had left written instructions for after his death. And when I heard you were entertaining suits from the other dukes, and from Marlan, when I didn't receive any word from you . . ."

"I'm sorry," she whispered.

Alasdair kissed her forehead. "We should've talked of this before."

She rubbed her cheek against him. "We're talking now."

"Yes, when we should be sleeping. We'll face Marlan tomorrow. We need to rest."

He turned down the lamp and plunged the chamber into darkness.

But sleep wouldn't come. Even as Alasdair's breathing deepened and slowed Rhian stared at the ceiling, her mind relentlessly clear and tumbling with thoughts. Henrik. Lords Harley and Volant. Damwin and Kyrin. Helfred. Dexterity. The looming confrontation with Marlan.

If he refuses to yield to me is my cause lost? Must I ask the other nations to support me against him? And if I do that . . . will I lose more than I gain?

Suddenly the chamber was too small, its ceiling too close. She needed air. She was going to suffocate in here. Trembling, she eased herself out of Alasdair's embrace.

"What are you doing?" he muttered as she rummaged for her boy's clothing.

"Going down to the stables," she said, dressing. "I didn't give Invincible his late-night tidbit."

"Tidbit?" Groaning, he sat up. "Rhian—"

"It's his little treat. He'll be looking for it. I'll hurt his feelings if I don't go down."

Another groan. "Damned spoiled horse. All right. But I'm coming with you."

"*No,* Alasdair!" She laced up her shirt. "Please. I've not belonged to myself since I ran from the clerica. After tomorrow I never will. It's not that I don't want you. I just want myself more. For a little time. The last time. A few moments of fresh air, alone. A small simple gesture, feeding my horse. Like I did when I was still a girl and life wasn't so . . . difficult."

Slowly, he lay down again, his sleepy eyes understanding. "Don't be long."

"I won't," she promised. "Go back to sleep."

"I'll sleep when you're beside me."

Habit had her belting her knife around her hips. After

so long training with Zandakar she felt naked without it. Then she stamped into her short boots, shrugged on her coat and took an apple from the guest chamber's fruit bowl. "Back soon."

She trod softly downstairs and let herself out into the rear courtyard where the stables were. The inn and its other inhabitants were slumbering. It was late. Or early. Tomorrow was a handful of hours away. The air was cool but not unpleasant, the night sky deeply black and full of stars. Moonlight draped the world in silver gauze. Beautiful. So beautiful.

I've had no time for beauty. There's been time for nothing but running and fear.

Invincible tossed his head when he saw her, offended at being kept waiting for so long. She unsheathed her knife and cut the apple into quarters. "My apologies for the delay, sir," she murmured, feeding him.

The horse crunched his tidbit, head nodding in appreciation. Smiling, she smoothed his broad, satiny cheek. A whisper of sound in the shadows behind her. Hard hands clutching her shoulders, turning her. Grasping fingers around her throat. Invincible snorted and kicked at the wall.

"Miserable bitch!" her assailant spat on a cloud of bad breath. *"God's rank enemy beneath the sun! You poison this kingdom! In Marlan's name I send you to hell where the spawn of devils like you belong!"*

Ven'Martin.

Until the moment she felt the blade bite through cloth and flesh Rhian had no idea she'd used her knife. No memory of dancing herself free of her assailant, driving him to his knees and impaling him on tempered steel, just as she'd been ruthlessly schooled.

Kneeling with him on the cobbles, bathed in gauzy moonlight and close enough to kiss, she saw Ven'Martin's face twist in a grimace of shock and pain. His wolfish green eyes were blank with shock.

"But—but—"

With a soft sigh he slid off her knife and thudded on the cobbles like a sack of wheat falling from a wagon. A thread of blood trickled from the corner of his mouth. He blinked. Blinked again. His hands pressed the hole she'd made in his belly, turning scarlet. They spasmed. Spasmed. He coughed weakly, blood bubbles bursting. Smoothly, like poured oil, she rose to her feet, her knife-blade crimson in the moonlight, and watched the wasted life fade from his face.

You wei hesitate killing, Zandakar had told her. *You hesitate, you die. Belly soft. Strike deep, go up. Twist knife. Cut inside. Make bleed. Make die.*

Every time they danced the *hotas,* Zandakar would tell her that. At first the thought had made her queasy but after a while she'd stopped hearing the words. At least, she'd thought she stopped hearing them.

But I didn't. The words seeped inside me, soaking into my muscles and bones. And now I've killed a man . . . exactly as Zandakar taught me to.

Turning on her heel, leaving Ven'Martin like a slaughtered beast, she went back inside the inn. Trod up the stairs. Returned to her chamber, where Alasdair was waiting.

He'd lit the lamp again but fallen asleep. "Alasdair," she said, standing beside him. "Wake up."

He opened his eyes and stared at her blearily. "Rhian?"

The blood-smeared blade was still in her hand. She showed it to him. "Ven'Martin attacked me. I killed him. You'd best come downstairs."

As he gaped at her, speechless, she walked out of their chamber and along the corridor where Zandakar had been given a room. He'd wanted to stay awake all night again, guarding her, but she'd flatly forbidden it. *This is King-seat, Zandakar. I'm safe in my home.* She banged on his closed door and a moment later he opened it. He was wide awake. Still dressed. He looked at her face and then at the knife.

"You're a good teacher, Zandakar," she said. "I didn't think. I didn't hesitate. He attacked and I killed him."

Back along the corridor, Alasdair was shouting for her. Other doors were opening.

"Show me," said Zandakar.

She took him to the dead man. Other people followed them downstairs till the courtyard was crowded. Alasdair. Zandakar. Her other bodyguards. The innkeeper. His stableman. Rudi and Edward in their nightshirts. Adric, still dressed. Ursa. Warm light from torches and lanterns chased away the silver moonlight.

Ursa pressed her fingers to Ven'Martin's throat then looked up. "Yes, he's dead, I'm afraid."

"God have mercy!" That was Helfred, arriving. "It's Ven'Martin. Why is he not dressed in his vestments? What is he doing here? Your Majesty, what *happened*?"

"He tried to kill me," she told him. Told everyone listening. The knife was still in her hand.

"*Kill* you?" Helfred stared. "Your Majesty, this is

Ven'Martin. Vestments or not he's a sworn man of God. What you say—it's not possible. There must be some mistake."

Ven'Martin's blood had dried a sticky dark red on the blade's honed steel. "You don't believe me?" she asked, her gaze fixed on it. "You think I killed him for sport, Helfred? Do you think I was *bored*?"

"No, Your Majesty, no—but *murder*? *A venerable*? It confounds understanding! Did he *say* anything? Did he—"

She closed her eyes. Heard again that rasping, hate-filled voice. "*In Marlan's name I send you to hell where the spawn of devils like you belong.*" She opened her eyes again. "I'm sorry, Helfred. This is your uncle's doing."

"*No!*" said Helfred, stepping back. "That's not possible. Marlan may be misguided but he would *never* stoop to murder. It is strictly against God's law!"

"God's law?" said Alasdair, his face livid with fury. "It's plain our prolate recognises no law but his own ambition. All but a few of Ethrea's people are with the queen. His chaplains proclaim her. He must know she'll face him in the capital tomorrow where all of Kingseat capital will shout her name. This was his last desperate attempt to defeat her."

A hurly-burly of voices, then, as Helfred and Alasdair and the rest added their clamour to the clamour in her mind.

This man is dead because I killed him. At last I am a killing queen. Is Zandakar proud of me? He must be proud . . .

"*Enough!* Have you doltish men eyes in your heads? Can't you see Her Majesty is wilting?"

Ursa. Her harsh demand silenced the uproar. Alasdair stepped forward. "Rhian?" he said, gently. "Come inside. Let us do with the venerable what must be done."

"If Marlan sent Ven'Martin here then his soul is surely damned," she whispered. "Or am I damned for killing him? Oh, Alasdair. I've killed a man of God."

"Rhian . . ." Alasdair's voice was anguished. "Please. Let me take you inside."

"Wei," said Zandakar. "I take her. I talk to her."

Alasdair turned. *"You?* I don't think so. You are the cause of this. You're her bodyguard, you're supposed to be, yet you didn't prevent this attack. She's killed a man who *you* should've killed. His blood should be on *your* hands, Zandakar. Not hers."

If the harsh words hurt him, Zandakar didn't show it. "Alasdair king has killed a man?"

"What?" Alasdair shook his head. "No. I've never killed a man. How does that matter? I am her—"

Zandakar's eyes were so pale. So pure. "I talk to Rhian, Alasdair king."

Silence, as the two men stared unblinking at each other. Rhian turned her head, distracted by movement. Dexterity had joined them, though he was still far from well. She looked at him, her miracle man. The toymaker who'd given her dolls and puppets, who'd mended her rocking horse and let her weep on his breast. He nodded, so slightly. His face was shocked, his eyes bleak.

"Alasdair," she said. "Please. Take everyone inside. I think I must talk with him out here. Alone."

Her words went through him like the blade of a knife. She saw them slice him. She saw him bleed. "Fine," he said curtly. "Your Graces? With me!"

"Your Majesty," said Helfred. "I beg you. Ven'Martin cannot lie here like a butchered hog. He must be laid out properly and prayed over. He—"

She rested her hand on his arm. "He will be. Have the innkeeper show you to his coldest cellar. Make what preparations you think are fit. Ven'Martin will be brought to you there."

"Majesty—"

"*Go,* Helfred! Before I—" She bit off the unwise words and swallowed them, though her throat was so tight. "Go."

The inn's yard emptied, Ursa scolding as she saw Dexterity on his feet. Too soon it was only herself and Zandakar . . . and dead Ven'Martin. Zandakar dropped to one knee beside the man she'd killed and bared his death wound to the brilliant night sky.

"Good stroke," he said, nodding. "Quick. Clean."

She shrugged, trying to pretend she didn't feel deathly ill. "Didn't I say you've been a good teacher?"

He stood. "Rhian good student."

"Papa always said so. He was proud of my accomplishments. I wonder if he's proud of me now . . ."

Twenty-seven years a king, Papa, and you never killed anyone. I'm not even crowned yet and there's blood on my hands. Blood because I wouldn't capitulate. Because I wouldn't accept the future you decreed for me. And now will a kingdom be punished for that?

Zandakar reached out, touched the base of her throat. His fingertips woke pain there. Ven'Martin's choking fingers had bruised her. "Man hurt you. *Wei* knife?"

"I don't think so. He didn't try to stab me. He wanted to strangle me." She shivered, remembering. "His eyes,

Zandakar. And when I stabbed him—when I stabbed him—"

"*Wei yatzhay* man dead, Rhian," said Zandakar, sternly. "Rhian *yatzhay,* Rhian stupid."

"All right then," she said, flinching. "I'm stupid. Because I am *yatzhay.* I'm *yatzhay* he's dead. I'm *yatzhay* I killed him." She felt her stomach heave. "I'm *yatzhay* I knew what to do when he attacked me."

Zandakar's eyes narrowed. "You ask me train you."

"I know I did!"

"I *wei* train, you die. *Zho?*"

"*Zho!* But does that mean I should be glad I killed him? Should I be *happy* I'm like you, a blooded, bloody warrior? I mean, you've got what you wanted. Rhian the killing queen. Are *you* happy?"

He said nothing.

"*Answer* me, Zandakar! Are you *happy* now?"

He stood in the moonlight and the light from the torches, his hair shimmering the most unnatural blue. He was dressed like an Ethrean but he still looked foreign. Exotic. His eyes were unshadowed. She saw his heart clearly.

He smiled. "Happy you *wei* dead. Happy I save you."

Oh, Alasdair . . . "How many men have you killed, Zandakar?"

He stopped smiling.

"I want to know," she persisted. "How many? A handful? Tens? Hundreds?" Still he said nothing. *"More?"*

"I am warrior, Rhian. Warriors kill."

"How old were you the first time you took a life? Do you remember?"

Thoughts flickered across his untranquil face. Then he

nodded, as though answering a question only he could hear. "I kill first man when I am twelve *intza*. I think you say years."

She swallowed. "God's mercy. You were a *child*. What were you doing, killing at that age?"

"Training to be warrior."

By killing someone? *Dear God. What kind of people does he come from?* "This man you killed. Who was he?"

"Criminal."

"You remember that?"

"*Zho*. I remember."

Surely it must be hard to forget, executing a criminal at the age of twelve . . . but she suspected he remembered a great deal more. *How long has he been hiding himself, I wonder?*

"And how did you feel after you killed him?"

He pulled a face. "Not good, kill that man."

Her own belly was still roiling. All the red wine she'd drunk earlier, sloshing around. It was a miracle she hadn't lost it in a great heaving. "And yet you killed again. Many times. More times than you want to tell me about." A shudder ran through her. "I never want to kill again, Zandakar. I didn't want to kill *this* time. I didn't say to Ven'Martin: *Fiend! You must die!* He attacked me and I stabbed him. I didn't think. I didn't question. I had my knife—*this* knife—" She held up the blade and watched the dried blood drink the moonlight. "I thrust it deep into his belly. I twisted it, to cut him inside. And then I knelt beside him and watched him die." Some sound broke from her throat, then, horrible and harsh. Her fingers opened.

The knife clattered on the cobbled ground. "Dear God, it was *disgusting*. I *butchered* this man!"

Zandakar shook his head. "*Wei,* Rhian. You die or man die."

"No! I could've shouted for help. I could've run. But Zandakar, I *didn't*. I *killed* him. It was instinct, like—like breathing. Dear God, after everything I've said and done to avoid violence between Linfoi and here. And yet *I'm* the one who's spilled the first blood. *I'm* the one who's tarnished the crown." There were hot tears on her skin. Inside she was freezing. "I wish I'd never learned a single *hotas*. I wish Dexterity had left you on that ship."

"Rhian . . ." Zandakar put one hand on her shoulder, standing so close she could feel his body heat. Her heartbeat quickened. "You not learn *hotas* you dead now," he said. "You not kill bad man? Bad man kill you."

And here they were again. *Kill or be killed*. His song without ending ever since he'd found the words.

With the softest of touches he wiped the tears from her cheeks. "Rhian die, what happen Ethrea?"

And that was the hideous question, wasn't it . . . If she died what would happen to the small precious kingdom she'd inherited against every expectation?

"Zandakar . . ." She hunched her shoulders against the cool night air. "I need to ask you something else. Something important. And don't tell me you can't remember because I think you can."

His eyes flickered with shadows again, with thoughts he would not share. "Ask."

"Have you ever killed a man who wasn't a criminal or trying to kill you in battle?"

He flinched, as though she hadn't dropped her knife but pricked it to his ribcage.

"Dear God . . ." She stepped back. "You *have*." *Oh Alasdair, Alasdair.* "Zandakar, who *are* you? Should I be afraid?"

His ice-blue eyes were liquid. "*Wei.* Zandakar *wei* hurt you. I teach you *hotas* so you keep safe."

If she picked up her knife and pointed it towards him, something would change between them that could never change back. Her fingers hummed to pick up the blade. She gripped them behind her until her knuckles cracked.

"Are you *yatzhay* for that, Zandakar? Are you *yatzhay* for killing an innocent man?"

Please God, please God . . . don't let him say no . . .

Zandakar nodded. "*Zho. Yatzhay yatzhay.*"

A deluge of relief, swamping the fear. *He's not lying. He's sorry. He's not a monster, he's just a man.*

"Do all the boys where you come from learn to kill when they're twelve?"

"*Wei.* Only warriors."

"What of the girls?"

"*Zho.* Girls warriors."

Of course they were. It had never occurred to him she could not fight . . . or kill.

Bending, she picked up the knife. It was heavy in her hand. Heavy with blood. Heavy with memory. If she closed her eyes she'd feel the give of flesh before steel, hear the soft exhalation of life fleeing the body.

I thought I was done with being reborn. I was mistaken. Tonight sees yet another new Rhian.

"Rhian . . ." Zandakar sighed. "You want be queen? This is queen. To kill bad men and be *wei yatzhay.*"

Slowly, so slowly, she raised the knife before her eyes. Made herself look at the dried blood, the edge on the blade. "It may be queen where you come from, Zandakar. Since the time of Rollin it has not been our way. And if I change that . . . if I turn back the clock . . . something will wear my face but it won't be *me*." She shifted her gaze to Ven'Martin's stiffening corpse. "He was wrong to attempt my life. *I* was wrong to take his instead." She dropped to her knees and let one hand rest palm-down on the man's unmoving chest. "I forgive you, Ven'Martin. I hope you can forgive me." She looked up. "Dance your *hotas* if you must dance them, Zandakar. They are part of you, I understand that. But from this moment you'll dance them alone."

"Alone?" Zandakar frowned. "Rhian *wei* dance *hotas*?"

"No. Not any more."

"Tcha! Rhian dance *hotas*," he said, his voice sharp with irritation. "Rhian *good* dance *hotas*."

"That's the problem," she whispered. "That's why I must stop."

Because I'm more than good. I'm very good. And because a part of me likes them. A part of me exults in my skill with a blade. A part of me—God have mercy—is not sorry Ven'Martin's dead.

Across the inn's courtyard, the sound of a door opening. "Rhian. Aren't you done yet?"

Alasdair.

"Yes. I'm done," she said, and stood. "*Yatzhay,* Zandakar," she told him, softly. "*Yatzhay* and thank you. For the second time you've saved my life."

"Rhian, please," said Alasdair. "Helfred's waiting in

the cellar. Let Zandakar take Ven'Martin to him. You must get some sleep before we ride in the morning."

He was right. Dawn was close. "Will you clean this?" she said, and held the knife out to Zandakar. "Keep it after, if you like. Or if you don't, throw it away. I have no more use for knives."

The request distressed him. "Rhian . . ."

"Fine," she said, and tossed the blade aside. The sound it made hitting the ground a second time was loud and final. "Take Ven'Martin's body to Helfred. *Zho?*"

His ice-blue eyes were touched with anger now. "*Zho.*"

She turned towards Alasdair then turned back. "Please. See to the knife."

"*Wei,*" he said. "Your killing. Your knife. You clean. You throw away."

His arrogant refusal roused her own anger. She opened her mouth to chastise him . . . then closed it.

Damn him, anyway. He's right. Papa would say the same thing and not so politely.

She retrieved the knife that had killed Ven'Martin. Washed it clean in the yard tub. Dried it on her shirt then laid it neatly on the dead man's breast.

Here is the first and the last of my killing. Whatever I am, whatever I may be, I will not be Queen Rhian with a blade.

"Are you all right?" said Alasdair, his voice tightly controlled, as they returned to their guest chamber. They were alone, though light shone beneath every door they passed.

She nodded. "I'm fine."

He ushered her into their room and closed the door behind them. "Rhian—"

"Alasdair, please," she said, her back to the window. "I needed to talk to him. Zandakar understands."

"And I don't?"

All the warm pleasure between them was drowned in blood. The soft kisses, the tender touchings, cut to pieces in the silver moonlight. "I know you want to."

"But you're saying I can't."

In his eyes she could see his heart breaking. Could he see hers, broken already? "Alasdair . . . you've never killed. How can you possibly know what I'm feeling?"

"I'd know if you'd tell me! But you'd rather tell *him*!"

"Do you know what I'd *rather*?" she shouted, her brittle self-control shattering. "I'd rather Ven'Martin wasn't dead. But he *is* dead, Alasdair. He's dead because *I killed him*. And nothing can undo that. No words can bring him back. So can we go to bed, please? One way or another it's been a busy evening and, as you say, I really need some rest."

"My God, Rhian," Alasdair whispered. "You're a stranger. I don't know you any more."

He opened the door, then shut it quietly behind him. The latch's soft catching was more terrible than the loudest bang.

She closed her eyes against a fresh welling of tears.

That's all right, Alasdair. I don't know me either.

CHAPTER THIRTY-SEVEN

Helfred found the letter from Marlan in the pocket of Ven'Martin's unlikely old coat.

After stripping the corpse and washing it free of blood and the voided wastes of violent death, he methodically inspected the discarded bloodstained clothing to see if he might find an explanation for this horrible event.

There had to be one. His uncle would never send a man of God to do murder. Ven'Martin had acted of his own wicked volition. Or perhaps he'd lost his mind. Or been a dupe. Yes. Someone else, Damwin or Kyrin most likely, had convinced Ven'Martin to attempt this heinous act. But it wasn't his uncle. It couldn't be.

And then his fumbling fingers touched the folded parchment.

Venerable Martin, my beloved servant in God, read the note. It was his uncle's exquisite handwriting. The hope of trickery was dashed. *I pray this finds you strong in faith and unblunted in purpose. Know that I trust you above all men. Indeed, you are as my own right hand, indispensable to the wellbeing of my body. Ven'Martin, Rhian's evil overwhelms God's light. Her corruption corrupts us. The Church of Rollin is in the shadows and, fought to a standstill, I am on my knees. Only you can save my soul. Only you can save God's Church and our sweet Ethrea from the scourge of this self-proclaimed queen. Rollin admonishes: it is sin to take a life. But I tell you as God's prolate: he who takes life in his service is blessed. Ven'Martin, I beg you. Save God's Church from this wicked woman. Save Ethrea. Save me.*

After some span of time, some uncounted passing minutes, Helfred refolded the letter and pushed it into the pocket of his chaplain's robe. Surrounding him in the chilly cellar, wrapped hams and cheeses and other perishable things.

If I touched them now they'd turn to stone.

Was he a fool, to feel so utterly betrayed? Ever since the clerica he'd known his uncle was . . . flawed. Why then was he bludgeoned with grief to learn how deeply those flaws had scarred him?

Because ambition is one thing. It can be tempered. Channelled correctly it can even work for good. But a man of God who'd suborn murder to serve his own ends . . .

Odd, but if Marlan had attempted Rhian's life himself he doubted the pain would burn so fierce.

It's the corruption of Ven'Martin that makes me want to weep. The twisting of his faith and the curdling of his soul.

He pressed cold lips to Ven'Martin's colder brow. "God forgive you, brother," he murmured. "You were sorely led astray."

He'd never dressed a corpse in a winding-sheet before. That was the work of Ethrea's devouts. Chaplains came after, to bless and sanctify the body with the right words and incense. He didn't even have a proper winding-sheet to hand, only clean bedlinens from the inn's housekeeper. Plain cotton, wearing thin here and there.

A small sin, not to give the best sheets to the dead.

It was a clumsy business, tearing them into long strips and binding Ven'Martin's lax, soul-fled body. The knife-slit in his belly was so obscure. An inch wide, no wider. One little incision and his life had leaked away.

Why did I think this death would have a greater fanfare?

It felt like a mercy to cover Ven'Martin's face with clean cotton. Faceless assassins were less frightening. Less . . . real.

Is not God omnipotent? Is he not a force against evil? How then did evil come to touch us so close? How have two sworn men of God smirched their souls so completely and brought such disrepute down on his Church? Is God powerless to prevent such infamy? If he is, what does that mean? Have I devoted my life to a phantom? An empty shell?

Aching with misery, steeped in despair and harsh questions without answers, Helfred knelt on the chilly flagstoned cellar floor and tried to console himself with prayer. His muscles stiffened. His fingers numbed. The tip of his nose felt like a chip of ice. But prayer had deserted him. All he had left was bitter disappointment.

When men of God turn to evil what hope is there for the world?

Then a warm breeze stirred the hanging hams and cheeses. A faint voice whispered . . . *Helfred. Don't lose heart.*

He was so startled he fell over.

"Who said that?" he demanded, flailing like an infant, or a turtle on its back. "Who's there?"

Helfred, have courage. Follow your convictions and keep the faith.

His fingers found the edge of the trestle table set up for Ven'Martin. He pulled himself to his feet and stared round the cavernous cellar. "Who *is* that? Is it—are you—*Hettie*?"

Helfred, you mustn't abandon this cause. If good men turn from a righteous fight how then can good hope to triumph?

"Hettie or not, I demand you show yourself! Immediately!"

You've a purpose, Helfred. You've great work to do. A great sacrifice to make so God might not be defeated.

The voice was much fainter now. He could hardly hear it. "What do you mean, a great sacrifice?" He spun around, trying to see every corner of the cellar at once. "And who could possibly defeat God? God is God, there is no greater power—is there? *Is* there?"

But he was alone. Alone with a dead man and cheeses and hams.

"God have mercy," he muttered. "I'm losing my mind."

He remained in the cellar with Ven'Martin, praying.

God, show me the path to take. Show me how to serve you. Show me what I must do to save my uncle from the darkness. Show me how I can return him to your light.

He heard no more strange voices. No more breezes stirred the cellar. His heart, so disquieted, found its peace again. And when the innkeeper came down to him with a message that it was just on dawn and he was wanted by the queen and her council . . . he knew without a whisper of doubt what it was he had to do.

"What?" said Duke Edward. "Man, are you *salt-brained*?"

"Edward," murmured Rhian. "Temper your language."

"Forgive me, Your Majesty," said Duke Edward, pink with emotion. "But Chaplain Helfred is salt-brained if he thinks to march into Marlan's clutches and survive the encounter with a whole skin!"

Helfred stood before Their Majesties and the dukes, who were seated round the public dining room's long table. The queen looked sleepless, the king like a bow-string pulled too tight. They sat side by side . . . yet separated by a distance as wide as the river.

Zandakar stands between them. He is hazardous, like rocks.

He cleared his throat. "Your Grace, you may call me *salt-brained,* you may call me *daffy-doddled,* you may call me any uncouth epithet you like. But the fact remains that Venerable Martin lies dead beneath us in a cellar. He must be returned to the bosom of the Church so he might be reposed and prayed for and buried."

"Buried with holy rites?" said King Alasdair. "Within the precinct of a church? *Ven'Martin?* Are you *mad,* Chaplain, to offer such an insult to Her Majesty's face?"

The three dukes were glaring, grossly affronted by the idea of Ven'Martin receiving any kind of grace. Clearly they wished him tossed nameless in a deep hole dug by labourers in an unknown field.

He kept his hands clasped loosely before him. "Your Majesties . . . Your Graces. I appreciate this is a difficult morning. I imagine we have all struggled overnight with Ven'Martin's death. However—"

"However?" said Duke Rudi, pugnacious. He was like a Keldravian fighting dog, overmuscled and swift to the throat. A good man for Rhian to have on her side but wearisome when it came to tempering with common-sense. "There's no *however* here, Chaplain. Ven'Martin was a conniving would-be killer, sent here by Marlan to butcher Ethrea's queen. He was *filth,* man. He was—"

"Your Grace, please," said Helfred quickly. "While we must deplore Ven'Martin's actions it's not your place or mine to condemn him out of hand. He's a son of the Church. Only the Court Ecclesiastica can assess his culpability."

"And who is it heads your precious Court?" sneered Duke Adric. "I believe it's the prolate, is it not? I think I see a problem there, Chaplain, since it was the prolate who sent Ven'Martin to kill the queen."

God save me, God save me. The letter from Marlan burned in his pocket. If he showed it to them they would never let him go. They would use it to bring Marlan crashing down from his great height . . . and in doing so might well destroy the Church too.

I cannot allow that. God's Church must survive.

"That is what Ven'Martin said," he replied. "But the word of a dead man is not proof, Your Grace. I always suspected Ven'Martin's devotion to my uncle was of an order inclining him to . . . rashness. When I return his body to the capital I shall request an audience with the Court Ecclesiastica and tell them of his claim. The Court will investigate. It's empowered to judge even a prolate. If I can convince them my uncle has—has—"

"Lost his reason and run amok?" said the king. "You're a fool, Helfred. Marlan will deny everything and the Court will never support you over him."

"Helfred . . ." Rhian cleared her throat. "You can't go. The Court Ecclesiastica has declared you anathema. If you show your face to its members or your uncle . . ."

He'd known it from the moment she'd said Ven'Artemis had come for him, but even so the words were a blow. *Cut off from the comfort of the Church . . .*

Echoing faintly in his memory, that strange, unknown voice: *Helfred, have courage. Follow your convictions and keep the faith.*

Was it Mr Jones' Hettie . . . or just his own frightened heart? And did it really matter? The advice was sound.

He bowed. "Your concern for me is humbling, Majesty. But how can I ask the people of Ethrea to defy Marlan and his Court if I'm not prepared to defy them myself?"

She had no answer. She knew he was right.

"Besides," he added, "Ven'Martin's body cannot remain in the cellar. Nor can you take it with you when you leave. You must distance yourself from what transpired last night, Majesty."

"I can't pretend it didn't happen, Helfred! I can't pretend I didn't—" Uncomfortable silence, as Rhian fought to retain her composure. "I can't pretend."

Poor child. If only he had time to counsel her. "Majesty, of course not. But neither can you allow this tragedy to divert you from your greater purpose."

"He's right," said Duke Rudi. "Old Scooton has a chapel and a bevy of venerables who support the queen. Why can't we—"

"*No*, Rudi," said Rhian. "Telling Old Scooton's venerables who Ven'Martin is and how he died would create more problems than I have time to solve. And we can't see him buried under false pretences. Not only would it be wrong, we'd be undone soon enough. We've sworn the innkeeper and his staff to silence but news like this finds a way to spread."

As the dukes muttered amongst themselves, and Rhian exchanged dark looks with the king, Helfred took a step closer to her.

"Your Majesty, you must see there is no other course of action. Let me return to Kingseat with Ven'Martin and do what my vows demand must be done for his soul."

"Oh, Helfred . . ." Rhian sat forward, eyes intent. More than ever she looked her father's daughter. "I've already kept you safe from Marlan once. Now you want me to hand-deliver you?"

"I want you to be a great queen," he said. "Your father spent his life keeping state and Church apart. You've defied Marlan to see that legacy kept alive. Queen Rhian, this is Church business. It's my spiritual duty to take Ven'Martin home and see that he's prayed for so his soul might be cleansed. If you are the queen you think yourself to be, you'll not presume to interfere with that."

As her council gasped and muttered Rhian gave him a faint, mocking smile. "And there speaks the Helfred who once drove me to distraction. I was beginning to wonder where he'd gone." She glanced at her council. "Gentlemen, I would have private speech with my chaplain."

Reluctantly obedient, the king and the dukes withdrew. As soon as they were alone Rhian leapt up from her chair and began to pace her makeshift council chamber.

"I could forbid you leaving, you know," she said, glar-

ing at him. "I could truss you hand and foot and toss you
into that wretched peddler's van. I could tie you to the tail
of Zandakar's horse."

He nodded. "Yes, Your Majesty. You could. But you
won't."

"Oh, won't I?" she demanded. "For a pimpled, outcast
chaplain you're terribly sure of yourself."

He touched his freshly pustuled chin, suddenly self-
conscious. "Ursa gave me some ointment. It doesn't seem
to work."

She banged her fist on the table in passing. "This isn't
only about Ven'Martin's soul, is it? You think you can
save your uncle."

Yes indeed, she was her father's daughter. Shrewd. Astute. A keen judge of men's hearts.

"If I say yes, will you call me disloyal?"

"For not abandoning your family? No. Of course I
won't. But Helfred—" Rhian stopped her pacing. "You
have to know he can't be redeemed."

"I do not know that, Majesty. Nor do you. And to claim
otherwise is arrogance unbecoming to the Crown."

Her chin came up, her eyes glittering with temper.
"Lecturing me again, Helfred?"

"Indeed, Majesty. When it's warranted."

Hipshot against the table she considered him, brooding. "You can't honestly believe you've a hope of swaying
Marlan from his course against me."

"Your Majesty . . ." He spread his hands wide. "I honestly believe God wants me to try. And since it seems
we're in a new age of miracles—who knows? With his
grace I might yet avert a bloody, destructive confrontation
between you."

"You might. But I doubt it. And I can't give you unlimited time to try. The longer I stay here the more dangerous is my position. I *must* push on to Kingseat, Helfred. I must reclaim the castle and take hold of my crown." Rhian shivered. "Or lose it, I fear. I am endangered by more than Marlan. The great nations will not stay their hands forever. I'm amazed they've stayed them for as long as this."

"They respected your father, Majesty," he said. "As his daughter, they respect you. And whatever you wrote to them, they respect that."

The look she gave him was almost grateful. "I'll stay here one more day, Helfred. You have that long to change your uncle's mind. But by noon tomorrow I will be on the road for Kingseat."

One meagre day? It wasn't enough. But he could see she'd not grant him more. He bowed. "Majesty."

She began pacing again, like a high-mettled mare constrained in its box. "You must know meeting with Marlan might put you in danger of your life. I've already killed one man. I don't think I could live with myself if—" She flung him an angry, anguished glance. "I might not like you, Helfred, but I don't want you dead!"

"I'm aware of the danger, Your Majesty," he said. "I cannot let it deter me."

"Damn you," she said quietly. "I liked it far better when you were just a prosing bore." She sighed. "Very well. Go."

He was at the door when her voice stopped him. "No. Wait."

He turned. "Majesty?"

Her searing pain had been thrust back into hiding. She looked like a queen again, austere and self-controlled.

"If you can be foolhardy, so can I. When you see Marlan give him a message. Provided of course he doesn't immediately throw you in a cell."

"Certainly, Majesty. What should I tell him?"

"That I have no desire for conflict between us. For Ethrea's sake, for the sake of its Church and its people, I am willing to forgive his crimes against me. He can't remain prolate, but I'll take no action beyond that. In the name of peace I'll see him discreetly and comfortably retired. He'll want for nothing, he has my word."

He blinked. "Majesty, you are . . . magnanimous."

"No, Helfred, I'm practical," she said, grimacing. "No good purpose is served in airing *this* dirty linen. I'll have troubles enough convincing the ambassadors I'm capable of keeping their masters' many interests safe without making my first act as queen a declaration of war on the Church."

It was a bold move. A clever move. "Your Majesty, I'll tell him. But I must be honest with you . . . I doubt he'll agree."

A small smile, unsettling and most definitely unamused, curved Rhian's lips. "Well, Helfred, that's his choice. And his misfortune if he's stupid enough to turn me down."

It took him less than half an hour to be ready for the journey. During that brief time he hid Marlan's letter in the peddler's van. Faith in God he might have, but to take such incriminating evidence with him to his uncle's palace would be the act of a naïve fool.

Marlan's words are blazoned on my heart. If I must I'll quote them to him and he will know I do not lie.

The innkeeper gave him one of the inn's light carts and a carthorse for the journey. Together they saw Ven'Martin's body placed in the back and covered with burlap to confound curious, prying eyes.

With a puffing grunt Helfred climbed onto the driving seat, picked up the reins and slapped them on the sleepy horse's rump. By Rhian's order no-one gathered to wish him godspeed. His departure was to be discreet and unremarkable. But as the cart rumbled forward he looked over his shoulder and up at the inn . . . and caught a glimpse of Rhian at a window, her face half hidden by its muslin curtain. When she realised that he'd seen her she nodded once. So regal.

The last thing he saw, as he left the inn's courtyard, was her small strong hand pressed against the window's glass.

Nearly three hours after leaving Old Scooton he reached his final fork in the road. Continue straight ahead and he'd end up in the capital. Turn left and cross the Ethling riverlet and he'd find himself at the Prolates Palace gates. He turned left, his heart thudding. The breeze was brisk and salty, coming in off the distant harbour. It was still full of ships. Trade continued unaffected, it seemed.

That will please Her Majesty. God willing, once Marlan's dealt with, life will swiftly regain its balance.

Thanks to the duchy's soldiery the road was clear now, so close to the castle and his uncle's palace. For most of his journey he'd had to push his way through gathered and gathering crowds. Word had spread from Old Scooton that Rhian was coming. Her eager subjects had plagued him with questions, clamouring to know if she came close behind.

He'd pleaded ignorance and forged his slow way onwards.

Does Marlan realise the depth and breadth of her support? Does he understand how the people love her? Or does his own hate blind him to the truth?

He was terribly afraid his uncle didn't realise, or if he did simply didn't care. And if that was the case, what hope did he have of making Marlan accept Rhian's unexpected and generous offer?

Dear God, give me wisdom. Dear God, give me strength. Please let me reach him and turn this kingdom from the brink.

There were six Kingseat soldiers at the Palace's rear gates. Never in its history had soldiers been stationed there, barring the entrance of God's chosen servants. For a moment he could only sit in the cart, blinking furiously to clear his blurred vision.

"What do you want, Chaplain?" their commander demanded. "Do you have official business or have you come to gawk?"

It was on the tip of his tongue to reprimand the man. But that would be foolish, so he breathed out his offence and let his face settle into a kind, harmless smile.

"God bless you, soldier. I'm Chaplain Henry from Daylesbury parish. I'm come to serve a spell in the palace archives. God bless me, it's an honour. Would you look at the beautiful building? I declare I'm so moved I could lead us all in prayer right this mome—"

"Get on," said the soldier, waving him past.

"God *bless* you, soldier," said Helfred, and hurried through the gates before the man changed his mind.

In the palace stableyard he took a young groom aside. "Stand with this cart, man," he told the lay-servant. "Don't let it out of your sight . . . and don't look in the back. If anyone asks it's the prolate's private business. God bless you and keep you. Disobey my instructions, you'll imperil your soul."

"Cha—cha—chaplain!" the groom stuttered. "I won't!"

Walking into his uncle's ecclesiastical residence was the most terrifying thing Helfred had ever done. Every breath was a prayer, every step a beseechment.

God give me strength. God give me courage. God give me the wisdom to prevail. God give me strength . . .

He was so scared he wanted to vomit.

His arrival was noticed immediately, of course. Doubtless he was notorious by now. As he entered through the palace's elaborate doors, as he crossed its vast marble entrance hall, as he trod the sweeping staircase up to the first floor, hostile gazes and agitated whispers followed him. He ignored them. He'd known he'd have no friends in this place, not even one or two clandestine supporters. Venerables and chaplains, modestly robed devouts, they all glared and muttered and kissed their thumbs at his passing. Prayer beads rattled. He wished he could rattle his own.

He found his uncle in the library.

"So," said Marlan, standing before his enormous oak desk. "My prodigal nephew is returned to the fold." He extended his hand, expecting it to be kissed.

Helfred halted before him and did not kiss his hand. "Your Eminence."

The strain of the past weeks showed plainly upon his uncle's face. Marlan's cheeks had lost flesh and his blood-shot eyes were sunken. Ringed with shadows. He looked unwell.

I have done this to him. In helping Rhian I have brought him so low. But I have no regrets. God, give me strength.

His uncle's outstretched hand clenched into a fist. The holy ring on his finger winked in the afternoon sunshine filtering through the tall, leadlight window.

"Why are you here, Helfred? Do you come for my forgiveness? If so, you have wasted a journey. I told you once, our blood-tie will not absolve you from blame." He lowered his arm, eyes burning with hate. "You traitorous lickspittle little turd, you must have the intellect of a flea to come into my palace. After all you've done? With anathema pronounced upon you? The intellect of a *flea*."

God give me strength . . . "Your Eminence, I come with an offer of clemency from Her Majesty."

"Her Majesty?" said his uncle. A small muscle flicked beside his spider-veined right eye. He was surprised. He was waiting for news of her death.

"Yes, Prolate," said Helfred, his mouth shrivelled dry. "Cease your unlawful opposition to her reign and she will forgive your many manifest sins. You will be permitted to retire from the prolateship and—"

"She forgives me?" said Marlan, incredulous. "Rhian the harlot? Rhian the whore? That unrepentant disobedient degenerate bitch forgives *me*? And you presume to bring her insult *yourself*?"

"It is no insult, Marlan, but a generous—"

His uncle's brutal hand struck him across the face, its ring splitting his cheek wide where once before a whip had cut it. Scarlet pain blinded him and blood slicked his skin.

"Are you *deranged*?" said Marlan, his hand raised for a second blow.

God, I asked for wisdom . . . "She is Eberg's heir, Prolate." Rollin's love, his face *hurt*. "Released from her wardship and married legitimately, by me. I was not pronounced anathema then so you have no grounds to deny her estate. You cannot supplant her, Marlan. She is beyond your—"

With a wordless snarl Marlan lunged towards him, a killing rage in his face. Helfred leapt back, one arm raised in fruitless self-defence.

"Ven'Martin's dead, Uncle!" he cried. "Your plot to murder Rhian has failed!"

Marlan halted. *"Dead?"* The furious colour drained from his cheeks. "What do you mean? How is he dead?"

God give me courage . . . "Her Majesty killed him as he tried to kill her . . . on your orders."

"She *killed* him?" For a moment it seemed as though Marlan might stagger, might lose his balance and have to seek support. Then he rallied, his spine stiffening. "I gave no such orders," he said, turning away. "Helfred, you cannot save yourself with wild accusations. You—"

"I've read the letter, Uncle," he said, his voice perilously close to breaking. *He never once saw the face of God. All he saw was his own ambition.* "I have it in a safe place. If you refuse Rhian's offer to stand down as prolate I will be forced to make it public. I do not want to do that.

I give you my word it will never see the light of day, provided you do as Rhian desires. You can retire to the family estate. I'll come with you. We can pray together for as long as you require. Months. Years. I don't care. You've lost your way but I can help you find the light again. The light of God's love and his merciful grace. All you must do is accept the truth: Rhian is your queen, the rightful queen of Ethrea."

"She is no queen of mine!" spat his uncle and turned. *"Sergeant! To me!"*

The library's closed door flew open and a Kingseat garrison sergeant came in, flanked by four soldiers. Their swords were unsheathed, the blades bright and sharp.

Caught between them, Helfred backed up to the nearest bookcase. "Please, Uncle, don't—"

"I am *Your Eminence* to you, cur!" Marlan snarled. "Sergeant!"

Helfred swallowed a moan. *Duke Edward was right. I was salt-brained to come here.* "Your Eminence, in Rollin's name, consider what you do next! Rhian is the lawful queen, all Ethrea knows it! And she is surrounded by signs and miracles. She—"

"Signs and miracles?" Marlan grabbed him, fingers clutching worn fabric, dragging his disowned nephew close. "I say these are *sorceries*. I say the bitch dabbles in foul unclean heresies. She is a polluted drab, Helfred. And you are polluted by your own mouth, supporting her. You are rotten refuse in the muck!"

God, God, give me strength . . . "There are no sorceries in Rhian's court. For you to claim so, Eminence, and deny innocent Ethreans the comfort of God because they would acknowledge the kingdom's true queen, that is a

grievous sin. Do not stain your soul so. Recant this untruth. Would you imperil yourself further in the name of
thwarted ambition?"

"You *lecture* me?" said his uncle, choked with disbelief. "You pustuled pimpled vomitous excrescence, you
dare?"

"I must, Marlan! I've come here to save you, to stop
you from—"

With a shout of rage his uncle hurled him to the floor
and began beating him about the face and head, open
slaps and fisted blows. The cut on his face opened wider,
spewing fresh blood.

"Prolate, have a care!" shouted the sergeant. "Dead
men are a poor source of information."

Close to mewling with fury Marlan staggered back.
Half sprawled across his desk, his habitual urbanity abandoned, he breathed like a winded bull as he struggled to
regain control.

Helfred, his body bright with pain, sat up slowly and
lowered his sheltering arms. *God. Dear God. I thought
you wanted me to come here. I thought you would help
me help him see the light . . .*

Marlan straightened. Now his face was chalk-white.
The tic beside his eye spasmed out of control. His eyes, so
sunken, blazed with unholy zeal.

"I know the bitch is in Old Scooton, Helfred. When
does she plan to ride into Kingseat?"

He made himself meet Marlan's frightening glare.
God, God. Have you abandoned me? "That is the queen's
business."

Marlan growled. "There is no queen in Ethrea."

Shakily, Helfred pushed to his feet. "There is. And you

will meet her. But you don't need me to tell you when Rhian will come. The people will tell you. Their cheers will bring this palace roof down upon your head."

"Really?" said Marlan. His smile was unnerving.

He couldn't help himself, then. *He is venal and hateful, but how can I call myself a chaplain and not try to save him?* "It's not too late, Marlan. End this. I will help you."

"It's already ended, you fool," said Marlan, and laughed. "Damwin and Kyrin's soldiers stand ten deep on the borders. If your precious Rhian should change her mind and try to turn back, she'll find herself cut off from the north and the treacherous duchies who've unwisely taken her side. She can only run forward now . . . into my embrace."

Memory assaulted him. Rhian on her knees in the clerica at Todding, her blue dress turning red with blood. His uncle's face, eyes gluttonous for her pain.

I have failed her. I have failed.

He turned, despairing. "Sergeant . . . uphold the law!"

"I am," the man said. "Prolate Marlan was appointed the kingdom's caretaker by the King's Council. The King's Council has not reversed that decision."

"There *is* no King's Council! He's thrown half of it in prison!"

"I threw traitors in prison, Helfred," Marlan said. "It's where traitors belong. Take him to the castle cells, Sergeant. Cast him with Linfoi and those other damned men. Let them tell him how he will be pulled apart and every sinew examined for evidence of his crimes. Let him wait in trepidation for my judgement to fall."

"Prolate," said the sergeant.

Two of the soldiers took Helfred by the arms. Almost weeping he tried to step forward but they restrained him. "Marlan, don't do this. In the name of all holy things, in the presence of the Living Flame, Rhian trucks with no sorcery. She *is* God's chosen queen. Turn your feet from this path of destruction that you tread. Open your heart to the message God sends you. It is not too late to admit you are *wrong*."

Marlan smiled. "Get him out of here, sergeant. Before I forget I am a peaceful man of God."

CHAPTER THIRTY-EIGHT

The kingseat soldiers dragged Helfred from the palace like a cat-killed rat. Heedless of his protests they tossed him into an enclosed wagon and drove him to the castle. As they hustled him inside through the imposing front doors he tried to tell them about Ven'Martin's abandoned body.

One of the soldiers cuffed him on the side of the head. "Shut your yap."

The casual violence was frightening. Before Eberg's death no soldier in Ethrea would have dreamed of striking a chaplain. They'd have thrown into prison any man who dared.

And now here they are throwing me into prison. The world is turned topsy-turvy. Dear God, put it to rights.

The castle echoed with an absence of people. The soldiers marched him through empty corridors, down empty staircases, past empty rooms. When he demanded to know what had happened to the royal staff he was cuffed so hard he saw a rainbow of lights. He didn't try to speak again.

The castle cells, disused for so many years, had been dug centuries before below the castle's ground level. No windows. No fresh air. Just darkness and despair.

His surly escort shoved him into a small cell lit by two smoking lamps hung high on hooks. It was already occupied. Two scarecrow men huddled each in a corner. A third lay on his side, his back to the world.

As the key turned in the door's lock behind him, such a dreadful, final sound, Helfred pressed his sleeve to his nose and mouth. The cell's floor was patchily covered in ancient, slimy straw. The stench was unspeakable.

"I know you," said one of the scarecrows. "You're Marlan's kin. Princess Rhian's personal chaplain. Helfred." His voice was a think croak, rusty with disuse . . . or screaming.

Helfred winced.

Do not think of screaming. Rhian is coming, she will get you out of here. Or Zandakar will, if she gives him the order. I'd like to see those guards slapping Zandakar on the head.

He peered at the speaker through the miserly gloom. He knew that voice . . . thought he knew that voice. "Lord—*Volant,* is it? The Duke of Arbat's man?"

The lord, gaunt and unshaven, nodded. "Volant. Yes."

Appalled, Helfred stared at him, afraid to take another step. Afraid of what he'd set foot in, this place was so grossly rank. Eberg's councillor looked terrible. His fine clothes, the satins and velvets of his rank, were stained and stinking. Rotting in places. His filthy hands were scabbed. Dried blood matted his beard and hair.

"Oh, my lord," he said. "It offends me mightily to see you brought so low. But you must take heart. All of you, take heart. Her Majesty is coming and as God is my witness, she will see you safely out of this place."

With a pained exhalation, Volant sat a little straighter. "Man, you're raving. Harley, d'you hear this? Marlan's sent us a madman to take the food from our mouths."

The man in the other corner stirred and looked up. Helfred nearly cried aloud, recognising him. Bluff and boisterous Lord Harley, stubbled and manhandled and sunk to extremity.

"My brother will hear of this," said Harley, the palest echo of his loud, rude self. "When Edward's told how I'm mistreated there will be rough words." A sob escaped him, and he covered his face with broken fingers. "Edward will send for me. You'd best be gone, knave."

Volant's gaze was contemptuously pitying. "You must excuse my lord Harley. He's not quite himself."

Perilously close to weeping, Helfred looked at the cell's third occupant. It must be Henrik Linfoi, the king's uncle. He was so still. Shadows covered him, and a threadbare blanket. Was the man living or dead?

If he's dead, God have mercy on the marriage. Helfred moved gingerly to him, and dropped to a crouch. "My Lord Henrik? I have word for you from the king."

Henrik Linfoi's eyes opened. "Eberg?" His voice was a mumble, the word slushing through split, swollen lips.

"No. Eberg is dead, my lord. Don't you remember?

Your nephew Alasdair is king now. He's married to Queen Rhian."

"You won't get sense from him," said Volant, with another wheezing laugh. "Lift that lice-infested rag they call a blanket and see what your precious uncle does to innocent men."

Helfred looked. His belly rolled, protesting. *When the king sees this he will lose all reason.*

"You're not lying, are you, or brain-fevered?" said Volant. "Eberg's stubborn brat is queen? She's made the Linfoi cub her king? Marlan said it but who'd believe that bastard? He'd say anything to put himself in power."

Helfred frowned and dropped the bloodstained blanket over Henrik Linfoi's maltreated body. "I'm a man of God, my lord. I do not lie."

"Ha. Your uncle calls himself a man of God. Here is his handiwork." Volant sneered. "Scriptural, is it?"

With a cracking of his joints, Helfred pushed to his feet. "I have no words for what this is, My Lord."

"So. Rhian is queen," said Volant, brooding. "And my duke supports her?"

"Yours and Lord Harley's. And of course Lord Henrik's son, Ludo. He's been made Duke of Linfoi."

"While Damwin and Kyrin have sided with Marlan. I wish to God Rudi had done the same."

"You should not say so, my lord. The dukes of Meercheq and Hartshorn are in grave error." *And they're poised with their soldiers at duchy Kingseat's back. At Rhian's back. If Marlan should tell them to cross over their borders . . . if he should order them to raise arms against her . . .*

"Hold on to the contents of your stomach, Chaplain,"

said Volant. "If you hadn't noticed, it stinks enough in here."

"Indeed," said Helfred. "You should speak to the staff."

Lord Volant stared at him, then broke once more into that harsh, wheezing laughter. Then he started coughing. "A man of wit! Well, that won't last long." He waved a hand. "Might as well make yourself comfortable, Chaplain. Barring a miracle, I doubt you'll see the sun again."

Mouth pursed, skin crawling, Helfred picked his way across the unspeakable floor and lowered himself, wincing, to the wall opposite Lord Harley. The councillor from duchy Morvell muttered something incomprehensible; it seemed almost certain his mind was overturned.

Poor soul. Perhaps when he gets here Dexterity can heal him.

The cell was chilly, and there was no fourth blanket. He hunched himself inside his robe and let his chin sink onto his chest. His cut, beaten face was hurting abominably.

"We must not lose hope, my lords," he said, as though they'd asked his opinion. "When Queen Rhian comes to Kingseat she will put all to rights. We will be released from this dreadful place and you'll receive restitution for your sufferings."

"Who do you think to convince, Chaplain? Us or yourself?" said Volant. Then he grimaced. "Well, if she is coming it had better be soon or she'll come too late for Linfoi and Harley. Maybe too late for me. I've an ague in my chest. I'm coughing up blood." He hawked and spat into his hand, then showed the red-tinged sputum as though to prove the point.

God give me strength. I shall leave this place diseased . . .

"My lord, with God all things are possible," said Helfred. "You have not seen what I've seen, you have not been blessed with the sight of wonders performed in Rhian's name."

By a lowly toymaker, but I shan't be mentioning that.

A fervid light shone in Volant's muck-encrusted eyes. "You believe it, Chaplain? That Eberg's brat is the true queen of Ethrea? That she'll put right what's gone wrong?" His voice cracked. "That she has the support of God himself?"

Helfred let himself smile even though it hurt his face. "My lord, would I be here if I did not?"

Marlan stood in the palace stableyard, staring at Ven'Martin's cold unwrapped body. He'd dismissed the boy guarding the cart and no other servant was so rash as to approach. This was a private moment. He was privately enraged.

You let me down, Martin. You let the bitch kill you.

The slit in Martin's belly was small. Innocuous. A single knife-thrust. Clean. Restrained. No other signs of struggle. No bruises. Just one wound. There must be a great deal of damage within.

And Rhian inflicted it. Eberg's brat, adept with a knife? I did not expect it. I am . . . displeased.

His fingers clenched and unclenched. He longed for someone to strike.

So, Rhian. It is war between us. I was prepared to be magnanimous. I was prepared to let you live. But you have pricked me. You have drawn blood. So you shall have blood, girl. Blood until it chokes you. Blood until you drown.

He looked at nearby Idson and beckoned him closer with a raised eyebrow. Idson came. So well trained.

"Your men stand ready?"

"Prolate, they do."

"The runners on the road between here and Old Scooton. They stand ready?"

"Prolate, we will know when she makes her move towards us."

He turned his back on failed Ven'Martin. "She will avoid facing me for as long as she can. Instead she'll lead her misguided followers down into the city in the hopes of whipping up further support."

Idson scowled. "She'll not get that far. We'll cut off her access before she even—"

"No," said Marlan. "Let her come. I will be waiting for her with the Court Ecclesiastica. Her defiance has been public, Idson. Let her defeat be public also." He smiled. "Keep your men well out of sight. Once she and her rabble have set foot on Kingsway, close the army of Kingseat behind her. She'll not escape my judgement twice."

"Yes, Your Eminence," said Idson. "And if she should offer any resistance?"

That would be too much to hope for . . . "What do you think, Commander?"

Idson was pale, but he seemed resolute. "Princess Rhian is in defiance of the King's Council. She has not been crowned, she cannot call herself queen. If she offers my men violence they will draw their swords."

Marlan nodded. "Precisely. Without hesitation or regret. One last thing, Commander. The ambassadors' residences?"

"Secured, Eminence," said Idson. "I have men at their gates and in the streets of the ambassadorial district. Every ambassador is reported in his home. Not one will set foot past his door until your permission is given."

"Well done, Idson. You may go."

Alone with Ven'Martin, that bitter disappointment, Marlan considered his final move, his containment of the trading nations' ambassadors.

They would protest, vehemently. There would be angry words. Lofty letters. Threats of hot air. It would all come to nothing. They needed Ethrea to live.

They think they have power here. Tzhung-tzhungchai thinks it has power. Tzhung-tzhungchai is mistaken, as are they all. Rhian is mistaken. I am the power in the kingdom of Ethrea. The sooner they accept that, the happier they'll be.

Marlan swept from the stableyard, leaving Ven'Martin to rot.

Slowly, carefully, Rhian smoothed the creases from the note she and her council had just received, telling them of the soldiers massed along the duchy Kingseat borders with Hartshorn and Meercheq. More soldiers were stationed at the river-stations, halting every barge. All travellers attempting to cross out of Kingseat were being turned away. Travellers trying to get from Hartshorn and Meercheq into Kingseat were turned away too, after being told they could blame Rhian and her stubborn rebels. Families sundered . . . businesses put at risk . . .

She wondered if the men watching her could hear her

heart beating. Beyond the chamber's windows, dusk was fading fast. It was almost time for dinner. Her last council meeting before Kingseat capital would need to conclude soon.

She looked up, her face schooled to confidence. "It doesn't matter. We were never going to turn tail and run back north. Let Damwin and Kyrin sit on their arses at the borders. Better there than nipping at our heels."

Edward glared at her. "Except with one word from Marlan they'll not be at our heels, they'll be looking to rip out our *throats*. And not even you and your Zandakar can dance your knives through two ducal armies!"

"He's not my Zandakar," she told Edward, coldly. "Mind how you address me, Edward. Fear is no excuse for bad manners."

Edward leapt to his feet. "*Fear?* Are you calling me a *coward*?"

She sighed. "Oh, sit down, Edward. Don't be tiresome."

"He has a point, Rhian," said Alasdair, as Edward resumed his chair in affronted silence. "If Marlan decides interdict isn't enough . . ."

"He knows already it's not enough, but I don't believe he'll resort to open violence."

"Rhian!" said Alasdair, exasperated. "He sent a venerable to kill you!"

"In secret! Which is very different from sending an army," she retorted. "He's trying to intimidate me with a show of force. *And* he hopes to turn the people's hearts against me by interfering with their daily lives. It's a desperate move, gentlemen. One that's doomed to fail."

"You hope it's doomed," said Rudi. "But hope never

sharpened a sword, Your Majesty. You hope Marlan will leave Damwin and Kyrin stationed at their borders, and maybe he will, but even if he does—the fact remains they stand between us and the soldiers of Arbat, Morvell and Linfoi, who could be rallied to your cause if it proves they're needed. Leaving you and Zandakar aside, all we have is our small combined escort and it's woefully insufficient to protect us or force Kyrin's and Damwin's armies to stand down. Which means the people of this duchy are penned like sheep. And it won't take long for the sheep to start complaining. You will look powerless, Your Majesty . . . and so will start the beginning of the end."

Not if I can help it. She folded and refolded the wretched note. "There's still Kingseat's garrison. Every last man of them approved by my father and loyal to him. Loyal to my House."

"I'm sorry," said Alasdair. "I don't think we can count on them. You've not been crowned yet and you're a woman. These are soldiers, not scholars or lawyers. They see the world simply. Even if some of them do support you, Rhian, we can't assume they'll draw swords on their fellow guards."

She tossed the note on the table before it shredded in her fingers. "You're probably right. But as I said, it *doesn't matter.* Because even if I *could* gather more soldiers to my banner I tell you plainly, gentlemen, *I wouldn't.* I will *not* have a pitched battle between ducal armies. Ethrean against Ethrean? It's unthinkable. A civil war in my name would only prove every wicked thing Marlan says to destroy me. I might as well hand him my knife and invite him to stab me himself."

Her words made them flinch, as she intended.

Beside her, Alasdair jabbed his quill-point into the sheet of paper before him. Adric kept his gaze on the table but she could tell he was in wild disagreement. He was such a hothead. His father and Edward exchanged looks.

"Well?" she said, challenging them. "You're my council. Counsel me. Am I *wrong*?"

"No," sighed Rudi. "Your Majesty, you're not wrong. If we must be at war we need to ensure it's a war of words, not swords and pikestaffs. Our best weapon is the people's love for you and their belief that you are God's choice for the crown."

"What would seal this for us is another miracle," said Adric. "Maybe two. Or three. In the right place, at the right ti—"

"*No,*" she said. "It's out of the question. Mr Jones is not well enough for any more miracles."

"He's been resting for days now," said Adric, undaunted. "Physicked round the clock. Surely—"

She banged her fist on the table. "Are you *deaf* all of a sudden, Adric? Or so lost to your duty you would argue beyond your place? Have I erred in your elevation? Are you too green to be a duke?"

"He's only saying what the rest of us are thinking!" said Rudi, defensive. "Jones might be our only hope of—"

"And what about me?" she said. "I thought *I* was our hope. Mr Jones has been invaluable but *I* am Ethrea's queen. If I can't rule without a toymaker as my court fool, bursting into flames to amuse the crowds and distract them from the fact I'm a lowly inadequate *woman,* then clearly I don't deserve to wear the crown!"

"That's not what we're saying, Your Majesty," Edward murmured.

"Yes it is, Edward." Rhian slumped in her chair. "And I'm saying it too. Once this is over, if the crown is still mine, it must *be* mine. I must have *earned* it. It's not enough to be Eberg's daughter. It's not enough that Mr Jones bursts into flame. *I* have to prove I'm worthy of ruling. I have to prove I deserve to be queen. So. Tomorrow morning I'm going home to Kingseat capital and I will prove exactly that. And when I am in my castle, with my standard flying over its battlements, the soldiers *and* the people will know their queen is on her throne. They will know there is peace in Ethrea. They will know their world is safe once more. *Then* shall I entertain the ambassadors and they too will know they have nothing to fear."

"And what about Marlan?" said Alasdair, his arms folded. "If you think he'll meekly hand you the crown without a word of objection—"

"You don't know he won't!" she said. "I have faith in Helfred. He may yet find a way to persuade his uncle that the time has come to stand aside. God knows he's persuasive. He persuaded me not to kill him any number of times!"

The look he gave her smouldered. "Letting Helfred go back to the capital was foolish and short-sighted. Either he'll convert to his uncle's cause or his uncle will find some way of exploiting him to harm you and I fear you are so tender you'll throw yourself away for—"

"Gentlemen," she said, standing. "His Majesty and I have private matters to discuss. Be so good as to withdraw. We will leave for Kingseat capital at dawn."

The dukes filed out in silence, their faces averted. The door closed behind them.

She turned on him. "Alasdair, are you *trying* to destroy their confidence in me?"

"Of course not," he said, and shoved out of his chair. "I just want you to think before—"

"Think? My God, I do nothing *but* think! I have so many thoughts chasing round in my head I'm in danger of losing my mind altogether!"

"Then perhaps instead of thinking you should talk!" he retorted. "Talk to me. Your husband. The man you made king."

"Would there be any purpose? You disagree with every choice I make! We don't have conversations, we have running arguments!" She clutched the back of her chair and watched him stamp around the room. "Nothing I do is right as far as you're concerned. Every decision I make is *wrong*. I was wrong to trust Zandakar, I was wrong to learn the *hotas,* I was wrong to send Helfred home, I was—"

"God *save* me!" shouted Alasdair. "You stupid wench! Can't you see I'm *scared* for you?"

"Well," she said, unsteadily. "That was a tender declaration."

He crossed the carpet in three swift steps, seized her arms and dragged her out from behind the table. In his eyes, behind the anger, something frantic struggled for release.

"I'm scared for you, Rhian," he said, his voice close to breaking. "We've been married scant weeks. I've made love to you twice. You're my *wife* and you won't let me protect you. What kind of a husband doesn't protect his wife? What kind of a king doesn't keep his queen safe?"

"Oh, Alasdair. Tell me, truthfully. If our positions were

reversed. If you were the lawful ruling king of Ethrea, and you had married me and made me your queen, and somebody tried to take your crown away. Would you let *me* protect *you*? Would you hide behind my skirts?"

"But Rhian, that's—"

"*No.* It's *not* different. The crown is neither male nor female, Alasdair. The crown is itself—and whoever wears it must stand alone. By blood and birthright I am Ethrea's queen. You are king by marriage. You will always stand behind me. Accept that now, once and for all, or walk away from me . . . and I'll rule alone."

"You'd do that?" he whispered. "You'd let me go?"

She nodded. "Yes. I'd have no choice."

A harsh, heart-pounding silence. Alasdair walked to the window and pulled the curtain aside. "I wouldn't let you."

"*You'd* have no choice."

He let his head rest against the casement and stared into the darkness beyond the glass. "Do you suppose Henrik's still alive?"

"I hope so."

"And Helfred?"

"I can't imagine Marlan would murder his own sister's son."

"And I'm afraid there's little our good prolate wouldn't do, now he's had a taste of power."

He sounded . . . defeated. Softly she walked to him and pressed her cheek against his back. She could feel his heart, racing too fast. "You're forgetting something important, my love. Marlan may be the prolate but I have God on my side."

He tensed. "Rhian—"

"Alasdair, I'm serious!" She stepped back, and tugged him round to face her. "From the beginning I've been sent signs, given portents. I was given *Dexterity,* and his miracles. I was given Zandakar, who's twice saved my life. I have to believe God *wants* me to be queen."

"Maybe God does want it," said Alasdair. "But God doesn't always get everything he wants. Sin exists, Rhian. Terrible crimes are committed. God can't want that, but . . ." He shrugged. "Still, they happen."

"And when I am crowned queen, and we are happy in our castle, I will devote my life to righting those wrongs. But first I must reach my castle, Alasdair, and to do that I need you. I need you to trust me. If my own husband won't trust me, why should my kingdom?"

So gently, he kissed her. "I do. I trust you."

She met his gaze steadily, though her belly churned. "Words are easily come by, Alasdair. I'll believe it when you show me. Speak to me in another council meeting as you did here tonight and I'll ban you from attending for the rest of your life. Do I make myself clear?"

For the longest time he looked at her. She was no longer able to read his eyes. They were blank, like shuttered windows. *Oh God. Oh Papa.* Then he kissed her again, and her own heart resumed beating.

"As you say, Your Majesty," he said, faintly smiling. "Now shall we find some supper? Or would you rather go straight to bed?"

They were ready to leave Old Scooton just after dawn. It was an anxious Edward who came to fetch her from the dining room. He was a bluff man, but a good one. Never since pledging his loyalty had he spoken of his brother

Harley, paying Marlan's price for his support of a queen. Nor had he once treated her like a wayward child, even though he was old enough to be her father.

"All's done, Majesty," he said, standing in the doorway. "We can ride out at your pleasure."

"Good, Edward. Thank you." She looked down at herself, at her worn boy's clothing. "I wonder if I should change into a dress?" she mused. "Marlan might fall down in a spasm if he sees me attired like a king."

The thinnest of smiles curved Edward's lips. "We can only hope."

That made her laugh . . . and all of a sudden, she felt a lot better. *I wanted this, after all. I wanted it. I fought for it. God help me, I killed for it. Am I going to shy away from it now?*

"I'll be there directly, Edward," she told her duke. "And Edward—"

He straightened out of his bow. "Majesty?"

"Thank you. Accepting me as your sovereign hasn't been easy, I know. But you've honoured the law. You've honoured right above ambition. Assuming I'm still queen by the end of the day, I promise I'll not forget it."

He cleared his throat, roughly. "This is God's will, Your Majesty. You're Eberg's daughter. If your name was Robert instead of Rhian none of this would be happening. And you've shown us all that you're pluck to the backbone. I follow you gladly, and so will my House."

"Thank you, Edward. That means a great deal."

"As for marrying Linfoi," added Edward. "You made the right choice. I only offered Shimon because I didn't have anyone else. Never thought you'd choose him. He's a little boy . . . and a pain in the arse."

That surprised a shout of laughter from her. "Oh, Edward! That's outrageous!"

"I know," he said, grinning. "But it's true." He sobered. "I'll tell the king to expect you."

The door closed behind him and she was alone. She looked around the plain panelled dining room, witness to a thousand passing travellers. It wasn't a chapel but it would have to do. She knelt, and bowed her head.

"I don't have Helfred to lead the Litany," she murmured. "And believe it or not, God, it doesn't feel right to say it without him. But if you love me, never tell him I said so."

A warm silence settled over her, easing the tension singing through her bones.

"God, you sent Zandakar to save me and Dexterity to light my way. I have to believe that means I can be queen, that I can be a *good* queen, even with my myriad faults. Today I'll face my greatest test. My greatest enemy. A man who wishes me such ill. A man who professes to speak with your voice, to interpret your wishes. He's a liar. We both know that. Please, I beg you, let the world know it too."

The warm silence cradled her. She felt for a moment like a little girl again, settled on her father's lap with his strong arms around her, holding her close and safe with love.

Tears filled her eyes. "Oh, Papa, I miss you. And Ranald. And Simon. How can the sun rise on a world without you in it?"

For one dark moment it seemed the resurrected loss would overwhelm her, just when she needed her bloody-minded stubbornness most. Then she felt, for an instant, lips pressed against her brow. Heard a distant voice whisper: *Be strong, Rhian. Be unafraid.*

"*Mama?*" she gasped. Lurching to her feet again, she stared around the room. It was empty. No distant voice answered. She was alone . . . and it was time to leave.

Stepping out to the inn's rear courtyard, her breath was stolen by the faces waiting there. Alasdair. Edward. Rudi. Adric. Her stalwart council, a new family of a sort. Waiting with them, the miracle that was Dexterity, weak and unsteady on his feet, supported by his tart friend Ursa whose astringent advice had helped her so much.

And Zandakar. Oh, Zandakar. Her strange friend. Her unlikely saviour. The biggest mystery she'd ever met.

Behind them, the rest of her travel weary company. Soldiers and ducal retainers, plain people of Ethrea, whose simple unquestioning loyalty humbled her. What she did, she did for them.

She had no great words. A stirring speech was beyond her. All she could do was smile, her fisted hand pressed hard to her heart.

"God bless you all," she said, her voice catching in her throat. "Let's ride to Kingseat, shall we? We have unfinished business there."

CHAPTER THIRTY-NINE

By the time it reached Kingseat capital, Rhian's royal party had become a people's army.

The citizens of Old Scooton were the first to join. Led by three of the township's venerables and its entire council, the men, women and children of Old Scooton abandoned their fields, their homes, their shops, the schoolroom. On foot and on horseback, on donkeys and in carts, they fell into step behind the soldier escort and ducal retainers, shouting and laughing, fierce in their love.

"Oh, Alasdair," Rhian whispered. "Should I send them home? If even one should get hurt on my behalf . . ."

"Send them home?" Riding close beside her, he took her hand and held it tightly. "You'd break their hearts. They adore you, Rhian. You are their queen and they've made themselves your champions. You can't send them home. They are the best weapon you'll ever have against Marlan and his lies."

He was right. She knew it. And to prove it further, as they continued the journey from Old Scooton to Kingseat capital, more and more of duchy Kingseat's people rushed to swell the ranks of her retinue. Venerables, chaplains, farmers, teachers, grocers, chandlers, fresh-faced mothers and grey-haired goodfathers, all lining the roads and laneways of duchy Kingseat to see her, to shout her name, to swear their allegiance to Rhian, Eberg's daughter. As the royal progress swept by them they swept along with it, determined that Rhian would be their queen.

It seemed she'd been granted another miracle.

The shouting woke Dexterity, sleeping fitfully in the peddler's van.

"What is it? What's happening?" he mumbled, sitting up. "Ursa? Are we there?"

"Not yet," she said, sitting on the bench reading a book. She turned the page. "Go back to sleep, Jones."

"Sleep?" He scrubbed his hands across his stubbled face. "Who can sleep with that racket? And anyway, I've been sleeping for days."

"And you'll sleep for days more if I've anything to say on it." She put the book down. "Did you see yourself in the mirror this morning? Death warmed over sideways, that's what you look like."

And what he felt like, despite Ursa's nonstop physicking, but he wasn't about to tell her that. "I'm fine. I'm much better."

She snorted. "You're not dead, Jones. It's not the same thing."

No, it wasn't, but if he agreed with her she'd only take that for permission to continue her aggressive care of him. He wasn't ungrateful . . . but he wasn't used to her hovering, either. Wasn't used to the fear in her eyes. It was horribly unsettling, and he'd had enough unsettlement for now.

Pushing his blanket aside, he coaxed his feet off the sleeping-shelf and onto the floor. The din outside the van was extraordinary.

"What *is* that, Ursa? Who's making that noise?"

"We've picked up a few strays along the road."

"A few? Sounds more like half the duchy."

"You're not far wrong," she said. "The people have rallied to Rhian's cause."

He felt a burst of relief, warm as summer sun. "That's good. That's wonderful. She's winning the fight. Don't you think it's wonderful?" he added, seeing Ursa's frown.

"I suppose," she said. "But I can't help wondering

what'll happen when we do reach the capital. There's soldiers there, Jones. Marlan's there, with his cronies. I doubt he'll think Rhian and a rabble of subjects is anything to dance a jig about."

"He won't attack the people. If he does that, he's lost."

Ursa sighed. "He might not have to, Jones. One wrong word, one shove at the wrong time . . . trouble's started from less than that. I should know, I've had to stitch up the results." She picked up her book, smoothed a finger along its creased spine. "No sign of Hettie, I suppose?"

He shook his head, trying to ignore the clutch of panic in his belly. *She hasn't deserted me. I'm not alone. She did say she wasn't always able to come.* "No. But I'm sure I'll hear something if it's important enough."

"Of course you will," said Ursa . . . but she didn't sound convinced. Then she shook her head. "Rollin's mercy, Jones. Can you believe the things we've seen and done since the day you bolted into my workshop, convinced you were victim of some exotic brain-fever?"

Could he believe them? Hardly. He'd *lived* them and found himself half-convinced it was a dream.

And if Hettie's right the dream's not over yet. There's greater danger still looming on our horizon. The thought was enough to freeze his blood. *I'm exhausted, Hettie. Please don't ask me for anything more. Please let me go home to Otto and my toyshop. Let queens and kings and warriors shoulder Ethrea's burdens now.*

"What is it, Jones?" said Ursa, alarmed. "Are you having a spasm? Have the megrims returned?"

"No," he said, and managed a smile. "As you say, I'm still weary. I just need more rest."

He stretched out again and closed his eyes. Let the

sound of all those people cheering Rhian wash over him, in the hope they'd wash him into sleep.

But sleep eluded him. Instead his mind raced. Rhian. Marlan. Zandakar. Garabatsas. His burden of secrets. Truths concealed, as good as lies.

Please come back, Hettie. I don't know what to do.

Marlan stared at the hastily written note Idson had sent him, then at the garrison runner who'd brought it.

"An *army*? Is the man *serious*?"

The runner paled. "Eminence, I don't know what else you'd call it. There must be thousands, all trailing the qu— Princess Rhian and her retinue. They'll reach town within the hour."

"They'll do nothing of the sort," he snapped. "Return to Idson. Tell him to assemble his soldiery across Kingsway, near Castle Bridge. I will bring the Court Ecclesiastica to join him in due course. Rhian and her rabble will be apprehended before they set foot in the township, in full sight of the castle she will never enter again."

"Your Eminence," said the runner, and bolted.

Marlan climbed the stairs up to the Court chamber, seething.

That bitch would challenge me with rustics? With cowherds plucked shit-stinking from the byre? I should have beaten her harder. I should have beaten her to death.

He flung open the Court chamber doors, startling the assembled Ecclesiastica.

"Brothers!" he cried dramatically. "What we feared has come to pass. Blasphemous heretical Rhian has bewitched the populace. She and her rabble approach us now intending no good works. We must ride to meet her. We must throw her in the dust!"

As one man the Court Ecclesiastica stood. As one man it shouted: "God save Prolate Marlan! May Princess Rhian burn in hell!"

"Look, Rhian," said Alasdair, pointing. "Kingseat Castle. You're home."

She was already looking. She knew this rising road like her face in a mirror. Every turn, every dip, every stone, every tree. The avenue they rode along, running beside the Ethling riverlet, had been her playground from the time she sat on her first pony. She and her brothers had raced each other here through all the long hot summers of childhood.

She knew exactly when to turn her head so Kingseat Castle would fill her eyes.

Majestically cradled in the open space created by the river Eth's splitting in two, the hereditary seat of the House of Havrell dominated the land. Its grey and cream stone blocks were bathed in bright sunshine. Its dozens of windows winked in the light. Rhian swallowed tears to see it. Was it her imagination or could she smell her mother's gardens perfuming the breeze? No Havrell flag flew on the battlements, but she'd soon remedy that.

Some way ahead was Castle Bridge, that crossed the Ethling and led into the castle grounds. She had to breathe hard for a moment, so overwhelming was the urge to abandon her retinue, abandon her people, and send her stallion galloping over it.

I'll sleep in my castle bed tonight. Let that sweet promise sustain me through what is to come.

Alasdair said, "Soon, my love. We'll reclaim the castle soon. Then no man will ever force you from it again."

She gave him a brilliant smile. "Nor woman, either. Our children will play here, Alasdair, and our children's children. It will be our family's home until the end of time."

They were riding so close together he could rest his hand on her knee. "It's nearly over," he said softly. "Only Marlan to subdue."

Yes. Only Marlan. "Thank you for standing with me. Thank you for believing."

His fingers tightened, caressing. "I've believed in you from the first day we met."

"I think if you didn't," she said, covering his hand with hers, "we wouldn't be here."

Trailing behind them, the brave, hardy people of Kingseat who'd refused to let weariness, blisters, thirst or heat sway them from seeing her all the way home. She loved them so much she had no words to express it. Perhaps some three thousand good souls . . . if it beggared her Treasury she'd find them a fit reward.

"We should stop soon," said Alasdair. "We must decide how best to enter the town, given—"

He broke off as a shout went up behind them. It was Zandakar. *"Rhian! Wei!"*

She twisted round in her saddle. "What? What is it?"

He kicked his stallion alongside her. His eyes were wide, his nostrils flaring. "Rhian *wei* smell? Rhian *wei* hear? Many men! Many horses!" He pointed ahead. "There!"

Even as he spoke, the sound of a horse neighing. Another horse joined it. One of their own horses replied.

Then a chorus of whinnies. Zandakar was right. *Many men.* The dukes jogged their own horses up to join her.

"Marlan?" said Edward, his eyes slitted, his face grim.

"It has to be," she replied, her belly tightening.

"He doesn't dare risk letting you into town," said Rudi. "He knows its citizens will rally to you, just like the rest of the duchy has."

Twisting round in her saddle again, she looked at the great horde of her subjects walking in her wake. Surely it was her duty to keep them safe.

"This is their kingdom, too, Rhian," said Alasdair, softly. "They have the right to fight for it. They won't thank you for denying them."

He was right. She couldn't deny them.

But if Marlan spills a single drop of their blood not even God will save him from my revenge . . .

She looked at Zandakar, silent beside her on his beloved Didijik.

I've missed him. I've missed dancing my hotas. I've missed laughing with him as we trained. Somehow, without meaning to, I made him my friend.

"I don't want bloodshed if it can be avoided, Zandakar. They must be the first to offer violence, *zho?*"

He nodded. *"Zho."*

"Bring the rest of the escort up with my bodyguards. Do not so much as *touch* your blade without a sign from me."

"*Zho,* Rhian *hushla,*" he said, and wheeled Didijik away.

She looked at Alasdair. "Well. Are you ready?"

The smile he gave her was reckless. "Not at all. Are you?"

Her answering smile was knife-edged. "Oh, Alasdair. I am."

She led her people onwards, around the avenue's next sweeping bend. It took them out of their shallow valley . . . and revealed the extent of the force ranged against her, cutting off her access to the township beyond.

Marlan was dressed in his most impressive vestments. Ropes and rivers of gold shone in the sun. His eyes were a cold glitter. In a show of humility, he bestrode a white mule.

You humbug. You mockery. You haven't drawn a humble breath in your life.

Behind him stood the Court Ecclesiastica, splendid on horses, their vestments almost as grand. Ranged on either side of them, Commander Idson and some one hundred skeins of mounted Kingseat guards, unsheathed swords in their hands. It broke her heart to see them. They should have been standing for her.

Helfred sat beside his uncle, mounted on a donkey. His robe was putrid, his hands bound before him with rough rope. Even at a distance she could see his mouth was gagged, his face swollen, cut and bruised.

Rhian pinched her lips tight. "Gentlemen," she said, not taking her eyes from the prolate, "I'm going to speak privately with Marlan. Alasdair, ride with Zandakar and our armed guard. Be ready to react if there's foul play. Edward, Rudi, Adric—fall back to the people. Make sure they don't panic." As Adric tried to protest, she held up one clenched fist. "*They are your people too, Adric!* Prove to me you're worthy of them!"

Without waiting to see her orders being followed, she nudged her horse into a slow canter . . . and rode to finish things once and for all.

"Prolate," she greeted Marlan, drawing rein. "You stand in my way. Take your Churchmen and your misguided soldiery and yield this royal road to me. I would ride into my capital and be greeted by my people."

Marlan spat on the ground between them. "No."

Unsurprised, she looked more closely at poor battered Helfred. "So much for family feeling. You do my chaplain a grave disservice. He came to you in good faith with my offer of clemency. I am not encouraged by the manner of your reply."

Marlan's lip curled in a sneer. "It is not my intention to encourage you. You are an abomination in the sight of God. Your disobedience is grievous and damages this kingdom." He pointed past her to the people of Kingseat, shifting and pushing to see what was going on. "Look at the souls you've ensnared in your wiles. They are all denied God for you. They will die in the dark. Were he alive your father would bleed at what you've done. You and your . . . *husband* . . . will surrender into my keeping and face the righteous wrath of my Church."

Ignoring him and his preposterous pronouncement, she smiled gravely at Helfred. "Chaplain, your sufferings on my behalf will never be forgotten."

Unable to speak, Helfred nodded, blinking.

Marlan's fist crashed against the side of Helfred's head. "This offal is not for you to thank or notice! Henceforth you will see *nothing* I do not permit you to see!"

She throttled fury. "Marlan, you have no authority over me. I am Ethrea's queen and you are *my* subordinate, not the other way around. From the day you took office you tried to circumvent my father. If not for him you'd have strangled Ethrea in your greed for wealth and power. You failed to defeat Eberg. You have failed to defeat me. Prolate Marlan, I relieve you of your duties. You are not fit to be prolate. You are not fit to keep swine."

"And you are a *harlot*! Not fit to rule a *midden*!" Marlan was spittled, panting with rage. *"Idson! Take her!"*

"No!" Rhian screamed, wrenching her horse round on its hocks. At Marlan's cry Alasdair had spurred forward, Zandakar two heartbeats behind, her lethally trained bodyguards and her soldier escort hard on their heels. *No—no—no—no—*She turned back to Idson and his men, closing in. "You fools, don't die for Marlan—get back—sheathe your—"

It was no use. The sane world disappeared in a clash of swords and horses and pain. She didn't have a sword, she only had a knife, men were shouting, howling, she heard horses roaring, Marlan cursing, Alasdair's voice crying *"Rhian! Get away!"* She was bleeding, or someone was bleeding, there was blood on her arm and on her horse and on her blade. She was trapped in the madness, sliding from the saddle. If she fell in this chaos she'd be trampled to death.

And then an enormous cry went up, not from the battling soldiers . . . but from the people of Kingseat who'd come to witness her triumph. It was echoed by the most venerables of the Court Ecclesiastica.

"A miracle! A miracle!"

The words halted the battling soldiers mid-slash. Or maybe it was God who halted the bloodshed. Broke the combatants apart and dropped the swords from their hands.

Panting, weeping, Rhian half-fell, half-slid from her horse into the road. Idson's soldiers were falling to their knees. Her own soldiers, well-used to burning men, backed their horses away and waited, unperturbed.

Wreathed in sweet flames, Dexterity walked into their midst.

"Shed no more blood in a cause without merit," he proclaimed, his voice subtly changed as it always changed when God set him on fire. "Let brother not slay brother for the man who has lost his way. Let your hurts be healed, let your hearts fill with peace . . ."

He waved one incandescent hand. Every soldier cried out as their battle-wounds were mended. Rhian felt the heat flash through her, felt the pain in her slashed arm and thigh vanish.

Oh, Dexterity. You have saved me again.

The toymaker spread his arms wide, and the unconsuming fire flared to new heights. Marlan's white mule panicked, throwing him to the ground. With a snarl the denounced prolate lurched to his feet.

"Trickery! This is trickery!" he shouted as his venerables fell back, amazed. "You credulous fools, she turns to hedge-witchery and heathen practice to make you believe she is chosen by God! This is *nothing*. This is *nonsense*. Look at that man there, a man with blue hair!" His shaking finger pointed at Zandakar, side by side with Alasdair. "He is behind this, you can be sure of it!" He swung round to Idson, who stood transfixed. "Arrest her, Commander! Do you hear me? *Arrest her!*"

But Idson, ignoring him, slowly dropped to his knees.

Dexterity halted an arm's length from rage-spittled Marlan. "O Man, you must listen," he said. "Turn aside from your wickedness. Repent your black sins. Rhian is God's chosen, she is the true queen of Ethrea. Acknowledge her sovereignty before you are condemned."

"Her *sovereignty*?" Marlan was screeching, his urbane mask stripped away. "I acknowledge her bastardry! She's a bitch and a whore! She is queen of nothing but shit! And *you*. What are *you*? Some tricked-up pretender set to frighten little boys?"

"Prolate Marlan, be wary." Dexterity's voice was sorrowful now. "You stand on unfirm ground. God watches you . . . and God despairs."

Marlan was almost dancing in his fury. "God? God? You fool, there is no *God*! There is man and there is nature and in between a paper shield, the desperate scribblings of other fools who can't bear to live alone!"

His outburst shocked cries from the Court Ecclesiastica. Helfred was staring, still safe on his donkey, tears running unbridled down his face.

"Marlan, I command you, say nothing more!" said Dexterity. "Unless you wish to ask Rhian's forgiveness and the forgiveness of that power you so wantonly deny."

Marlan laughed, then looked around him at his venerables, who were kissing their jewelled prayer beads and their Rollin medallions. "You credulous cretins! Can't you see this is mopery? This is *illusion* and you are stupid to give it credence! Look! I shall prove it! I shall show you the *truth*!"

Rhian saw what he intended a heartbeat before he did it. She hated him, passionately, but still she leapt forward. "No, Marlan! *Don't do it!*"

But Marlan ignored her, as he'd always ignored her. He seized Dexterity by the hand . . . and burst into flames like dry kindling in a firestorm.

Unlike Dexterity, he was not protected by God.

When it was over . . . his last hideous screams faded to silence . . . and she'd finished retching herself empty of bile . . . she staggered to where her prolate had burned.

All that remained of him was a scattering of ash. Even as she stared at it, a warm breeze sprang up without warning . . . and the ash was blown away.

Still serene, still inhuman, Dexterity drifted to Helfred, who had tumbled from his donkey and was kneeling on the ground. Dexterity's burning finger touched his bindings and his gag. They fell to pieces and he was free. Then Dexterity's palm touched Helfred's hurt face and it healed in an instant.

Dexterity smiled. "Chaplain, be upstanding."

Dazed and silent, Helfred stood.

"Helfred, you are God's chaplain no longer. For your service to him, for your service to Rhian, be now Ethrea's prolate . . . despite your tender years."

Rhian choked. *My prolate? Helfred? Oh no . . . don't I get a say?*

Next, Dexterity looked at the venerables of the Court Ecclesiastica. To a man, without speaking, they slid from their horses and abased themselves in the road.

"Proud servants of God, you let yourselves be led astray. Here is your new prolate, who will keep your feet upon the righteous path. Here is your queen, who is lawful in God's sight. You are forgiven. Do not misstep again."

The venerables gabbled promises and kissed their prayer beads again.

"Rhian of Ethrea . . ."

She stepped forward, aware of Zandakar watching. Of Alasdair watching, letting her stand alone as Ethrea's queen. Aware of her dukes and her people, crowding closer, awed and hushed and knowing they witnessed history.

"Rhian of Ethrea, this is your time," said Dexterity. "A darkness is coming. You are tasked to defeat it. The free world trembles. Its fate is in your hands."

"*What?*" she said. "What darkness? What do you mean? How can the world's fate be in *my*—"

Like a snuffed candle the golden flames extinguished. Blinking, Dexterity stared around him then began his familiar slow collapse. Rhian caught him in her arms before he touched the ground.

"Let me through there! Let me through!" a sharp voice demanded over the excited mutterings of the crowd, and then Ursa joined them, carrying her physick's bag. "Jones, speak to me. Jones! What's your name?"

Dexterity frowned muzzily. "Jones, I think. Isn't it?"

"*Jones!*"

He moaned. "Yes, I'm here, Ursa. Please. Don't shout."

"It's all right, Your Majesty, I've got him," said Ursa.

She was so protective. God bless her for it. Rhian eased him into the older woman's arms, then turned as she felt a hand touch her shoulder.

"Oh, *Alasdair*!" she whispered, and let him pull her to her feet. "Did you hear that? My God, what does it mean?"

They were surrounded now by a babble of noise. As though Dexterity's collapse had broken some spell, the soldiers and the people and her own retinue milled and marvelled and laughed and cried.

Before Alasdair could answer, another hand touched her. This time it was Helfred. "Your Majesty—forgive me—"

She eased herself out of Alasdair's embrace. "Yes, Chaplain?" She shook her head. "Or should I say *Prolate*?"

He had the grace, at least, to look embarrassed. "Your Majesty . . ."

"Never mind, Helfred. What do you need?"

"I need Ursa," he whispered, and cast a glance towards her dukes, who were battling their way through the crowd to join them. "It's the councillors. In the cells below the castle. Henrik Linfoi, Lord Harley . . ." His voice trailed away.

"Henrik?" said Alasdair, his face darkening. "Did Marlan hurt him? *Helfred*. Did Marlan—"

Helfred nodded. "Yes."

Rhian took Alasdair's arm. He felt turned to stone. "I'll fix this, Alasdair. I promise." She looked for Idson, saw him hovering nearby. "Commander!"

The chastened Kingseat commander dropped to one knee. "Your Majesty. Forgive me. I—"

"Never mind that now!" she said, not caring for his shame. "I have several tasks for you. Send word to your soldiers in the town. They are to stand down at once and return to their quarters. You and your men here will ride with me on my progress, except for three guards who'll take my physick to the castle cells." She smiled, not kindly. "I think you know why."

"Yes, Majesty," Idson whispered.

"Yes, indeed. Ursa!"

The physick looked up from tending to Dexterity, who sat on the ground, his face washed pale, his hands trembling. "Majesty?"

"Go to the castle cells with the guards Commander Idson gives you."

She frowned. "But—"

"*Go now.* Once you have seen the men imprisoned there, tell the guards what you must have to do your work. They will obey you implicitly—" She turned. "Won't they, Commander?"

Idson nodded. "Yes, Your Majesty. Madam Physick? If you'll come with me?"

With a last anxious look at Dexterity, Ursa picked up her bag and followed the commander.

Rhian took a deep breath and let it out, hard. Dear God, this was too much to think of, too much after so long exiled from her home. She looked at her dukes and steeled herself to remain strong.

"Your Graces, your council kinsmen are held in the castle. When our business is concluded you shall see them, never fear. *Do not argue!*" she added, as Adric opened his mouth. "Instead inform our soldiers and my bodyguards that we will shortly resume our progress into the town. Helfred!"

He offered her a small bow. "Your Majesty?"

"You and your Court Ecclesiastica will also join my progress. Afterwards you'll repair to the Prolates Palace. You have much work ahead of you in the healing of this kingdom. Might I suggest your first order of conduct is to remove all interdicts *immediately*?"

"Be assured we shall, Majesty," said Helfred.

"Then be so good as to organise yourself and your venerables. I wish to depart in a very short time."

Another small bow. "Certainly, Your Majesty."

Bemused, Rhian watched him collect the white mule from the soldiers who held its reins, go to mount it, then stop. Hand the reins back and instead retrieve the donkey.

To her great surprise she felt herself swamped by an enormous wave of affection. "God bless you, Helfred. You've come a long way."

Perched on the pathetic little donkey, he nodded. "As have you, Majesty. With much further to go."

A cold shiver touched the nape of her neck. *A darkness is coming. You are tasked to defeat it. The free world trembles. Its fate is in your hands.* She didn't know what that meant. She would have to find out. But that would have to wait, for now.

"Zandakar," she said. "Put Dexterity in the van and drive to the castle. See him made comfortable in a chamber and sit with him until we return."

Zandakar pressed his fist to his heart. "*Zho*, Rhian *hushla*."

Head spinning, she looked at Alasdair. "Is that it? Is that everything? Or have I forgotten something important?"

Heedless of who was watching, he stole her breath in a kiss. "No, Your Majesty. Not a thing."

She smiled, her heart lifting. "Then I think it's time we finished what I started . . . don't you?"

She rode through the capital's streets with Alasdair and the dukes and Prolate Helfred and the venerables and a solemn escort of Kingseat guards . . . and the dear sweet

Kingseat Ethreans who'd refused to desert her. Her father's people—*her* people—spilled out of their homes and shops and schools, choking the streets and laneways to see her . . . and their joyful cries rose into the blue sky.

"Queen Rhian! Queen Rhian! God bless our Queen Rhian!"

Late the next morning, in her castle, with her standard flying proud from the battlements, magnificent in sapphire silk brocade and her mother's dragon-eye necklace and earrings, she met with her husband, her dukes, Dexterity and Ursa in a silk-panelled room more comfortable than the council chamber.

She was considering having that room locked for good.

So many matters of state to deal with. So many crises. So much wrong to put right. Not the least of which was recovering all the banished castle staff, especially Dinsy.

Her mistreated councillors were still too ill for her to visit. None of them would die, said Ursa, though it was doubtful Henrik Linfoi would ever walk again. Dexterity, it seemed, had tried to heal him . . . but he was without miracles. His powers had burned out.

What he felt about that could not be read in his face.

All the ambassadors were demanding to see her. She told Alasdair to draw up a schedule, commencing that afternoon. There was still the problem of Damwin and Kyrin but before she took action she'd give them time to come to her of their own accord. Not too much time, though. She wasn't feeling that generous. The Church, for the moment, she could leave to Prolate Helfred. He and the Court Ecclesiastica, his note said, had reached an understanding.

Helfred, my prolate. Oh God, your sense of humour . . .

"Lastly," she said, sweeping her gaze round the table, "there's the matter of my coronation." Her hand covered Alasdair's. "*Our* coronation. I—"

On a spine-chilling breeze the chamber's double doors blew open. A man stood on its threshold. Rhian stared. He was tall. Well-muscled. Clad in silk of peacock blue. Amber skin. Deep brown eyes. Long black hair. His face a miracle of bone. She'd seen a painting of him once, and never forgotten it after.

"Greetings, Your Majesty," said her uninvited guest. "Apologies for the intrusion . . . but our business cannot wait."

She stood behind her council table, so pleased she wore her mother's rubies. "King Alasdair . . . Your Graces . . . my friends . . . I make known to you His Imperial Majesty Emperor Han—of Tzhung-tzhungchai."

The emperor bowed. "Majesty, I received your letter."

She would *not* be intimidated by him . . . "As I recall it wasn't an invitation."

"Not . . . apparently," said the emperor, amused. "I read between the lines."

Emperor Han was not alone. Three men stood behind him, and they made her skin crawl. Emotionless faces, long black moustaches plaited with bone. Longer fingernails, carmine-red and curving. Sorcerers. Witch-men of Tzhung-tzhungchai, feared throughout the known world.

In Rollin's name, what is this? Why have they come here? Is this the danger that Ethrea faces? God help me, I can't stand against witch-men.

Alasdair and her dukes still did not move, but she could

feel their terrible tension. How deeply did she love them, that they sat and waited for her signal. Ursa and Dexterity sat staring, too.

"Emperor Han," she said politely, as though they were meeting at a tedious trading nations' reception. "There are guards in this castle whose purpose is to prevent interruptions."

"Your guards are unharmed, Majesty," said Han, equally polite. "When they wake they will feel no ill effects."

Ridiculously, she wanted to laugh. *And so I am chastised for the drugging of the clerica* . . . "You say we have urgent business?"

"Sun-dao," said the emperor. "The man is not in this room. Is he in the castle?"

"Yes," said the witch-man on his right.

"Man?" She frowned. "What man is this?"

"A black man," said Han. "With blue eyes and blue hair."

Zandakar. "Unusual. What is this odd man to you?"

"Your eyes tell me you know him," said Han. "What is he to *you*?"

Her chin came up, defiant. "A friend."

"Ah," said Han, softly. "Then the new queen of Ethrea is deceived, or friends with hell."

Now she did laugh. "Don't be absurd."

The witch-men hissed loudly, eyes rolled back in their heads. Then Sun-dao stepped forward. "That one," he said, pointing at Dexterity, his eyes still slivered white. "That one is marked, Emperor. That one bears a sign."

She turned. "What is he talking about?"

Dexterity leaned back, alarmed. "I don't know, Your Majesty."

"He is marked!" said the witch-man Sun-dao, and clenched his fist above his head.

A cold wind sprang up, lashing around Dexterity. It plucked him from his chair, tugged him gasping across the chamber.

"Emperor Han, enough!" Rhian shouted as her council erupted into protest. "How dare you assault one of my people!"

Emperor Han ignored her, and so did Sun-dao. Dexterity staggered into the witch-man's embrace. The witch-man tore his shirt laces open and plucked from around his neck a wooden carving strung on twine.

"He is marked," said the witch-man, and held the thing aloft.

Dexterity was ashen-faced and trembling. Rhian raised a hand slightly and her dukes subsided. Alasdair subsided, but it was a close-run thing. "What is that?"

"It is a *scorpion,*" said Emperor Han. "The symbol of a false god that is poisoning the world. Any man who wears this sign is not a man who can be trusted."

She looked at Dexterity. "Dexterity? Do you know anything about this?"

"No, Majesty," he said, but would not meet her eyes.

God help me. He's lying. "You do. Where did you get it?"

"He got it from Zandakar," said Ursa. "Zandakar carved it, and—"

"No, Ursa! *Don't!"*

"Don't what, Jones? Tell the truth?" Ursa's hands slapped hard on the table. "After all we've been through to put Rhian on the throne, now you want me to start telling her *lies*?"

Rhian looked at the man she'd thought was her friend. But friends didn't lie to each other. They didn't keep these kinds of secrets. "Alasdair, I believe you'll find Zandakar in the stables."

Alasdair slipped from the room, his hand touching hers briefly as he passed. She could barely feel him. Her flesh had turned to ice.

"Emperor Han," she said, in her mother's dragon rubies. "What else can you tell me of Zandakar?"

The emperor clasped his hands. "He is of a mighty warrior race who cover the innocent earth like a plague, burning and killing and consuming everything in their path. The far east is lost to them. Now they look west. Their leader is a black man with red hair who serves their false god without mercy. A killer of thousands. A destroyer of cities, and nations, and hope."

"And how do you know this?"

"Sun-dao is a seer," said Emperor Han. "No man living hears the wind as he does. The wind blew visions to him. The wind whispered a name. *Mijak*. The wind told us we must come here and find the man with blue hair. That he is one of these warriors, with much blood on his hands."

The chamber was full of sunshine. All she could do was shiver. "I see." She turned to Dexterity. "Is this true?"

"Hettie said I wasn't to tell you," he muttered. "Hettie said it wasn't time for you to know."

"Hettie said?" She shoved her way around the table and took handfuls of his shirt in her cold hands. *"Hettie said? Mr Jones, how could you?"*

"I'm sorry . . . I'm sorry . . . I only did what she said."

"What do you know about him? What should I know?"

Mr Jones looked at her with grief-stricken eyes. "That

he's a good man. That he's *yatzhay*. That you need him or we'll be lost."

She let go of his shirt and pushed him away. "Oh, God. *Dexterity*." With a teeth-grinding effort she regained her self-control. "What else did Hettie tell you? What has *Zandakar* told you? Whatever that is, you're going to tell *me*."

"All right," Dexterity whispered. "But only you. And only if you promise—"

"Rhian," said Alasdair, coming through the door. "Here is Zandakar."

He walked behind Alasdair, so handsome, so easy. Such graceful power in him, such pained love in his eyes. He saw her and stopped, his fist punching his breast. One glance he flicked at the emperor and the witch-men, but all he cared to see was her.

"Rhian."

She looked at him in silence and let him see her face, her real face, with her cold hurt heart laid bare.

"Mijak," she whispered. *"Mijak,* Zandakar."

"Yatzhay," said Dexterity. "I didn't tell them. They knew."

Zandakar said nothing but his ice-blue eyes filled with tears.

"And so you are answered," said Emperor Han. "Queen Rhian of Ethrea, let us sit, as rulers do. You and I have much to discuss."

MIJAK

Hekat stood on a hilltop and listened to the wind coax silver songs from her godbells . . .

The god is singing, it is singing, it sings Hekat in the world.

Below the hill spread the conquered city of Jatharuj. One more conquered city in the land once called *Icthia*. Now there was no more land called *Icthia*. Like Shavay, like Totti, like Malk'n and Dardann, the land of *Icthia* was Mijak. Its people were dead, or turned into slaves.

Every land is Mijak. Even if a land does not know it, that land is Mijak and its Empress is Hekat.

In her weary body, such a sound of groaning. The sun was still high, Vortka would not heal her till it fell into the ocean. Four fingers from now, she must groan four fingers more. Groan silently, groan without tears, groan and walk as though there was no groaning. Let the ocean take her groaning, let it drink her cries of pain and spit them out as foam that flew upon the breeze.

Aieee, god, the blue ocean. A lake as big as the sky, Mijak could drown in it. Hekat could drown, she comes from the desert. She comes from the savage north where oceans are red, where they are made of sand.

Two fat godmoons since they had come to this ending place, where the land stopped and the water began. Water that was full of salt, no horse could drink it, no better than poison. There were godhouses in Jatharuj now, there were godspeakers and sacrifices. Because she had come here the god was in this place, it was not here before she came. That was her purpose, she brought the god. The god of Icthia was conquered, all its priests bleaching bones in the sun. Their blood was gone to feed the true god, Mijak's god. The god in the world. The blood of slaves and sinners was more pleasing than any blood of lambs and doves. The great desert had taught her that, she taught the godspeakers this new, great thing. They gave the god strong blood, when Vortka would let them.

Vortka did not like the strong blood. He was growing old and soft. He said only the useless and dying slaves could be given to the god in blood. All other blood must come from the sacred beasts of Mijak. He was high godspeaker, and every newsun and lowsun he silenced her groaning with his crystal. She had to listen, she wished she did not groan and need him.

When I have given the god all the world, the god will stop the groaning in my body. Let Vortka beware then, for dancing Hekat will return.

So long now since she had danced with her snakeblade. In her dreams she danced the *hotas*. In her dreams she was young and lithe. In her dreams she danced with Zandakar, he was a small boy and she was his life.

Far behind her on the high hilltop, so far, Et-Raklion and Mijak lay beyond the demon desert and the conquered lands and the meek Sand River. Dry, dusty old Mijak, emptied of everything but cripples and goats. Mijak's people and their slaves were in the world, in the new green lands that were Mijak for the god.

Soon the whole world would be Mijak for the god.

Hekat the Empress, godtouched and precious. I am giving the world to the god.

And in the god's world somewhere there was Zandakar, her only son. She would find him, they would meet. She would forgive him, and Dmitrak, Spawn of Nagarak, would bleed and feed the god.

Hekat the Empress and the warlord Zandakar. Born to rule in the world for the god.

Conquered Icthia was a sailing nation. In the city of Jatharuj, spread out before her, were many boats that sailed the wide ocean. Not enough for her whole warhost, it numbered tens of thousands, but the slaves of Jatharuj were building her more. Other Jatharuj slaves taught her warhost how to sail them. She stood on this hilltop with her godbells singing silver and watched her warhost learn to sail those boats.

And when they have learned, when they ride the boats as they ride their Mijak horses, when there are enough boats to hold all the god's mighty warhost, they will sail across the ocean taking the god into the world. Hekat will sail with them. Hekat, Empress for the god.

The boats of Jatharuj had new masts, they were godposts, the god's scorpions drank the keen salt air. They drank the air, they tamed the ocean. Sailing on the tamed blue water with the god and its scorpions was Dmitrak, with red hair. Until she found Zandakar she needed him breathing. Until she found Zandakar he was her son, he was the god's hammer for striking the world.

Already Dmitrak had used the god's power to sink

trading boats from other lands, boats which had sailed into Jatharuj as though they were welcome here. The men on those boats who did not die were now slaves. They came from lands known as *Slynt* and *Arbenia* and *Tzhung-tzhungchai*. Lands who were conquered, though they did not yet know it.

Aieee, god, I admit it, Dmitrak has his uses. Vortka high godspeaker, he has his uses also. Vortka is chosen, he lives in your eye. You keep him alive for me, so I might be spared groaning. He is my old friend, I have feelings for him. I never said I do not. Though he makes me angry I will not smite him.

Do not ask the same for Nagarak's spawn.

In the warm light, in the wind singing silver, she closed her eyes and saw blue hair, saw blue eyes, saw Zandakar dancing. She danced with him and he was not a child.

I am coming, Zandakar. I am coming to find you. I bring the god with me . . . and we shall rule the world.

ACKNOWLEDGEMENTS

Tim Holman and Darren Nash: my champions!

The super-fantastico Orbit US/UK team: where would I be without you, guys?

Julia Denos, cover artist, and Peter Cotton, designer: you both rock! And Mark Timmony, who's cursed with my maps.

My selfless and dedicated beta readers: Glenda, Mark, Elaine, Pete and Mary.

Ethan, my agent, who copes admirably with this control-freaking writer.

My dear friends, who put up with my extended absences as I write.

The fans who've been so kind to email and say my books have entertained them.

The booksellers who point new readers my way.

Lastly, my parents, who still don't get what it is that I do but continue to support me anyway.

In Memoriam

Robert Jordan, author of the genre-changing Wheel of Time series, who departed this world too soon, leaving many broken hearts behind him.

extras

orbit

meet the author

KAREN MILLER was born in Vancouver, Canada, and moved to Australia with her family when she was two. She started writing stories while still in primary school, where she fell in love with speculative fiction after reading *The Lion, the Witch and the Wardrobe*. Over the years she has held down a wide variety of jobs, including horse stud groom in Buckingham, England. She is working on several new novels. Visit the official Karen Miller Web site at www.karenmiller.net.

introducing

If you enjoyed
THE RIVEN KINGDOM,
look out for

HAMMER OF GOD

Book 3 of the Godspeaker Trilogy
by Karen Miller

S he was barely aware of the servants and courtiers who
acknowledged her passing as she left the castle. They
bowed, she nodded, some words were exchanged. Like
her father before her she refused a cloying coterie of attendants and discouraged hangers-on at court. If she wanted
company she called for it, otherwise everyone knew she
was to be left alone.

The weight of their gazes as she walked by was as
heavy as any crown devised.

Outside, in the privy gardens that ran along the edge of
the hill overlooking Kingseat township and the harbour, the
sunshine was mellow. Warm as a mother's breath against

her skin. She let her fingertips touch drooping, perfumed blossoms. Resisted what she knew she must consider and flirted, for a little while, with memories of simpler, happier times.

And then she stopped, because she was no longer alone. The eldritch sense that had served her all her life told her who it was. Without looking over her shoulder she said, "Emperor Han. I know for certain this time there was no invitation."

The Emperor laughed. "I took it for granted you would be pleased to see me."

"Did you indeed?" she said, and turned to confront him. "Well. That was very presumptuous of you."

He bowed. "It was, Queen Rhian."

Head to toe he was dressed in black silk: high-throated, long-sleeved tunic, narrow pants. His long black hair was tied back from his extraordinary, ageless face. His dark brown eyes were watchful, and amused. He wore no jewellery, no trappings of power … but even a blind man would not mistake him for a commoner.

Rhian considered him. "How did you gain access to my privy gardens?"

"Does it matter? I am here."

"Are you an emperor or a witch-man?"

His eyebrows rose, two beautiful black arches. "Perhaps I am both."

"And perhaps you could answer me like an honest man, instead of playing silly word games as though you were a child!"

That surprised him. "You are bold, Queen of Ethrea."

"And also quite busy. Was there something you

wanted, Han? Or are you simply bored, and seeking a diversion?"

He hadn't given her leave to address him as an intimate. She'd committed a breach of protocol.

So we stand evenly matched. Witching himself here was just as rude. If that's what he did. And I can't think of another explanation. He's hardly inconspicuous.

Instead of answering, Han looked her up and down. His dark eyes gleamed; it might have been appreciation or even condemnation. He was impossible to read.

"I have known many queens, many empresses, many . . ." He smiled. "Women. Do you dress like a man in the hope other men will accept your rule, or is it that being a woman isn't enough for you?"

She looked down at her not-very-queenly clothing: leather huntsman's leggings, a leather jerkin, silk shirt. On her feet leather low-heeled half-boots. Strapped to her left hip, a knife once cherished by her brother. Its hand-polished hilt was set with tiger eye, Ranald's birthstone. Her fingers often found it, and touched it, remembering.

"Han," she said, looking up again, "you must think me witless if you believe *I* believe you're here to comment on my choice of attire. How can I help you? What do you want?"

He plucked a fragile pink ifrala blossom from a nearby flower bed and held it to his nose, delicate as any lady-in-waiting. Breathing deeply, he smiled. "Your mother had a sweet touch in her garden, Rhian. I remember she made ifrala perfume every spring."

She blinked. "You knew my mother?"

"Briefly." He opened his fingers and let the blossom drift to the grass. "Rhian, why have you not convened a meeting of the trading nations? Do you think this *Mijak* will change its mind? Or, like a little girl, do you hope that if you close your eyes tight the spirits and demons will not see you in the dark?"

Spirits and demons. *There are no such things.* "If you're so certain I'm wrong in waiting, Han, why have *you* not summoned the trading nations yourself?"

"If I were the ruler of Ethrea, I would."

She folded her arms. "Why should I trust what your Sun-dao has to say? Why should I trust you? I don't know you, Han. I only know your reputation, and the reputation of mighty Tzhung-tzhungchai. You swallow nations as I swallow a plum. Perhaps I'm the pit you think to spit out in the dirt."

"Rhian, Rhian . . ." Han sounded sorrowful. "Don't disappoint me. The Tzhung empire has swallowed no-one for nearly two hundred years. You know that. And you know my witch-man speaks the truth. The truth rots in your dungeons. It yearns for the light. It dreams of a dead wife. Zandakar is the key to defeating Mijak. How long will you leave him a prisoner when your life, and my life, and as many lives as there are stars at night depend upon him? How long will you deny the only truth that can save us?"

"Zandakar is my concern, not yours," she said, turning away.

The Emperor sighed. "Before Mijak is tamed you must tame your disobedient dukes. The dukes are why you do not convene the trading nations. They are why you stand before me, bound hand and foot and helpless as a child. Until the dukes are tamed your crown is in danger. Zandakar is also the key to their downfall, and you know it.

There is so little time until there is no time at all, Rhian. Will you let pain and pride waste these brief moments?"

"Be quiet!" she snapped, spinning to face him once again. "Who are you to come here uninvited and tell me how I should rule and who I should see? If time is so brief, if I am so helpless, take your Tzhung fleet and sink Mijak on your own!"

Han smiled. His eyes were flat and black as obsidian. "If the wind desired it, girl, then so it would be and my empire would flood with the grateful tears of the saved. The wind does not. It blows me to you."

I never asked it to! I never asked for this!

"The wind does not care," said Han. "And neither do I. Deal with your dukes, Rhian."

Still fuming, she glared at him. "How?"

"You ask for my help?"

"I ask for your opinion!" she retorted. "My father taught me there is no shame in seeking counsel of a wise man. You are an emperor. I assume you've had some experience of—of—uncooperative vassals."

His cold eyes warmed. He was amused again. "Yes."

"Well, then?"

"Rhian, there is nothing I can tell you that you do not already know. The wind has made you a warrior. No breathing man can fight the wind."

Perhaps that's true. But this breathing woman can certainly try.

"You can," said Han. "But you won't."

Was he inside her mind now? Or was her face less schooled than she liked to imagine? He infuriated and frightened her like no-one else she knew. "I don't want to shed their blood, Han."

He shrugged. "Want means nothing. Need is all."

Tears burned her eyes, then, because she knew he was right. Hand on her knife-hilt, she blinked them away.

"Go," said the Emperor of Tzhung-tzhungchai. "Do what you must, Rhian. Do it quickly. And when you are done, I will be waiting."

8/14 (10)   11/11 (5) 8/11